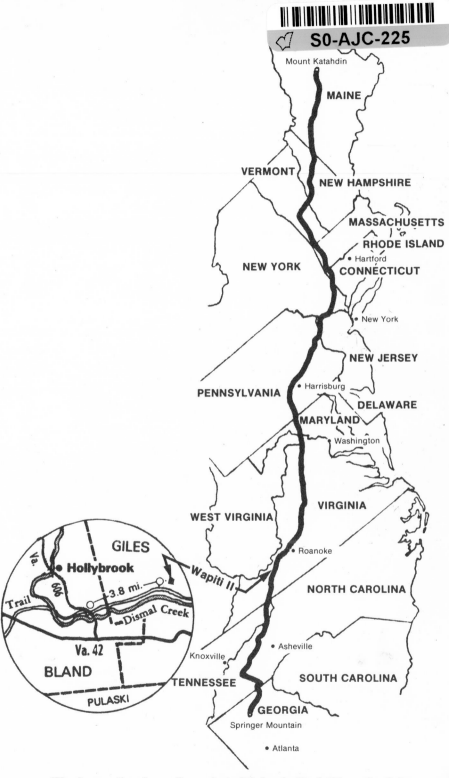

Mount Katahdin

MAINE

VERMONT

NEW HAMPSHIRE

MASSACHUSETTS

RHODE ISLAND

• Hartford

NEW YORK

CONNECTICUT

• New York

NEW JERSEY

PENNSYLVANIA

• Harrisburg

DELAWARE

MARYLAND

• Washington

WEST VIRGINIA

VIRGINIA

• Roanoke

NORTH CAROLINA

• Asheville

Knoxville
•

SOUTH CAROLINA

TENNESSEE

GEORGIA

Springer Mountain

• Atlanta

GILES

Va.
606

• **Hollybrook**

Trail

3.8 mi.

Wapiti II

Dismal Creek

Va. 42

BLAND

PULASKI

**The heavy line from Georgia to Maine is the full length of the
Appalachian Trail.**

MURDER ON THE APPALACHIAN TRAIL

Books by Jess Carr

A Creature Was Stirring & Other Stories

The Falls of Rabbor

The Second Oldest Profession: An Informal History of Moonshining in America

The Saint of the Wilderness

Birth of a Book

The Frost of Summer

The Moonshiners (In paperback, Millie & Cleve)

Ship Ride Down the Spring Branch & Other Stories

How A Book Is Born (for young people)

A Star Rising

MURDER ON THE APPALACHIAN TRAIL

A Novel By

Jess Carr

Commonwealth Press   Virginia

MURDER ON THE APPALACHIAN TRAIL
by
Jess Carr

Library of Congress Catalog number: 84-072458

ISBN Number: 0-89227-106-X   31499

The author is grateful to the following corporations and individuals for permission to quote material as noted below.

Sam Fox Publishing Co., for permission to use words from *The Happy Wanderer*.

The Richmond Organization for permission to use words from *Turn! Turn! Turn!*, © Copyright 1962 Melody Trails Inc., N.Y., N.Y., adaptation and music by Pete Seeger.

The untitled poem used at The Homestead memorial service for Bob Mountford and Susan Ramsay, with the lead line. . . *do not stand at my grave and weep* . . . was, after a diligent search by the author, assumed to be by an unknown author and uncopyrighted. If contrary information later comes to light, proper credit will be given in a subsequent edition.

Quotes from other published works, listed below, are in the public domain, but are here identified: Wordsworth, "The Tables Turned," from *The Poetical Works of William Wordsworth,* New Haven, 1836; Robert Frost, "The Trial by Existence," from *"A Boy's Will,* New York: Holt, 1915; Antoine de Saint Exuperty, *The Little Price,* Paris, 1886; *The Brothers Karamazov* by Fyodor Dostoevsky, translated from the Russian by Constance Garnett (New York: Macmillan, 1923); Henry Wadsworth Longfellow, "Nature," from *The Collected Works of Henry Wadsworth Longfellow,* edited by Horace E. Scudder (Boston: Houghton Mifflin, 1886).

Quotations from the Bible are from the King James version, and The Living Bible version.

Commonwealth Press, Inc.
415 First St.
Radford, Virginia 24141

Printed in the United States of America

Dedication

For all of those pursuers of dreams
who aspire to the noble title of
End-to-Ender on the Applachian Trail

INTRODUCTION

Like an enormous sleeping dragon, the Appalachian Mountain chain sprawls over a two-thousand-mile north-to-south corridor of the eastern United States, crested by a wilderness path now known worldwide as the Appalachian Trail. Passing through fourteen eastern states, eight national forests, and two national parks, the Trail starts (most end-to-end hikers use the south-to-north direction) at Springer Mountain, Georgia, approximately 3,800 feet above sea level, reaches its 6,600-foot pinnacle at Clingman's Dome, Tennessee, and ends on Mount Katahdin, Maine, at 5,267 feet.

When the white man first set eyes on the New World, the short segments of Appalachian Trail bore evidence of occasional use by the Indians; and parts of it served the earliest settlers of North America. But in today's concept of recreational and adventurous foot travel, it had its beginning in 1922 when a one-mile stretch of trail was cut in the Palisades Interstate Park in New York.

The Appalachian Trail seems to have been born of a dream in the mind of Benton MacKaye, —a forester, author, and philosopher. The first person to hike the entire Trail was Myron H. Avery, who started his trek in Maine in the 1920s and, walking only sections at a time, finally completed the full course in 1936. Like MacKaye, Avery was a man of many interests; he was elected to Phi Beta Kappa at Bowdoin College and received a law degree from Harvard University.

Avery's adventure established a standard for millions who have followed him. The trail has become as much a spiritual and philosophical pilgrimage as a physical one: a journey into Self, a renewal of the age-old belief that Man and Nature are one, that in earth's quiet peace can be found, and that a new vitality of body and mind is waiting at the end of the trail. More and more the deep-thinking, socially sensitive man and woman are drawn to the Trail as Avery believed they would be.

Even so, the challenge of the two thousand miles of wilderness pathways was formidable. By 1972 fewer than one hundred "end-to-enders" had hiked the full distance within the year. By 1980 the number had not reached six hundred. Hiking the Appalachian Trail, a hiker found, was slow going indeed: fifteen to twenty miles a day was the average through rain, sleet,

1

snow, and powerful winds on the mountain crests as one dodged fallen trees, fought off wild dogs (sometimes in packs), went hungry, or missed a vital stream of water. The hike took a raw kind of courage, an unbelievable physical stamina, and a sixth sense that defied description. The most intelligent of male and female hikers found themselves almost hopelessly lost on occasion in spite of the frequent "white blazes" by which the Trail is marked.

The Appalachian Mountain system is punctuated in many places by successive mountain groups and approximately parallel ranges separated by longitudinal valleys. Occasionally the Trail becomes easy when it follows established highways for short distances; at other points, it seems to climb a rock cliff or, at best, to require a climber to pull himself up the side of a mountain incline hand over hand, balancing a fifty-pound pack on his back—a pack that must not be lost or seriously damaged, for it is his sole sustenance.

As the Appalachian Trail enters Virginia, the hiker begins his approach to the one-third point of its total distance. More than five hundred miles of the Trail traverses the Commonwealth—double the distance in any other state; and that long stretch is considered by many hikers to be one of the most beautiful sections of the journey. In the spring of the year, it is an exquisite fairyland. At the lower heights, the hiker is treated to green, sometimes fog-enshrouded forests, blooming dogwoods, leaf-carpeted pathways, massive boulders and smaller rocks covered in colorful fungi, lichen and velvety moss, virgin timber from massive oaks to perfumed hemlocks, a scattering of spring violets, blooming berry bushes, plus wild strawberries, wild phlox and other ground covers, and—most colorful of all—wild flame azalea and endless rhododendron. Below the Trail, one sees a checkerboard of lush green valleys broken by plowed fields, often parceled off by serpentine split rail fences and rippling creeks and rivers.

Not infrequently a homestead from the eighteenth century comes into view, its gray weatherboarding curling outward to the sun; nearby a less-well-built barn appears to be collapsing. But as the dense forest obscures the sight a picturesque cascade looms ahead, its potable water dropping forty feet down jagged limestone, in a muted happy song. The foliage grows thick, and the smells grow sweeter with wild ginger, sassafras, and long-needle pine. Without warning whitetailed deer leap across the trail, casting looks in passing that clearly establish just who is the intruder. Soon from a high peak, a village comes into view. A creek winds in a half-moon around the settlement and meanders down the fertile valley. In the distance a church steeple stands high above the white frame houses. Soon that too passes from view, and the trail to dip before another ascent begins. The face of the new terrain seems friendly somehow as if it is home to something other than the numberless snakes, opossums, skunks, wild turkeys, raccoons, foxes, squirrels, and occasional bears that call the great Appalachians home.

All this begins to explain the lure of the Trail. Many hikers confess to a sort of vertigo when heart, senses, and vision take flight. The soul floats aloft while the feet sink into the moss-cushioned earth. The mind soars to great heights and the intellect is sharpened until the truth of Wordsworth's *The Tables Turned* rings clear:

> One impulse from a vernal wood
> May teach you more of man,
> Of moral evil and of good,
> Than all the sages can.

After traveling approximately eighty-five miles into southwestern Virginia, the hiker approaches Jefferson National Forest. The entry point is not an imposing series of arches in the Roman tradition but rather a narrow road paralleling Kimberling Creek and announced by a carved wooden plaque, compatible with the rustic surroundings. No village here; the nearest village—Hollybrook—is three miles away to the northwest, and close by are places like Rabbit Squat, Lick Skillet, and The Wilderness. Here, however, there are four or five houses, a country store, and across the road from the store, a large sawmill operation. Separating store and sawmill is Route 606, a narrow paved state highway running northwestwardly through the county of Bland. Twelve miles farther along, Route 606 intersects with Interstate 77. In two dozen miles more the Interstate crosses the line into West Virginia near Princeton; then it becomes the West Virginia Turnpike, a scenic thoroughfare leading to West Virginia's "billion-dollar coalfields."

Trent's country store near Hollybrook is especially welcome. There lies the opportunity to buy a pint of ice cream, to get a few bandaids, to sip leisurely on a cold Coke, and to get the latest local and world news. If the lunch break or quitting time has arrived, there is the opportunity to mix with the mill hands. Sometimes the denim-clad locals have to be drawn out, taking their good time while shifting a cheekful of Levi Garrett chewing tobacco from one side of the mouth to the other. Generally they are friendly to hikers though on occasion some will admit to curiosity about why a professor from Harvard, a social worker from Maine, a nurse from Charlotte, an engineer from Pittsburgh waste their time on a two-thousand-mile hike—or, for that matter, a ten-mile hike. It is soon evident that these rural Virginians live close to the soil have simple tastes and unsophisticated lives. Though in some ways the times have engulfed them—four-wheel-drive vehicles equipped with stereos and CB radios are common—their philosophy of life is still that of their forebears. It is Baptist, Methodist, Christian, or Pentecostal Holiness church on Sundays, family clannishness, heated politics, love of the land, and a general—perhaps fatalistic—acceptance of their lot. Sometimes they enrich their lives by offering food and sleeping quarters to a tired hiker.

If any of them ever feels hostility toward a Trail hiker, it's a minor concern: climbing a wire fence, leaving a farm gate open, frightening a farm man or a woman by a sudden, unannounced appearance at darkness or dawn. Sometimes a female hiker raises local eyebrows (or temperatures as the case may be), by appearing at the country store braless in a sweat-saturated T-shirt.

For the most part, the lush little valley is a community at peace. But not always. Nearby is the Bland Correctional Farm, a state institution for short-term prisoners who work on the Farm raising livestock, vegetables, and crops, thereby paying their keep. Prisoners escape now and then while they're working in the fields or dairy barns, and the bloodhounds have to be put to use. Once in a while, a runaway turns hostile and murders or maims someone. It's a cloud under which local residents hate to live. They especially hate the thought that many of the prisoners came out of big-city backgrounds where ghetto life and jungle-like upbringing made them morally bankrupt. But in any event "The Farm," provides local employment in the way of guard positions, administrators, clerks, secretaries, and mechanics. Bland County has no railroads and fewer than a dozen small industries, none of which employs more than a hundred and fifty people. And the bulk of the vast timberland has long been cut out. Neighboring Giles, which shares a common border within Jefferson National Forest, enjoys railroads and a larger industrial base, but the western part of the county is rural and mountainous.

Bland and Giles Countians more and more have found themselves commuting far outside the county to find work. For some, it is an injury to their Scotch-Irish pride. The twentieth century has caught up with them, and county officials find the financial going increasingly tough. At times it is difficult to maintain the school system according to state standards in counties without a large industrial base while still coping with a populace long accustomed to low real estate and personal property taxes. County supervisors for years have felt the increasing pressure of public need versus tight-fist land-holders who vote the status quo.

During the 1930's manganese ore was discovered in the area, and great hope prevailed that east Bland and west Giles had struck it rich at last. The hope was in vain; many of the deposits turned out to be of low grade, and the richer veins petered out after the Korean War period. With government permission some of the ore was mined in Jefferson National Forest. But in the end it seemed as if Nature herself had plotted against a hoped-for industrial boom. For all the disappointment, there were those who breathed a sign of relief that boom times hadn't come and that they could maintain a way of life a century and a half old.

It is a strange world, no doubt, to hikers from New York, Baltimore, Washington, Miami, or Boston; yet it is in perfect accord with the spirit of the Appalachian Trail. Was not tranquility in the heart of breath-taking natural beauty one of the goals of every hiker as he shouldered the heavy backpack and enter Jefferson National Forest in earnest? In what other surroundings could there be any more peace and assurance of mind?

Inside the forest, scarcely two miles past Trent's Store, the trail runs parallel to Dismal Falls, a naturally formed rock cliff of broad limestone, layer upon layer, jutting in irregular and jagged patterns over which tons of

4

water spill and churn ferociously to a deep pool below. In the quietness of the wooded world in the spring when Dismal Creek is flush, the melodious sound of the rushing water can be heard a mile away. The falls is awesome in its beauty and power, and the onlooker finds himself frozen before it. Patience may be rewarded by sight of a deer, a raccoon, or more rarely a bear coming to water. The tired hiker with boots removed, comfortable seating found on a poolside rock, and sweaty toes dangling in the chilled water, is assured of instant renewal. For the playful hiker who wedges bits of a biscuit between his toes, literally hundreds of mountain trout minnows nibble until the bread is gone; that is, if he can hold convulsive laughter in cheek while the hungry minnows eat, causing an involuntary twitching at the ankles that runs up the legs into the spine.

Other sights await the hiker, and endless side trails marked with blue blazes divert him—all along the Appalachian Trail. With the hiker back on the trail proper, the map shows an upcoming shelter/lean-to called Wapiti. Beyond it and in recent months, an improved shelter called Wapiti II has been constructed by the Forest Service. The new location is just inside the Giles County line, approximately twenty miles from Pearisburg, the county seat.

It is doubtful that more than a few thousand people in the entire world had ever heard of Bland and Giles counties, Virginia, much less Wapiti II, until in late May of 1981 when this section of the Appalachian Trail made national headlines. Hikers far removed from civilization—Trent's Store and the wail of sawmill activity—were on their own. Seemingly no one heard three quick shots or the shrieks that must have preceded the repeated stabbings with a knife. Perhaps no one who heard would have believed, for no such thing had ever happened across the five-hundred-mile Trail in Virginia; and only once had a violent death occurred along the two-thousand-mile length of the entire Appalachian Trail.

There had been rain those two fateful days, but it had not washed the telltale stain of crimson from the greyish-brown bark of a tree nor cleansed the green moss and winter's leaves of the same horrible blemish. On the wooden floor boards of Wapiti II, more blood had been spilled, but the killer or the killers had attempted to obliterate it with dirt, ashes, and charcoal.

Even before the manhunt for one or more crazed killers had formally begun, the peaceable citizens of Bland and Giles—perhaps the whole of Virginia—wondered whether their beloved land would ever be the same again. Days later, like the rest of the nation, they stared wide-eyed and unbelieving as the press and television proclaimed, "Two Young Maine Social Workers Murdered on The Appalachian Trail."

It was the escaped-convict pattern all over again, although now, there *were* no escaped convicts. Nevertheless, the feeling was the same: the sudden start at the most commonplace noise; the fitful sleep; the shotgun, the rifle, or the pistol within easy reach; the securely locked doors; the super caution at the approach of every stranger; the refusal to answer a

5

late-night doorknock; the gathering of children before dusk; the purchase of more guns and vicious guard dogs. But somehow, the people themselves had been responsible this time. The host-guardian obligation was theirs. It was the unwritten code for all decent men and women of all time. Even a stranger in their homes or upon their land was a guest to be protected or a potential friend to be sent on his way food-filled, rested, merry. Their ancestors had practiced the same hospitality.

What animal had shattered this ancient tradition with such unspeakable blood-letting and with what motive? How could two beautiful young people in the prime of their lives and ostensibly on a fund-raising hike for a retarded-children's home, and a home for troubled juveniles, have provoked in any way such a heinous crime? What unfathomable horrors yet lay ahead for other unsuspecting hikers if the killer or the killers went uncaptured?

And what if the murderer was not some deranged "foreigner" who killed in cold blood but was rather an area citizen whose hostilities could no longer be held in check? If so, did he—or they—still lie in wait for another opportunity—even for innocent children, perhaps? Or was his obsession focused on those traversing the Appalachian Trail?

CHAPTER I

At last the dream was coming true. Robert Tatton Mountford, Jr., had dreamed the dream for more than ten years. He'd just turned twenty-seven on February fourth of this year, 1981, but the burning ambition to hike the full two-thousand-mile length of the Appalachian Trail had begun in his senior year of high school at Dover-Foxcroft Academy in the small Maine town of the same name where he'd spent nineteen of those twenty-seven years.

It seemed now in retrospect that he had been in training for the big hike most of his life. At Dover-Foxcroft Academy he had played basketball, had been a member of the wrestling team, had been voted the school's "Most Valuable Golfer," and had served as co-captain of the championship football team. All these activities had contributed to the development of his powerful five-foot-nine, one-hundred-ninety-pound body. In mental, artistic, and social growth, too, he had some impressive credentials: freshman class president, four-year member of the school band and trumpet soloist, four-year member of the school choir and occasional baritone soloist, organizer and leader of his own dance band, member of the Key and Varsity clubs, and president of the Student Council in his senior year.

At Bryant College in Rhode Island, skipping an offered football scholarship, he had set his sights on a business degree after which he would enter his father's insurance business. But during his first year at Bryant, he had decided that his future was not in doing business with people but in getting to know them and in learning to see inside them.

The next year he had entered the University of Maine, Orono, in pursuit of a degree in psychology. Here the books had come first; yet he had been able to carry spare-time jobs, work in trips to Russia and to England, and keep in trim shape with golf, tennis, handball, racquetball, and frisbee throwing. Tennis, swimming, waterskiing, and jogging had occupied the summers. Fall and winter had been good times for hiking, lengthy down-river canoe trips, scaling his favorite place in all the world—Maine's own Mount Katahdin—and, more recently, ice climbing when the weather got cold enough to freeze a solid sheet of ice to the face of various pinnacles and all that stood between the climber and a five-hundred foot drop was a length of nylon rope, a good set of cramponed boots, and a sharp ice axe. But the death-defying danger was a part of the thrill of it. All his life he had wanted—needed—challenge, with or without danger. It was as much a part of his psyche as any other factor in his being.

And now, as the little '79 blue Ford Fiesta sped down Interstate 95 toward Boston, Bob Mountford headed for the greatest—and most dangerous—challenge of his life. He was trying to sort out and neatly package the diverging emotions and expectations that swirled inside him: the once-in-a-lifetime adventure ahead, the madness and ecstasy just past, the warmth beside him of Jackie Hilton—his driver now but his lover a few hours ago.

Jackie and her four-year-old daughter Jennifer would see him to Boston to the Amtrak train for Anniston, Alabama, for a rendezvous with his aunt and uncle in Gadsden and then on to Springer Mountain, Georgia, the beginning of the Appalachian Trail. His plan was to hit the trail by April 1. Today was Friday, March 27.

He had been too exhausted and distracted to drive when he and Jackie and Jennifer had left Ellsworth, Maine, four hours earlier for the drive to Boston. He and Jackie had announced their plans to marry at Christmas; but now marriage was off. For Jackie it was a relationship balked by old history, old hangups, uncertainty in an unpredictable world, and complicated by time apart and personal problems. Their situation was one of the many things the solitude of the Appalachian Trail would help clarify and put into proper focus, Bob hoped.

He looked across at Jackie's delicate profile in the pre-dawn light. They had had little sleep, but she held her small head, rich in luxurious brown hair, erect, a look of warm fulfillment on her face. He felt the same afterglow overlying his excitement at nearing the start of the Trail. Jackie! Although the engagement had been broken, their love life had suffered little interruption. Late the previous evening and into the hour past midnight, they had made love. And they had lain there daydreaming and fantasizing about what a wedding would be like on top of Mount Katahdin, she in a long white-trained dress billowed by the winds and the two of them lifted up into the magic-carpet clouds and floating away to the Himalayas or the Alps.

This last evening and morning together before he left for Boston had begun when Jackie picked him up at the Holiday Inn in Ellsworth. He had stopped by the motel to tell his mother goodbye. "Mim," as everybody called her, was the Director of The Little Red School House in Dover—Foxcroft, a school for retarded children—and some adults, too, up to age, forty; and she had come to Ellsworth to attend a meeting on Maine's Pre-School Pilot Program. After he had told her goodbye (he had told his dad goodbye the previous day) he had gone with Jackie to her apartment.

At her place Bob had engaged Jennifer in a songfest and a round of game playing. When both grew tired, the three of them had caught the tail end of a movie on TV. Afterwards, Jackie fed Jennifer and put her to bed.

Once alone, she and Bob had sat just looking at each other until slowly, they arose, felt the magnet-like pull of their mutual need, and retreated to her bedroom. The hunger of days apart had burst upon them like soaring rockets.

Some time later, Jackie got up to make sure Jennifer was covered and sleeping comfortably. They all needed rest before the long trip to Boston. Bob, too, began to doze off and she began the preparation of their own dinner. Later when she shook him awake, he got up, sniffing the aroma of charbroiled steaks. The small table was spread with her best china, reflecting gold candlelight; and no less a glow was in her eyes. Jackie's eyes. They were so warm as to melt anyone who looked into them—cocker spaniel eyes he called them—soulful brown, green-flecked. And she was delicate at five-three and a hundred-six pounds. All her features were small but in near-perfect proportion: sensitive lips, high cheek bones, smooth olive complexion, a dainty neck, small firm breasts, shapely hips and legs, delicate ankles and feet.

They ate their dinner, lingering over wine. Conversation lulled; their eyes were locked together. This reunion had reached an intensity neither of them had expected. A last hurrah? Bob knew only that their broken engagement was somehow separate and apart from the way she felt about him at this time and at other times; his only course was to be patient until she had worked it all out in her own complex mind. She had indicated a need to see others in the process of sorting out her own feelings. And when he returned from his journey along the Appalachian Trail, she might be gone.

They emptied their wine glasses and by unspoken mutual consent went hand in hand back to the bedroom. She left him briefly to fetch an ice bucket and champagne. She had bought it special—and another bottle for the Boston train station parting—at the supermarket in Ellsworth while she was selecting the steaks. After she had poured, he held the first sip to her lips. She savored the bubbly liquid; after she had swallowed, the moisture still glistened on her lips. She hadn't the chance for a second sip then; he pulled her down fiercely and soon the rockets blazed all over again between brief pauses for more champagne. And again he had dozed off—spent, dazed—and she had shaken him awake. It was 1:30 A.M. Time to dress, carry Jennifer to the car, and head for Boston.

The little Fiesta hummed along the Interstate at an even sixty. He liked his car; Jackie would take good care of it in his absence. He reached over and laid his hand on her knee.

"You're a good driver," he said softly.

"Of course. And you don't have to talk so softly. You know how soundly Jennifer sleeps."

He looked back. Sure enough, the child hadn't even realized she had been taken from her own bed and transferred to the hatch section of the Fiesta, a space crowded somewhat by his suitcase and hiking gear. His eyes lingered as occasional car lights and the brightening dawn illuminated the child's face. It was an angelic face, bathed in soft brown curls. He loved that little girl almost as if she were his own. He could be so damn sentimental and tender at times—something he had to guard against on occasion lest the fatherhood bug bite him for real. He adjusted Jennifer's blanket and turned back.

"She's dead to the world."

"With my hectic life, she's adjusted and come through like a good little trooper," Jackie said.

"She needs stability. Jackie, when I get back from the Trail, I want a firm decision from you. No more dodging around."

"I'm not dodging around, and you know it. But there's so much I've got to work through."

"One fouled-up marriage isn't the end of the road. And everybody goes through the custody thing."

"It's more than that. It goes back a lot longer than that. And we've talked about it a thousand times! Let's not spoil it. Okay? We agreed ___ "

"Okay," he said, and turned on the radio.

They rode along to the tune of James Taylor's *Mill Worker* for a while, and Jackie's head began to nod. He poked her gently in the ribs.

"Wake up."

"I wasn't asleep, dammit!"

"You were nodding. Want me to drive a while?"

"I don't trust you. You're so charged up, you'd put us up a Greyhound's rear end."

It was the truth. He had always been excitable. Since grade school when an idea or a goal seized him, he had wrestled it as he would wrestle a bear. Robert Mountford, Sr., had long voiced a family motto: "There are sitters in the world, and there are doers. The Mountfords are going to be doers!" And so it was.

Yet it was still not entirely believable that Bob was going to walk the Appalachian Trail even though he had read many news stories about his impending trek. Most of the newspapers and many of the TV stations on the east coast had played up the adventure-in-the-making until he had become a sort of regional hero—a receiver of fan mail. It was more attention than one would expect a run-of-the-mill-hiker—even a 2,000-mile hiker—to get.

But this man was no run-of-the-mill hiker; he was the leader of a Cause. His mother's pet project, The Little Red School House, desperately needed funds for expansion. And Bob Mountford about to tackle the Trail, had asked the people of Dover-Foxcroft to sponsor his hike as a sort of walkathon in which they would contribute a minimum of one cent per mile per person and twenty dollars each if he made it all the way. All funds would go to The Little Red School House.

He had used the same idea and approach at The Homestead in Ellsworth, Maine, where he had worked until time to start his six-month jaunt into the wilderness. The Homestead, like The Little Red School

House a private, non-profit institution, was a residential treatment center for adolecents, situated outside the city in peaceful country surroundings. Though partly supported by the State of Maine, it could use more financial resources in helping troubled youngsters to overcome their self-destructive behavior and to adjust to responsible adulthood.

Pledge cards and publicity had gone out from both towns and both schools. Financial pledges, beginning moderately, had gone as high as twenty cents a mile. His excitement mounting, Bob hoped that the twin projects would gain momentum as he walked from Georgia to Maine and as the media kept the public abreast of his progress.

It was all very heady, and the undertaking had become a sort of new weight upon his back even before he had set foot on the Appalachian Trail.

"I've got to have some coffee." Jackie broke his reverie.

"Okay, but why're you sleepy? I feel great!"

She gave him a sheepish grin.

"Some people give and others take, I guess."

"You *are* a sweetie." He squeezed her knee until she flinched. "I'll throw in doughnuts and eggs if that's what it takes."

"Just coffee. Are we getting there?"

He lit a cigarette and looked out into the brightening dawn and oriented himself.

"Thirty or forty miles more. There should be a restaurant turnoff just ahead."

Bob brought coffee to the car since they couldn't leave Jennifer alone, and it revived them. Travel was slower as they approached the city. Fog, rolling inland from Massachusetts Bay, lowered visibility. Bob looked at his watch. They had time to spare. The fog hung with them until South Station loomed out of the mist, a dirty greyish brown, like some gigantic boulder reaching through the clouds. Parking room was plentiful since they had beaten the first big wave of commuters.

While Jackie began to arouse Jennifer gently, he got out and felt the first blast of chill air. The moisture-laden fog and the March breeze coming from the bay penetrated like a splash of ice water. It still felt like February. Georgia suddenly had more appeal than ever. Little wonder most hikers walked from south to north. Going with the spring season made a lot of sense. A second icy gust hit him, and he let out a Tarzan yell. Jackie cracked open the car door:

"My God! Do you want to wake all of Boston?"

"They ought to be up anyway—seeing me off."

"Jennifer and I will have to do—and you scared the wits out of her. She's not very wide awake yet."

Jackie cuddled the child in the front seat, and Bob removed his suitcase and hiking gear. He swung the backpack over his shoulder, interlacing his arms as if he were beginning the hike then and there. Next, he strung his hiking boots over a post of the pack, grabbed the suitcase in his left hand,

and reached for his walking stick with the other. He wasn't about to leave that walking stick. He had cut it himself in the Maine woods. It was not only his trail stick—solid hardwood; it was going to be his defense against the damnable dogs and timber rattlers that posed a threat to every hiker on the Appalachian Trail. He ambled off to check his belongings while Jackie got Jennifer dressed and sociable.

Inside the station there were more waiting passengers than he had expected to see. He turned his backpack and suitcase over to a lethargic baggage handler who checked them through without a word; then, holding his walking stick, he headed back toward the waiting area. South Station so early in the morning had the feel of a mausoleum and the look of a medieval cathedral: vaulted ceilings, echoing walls, drab coloring. It smelled of antiquity and played host to pigeons jetting through the high places. He looked up at a greyish white bird making a circle and remembered an old two-bird cartoon: "I'm going to put all on Princeton." He chuckled at that, drawing a strange look from a ragged old man going by. It suddenly occurred to him that he looked little better in his wrinkled brown corduroys, Chuck Roast jacket, and scuffed Dexter Casuals.

The waiting area looked like an auction room full of worn church pews. Instead of sitting down, he twirled his stick like a baton. Maybe it would work. He could knock off the wild dogs as if they had stuck their noses into a whirling fan, make them go away, or whack their tails off. Grampy Rideout—his mother's father who now lived in a trailer behind the Mountford home in Dover-Foxcroft—had told him as a child that to cut a dog's tail off would kill it.

"No, Grampy," Bob had argued, "it won't. Haven't you ever seen a bobtailed dog?"

"Sure it will, Bobby. Sure it will—if you cut the dog's tail off behind its ears!" Grampy Rideout was like that. Grampy would've come along on the Appalachian Trail at the drop of a hat even though he was seventy-three.

Jackie and Jennifer headed across the dirty, drab floor toward him. Jennifer, wide awake now, sprinted ahead, and he laid his stick down and prepared to catch her on the run as he often did. Jackie was grinning and brown-bagging the bottle of champagne she had brought from home. In the light she didn't look much better than he. She, too, had on faded corduroys, a cotton print shirt, and a green windbreaker as worn as his own. He hoisted Jennifer and gave her a squeeze.

"Not too hard," Jackie teased. "Let me take her to the bathroom first."

A few commuters started to come in. They looked almost as dour as the baggage clerks, and a few were still yawning. He felt guilty somehow watching them. Today was simply a routine—and possibly dull—day for them. In a few days he would be atop Springer Mount, christening his walking stick in soft Georgia soil and heralding, witnessing, smelling, feeling the sweet glorious spring. He wanted to give the Tarzan squall. He wanted them to feel what he was feeling.

Jackie and Jennifer came back. Jackie was minus the brown bag, but she had something wrapped in her jacket.

"We'd better check this out in a hurry," she said mischievously. "The commuters will be coming in for real in a few minutes."

Her soft eyes were aglow as she inched the neck of the bottle out of the coat-nest. Still standing, he twisted wire, foil, and plastic cap free, and the pop resounded into the high ceiling and echoed back. As a dozen heads turned, Jackie and Bob feigned innocence, shoving the bottle out of sight. Jennifer soon betrayed them by playing pool with the cap and Bob's walking stick. As long as she didn't play golf, they were safe. When inquisitive eyes had turned back to newspapers, he took a long swig. Then Jackie. Then Bob. Then Jackie began to giggle. He pushed her playfully back to a bench. When next they turned the bottle up, he saw a policeman casting a suspicious eye at them.

"Dammit, why didn't you think of coffee cups?" he playfully groaned out of the side of his mouth.

"I can go and try to find some."

"No, it's more fun this way."

Jackie giggled again like a schoolgirl—and Jackie didn't giggle. She was thirty-three years old. Both were acting like sophomores. With the way clear again, he chugalugged a quick one and almost choked. This time Jackie laughed with that same warped sense of humor he had come to know well. He could see the headlines now: "Trail Hiker Chokes to Death on Champagne Before Leaving South Station: All For Naught." Jennifer had cueballed the cap halfway across the waiting room floor. He went to turn her around.

"Why we here, Bobby?" she asked. "Where you goin' on th' train?"

"To Alabama. And then to Georgia. And then take a long walk in the woods."

"You comin' back?"

"Of course, I'm coming back. You don't think I'd leave *you*, do you?"

"I don't want you go, Bobby. I want you stay here."

Jackie was half-reclining, propped up by an elbow. On empty stomachs both were feeling the alcohol.

"Save some for me," he said, reaching for the coat.

"I could lie right here and sleep for a week."

"Well, don't. And you and Jenny get a good breakfast after I'm gone. And lots of black coffee."

"I'm not drunk. Just feelin' sooo good. Soooo lovin'."

"I could have got Pullman quarters if they had such things on the Amtrak," he said, taking another swallow.

"How I wish . . . !"

"I still think you could have arranged it and gone with me. Don't say I didn't ask you. Think of the fun you'll be missing."

"You know I couldn't. My new job. No earned vacation yet. No extra money. But I will definitely ride down with your parents when they rendezvous with you at Easter. Bob, you never did tell me why you asked Susan Ramsay to join you on the trail."

"She's just a friend and co-worker. You know that. Besides, several of my other co-workers are joining me on the trail at various points. Neal and Sandy are going to be a week behind me, going the full distance. Some of the others are going to hook up when I get to New Hampshire."

Jackie reached for the rolled-up coat.

"You're sure it's just a friendship—Susan?"

"That's what I said. Besides, aren't you the one who wanted a little more rope? 'Maybe I need to see others—to get a new perspective,' I believe you said?"

"Yes, I guess I did."

The bottle was almost empty. He took a final swallow and let Jackie kill the rest. She had grown silent and more sleepy-looking. He was getting a little intoxicated himself. He stood up to help shake it.

The whole area was getting a big influx of commuters, and too many of them were finding the aftermath of the champagne party highly interesting. Jennifer had poked her cueball all the way back nearly to their bench. Without warning she took a swing at the bottle cap and missed, and the arch of the stick missed the nose of a smartly dressed businesman by the slightest hair. The look he gave them would have roasted chestnuts. Jackie grabbed the stick and handed it to Bob.

When the train was called, she admonished him to have something to eat on board.

"If you had really been thoughtful," he said, "you'd have packed me a little ham on rye, some boiled eggs and pickles, and a banana or two."

"Haven't I always been thoughtful?" She dropped it.

"Yes, always. My thoughtful Jacqueline." He kissed her suddenly on the bridge of the nose.

Although Jacqueline was her proper name, he used it only at times of serious endearment or when he chastened her for something. Which was it this time? She wondered. All was not right between them. She was sending him away with some fear in his heart—some uncertainty that she honestly couldn't assuage at the moment. She needed time. And Bob Mountford, she believed, had deep-seated fears about many things that he tried to conceal from even those nearest and dearest to him. She knew this, and he knew that she knew it, and maybe that was part of the undertone in his voice. Perhaps he thought she wouldn't be around when he got back.

She wrapped her arm about his waist as they walked toward the platform. He finally encircled her waist with one arm and with the other hand clacked his walking stick on the floor like an old man. With Jennifer in tow in Jackie's other hand and with all of them swaying slightly, they must have looked like a family out of Boston's slums. They walked slowly, jostled now and then by rushing commuters. Strangely, Jackie felt her eyes start to mist. She would see him in six months. What was the big deal?

At trainside, he kissed Jennifer first and hoisted her high one more time.

14

He turned to Jackie and kissed her hard and long. When he finished, she responded in like manner. His bristly mustache—nearly a walrus except that he had clipped the corners severely—sanded her nose and upper lip, and his beer belly prevented her from snuggling as close as she wanted to be. He was badly overweight, but the Appalachian Trail was going to cure that. She backed away and gave the bulge a maternal pat. He put a finger over her lips.

"No snide remarks. I told you I'd take it off. Going from a hundred-ninety down to one-seventy."

"Don't overdo it. I don't want you coming back a skeleton." Playfully she tugged at his ear with the miniature earring in it. "Pawn your gold if you run out of money—or call me, and if I've got it, I'll send you some."

"I'll make it. Can always hire myself out to some moonshiner if need be."

He started to board, fingering the earring as she had done. That symbolic earring. How he wished ole Sean Stitham could be going with him on the Trail! Sean was the best friend he had—going all the way back to their D-F Academy days. And the earring had been his and Sean's mutual idea. Sean would be graduating in May from med school at Vermont University. Hence, Bob's ear had been a practice run. But more importantly, the gold object had been his and Sean's anti-macho statement. A sort of private joke between them. And Sean had thought the decoration would help Bob stand out on the trail.

When he had seated himself and positioned his walking stick at his knees, Jackie was holding Jennifer up to the window. The child threw him a kiss, and he threw one back. Jackie threw one too, and he returned it with some foreboding. As the train began to move, he relaxed and let his head fall back on the headrest, savoring the image of Jackie and Jennifer, little knowing that he would never see them or his beloved Maine again.

CHAPTER II

Before they left Boston, Jackie treated Jennifer and herself to a hot breakfast—scrambled eggs and link sausage—and for herself lots of black coffee. Wine made her so laid back—so peaceful with the world. Maybe that was good medicine. She had decided to continue south on I-91 and visit her parents in Providence before heading back to Maine. Going home was not always a happy affair. Old conflicts had a way of surfacing at the wrong times. But her middle-class parents needed her support now more than ever. Her mother had suffered a stroke, and her father, a machinist, was ill prepared to work long hours and maintain a household with a sick woman.

She was back on the interstate before realizing she hadn't called the Mountfords to tell them that Bob was on the train and headed south. Lord, the love in that big old Dover-Foxcroft house! On every wall were photographs of ones loved and cherished. There were photos of Bob and his two brothers and two sisters in every step of development. And pictures of Bob Senior and Mim in every stage of their lives, including candid shots at conventions or on vacation and photos of parents, grandparents, friends of today and yesteryear. All that, and a constant aura of warmth, concern, genuine zest for life. Jackie loved Bob Senior and Mim Mountford with a special tenderness, and she believed that they returned that love. Still, the broken engagement had left them puzzled; and it was not the kind of thing that Jackie—or perhaps even Bob Junior—could satisfactorily explain.

Jennifer rose from the back seat and tugged at her mother's hair.

"Mommy, is Big Bob coming back? I miss him."

"Of course, he's coming back, Honey. You'll be five by then. Maybe he'll bring you a birthday present from down south. Lie back down and sleep. We're going to see your grammy and grandpa Roy before we go home."

She had not even liked Bob Mountford at first. She had met him when he worked at the Department of Human Services in Ellsworth, where she too had just landed a place in May of '79. The Department was housed in an old peach-colored boathouse, on the Union River, hardly qualifying as executive quarters of the first rank. Nevertheless, she had been excited, it was her first full-time job since 1975.

Bob Mountford had hardly made her feel welcome. In those first days at work when she had sought his advice, he had given it in a strictly professional way, but there was a chilliness in his manner as if he felt himself intellectually superior. But he was obviously top flight in his job as a Children's Service Counselor. In working with abused children and their parents or guardians, Bob could meet them on any level, and talk the same language. And he usually drew immediate respect from them.

For two weeks after she had begun work, there seemed to be no thaw in the cool distance he kept. Many times when she would ask a legitimate question, Bob would say smartly, "Go ask Paul," meaning Paul Labun, the Director of Children's Services, whose office was in the same building. A graduate of St. Francis Xavier, Paul was a good-looking guy of small stature, relatively easy-going in most situations. He seemed almost to enjoy seeing her batted back and forth between himself and Bob.

Days later Bob had nearly gone to sleep at the wheel of his car and rear-ended a dump truck. The car was totaled, and he was taken to the local hospital for repairs. When Jackie saw him on his first appearance at the office, he was somebody else again: foot in a cast, eyebrow and face cut, and a steady groaning as if every bone in his body had been broken. And before Jackie had gotten used to his appearance, Paul took him to Bangor, where his address, the office was told, would be in care of somebody named Joanne Irace until he could get in touch with his parents and borrow a family car.

Jackie was to learn later that Joanne Irace had been Bob's friend during his University of Maine days.

When he came back to work, still on crutches, Jackie found herself chauffeuring her ranking co-worker about the area in the line of official duty. He was less aloof now and her respect for his skill and professionalism turned into admiration as side by side they worked with every facet of human degradation: incest, child-beating, neglect, heart-rendering hunger, filthy living conditions, desertion, drugs, child prostitution, alcoholism, torture—the whole gamut. Sometimes she would almost weep at Bob's tenderness with children—and adults too—when all seemed hopeless for them.

She began to feel a growing personal warmth for him. She wrestled with this feeling because she was still married though as far as she was concerned her marriage to Bob Hilton had been dead for more than a year. Getting the job at Human Services had been the beginning of her attempt to earn needed money and rescue her self-respect. She had worked here and there at substitute teaching, waitressing, clerking since her marriage to Hilton in September of 1975, but she had never made full use of her degree in psychology and elementary education from Rhode Island College or her M. Ed. from Boston College. Now life itself had new meaning. She bounded out of bed each morning with fresh enthusiasm.

Regarding Bob Hilton and herself, marriage had ruined a once-beautiful relationship. He had been so totally different during the early days. They had taken some cross-country camping trips, had shared countless unforgettable experiences. Hilton had been loving, attentive and undemanding and at the time appeared to have it all together. His background was New Jersey upper middle class, his parents liberal Unitarians, and she had seen in him someone to look up to. But *her* family had had a hand in spoiling it all.

Now, as she drove down the Interstate to Providence, that old feeling of bitterness began to come back more strongly. Her family had been all too conscious of the two previous living-together relationships she had had before Hilton. It was time she settled down, they said, and had a family.

Jackie slowed the car momentarily and looked back at her daughter, peacefully asleep. How she loved that smart little urchin! Jennifer was the one really good thing that had come from the ill-fated marriage.

After her divorce from Hilton, she and Bob Mountford had taken positions at The Homestead Project in Ellsworth.

Bob rented a house in Surrey in early June of 1980, not far from their work, and she and Jennifer moved in permanently with him. It was a glorious honeymoon cottage, a remodeled garage that had once been a carriage house to a larger estate but surrounded by natural beauty: woods, a lake, fields of blooming spring flowers. Jennifer loved boating on the lake and roaming the fields, and Bob became the model surrogate father. They were a happy family at last.

A tractor-trailer load of canoes came up from behind her, veering to the passing lane, and went barrelling down the interstate. Jennifer stirred, roused by the noise, then fell back into peaceful slumber. The canoes reminded Jackie of their first family purchase during those early days at Surrey. They had bought their own canoe—a good quality brand of tough, treated fiberglass.

The new canoe had received a lot of bumps and scratches in a hurry. Their first big trip was a ten-day journey down the Allagash River. It was an unforgettable experience, overwhelming with awesomely beautiful clouds set in an azure sky, cooking over a popping, aromatic open fire on the riverbank, sleeping in Bob's arms beneath tall spruce trees.

An unforgettable adventure! It had given her and Bob more than they had ever had before: ten days of intimacy in the silence and serenity of the wilds when they had become truly one, not only in a spiritual sense but in a physical sense totally dependent upon each other. They had been alone in the world to love and laugh and face real danger. All this had been enough, but a few days later she, Bob, and Andy (Bob's friend from The Homestead) had gone out near Bangor for a rock climb up Chick Hill. It was a tough ascent—five or six hours of it. Exhausted at the top, but exhilarated to near intoxication, Bob had called out before God and everybody: "Marry me, Jackie; marry me, my sweet Jacqueline!" The echo of his deep voice drifted into infinity, and she wasn't sure of the seriousness of the proposal in such a place, especially in the presence of a third party. Afterward, the three of them went eating, drinking, and dancing at the Stable Inn. They stuffed themselves, practically floating with imported beer, and both men danced her breathless. Again with deadly seriousness Bob proposed.

That night as she lay in his arms, she wrestled with this dilemma: she loved him, but would it all be spoiled again? She wasn't really ready for marriage. She cared about her former husband and his welfare. A quick remarriage on her part would be just one more blow to his battered psyche.

There were other reasons for hesitation. Was Bob Mountford really ready for the confinement of marriage? She knew deep in her heart that *she* was not. Bob had experienced two great loves in his life; she was number two. First had been Joanne Irace. And, Jackie believed, Bob still loved Joanne.

Jackie stalled. Bob became even more loving and considerate; he endeared himself more every day to Jennifer. The pressure became unbearable. She *had* accepted his proposal with a nagging fear and uncertainty in her heart but with a measure of joy as well.

The time they had chosen to announce the engagement to his family was Thanksgiving weekend; it was no ordinary holiday for the Mountfords since it was to be celebrated in Texas. Nearly all of the children had told their parents in advance that getting together for Christmas was out of the picture. Bob Senior and Mim and two of their children had come up with the idea of a combined Thanksgiving-Christmas get-together at the homes of their second eldest son, Scott Michael and his wife-to-be Gail, and second eldest daughter, Catherine Mountford Lykins and husband Tom. Both couples lived in Houston. The other two Mountford children, Carolyn Mountford Carver, with her husband Dan, and Steve Mountford, single, Orlando, Florida, would join Bob Senior, Mim, Bob Junior, and Jackie in Houston—a family reunion if ever there was one.

Bob Senior and Mim, Jackie had learned, urgently wanted this reunion. It was more than simply a desire to share family love and togetherness. Bob Senior voiced loudly his opinion: they all needed more of the sustaining power that members of families provided one another.

Bob Senior had cut a small Maine spruce for the Christmas tree. With the Mountfords in Houston and gift packages under the tree, it was the most joyous and high-spirited of celebrations, first at one home and then at the other where the combined guests had been parceled out. There was a night on the town; there was a trip for Grandpa and Grandma with the Lykins children to the zoological park; and finally there was a family gathering whose impact no one had anticipated—and no one now would ever forget.

Before leaving Dover-Foxcroft, Bob Senior had called several times to Houston, seeking a special kind of church in which his whole clan could find instant refuge and spiritual renewal as a culmination of their time together. The spiritual lives of his children had gone awry, he felt, and he spoke of this to them tactfully, sensitively as a loving and understanding father. They had all been reared in the Episcopal church, and more recently, after a personal "born-again" experience, he had become active in the charismatic Episcopal movement—those of the faith with a more fundamentalist leaning. He was now a lay reader in the church, having been licensed by the district Bishop. Calling Houston, he had tracked down the location of The Church of the Redeemer; and here he now took his entire clan. It was a large church in an older section of south Houston, a working-class area whose people obviously took pride in their neighborhood. The building and the grounds were well kept. The ivory-greyish masonry structure with an ancient-looking belltower presented a facade of welcome with a massive arch-in-relief within which was a large Christian cross. If Jackie and Bob's brothers and sisters had not known that the Church was charismatic in philosophy, they soon found out. No sooner had they approached the great double doors than they were met and lovingly embraced in welcome by numerous church members. Instant love! At first it was strange, if not chilling, to be so held by strangers, Jackie had thought. Soon, however, that sincerely intended warmth and welcome began to eddy through her as she observed that it did through them all. Bob Senior and Mim were smiling with an understanding that Jackie knew she and the others did not yet fully share. The more Jackie watched Bob Senior, the more she realized his plans were working to his satisfaction.

Once inside the church she felt strangely at home and felt that the others did, too. Bob held her hand; she could feel warmth and the race of his pulse. The sanctuary was not quite full, but already some quality of reverence and worship had taken over. Behind the altar was a massive painting of Jesus Ascending; below Him encircling the ground under Him, there were mixed races of people looking upward. The choir sang. A minister began to speak, and another minister stood at his side, translating into Spanish for the mixed audience.

Jackie followed the sermon for a few minutes before, consciously or unconsciously, blocking it out. Some hint of panic within her began to do battle with the earlier peace. In a moment she felt tears trickle down her cheek. She looked at Bob, not totally certain of how he was responding; then side glances revealed that they all had begun to feel something that moved them deeply.

She was glad when the service was concluding. Something in her was collapsing; the very walls seemed close and she had the urge to run down the aisle to sunlit freedom. And Bob was silent. Vaguely—perhaps from Mim or Bob Senior—she remembered something about a strange spiritual experience Bob had undergone while at the University of Maine with Joanne Irace, and she could see in his eyes that he had been remembering something of great importance. But then Jackie wanted only to get out of the church and to get away from the arms that were more crushing on departure than they had been on entry.

As all of them prepared to drive to a restaurant for Sunday lunch, almost nothing was said. Something had happened. Jackie couldn't quite explain what it was, but all of them—all but the grandchildren— had been deeply shaken. At the restaurant they seemed submerged in some need for self-examination. Jackie's eyes started to spill over again. Nothing in her Catholic upbringing had prepared her for this day. Before the day was over and the time came to drive from Texas back to Maine, the old fears began to return. She wasn't ready for marriage again. The old hurts needed more healing. She didn't mention any of this to Bob, but all the way from Texas to Maine she wrestled with it.

"Mommy, I'm thirsty." Jennifer suddenly broke the reverie.

Jackie looked at her watch.

"Can you hold out thirty more minutes, Honey? We'll soon be at Grandma's."

"If you hurry ___ "

"Crawl over and sit with me. We'll turn on the radio and make the time go faster."

They had been back at Surrey for a week when she told Bob she couldn't go through with the marriage. At first he was surprised and hurt and then angry and bitter. And a time or two she feared him in a physical sense. She was a mouse under him; one squash of his mighty paw ___ Finally, he accused her of dishonesty and of leading him on, toying with his feelings.

In early December Bob had decided to split. He got an apartment in Bangor which he shared with two University of Maine students. Working with him at The Homestead became awkward; but luckily another position she had applied for earlier was opening up. Later in December, she resigned from The Homestead and prepared to move to Livemore Falls to become guidance counselor at the junior high school. Temporarily, she would live with a cousin while she was looking for her own place.

She and Bob continued to see each other but less frequently. Nevertheless, Bob—and the elder Mountfords—invited her to Dover-Foxcroft for the week before Christmas. There was some hesitancy in accepting the invitation, but she felt that the Mountfords perhaps expected some explanation from her about the broken engagement. It turned out to be a pleasant interlude except that in the Mountford household she and Bob were not allowed to share the same room. The day before Christmas she left to pick up Jennifer at Bob Hilton's apartment in Ellsworth and to go on to Rhode Island for Christmas with her own parents. By December 30 she and Jennifer were back in Ellsworth, where Jennifer was again left with her father so that father and daughter might spend New Year's week with his parents. Afterwards, Jackie had driven back to Dover-Foxcroft as she had promised earlier. The Mountfords' loving hospitality never wavered, no matter who or how many had invaded the big old house with the wood stove in the kitchen to which everybody seemed ultimately to be drawn.

A surprise awaited her arrival: Susan Ramsay from The Homestead had also become a houseguest. Was this of Bob's way of sending a message or just a gesture of friendship? Jackie neither saw nor sensed anything to indicate it was more than a friendship. In any event the three of them began to make the rounds of New Year's Eve parties. First they had gone to a party at the home of Sean Stitham's brother and then to another Stithams' friend's house; then next day they had gone to another, and still another, until she was food-logged, booze-logged and people-logged. On January 2 the three of them had gone to Squaw Mountain for cross country skiing. It was a great day of head-clearing exercise, topped off around the resort bar during which they had played guitars, sung the old songs, drunk in the warmth of fire and human personality. Bob Mountford was in heaven in the presence of good friends, good food, and good drink.

But now at Dover-Foxcroft Jackie had the feeling that maybe she didn't belong anymore. Bob still didn't understand her hangups. His frustrations sometimes culminated in yelling sessions during their few private moments. At times he overpowered her, both physically and emotionally. Her problems were only imagined he would insist and she wondered whether they were. But a new element had been introduced: just how did Susan Ramsay fit into all this? Never mind. Jackie, too, had felt the need lately to see other men—to sort it all out from a new perspective. To tell the truth, Bob Mountford had not filled all the voids in her life; and she had long suspected the special place in his heart that Joanne Irace occupied.

For the remainder of January '81, she and Bob saw little of each other. On January 22 Bob's grandmother Rideout, Mim's mother, died. Although Bob had always been much closer to his grandfather—his grandmother at age 73 still being too much the "don't-do-this, don't-do-that" type—he nevertheless suffered deep remorse over the death, and Jackie went back to Dover-Foxcroft a week later to console him.

The consolation session turned into renewed passion. Having been forbidden to occupy the same bed with Jackie at the Mountford home, Bob rented a hotel room. He there shed latent tears over the death of his grandmother. Still, these quiet, private moments with Jackie had been a release for him and had fanned the fading fire of their own relationship. Their lovemaking had been beautiful, unusually satisfying. Jackie had gone back to Livermore Falls feeling that she had reached another new beginning, or, at least, a different plateau.

In February, Bob came down and helped her move into her new apartment. During March they were together almost every weekend. There were shopping trips to Eastern Mountain Sports in Lewiston for the Appalachian Trail hike that Bob had been planning for nearly a year with side trips for maps, books and hard-to-find supplies like the small canisters of LP gas for Bob's trail-sized cooking stove. Finally the fleeting days of March had passed in a rush of excitement and last-minute planning for the trail launch. Nothing was left undone except Jackie and Bob themselves.

When they pulled up to the modest frame house of her parents, Jackie noticed that it needed painting, and winter's leaves had come to nest in deep rows against the sides and the front. There was something old and drab-looking about the place; yet the structure was not that ancient. Maybe it was her own mood settling in. She braced herself and got out of the car. With Jennifer's hand in hers, she paused halfway up the walk. She stiffened her spine and mentally repeated the words: patience, restraint, kindness, love. At the door she remembered also to call the Mountfords in Dover-Foxcroft and tell them that all was go.

CHAPTER III

The train rolled into the Anniston, Alabama, station shortly after 11:00 A.M., and Bob found Jane and Leonard Jones waiting to greet him. Jane, his mother's sister, was a top-flight nurse, who occasionally contributed to her professional journals; she could juggle many tasks with equal skill. Leonard was a big guy, six-three, two hundred pounds, dwarfing his wife by three-quarters of a foot.

Bob dropped his gear, gave his attractive, brown-haired aunt a bear hug, and reached for Leonard's meaty hand. Except for a bald spot beaming through Leonard's black hair, his uncle still maintained the look of young manhood and athletic fitness.

"You didn't have to squeeze the breath out of me!" Jane exclaimed.

"He's trying to show you what good shape he's in for the Trail," Leonard said.

"Right on!" Bob agreed. "I'm cocked and ready. See my walking stick? Cut it myself out near Sebec Lake."

"How could we miss?" Jane chuckled. "You look as if you're ready to hit the trail right now." Her eyes focused on his earring, but she said nothing.

"Not quite," Bob said. "I'm getting the sniffles; I'll need one of Leonard's thick charbroiled steaks to get myself in top form."

The banter was easy as the three of them walked out into the warm Alabama sun. Leonard helped load the gear into the Chevy Caprice, and they were off to Gadsden proper and to Jane and Leonard's spacious, stone-and-wood home atop a mountain overlooking the city.

After lunch on the patio in the warm Alabama sun, Bob began to feel travel fatigue and sacked out. The next thing he knew, his cousin Len Junior was pouncing on him. He had slept until dinner time.

"Easy on the ribs, Lenny! I may have to wrestle a bear."

At a big sixteen, Lenny was pretty tough in his own right.

"You look like a bear yourself. Where'd that soup-strainer come from?"

"Oh, the mustache. I didn't have that before, did I?" Bob sat up, stretched, smoothed the long hairs under his nose, brushed back the hair that always tumbled over his head like an unruly mop. "You ain't seen nothin' yet. I'm going to grow a full beard on the Trail. I'll probably look

24

like a long-lost Paul Bunyan by the time I walk back to Maine."

"Wish I was going with you. School is dull as last year's news."

"Come up to Maine next summer, and we'll take a canoe trip."

Lenny's eyes brightened. "It'd have to be before the last of August. Football practice starts early."

Jane called, and Bob padded barefoot to the kitchen. She was prettily dressed in a fuchsia peasant tunic and blue slacks. Like his mother, she had big brown eyes. Even at forty-two she was still a striking woman.

"I didn't know this was a dress-up affair," Bob said. "Guess I'd better get out of these jeans and get some shoes on."

"Forget it.

Jane handed him a drink, and he wandered out to the patio where Len was turning the steaks. Bob felt the cold of winter in the patio stones. He sat down and propped his bare feet on the railing.

"You took me at my word, didn't you? Jeez, I didn't mean to write my own menu."

"We gotta do our part to put the red blood cells in you." Len chuckled. "What is that stuff you hikers subsist off of? Gork, or some such mixture?"

"GORP—it means a mixture of Grains, Oats, Raisins, Proteins."

"You already loaded down with the stuff? How you going to get your supplies?"

"I've got my initial supply with me. Mom and Dad are sending me mail drops all along the route. We've got it timed according to my needs and daily progress. I go off the Trail at predetermined post offices."

They moved inside to eat. It was two days short of April first, and the night air was chilly.

After dinner, Bob enlisted Lenny's help, and the two of them spread his supplies around the spacious living room floor for checking and sorting. With Leonard and Jane observing, the scene took on the look of Christmas morning around the Yuletide tree. Jane left to get two small packages.

"Our contribution," she said with a grin. "Call it our bon voyage present."

Bob unwrapped them. "A pedometer! A snake-bike kit! Thanks! Now I can calculate how fast the snakes are chasing me? And if the reptiles win the race, then I use the second gift ___ right?"

"We hope you don't need that gift," Leonard said, "but just in case ___ "

"Any snake that bit Bob would probably die from hydrophobia," Lenny quipped.

"Careful, Cousin," Bob warned. "I may cancel that trip down the St. John River I promised you for next summer!"

Bob sorted through the smaller items and withdrew a detailed sketch of his backpack. It was numbered from one to nine, each figure designating a section of the pack into which specific items would be placed.

"This way, I'll always know exactly where things are located. Won't have to unpack everything to find a given item," Bob explained.

"Are you always so meticulous?" Jane said.

"My critics say so. I'm supposed to drive people nuts about such things."

Bob invited them all closer to view his diagram. Into area No. 1 would go food, pots, cooking stove, personal items, camp moccasins, pile coat, soap, hat and gloves. Area No. 2 would contain extra outer and under clothes, socks, rain suit, gaiters, bandanas; area No. 3, journal, headlamp, writing paper, ball point pens, and spare bulbs and batteries for the flashlight; area No. 4, maps and guidebook, spare plastic bags; area No. 5, two 1-qt. water bottles, spoon, pot holder; area No. 6, two cans of cooking fuel for the stove, and related items; area No. 7, bottle of vitamin C and one of multivitamins, insect spray, can opener, safety pins, cigarette lighter and extra book matches; area No. 8, medicinal tape, first aid kit, candles, extra camera film, thread and needles; area No. 9, sleeping bag, pad, tent, ground cloth, length of rope, sierra cup, and compass.

Lenny handed over each item Bob called for in the packing. Each was already a precious possession with a history. Jackie had trudged with him to a dozen places in Maine, searching out the brands he wanted. He had bought most items at Eastern Mountain Sports in Lewiston; but he had wanted custom-made hiking boots, and these he had purchased at Winterport Boot Shop. He had purchased a Camp Trails backpack, a Pocket Hotel tent, a Buck Knife, a Silva compass and a Chuck Roast jacket. He had confidence in all his gear.

The living room floor began to clear. He saved his Bible until last in order to pack it for easy access. He leafed through it a moment.

"Want to hear my first hiking verses?" he asked.

"Just don't pass the collection plate afterwards," Lenny said.

"Don't be irreverent!" Jane scolded.

"Read on, Preacher Bob," Leonard said.

Bob laughed. "O ye of little faith. Would you believe that my aptitude tests at the time I entered Maine U. showed that I was well suited to the ministry? Social work was second. Okay, here's my first hiking verses." He turned to Isaiah 55:12 and read: "For Ye shall go out with joy, and be led forth with peace: the mountains and the hills shall break forth before you into singing, and all the trees of the field shall clap their hands."

They were all quiet for a moment, obviously as moved by the ancient, beautiful words as he had been after searching out and reading them for the first time himself. He closed the Book and packed it away.

"Now, Auntie, if you'll hold on to this old suitcase and the clothes I don't need until Mom and Dad come down at Easter, I'll be all set."

"They'll stop somewhere along the way and meet you near the Trail? Is that the plan?" Jane asked.

"Yes, and Jackie's coming with them. She's going to hike with me for a few days. It'll probably be somewhere in Tennessee. I'll have to come off the Trail and call to set it up."

It was Tuesday, March 31. The sky was clear and the most vivid blue he could remember. The temperature was already in the 60s as he stepped out on the porch to tell Jane and Lenny goodbye.

Jane hugged him tightly.

"You did pack bandaids and toilet paper?" she asked like a mother hen.

"Always the nurse, aren't you, Auntie! Yes, I've got all the little comforts of home tucked away." He kissed her cheek.

Bob shot out a quick hand to Lenny's shoulder.

"Hang in there, Sport, and don't forget our plans for next summer. You'll like riding the rapids of the St. John's."

"I won't forget. See ya. Don't do anything stupid ___ " Lenny's voice trailed off.

Later, when he and Leonard headed out of town toward the Georgia border, Bob noticed on a bank sign that the thermometer had climbed nearly to seventy degrees. It was a good omen. God and the whole world were smiling on him. It was only thirty miles or so to the border, and scarcely another fifty or sixty to his take-off point. He was chain-smoking and he felt himself leaning forward with every passing mile. He could sense Leonard watching him from the corner of his eye.

"You can crawl out on the hood, but I don't think it'll get you any farther faster," Leonard said.

Bob leaned back and took a deep drag on his cigarette.

"I still can't believe it," he said. "It's so damned unreal."

Leonard turned off the highway into Amicalola State Park and headed toward the Visitors Center, where a large number of tourists and hikers had already gathered. Late March and early April were popular times to begin the jaunt into the wilderness. Bob knew, however, that for every thousand hikers who began the Trail, nine hundred would give up after a few score miles, and the remaining one-hundred out of the number would go most—or all—of the way. He would be among the successful ten-percent. Of that there was no doubt.

He spent a brief time at the Visitors Center, checking posted maps and info bulletins, seeking any late news about Trail happenings. Once they were back in the car, Leonard drove to the closest vantage point for Bob's entry onto the Trail. It was 10:30. Bob jumped out of the car as if it were aflame. In the distance the little he could see of Amicalola Falls made it look formidable indeed. The rock cliffs looked as if they were stairsteps into the heavens. In spite of the warm weather, the trees had no leaves yet, and the mountainous terrain appeared stark.

Leonard was soon at his side.

"Wanna forget the whole thing?"

"No way, man. No way. It's calling me already. Help me with my pack."

Leonard wanted to wait and watch Bob's ascent from a distant high point. They agreed that Leonard should drive up the mountain and hit the Frosty Mountain Fire Road shown on the map. It was five miles or so away, and Leonard would have a two-and-a-half-hour wait for Bob's appearance out of the trees, but he insisted.

"Let business wait," he said. "I don't see this kind of thing every day."

Bob adjusted the fit of his hiking boots and stood up. Leonard helped him thread arms into the backpack. When that, too, was adjusted to his liking, Bob arched his back and checked the balance. He felt the way he supposed an ancient gladiator ready for battle might have felt, and his walking stick was his spear.

"Well, Unc, I'm off to the wilds! Thanks for everything."

"Take care, Bob, and good luck. Don't forget to sign in on the register."

"What do you think I am—some greenhorn?"

"Just thought you might be a little excited. Take it easy, now. Don't overdo it. I'll be watching for you."

"One more thing: I won't need *these* any more." Bob tossed the pack of cigarettes onto the car seat.

"You mean it, huh? You put me to shame," Leonard said.

"Yep. See you on the mountain."

Leonard pulled off; and after a few moments of orientation, and emotional conditioning, Bob took his first steps. There were hikers in front and behind him, their blue, orange, yellow, and sundry colors of backpacks standing out vividly against the nearly colorless terrain. A large number of tourists and others cheered the hikers onward. It was a good beginning.

The old adrenalin was already pumping. Bob could feel the shock and surge of it infiltrate his whole system. It was the driving force of a soldier in battle, the real power of an athlete on the fourth down with two yards to goal, the nectar that turned ordinary men into supermen.

The new boots felt good and clung effectively to the well-trodden soil and sharp rocks, and indeed the trailway was as straight-up as it looked. On a firm ledge he stopped to readjust the backpack harness. It was tight. An uphill pull flexed his back and stomach muscles and pushed uncomfortably against the confinement. He took the opportunity to rid himself of one more thing: his blood-pressure pills. Walking toward a wet-weather branch, he tossed the container and saw it splash. Somewhere farther along, he supposed, the pills would wash out into the Atlantic. Let the blood pressure of the sharks be lowered. The Appalachian Trail would be all the medicine he needed.

As he walked upward, it occurred to him that he was not really walking alone. There were countless people who had had a part in this journey: with the train ticket from his mom and dad; the calls from his sister, Carolyn, and brother, Steve, in Orlando, and Scott and Cathy in Houston; the back-up support from all the people at The Homestead; well-wishing phone calls from a hundred friends including Joanne and Debbie; Jackie's unforgettable send-off and Jane's and Leonard's hospitality. Greatest of all, perhaps, were the hundreds, if not thousands, of well-wishers who had pledged to the fund-raising for The Homestead and The Little Red School House, and who would be watching for news about his weekly progress. For some reason he felt the presence of Joanne Irace very strongly. She must be praying for him. Yes, that would be it. Joanne was a deeply devout Catholic, whose faith awed him at times. It was strange how the two of them had come together at the University of Maine — Stranger still how Joanne's religion had come between them as well as being a bond that afforded them something special.

His thoughts turned to Jackie. It was now after 11:30 A.M. She would be in her school office at Livermore Falls, counseling kids with problems. (Who *didn't* have a problem?) Jennifer would be in kindergarten, her child's mind alert, as usual, to everything around her.

Another mile, and his head cleared. Any hint of sniffles was gone. The smells of pine needles and rich earth invaded his senses until the last vestige of tobacco taste was gone. Soon he was passing by Amicalola Lake above the falls. Upward, ever upward. His legs and body were responding like those of a fine race horse.

He overtook a middle-aged hiker ahead and called out: "Your first long hike?"

"How did you know?" the middle-aged man called over his shoulder.

"I can tell by the way you're already puffing!"

"Yeah. I'm used to pushing a pencil—not one foot in front of the other—uphill."

"Cheer up! You've only two thousand miles to go."

"Oh God!"

Bob passed, and after a few yards he looked back. The hiker had sat down. He looked as if he were about to cry.

When 12:00 o'clock came, Bob stopped to have a breather and to retrieve a fistful of gorp from his pack. He washed the tasty, strength-giving mixture down with a swig of water from his plastic bottle. The liquid was almost lukewarm—a condition he would have to get used to. Strangely, he felt possessed of more stamina than when he had begun.

At 1:20, a section of the Frosty Mountain Fire Road came into view. It was another half-mile before he saw Leonard's car. His uncle was stretched out on the hood soaking up the sun. Coming closer, Bob tuned up his vocal cords on the first verse of "The Happy Wanderer," one of the trail songs he and Jackie had practiced on their guitars.

"I love to go awandering along the mountain track / And when I go I love to sing / My knapsack on my back ___" he sang at full volume. Leonard sat up and waved across the distance. The two of them had already said their good-byes, and Bob travelled on without moving closer.

Late in the afternoon a rustic sign announced his arrival on Springer proper. He signed the log—stored and protected in a sort of mailbox—and noted the elevation as posted: 3,787 feet above sea level. He took his turn and lingered, reading the register. There were names from two dozen states. Scores of people were already ahead of him. A dozen or more lounged about, talking, taking photos, or nursing sore and blistered feet that had already begun to take a toll. He took some photos of his own, and chatted briefly with two guys from a college in New Jersey. He wasn't yet in the mood for in-depth conversations. He needed to make some sort of mental and emotional transition first.

The transition had something to do with leaving behind the problems of The Homestead and its "members"—they were not called inmates, students, or juvenile delinquents. Another part of it was taking his distance from Jackie, coming to terms with how he really felt about Joanne, dealing with a growing closeness between himself and Susan Ramsay, of learning what the future held for a twenty-seven-year-old man who hadn't yet settled down.

And—the part of the transition was his anticipated confrontation along the Appalachian Trail with that Supreme Spirit Being—who had twice made Himself known to Bob Mountford, Jr.,—that mankind called God or Allah, Jehovah, or Yahweh. Bob's surrender to Nature, the yielding of himself to the strength of earth, his drinking in the tranquility of the Trail—all of this was a part of the transition.

He moved out in search of shelter for the night. He found a lean-to occupied by Don Farrell and Mark Guilmette from Massachusetts. It was instant friendship. Tomorrow he would make it to Gooch Gap early, but for today he wouldn't push too hard. He would break in his muscles gradually, fix a good supper, lie in his sleeping bag under the stars and allow the wondrous wilderness to take him into her womb. By dawn, he would be reborn.

CHAPTER IV

According to plan Neal Chivington prepared to leave Ellsworth for Springer Mountain, Georgia. By his calculations Bob Mountford would have almost a week's head start on the Trail. Neal had met Bob when they worked at The Homestead. Neal had resigned as head counselor four months previously, and he was in no hurry to begin a new job—at least until he had experienced the adventure he had planned along the Appalachian Trail and could list himself among the end-to-enders.

Neal realized that he didn't have the ideal build for a hiker. He was built more like a basketball player, slender at six-five; the weighty backpack would take a heavy toll on his long spine over the long haul. He still possessed most of his long reddish-blond hair, and at thirty-four his health was good; his stamina, up to par.

Going along on the hike would be Sandy Skinner with whom Neal had had a two-year relationship, and Sandy's brother Steve. In her late twenties, Sandy worked at a health food store in Ellsworth. Short in stature, she had long black hair that she sometimes wore in a single-plaited pigtail. Her dark skin contrasted with Neal's fair complexion. Wearing that black pigtail, Sandy looked like a pretty Indian maiden; and her sunny disposition and good health would make her a good companion along the trail. Neal knew they looked like a Mutt-and-Jeff pair, but both of them took the jibes in good humor.

Sandy's brother Steve was younger than Neal and Sandy, and though he hadn't attended college yet, he was a bright, idealistic young man. He had, in fact, some leanings toward the ministry or, perhaps, toward social work, where he hoped that he could influence the formative years of the underprivileged young. His religious leanings tended toward the charismatic movement gaining momentum throughout the country. Steve Skinner would be another good traveling companion on the Trail. He was just under six feet, a solid one-sixty pounds with Sandy's same hair and skin coloring. He was a solid outdoorsman. He worked with his father in the remodeling/painting/residential construction business in Everett, Massachusetts, and as a result he was already muscle-hardened.

Neal hadn't attended the University of Maine as Bob had; he had taken his degree at a college in Flagstaff, Arizona. He and Bob liked each other

31

from the moment they met at The Homestead. Not everybody took to Bob Mountford instantly; new acquaintances were sometimes made uneasy by a display of his sharp intelligence. But Neal admired him, and learned from his vast store of knowledge and worldly experiences.

Bob questioned everything. He would argue just for the sake of argument, splitting hairs with deft skill and amusement until he had opponents screaming. Yet behind it all was an aura of insecurity. Bob played the preppie at times and could be childish. He loved old comic books and could mimic characters from old-time radio and TV shows with side-splitting skill.

Bob had a great sense of humor, but he could be obnoxious at times. At work he would play the role of executive director with comic exaggeration. He would break the rules and steal food from the refrigerator and swear with utmost seriousness that he had seen so-and-so do it; then he would confess later his "sin" and go into the most long-winded explanation of just what made him do it. Neal still considered him one of the best counselors The Homestead had ever employed. When it came to crisis intervention and conflict resolution among the "members," Mountford was solid business. Rarely was his quick judgment, his immediate response in a crucial situation seriously flawed; when he did make a mistake, he accepted the responsibility and learned from the experience.

Aside from Neal, Sandy, and Steve, others would not be following or joining Bob on the Trail for several weeks. Susan Ramsay would head for Virginia in early May. Neal didn't know the degree of attachment between Bob and Susan. He knew only that they spent time together after work cross-country skiing, jogging, and hiking; that they were mental and physical equals, and that they loved to sing and play their guitars together. A likely romance in the formative stages, he guessed.

Neal, Sandy, and Steve had intended to leave Massachusetts on April 1, but they had missed the train and headed south on April 2. They arrived in Georgia on April 3, had a big brunch at a restaurant, hitched a ride to a better vantage point for hitting the trail, and put boots to soil.

They hiked from Nimblewill Gap, some two and a half miles, to Springer Mountain, and then another three miles to Cross Trails lean-to. Not a bad beginning. While looking at the Appalachian Trail register, they noticed that Bob Mountford had signed in on March 31. They were just three days behind him.

CHAPTER V

Peggy Wheeler and Isaac "Ike" Charlton prepared to leave Princeton, West Virginia, on April 7. Both were happy to rid themselves of the hustle and bustle of city life and all its problems for the peaceful lure of the Appalachian Trail. Each of them, Peggy knew well, had many reasons to put life on the shelf for a time and do some soul-searching. There had been times in the last two or three years when she would have liked to chuck the whole business of school, men, career—everything.

She was still as far from a career decision as she had been that day in 1977 when she had enrolled at Concord College, Athens, West Virginia, a four-year school with a student body known for instant friendliness. At college she had begun her studies with a career in medical technology in mind. The choice soon proved wrong, and she had then decided to go into fashion merchandising. That, too, had lost its luster by her third year. In the end she had dropped out as her interest in university education waned.

Her current male interest and hiking companion had gone through frustrating problems of his own. Ike Charlton, after his football-playing days at Beaver High School, Bluefield, West Virginia, had gone to work with a nearby Virginia laboratory. A "rat tester" he had called himself, but he hadn't stayed there long enough to reach any degree of real interest or advancement. Drafted into the army in 1966, he had become a military policeman with duty assignment in Korea. It had been only a two-year hitch in Seoul and, for a brief while, the historic area of Panmunjom.

Peggy had known Ike for years in their suburban neighborhood. But Ike had been an "older man" then. Since she had moved back to her father's house in August of '80 from the dorm at Concord, that ten-year age difference seemed unimportant. Ike was thirty-two. She had discovered him to be basically a quiet, gentle man but a man capable of great wrath if the occasion called for it. He was also big-bodied at nearly two hundred pounds with huge shoulders, strong arms, and powerful legs; he was still the athletic tackle he had been on Beaver High's football team. One thing had changed, however; he had gone mod and sported a bushy, deep brown beard under a mop of thick, unruly dark hair. His broad face and square chin took on a sort of shaggy look but not unattractively so. Ike had never claimed any credit as an aspiring scholar, and intellectuals turned him off.

He liked the simple life, and found himself more and more inclined to work with his hands. That inclination had led him to take a job with a local building supplies company after he was discharged from the army in 1968.

But in 1971 he had found his real niche: stone-masonry. He would spend hours telling Peggy how this craft fulfilled something in him and how the laying of stone was like putting the jigsaw puzzle pieces of one's own life together. A God-like occupation, he would say, taking earth's elements and making something lasting and beautiful from them. And he liked the feel of the sandy, wet mortar and trowel in his hands though it roughened his flesh and swelled his knuckles and sinewy fingers. Peggy had seen some of his work—the facade of a commercial building, lobby planters, fireplaces, monuments, even stone walls and fences, and she had caught the essence of his creativity in the craft that he loved.

In some ways, however, both had felt themselves to be stagnating. Both had tasted the reputed glories of the drug scene and found it vastly over-rated. Perhaps they had entered the "in-between stage," the "awkward age," when one's place and direction were muddied by a multiplicity of things, sometimes tangible, sometimes intangible. Each of them had even developed a weight problem.

At a hundred and fifty-seven pounds on a five-foot-seven frame, Peggy knew that her chubbiness was fast headed toward that dreaded condition called fat. Ike didn't need the beer gut that had begun to hang over his belt either.

These were only a few of the reasons the Appalachian Trail had beckoned with some sweet silent call.

On April 8 they arrived in Georgia at Amicalola State Park. They took the difficult route via Amicalola Falls to Springer Mountain and on April 9 reached the summit. From 3,800 feet above the level of the Atlantic to the east, Peggy jokingly told Ike that they had reached Mount Olympus and that she would christen him a bearded Zeus.

Peggy was proud of her creamy complexion, long coppery blond hair, full figure, and the face others called attractive. But the fat had to go. How many times she had looked into her full-length mirror, stared into her own eyes, saying, "Cool it, kid." Then new frustrations would come—the deteriorating home situation, low grades, men problems, career decision—and she would go on another eating binge.

The lofty splendor of Springer Mountain was difficult to leave, but next morning at sunrise they broke camp and headed northward. Rain had obviously fallen some days before; the soil was soft, and the leaves of winter along the trail were not crunchy. At such an early hour, the sun rising in the east cast eerie shafts of light through the trees, and an occasional cloud of mist hanging low in the mountain valleys gave the illusion of fairyland. Fallen trees along the footpath looked like monstrous sleeping serpents. Peggy was walking ahead, and the thought of reptiles caused her to stop. She was deathly afraid of snakes.

"What's the matter?" Ike said, catching up.

"Those dead logs look like overgrown copperheads. And the way the sun plays in and out between the standing trees makes some of them look as if they were moving!"

"Man, what an imagination you've got! But wait 'til we get to Tennessee. I hear they've got timber rattlers there as big as my leg!"

"Oh, God. Are you kidding me, Ike? You walk in front!"

"That wouldn't be good. Those rattlers like to sneak up from behind like a junkyard dog and bite you in the heel!"

She was practically dancing, looking in all directions for some unseen menace. He laughed a deep guttural laugh until it echoed through the trees, and she knew he was piling it on thick.

They each had a swig of water and took a fistful of gorp to munch on as they walked. Farther along, they could see two hawks soaring effortlessly between the peaks of two ridges. Their underbellies looked like pure silver as with unbelievable skill they rode the updrafts, soaring higher and higher until they paused, adjusted their wings, and rode the downward current like an earthbound jet. Again she stopped, marveling at the soul-stirring sight.

As they started off again, two other hikers overtook them. One paused long enough to reach into his jeans pocket. He extracted a handful of something whitish and shiny. He dropped a couple of the small objects to the side of the footpath and grinned.

Peggy came closer and looked down:

"Seashells?"

"Yeah." He laughed. "Can't you just see some of these land-locked end-to-enders walking along and seeing one of my souvenirs and wondering how sea life existed three thousand miles up on a Georgia mountain? It'll blow their minds!"

He hurried off, laughing at his own flimflam.

"I guess it takes every kind to make up a world," Ike said.

"Somebody told me once that the Appalachian Trail was like the crossroads of North America. Now I can believe it."

By the time they reached Neel's Gap, late afternoon on April 13, Peggy had begun to feel as grimy as a coal miner. This particular resting point along the trail did have a few touches of civilization: a country store/house offering supplies and souvenirs, cabins and rooms with showers nearby, and an exit off the trail via U.S. Routes 19 and 129. A number of hikers were laying over, and Peggy began to think that getting under hot water and soaping down would be an hour's-long wait-in-line proposition. They bought some food in the store and asked the clerk the distance to the nearest motel. He told them but added, "You'll be lucky if they're not full up. Seems like everybody hits the Trail in April."

Peggy sighed. "If I don't get some dirt off, somebody's going to have to scrape me."

"You're welcome to use our shower," a voice from behind sang out.

Peggy turned to face a red-haired, slightly balding man in his mid-thirties with friendly blue eyes and red mustache.

"Follow me. You can rest and freshen up at our room. We're going to take it easy a day or so," he added.

As they left the store, Peggy introduced herself and Ike, and Rick Davis introduced himself. At the rustic cabin room, Davis introduced Rita, his wife. Rita—long, silky blond hair—was slender and just a shade over five feet tall. Hardly the epitome of the athletic trail hiker, she was petite and pretty. She appeared to be in her late twenties.

"So—are you two going the whole way, or just weekend hikers?" Rick asked.

"We'd like to go the whole way," Ike said, "but we're takin' it day-by-day. I've had a bum foot, and so far, no problems, but we'll wait and see."

"Welcome to the club," Rita said. "Rick's having problems with his knees. Don't know how long we can hold out either."

Rick looked to be in good athletic form, Peggy thought. His under-six-foot body was well toned, and she would bet that he played tennis.

Conversation raced in the quick camaraderie that prevailed among most trail hikers and was one of the unforgettable rewards of the whole experience.

Peggy got clean clothes from her backpack and hit the showers first. Sheer heaven! She even found herself singing a hiking song, and through the wall she could hear the three others joining in.

By the time Ike finished his shower, she had learned even more about these Davises. Rick was a designer of computer systems in Florida, and Rita worked as an administrative assistant with the telephone company. Obviously they were the kind of loving, with-it professional couple that Peggy could admire and hoped one day to be like. They had done all kinds of fun things together and had planned a cross-country motorcycle trip for some time in the future. Peggy listened to their stories of various adventures with appreciation and awe. The give-and-take was so warm and open that Peggy felt as if she had known the couple all her life. Such an atmosphere prevailed along the AT. She and Ike—from the moment they had ascended Amicalola Falls met one after another who had somehow enriched their lives. At night, it was even better, for there were long hours in which to bask in the warmth, and life story of other human beings.

"I guess we should keep a diary," Peggy said., "but neither of us is very good at converting feelings and nature scenes into a few scribbled words."

"We always carry one," Rick said. "It's fun—even years later—looking back on the littlest things that happen."

"Yeah—and some people *insist* on being included in our diary," Rita chuckled.

"Yeah," Rick took it up. "While we were getting ready to leave Hawk

Mountain shelter a few days ago, a strange-acting guy about Ike's age came up and asked me for my diary so that he could write in it. He had the weirdest look in his eyes, and I didn't know whether he was spaced out or not. I got the creepiest feeling, but I handed it to him and he wrote in it in big bold letters his name, address, some macho slogans, and one final great swirl of the pen point. The guy's whole manner was eerie. It was more of a feeling than anything he did. Anyway, when he handed my diary back, and we turned to go, I actually sensed his coming up behind me, and I pushed Rita away from me and turned to meet him. I've never been attacked from behind, but something in me said, 'Watch out!' I actually jumped, and there was a sinister gleam in his eyes as if he had planned to do something—or had already mentally done something to me that he got a special kick out of. Something in my head kept saying, 'Don't let that guy stay behind you.' "

"Glad we haven't met anybody like *that* on the trail," Peggy said. "I've known a few of that kind, and once is enough, believe me."

"This guy leave the trail, or is he ahead of us?" Ike asked.

"He's ahead," Rita said. "We ran into him again at Gooch Gap two days later. Needless to say, we stayed clear of him and let him gain distance.

"There were some other strange things about him," Rick mused. "For instance, he ate his food with a stick/spoon, and he had the regular kinds of canned foods and whole potatoes—not the compact, quickie stuff most of the hikers use. It was as if he had run for the AT in a hurry and had forgotten to bring eating gear and the right type of food. And another thing: it's rare to see a hiker carrying more than a forty-pound load. This guy, by his own admission—or brag I should say—was carrying a ninety-five-pound pack!"

"What did he look like?" Ike asked. "Just in case ___ "

"He was real macho," Rita intoned. "Not quite six feet maybe, but well built. Medium brown hair, grey or hazel eyes, rather good-looking. There was something about his smile, too; it was slow and a little arrogant. Am I getting it right, Rick?"

"Yes, and there was something a bit too military about him. In fact, he was wearing an army fatigue shirt. Sergeant's stripes, I think. I noticed him flexing his muscles a time or two. He was in excellent physical shape."

Some kind of resonance began to tickle Peggy's spine; she didn't know why or what kind, just that she was on some kind of wavelength.

"Did he have a sleeping bag or other regular stuff?" Ike asked.

Rick pondered a moment.

"Yes, I think so. A green cotton sleeping bag as I remember it. But there was something else that was odd. As you know, hikers don't usually carry a hatchet. This guy had a big long-handled hatchet hanging from his belt on one side and a big hunting knife hanging down the other. That knife alone looked lethal enough to pin a deer to a tree and gut it."

"But we never could figure out why he had a fishing reel," Rita added.

"Maybe he figured to be in the woods a long time, and if he ran out of food, do a little trout fishin'," Ike said.

"Who knows?" Rick said. "I've never had such a strange instinct about a person. It chills me to think about it, but I wonder if he had a weapon in that oversized pack."

For a moment the conversation ran down, and certain key words echoed in Peggy's head: Army. Macho. Arrogant smile. Muscle-flexing. Sinister aura. Military. Brown hair. Gray eyes.

"We'll keep our eyes out for him," Ike said. "Probably just a space cadet."

"I don't think he was on drugs," Rita said. "Rick . . .?"

"I don't really know. Well, enough about Ned Shires, 'the ninety-five-pounder,' as he called himself. Anybody want something to drink?"

Peggy couldn't answer, couldn't even make her throat produce a gurgle. She felt the blood drain from her face until the skin seemed to grow cold. Ike's eyes were glued to hers. *Ned Shires.* That name was as familiar to him now as it was to her. It was a name she had hoped never again to hear.

"I said, did anyone want something to drink?" Rick repeated.

Rita's eyes had already met Peggy's, and Peggy could see in Rita's face a mirror of her own shock and fear. Rick seemed to see both faces simultaneously.

"What's the matter?"

Peggy still couldn't speak. A lump the size of a golf ball stuck in her craw, and her heart banged against her chest until surely everybody could hear it.

Rita sprang to her.

"Peggy—what's the matter? What's wrong?"

"She knows this Shires guy," Ike said. "Used to date him . . . and he bruised her up a few times."

Peggy's body began to tremble, blood returned to her face which grew hot. She lit a cigarette and tried to steady herself.

"Let me see where he signed your diary," she managed to whisper.

Rick got it quickly.

"Yes, it's him," she said haltingly. The signature was all too familiar.

She handed the diary back as if it were a death-notice telegram.

Rick's voice went flat. "Is this guy supposed to be following you or something?"

"I guess he is. I thought I was rid of him forever—but I guess not."

"But how did he know you were going on the Trail?" Rita asked.

Peggy tried to respond. She had started to tremble again. Ike took both her hands in his and answered for her: "The two of them talked about doin' the Trail together some time back."

Her composure returning, Peggy said: "After Ned and I split, he kept calling me. Wanted to know if I still planned to do the AT. I told him I was, but that I had somebody else now."

"Tell 'em the rest," Ike said.

"I think he's been following me around my home town. Some friends and acquaintances say they've seen him in Princeton on several occasions. He'll harass me to the ends of the earth."

"No, he won't," Ike said. "I'm a peaceable man, but if he tries anything I'll strangle the bastard with my bare hands. I can be gung ho military too ____ I was in the MPs."

"You might not get a chance with bare hands," Rita warned. "This guy may be planning to wait in the bushes for you. Is Ned Shires like that, Peggy?"

"He's a fighter. He's taken guys twice his size. Ned was one of the youngest sergeants in the army. Made it at twenty. Spent six years in Europe—took everything the army offered. Jump school. Everything. And he keeps his body tuned like a champion weight-lifter. He'll never let me go. He'll kill me first."

Rita placed a comforting hand on Peggy's shoulder.

"Don't say that. It's something he'll get over. Men can be so stupid."

"He won't get over it. It's more complicated than jealously. He wants possession of me—my mind, my actions, my body ____ everything."

Will it never end? Peggy thought. Obviously, his hate/love for her was festering like a boil in his gut, and eruption could take any number of forms. Ironic. The Appalachian Trail was supposed to be peace personified, and here she sat shaking. She fought it off:

"I'll have that coke after all.'

"Would you think about going off the Trail? Going home?" Rick asked.

"I'm not afraid of him," Ike interjected. "Maybe we ought to meet this thing head on."

"You're not a fighter by nature, and you know it." Peggy reached again for the big hand that offered assurance. "I don't doubt you could give a good account of yourself, but you're not the vicious type."

"Leaving the Trail might not be a bad idea," Rita said.

"No," Peggy said stubbornly. "Who's to say he's not waiting for us to do that very thing? Or maybe he'd be waiting for me at home when I got back. And anyway—I won't let him ruin the trip Ike and I have looked forward to for months." We both need ____ "

"That doesn't matter," Ike said. "If you want to leave the trail, I'll go. No problem. I don't want trouble, but I won't run from it."

"We stay," Peggy said firmly. "I'm not going to hide for the rest of my days, and I've dreamed of doing the AT for half my lifetime. We can play it safe, however, by going off the trail for a few days and letting him get way ahead of us. We can check him on the trail logs ____ "

"But wait a minute," Rick warned. "Won't he get suspicious at the various shelters and lean-tos when he doesn't see your names on the log? Won't he know you're behind him—not in front?"

"No," Peggy said. "Obviously, he doesn't know where we got on the Trail. He must have started at the beginning, hoping to catch up with us.

Still, if he travels far enough and nobody has heard of us, he might get suspicious."

"Maybe you ought to wait a few days." Rita's eyes met her husband's with the same apprehensive look.

"The guy loves to hike," Peggy said. "He won't wait around. He'll want to get on with it."

"I can testify that he's got all the makings of a hiker," Rick said. "He took off up the mountain with that ninety-five-pound pack like it was a loaf of bread."

Ike gathered their things and helped Peggy on with her backpack. She took one last drag from her cigarette and ducked it.

Rita gave her a quick hug. "Be careful. I don't want to read about you two in the papers."

"And don't be reluctant to approach the authorities if need be," Rick warned. "I'm not so sure you shouldn't have already."

"Ned Shires can't hide," Peggy said, with more cheer than she felt. "Anybody he meets will remember him. He can be most charming if it suits him."

Neel's Gap was full-up with hikers, and they walked on toward Tesnatee Gap. As they approached Cowrock Creek, a note tacked onto a leaning pine tree caught Peggy's eye. It said: "The ninety-five pounder passed this way. Beware." She froze in her tracks.

"Oh, Ike," she said and her throat turned dry.

"Forget it. He's just playing games."

The Trail map indicated that Tesnatee Gap shelter lay ahead and that water was not far away. By Rick Davis's calculations, Ned Shires should be at least two or three days ahead of them.

At the camp site, the two seashell-dropping hikers already occupied the old log lean-to. The place looked time-worn, but it did boast a fireplace and scenic surroundings.

Once their own space was occupied nearby and their sleeping bags unrolled for pre-bedtime airing, Peggy used the stone fireplace to warm vegetable-and-potato patties. Ike made instant tea with spring water. It was a sparse meal, but neither of them seemed hungry. Ike said nothing, but his eyes kept watch over her as they ate in near silence. She knew this basically mild-mannered man would go after Ned Shires if she gave the word. But she hadn't; she didn't want him involved in old history if it was possible to keep him out of it. And Ike didn't know everything. She had told him much of it, but some things she couldn't tell just yet.

It was almost dark when she and Ike slid into their own sleeping bags. A chill hit her after she was snuggled in, and her body began to tremble again.

"You all right?" Ike's hand came over to touch her.

"I'm okay," she said softly, but then her teeth began to chatter. Renewed fear danced along her spine. She clamped her jaws until they ached.

She looked up into the starry heavens. The moon didn't look full, but a tree limb obscured her vision. As a little girl she had lain out like this many times on her family's back lawn, in the heat of summer, watching the fireflies.

Ike started to snore, and then a hoot owl tuned up. The bird's mournful tremolo sent new chills through her. She snuggled more deeply into the cozy fabric, but she couldn't sleep.

It was at Southern West Virginia Community College that she had first met Ned Shires. She had enrolled there in a business course after dropping out of Concord College near her home town. At SWVCC, she had taken a job in Logan with Nicole Ivey, the divorced wife of a local physician, receiving room and board in exchange for babysitting the Ivey children and doing light housework. It had been a good arrangement and Nicole Ivey—a professional nurse—had come to be more of a friend than an employer. Life with the Ivey clan had had its rough moments, but on the whole Peggy had learned a lot. Nicole had been an attractive, worldly-wise woman who could advise without being pushy and who could even be motherly with such skill that the impact hit weeks later.

Peggy had confessed to Nicole on one occasion that she—Peggy— "surely didn't win any prizes when it came to picking men." Nicole hadn't agreed, but she asked Peggy to examine her relationships and come up with the reason for her belief. Peggy had tried to do so but she honestly couldn't come up with a satisfactory reason why she had dated so many losers. Maybe she was too trusting. Not all of the men in her past had come up minuses, but she had had an inordinately high number of phonies, opportunists, dropouts—and one or two who bordered dangerously on the side of potential rapists.

Yet Ned Shires was in a class all his own. On that day in January of 1980 when she had met him in the SWVCC library, she would have pegged him the most serious student at the college. He was taking a course in French, and somehow he had seemed mature beyond his years.

The friendship had warmed, and they had begun dating. Within a week they had slept together. Lying in his arms, she had heard his life story: His childhood in Southwest Virginia, his love for the family farm; his turbulent high school days when he had learned to fight and beat to a bloody pulp guys twice his size, his father's professorship at a nearby college, his mother's public-school teaching position, his brother and two sisters, his poor academic record, and his entry into the Army after high school. He had "found" himself in the military, and for nearly six years—three of them in the paratroops— had served in Germany and Italy. He had hiked and gone sightseeing all across Europe, skied and had a love affair with an American ski instructor from Colorado. He had made some prize-winning photographs of historic places, had been discharged from service, and had come back to West Virginia to "find himself" again. He hungered for an education; he desired knowledge above all things.

The implied maturity had appealed to her. At first she had found in him a stablizing force that gave meaning to her own life, a sense of well-being her warring parents had never provided her.

It wasn't long, however, until the idealistic Ned Shires began to show another side. He had been out of school a long time, and buckling down to the books took a toll. When the going had gotten rough, his personality had changed. It was as if he had to take his frustrations out on somebody, and frequently it was upon himself. He had become a fanatic about physical fitness and glorified his own body.

Some days and nights he could be just plain weird, his thoughts so far away that she usually couldn't bring them back. When she could, he talked like some hodge-podge combination of Freud, de Sade, and Pope John Paul II. He could lecture like a college professor on psychology, sex, and religion—even combine the three topics into a perfectly plausible thesis that made more sense than anything she had ever heard.

Their sex life for the most part was ideal. Ned could sometimes be macho, but more often tender and considerate. He had learned that she liked a certain amount of ceremony, and he would bring wine, scented candles, and the right mood-setting records for bedside use.

But the bedside wine—and he drank little, considering himself almost a teetotaler—and the studies didn't camouflage a certain Jekyll/Hyde quality of his personality.

Gradually, Peggy had begun to recognize that he wanted to control her. He had always possessed a powerful presence—even older adults felt and sensed it—and sometimes he would have a strange look in his eyes. The way he could time a smile and a certain way he flexed his arms and popped his finger joints had an odd effect on her.

After meeting him, she had moved from the Nicole Ivey house to be nearer school and to get away from her young wards, who had begun to get on her nerves. She and some other girls had rented an old farmhouse not far from the college. It was a drafty old place, but it was cheap, located among scenic rolling fields, and it allowed a life style that made it unnecessary to answer to anyone.

There she had tried to break off with Ned gradually, and he had become pouty at best and furious at worst. Once, when she had a male friend from Princeton down for a visit, Ned had come out to the farmhouse for what she felt was a calculated confrontation. When she had demanded an explanation, he grabbed her arm, set her aside like so much garbage, and left bruises on her flesh that took weeks to go away.

As her fear of him mounted and her finances dwindled, she had taken the only sensible course left and gone home to Princeton, West Virginia. That should have ended it, but rumors and occasional sightings of Ned Shires in the Princeton area began to frighten her. Rumors—and possible sightings of an unwanted man on a public street—were hardly enough to report to the police. She began to wonder if she were growing paranoid.

By the end of 1980, she had found a job in a retail store, taken secret residence with family friends, and generally lain low. The nights had been the worst. Somewhere out there, she had imagined Ned Shires furious as a rabid dog, until the day came when he could either possess her completely or destroy her. But finally when Ike had come into the picture, life seemed normal again.

All had gone well until the day's fateful meeting with Rick and Rita at Neel's Gap. How could Shires have possibly known that she and Ike had planned to hike the AT on a certain date? To whom had she mentioned the trip other than her closest confidants? Maybe Rick was right; maybe Ned had shadowed her until she and Ike had begun to buy supplies. Perhaps he had even followed them on dates and they had been too occupied to notice. Did he see them leave town, headed for the Appalachian Trail? She replayed her every move and still drew a frustrating, maddening blank.

Whatever the details were, Ned Shires lurked somewhere in the shadows along the Trail. Did he really want to harm her, or did he merely hope to make her life so miserable that she finally did herself in—or took refuge in a mental hospital? Strangely, she had half-prepared herself for death. She couldn't share that with anyone—not even with Ike, but a part of her desire to walk the Trail was tied to the expectation of a premature death. The AT was in a sense a pathway into the unknown. But if what she feared did happen, she had not expected it on the trail. God would cry out against it. His wrath would know no bounds against those who would shatter the serenity and the beauty of His holy wilderness with bloodshed and violence.

The hoot owl raised his eerie voice from a more distant tree, and the sound began to subdue her restless mind like a double dose of tranquilizers. At last, all was turning as black as the silent forest about them, and the long-needle pine trees smelled so good __ so good __ so __ .

When she awoke under the rays of the rising sun next morning, Ike was already fixing breakfast, the others were gone, and she wandered down the gully to a private section of the meandering stream. The water had a sting of chilliness when she washed and the deeply inhaled morning air caused her lungs temporarily to ache. The forest was alive with happy sounds. A crow cawed in the distance, and she herself began to hum. It occurred to her suddenly: she *was* happy! The night had taken most of the fear away; the new day offered some kind of delightful promise. The feeling was so good she wanted to hold onto it, and certain intuitions had begun to creep into her mind, telling her just how she might retain the new sense of peace. They must leave the Trail for a few days in order to give Shires time to get farther away from them. The farther away he got, the less likely he was to backtrack, and the more diminished the chance that any through hikers would mention her and Ike to Shires in casual conversation. Travel time and distance calculation were a tricky business anyway. No hiker kept up the same daily pace. One day it could be twenty miles; the next, five miles or no miles. It depended on weather conditions, on every hiker's mood, his decision whether or not to leave the white-blaze Trail for a sightseeing blue-blaze adventure, or to go into some town for supplies, medical attention, post office pickups, phone calls, or simply to indulge in "civilized" life and gain new resolve for the continuing trek into the wilderness.

She spooned the instant breakfast Ike had prepared, and it was good. The powdered orange juice, mixed in cool limestone water, had a special zing. Her intuitions now solidly founded, she decided to lay it out.

"What do you think about getting off the Trail temporarily while we're still in Georgia? Put a little more distance between ourselves and him ___"

"Whatever makes you feel good."

"You're an agreeable soul."

"You know it."

"I thought maybe we could get off at Helen. Sack into a nice motel. Rest. Do a little sightseeing ___ "

"The motel sounds good," he said with a grin, "but what's at Helen?"

"They call it 'Little Bavaria.' Sort of a unique place, really. Tourists talk about it a lot."

Ike ate in silence for a moment.

"I've been thinkin'. Maybe we ought not to turn tail. Maybe it's time I helped get this thing straightened out."

"No, Ike, I don't want you involved. This was before you and me."

"You expect me to sit on the sidelines and watch forever?"

"It won't be forever. It's got to end."

"That's what I'm afraid of. I feel so damn helpless. And you can take some bastard's shit just so long."

"If we're lucky, maybe we'll never hear the name of Shires again."

She could see in his eyes that the statement didn't satisfy, but he said nothing more. She cared deeply for the big hunk, and she knew that he would do anything honorable to avoid bloodshed with anybody. She got up and tied the long strands of his hair, then plaited and tied the ends of her own until one long braid hung down her back. She wanted no flying tresses to get snagged by the underbrush.

They broke camp and headed for the Helen, Georgia, exit.

CHAPTER VI

Before a full week on the trail had passed, Bob Mountford was walking toward Montray Leanto near the Georgia/North Carolina border. It was April 5. During the previous night a downpour had come. At dawn although a gentle rain still persisted, he had struck out along the damp trail. The temperature was between fifty and sixty degrees, but the rainsuit kept him dry and warm.

Well after midday the sun popped out for real, though threatening clouds kept rolling over the horizons, and finally another shower began. The rain had made the fragrant earth soft; there was no sound of footfalls except on the rockiest ground.

As he reached the crest of a ridge, a magnificent rainbow welcomed him. For a moment he imagined that the arch reaching from valley to valley over an entire mountain had been fashioned just for him. It looked miles away; yet he had a childlike desire to reach it and to pass under, to be serenaded by some unseen angelic chorus, and then to find the pot of gold. Of course. How many children, he wondered, had done as he had in childhood and actually struck out for the variegated tail that dipped to earth where the treasure was, only to find that the brilliantly colored span seemed to move farther and farther away. Ironic how during the night he had been searching the Scriptures and had come across that passage in Genesis where God had sent His bow as a token of His covenant between Noah and all of mankind to come: a promise that destruction by water would never be visited upon people of earth again. An ancient Jewish myth? An oft-repeated Babylonian fable? Bob wished with a new desperation, made more urgent somehow by the awesome surroundings, that he knew the answer with certainty. How simple life could be—how void of all the petty frustrations of daily existence—if one could simply believe!

His eyes would not leave the splendor of the sights before him. And the aroma of the washed-clean earth seemed to invade his pores and filter into his lungs like laughing gas. Yes, he wanted to laugh, to cry out in joy, to make a gift of what he saw and felt to the whole world. Maybe he was getting giddy from the height. How high was he anyway? He knew that

Clingman's Dome, Tennessee, at 6,600 feet lay not far northward. He reached for his Trail map and a fistful of gorp.

"Are you lost?" a voice called out from the rear.

Bob started. He hadn't heard so much as a twig break. He turned to face an older man closing the distance between them.

"No. Not lost," Bob said. "Just checking the height of my surroundings."

The man—in his early to mid fifties, Bob judged—offered his hand and a brief smile that was somewhat reserved: "I'm Frank Maguire."

Bob met the bright blue eyes of the lanky hiker.

"Bob Mountford here. Where you from?"

"Princeton Junction, New Jersey, and today I feel a long way from home."

"Compared with me, you're a local boy. Try Ellsworth, Maine."

Frank had already begun to grin at the word "boy." He said, "You know, I've come so near feeling like a youth again while I walk this trail that it either scares me or excites me. I don't know which. Anyway, at fifty-seven I'm definitely no boy."

"You do a lot of hiking? Shooting for the rank of end-to-ender?"

"What little hiking I've done up to now's been in New York State. The Adirondacks. And yes, I am hoping to go all the way."

"There's gotta be a story in this somewhere." Bob grinned.

"Guess so. Isn't there always? Mind if I walk with you? Thought I'd try and make it to Montray Leanto and sack in for the night."

"Glad to have you. That's where I was heading when that stream of diamonds just about hypnotized me."

Frank shared the vision of the rainbow and said: "Seems like we ought to play "The Star Spangled Banner," "God Save the Queen," "I'm Always Chasing," or something appropriate."

Bob laughed, but Frank was deadpan. Bob could already see a quiet self-confidence in this man.

"There is some music coming up behind us," Frank added, this time with a chuckle. "There's a couple of guys from New Zealand back there. Luigi and Beni something-or-other. They work in a butcher shop, I think somebody said, and are as wild as a pair of bush kangaroos. They've got a portable tape deck with them, and every once in a while the trees and rocks vibrate with sounds of the Rolling Stones."

"And I came for peace and quiet," Bob said in feigned disgust. He picked up his walking stick, adjusted his backpack harness, took a mouthful of gorp, and headed up the trail. Visibly weary, Frank followed.

"Planned this hike a long time, or just got on spontaneously?" Bob called over his shoulder.

"I've dreamed about it since I was a teenager. Never had the time before to go the full route. Got time on my hands now."

"Retired? From what?"

"Police work. Used to be police chief of Princeton Junction."

Bob stopped dead in his tracks and turned around.

"No kiddin'. My maternal grandfather was police chief of Millinocket, Maine. He's retired now and lives in Dover-Foxcroft, my home town."

"Hope he had it easier than I did. We had everything from tombstone thieves to the Mafia. And this drug thing is like the plague. Crazy. I'm glad I'm out of it now."

"What're you going to do with your time besides doing the AT?"

"Think I'd like to refinish and sell antiques. Maybe build myself a new house too. With my own hands."

Bob turned and started off along the trail again, continuing the conversation: "Build yourself a log cabin somewhere. In a setting like this. Or do you have a wife and family to consider?"

"My kids are on their own. No wife at the moment. We're split up. Don't know whether the new lady in my life would go for it or not."

"Welcome to the club." Bob chuckled. "I've got a few women problems, too. Heavy, man. Real heavy. And I haven't even been the first time around."

"Wait'll you've been there twice and sweating out number three."

Bob glanced over his shoulder. At about six feet and slender, the ex-chief would still be attractive to women. There was a rugged handsomeness to Frank's face and a certain mystic quality about him, by which one sensed that a man knew more about everything than he would ever tell anybody.

"So, you've got a reluctant, almost bride-to-be on your hands?"

"Something like that," Frank grunted.

"Same with me. Except my situation's more complicated than that."

For the moment Bob didn't pursue the conversation further.

It was late afternoon when they reached Montray Leanto and set up camp. Bob volunteered to fix supper for both of them and Frank didn't argue the point. Bob unpacked his stove and cooking gear and lined up the ingredients for the meal on a well-weathered log. His cooking fuel was dangerously low, and he asked Frank whether he had fuel to spare. Frank got it and sat down to observe the proceedings.

"What's all that?" Frank pointed at the row of condiments Bob used to jazz up his trail food. "And what a pot, for God's sake! You used to cooking for a boy scout troop?"

Bob laughed. "I like to do it up right. Amazing what a little olive oil and cheese sauce and some exotic spices will do. And don't knock the contents of my big pot until you try it. Cooking's one of my hobbies."

Frank watched intently while Bob made a sort of quickie stew from various packets, sprinkled it with this-and-that shaker, heated it, and poured it over cooked rice. While the mixture cooled, Bob made hot tea. The weather wasn't threatening now, so there was no need to take shelter in the leanto just yet. Besides, the aroma of their surroundings seemed compatible with the rich smell of the food, and Bob placed the spread along a rock ledge, where he found a dry seat.

Frank dipped in, and a broad smile creased his face after the first bite.

"Real good. You ought to open up a French restaurant somewhere. What do you do besides cook?"

"Social work. doing adolescent counseling, crisis intervention, outdoor therapy. That kind of thing."

"Juvenile delinquents?"

"Yeah. A secluded residential treatment center kind of setting."

"I've done a lot of work with kids myself. Community projects and police projects. Rewarding work. Sometimes wondered if that wasn't where I really belonged."

"Well, it's rewarding. Lot of human wrecks out there, but most are salvageable with a lot of hard work and old-fashioned caring. Where has love and compassion disappeared to in this mixed-up world anyway?"

"You're asking the wrong man. Guess I've worked with the dregs of society too long. I've got a warped view now, and I don't like it worth a damn. I want a new beginning. That's part of what this hike is all about."

"Is *anybody* on the Appalachian Trail normal? I think maybe we're all basket cases."

Both laughed and dipped into the big pot for seconds. Frank poured more tea and said: "So what's your problem? You can't be over twenty-five or six. That's too young to have any serious problems."

"I'll never see twenty-six again, and I'm getting a little panicky. Maybe I ought to be settled down by now. Wife. Kids. Career. Always have liked kids. My peers say I've never left that category myself."

"Did you mean that you've got a reluctant fiancee, too?"

"Yeah. Jackie and I have an on-and-off kind of thing. She's not sure, and I guess the truth is maybe I'm not either. She's supposed to meet me in Tennessee and hike a distance. And I can't forget Joanne, a girl I dated at U. Maine. She haunts me night and day. It's as if she has been walking with me along the trail. And I've sort of a new thing going with a girl I work with, who's going to meet me in Virginia for a few days of walking together."

"Jeez! A running soap opera along the Appalachian Trail! My problems seem dull in contrast."

"Just one does make it simpler. What's her name?"

"Adele. She's somebody very special. When I finish the AT, she's going to give me an answer. If it's a 'yes,' I want to relocate in Pennsylvania, build a new house, and make a new start."

Conversation lulled after each had gone into more detail about his own career, and Frank wandered off through the trees as if to be alone with his thoughts. Bob busied himself with cleaning up from the meal and washing the utensils. He swept out the leanto, with a broken bough from a pine tree, and unrolled his sleeping bag to air. Retrieving his Bible from the backpack, he sat and propped his back against the west corner of the leanto where the fading light was best. Each night along the trail, he had read one or more chapters of the Scriptures and before retiring had selected what he called a "hiking passage" with which to begin the new day. Strange how the

48

Book he had disdained, earlier in his youth now struck him as both perpetually new and startlingly wise. For the hiking passage he always sought a new nature theme. Tonight after a lengthy search, he hit on the first part of the nineteenth Psalm:

The heavens are telling the glory of God;
  and the firmament proclaims his handiwork.
Day to day pours forth speech,
  and night unto night declares knowledge.
There is no speech, nor are there words;
  this voice is not heard;
Yet their voice goes out through all the earth,
  and their words to the end of the world.

In them he hath set a tent for the sun,
  which comes forth like a bride-groom
leaving his chamber,
  and like a strong man runs its course with joy.

Its rising is from the end of the heavens,
  and its circuit to the end of them;
  And there is nothing hid from its heat.

The law of the Lord is perfect,
  reviving the soul;
The testimony of the Lord is sure,
  making wise the simple.

He re-read the words until he was sure of their meaning, hardly conscious that he was audibly repeating most of the lines. New dimness fell over the page, and he looked up. Frank stood between him and the hazy horizon. Frank looked around and took a last drag from his cigarette and ground it out in the moist soil at his feet.

He said, "I didn't mean to leave you with the mess. After the good vittles, dish duty's the least I could have done."

"No sweat. You handle a breakfast."

Bob marked the place and closed the Bible. Frank's exhaled smoke still hung in the air, and Bob wanted to gather it all into his own lungs, so great was his nicotine hunger.

"Man! I need a cigarette ___ "

"Why didn't you say so? I've got half a carton. Here. Take what's left and I'll get a new pack."

"No—I can't do it. Gotta sweat it out. I quit back at Springer. Was smoking like a fiend."

"Tried to get myself to quit a time or two. Tough. If you change your mind, help yourself."

Bob started to read again to get his mind off the terrible craving. Frank, sitting down across from him, asked gently: "Planning to teach a Sunday School class at the next hostel?"

"No. Just trying to zero in on the Big Picture. Call it objective research."

"Thought maybe I'd hooked up with a Jesus freak in disguise. Didn't know whether to run now or wait until morning."

"Wrong tag, Chief. I'm just a wayward pilgrim, trying to find The Way. You a church man? Read the Book?"

"Sometimes. Was brought up a Catholic. A little lapsed now, I guess."

"But you're a believer?"

"Yeah. That hasn't changed."

"I was brought up an Episcopalian, but the truth is I'm not much of an institutional man. We've lost both the beauty and the purity of worship. Somewhere along the way it got bogged down in isms and popular tradition. I've felt more here in the wilderness than I ever thought possible."

"We're all looking for renewal, I guess. Still a lot of question marks."

They talked on until there was scarcely enough light to get their possessions in order and sack in. The sandman visited Frank in a hurry, but Bob's mind was occupied with the coming of Easter. If all went well, his mom and dad would be coming south, dropping Jackie somewhere in Tennessee before going on to Jane's and Len's in Alabama and picking Jackie up on the return. If the timing worked out as he had planned, he and Jackie would be walking together in the Great Smoky Mountains National Park. Thunder sounded somewhere in the distance. Maybe rain again tomorrow. He sank deeply into the warm embrace of his sleeping bag.

The morning broke with an overcast sky, and the air was cold. Bob felt his nose to make sure it wasn't frost-covered. He dreaded crawling from the sleeping bag, feeling the delicious warmth dissipate from his body. He looked around. Frank was already up; in a moment the aroma of coffee wafted over and teased his nostrils. Frank was doing it up right. Suddenly there was no reluctance to get up. Bob bounded from under the leanto.

"Man, you really know how to start the day! Got any maple syrup for those pancakes?"

"Yeah. A little bottle of Log Cabin. Hungry?"

"Always. Ever notice how much better food tastes outdoors?"

"Seems that way."

"I'm not going to do much more cooking until I get some fuel. I need to go off the trail today anyway and call home. Check on my folks' plans about coming south. I'll tell Mom to get me more cooking fuel to my mail drop in Hot Springs."

"I'll share more of mine with you."

"Thanks, but no point in your running low. I knew I didn't have enough, but in the rush of things it slipped my mind."

They broke camp, and when midday arrived, they had reached Dicks Creek Gap where U.S. Route 76 provided an exit off the Trail into town.

"Sure you won't come with me for a little taste of civilization and some restaurant food?" Bob asked.

"No thanks this time. I've got enough civilization to hold me a while."

"I'll catch up with you along the way. Don't wrestle any bears."

"Take care. See ya."

Frank walked on, and Bob headed for the highway. As he came out of the woods three hikers were standing near the roadside. He saw the traditional Trail friendliness in their faces.

"I'm Bob Mountford from Maine."

"And I'm John Linnehan from Florida." The eldest member of the three had a slight Boston accent.

Linnehan, like Frank Maguire, appeared to be in his mid-fifties, tall, relatively slender, and the fringes of brown hair peeping from under his hiking cap looked sparse indeed. His cocoa-colored eyes showed instant perception.

"I'm Patti Hydro from Maryland." The younger of the two women stepped forward.

She was small, and her brown hair was cut short. Her smile was quick and genial; her complexion reflected a healthy glow. Late twenties, Bob guessed.

"And I'm Jean Tierney also from Maryland." The second slightly taller woman showed a puckish grin framed by a pretty face with high cheekbones and a petite nose. Her hair was as short as Patti's but darker, and she would be in her late thirties or early forties.

"So? Are we all heading for town?" Bob asked.

"Just Patti and me," John Linnehan said. "I've developed a good case of tendonitis in my knee. My wife has our supply of Bufferin back at the motel in Helen. She had to get off the trail and rest up a while. Patti and Jean are low on food, so Patti and I decided to hitch in."

"Then I'll wait here with Jean for a while. Three would scare off a possible ride," Bob said. "I'll hitch in after you two leave. Need to buy a good supply of Twinkies. Been mentally tasting them for miles."

"I can tell right now you're a loose spirit just to hitch into town for a supply of Twinkies," John said.

"I need a few supplies, too ___ and to use the phone," Bob added.

"How many miles are you doing?" Patti asked. "You look like a pro."

"About fifteen a day, average," Bob said. "But I think I'm in shape now to go for twenty or twenty-five."

There were sighs of appreciation all around and Jean said, "We're straining to average ten or twelve. You must be experienced."

"I think we're outclassed," John said; then he and Patti went on down to the edge of the highway.

Bob and Jean watched from the bushes so that they would not frighten a motorist from stopping. "Is John going all the way on the AT?"

"He says so. If he can get his knees and Martina, his wife, in condition. She came down with blisters. They're a super couple."

"Are all of you traveling together?"

"Sort of. Patti and I and our friends, John Jurczynski and Peter Butryn, from Schenectady, met Linnehan at Addis Gap Leanto after his knee started acting up."

"Butryn and Jurczynski going on?"

"Yeah. We told them we'd catch up."

"Tell me about Linnehan," Bob said.

"He's a real estate broker from Sarasota. Martina teaches kids with learning disabilities."

"Can't wait to talk with her. We'll have a lot in common."

Bob talked about his own work, and learned more about Jean's background. She was, she told him, a naturalist, working under various jurisdictions in the State of Maryland. Patti, he learned, worked for the telephone company and lived in Marlboro, Maryland. The hitch-hikers, however, were making no progress at all. Half-hour passed; one or two cars went by without so much as slowing.

The hitch-hikers gave up and came back. John was walking painfully.

"This is no time for false courtesy," Bob insisted, fishing in his backpack. "Here. Take these. I can get more later."

He handed John six packets of extra-strength Tylenol.

"I can't do this," John said. "You might need them yourself."

"Forget it. Now get a dose down your gut, or you won't make it to the next leanto," Bob commanded. Belatedly he realized he had sounded too harsh, but Linnehan was grinning. He took the medicine and washed it down with water from his drinking bottle.

"I think I'll try it to town on my own," Bob said. "Maybe a handsome, intelligent-looking lone hiker will have better luck."

"If you meet anybody like that," John replied, "tell him to try it and let us know the result."

The triple laugh was on Bob, but the good sound of it was an excellent way to part company.

"Catch up with us when you can," Jean called as Bob walked away.

Later that day, Bob caught up with the same threesome and pitched camp with them at Plum Orchard Gap. There he also met six-foot Peter Butryn bearded, heavily built, with dark-patched blond hair and piercing blue eyes; John Jurczynski was equally athletic-looking but smooth-faced. Jurczynski had long, curly, sunbleached blond hair, greenish-blue eyes, and a ruddy complexion. Both men looked to be in their mid-twenties. Working with Peter setting up camp, Bob learned that Peter was an environmental technician who had hit the trail to work through some career decisions. Later he learned that Jurczynski had come from California where he had been a grounds keeper for the state after attending college two years; then he had biked to the East.

That night around the campfire they all shared food, and again Bob took a ribbing about his oversized pot. The jibes slowed, however, when they tasted his AT goulash.

When everybody was stuffed and couldn't move from the comfort of the campfire, Bob got a few of his walkathon pledgecards from his pack.

He stood so that the firelight would be between himself and his listeners.

"Now that I have a contented, captive audience, I should like to offer you each the chance of a lifetime. The chance to invest in humanity. The opportunity to donate a sum large or small to The Little Red Schoolhouse and The Homestead Project, both in the great and glorious state of Maine."

"I thought snake-oil salesmen went the way of the oxcart," Linnehan chided.

"Just a moment, sir." Bob waved a commanding hand. "Snake oil would help, but the deserving, lonely, handicapped people of whom I speak need, much, much more. Allow me to continue."

He went on to give the background of his mother's pet project and the history of The Homestead Project. Then he passed out the pledge cards.

"I'm convinced and ready to make a pledge," Linnehan said, "but who's this convict whose picture is on the cards?"

They all held their cards closer to the firelight and saw Bob's photo— complete with walrus mustache—imprinted there.

"No question about the worthiness of the cause, but who carries surplus money on the AT?" John Jurczynsk said. "I'll keep the card and send some when I get home."

"No rush," Bob said. "Save your pennies and send them at your leisure. All donations appreciated whenever sent."

The rest of the group got caught up in the worthiness of the cause; after hearing more background, each promised to send money from home.

The camaraderie lasted long around the fireside until the cherry-red coals started to fade. Darkness was fast approaching. Bob got up and laid his ground cloth on the earth between the campfire and the shelter.

"You sleeping out?" Linnehan asked.

"Yep. Any better shelter in the world than the star-studded heavens? The man in the moon grinning down at you? The big dipper tilting to pour a cup of celestial nectar?"

"Very poetic," Linnehan said, "but you didn't mention the big-mouthed bear who might also have visions of morsels-of-Mountford in mind."

"I come from a long line of bear fighters. No problem."

"I think I hear a tall tale coming on," Jean said.

"Not one of those," Patti groaned.

"Okay, have it your own way," Bob said. "If you don't want to hear the most stupendous bear tale in history, the many times my crusty old maternal great-grandfather nearly lost his dear life, then I'll be silent."

Bob paused for effect, but when the quiet was unbroken, he resorted to the gimmick of two-way conversation with himself.

"Tell us, Bob." "You really want to hear?" "Oh, yes! It sounds exciting."

"It is, I promise." "We can't wait. Hurry!" "Give me a moment to gear up, please!" "The anticipation is killing us." "All good things bring momentary suffering." "Get on with it!" "Okay here goes!"

"I'm not sure I'm ready for this," Peter said.

"I think it's going to be more of a shaggy dog story," Linnehan said, "but let the guy get on with it."

Bob took the tale-teller's stance, and began: "Well, my maternal grandfather, who lives with us in Dover-Foxcroft—and whose name is really Lloyd, but we call him Bill—used to keep all of us Mountford children entertained with tall tales his father, whom everyone called Dirty Bill, passed down to him. Now my great-grandfather Rideout used to be a woodsman in the wilds of Canada and northern Maine. He stayed in the woods for months on end, and I don't have to tell you how he got his nickname. And Dirty Bill was always running headlong into bears. One time when it was illegal to kill bears in Maine, great-grandpa, hungry for some good hind quarter, captured a big brown with his bare hands, wrestled it into the Saint Lawrence, swam with it across the river into Canada, and killed it barehanded there."

The guffaws shattered the night air.

"Don't you doubt all this for a minute," Bob warned. "It's all the gospel. Well, on another occasion Dirty Bill was cutting timber on the other side of the state, near New Brunswick, and two big she-bears hemmed him in against a rock cliff. The situation was hopeless. Dirty Bill said his last prayer. Then he got an idea. He lunged at both she-bears with his powerful arms outstretched, and when the bears opened their mouths to devour him, Dirty Bill rammed his arms down their throats through their stomachs and caught them by the tails and turned them wrong side out."

The audience outhooted the whole owl population for miles around.

"But Dirty Bill outdid himself," Bob went on. "He didn't reckon with the fact that those she-bears were pregnant; when he had turned them wrong side out, two dozen little cubs started running all around the place. It was too late then. He tried turning the mama bears right side out again, but it didn't work. So for a whole winter Dirty Bill had to stay in the desolate Maine woods caring for all those little cubs. He took rubber gloves and fashioned nipples with the fingers and fed the cubs maple syrup to keep them alive until spring."

Gales of laughter swept over the tired group, and each headed for his sleeping bag.

With his lower body snuggled deep in the warm wrapping, Bob donned the miner's lamp he had brought along for night reading and searched the Scriptures for the next day's hiking verse. He read a little from The Song of Solomon, and half-way through the second chapter his eyes fell on verse twelve: *The flowers appear on the earth; the time of the singing of birds is come, and the voice of the turtle is heard in our land . . .*

The verse seemed beautifully appropriate. The birds had sung along every mile of the trail and soon the lush rhododendron would burst forth with magenta blossoms; woodland fields would be colored with wild phlox, but what does a turtle's voice sound like? Bob removed the headlamp and lay down to sleep, but his mind was churning. Camp was utterly quiet. Something in him rebelled against questions left unanswered. Finally, he could stand it no longer.

"Hey, Linnehan! Do turtles have voices? Y'know—calls, cries, barks?"

Some kind of grumbling came from the older man's direction; then a sharp Bostonian voice split the air: "If they did, Mountford, they'd say, 'Shut up and let your friends sleep'!"

"Yes, they make kind of a gurgling sound," Peter called out. "And don't ask me to minic one. I'm bushed."

"Goodnight, Bob," Jean called out with ingratiating sweetness.

"Goodnight, Jean. Goodnight, Patti. Goodnight, John J. Goodnight, John L. Goodnight, Peter. Goodnight all . . ."

". . . *shut up!"* A chorus of mixed voices rent the air.

Bob sank as low in his sleeping bag as his big body would allow. He just didn't know about these grumpy people after all. High in the heavens a million stars blinked; it appeared to him that the moon, smiled approval that he had enriched his life with the personality of these new friends.

CHAPTER VII

The rising sun bathed the quiet land with an orange glow. The sky was clear; the air still and brisk.

Bob was the first one up. He paid nature's call deep in the woods and returning saw two whitetailed doe coming to water. What delicate, yet magnificent animals! How quick their dignified walk could turn into ballerina-like leaps that seemed to defy gravity!

Back at the fringes of the camp perimeter again, he began morning calisthenics. He could feel his blood surge, his body come vibrantly alive. He wanted to give his Tarzan squall, but only a couple of the others had begun to stir. Exercise completed, he spotted a big rock nearby and stood upon it for another sometimes-morning ritual.

Like a Roman orator, he cleared his throat and began: "Coniferous. Consistorial. Dramaturgically. Dyslogistic. Encomiastical. Fanfaronade. Fetiparous. Globuliferous. Graminivorous. Homochromatic. Idiosyncratically. Jurehumano. Keratogenous. Knighterranty. Luminiferous. Macrography. Mansuetude. Philopena. Philoprogenitive. Philo . . . "

". . . what in Caesar's name is going on out there?"

Bob turned and saw John Linnehan poking his balding head from under the leanto. His eyes looked propped open and wild.

"My vocabulary exercises," Bob called back. "New words I'm learning to use."

"Before breakfast?"

Bob quit and joined Peter and Patti, who had begun meal preparations. The cooking fire was soon roaring. Where a group was concerned, one fire saved everybody's stove fuel.

"If you do *that* many word exercises until the end of the trail, you can write your own dictionary," Patti said.

"Maybe," Bob agreed, "but I won't be going the whole stretch at one time. I've got to get off the Trail in Pennsylvania. We have the Maine Special Olympics in June. I promised Mom I'd help. It's not just for her kids. Retarded youngsters from all over the state participate. It's a real big deal. A couple of thousand kids doing some amazing things."

"That's fantastic," Peter said. "I've never seen anything like that."

56

"The best part," Bob said, "is watching the sheer joy—the sense of accomplishment in the participants. Seeing a deficient kid carrying that torch makes you want to stand up and cheer."

The three of them talked on about The Little Red Schoolhouse and the problems of the retarded in general. Funny, Bob thought, how people everywhere responded so positively when that particular social problem was mentioned, but action and contribution lagged far behind sympathy.

"Come and get it!" Peter yelled. "Hot oatmeal and powdered milk. Three dollars a head. Two-ninety-five if you bring your own sugar."

The three missing bodies appeared from different directions.

"Oatmeal?" Jean cried. "Why not link sausage, scrambled eggs, hot apple sauce, hominy grits, hot biscuits, and blackberry jam?"

"Dreamer," Peter said. "Oatmeal will stick to your ribs. We've got some rough territory to cover in the next two or three days."

There were groans. Everybody knew that some straight-up mountain terrain lay ahead.

Patti served hot tea after each had filled his cereal bowl. As his contribution Bob steamed some of the dried fruit he had brought along. They all sat Indian style. The air was still brisk enough for the fire to feel good even through a down vest or a jacket.

"Speaking of bread," Bob said, "I know of a lady in Wesser, North Carolina, who makes sourdough bread. She doesn't know it, but I may just pay her a visit."

"You're excused if you'll bring us some," Peter said.

"On the other hand," Bob added, "I'm fighting the battle of the bulge already. Want to drop twenty pounds. Haven't made ten yet."

"Wait'll you face the Nantahalas and Albert Mountain up ahead," JJ said. "You'll drop excess body fat like a fasting guru."

"Even if you just fall and roll back you'll be firmed up," Linnehan cracked.

A ripple of laughter made the rounds. And on the trail every amusing little incident seemed funnier—exaggerated until the mildly comical became hilarious.

"Jeez! These mountains are anthills," Bob insisted. "Try going a half mile up the face of a cliff—on a rope, hand over hand—trying to get an occasional spike in a crevice."

"That I'd like to become more proficient at," Peter said.

"You're hereby invited. All of you. If you haven't seen Maine, boy, you've really missed something. Give me Mount Katahdin, and you can have the rest of the world."

"Now that we know the Maine State Chamber of Commerce sponsored Bob's trip, anybody interested in seeing North Carolina?" Linnehan offered.

They pitched in for the cleanup operation. JJ doused the fire, and everyone began to ready his gear.

"Everybody sign in on the log?" Jean called. "Last chance."

Peter and JJ led off with Bob and Linnehan following. Patti and Jean brought up the rear. The first rule of the trail was that a slow hiker didn't hold a faster one back. JJ and Peter started to string out; so did Bob and Linnehan. As Bob looked back, Patti and Jean were already fifty yards apart. Everyone was beginning to find his own stride.

Later in the day, when the first steep mountain had been traversed, one by one they came in to Muskrat Creek shelter for a breather and for more than the water and gorp each had probably had along the way. The sun was not unbearably hot, but for long minutes every heart raced from the stairstep climb into Nantahala Mountains.

While they were signing in on the Trail register, somebody noticed that an earlier hiker had penned the lyrics of Cat Stevens's "Eleven Miles From Nowhere." Bob read the lyrics aloud, and in a moment the group took up the chant. Like a backwoods version of a Lawrence Welk quintet, they began to sing the song for real. As Peter's and Bob's froglike basses mixed with JJ's and Linnehan's whiskey tenors and Patti's and Jean's sopranos, the performance slid smoothly down the mountainside and petered out in the hollows.

"No chorus of mountain goats ever sounded better," Linnehan said.

"Yeah. It was good enough to curdle the moonshine in these parts," JJ said.

"Speaking of shine," Bob said, "you suppose there's any place around we could get a little white mule or mountain dew?"

"Forget that stuff," Linnehan said. "It's probably distilled out of a rusty car radiator anyway. What I've got a taste for is some good cold beer."

"You're out of luck, guys," Jean said. "The map says we're miles from nowhere. The next town of any size is Franklin; if that vision of suds is to come alive, we'd best hit the trail."

Bob led off and the group trudged on more deeply into Nantahala National Forest, each again finding his own pace, thinking his own thoughts, dreaming his own dreams.

The day grew hotter; the climb, ever upward. The great Appalachian chain was a thousand worlds in one, each offering surprise and reward of a unique and unforgettable kind. By three-thirty that afternoon, the whole party reached Standing Indian Leanto. The location was an especially pleasant resting area with a good view, a large picnic table, and pure water nearby. And it had another feature: Frank Maguire.

They all sat around the picnic table, each bringing his trail diary up to date and generally relaxing with a cup of hot tea. Frank was having a leisurely smoke, and again the delicious aroma of burning tobacco invaded Bob's nostrils. Bob actually began a concentrated effort to breathe in the second-hand fumes and took a round of ribbing about his "weakness." The more they chided him, the more Bob could taste the rich tobacco. Finally he could wrestle with his urgings no longer.

"I've got to have a butt! For God's sake, Frank, give me just one!"

"No. You told me not to. You said you really wanted to quit."

Everybody around the table was nodding agreement with Frank.

"We've all just voted 'No,'" Linnehan said. "Bad for you. Just think: The Great American Athlete succumbing to the evils of the weed, allowing his strength to be dissipated, his lungs to be contaminated. Shame! Shame!"

"I'm going crazy!" Bob insisted. "Damn it, Frank, just one. I'll give you five bucks for just one!"

With stoic calm Frank pulled one from the pack and handed it over. "Knew you'd never hold out. Had a bet with myself about it."

Bob lit the Camel, sucked the first drag down deep, felt his toes tingle. "Aaaahh," he exhaled slowly.

"Hooked again." Patti laughed.

"I've got to make note of this tragic day," Jean said, as she started writing again in her diary.

"Another good hiker bites the dust," JJ added.

"And I really believed Bob had unshakable resolve." Peter sighed.

"Blessed is the man that endureth temptation . . ." Linnehan threw back Bob's earlier quotation on the subject.

"Dammit!" Bob exploded. "I'm going into the woods and smoke alone."

After they had had a kind of community supper, the harassment died down, and he and Frank blew smoke rings at each other across the table. Bob thought the after-meal smoke was the best he had ever had, save for that time he explained, when he was an exchange student in Russia and had run out of American cigarettes and had to switch to foreign brands. Then someone had come up with a pack of Chesterfields, and he was in heaven again.

Dusk was ending when they finished talking and began to ready sleeping bags and to lay claims to space. Because the leanto wouldn't accommodate everybody, John Linnehan was the first to volunteer to sleep outside.

Bob scoffed. "Your knees would lock up for sure with rheumatism! We'd have to sit on you in the morning to straighten you out!"

"Watch your sassy mouth, boy! I'm keeping up and you know it!"

It was true. Linnehan's strength was amazing.

A grumble of thunder resounded in the far distance. Bob hoped no rain would come for a day or two. Mount Albert, which they faced on the morrow, was obstacle enough bone dry. Wet, the straight-up climb would be treacherous indeed. "Lord, let it be dry tomorrow," he whispered, realizing that the simple request was his first prayer in a very long time.

As if the prayer had been answered, the dawn broke clear, not even a hint of the early-morning fog that was so common in the higher elevations was in view. The sky was cloudless, and just a hint of chilliness existed in the air.

"Hey, you clowns! Get up! There's a whole new world out there! Mount Albert awaits you!"

"Quiet, Mountford!" Patti's groggy voice protested. "I'm sacking in. Not going. This bag feels good _____ "

"Like fun you're not! We can't go on without *you*."

He sprung to the opening of the leanto.

"Get lost!" Jean managed a low groan.

Frank was wide awake, half out of his bag, twin ribbons of smoke coming out of his nose.

"Don't tell me you're debating this challenge, too?" Bob said.

"Not debating—just remembering what somebody told me. Getting to the top of Albert Mountain is hand-over-hand work. I think you four had better have lots of beans and cornbread for breakfast. I'm staying here."

The rising sun had barely cleared the eastern treetops when Bob, Peter, Linnehan, and JJ hit the trail once more. Linnehan and Peter led off. It suddenly hit Bob how much a backpack-laden man looked like a moon-bound astronaut loaded with scientific equipment. Another thing that registered belatedly was the mild similarity of looks and build between Peter and Neal Chivington. Bob hoped that Neal, Steve, and Sandy would catch up, but the chances were good that they were at least five to seven days behind. At the next Trail register he would leave his Maine friends a note anyway.

That this day was going to be an unusual one was soon proven when Peter ahead on the trail called back through the trees: "Look out! The "thing" is coming toward you!"

Bob looked up and saw a strange animal barreling down the trail toward him. At twenty yards its grotesque foaming snout, steely tusks, and dumpy body told him that it was a wild boar. Bob readied his trusty walking stick, but the speedy little monster veered off the trail into the underbrush. He had expected wild dogs, but wild boars? He stopped to draw a deep breath, felt his heart racing in his chest. His knees grew weak and down he sat.

JJ, coming into view, said, "What was that I heard bulldozing through the underbrush?"

"You won't believe me."

"The Abominable Bushman?"

"A wild boar."

"No kidding. You haven't been chewing ivy leaves or anything?"

"I kid you not! It was a ferocious-looking hog with ratty hair and a mouth like a chainsaw!"

JJ laughed.

Bob, still nearly breathless, said, "I didn't know there were such animals in North Carolina. Never heard of it."

"Well, seeing is believing. Sure it wasn't a deer?"

"Dammit, it was a big pig in high gear, I tell you. Wait'll we catch up with Peter and Linnehan. They'll tell you. Peter called out and warned me."

"Good thing Patti and Jean didn't run up on that thing. They'd have set a world record in tree climbing."

Thinking about that sent Bob into spasms of laughter. For a moment before, he himself had been heading for a tall oak. With a shudder he hoped that the animal wasn't rabid or that he wouldn't turn back on them.

Bob and JJ caught up and the four of them rested, compared notes on what they had seen, and recharged their batteries with a generous helping of gorp. Again Peter and Linnehan led off; Bob and JJ soon followed.

The fearful symmetry of Albert Mountain became more forbidding with each step. At points Bob could see Peter and Linnehan far above him, and Linnehan was indeed using his hands to overcome the steep grade. This section of North Carolina reminded Bob of the most rugged sections in Maine. But the exertion was good. As the air on the upper heights grew thinner and colder, the sweaters and the light jackets they had all worn that morning felt good. The trees were many days away from leafing out, and the barren mountain offered little cover from the rising wind.

Barren or not, the mountain had a unique beauty. At points vast boulders appeared to be stacked one upon another as if some colossal stonemason had laid them there among the scrubby trees—trees too near the frost line to grow big and tall. Depressions like great wounds or pockmarks in the rocky earth were nesting places for odd-looking fungi and lichen. Rotting fallen trees and slowly decaying stumps provided natural fertilizer and homes for burrowing animals. Abundant fallen leaf cover did the same, and helped, along with the millions of spidery roots, to protect the land from catastrophic erosion. Nature's engineering at its best.

The firetower on top soon came into view. A little while later, he saw Linnehan and Peter make the summit, and both climb up toward the observation room. Suddenly, he felt a new burst of energy; he wanted to do the same, stand on top of the world and feel euphoria of body and soul.

The vantage point achieved, he found the view breathtaking. The earth's contours spread for miles in all directions, before fading into a hazy infinity. When he too had gained the observation room, Peter and Linnehan were still puffing from the climb.

A ruddy-faced forest ranger looked mildly amused at the hikers surrounding him and said to Bob, "I watched you. You came up that grade like it wasn't there. I can tell you right now, you're an experienced hiker!"

Bob confirmed it with a grin and instantly felt the warmth of this North Carolinian with his friendly drawl.

"Show us where Franklin is," Linnehan said.

The ranger pointed a leathery hand north-eastwardly. "Over *there*. To the right of that ridgeline."

"Oh, boy!" Linnehan said. "I can almost see that tavern on Main Street. Beer. Good, cold, foamy, delicious beer! I can taste it now."

"You don't see no tavern in that town, my friend," the ranger said. "That town's dry as a bone. This county can't sell alcohol. Dry as a bone from east to west, I tell ya."

Bob went into gales of laughter. Linnehan's face was like a slapped child's.

"You'll just love the iced tea in Franklin," Bob said. "Beer's bad for you anyway. It's like cigarettes and wild women."

Even the ranger could hardly suppress a grin.

There was a general picture-taking session then, and finally Peter wanted a photo of himself alone, the sweeping North Carolina mountains and valleys as a backdrop behind him. The pinnacle he stood on was so high that a hurricane fence guarded the perimeters of the lofty boulders. The gigantic rocks were so ancient-looking that the wind-and-storm-cut etchings looked a million years old.

The rigorous climb and the descent gave birth to voracious appetites, and the four of them set up camp well before dark at Big Spring Leanto. When they bedded down under tents, Bob knew that nobody needed a nightbird's song to end this day.

Next morning the rain they had feared seemed to be on the way. The sky was overcast, the land bathed in browns and grays. The whole crew save for Frank Maguire had planned to go into Franklin. Frank would either wait in camp or walk on as it suited him. More and more Bob was seeing the loner—the individualist—in Frank, and he wanted to get to know the ex-chief better.

Linnehan had more reasons than anybody to get into Franklin in spite of its dry status. Martina had agreed to rendezvous with him there.

They broke camp and were on the trail by seven-thirty. Within the first mile a gentle shower began, and before they got to Wallace Gap, a steady downpour was upon them. Debate arose as to whether this vantage point was best for hitch-hiking into Franklin. Peter and JJ decided to stay and try their luck. Bob and Linnehan hiked on toward Winding Stair Gap three miles away to try a new highway.

Bob kept a fast pace and had to stop at intervals for Linnehan to catch up. The rain kept pouring down, and the temperature had dropped at least to the low forties.

Arriving at the gap and Highway 64 by 11:30, they found the wind and the rain even more savage. The wait for a ride along the highway became increasingly miserable, and Bob began to worry. The possibility of getting hypothermia was real especially in John's case. Bob suggested that his hiking partner put on his down jacket and offered him gorp for nourishment.

For an hour and a half they stood along the highway. No luck. "You'd never wait this long in Maine," Bob said. "People at home recognize the backpackers and are eager to help them."

A few minutes later JJ and Peter showed up. They had no luck either. Everybody was suddenly feeling down. And being wet and cold didn't help any.

As they all waited longer, Bob suggested a rock-throwing contest. He set some roadside soft drink cans on a post, and each took turns at fifty feet. A fifty-cent pool was established for the winner. After they had repeatedly tried without hitting the target, a flatbed lumber truck came down the highway and stopped.

Linnehan was shivering, and Bob insisted that he ride in the cab. The remaining three threw their gear on the truck bed and climbed on. For a few miles the rain slapped and stung their faces like flying sand; then, mercifully, it stopped.

At the major intersection in Franklin, they all got out and headed for the motel in which Martina (having arrived via bus) was supposed to be lodged. Bob was sure that Dirty Bill had always looked like an usher at the Ritz in contrast to the four grimy bodies that now made a mad rush to Martina Linnehan's room.

Martina, only slightly shorter than John, opened the door and let out a little cry before gathering her soaked husband to her breast. She was a slender, pretty woman in her forties, most likely. Her warm brown eyes were aglow, and Bob could see in her a person naturally affectionate.

After a few brief niceties, Bob, JJ, and Peter left the room, rented one of their own, and fought like school children to get into the shower. Civilization at last!

CHAPTER VIII

Having showered and relaxing on the bed, Bob, JJ, and Peter had the unexpected thrill of seeing some of the space shuttle events on TV. It reminded Bob that no matter how much he and the others were enjoying the peaceful and scenic life of the Applachian Trail, other things no less exciting were going on.

Space probes or not, bellies begged for filling, and they headed for the local barbecue pit. Spectators soon got the idea that some kind of eating contest was going on. Bob noticed that they were the center of attention; a few people had begun to stand and look.

"They just don't know how long it's been since we've had baths and french fries!" Bob cracked as he shoveled on.

On the way back to the motel, they picked up picture postcards and snacks for later evening and then stopped by the Linnehans' room. Showered and dressed in clean clothes, Linnehan didn't look like the same man. Martina, too, had freshened up and looked delightfully feminine.

"*Now*, you look too much like the real estate executive," Bob said. "I don't know whether we're going to take you back on the trail or not."

"Correction. Take *us* back. Martina's in fine form now. She'll probably walk me to exhaustion."

Within the hour Patti and Jean knocked and entered.

"Where's Frank?" Bob asked.

"He was getting ready to head north when we left," Patti said. "Still waters run deep."

"We'll catch him somewhere along the way," Bob said. "Want to get to know him better."

The room was small, the TV set only mildly below blaring, and two or three different conversations were going simultaneously. Martina visited with each of her guests briefly, entertaining—sans spirits—with the same poise and charm she might have at home in Sarasota.

"John can't talk enough about you," she told Bob. "He says that you are a brilliant conversationalist and walking encyclopedia. He says, too, that you keep them all in stitches, know all about politics, read the Bible to them, cook like a French chef, and have the last word about sports, hiking and outdoorsmanship."

"I confess only to telling him that I read *National Geographic* religiously."

"Obviously you read everything. But that's not what impresses me most. He tells me you're in social work—that your mother is the director of a home for retarded children. Perhaps he told you that's my calling too."

Martina elaborated on the sixteen years she had spent in special education work among the learning disabled in Florida and elsewhere. Bob revealed his own briefer past and experiences. The night was too short to cover all their mutual interests.

"I look forward to talking with you more on the trail," Martina concluded. "I think you can tell me a lot."

The guys walked the girls to their room; then getting back to their own, Bob busied himself addressing postcards. For his parents he selected one with a color photo of purple rhododendrons in full bloom and wrote final instructions for their—and Jackie's—rendezvous with him at Easter. It was working out beautifully. They would have the drive down scenic Interstate 81 into Tennessee, hit Interstate 40 toward Knoxville, and after a short jaunt on state roads they would head right in to Great Smoky Mountain National Park headquarters.

Hard to believe that April 19, Easter, was just nine days away. It now seemed an eternity since he had held Jackie in his arms, felt her small, yet incredibly strong, body yield to his own. The thought continued to warm him as he wrote and addressed one postcard after another.

Next morning after breakfast of sausage and pancakes, Peter wanted to make a dash to the local health food store for some sunflower seeds, and Bob and JJ went along. Like many hikers, Bob liked to munch on the tasty and nourishing seeds; now was a good chance to get some along with a fresh supply of specially ground condiments.

When they got back to the motel, Linnehan and Martina were all set, and the five of them hired two taxis for the trip back to the trail. The girls had decided to stay in town longer and hit the trail later in the day. Linnehan, Martina, and JJ took the first cab. Bob and Peter had hardly closed the rattly door of their own when Bob found himself in verbal combat with their driver. Bob ribbed the wiry-haired Carolinian about the dry status of the county.

"We're stampin' out sin," the cabbie said with a wry smile.

"You don't ever make a little run across the county line and bring back a load?" Bob prodded.

"When the money's right, I've been heard of doing such a thing."

"Shame," Bob said. "And right here on the fringe of the Bible Belt."

"The people around here always vote liquor down?" Peter asked.

"Yep, and a few of the moonshiners help 'em."

They had cleared the town limits when the driver asked them what life was like on the Trail. Peter shared some of his experiences.

"Everybody tells me somethin' different," the driver said. "I haul a lot of hikers that come in for a rest. Some of 'em don't go back—get wore out, discouraged or somethin'. By the way, one feller told me there's a lot of good-eatin' ramps between here and Wayah Bald. You ought to try some."

"Ramps? What are ramps?" Bob asked.

"You've never heard of ramps? They're like wild onions. You can eat 'em. Cook with 'em."

Bob asked for a description of the plants and instructions about how to look for them. The explanation was lengthy, and the driver finally concluded; "When you eat 'em raw, they'll stay on your breath for days. Last time I tried 'em, my wife said I could sleep in the basement. She said she'd just as soon sleep with a Jersey bull as a man with ramps on his breath."

Back at the Trail intersection the driver helped get the gear from under the tied-down trunk lid and offered a final bit of advice.

"When you find them ramps, peel the outside skin off good, or they'll set you afire plum down to your balls."

They promised to take the advice, chipped in to pay the fare, and threaded arms into their backpacks. They soon caught up with the other three.

Back on the trail Bob, JJ, and Peter hiked ahead, leaving Linnehan and Martina to bring up the rear. Martina would have to take it easy until her body was accustomed to hiking again.

At midday when the three of them had come to a rest stop and paused to have some gorp and sunflower seed, Peter said, "Maybe that rebel was pulling our leg. Seems to me I read somewhere that ramps grow only in West Virginia."

JJ was making wide circles around the place where they sat. Spreading out, he investigated a moist, flat area—and he called to Bob.

When Bob and Peter reached him, JJ was holding aloft a flat-leafed, onionish-looking plant whose aroma told Bob instantly they had struck pay dirt. Bob pulled a few of the plants for himself.

"They look like wild leeks I saw in the lowlands in Scotland," Bob said. He pulled several handfuls, tied them at the tops, and hung them on the framing of his backpack. He pulled another to taste.

His mouth was quickly afire in spite of his peeling away the outer skin as he had been instructed. He spat the stringy matter to the ground.

"Hot as hades! Wild garlic, it should be called."

JJ and Peter couldn't resist making their own test, but they almost lost their breakfast.

"I'm still going to take a mess," Bob said. "I'll make us a stew tonight and spice it up a little. We'll call it Appalachian Trail Ramp Stew. It'll start a trend. Probably be on the menu at the Waldorf in a year or two."

"Don't hold your breath," JJ said. "Or maybe you'd better. How about walking a mile or two ahead?"

That afternoon they arrived at Wayah Bald and set up tents near a massive stone structure that was both a monument to one John B. Byrne, former supervisor of Nantahala National Forest, and observation tower.

Outside stairs wound upward along the rock wall to a viewing platform that allowed a three-hundred-sixty-degree sweep of the terrain. Once they had gained the dizzying height, Bob, Peter and JJ stood in breathless wonder for a long moment. Peter looked at his Trail Guide.

"Five thousand, three hundred and thirty six feet. We're standing over a mile high!" Peter exclaimed.

JJ searched his own Trail Guide and pointed north.

"That far point—that's Mount Mitchell. Highest peak east of the Mississippi."

The incredible view wasn't limited to the north. To the south and southeast, they could see the mountains of Georgia and South Carolina.

For an interminable time they remained there like a group of kids on the observation floor of the Empire State Building.

"Didn't know there was so much thinly populated land in the whole world," Peter mused.

"Those trees sure would build a lot of houses," JJ said.

"Of course, you'd have to come to Maine to see really tall timber," Bob added.

"Right now I'd settle for scrub brush if it'll burn," Peter said. "I'm getting cold."

The wind did have a penetrating chill, and sweaty bodies felt it quickly. Bob, taking a final glance southward, thought he caught a momentary glimpse of the Linnehans crossing a clearing.

"I think our companions are on the way. I'd better get busy with my Appalachian Trail Ramp Stew."

After the campfire was going just right, Bob got out his big pot and inventoried their collective supplies. A stew was out of the question since a shortage of ingredients prevailed, but he was determined to use the ramps in some way. Finally the idea of cooking some "campfire" hoagies struck him. They didn't have sirloin beef strips, but they did have plenty of beef jerky. Bob had tomato paste for his occasional spaghetti making, and he had bought cheese and cheese oil in Franklin. The normally-used green pepper was out; but as for the required chopped onion, the ramps would, he hoped, be the perfect substitute. For hoagie buns they would have to make do with English muffins.

When the whole concoction was ready, he placed a layer of muffins in foil, covered them generously with the combined ingredients, added cheese topping, sealed the foil, and placed the separate servings in the warm outer ashes of the campfire. JJ and Peter had held their noses throughout the whole operation, pointing all the while to buzzards circling overhead. When he was sure the warm ashes had melted the cheese, Bob retrieved a serving and peeled back the foil. The aroma was like a whiff of atomized Texas Pete carried on the breeze from a chicken house. When it cooled, Bob bit in.

"Fantastic!" he proclaimed just before his eyes started to water.

"Do I dare?" Peter reached uncertainly for his helping.

JJ plunged in without comment, but Bob saw him close his eyes before taking a bite.

All three of them were hitting the water bottles heavily when Martina and John came over the rise. Linnehan had hardly set foot inside the camp perimeter when he sang out, "What are you burning on the campfire, dried cow dung?"

"Appalachian Trail Campfire Hoagies 'n Ramps," Bob said. "Come and try some."

Martina was more curious than her husband, but she nibbled cautiously. Linnehan smelled his momentarily and rolled his eyes.

"I'm trying to identify it. I remember once in Boston taking a short cut through an alley. Some wino had left a rolled-up codfish in an old boot."

"That's it!" Bob growled. "I resign as camp cook. No appreciation."

"Don't give up yet," Linnehan said after taking a bite. "We'll give you a second chance. Somewhere up ahead there'll be some brook trout. And if you can make hush puppies, you're redeemed."

After the meal was over, they all went up to the observation platform and stood there until the sun had disappeared behind the western horizon.

"Have you ever seen a sunset at sea?" Martina asked Bob.

"I spent part of a summer once in California and saw the sun go down over the Pacific; I guess that's close."

"So—what were you doing in California?" she prompted as they walked back to camp.

"It's a long story. My hometown friend, Sean Stitham, and I—took part of the summer of '76 off to see the country."

"And check out the girls of California, no doubt?"

"That, too, but it was more than that. We saw a lot of Stinson Beach, and were royally entertained by Sean's friends. We did some backpacking in Yosemite National Park, and after that it was time to head home."

Back at the dying embers of the campfire, Martina, asked, "This friend—Sean—is he as good a backpacker as you?"

"Sean's good at anything he seriously tries. In many ways he's a genius. More than a little bonkers at times but still a genius. He's going to be an outstanding physician some day."

"Did the two of you do any hiking east of the Rockies coming back?" Peter asked.

"We didn't come home together. Sean stayed on, but I had to get back to earn some bucks for fall quarter. I hitchhiked. What a catastrophe! I was broke again and hooked up with a con man selling 'loyalty certificates.' "

"I think I hear a doozy coming up," Linnehan said.

"This is no tall tale," Bob insisted. "This guy was the only chance I had. Anyway he had a bunch of loyalty certificates printed up. You know, the kind of thing that says, 'This is to certify that blank is a Loyal American, dedicated to the Flag and all that this Great Nation stands for; and so forth.' And aside from the certificates, the guy had boxes full of surplus World War II ribbons. So my job along with his was to buttonhole a not-too-intelligent-looking Hoosier, sign him up on the certificate, pin a ribbon on his chest, and collect five bucks. It shames me now to admit it."

"I always knew there was a touch of the shyster in you," Linnehan chuckled. "Okay, How much did you make?"

"Ninety-six dollars in one day and night. In a beer hall. I got eight half-drunk guys in a row."

"And they were probably old vets. Shame on Mountford," somebody chided.

Bob took such a ribbing he was soon sorry that he had told about his hard-luck hitchhike.

Afterward, when he had donned his miner's lamp for Scripture reading, a real sense of guilt came over him. It was not out-and-out thievery. The "contributors" had got a fancy piece of paper and ribbon for their money, but they had been conned.

His pricked conscience continued to disturb him. What was it about the purity of the Trail that made a person look more deeply into himself?

When dawn broke, Peter was the first one out of his sleeping bag. Bob's slumber was suddenly interrupted by Peter's shrill voice.

"The little beasts cleaned me out! Ate the last one!"

Bob scrambled to his feet as did the others.

Peter stood over his stuffsack, pointing at the hole a mouse had made. All the sunflower seed was gone save for a few hulls the rodent had left on the ground in his hasty retreat.

Collective laughter was instantaneous, but Peter squatted beside his perforated gear in disbelief.

"We'll send out a posse if you say so," Bob said, "or we'll share our supply until you can resupply yourself."

The gesture helped, but Peter ate breakfast in disgusted silence.

Over a second cup of hot tea, Martina wanted to hear more about The Little Red School House and Bob's work at Homestead. He talked at length; then he heard more of her own experiences. Finally she said, "You're a very special guy. Wish we could walk all the way with you and continue these good talks, but I can't keep up and I know it."

"Maybe you'll catch up somewhere along the way. If not, come by my parents' home before you head back to Florida. You'll be like one of the family. John knows all the particulars . . . and Dover-Foxcroft is not far from the end of the trail."

Martina thanked and embraced him, and after they had all broken camp, Bob shook hands with Linnehan in case they should not see each other again.

"What kind of ridiculous ceremony is this?" Linnehan said. "Haven't you ever heard of the Tortoise and the Hare? We may beat you to Maine!"

"You could at that—but just in case. Take care. You're a helluva guy. I won't forget you.

Peter and JJ loaded up, and Bob shouldered his own backpack. The sun winked over the endless ranges to the east: spring was definitely in the air.

"We can make it to Wesser by day's end," Bob challenged. "Sourdough bread at last."

"Maybe, but a big-mile day," JJ said. "Why rush it?"

"I think JJ hopes Patti and Jean will catch up," Peter said low.

Bob had observed JJ and Patti beginning to hit it off earlier, and if the Californian wanted to hang back, that was his decision. As for himself, Bob itched to cover some ground. He led off.

Before passing from view, he turned one last time and waved. Now that he was removed from them, some feeling told him that he probably never would see the Linnehans again. It was a saddening thought, and yet it was a part of trail life. The realization of it made him lengthen his stride all the more. His body seemed bursting with vigor, his senses suddenly sharpened to sights and smells. No one would outwalk him today. Already he was leaving JJ and Peter behind, but it was just as well. He needed some solitude; he wanted to savor the thought that Jackie would soon be with him in the Great Smokies. Jackie loved the outdoors no less than he. And small as she was, she was incredibly strong and had amazing powers of endurance.

The Trail dropped sharply into Burningtown Gap, more than a thousand feet lower than the scenic perch atop Waylah Bald. The valley ground offered new sights. The hardwood timber grew taller, and here and there a few first-growth chestnuts survived. Flame azalea bushes were not long from blooming, and a variety of ferns—some deep green, others nearly a pea-green—grew lushly in fertile soil. The aroma of rich earth was indescribable; Ben Creek meandered peacefully down the valley.

He crossed an overgrown field and ascended to the north ridge of Burningtown Bald. He paused at Cold Springs Leanto, noting in the Trail Guide that the shelter had been built by the old Civilian Conservation Corps back in the '30s. So many, over so long a period of time, had made the AT possible, he thought. How can I leave the Trail better than I found it? A spring was nearby, and he drank the fresh water and filled his canteen. He ate some gorp at the picnic table before walking on past enormous oaks and sparse undergrowth.

Copper Bald loomed next and beyond it Black Bald: vast protruding bald mounds like breasts, reaching for the heavens.

By the time he had reached Wesser Bald late in the afternoon, he began to feel fatigue. It was a tough section of trail—up and down one mountain or "bald" after another. He rested and ate a couple of granola bars; the view itself was enough to give him strength. He visited the fire tower, and the panorama stretched beyond the Nantahala Gorge to the Great Smokies. The tower map confirmed that he had reached the northernmost peak of the Nantahala mountains. In two or three days he would be nearing the Tennessee state line.

It was still six or seven miles to the village of Wesser and he trudged on. Descending the mountain via the switchbacks along the ridge, the trail ultimately wound along Wesser Creek past an occasional house. Here in the fertile valley at the lower elevations, spring growth was more evident. Dogwood, bellwood, and a black locust or two had started to bloom. Budding red maples provided an arresting contrast, and in spots along the creek bluets made a colorful carpet. Violets, trout lilies, and painted trillium grew here and there.

A little farther along he approached a ramshackle frame house that didn't look lived in, but an old woman, her white hair neatly contained in a bonnet, stood in the plowed soil of a garden. She bent periodically, planting some kind of seed. Bob walked over.

"Planting time, huh?"

She straightened slowly and arched herself backwards as if to ease off a crick.

"Yep. See my onions? Plantin' some more lettuce now."

"I'd love to be around when your tomatoes and sweet corn come in."

She studied his face and took note of his backpack.

"Why aren't you busy plantin' your own garden 'stead of walkin' 'round with that *thing*?"

"I'm from Maine. We don't plant gardens quite as early as you do."

"From Maine, huh? Good potatoes come from up there."

"Yes, Ma'am."

"Why so many of you younguns waste your time walkin'? It's gettin' like a super highway 'round here."

"It's the only way a lot of city people ever get to see your beautiful country."

The wrinkled brow unfurled slightly, and for a moment Bob thought she might invite him in for a ham biscuit or a glass of iced mint tea. If you could believe old history, few rural people were hospitable to hikers; but maybe things were gradually changing.

"I'm wasting time jawbonin'," she said. "I'd better get back to work."

She bent down again before he conceded loss of the diplomatic round.

"Good luck with your garden. Hope you have a good season."

The woman grunted something, and he walked on. With every step the imagined ham biscuits tasted better. Greater fatigue and ravenous hunger overtook him for real by the time Wesser Creek Leanto came into view. The wire-enclosed site had a double fireplace and a cold mountain spring, and the bunks in the leanto looked especially inviting.

In minutes he had a campfire going and heated a rice-and-gravy dinner with some tuna fish added. All the meal lacked was a hunk of sourdough bread. But the village of Wesser would have to wait until tomorrow. Rested and hungry once more, he would descend on the outdoor center restaurant and have that famous dinner known to hikers and boaters far and wide, "the river runners special." Then he would be ready for the jump-up out of Wesser and the treacherous trail around the rim of the Nantahala Gorge. One slip and you could fall forever, someone had said, but every mile moved him closer to Fontana Dam and the Great Smokies!

CHAPTER IX

Bob Mountford, Sr., picked up the ringing phone in his combination study/insurance office. The exuberance of Bobby's voice was unmistakable. Father listened to the outpourings of son for ten minutes before there was a pause.

"No, your mother's not here. Did you get your mail drop at Fontana Dam okay? The next one's already on the way to Hot Springs . . ."

Bobby cut the conversation short with the question his father had been dreading.

"I know it's going to disappoint you, Son, but we're not going to make it south. I've got an important business meeting and an insurance conference I simply can't miss. Jackie can't go either. She's had a financial emergency _____"

Bobby broke in.

"No, it's not herself or Jennifer. Something to do with the house. She told your mother all about it. We offered to pay her way, but then our part of the thing fell through. We'll get ourselves together and meet you farther north along the trail in June. Jackie's determined to hike with you."

He could hear Bobby's sigh, sense his spirits sag. Even his voice seemed to drop a tone.

"All the eastern newspapers and a lot of TV stations are reporting your progress. We gave them copies of your Trail schedule. Money's coming in for the school in trickles, but wait'll you come down Katahdin!"

As if challenged anew, Bobby perked up. He began to elaborate further on the trail experience and all the people he'd met, until Bob himself began to feel the thrill and the physical drain of the experience. When Bobby finally rang off, Bob had the most compelling urge to throw business to the winds, drop everything, and stuff his own backpack for travel.

When Mim returned from her errands, he found himself crying out in joy: "Bobby's reached Fontana Dam near the Tennessee line. He's eating up that defiant old trail!"

Mim grinned as broadly as he himself was doing.

"Almost to the Great Smokies. The dream really is coming true."

"Of course! Don't dreams always come true in the Mountford household?"

"Not always," she said. "I can remember a few times . . . "

He wrapped his arms around his bride of twenty-nine years and kissed her on the forehead. She was prettier now at forty-seven than she had ever been, her dark brown hair revealing but few grey strands, her olive complexion still firm and smooth. Although she came from French stock, Mim had the coloring and the features of the Spanish. Her bearing, however, was inclined toward reticence and humility though she could show a healthy burst of temper when the occasion called for it. Across the years she had been a better wife than he had been a husband. But that was old history now. They had at last reached a plateau of marital harmony that was rare among older marrieds.

"Was Bobby very disappointed about our not coming?" Mim asked.

"Yeah, it hit him pretty hard, but I told him we'd work out something for farther along the trail."

"Won't make my day any easier knowing we've let him down," she said, gathering up an armload of coloring books.

"You've waited on the children hand and foot for all their lives. Now don't be getting a case of the guilts."

"Coming by school today?" Mim asked, leaving.

"Maybe between appointments. I've got a pretty full day."

"Anything special you'd like for dinner? It is sort of a celebration day, you know."

"Let's eat out and do it up right."

Mim smiled slowly, the curve of her thin lips revealing her good teeth and a particular expression he had come to know so well.

"You'd like to have gone with him."

"Yeah, I really would. I'm still a little caught up in the thing."

She came closer, bumped his knee cap with her own, and looked into his hazel eyes.

"You think those forty-eight-year-old legs could do two thousand miles of wilderness?"

"Sure! Why not? Am I really any different from the handsome, virile football player you fell in love with?"

She patted the expanding middle-aged gut on his five-foot-nine frame.

"You didn't have this as I recall."

"Other than that, I'm in top form! One hundred seventy pounds of sheer muscle. I could do it. I may just show you some day."

"One Mountford on the Appalachian Trail is enough. I'm already envisioning rattlesnakes and hungry bears nipping at Bobby's heels. Don't give me more cause to worry."

"Typical mother! No need to worry about Bobby. He's man enough to handle any kind of situation. Now off with you."

Mim backed her car down the drive by his window, and he waved. The Little Red School House was a vital part of her life. Since 1967 she had been a supporter and volunteer; from 1972 to 1979 she was an active teacher; during 1979 she became Executive Director. Mim's work was not

73

now strictly administrative, for she still found time to teach ceramics, woodworking, and leatherworking as well as the ABC's of learning. Bob Senior too had contributed volunteer work and business advice; Bobby had played a part across the years by frequent appearances at the school for impromptu concerts with his guitar. The students loved to hear him sing and play "Puff the Magic Dragon"; they would beg him to play it over and over. And the annual Christmas sale of handcrafted items took concerted family effort to bring it off successfully. In fact, The Little Red School House had been a project of highest priority for the whole Mountford family since they settled in Dover-Foxcroft in 1967.

Both Bob and Mim had been born in Millinocket, a mill town some sixty miles north of Bangor. The community was a company town with only two roads—one coming in, the other going out—and had a duke's mixture of Italians, French, English, Poles, Russians, and Slavs. The one thing all of them seemed to have in common (the males, at least) was a love of alcohol. Bob's father, Floyd Mountford, had been employed by the Great Northern Paper Company as so many of the townspeople were. Floyd Mountford, however, had kept a job only by the skin of his teeth. He had been an alcoholic since the age of sixteen, and the drinking eventually caused the breakup of his marriage. Bob Mountford was rescued, when he was six, from his parents' strife-wrecked home by his paternal grandmother Gertrude. He rarely saw his father, who was usually up to some mischief like bootlegging or hustling a quick buck in some other way. Once his father had sneaked over to make some home brew in Granny's bathtub, and Bob had been scalded during the process.

In high school Bob became a topnotch football player, helped support himself with an early morning milk route, and delivered the *Bangor Daily News* to boot.

He and Mim were married while still in high school. Bob, a senior, was seventeen, and Mim, a junior, one year younger. Although Bob managed to graduate, it would be twenty years before Mim would get her G.E.D. and then go to University of Maine at Farmington for an associate degree.

The babies began to arrive and Bob found himself working in the dreaded picroom of The Great Northern Paper Company.

Mim was happier in her new role than he was in his; she found contentment in her housewifely duties and motherhood. Bob loved his wife, but at the same time he was unwilling to give up the nocturnal activities with his old drinking buddies.

Their third and fourth children were born in 1955-56, and the pressure was really on. Bob had come to dread—if not hate—going to work at Great Northern. And now Granny Gertrude's (with whom they lived) health began to fail. She died in March of 1956, leaving her property to the grandson she had adored and reared. A little guilty, Bob recognized his beneficence as his first big break: he would sell out, move from Millinocket and start a new career free of the grime and sweat of the Great Northern picroom.

The new job was with Metropolitan Life Insurance Company. He prospered, and was ultimately moved to Dover-Foxcroft, Maine.

On their first house-hunting trip to Dover-Foxcroft, they heard of a house that met their requirements of "dream home" in almost every respect: a big two-story frame that welcomed them like old friends. It had a huge, flat yard, and a good barn, which in the Maine tradition, was attached to the back of the house. It had four bedrooms, a bath on each floor, and a good downtown location. The sale was finally consummated at the unbelievably low price of $12,000. What man in all the world, he asked himself, could buy such a house for less than his annual salary?

Yes, God had been good to the Bob Mountford family. But Bob Mountford had not been so loyal to his Creator. This knowledge had begun to prick his conscience as each year brought more and more success. It wasn't that he hadn't been aware of God's existence. Both he and Mim had been reasonably faithful in church attendance since childhood: he under the thumb of Granny Gertrude and her Episcopal cohorts and Mim under the influence of her nominally Catholic mother and lapsed-Baptist father. But in his earlier years especially, he certainly had not lived the life of a consecrated Christian. And reminders about his spiritual condition came from the strangest places. In town Al Tompkins, an old street evangelist everyone thought of as a kind of twentieth century Isaiah, latched onto him at every opportunity. Bob couldn't count the times that grizzled, sepulchral-faced old prophet had thrust a bony finger into his face quoting: "Now is the day of salvation . . . "

The blessings had continued unabated. Or was it that he had become more and more aware that so many seemingly routine things were indeed gifts of God? By 1973 his feelings of alienation from God, his frustration about religion in general, and a host of other factors had brought him to a point of spiritual and emotional crisis. For one thing there had been more serious problems with some of the children during their high school years—problems that should never have happened had he given them the spiritual guidance that a father should have given them. For years now the Holy Spirit had been calling him patiently, lovingly. Or was he going off the deep end in some twisted, delusion of mind and emotions?

In the spring of 1974, he could stand his spiritual frustrations no longer. Alone in his and Mim's bedroom he had knelt and prayed a prayer the likes of which he had never prayed before. He had laid before his Lord everything that had troubled him for a lifetime. Even the most minute thing. He had concluded the prayer (it had left him in saturated clothing so great was his sweat) with the pleading: "If You are real and if following the Christ is not a cruel hoax upon mankind, then show me ___ "

He had gotten up from the floor, but once he was on his feet, it was as if paralysis had set in. His body was melting with heat and his lips started to move of their own accord. The sounds coming from his mouth were unrecognizable. The soft utterings were melodious and even, but he did not recognize the words as having intelligible meaning. The utterings ceased as unexpectedly as they had begun. Then he stood there shaking until he moved to the bed. His strength gave way, and he collapsed face down.

When, still shaken, he had stood up at last, he wondered how this unexpected phenomenon could best be explained to his family, his fellow church members, his friends. Or should this special awakening be kept secret? It must not be, he concluded.

Mim knew him better than anyone else in the world. Still, it was not as easy to share the event with her as he thought it would be. The children believed in the validity of his experience because he said it was valid, but it changed nothing in their view of spiritual matters. And in the cases of some close friends the revelation only invited strange looks. A handful of people understood. A smaller number had undergone the same experience. Before long, he was hearing mutterings that "Bob Mountford is getting too evangelistic ___"

Thinking how best his new direction could be channelled, Bob spoke to his bishop. Their conclusion was that Bob should become a trained lay reader, and, if he chose, to work among the fast-growing charismatic branch of the Episcopal church. In July of 1974, after Bob's completion of study and special training, the Bishop licensed him as a lay speaker and he appeared in some Maine church almost every Sunday. His new self was not, however, proving a complete blessing. Was he now a full-fledged hypocrite? He knew that he had been guilty of trying to force his beliefs upon his children. He had been told of a new arrogance in himself. Yet there had been too much joy in his soul to keep quiet for long.

He and Mim had begun reading the Bible to each other as they traveled about. And they read every book on theology, religion, evangelism, and Christian history that they could lay their hands on. They did grow, not only in spirit but in their love for each other and in their concern for the spiritual and general welfare of their children. But Bob wondered just how much he could change the lives and the directions of his children at such a late date.

He and Mim kept up their studies and travels. In early 1977, he decided to leave Metropolitan and go it alone as a general agent, working out of his home. In this way he would be better able to carry out his lay reading and personal evangelism and to enjoy the renewed and refreshing relationship with his wife. In retrospect he wondered how she could forgive him for some of the things he had done to her—especially in the early years of their marriage. He would make it up to her, and they would fall in love all over again.

That spring a strange thing happened. Bob had long hoped and prayed that his own spiritual renewal would be felt among his children, but he had seen little evidence of it. Now Bob Junior called from the University of Maine, Orono, to recommend a film series he had just seen at the University, based on Dr. Francis Shaeffer's, *How Should We Then Live?* And Bob Junior was bold enough to proclaim that he had had a spiritual awakening of his own from viewing the film and that he and his girl friend,

Joanne Irace, had knelt by her dormroom bed and recommitted their lives. Bob Senior counted that call as one of the happiest events of his life.

He and Mim were familiar with the writings of Dr. Schaeffer, and in Boston the following year they had the opportunity to see his *How Should We Then Live?* for themselves.

As time passed, he and Mim were painfully aware that not all of Bobby's personal life reflected the recommitment allegedly made. But their son was still searching; that was a part of what the Appalachian Trail trip was all about. They realized, too, that their children's generation had an entirely different standard of values from their own. Still, one of Bobby's reasons for taking his Bible along on the Appalachian Trail dated back to his and Joanne's viewing of that powerful film. The news media had well publicized Bobby's taking of that one Book, but they couldn't know all the reasons; they didn't know that Bobby had undergone a second spritiual experience in Houston in which the whole family had participated and experienced some powerful awakening; and the experience, they all had agreed, carried with it an undertone of foreboding—though no one could explain his disquiet.

Neither did Bob discount the influence that Al Tompkins had had in Bobby's life, for the old street evangelist didn't discriminate; in town, he buttonholed young and old, black and white. And old Al had for years preached the wrath of God and the coming Judgment to all the Mountford children along with the remaining populace of Dover-Foxcroft.

The doorbell rang, interrupting Bob's long reverie.

At the front door, he greeted Verner "Sody" Soderstrom. Sody was more like a member of the family, who, now retired, made the Mountford home a regular stopping place.

Sody headed for the kitchen stove, and shook the coffee pot to determine its contents. Bob got cups from the cupboard and pulled up a couple of chairs.

Bob poured, Sody gave a little shiver.

"Don't think spring's ever going to come. Cold as blazes out there."

"You should have gone south with Bobby."

"Heard from him already?"

"He called a little while ago. He's coming into Tennessee."

"The papers and the TV sure are blowin' it up." Sody grinned.

"I guess it's the biggest thing that's ever happened in Bobby's life."

"Like to do something like that before I get old and worthless."

Bob looked into Sody's one good eye. The statement was a sincere one, he concluded, in spite of the fact that Sody could hardly walk from one end of town to the other.

"It'd be a formidable task. Mim's already told me I couldn't make it, but I may just do it one day to prove her wrong."

Sody emptied his cup. "Don't believe there's a man alive—that considers himself a man—that hasn't dreamed of walking the Appalachian Trail all the way."

"Maybe, but less than six hundred a year actually do it."

"Bobby will do it. I never knew a kid with any more determination, and I've lived around here a long time."

"Sody—Bobby has a problem that not even his mother knows about. It's high blood pressure. And it's worse now that he's overweight. And he smokes like a fiend. Frankly, I'm a little worried about what two thousand miles up and down mountains might bring on. And I can't let her know that he told his girl friend he was going to throw his blood pressure pills in the nearest creek once he hit the Trail."

Sody got up and filled his cup again.

"Don't believe there's any cause for worry. Honestly don't. I've read volumes about it. There's something about traveling the AT that makes a new man or woman out of every hiker. Mark my words."

"I hope you're right, Sody. Nothing would make me happier than to see my son come down off Mount Katahdin a new man in body and spirit."

CHAPER X

For the first time since hitting the Trail, Bob felt downhearted. The news that Jackie and the folks were not coming hit him harder than he could have predicted. They had agreed to meet in June but that was a long time to wait. He trudged onward, but for miles the shadow of depression followed him.

The stopover at Fontana Dam had been a time of reunion with old hiking companions and a time of meeting new ones; now he felt the urge to head deeper into the Smokies alone. His backpack was filled with new supplies, thanks to his mother's mail drop at the Fontana Village post office; he had caught up on promised correspondence to co-workers in Ellsworth and numerous other friends; his body, at least, now felt cleansed and stronger than ever. Fontana, by usual Trail standards, was almost too luxurious. The spacious shelter was new-looking—a $30,000. building according to some—and the nearby showers appeared to be marble-lined. The 480-foot-high hydroelectric dam that impounded the Little Tennessee River, thus creating Fontana Lake, was a picture to linger over. The cafeteria and well-stocked grocery in the village three miles removed had been enough to substitute for the comforts of home.

Now, however, as he trekked northward, such creature comforts were a fading memory.

Nearing Siler Bald, the Trail passed through magnificent hardwood forests and grass-grown ridges. In spots, Indian paint brush, wild iris, and lady slipper—dotted the landscape. The very silence—save for the crunch of his boots—seemed to give utterance to some sweet, barely audible song. Virginal earth. Smiling mother. Yielding herself to the dreams and longings of every hiker.

At Siler Bald Shelter he pulled in for the night. Nine of the twelve built-in wire bottom bunks were taken by eight high school kids and their counselor. Just before dark two guys from Vermont came in and the house was full. The site practically straddled the North Carolina/Tennessee state line as did most of the Trail throughout the Smokies. Bob made friends quickly with the kids but felt a little demoralized at being addressed as "Sir." Nevertheless, he saw in the exuberant youths an earlier portrait of himself.

Once he bunked down, it was clear that there would be little sleep. The kids whispered and half-heartedly muffled giggles. It was evident also that they eagerly awaited the visits of the bears that were so commonplace in the area. Hikers in the Smokies were warned at every turn against sleeping out-of-doors, and the Park Service, for the most part, had bearproofed the various shelters with heavy-gauge wire screening.

At every foreign sound outside the shelter the kids' flashlights came on like so many fireflies. Once it was a deer running through camp. Later a skunk's gleaming eyes reflected the intruding light; then it went back to scrounging for tidbits of bread or beans.

Just before dawn a gentle rain began to fall. At daylight one look outside told Bob it wouldn't be the best of hiking days. But neither was the overcrowded shelter the best place to wile the hours away until sunshine came again.

The others had hardly stirred from their warm sleeping bags when he shouldered his backpack and headed north. The upper treetops and the high elevations in every direction had a glassy sheen. Ice. On loftier pinnacles the whiteness suggested a skift of snow. At ground level the temperature had to be in the thirties. The realization made him shiver although he had donned rain cape over jacket.

At Loggy Ridge the drizzle stopped. He removed the rain cape, shook it dry, and rolled it for storage. Retrieving his cooking stove, he heated chicken noodle soup for breakfast. Plenty of fuel now after the Fontana mail drop. No more bumming from Frank Maguire. Turning his vision toward Clingman's Dome in the distance, he wondered whether Frank, Renate Lillifors—a German divorcee they met at Fontana—and some of her Michigan friends had been caught in the icy rain before reaching Newfound Gap, still farther up the trail. He should have gone with them. Compared with him they were amateurs in wilderness survival, but he had wanted to stay over at Fontana, do his mail, wash his clothes, make phone calls, and sweat out his disappointment.

By mid-morning he began the ascent of Clingman's Dome. The fire tower in the distance still looked ice-covered, and the summit of the Dome lay under a frosting of snowflakes and sleet. The whole scene looked like a monster wedding cake done up with all the trimmings—including abundant mountain cranberry plants as part of the decoration. He wondered how woodland flowers and plants already blooming could survive the cold and ice.

Before reaching the summit the trail became slippery, and without his walking stick he would have fallen flat on his butt a dozen times. He rested a moment, adjusting the red bandana tied around his head. In chill air all skilled hikers wore some kind of covering to keep their heads warm, giving it enough slack to allow air to circulate and help dissipate the sweat. His garb reminded him of what old Thomas Lanier Clingman might have looked like 150 years before, when the crusty Civil War general, U. S.

Senator, and mining prospector had explored these magnificent mountains that now bore his name.

The sign on top said: "Highest point on the Appalachian Trail—6,643 feet." Only a handful of people were about on so miserable a day. Soon they headed toward the side trail leading to the observation tower and the entire mountain was his. At least he thought so until seeing a movement in the wet, snowy leaves. A terrapin. How could the clumsy, pokey turtle have gotten this high up under its own power?

There was hardly enough snow to gather a handful, but he tried. The trees still retained their icy covering, a painted fairyland of straight and twisted shapes, in browns and grays and whites. Balsam fir added green, but the branches seemed to be weeping. Silence lingered with such eloquence that his own heart threatened to stop. Why could he not stay here forever, sort out his life and commune with God and nature, become friend of every living thing, pledge himself to Martin Buber's "I-Thou" relationshp to all things in life and thus experience total harmony within

Ice. Snow. Cold. Memories. Once there had been a terrible scene with Joanne on a cold, snowy winter night. They had been to a party in Ellsworth. He had had a few too many beers. Taking her back to the University at Orono, he had driven northward along Route 1A like a speed demon. Joanne became terrified as she always did when he drove fast. She had begged him to slow down, and when he didn't, she had asked him to let her out. He had brought the car to a spinning halt on the icy road. Joanne got out. As her form became obscured in the powdery downpour, he drove off. The temperature was near zero, and her heavy coat lay on the back seat. For two miles he drove on and then turned back to pick her up.

She stood by the roadside, her posture as regal as a queen's—cold fury in her eyes. He pleaded with her to get back into the car, but she refused. She was shaking violently. When he promised to slow down, she got in, but some terrible, unmendable damage had been done. She wept softly as they drove along, and the cute little trick he had perpetrated quickly turned to self-shame. It had been just one more signal of the beginning of the end.

But had it ended? If so, why did he still write to her, engineer little ways to see her, and call often, always signing off with "Joanne, I'm going to marry you some day." The truth was that her spirit, her memory, had been with him from the beginning of the hike. He knew she was praying for him. He could actually feel it. But maybe in a way Joanne's personal, philosophical, and religious purity had been part of the problem.

He had met Joanne Irace at the University of Maine in Orono in the fall of 1976. She was five-five, a hundred and fifteen pounds; she had long dark hair, dark eyes, and a beautiful Madonna face. It had been a casual first meeting. He had dated Cindy and Barbara on Joanne's hall, and sometimes they went out as a threesome or foursome. Joanne made no bones about the fact that he came across to her as arrogant and forward, cocky, loud, and unbearably self-confident. But she had mellowed when she saw under the shield; she even grew to laugh at his twisted Woody Allen sense of humor. Still, it was a case of introvert versus extrovert. And she was methodical, cautious, patient; he was always in a hurry, whether it was writing, walking, driving, or just plain living.

The relationship deepened slowly. It was a year before she responded to him in a romantic sense. It had been slow going, but he had gained ground in little ways. As beautiful, talented, and intelligent as she was, Joanne needed upbuilding and reassurance. Boosting her self-concept was a pleasurable thing to do, and she told him that of all the people she had ever known, he alone had the ability really to listen. She had the idea that her hair lacked luster or that her hands were ugly or that her legs were too fat. It wasn't an act, and he loved dispelling such hangups. And when she changed majors at school—from business to education—he countered her doubts again. "No, all the dum-dums don't go into education," he had assured her; and she was a born teacher.

He had been visiting friends in the dorm one night, and at 11:30 Joanne was sitting out in the hallway studying in order not to disturb her roommate's sleep. Heavy into philosophy, she was having trouble grasping some theories. He explained them to her, and they had spent the next two hours discussing secular philosophy versus the Bible—Plato versus the apostle Paul. At nearly 2:00 A.M., she asked him to leave since she had an early morning class, and he asked to kiss her goodnight. She consented. The slow, lingering warmth of her mouth was unlike any sensation he had ever before experienced. In those sweet pure lips there had been some charge of electricity that had lasted for weeks.

"Going out" with Joanne was often a campus movie, play, or concert. In her sensitivity he found a seemingly fathomless range of understanding and feeling. Sometimes in the middle of a classical concert, her concentration would be so rapt as to make her oblivious to surroundings. Watching her classic profile, he could sense her riding the crests and suffering the valleys of the great compositions until she was lost in the music, and great silent tears trickled down her cheeks. She loved many of the rock bands, too, and most of the in-between music as did he.

Their woods walks together in the fall were replaced by cross-country skiing when the snows came. Sometimes they drove to Dover-Foxcroft and helped his father saw and stack firewood. Joanne loved stacking wood to the point of fanaticism. That simple physical task fulfilled something in her that defied his understanding; long after fatigue had set in for him, she would be raring to go off and climb local Boarstone Mountain.

On Sundays in Bangor, they went to St. John's Episcopal Church, and often attended Bible study classes. Though Joanne had been reared a Roman Catholic, her Catholicism had been at first as nominal as his practice of the Episcopal faith. But she had long been practicing a more deeply committed prayer life. She shared the minutest details of her daily Christian pilgrimage, and he was profoundly moved by her sincerity. It was as if she recognized more and more that without nurturing the spiritual side of her nature as well as the secular side, she was an incomplete person. She recognized as a practical fact that she was a child of God, truly felt that father-love and wanted to respond to it with greater obedience each day. That simple faith, and a growing awareness of the constant presence of Jesus in her life, generated in her countenance some mysterious yet radiant glow. He had not arrived at this level of spiritual maturity, but after a time with her, he wanted to.

Sometimes they would study their Bibles together, having long talks about theology and world religions, compare at great length philosophers both ancient and modern, and finally pray together.

But Joanne was no prude. Passion emanated from her being until he could feel the vibes across the room. And as their commitment deepened, his desire for her became overwhelming. He had every reason to believe she shared this feeling, and yet she was able to pull back from the brink of sexual temptation in some touching, uncanny way that left both of them stronger than ever. They talked endlessly about their dilemma, but it was clear that serious sex, as far as Joanne was concerned, was too great a gift to despoil and cheapen outside of a mutually committed marriage relationship. There was a side of her that suffered agony in such a decision, but he respected, perhaps even loved, her more for her resolve.

In the summer—between the demands of his various part-time jobs— they spent hours walking along the beach picking up seashells and rocks, cooking and making bread together, and taking long woodland hikes. He composed songs about her and accompanied himself on his guitar; they read classic literature aloud, drank gallons of coffee at the Bear's Den on campus, watched sports on TV, watched and criticized Phil Donahue, attended cookouts and parties with friends, made up word lists for vocabulary improvement, fished, and studied the Bible.

By fall—his senior year—he loved her so deeply the subject of marriage could not be pushed from his mind. At the same time there were practical considerations. There was school to finish, and he had little money of his own. In addition Joanne was two years behind him in school. Nevertheless, they talked often about wedding plans. He even worked on a design for their house, a modest design of native wood with a big woodburning stove in the center of an open floor plan.

He kept up his penny-poker-playing, ice-and mountain-climbing with male friends, but there was a terrible void for him in her absence. In so many ways he felt incomplete when she wasn't along to laugh, to share, to just be Joanne.

Later that winter something had happened that seemed now a kind of special consecration of their love. They had attended a film put on by the Intervarsity Christian Fellowship, a version of Dr. Francis Shaeffer's *How Should We Then Live?* The film was both a sermon and a philosophical treatise. Dr. Shaeffer was obviously a devout Christian and theologian, but he was also a competent philosopher and historian. Bob had sat there spellbound. For once he was hardly conscious of Joanne except for times she squeezed his hand. Dr. Shaeffer reviewed the great philosophies and philosophers of history until they seemed a living presence. Then with equal skill he drew parallels to the wisdom of the Prophets and the Holy Scripture and showed how nations without moral absolutes had crumbled into dust. He had not disdained the wisdom and thought of Man, but had pointed out its limits in the light of Biblical truth. In the final analysis Dr. Shaeffer seemed to say that the collective wisdom of mankind had finally been personified in the Author and Finisher of all Wisdom, Christ Jesus. But talk of mere wisdom faded in the greater light of Christ's sacrificial love, the gift of unearned Grace, the pardon for sin without payment; the impossibility of a harmonious and happy life outside of God's will.

Whatever depth of commitment to this ideal Bob had lacked, he rectified that night. He and Joanne went back to her room, knelt by her bed, held hands, and prayed long and fervently. They asked forgiveness of their sins past, present, and future; they asked for the in-dwelling of the Holy Spirit and for a guiding hand as they struggled daily to lead Christian lives.

That same year he went to work part time as an attendant at Bangor Mental Health Institute. He needed more spending money and could lighten the financial burden on his father as well. It was tough working, studying, attending classes, having enough time for Joanne. On the night shift, he sometimes fell asleep on his feet. Other nights, drama awaited. One weekend a patient came dangerously close to stabbing him to death. He loathed the job; the lack of serious attention to patients' needs saddened and disgusted him. The oversedation in place of therapy and tender care was a monumental tragedy.

There wasn't enough money to go ahead with marriage plans. Sexual frustrations had not disappeared even in light of deepened spiritual commitment, but he hung on. Joanne's superhuman resolve seemed only to make her more beautiful and more radiant.

Toward the end of the school year, little differences that they kept under control by mutual compromise began to surface more often. Bob enjoyed large, loud parties with rampant drinking and hordes of strangers; Joanne preferred small gatherings in the company of close friends, warmed only by reasonably sedate behavior and slowly sipped wine. She lectured him both sweetly and harshly about his smoking. He had always been a big eater; that too became an issue. He was developing a minor weight problem, and his love of beer compounded the problem to the extent that Joanne couldn't drop the issue. Blood pressure problems came next. Their church-going and Bible readings also began to suffer. It had become easier not to make the effort and just go to the movies. His driving fifty in a thirty-m.p.h. zone bugged her, and the outing was ruined. Finally they realized that their underlying personality differences had begun to drive a wedge between them.

Graduation day came, and a vacation trip had provided a time of respite and reappraisal. No matter how he cut it, Joanne was the most vital force in his life. In spite of her little hangups, she was a rare gem, an exquisite perfume that inflamed, intoxicated him.

With a greater need than ever for each other, they tried to make a fresh start. He found work at State of Maine Human Services in Ellsworth, and at nights and on weekends he kept the road hot between Ellsworth and Orono. Then the cracks started to show again. When winter came, there was that terrible scene: Joanne getting out of the car and running into the snowy darkness.

He began to see her less and spend more time with Paul Labun, his boss at Human Services, and other local guys—playing poker, or having a few late-night beers. Joanne couldn't understand why he preferred nights out with the guys in preference to her company. The truth was that he couldn't really tell her. He was changing somehow, and he didn't know all the reasons. Though her religious faith and commitment deepened all the more, his seemed to be waning. He didn't regret his commitment that night by her bed, but he felt increasingly uncomfortable when it was obvious that she was reaching still another, higher plane.

Then he wrecked his car on the way to work, banging himself up pretty badly. Once out of the hospital, he wanted to go to her for rest and recuperation. That event, however, was to be momentous. Still too patched-up to drive even though he had returned to work, he started making his work rounds with Jackie Hilton as chauffeur. It was as if there were two of him: one beginning to respond to Jackie; the other unwilling to let go of Joanne.

Some time later Jackie gave him a marijuana plant. Joanne, when he told her of it, exploded: "What do you plan to do with it? Smoke it?" Maybe he yelled back, "Yes"; he didn't remember. They yelled at each other too much. And nights out at Intervarsity programs or fellowship group discussions began to turn him cold. For one thing the students by then seemed too young and immature. And Joanne moved to a new dorm and surrounded herself only with practicing Christian friends; he felt that was a little stifling.

Yet, in the final analysis neither could let go though time between dates lengthened, a prolongation of the agony. Between times he would call and they would open and attempt to close the wound. Finally he would ring off with, "Honey, I'm still going to marry you some day."

His relationship with Jackie became more serious. He saw Joanne less and less, but several weeks later when he learned that she was ill, he went to her. On arrival he kissed her with longing without concern for "her germs" and felt a momentary surge of renewal in her arms. He stayed a long time and ended reading to her. Jackie had given him a copy of Antoine de Saint-Exupery's *The Little Prince,* which had touched the deepest chords in his being for reasons that were not easy to explain. Part of the appeal was the poetic tension the work generated, but beyond that it gave birth to a sense of serenity in his own soul that few books ever had given him.

As he sat reading it to Joanne, a sadness much greater than he had ever experienced in prior readings came over him and he began crying. He was coming to the end of the book; the Little Prince was going away forever and was very sad because his earth flower had to be left alone to fend for itself upon the hostile earth. Bob remembered those closing lines as he remembered his own name and remembered the sound of his own voice reading the lines to Joanne: "You know—my flower . . . I am responsible for her. And she is so weak! She is so naive! She has four thorns, of no use at all, to protect herself against all the world . . ."

"You're my flower, Joanne," he said. "I nurtured you and made you my princess; I dreamed that your soft petals would always stroke my cheek and that your sweet essence would live forever in me."

Both of them wept together. Yet without a spoken word, each knew that this tender moment was only a postscript to an old letter.

Months rolled by in which there was little communication. At last he heard that Joanne was seeing someone named Steve.

Then during the week of his departure for the Appalachian Trail, she called to wish him well and to ask him to write a letter of recommendation for a job opening. "I'll be thinking about you and praying for you," her soft voice promised, and the old yearning had come back. He could hear her breathing, and feel his own heart pounding, but words wouldn't come, and the line finally went dead.

Joanne's prayers—they followed him like his own shadow, creeping over him like summer warmth. Sometimes he half expected her to emerge from a grove of trees dressed in flowing whites, the breeze billowing her gossamer sleeves until she floated weightless into his longing arms.

"Are you asleep or just frozen to that stump?" someone called.

Bob looked up, but it registered belatedly that he was the one being addressed.

"Are you sick or anything?" the young park ranger asked. "You've been sitting there so long ___ "

Hopping up, Bob rolled the rain cape and stored it.

"Not sick, but well tranquilized," he quipped. He spread his arms as if to embrace the mountain. "You don't see something like this very often."

"This time of year we don't need it. We were afraid the power lines might have snapped, but they haven't."

The ranger walked off, and tourists were beginning to arrive at Forney Ridge parking area. Soon they too would be climbing the tower to see the expansive fairyland. If he was to be on his way, he would have to beat them to the punch.

As he gained the tower, his every breath sent forth a white cloud. Then the sun peeped out of the gray sky; in minutes tinkling ice began to fall. Ice against metal, ice against wood, ice against stone, ice against ice. With the exercise of a little imagination, the combined sounds became a delightful melody. His eyes swept the panorama: endless balsam fir trees, shedding their burden of ice and snow, released their overladen boughs until the effect was like a million eagles readying wings for flight. Sun rays darted to earth and pierced ice diamonds, splattering into countless multi-hued prisms. The landscape cleared as if a vast curtain had been drawn back. Bob gasped at the awesome wonder of it.

The suggested symbolism hit him slowly. Behold, your inheritance if __ Here he was higher above earth (with his feet still on the ground) than he had ever stood, and seemingly the whole world was laid out before him. But so, too, did the crown of his head reach for the heavens. Some kind of eerie awareness seized him as he tried to rid himelf of all impediments and let his mind float free. The sun warmed him as he stood there. The ice-melody rang in his ears with exaggerated sharpness. Soon his eyes shifted from terra firma to the clearing azure sky. The need to stand still and simply listen with a deeper concentration than he had ever exercised took root deep in his being. The very Spirit of God seemed to engulf him.

"What do You ask of me?" he whispered.

He waited until the stillness was shattered by laughing, wonder-filled tourists approaching the tower; then he began his descent.

The tower experience was his third __ different and yet not different from the one kneeling at Joanne's bed, and miles removed from the one in Houston at The Church of The Redeemer, but still the same. He wondered whether he should share this latest spiritual experience with friends farther up the trail. "Yes," he decided, "he would."

He hit the Trail once again. Mount Collins would be a good place to stop for lunch. And if he could make Newfound Gap or Mount Kephart by day's end, he would be halfway through Smoky Mountain National Park.

CHAPTER XI

By April 24 Bob was well inside Pisgah National Forest with Hot Springs, North Carolina, dead ahead. On approach the Hot Springs hostel looked first class and sported a big sign displaying the AT emblem and an added "Welcome" painted in bold white letters. Frank Maguire, Renate Lillifors, Peter, JJ, and half dozen others lounged about the patio area.

"We beatcha," Frank goaded. "Is the old boy losing steam?"

"Maybe he took a short cut," Peter jibed.

"Ease up, guys. Can't you feed me a charbroiled T-bone and some fries before you lash into me?" Bob pleaded.

"Vhat do you vant served with it? Shrimps and champagne?" Renate asked playfully.

In spite of lengthy residence in the States, the German girl still had trouble with the W's.

"Any kind of food and lots of tender loving care," Bob sighed.

Renate laughed. At twenty-four, she was pretty when she smiled, but a serious expression gave her a sad, forlorn look. During their rest stop there Bob had learned at Fontana that she had worked in Michigan for five years with the mentally retarded. He had hit it off with her immediately, finding her both interesting and worldly wise.

Trail camaraderie and tale-telling were soon fast and furious. When Bob ran down, he lit a cigarette.

Woody Rambo, a tall, well-built Pennsylvanian, recent college grad in criminal justice and corrections, said, "It's a little unusual to see a through hiker who smokes. Frank too."

Bob blew a smoke ring in Frank Maguire's direction.

"Yeah. We fiends have to stick together, don't we, Frank? We're kind of a minority."

After a refreshing shower, Bob joined some of the others for a trip to the town post office. Another mail drop from Dover-Foxcroft awaited as did a letter from Joanne. He read it quickly on the spot and savored it once again in the hostel study. Renate peeked in on him.

"I recognize the look," she said. "Vords to varm the heart. You are a romantic. I could tell the first time ve met."

"When we all get back from dinner, you can share all such little insights with me," Bob said. "For now, let's hit every pizza parlor and hamburger joint in town."

Later that night the hostel was brimming over. The Keewee brothers—Beni and Luigi Paroli—were from New Zealand. John Smith, lawyer aspirant, and wife Candy Lakin, a nurse were from Michigan. Other hikers were John Pearson, retired Lieutenant Colonel, Corps of Army Engineers, from Hawaii; Don Ferrell, retired Hydrologist with U.S. Geological Survey, from Massachusetts; Dave Tice, Master's candidate in Engineering from Virginia.

At 10:00 the conversations were running down, and Bob went to the study to write a letter to Joanne. How did one tell another what a Trail experience was like? It was best, he supposed, to say it simply. Leave the poetry and the philosophy to the poets and the philosophers.

Dear Joanne,

Very happy to get your letter! I'm staying here at a hostel run by Jesuits in a beautiful small town with mountains surrounding us. I've walked 268 miles since I started in Georgia on April 1. The southern Appalachians are gorgeous!

He told her about life on the trail:

I've met a dozen or so wonderful people whom I keep passing and vice versa along the trail. It's sort of like a small community. They're from all different areas, backgrounds, and ages—and all walking Georgia-to-Maine for different reasons—different hopes and goals. I walk my own pace each day, and although I'm frequently alone, I'm never lonely. I do miss my family and friends and job from time to time, but this is such a beautiful and pleasurable adventure that I'm very happy . . .

I'm afraid I can't convey the whole experience of hiking the AT in a letter, but I look forward to seeing you (wherever you may be) in the fall and sharing some of this rich adventure with you.

Perhaps you'll be a bona fide employed school teacher when I see you next! Any child in your class will be fortunate to have you for a teacher—you're so warm and gentle. I miss you and think of you often . . .

If you wouldn't mind, I'd enjoy it if you'd write once a month and give me a brief rundown on current events (like local feasts and banquets).

He described the hostel:

It's located on the edge of town at the foot Deer Park Mountain. A small winding road swings into town in front of this large, all natural wood beamed log cabin—I'm in the study writing this—a large room with a wood stove, couch, chairs and table—there's a small pantry and kitchen in the next room—then a small cement patio with a roof connecting to a large wing where everyone sleeps. Twenty-four people can stay here—there are seven bedrooms—two of which are reserved for retreats. There's a beautiful lawn with huge oak trees near the road. Next to the hostel is a small chapel, and next to that is a big beautiful mansion which is the Jesuit residence. You'd love it here—people are so friendly. Well—I've got to hike eleven miles to the next leanto, and it's going to be a perfect hiking day come morning. Thanks so much for writing and please keep in touch.

     Much Love,
     Bob

As he was sealing the envelope, Renate's robust figure was framed in the doorway. She had on clean jeans, her long blond hair still wet from her shower.

"You talk yourself to death, and now you scribble all night."

"A couple of short notes, and my duties will be done."

"You haven't told me much about yourself. Your vork. Your reasons for valking the Trail. You seemed distracted at the Fontana Dam place."

"Had a lot on my mind. Some disappointments."

"I vould like to listen."

"And so would I. Start by telling me what it was like in Germany during the 1960s. And what American GI later stole you away and brought you to the good ole USA. I believe you said that you're divorced now."

"Yes. So many complexities. But my friends from Michigan brought me to the Trail. Is good, no? To sort out one's life in the voods?"

"Very good. There or here. Sit down. We've got all night."

Daylight had scarcely arrived when there was a scramble for the showers and talk of the waiting trail. Bob savored the hot water, wrapped his body in a towel and his head in still another, and made the rounds. Frank, Renate, Woody Rambo, and others laughed as he addressed them gravely in what he considered his best Arab sheik accent.

"Today, O Favored Ones, the price of oil will be five hundred—no, four hundred—petrodollars per barrel. Perhaps I shall make it three hundred. I feel very generous. Praise Allah. Praise Mohammed. Praise Mecca."

When Woody stopped laughing, Frank said, "I don't know whether Renate and I want to hike with you today or not. They have places around here called the Funny Farm."

"Ve von't tell anybody ve know him if Rangers come along."

Shortly after sunrise, the three of them hit the trail.

On the night of April 25, they reached Spring Mountain Shelter and introduced Renate to the joys of carrying water and washing pots and pans, for which they rewarded her with M and M's.

Three days later They had arrived at Sam's Gap early in the afternoon. The AT took a big horseshoe loop in the area and crossed over U. S. Route 23.

"We're close to Thomas Wolfe country from here," Bob said. "Asheville is just south of us."

"This Volfe is a friend of yours?" Renate said.

"He was a famous writer in the area—throughout the world in fact."

"Author of *Look Homeward, Angel,*" Frank added.

"Well, listen to this," Bob said. "A literature-wise flatfoot!"

"Don't give me too much credit. Somebody was talking about Wolfe and Asheville last night. You can go there and see the family homestead."

When Peter, JJ, and Dave Tice arrived later, Peter handed him a news clipping. It was a *New York Times* story about Bob's walkathon. Bob perked up.

"Where'd you get this?"

"Mother sent it with her letter."

"No kidding. I didn't know the press was keeping up with me so well."

"I know Bob Kane—the editor of my hometown paper—personally," Dave said. "Want me to talk to him about running your story in the *Pearisburg Virginian-Leader?* Maybe raise some extra funds for The Little Red School House?"

"Sure. Why not?" Bob said. "Anything to help the School kids."

As per agreement Peter, JJ and Dave Tice later rendezvoused with them at the Pizza Hut in Erwin, Tennessee, for an "all-you-can-eat" reunion. Bob and Renate had lost Frank temporarily, and some kind old man had rendered taxi service until they found the ex-chief. It was a welcome treat. The walk from Sam's Gap to near Erwin had been rough and twisting. The Trail still rode the arched back of the Tennessee/North Carolina state line at a height of thirty-five hundred to four thousand feet. Cherokee National Forest lay to the west; Pisgah, to the east. In the lower elevations blooming trees and bushes now painted a colorful woodland mosaic.

"Eat well, my friends," Frank said between bites. "Roan High Knob will soon be staring you in the face."

Bob didn't need a reminder. He had read his guidebook. Roan High Knob climbed to an elevation of over sixty-three hundred feet.

When conversation lulled, each took turns pumping quarters into the juke box. After a while Renate took it over, playing Bob Seeger songs exclusively.

The repetition soon grated. Bob yelled over," You got a one-track mind. Play something else!"

Next time Renate played *"I Must Admit It's Getting Better"* and Frank looked up, grinning:

"I think she's trying to send you a message? Is it?"

Bob, choking on his pizza, drew a laugh. He and Renate had hiked alone at times; he knew there were suppositions abroad.

"How can I help it if they all want me?" he questioned.

The guffaws resounded around the table. Renate came back."Are ve almost over the mountains? My feet and legs are not vorking vell. They hurt."

Frank rolled his eyes. "I was just reminding these boy scouts that soon we are going up nearly a mile and a quarter into the sky."

Renate wanted to spend the night in the comfort of a motel and rest up for the ordeal. Bob and Frank agreed, but Peter, JJ, and Dave hiked on.

To make matters worse for Renate when they did finally reach the Roan Mountain area, the temperature had again turned chill, and a shallow snowcap adorned the vast pinnacle. At the top Dave had left a note saying that he had slept alone there in the cold wilderness. Rugged individualist, Bob thought with appreciation. He liked Dave Tice. Maybe farther along the way, he would get to know the big blond-haired, red-bearded Virginian better.

When they reached Elk Park, Bob was disappointed to find that Dave was leaving the trail to meet his brother John. The reunion turned out to be a short one, however, and Dave caught up at Morehead Gap shelter farther along.

They were only a few days from the Virginia border, but Renate was having serious foot and leg problems. Next morning Frank and Dave walked together, and Bob stuck with Renate. Some miles later a farm wife called to Bob and asked if she could serve them breakfast. Wonder of wonders! Could she!

Filled with eggs, fried ham, grits, hot biscuits, and coffee, he and Renate hit the trail again, singing.

But by the time they reached Watauga Lake, Tennessee, Renate was ready to throw in the towel. They went swimming in the chill water and played tag under the waterfall, but Renate still wasn't revived. The pain—not to mention blisters—had become unbearable. She would have to see a doctor in nearby Elizabethton, but she wasn't giving up.

"I vill hitch a ride and meet you in Damascus," she promised.

Alone again, Bob picked up the pace. He was soon outwalking both Frank and Dave, leaving them far behind. There was a new zest in him. He had received letters from Homestead coworkers, and just as many from youngsters there, at last mail drop, all cheering him. In his imagination he had begun to smell the green Virginia countryside. May had come, and Susan Ramsey would be making preparations to meet him. Strangely, some of her facial features escaped him. Trail life did strange things to the mind. Nevertheless, he felt his heart surge; his steps northward toward Damascus quicken.

CHAPTER XII

Dianne Collins, head counselor at the Homestead, was both glad and sorry to see May 1981 arrive—glad because her friend and fellow counselor, Susan Ramsay, desperately needed a vacation. But Susan's absence, though temporary, would leave a void at The Homestead. Neither was "the home" quite the same with Bob Mountford gone. He had been on the Appalachian Trail for a month now. Susan was scheduled to rendezvous with him along the trail at Damascus, Virginia, on May 9, but first she had planned a surprise visit to her parents' home in Aurora, Ohio, a small town south of Cleveland. She had told Dianne that her parents had planned a visit of their own to Maine—to celebrate Susan's twenty-seventh birthday on May 27. And Susan had expressed concern that her visit might preempt those plans. En route home, Susan had also planned an overnight stopover at Oberlin College in Ohio to attend the recital of a friend and to see a number of Michigan and Ohio friends who would be at the affair.

It would be impossible for Dianne to forget the first time she met Susan Ramsay. It was in 1979. Susan was a candidate for a master's degree in art therapy at Vermont College of Norwich University at Montpelier. Advisor Jane Gilbert of VC had directed her to The Homestead as a likely outlet for some practical application of her art therapy training and as a place of rich source material for Susan's master's thesis. Thus Susan had arrived at Ellsworth to look over The Homestead operation.

On that occasion Susan was dressed like a ragamuffin in ratty-looking faded green slacks, an old unironed blouse of clashing colors, and sandals that didn't match. She was a big girl of five-seven or eight, weighing maybe a hundred-fifty or sixty pounds. She wasn't really fat—just big-boned and naturally large. But she had a pretty, almost childlike, face, a full figure, long coppery blond hair that hung nearly to her waist, and warm, brown eyes that hinted at constant mirth. Dianne resembled Susan in height and hair length, though her own hair was red, her eyes green, and her figure much slimmer. She had correctly guessed Susan's age to be near her own at twenty-five or twenty-six.

She had liked Susan instantly. And most everyone else had also. There was an open quality about the girl, and behind it an elfin demeanor. Susan seemingly doubted no one's honesty or integrity. Her trust bordered on naivete.

Aside from her academic credentials, Susan had had some equally impressive practical experience. She had worked at the Washington County Day Treatment Center and at The Group Home, both in Montpelier, conducting individual art therapy sessions. Long before coming to New England, however, her work among youth was well established: summer jobs during high-school days with her local city recreation department and during college summers at Interlochen Arts Academy, the University of Michigan's summer camp for exceptionally gifted students throughout the world. At Interlochen she had moved through the ranks of counselor, resident advisor and assistant ceramics professor. She had become skilled in pottery making/teaching, using her talents frequently for the benefit of retarded children. Her volunteer work before, during, and after undergraduate days was impressive: at University Hospital Complex in Ann Arbor, Michigan, she had worked with occupational therapists in games and activities for all ages; at Traverse City, Michigan, she had become a swimming coach for the handicapped; a camping chaperone, supervising and teaching art to mentally retarded girls. Wherever her talents could be used, Susan had volunteered them.

At The Homestead Susan needed all her abilities. The entire staff did. The troubled, sometimes unruly youth—both male and female—never seemed to let up for a moment. In contrast the physical setting of The Homestead was serene and beautiful. Located on the northern outskirts of Ellsworth the four primary buildings—the lodge, the schoolhouse, the library, and the group rooms—sat beside Graham Lake, a body of water created by a hydroelectric dam across the Union River. The twenty-six-mile-long lake was perfect for canoe trips and for swimming for those who could endure the chill water.

The buildings were constructed of natural wood. All of the rooms were as rustic inside as out, and some of them showed scars of vandalism, and inattention to general care. Keeping the place clean and orderly was a seeming impossibility.

But from the outside appearance a casual visitor might mistake the buildings and the grounds for an exclusive summer camp. A number of smaller buildings containing craft shops, athletic equipment, boats and canoes, chain saws and wood harvesting tools, tents, backpacks, and a host of other items lay at the fringes of the lodge. Approaching via the winding gravel road and gently rolling land, the visitor would be so awestruck at the natural beauty that it would register only belatedly that this was a house of correction: a residential treatment center for seriously troubled adolescents aged thirteen to seventeen. The treatment center was operated by a non-profit corporation, which looked to contributions as part of its sustenance.

Serving as office manager as well as counselor, Dianne had been one of those helping Susan with her orientation. Susan caught on quickly and, like Bob Mountford, went at problems with great enthusiasm and dedication. The "members", who had been through the usual outpatient mental health and criminal justice systems, needed more refined therapeutic treatment. Plagued with serious behavior problems, they could not cope with most ordinary life situations. Thus The Homestead developed a program that focused on group therapy emphasizing practical behavior and emotional honesty apart from mere intellectual understanding.

The Homestead plan was not to avoid stress but to create the kind of natural stress which provoked a response to which a therapeutic approach could be made. Like Dianne, Susan would find that a function of the members' irresponsible behavior patterns was that they masked the senses of weakness, inadequacy, and inferiority which most of them felt at a very deep level. The rewards for the counselor would come when a member took the gamble to reveal himself, at great personal risk, and grow from it. Of course, a great danger lay in counseling a member who took the risk and lost. Violence against self or a given counselor was often a result. Not many such explosive-prone young people wanted anybody to see "inside their heads."

Dianne had soon recognized that both Susan Ramsay and Bob Mountford quickly became masters in their work technique. She could be justly proud of all her co-workers and fellow staff members. With the rarest of exceptions, they knew when and how to give and to take. And all of them recognized that to remain sane under such work circumstances, they had to act a little crazy themselves on occasion. Mountford especially had the ability to create comic chaos and invent Abbott and Costello situations. With a little Woody Allen and Peter Sellers thrown in, he could change the dullest day into one of slapstick comedy, custom-made farce, and situational travesty. Mitch Gelber, Director of Treatment, was often a partner, and sometimes the object, of such antics.

At other times such antics were put in mothballs, and a night became a singing session. Bob and Susan could hold staff and members spellbound with vocal/instrumental renditions of James Taylor, Elvis Presley, John Denver, Jim Croce, Fats Domino, or Eddie Arnold.

Surprisingly, even the most sentimental of songs could sometimes provoke a member to initiate a confrontation. Maybe a memory of some kind would be triggered or an earlier, unpleasant encounter would be recalled. In any event the on-duty staff members were always ready for good backup help if a member or members showed signs of boiling over or needed "draining." At other times the "group room" was the only answer. It was a padded room with a punching bag and mattresses. There a member out of control could yell, scream, punch, stomp, and otherwise deplete his anger against the unseen "them."

The same Members vs. the Staff interplay continued out-of-doors where perhaps the reality therapy worked even better. There were long hikes, rock climbing, boating, work in the woods, survival training, to help build trust, dependency, and respect for one another, as well as depleting hostilities with physical exercise.

Susan Ramsay was able; she was sturdy and confident in her own strength. Once she had accompanied a group of members and counselors on a long wintertime hike. The snow in places was three feet deep. After the males had taken turns in the front ranks breaking a trail, Susan had insisted on moving to the head of the line and breaking trail for a two-hour stretch.

But the qualities in this young woman that moved Dianne most deeply were her unselfishness and her compassion. Susan was offered the job of Assistant Head Counselor in November 1980, and with the job came a nice raise. But Susan had learned that another counselor had been seriously considered for the position and privately appealed to Dianne.

"I'm deeply grateful for that promotion, and for the confidence you've shown in me; but for personal reasons I just don't feel up to the job at this time; and I'm happy doing just what I'm doing. The other person is well qualified; both of us know it; and that boost in income would sure help him over a hard place. Why not move him in—give me a rain check, if you will?"

And that, Dianne knew, was Susan Ramsay all the way.

Only a few times had Dianne seen another Susan: that part of her revealed a lot of pain and insecurity not quite successfully hidden away. When Susan had first come to Maine, she brought a man with her. The two of them had lived together twelve or fifteen miles outside of Ellsworth near the community of Bucksport. The residence, a rustic cabin belonging to a friend of Susan's, was along the shore of Penobscot Bay. Dianne had not known Alan McKelvy's name then, or had she an opportunity to meet him. Susan had lived with him little more than a month in Maine before he hightailed it back to Michigan. Susan had then moved into Ellsworth.

Susan's next lover was an older area man with two teenaged sons from a previous marriage. John, nearly forty, had fallen in love with Susan almost from the outset. Pressured about marriage, Susan had backed away from the tempestuous affair in a panic. She had settled in a two-room cabin on Graham Lake, some miles from her place of employment. Its wood shingles were painted barn red and its metal roof, forest green. Its most redeeming feature was a big picture window that looked out across the lake. There she lived happily with her music, painting, poetry writing, woodland hikes, and daily jogging jaunts. She also cut her own firewood. The two-room cottage looked little better than an oversized woodshed, but Susan had made it homey with her collection of books, prized antiques, wood-burning stove, handmade curtains, and guitar propped haphazardly in a corner. What the cottage lacked in luxury became secondary to the exquisiteness of the long view down Graham Lake and the picturesque Maine forests that surrounded her. The whole scene was Thoreau's Walden come to life again, and Dianne suspected that there was a lot of the female Thoreau in her friend.

It wasn't as if Susan had—outside of working hours—become a total recluse. She liked people at work and in town. She participated in the

Ellsworth Joggers Marathon, and she was a featured soloist in the area's Acadia Choral Society and in the Haydn Festival Orchestra presentations. Aside from these activities, Dianne suspected that Susan was happiest of all jogging alone along a woodland path, putting brush to canvas along the lakeshore or singing a ballad under a sweet-scented fir tree.

Dianne had not understood all this at first though she and her husband Tom, who was out-of-doors Activities Counselor, also lived and enjoyed the spartan life in a rural location not far from where Susan lived. In fact, Susan had approached Tom about buying five acres so that she could build her own log cabin. It had come out only gradually that Susan's background was upper middle class. How did a girl who probably came from a suburb of two-hundred-thousand-dollar houses adjust to a two-room shack? In the midst of the rural Maine woods? What transition, what shedding of middle-class values, what total disdain for material things had come about to mold this unique human being? And Susan was no old-time hippy; the work ethic was too strong in her. Nor was she anybody's Pollyanna.

Dianne and Tom often had fellow staff members to dinner in their unpretentious home, a home that had felt the skilled hands of her carpenter/woodsman/counselor husband and whose rustic beauty she too could take credit for. Susan and Bob—and others—came by often. It was in this setting that Dianne first thought that she saw something developing between Bob and Susan. Nobody at Homestead knew for certain the exact status of the relationship between Bob and Jackie Hilton, since Jackie had left Homestead, but Dianne and others had reason to believe that the affair—or engagement, or whatever it was—was on the wane. Evidently Susan thought so too, for she was soon beginning to make her play.

Dianne's home parties were often simple affairs of home-cooked food and good fellowship, warmed by a few drinks. As the evenings lengthened, Bob and Susan would sing and play together. Their repertoire ranged from the classics to the most "country" of country tunes. They were excellent entertainers; one sensed a personal harmony between them beyond the songs and the acting. Many of the staffers felt that Ramsay and Mountford were made for each other. They were well matched in education and intellect; both loved working with less fortunate people; both loved the out-of-doors, both were bright and witty, both loved music, art, and travel; and strangely in both was the same faint aura of personal insecurity.

But there was always the work; the strain of working with problem kids. All this had to do with why Susan Ramsay needed a vacation. Throughout April she had a particularly bad time of it. One of her wards—Karen a fifteen-year-old-girl—had slashed her wrists. To Susan it was as if her own sister had tried to end her life. They took the injured girl to Bangor Mental Health Institute, where Bob Mountford had once worked; Susan had for days suffered deep remorse over what she felt was her "failure" with the girl. And this was not the only evidence of strain and fatigue that Susan was showing. Something deeply personal was eating at her gut. Dianne would wager it was Bob Mountford. What was his status with Jackie Hilton? Had he been honest and above-board with Susan, or was the attraction only on her part? Would her reunion with him on the Appalachian Trail be the beginning of something or the end of something only Susan believed had begun?

On the misty morning of May 3, Dianne drove to Susan's cabin prepared to render taxi service to the Ellsworth bus station. She swung her car around beside Susan's avocado green Volkswagen. Her friend was as proud of that scarred old machine as if it had been a polished Mercedes. It had been Susan's parents' gift to her after graduation from Denison. When Dianne got out and rounded the cabin corner, Susan stood in the doorway, staring out across the lake. She was dressed in rumpled jeans and a long-sleeved cotton shirt, her long hair in one pigtail, and her feet sans shoes or socks.

"How are you?" Dianne knew it was a rhetorical cliche, but Susan had a strange look.

"Shitty," Susan responded.

Dianne had seen Susan the previous day at softball practice and later, at her usual daily jogging. So the problem wasn't physical.

"Our would-be suicide bothering you?"

"Among other things."

"She's doing okay. I got a report last night."

"She's angry at me for leaving her." Susan sighed.

"That's not altogether true and you know it. Now forget it. You need a vacation. Where's your stuff? Let's get going. You'll miss the bus."

Dianne stepped inside. Susan's hiking gear and a single bag sat in the middle of the crowded room. The rest of the cabin looked neater than usual, although Susan made no pretense of being a good housekeeper.

Dianne reached for the bag and an armload of hiking gear.

"Aren't you going to need more than this on the AT?"

"I've got some extra stuff at home in Aurora," Susan said. "I'll get my backpack in order there before I join Bob."

"Somehow, you don't look as happy about all this as I'd expected."

"I'm happy." Susan managed a brief grin. "But I'm scared, too. Don't know what lies ahead for Mountford and me. Gotta face McKelvy again too. He'll be at the Oberlin bash."

Dianne didn't ask questions although she knew that Alan McKelvy had left Maine abruptly. She also knew that Susan had taken a nose dive when Bob had left Homestead for the AT. She had gotten all emotional when she missed him at work and felt ridiculous afterwards. Dianne had taken her out that night.

Dianne took the first load to her car and returned. Susan had put on the most gosh-awful-looking socks imaginable, and her scuffy shoes were little better. Now she was searching frantically among her books.

"What've you lost?"

"There are some books I want to take along the trail. The Alexandria Quartet series. I've read *Justine,* but that leaves *Balthazar, Mountolive, and Clea.* Ever read them?"

"No. And can't you think of better things to do on the moss under the trees along the AT?"

Susan grinned broadly for the first time; then she laughed her girlish laugh.

"There'll be time enough for *everything* I hope. Bob took his Bible along. I need something to read, too. I sure don't want to be preached at; that would freak me out for sure."

"What's with him and the Good Book anyway?"

"Searching, I guess. Just like me. Wants to 'approach the Scriptures objectively,' he said."

Susan put her paperbacks in a brown bag and reached for her down jacket. She glanced at the unmade bed, laid her things down, and made it hurriedly. Her eyes lingered overlong on the flattened patchwork covering.

Dianne needed no interpretation of this touching scene or the longing in Susan's eyes.

Susan closed the damper on the stove and took a last look around.

"It'll have to do until I get back," she chuckled. "If I left it completely clean and orderly, and then a tree fell on me along the AT and I didn't make it back, nobody would believe I once lived here!"

It was so true Dianne had to laugh, too.

Susan locked the front door and handed Dianne the ring of keys.

"Take good care of my earthly paradise. The Volkswagen key is on the ring if you or Tom need it. Damn! I forgot to get you extra dog food for Silica."

"Forget it. I'll pick up some on the way back from the bus station. The kids will look after her. Don't worry!"

That was the understatement of the year, Dianne thought. Susan's canine—a mixed yellow lab and golden retriever—was the lodge mascot and was already comfortably housed there.

Susan veered off toward the water's edge and stood there. Dianne waited. Susan could be like an irresponsible child sometimes.

"Will you come on! You're going to miss your bus!"

Susan ran back, an urchin grin on her scrubbed-clean face.

"I was just recalling something. Do you remember this winter when Bob and I cross-countried down this frozen lake? He said something very strange but moving to me. He said, 'If the ice breaks, and we fall through and sink, will you ski on to heaven with me?' Wasn't that beautiful? I don't know why I thought of it just now."

CHAPTER XIII

Scarcely had the Ellsworth-to-Bangor bus cleared the city limits when Susan's eyes searched the landscape to the west. The bus was passing east of Bucksport. Shades of Alan McKelvy. Memories of a bayside cottage they had shared there not too long ago. Now, they were just friends. She would see him at Oberlin at the recital, he had written, but she wasn't entirely sure she would benefit from that reunion. God, the pain he had put her through.

Alan McKelvy was hundreds of miles away in Marquette, Michigan. But what was distance anyway when the mind took only microseconds to span a continent and when the heart warmed or chilled instantly with the ebb and flow of remembered moments? There were times she wondered whether McKelvy was burned into her being as irreversibly as a branding iron's imprint on animal flesh. It had been more than five years now since he came into her life. During the summer of '75 before her senior year at Denison, she had met him at Interlochen Arts Academy in Michigan. He was remote, sometimes in the extreme, but from the first she had sensed a gentleness in him. He was the kind of man that grew on you. His six-foot gaunt build, thinning brown hair, and full beard had given him a scholarly look, yet he had no such credentials. At mid-twenties he was an unschooled idealist in a world he was sure had gone mad. His one link to sanity had been his love of music and the arts. His mother was a professional pianist; his father, a musician/vocalist/businessman; his brother, an accomplished guitarist; and he himself was equally skilled, playing both contemporary and classic guitar. But that musical family, like so many American homes, had been devastated by conflict about which she knew only bits and pieces. In any event each McKelvy family member had gone his separate way.

Perhaps this extra element in McKelvy's sense of alienation had brought him and Susan together more quickly. And, too, they shared some deep concerns about the insane world in which they lived. Things like the Vietnam War, American materialism, the shallow lip service the country's industrial community was lending the monumental problem of pollution, and the broader ecological concerns.

Both she and McKelvy had been counselors at Interlochen Arts

Academy that next summer of 1976. It was a dream job and a welcome change of pace after she had graduated from Denison. Interlochen was a perpetual renaissance—a world within the world. The young geniuses of tomorrow gathered there each summer—bright youngsters from many countries. Who was to say that a Picasso, a da Vinci, a Rembrandt, a Donatello, or a Beethoven was not among them?

Common ground and a deepening friendship with McKelvy had soon grown into something more. Later in the fall they had taken a long walk in the countryside near Interlochen, complete with picnic basket and blankets. They had lingered long after dark, spread their blankets near a pond, and searched the starry heavens. The nights had grown chill by then, and the warmth of his slender body had felt so good. In moments she had yielded herself to his tender lovemaking, and then they had slept a delicious sleep in each other's arms under the fathomless sky.

That fall and winter she remained in Michigan working in a restaurant and at Central School in Traverse City.

In the summer of '77 both she and McKelvy were back at Interlochen, he as a counselor and she as an assistant professor of ceramics. They found a house a short distance from Interlochen near the community of Karlin, and there they began living together. "House" was stretching the definition. It was a twenty-foot by twenty-foot building covered with gray brick siding, a small screened porch to the rear, painted red. But before the summer was over, blight had begun to infest the garden of paradise. Loving and living with McKelvy began to take its toll.

She discovered that he shrank from even the smallest problems as a hurt child shrinks to its mother's knee. The larger problems he submerged in a sea of drug-induced forgetfulness. In that way she couldn't be the faithful companion. Something in her physical make-up could not tolerate drugs, causing her to react in the opposite way from the much-sought euphoria of colorful dreams and timeless ecstasy. Alan took almost every kind of drug, and she began to resent him for it, not because of the habit itself but because it magnified his weaknesses and provided a shallow, cowardly refuge.

"I know your name." The intruding small voice interrupted Susan's reverie.

Susan turned from the window. A silken-haired girl of two or three was struggling for a kneehold on the seat. Susan helped the chubby legs overcome the obstacle and drew the child to her. It was a role she expected to play more and more. Her sister Kelly was now a new mother with an eleven-month-old daughter; her brother Richard had an eight-year-old stepson to whom Susan had played "auntie." Still, "Aunt Susan" didn't seem to fit somehow. Both Kelly's and Richard's first marriages had failed, and each had remarried. And now the thought of marriage scared the hell out of her.

"I know your name," the child repeated like a broken record.

"And your name is Buttonnose!"

"My name is Melody."

"And where is Melody going?"

"On the bus ___ to some place."

"To Bangor? Boston?"

The child jumped down to ask her mother, seated directly across, but the woman corralled her youngest between her knees and the window.

The mere touch of that infantile flesh brought back memories of a different kind. At one point Susan was sure she was pregnant. McKelvy had panicked. And Susan had agreed that fatherhood would blow his mind for certain.

She was little better prepared for motherhood, and she had batted abortion and other alternatives back and forth like tennis balls. She also allowed herself the imagined joy of holding her own flesh and blood in her arms, rocking it, nursing it, growing to love it. In the end she arrived at only a slightly lesser degree of panic than McKelvy. Then it was over. One missed period and all was normal again. It was a hard lesson in remembering to take her pills, a lesson she vowed never again to forget. Odd though, how McKelvy's pleading blue eyes had flooded when he learned that a baby was not to be.

The rut they found themselves in seemed to grow deeper. McKelvy was doing nothing with his music, had bummed out at every turn toward furthering his education, and seemed more inclined each day to cling to her with an annoying dependence. She had given too much of herself already. She prepared to split and to go to the West Coast and through some connections there join the co-owners of a pottery shop in Portland. That's what she needed: to get her hands in the wet clay.

She decided to head west alone—just she and the "Bean"—her trusty green Volkswagen. Bawling and vomiting, she left Michigan with a bad case of diarrhea. At nearly ever small town stoplight, she penned McKelvy a one-line love note. She loved that eccentric bastard; but God, she had to get away or be smothered.

After six months she headed back east. Ill fortune struck. In Jackson Hole, Wyoming she had slammed into a herd of elk, and some of them had actually climbed over the hood of her car, smashing her windshield in the process. She had killed a cow elk and cried like a baby. She had had an accident on the way West also, and had taken a job at Talley's Restaurant in Rapid City, South Dakota, to earn money for repairs. Now she found herself in the same boat. It was back to waiting tables again while the body work and windshield replacement on the Bean seemed to take forever.

With McKelvy again at last, she had made a new beginning. Their passion-filled nights were something out of the romance books, and during his non-working days she had encouraged his guitar and voice practice and kept him off everything except pot.

But the new beginning hadn't lasted. He began to speak of going to California to join his brother John and form a new band.

Another tearful goodbye, and this time he had headed for the shores of the Pacific. In the aftermath she, too, had gotten a burst of ambition. Through a friend she had learned of a vacated pottery shop in Buckley, Michigan, and jumped at the chance to become a self-employed professional potter. It had proved one of the most challenging periods of her life; yet the experience had told her something about herself: she belonged to people no matter how fulfilling the exercise of her craft skills.

Her experiences had confirmed what she had instinctively known all along; her life must be devoted to the handicapped, to the needy, or to troubled youth. Ole Bud Ramsay, her dad, had been right after all. He had said, "If you ever get all your avocations channeled into a vocation, you'll be a smashing success." Overnight she had decided to enroll at the University of Michigan and take additional courses in psychology and advanced painting with the hope that when her finances improved she could go for a master's in art therapy.

Settled in Ann Arbor that September of 1978, she had lived alone in a small apartment for only three months when McKelvy reappeared. She had never seen him so forlorn and dejected. He and his brother hadn't made a go of it. The whole deal had been a real bummer. Their musical tastes were too much at odds, and Alan was crushed. For a time he had tried supporting himself through Manpower, doing everything from construction work to sweeping floors. There was nothing in his sensitive nature that prepared him for life's disappointments, and she found herself nursing his wounds like a pampering mother. He moved in permanently, and to augment their income she had taken a job as a waitress, taught gifted high-school students pottery making, and done some volunteer work with retarded kids. At the restaurant/supper club she had endured the grappling hands of sex-hungry males, heard the woeful tales of love-starved housewives, seen the highest and lowest of humanity, and met and worked with some of the most unforgettable of Dickens' characters.

It wasn't as if she had deserted her parents back in Ohio. With and without McKelvy, she had taken an occasional trip down to Aurora. The trips had not been without conflict. When she came back from Oregon, her mom and dad had spent two hours putting her through the wringer regarding her future and her "shallow sense of responsibility."

McKelvy never was sure he fitted into her home setting. During the Christmas of '77, she and McKelvy had been heavy into the anti-materialism movement, and she had created havoc by throwing out most of her Aurora possessions: things that by no means put a dent in the furnishings of her parents' hundred-fifty-thousand-dollar suburban home. She was sincere in her wish for humble poverty, and McKelvy had supported her, encouraged her. Still, it had hurt Bud and Ginny Ramsay. A few times she and McKelvy had gone with her family to their summer cottage at Au Gres on Saginaw Bay in Michigan. Those gatherings too had been less than successful when McKelvy took to the woods with his guitar rather than face a family situation. It was not that her parents were not enlightened. Most times they were more than kind to McKelvy, but they reminded him of traditional life styles that he disdained; part of the rot of American society.

In the winter of '79, life with McKelvy had begun to wear thin again. She was working as a potter, waiting tables, working with occupational therapists at University Hospital Complex.

They spent endless nights reviewing the commitment they had made. In spite of the glowing words, the soft phrases, the passion-filled nights, and all the tears, the lopsided nature of the arrangement hit her again like a sledge hammer. McKelvy was a luxury. Her real self cried out to serve others, not to play nursemaid to one beautiful, talented, sensitive, idealistic weakling.

So she had split again in what turned out to be the most important decision of her life: she had gone to Montpelier, Vermont and had begun her work toward a master's in art therapy at Vermont College of Norwich U. She had plunged into the program, made deep friendships among her fellow students and professors, and found time for more volunteer work at the Washington County Day Treatment Center; at The Group Home in Montpelier. In spite of the rush of activity, she hadn't forgotten McKelvy. He was so implanted in her soul that she had found herself talking aloud to him in the late hours of night. At such times she would grab a piece of paper and let if flow: "Sweet gentle man, I have your picture here beside me, and surprisingly it's been a source of latent, yet vivid memories. The result of those memories is not negative as summer and you were. You are still alive in my heart and an inspiration to me, and I continue to feel such love in my heart for you—and the man you are. You are pretty incredible, McKelvy."

Then had come Advisor Jane Gilbert's suggestion that she go to Maine and look over The Homestead operation in Ellsworth. The whole scene had been a godsend. All of her skills could be focused on a needy person. And the Maine woods—like her beloved family cottage on Saginaw Bay— would fill her being with beautiful thoughts and new creative energy.

McKelvy had come to Maine that summer, and they had made another beginning. The honeymoon had lasted just six weeks. McKelvy, she admitted at last, needed a mother more than a lover. He had matured enough to admit at last that he loved her but was "not in love" with her. She felt used. Hurt .and anger boiled like an erupting volcano. Then he was gone back to Michigan, and for days she had remained in seclusion, sorting it all out.

In time, when some of the hurt had gone away, she had looked upon the event as possibly the biggest growth step McKelvy had ever taken. She had then vowed that bitterness would not end their long friendship, and she had written to him. He had responded in kind, and so it was. When she got to Oberlin, it would no longer be a lover she was meeting but a friend, a dear friend for whose welfare and happiness she still cared unendingly.

The bus lumbered into the Bangor terminal where she would switch to an express for Boston.

Susan's seatmate on the crowded express was an obvious old wino gurgling and snoring like hell.

After McKelvy, what had driven her to John? For one thing, John, an Ellsworth resident, had seemed to appear at just the right time to help her pick up her shattered pieces. Had she, in fact, done a McKelvy switch? Was it she who then needed a father substitute to lean on—an older man with sons? It had been instant, mature love all right—so earthshaking, for him at least, that he had wanted marriage in a matter of weeks. That had freaked her out. She had run like a virgin from the devil and taken solitary refuge in her woodland cabin.

Before she had got her head screwed on completely, Bob Mountford had come upon the scene. He above all people had helped her come gently back to earth again. At first she hadn't liked him. He was cocky, too aware of his wit and intelligence, too confident in his work, and annoyingly good at everything athletic. He could also see through her as nobody else ever had. But there were pluses. They had soon discovered a mutual love for working with underprivileged kids; love for the out-of-doors, mountain climbing; music in general, and guitar duos in particular; good books; and good food and drink.

It was the most natural thing in the world that they started jogging together occasionally after work, taking a walk or swimming. And it was just as routine that he would drop by her cabin, pick her up, and they—and others—would all head for Dianne and Tom Collins' house for a round of beers, home cooking, and exuberant fellowship. Some of the sessions were like work conferences in which problems at Homestead were the main topic. Weeks at a time they would hardly see each other. She would be on a trip or camp-out with the members, or he would be similarly scheduled.

A great friendship grew from early days, one that had deepened until just a long conversation was a treat. She loved probing Mountford's fertile mind and loved equally sharing her knowledge and experiences with him. He would finally come across as aware and sensitive. A deeper relationship was out of the question. She knew of his commitment to Jackie and his lingering love for Joanne; he had shared parts of those love stories with her. Even so, something had begun to happen by the time Thanksgiving arrived. She bummed out when days went by and she hadn't talked to him or shared some event. Her daily jogs got longer. Two miles. Four miles. Six miles. She had tried burning up her frustration with physical exhaustion, taking long walks alone, writing poetry, composing songs and playing her guitar by the banks of Graham Lake, or painting landscapes that invariably had a lone hunter in the background who had the dark moppish hair and exciting physique of a Bob Mountford.

Then, a few weeks before Christmas, the inevitable had happened. She had invited him for dinner one night—both loved to cook—and Bob had concoted one of his fancy Italian dishes so spiced up with condiments as to set them afire at the onset. And then came glass after glass of wine. And the fire in her woodstove had crackled with the most soothing of melodies. As the night grew colder, she opened the stove's filler door. To the dancing silhouettes of flame upon the wall they made love, and when morning came, she still lay there against his hairy chest, held tightly in his powerful arms.

The day after, it was business as usual. Homestead problems. Back to her long walks and daily jogs. But within the week he was back in her bed again. She wasn't sure what it meant, if anything. In a little more than three months he would be hitting the Appalachian Trail. And Jackie might be meeting him somewhere along the Trail; he had said that, too. So much for the stories around Homestead that the Mountford/Hilton thing was waning.

Two weeks before Christmas he blew her mind. In one sentence he said it: "Meet me in Boston on December 27 and then we'll go on to Dover-Foxcraft for New Years and plan to hike a section of the AT with me."

Hearing it, she was freaked out; she had stood there like a wooden Indian. To this day she didn't remember giving him an answer. In any event she hurried home to Aurora for a couple of days with her family and then packed for Boston. At home she had undergone a real hassle over why a mere two days at Christmastime could be allotted to her parents; and her answer that she had to get back to "get her work organized" didn't help.

For two days and two nights in a Boston hotel, she and Bob had made love to the point of exhaustion. Groggy and tired or not, she put her best face on and had gone with him to Dover-Foxcroft. The only strange looks she received were from Jackie Hilton when Jackie had come back to Dover-Foxcroft from her own Christmas trip.

What kind of weird number was Mountford pulling anyway, she wondered; but they all became a compatible threesome—taking in the various parties and later going skiing, enjoying a songfest and banquet, and doing other fun things.

"Are we in Medway yet?" The wino, stirred, looked up.

"We're headed for Portland, Boston, and points south. You're on the wrong bus headed the wrong way, my friend."

"The hell you say!"

"You'll just have to wait and get off at the next stop. I'm sorry," Susan said consolingly.

"I gotta get to Medway—got some money comin' to me." "Why don't nobody care about a feller ___ what goin' to happen to me . . . don't nobody care!"

She walked up the aisle and talked to the driver, but there was nothing he could do until they were off the interstate. She came back and relayed the message. A string of oaths came staccato out of the wino's mouth, and then he started snoring. Always there was someone who needed loving care. She wondered whether she would ever have such an opportunity with the man who now meant as much to her as anybody else in the world.

CHAPTER XIV

On Tuesday, May 5, after the Oberlin bash was over, Susan called her sister Kelly in Aurora and asked her to meet her at Exit 6 on the Ohio Turnpike. Susan had a ride that far with Michigan friends who had also attended Stuart Grey's senior recital. Many who had been in the audience were Denison/Interlochen/Oberlin friends, and Susan was still floating from the camaraderie, good beer and champagne, and from having been packed umpteen deep overnight in Stuart's apartment afterwards.

Kelly was on schedule and took Susan back to Kelly's farmhouse on the outskirts of Aurora. Susan was instantly awed by the new carpentry work Kelly's second husband, Curt Sucher, had done on the place.

While Kelly paid the babysitter, Susan looked at new family snapshots. Kelly was older than Susan by two years, and the two of them had always been vastly different. Susan conceded that Kelly was the more attractive with silky blond hair, a pretty complexion, smooth face, and graceful, slender figure. Kelly had always been the more serious, more reserved; her outlook and personal philosophy were essentially traditional. Perhaps working with her father—the self-employed businessman—had made Kelly herself more businesslike. She and Susan had not always been close, but the passing years and shared joys and sorrows had brought them closer together.

After a little of the kitchen chatter died down, they sneaked into the baby's bedroom. Katie was asleep. Since Susan couldn't vent her nervous energy by cuddling her niece, she began to pace.

"Calm down," Kelly said. "Everything's going according to plan. Mom and Dad will be on schedule. Ever know Bud Ramsay to be late for an appointment?"

"You didn't blow my cover! What did you tell them?"

"That Katie and I, both, were running fevers and needed to be taken to the doctor. They haven't the faintest idea that it's anything else."

"Oh, God! They'll kill us both. You know how Dad hates to be pulled away from business matters, and with Mom, another member of the firm out, too."

"I had to sound sick to get them both out here, told Mom she would have to carry the baby."

Susan lay down on the extra bed and Kelly paced.

"How's it feel to be almost twenty-seven, *Aunt* Susan?"

"Cram it! I still feel like I'm seventeen!"

Kelly laughed.

"Well, I don't. Motherhood changes you. And all this—work."

"Regrets?"

"No. I've never been happier or more fulfilled. In Curt I've got a real man. You wouldn't believe the way he works. All day on the job as contractor and half the night here, remodeling our own home. But we're building something."

"Number One still working for Dad?"

"Oh, yes. And we're all still friends. Casey even comes to Mom and Dad's when we're there and plays with Katie."

"That's great. Must spoof him a little bit, though, to hold a kid that might've been his had your first marriage worked out."

"That's his problem. We should've just lived together for a while; then it would've been over. No marriage mess to undo."

"My philosophy exactly. Hey, maybe the twain's beginning to meet!"

They laughed like schoolgirls, and it was good.

"How's *your* love life?" Kelly came back.

"Good and bad. Up and down."

"This sudden yen to hike the Appalachian Trail fit in?"

"Maybe. Maybe not. It all depends."

"On what?"

"It's a long painful story with lots of jarring turns and dead ends."

"There's time to spill it all."

Susan sighed, bracing herself; but the sound of a car engine cut her short. "Afraid there *isn't* time. If my ears don't deceive me, that's the Bayard T. Ramsay & Company, Inc. Cadillac pulling up your drive."

Kelly went to take a quick look. She ran back.

"Right on! Now stay hidden while I fake a good case of the trots, kidney stones, and tennis elbow!"

Susan huddled in a corner. In the distance she could hear Kelly pouring it on thick, but her mother kept saying, "Something's going on! What's going on?" When her dad came in, Kelly began to drop the facade and simply asked to be followed. The thump of six feet coming down the hallway began to sound like a death march. Susan could hear her heart pounding. It had been months since she had been home. The prodigal daughter returns was the last thought she got off before her parents entered the room.

"SuSu!" Ginny Ramsay nearly screamed.

"I don't believe this!" Bud Ramsay's echo was only mildly fainter.

Susan flew into her mother's arms; then she freed a hand to reach for her dad. For a moment it was a three-way bear hug, and then reality hit.

"But we were still planning to come to Maine in three weeks!" practical Bud Ramsay said.

"I know, and now I've ruined it for you."

"Ruined? This is a bonus!" Bud shot back.

Ginny reached for her daughter again.

"It's so good to have you home. But you've almost given me a heart attack."

"You don't need that on top of your arthritis," Susan said. "How goes the spine and troublesome little joints?"

"If we don't discuss it, maybe it'll go away. Let's talk about you."

"Yeah, to what do we owe this nifty little surprise?" Bud asked. "In the old days I might have expected the soft touch . . . just kidding, Susypie."

"Oh, don't give up on me, Dad. All your financial lectures haven't bailed me out of my bad money management problems yet. I might just be on the make for big bucks—little bucks—whatever."

"She's been at Oberlin," Kelly joined in. "I picked her up on the Interstate after she left her friends."

"So—we're second best." Ginny affected a pout.

"No way. If Kelly'll put the coffee pot on, I'll tell you all about it."

Susan went into lengthy detail about the Oberlin affair, Alan McKelvy's presence, various reunions with this friend or that, but invariably the subject came back to Alan McKelvy.

"Are you telling us the McKelvy thing is over or not over?"

Susan searched her father's eyes a moment before answering. Bud and Ginny Ramsay had always tried to be polite to McKelvy, but they made no pretense at believing that this man measured up to the standards they had set for her.

"The romance is over, Dad, but we'll always be friends. We've shared too much to wipe the slate clean. It was great to see him, and we all had a fantastic time together. McKelvy has a lot more ability than any of you have ever given him credit for, and he's a lot more complex than meets the eye."

"I hope that he can get his act together," Bud said. "He does have potential."

"He's hoping to work with a senior citizens group in Marquette," Susan said, "and he can still pursue his music interests on the side."

"Okay, so Alan McKelvy's been put into mothballs," Kelly said. "Now what about this trek on the Appalachian Trail with Bob Mountford?"

"Who's Bob Mountford?" Bud said.

"A very aware guy at Homestead I've been working with for the last few months. He went to the University of Maine, did social work for the State a while, worked at Bangor Mental Health Institute, and did a lot of other things. He's been to Russia and speaks the language. Had a jaunt in England too, and God knows where else. He's quite a fellow. Plays guitar, sings. Great cook, and a man with a body and a brain. I agreed to meet him in Virginia and hike for a week."

"All this in one breath!" Ginny said.

"This sounds like it's going to be some passionate reunion," Kelly said, "or will it be just a handshake?"

Susan felt her face grow warm. She sipped at her coffee.

"I'm not sure. Maybe something in between," Susan finally said.

"Why keep us in the dark?" Bud asked.

"The truth is, I know how I feel, but I don't know how he feels. Besides, he's kind of engaged."

" 'Kind of ' engaged?" Ginny asked.

"Yes. He hasn't said much. Some of his friends think it's not working out and that Jackie—the girl—broke it off."

"So you're saying that this Appalachian Trail thing is supposed to clarify matters as well as being a vacation challenge?" Bud said.

"Something like that. But let's not oversimplify it," Susan cautioned. "It's not as if we've never done anything like this together. In Ellsworth we've hiked, skiied, mountain-climbed, swum, cooked, socialized, worked, and everything else together."

"Everything else?" Ginny picked up on the phrase.

"You know what I mean, Mom."

Ginny's eyes were unusually steady in searching her daughter's for a moment, and Susan wondered whether her hasty exit from Aurora during Christmas was now being more thoroughly and accurately analyzed. Her family had, she realized, not quite forgiven her for that.

"Bob took me back to his home in Dover-Foxcroft," Susan added. "We had three great days the week before he left for the AT. I want you to meet his folks when you come to Maine. They're really fantastic."

The subject of Bob Mountford began to die away after a few moments.

Ginny said, "Well, obviously there's nobody sick in this house—thank God. Why don't we all get our affairs in order and celebrate tonight? Kelly, can you and Curt make it?"

"We'll arrange it."

The next day while her mom and dad were at work, Susan struggled at getting her backpack in order. It was a Kelty in excellent condition and her hiking boots, long ago bought in Maine, were well broken in. She decided also to take along the expensive Pentax camera her parents had given her for Christmas. Later she'd go out and shop for a few small things and some food.

At 1:00 p.m., she used Ginny's car and met her parents for lunch. Afterward she went on tour of the offices of the Bayard T. Ramsay & Company, jobber-sales representative for a number of manufacturers involved in institutional and industrial supplies. In a dozen years the firm had come a long way to its offices atop the new bank building in the Aurora Shopping Center and to its impeccably modern, business-efficient furnishings—symbols of prestige and affluence that smelled of the same materialism that Susan normally disdained. Somehow this was different. Both her father and mother had worked hard and long for this success. Kelly, too, would soon be working full time for the firm and, of course, her brother Richard already managed the Indianapolis branch.

110

Heading for the parking lot, Susan looked back at the handsome masonry building, sorely tempted to go to the shopping center liquor store, buy a bottle of champagne, and break it across the building cornerstone. Bayard T. Ramsay & Company had arrived, but what a struggle it had been!

Bud and Ginny had met in 1946 as students at the University of Michigan and married in 1948. Neither had graduated; Bud had gone to work at once as a sales trainee for Union Steel Products. From 1950 to 1953, he saw service in the Marine Corps, where he had risen from Private Ramsay to Captain Ramsay, and Ginny—after Bud's Parris Island days— had made a home for them at Camp Lejeune and at Quantico Marine Base.

After his service with the Marines, Bud had gone back to foot-soldier sales work, moving from one corporation to another and upward to a spot as industrial sales manager. Moving out on his own, he had freelanced as a representative for several companies; and eventually he had bought out an independent company rep firm and proceeded to the formation of Bayard T. Ramsay & Company.

And now the company was on firm ground in Aurora. Susan, started the car and headed for a supermarket, where she bought a supply of dried fruit, cheese, granola bars, and instant breakfasts, raisins, grain cereals, and a good mixture of other foods to make her own variety of gorp; she bought also a small first-aid kit and extra film for her camera.

As she was on her way back to the car, a voice sang out behind her.

"Susan! Laura Susan Ramsay!"

She wheeled about.

"Mr. Mancine!"

He rushed to embrace her.

"You can call me Lou now. I'm no longer your guidance counselor. You did graduate Aurora High in '72 as I recall."

"Old habits. So. You're looking great. Haven't changed a bit."

"I'm still taking the flak and dishing out the same old Freud. What are you doing back in Aurora? Didn't I hear you were up in Maine doing social work or something?"

"Visiting my folks before taking a jaunt on the Appalachian Trail."

Susan told the story for the umpteenth time.

"The Cleveland papers carried a story about a Maine man who was planning a 2,000-mile walkathon on the AT as a fund-raiser or something—for a children's home as I recall."

"He's the one I'm walking with—not all the way from Georgia to Maine, of course. I'll just be on the Trail a week; then I'll go back to my job in Maine."

"Small world."

"Yeah. Isn't it?"

"You know, I've often thought about you. I'm not sure the school has ever been quite the same."

"Wow. Like you haven't had any problems since!"

Lou chuckled, and then it turned into a dual laugh.

"You and your cohorts weren't *that* bad," Lou added.

"You haven't forgotten the time we ruffled some official feathers about that underground newspaper we started?"

"I must admit that was memorable."

They continued reminiscences until they ran out of both breath and memory. Thomas Wolfe was wrong. You *could* go home again.

As she headed home through heavy traffic, the incident of the underground newspaper sprang from out of the past with fearful clarity. Her first really big life crisis. She had been a junior at Aurora High that year, and the Vietnam War, the free speech movement, abortion, drugs, sex education, and a lot of other issues were big among the students. But students were not then finding an outlet for their views; hence the clandestine paper had been born. For a while it had been the hottest newspaper in town. Then the walls came crushing in. Cornered, Susan and a friend confessed editorship. The son of a high-ranking school official, however, escaped punishment. He had been as guilty as Susan and her co-worker. Susan had been suspended from school for two weeks, and the black mark had ultimately worked against her when she applied to Oberlin and other prestigious schools. She withstood the onslaught of administrative crackdown at school with an iron will, but when her father came to school to defend her, she broke down and bawled like a baby. At first, Bud Ramsay had thought that his presence humiliated and embarrassed her. Only afterwards had Susan told him that she had been so moved by his defense and had felt so loved even amid the awkward circumstances that she had caved in like a crushed egg.

She stopped for a red light. On green, a guy coming from the opposite direction blew and waved. Was he—he looked like—Steve Jaremko, her old boyfriend from high school days? Good old Steve. She had few boyfriends at Aurora High; she was always chubby, even mildly fat; she had been on diets at periods and she had no illusions about sexpot attractiveness for herself. Nobody had outdone her in student activities, however. She was a class vice president, class treasurer, member of the Student Council, wrestling team's mat maid, and statistics keeper for the basketball coach; she participated in the girls' track, cross-country, and basketball teams, and in Junior Olympics; she was named Miss All American Girl; she was a member of the American Field Service Club, English club, glee club, chorus, and drama club; and her really big moment had come when she won the lead role in *Hello Dolly* during her senior year. That role had been one of such challenge that even now she wondered how she had risen to it. The standing ovations after each performance still rang in her ears.

As a climax to those happy days, she had one more unforgettable senior honor: Homecoming Queen. In between times she had taken guitar lessons from brother Richard; and summers had been just as full with work in the city Recreation Department's athletic activities and special programs.

She turned off the main drag and drove by the non-denominational church in Aurora, which she and her family had attended since her eleventh year. She had been baptized, however, at Covenant Presbyterian Church in Los Angeles during the brief time Bud Ramsay had been in California developing his sales rep contracts. Church had never been a big thing in her life, and in recent years organized religion had turned her off. It wasn't that she hadn't had meaningful spiritual experiences. Every hike in the woods was a meaningful spiritual experience as was the viewing of a hawk soaring majestically in the heavens.

She hadn't closed her mind completely to traditional religion; in fact, she had participated in services both far out and fundamental. One of the most memorable of the latter type came about when she had a long layover in Rapid City, South Dakota, on the way to Oregon, getting her banged-up Volkswagen fixed, and she had taken a job at Talley's Restaurant to raise funds. At Talley's she had become close to Betty, a waitress, with three kids and a husband; they lived in a mobile home with a little garden in the rear. Betty and her family were devout Pentecostals, and Susan had accompanied them to church one Sunday. She had not been prepared for the emotion-charged service, and yet it had reached some deep need in her being. The minister had preached on the Christian's need to develop holy respect for every person and every living thing. Only by doing so, he had declared, could one even begin to approach Christlikeness. "Right on!" she had almost been compelled to shout along with others of the congregation. She had thought a lot about Jesus the Christ across the years, but if He was not Mohandas Gandhi, Don Juan, Father Groppe, and Martin Luther King as well as the gentle Nazarene, then He did not really exist.

Susan turned onto New Hudson Road. Her family's big two-story wood-and-masonry home was impressive indeed. Its spacious lawn, majestic oaks, attached garage, screened-in rear porch, and stone covered patio were but minor enhancements to the main house itself. Inside, a lifetime collection of memorabilia and fine furniture graced the rooms. The large sunken living room with wood-burning fireplace and richly polished oak floor had been the scene of many a memorable family and community gathering and, Susan thought with a tinge of amusement, of more than a few family battles. Needless to say, one or two of them had been centered around—her. She had had her moments of rebellion though her parents maintained that Kelly had been the most unruly of their offspring. Susan knew—without being constantly reminded then and now by her siblings—that she had been the favored child of the threesome. With that warming and slightly guilt-ridden thought, she parked the car and delivered her purchases to the kitchen.

She laid the backpack items out on the breakfast table and sorted them out, mixed her gorp to her liking and packed it in plastic jars, and headed for her room upstairs to put everything in order. This would be her last night at home. Tomorrow she would board the Greyhound and be off for Damascus, Virginia.

113

As usual, the backpack threatened to burst at the seams, and she re-rolled the sleeping bag, rain suit, ground mat, and a few bulkier items. She held out one of the books *(Balthazar)* from the Alexandria Series that she brought from Maine to read on the bus. *Clea* and *Mountolive* she put with her packet of trail maps in the backpack for easy access. Her packing finished at last, she laid out in the hallway everything she would be taking to Virginia. As if the scene had caught her eye for the very first time, she looked down the long stairway to the first floor. Once, she remembered vividly, she had fled up those stairs to her room in tears. How many times she had run down from above in the heat of excitement or expectation! And she remembered once sitting on the top step envisioning herself descending slowly, elegantly, in a long white wedding dress. Bourgeois visions. Infectious materialism. Shitty traditionalism of the worst order. How insane and uncaring that any woman would spend a thousand dollars on a wedding dress when three quarters of the brides and the grooms throughout the world didn't have the price of a week's groceries or a bed of their own!

That thought had barely faded when she found herself walking farther along the lengthy hallway. She stopped at the open door of her parents' bedroom. A king-sized bed dominated the spacious interior, and a chest at the foot supported a good assortment of her mother's favorite books. Ginny Ramsay was an avid reader, and her sister had attained a measure of national status as a poet and short-story writer. By standards of the common man, the room was luxurious; to some, the whole setting might have looked like a suite in the Waldorf—assuming that they had ever seen one. Still, her parents' bedroom had been in earlier years her favorite room in the house. Her mother's taste in colors and furnishings was exquisite; yet there was some falsity in all of it. Number 77 New Hudson Road was another world compared to her two-room wooden cabin in the wilds of Maine!

Back in her old room she lay down on one of the twin beds. Her eyes searched the surroundings. Mementos were everywhere: reminders of the trip she and The Denison Singers had taken to Romania; trophies for athletic accomplishments; awards for musical and other artistic honors; souvenirs from her backpacking trip across Germany and Denmark the summer of her seventeenth year; a miniature sculpture commemorating her trip during '77 to Florence, Italy, to join friend Jan Waterson for a cultural holiday; a framed Denison graduation/baccalaureate program in which she had been the featured soloist.

A photo of Alan McKelvy stared back at her, his pained, pleading blue eyes set in a handsome bearded face, seemingly asking, "What went wrong?" Stupidly she felt her eyes begin to fill. She sat up and dabbed at the moisture with a tissue. Good old mom. Ginny always kept a box by every bed in the house.

Incredibly the seeping eyes refused to stop. She found herself giving way to weeping. What the hell was it? She didn't understand this shit. Didn't understand it at all. Something about this visit was playing tricks on her; that was it. Too many memories. Too much pain. Like skimming the topsoil from a cemetery and letting the corpses arise and walk. Lazarus, come forth! Death. Immortality. Heaven. Hell. Jesus. Mohammed. Buddha. Jehovah. Brahma. Madeline Murray O'Hair. Don Juan.

Her wristwatch said 5:10; Bud and Ginny would soon be home. The least she could do was to start dinner. After a quick shower she felt revived.

One quick look in the refrigerator told her that Ginny had planned a fondue dinner. It was a favorite way to dine in the Ramsay house. With two small skewers per person, one could keep a chunk of meat cooking in the pot of boiling oil while eating one just retrieved. Heating the cooking oil in the fondue pot would have to be a last-minute operation, and the tossed salad making should be postponed also to ensure crispness. Baking some large potatoes was all there was to do. She scrubbed them, set the oven temperature, and opened for herself a beer. Her parents were connoisseurs of mixed drinks, and her own tastes on occasion were similarly exotic. Maybe beer was best. The common man's drink. That, or good wine with good friends, sipped slowly while you watched their eyes begin to glow as one's own did.

At 5:35 the President and the Vice President of Bayard T. Ramsay & Company appeared. Ginny saw the set table, peeked into the oven, saw the beef chunks marinating in the bowl.

"I can't believe it, SuSu. You getting domestic!"

"Never," Susan said. "In Maine, I cook a pot of good old Boston baked beans on my woodstove, and it lasts me for days."

"All of a sudden that sounds good," Bud said and began to mix drinks for himself and Ginny. "Another beer, SuSu?"

She reached for it; tossing the empty can toward the garbage container, she missed. Ginny tried to stoop and pick it up, but her bend was more like a hula dance and her face grimaced.

"Your arthritis is bothering you," Susan said. "I'll get it. Isn't there anything the doctor can do?"

"Afraid not. Pills help briefly. Maybe a hike on the AT would unbend me."

"That'll be the day," Bud quipped.

"Well, I am taking you both on some long walks in Maine, so get yourselves in shape."

While her parents went upstairs to freshen up, Susan got down wine goblets and placed them around the table. Then, remembering she hadn't called brother Dick, she dialed the Indianapolis number. Kathleen, her brother's second wife, answered, and they chatted a few moments. Strange how Kathleen and Denise—Number One—had similar voice qualities, especially when they were excited. Dick finally came on the line, complaining that he was dripping water on the floor because some people had no respect and called other people in the middle of a shower. She responded that perhaps he hadn't identified the source of the water; that grouchy businessmen, weighted down and made prematurely old by the mad rush of capitalism, quickly lost control of their bladders. The repartee was flying when Bud and Ginny came downstairs and wanted to say a few words.

The two men began to talk business while Susan and her mother finished preparing the meal. Bud finally hung up.

"Nice going in Indiana," he remarked, joining the women at the table. "SuSu, your brother is becoming the epitome of the successful executive."

Richard had been a political science major at Brown University while Kelly had gone to Ohio State. Susan was not sure in her own mind that her brother was totally reconciled to life as a businessman. Still, she said nothing as they ate. She was thinking: "Make no waves or offer no contrary opinions; don't let this become an idealogical battleground and upset the harmony of this good homecoming."

They lingered over wine and dessert to talk of when an outing—including *all* family members—could be scheduled at the Ramsay cottage in Michigan. That possibility warmed Susan's heart. Her love of the outdoors had been born at Au Gres, their Saginaw Bay retreat.

"SuSu, if your master's degree is wound up by June, maybe we could all meet on the Fourth of July weekend and celebrate," Bud suggested.

"Sounds great. Just keep your fingers crossed that my thesis passes muster."

"What are you writing on?" Ginny asked.

"A thinly veiled setting at Homestead. Calling it, *Clark: The Artwork of an Adolescent in Residential Treatment.* It's been tough going. I'm not the greatest at articulating my thoughts and observations."

"You can do anything you set your mind to, Susypie," Bud said. "I've seen you buckle down and do the impossible before."

"Thanks for the vote of confidence, but when I don't show up at Au Gres on the fourth, you'll know your judgment is not always infallible."

The laughter was relaxing. Maybe they all were mellowing, Susan thought.

They cleared the table, mixed fresh drinks, and moved to the living room. Susan wandered about the room, looking at the family pictures, art objects, and memorabilia. At the rear of the room was a framed map of Au Gres and the Saginaw Bay area. As she had a thousand times previously, she searched for the tiny dot of landscape that identified their cottage. Funny how Fate worked. Had it not been for her maternal great-grandfather, Edwin Sims, they would never have set foot along this peaceful Michigan shore. Great-Grandpa Sims had bought five thousand acres in 1904 for one dollar an acre. The cottage Ginny now owned was built in 1938 and had been deeded to her in 1967 as a gift from her parents.

Ginny called from across the room: "You're getting itchy feet to hit the trail, aren't you?"

"You always had such an Evil Eye?" Susan laughed.

"We miss you, Susypie. I wish it could be like this more often," Bud said.

"Don't get sentimental on me, Dad. I'll flip for sure. I really don't belong here, y'know."

"Yes, you do."

"No, Mom. It's not me. I don't fit now. I'm Earth's child."

Soft-hearted Ginny choked up on her intended response.

"You've always fit," Bud insisted. "Who hasn't had his growing pains? So you don't think like the rest of us. More than not, you've been our breath of fresh air, you know. Maybe things will work out with this Bob what's-his-name. You could be a happy wife and mother this time next year."

"Don't count on it," Susan exclaimed. "Then or ever. If it happens, fine. If not, I don't need it to exist. Women are more now than brood sows and house slaves."

"No lectures, Susypie. I know your views, and I respect them."

Bud went to the kitchen for another round of drinks and came back with his granddaughter in his arms. Kelly and Curt followed.

"I'd begun to think you'd forgotten," Susan murmured. She took little Katie from her Bud's arms. "I really haven't had much time to hold her, y'know."

Susan wasn't aware of all eyes upon her until the room grew silent. While Bud served the newcomers drinks, she continued to cuddle the warm, pink child. At eleven months Katie was so beautiful as to mesmerize the onlooker. Four sets of friends in four different locations had recently become new parents, and Susan had already held two of those offspring. It was a good, yet a strange, feeling. She knew that a part of it was that time when she had thought herself pregnant.

Bud Ramsay's eyes were aglow, and he stood erect, towering over Katie. Susan had not really thought of him in grandfatherly terms. His tall, well-tailored physique was without a serious middle-aged spread, his dark hair not predominantly gray but thinning. He, was the epitome of the successful executive. An aura of dynamism and decisiveness clung to him.

Tiring, Susan shifted the infant in her arms.

Bud said, "Give her back to me for a while. I'll give you a rest."

Bud cooed at Katie like a sentimental first-time father. For all his businessman bluff and bluster, he could turn as soft as a kitten. Maybe, Susan speculated, that quality was one of the things that compelled her to love him so deeply—even to forgive him for those times when they had clashed and he had come down too severely.

The baby soon grew fussy, and Kelly fed her and put her to bed.

When she returned, Bud said, "Such occasions as this are all too rare in the Ramsay household these days. I want to fill our glasses and propose a toast."

Bud made the rounds and then lifted his glass.

"Here's to the Ramsays—and to Curt and Richard's Kathleen. May we each continue to aspire to the best that is in us. And when we must go our separate ways on the road to excellence, let us look back to those who love and sustain us, forgetting old hurts or new wounds, so that we hear our own personal drummers with clarity of mind and sincerity of heart."

"Hear! Hear!" the chorus chanted, the glasses clinked.

Ginny stood, wrapped her arm around her husband of thirty-three years. There were tears in her eyes as she kissed his cheek.

"You can be quite poetic, you know."

Kelly then proposed a toast of her own. "And here's to SuSu. May any snakes that bite her on the Appalachian Trail die instantly of blood poisoning!"

The good laughter died away to an uneasy silence. The reality was that another of a hundred goodbyes was at hand. Yawns and last hugs and caresses sealed the day's end. The grandfather clock in the hallway struck 12:00, measuring out each eerie tone with resounding authority.

In her room, now all too deathly quiet after so much togetherness, Susan reappraised this homecoming. Something had been present that had never been there in the same degree before: some invisible, but beautiful, bond that miraculously had grown deeper. Her father's toast still rang in her ears. Her father never ceased to amaze her. He sometimes seemed fathomless in revealing new and unexpected sides of his nature. But was she not describing herself as well? Who were the Ramsays her father had toasted? For that matter, who were the Coffins—her mother's side?

She had been too well schooled in family heritage not to know that there had been good stock—and bad—on both sides which had risen above the commonplace. Through her father she could claim descent from President James Monroe; her mother's ancestor, Tristram (Coffyn) Coffin, had helped to found the first colony on Nantucket Island in Massachusetts. But who was Laura Susan Ramsay? The question spun round and round in her brain like a repeating record.

In bed Susan found sleep evasive. For some unexplainable reason, an old poem she had written years ago came back to her: "She lived in the ocean/The sky was her home/The earth was her Mother/Her name is my own." It bugged her that she couldn't remember when and why she had written it. She got up, turned on the light, and seached her bureau for an old diary. The memory began to come before she actually found the section she sought. Then the exact page caught her eye. She had written the poem in November when she was marooned in Rapid City, South Dakota, in'77. Maybe there had been some carry-over emotions after the unusual church service with Betty. The diary pages continued almost to turn themselves, and then her eyes focused on the November 7 entry:

Can't shake religion from my body, my soul. I run away always—can't even talk to myself about it. Alluding to angels— Holy Ghost in spirit—cannot fathom gods—something more to it. Earth. I want to save people—I want to endlessly confess my sins to my people so I have pedestal image to live up to. Virtue-within. We keep who we are inside—if we are that blessed. Some of us live in earthly heaven, some of us live in hell. Some people die in misery and some people die in peace. Some people die for nothing, but the dying doesn't cease. And it doesn't quit inside, does it? I want to feel the earth in my hand moving. I become comfortable when I realize what I do I do— because of what I believe is right—helping people help themselves—a battle I am all too righteous in assuming. My ground of being is shifting—from God's to value confusion. Jesus—I can't ignore His message. And I realize again that this comfortability is all screwed up. I don't know what it means to be free—to dance through a day—spiritually. To love. My dreams are escaping me. And again I look to the children. Letting them dance through their day is a promise to my future—a blessing for today. Prayer. O now I pray. To be strong enough not to discount the individual need in lieu of a compromise in another. To have inner peace—and understand good and bad of humanity—and to share this physically-spiritually with another would be freedom enhanced. I don't think I can do it. I am my own betrayer. Weakness is easier and less painful. In the end I will know.

Tonight, now, I think about how I will end. I wish I knew how to really give. One tin soldier rides away from the battle.

One tin soldier rides away from the battle. The last line stuck in her consciousness. Why could not the tin soldier turn to flesh, wielding a steel sword and purple banner, and come charging back on a white steed ready to fight in quest of the Impossible Dream? She snapped off the light and got into bed.

She felt her lips part in the darkness, and her smile broadened and stretched her cheeks. She would have no white steed to ride on the Appalachian Trail, but perhaps it was best after all to approach the pinnacle humbly—on foot. Hadn't the Chinese—Confucius maybe—said that a journey of a thousand miles began with the first step?

CHAPTER XV

During late afternoon of May 8, Bob and Dave Tice arrived at Abingdon Gap shelter near the Virginia/Tennessee state line. Before dark Frank Maguire drifted in, too. They were all running low on food, but Damascus lay dead ahead, and the small town offered all the shopping variety they would need for replenishment.

At supper Bob ate two Kraft macaroni and cheese dinners though the most robust through hiker rarely had the capacity for more than one.

"Mountford's like a bear after six months of hibernation," Frank grunted, but he, too, was putting it away, and Dave was not far behind.

Bob had walked most of the day with Dave Tice. In discussing mutual career goals, they found that both had a love for children and young people, and Dave revealed that he had driven a school bus once in his native Giles County and again while he was an undergrad at Virginia Polytechnic Institute and State University. Earlier in the day as the two of them had been resting beside a highway, a school bus stopped to discharge a young boy. The child's mother had met the bus, and the four of them talked for nearly an hour.

It seemed to Bob that this was really what life ought to be about: the enrichment of one's experience with the person and personality of others, whether young or old, rich or poor, black or white. Maybe others didn't feel this way; yet most of the hikers all along the Trail had impressed Bob as intelligent, sensitive, caring people. He saw in them something very special.

By 5:00 A.M. they were up again, had instant breakfasts, and put shoeleather to soil once more. Bob mentioned that he would not be getting another mail drop from home until they got to Whitetop, Virginia, the next village along the AT after Damascus.

"When we get to Pearisburg, the next town on the trail after Whitetop, I'm taking Susan to meet a family friend of ours, Dr. Richard Desjardins at Blacksburg," Bob added.

"Small world," Dave said. "I know him! When I was at VPI & SU, I had an infection and had to see him at the college infirmary for a week or so. How long you known him?"

"As far back as I can go," Bob laughed. "He delivered me into this zany world. We were all from Millinocket, Maine."

"I didn't know you'd been born, Mountford," Frank said. "I thought the way you eat, you must've been hatched from a vulture egg."

"Some of us have it; others don't," Bob countered.

They began to split off then, each finding his own pace. Through hikers rarely walked together for long distances. Usually, they were a mile—or miles—apart, but the end of the day usually found various combinations of them pulling into the same campsite for the night. Thinking back, Bob realized that about a dozen people had traveled at roughly the same pace as he had. He knew that the Linnehans would never catch up, and he had no idea how far behind him Jean Tierney and Patti Hydro might be. He wondered also whether Neal Chivington, and Sandy and Steve Skinner were gaining on him or had also taken some offtrail trips or been otherwise delayed. In any event he had left them notes at various trail registers—notes apparently written by Woody Allen, Groucho Marx, Fidel Castro, Phyllis Diller, or combinations of such characters.

Still a couple of miles from Damascus, he took a blue-blaze trail downhill to a spring at an old abandoned homestead. The limestone water tasted sweet, pure, and cold. He marveled at the aura of life that still hovered about the ruins. He wondered how many years some farm housewife (or wives), before the days of electricity, had trudged from main house to springhouse, keeping the milk cool in big pottery crocks in the cold water. More important still, why had the family let the homestead die? Had invading Yankees—during "The Late Unpleasantness," as Southerners called the Civil War—brought devastation from which the family had never recovered? The whole Trail—the whole countryside—breathed the living history and the struggle of man to subdue nature and overcome misfortune.

The trail continued to drop as the town came closer. At the Virginia/Tennessee line the elevation on Holston Mountain had been scarcely over three thousand feet, and according to the trail map Damascus proper dropped to under two thousand.

Emerging from the woods, he descended gradually along a farm road to several barns and then through a pine thicket. Wild violets and dandelions were everywhere, spread out like a carpet of welcome.

Reaching town, he walked along U.S. 58, crossed an abandoned railroad bed and Beaverdam Creek, and headed for the hostel.

The building, an earlier-era two-story house painted grayish green with a big screened-in porch, could house sixteen to twenty hikers. It was called "The Place." The accommodation was owned by the United Methodist Church, which sat just across the alley behind it. As he crossed the grassy lawn, the porch looked crowded already. He parked his backpack and heard a series of affectionate catcalls. When the welcome died down, Frank and Dave begun to rub in his tardiness.

"What kept you? Thought you were the Trail speed demon," Frank said.

"I took a blue-blaze to an old homestead," Bob said. "Had myself a cold drink of spring water. Rested. Let my imagination soar. Whatsmatter, you turkeys got no sensitivities for history and nostalgia?"

A half dozen lit into him again, but he only half heard them. His eyes were searching for a particular face. Don Farrell, JJ, Renate, the "Michigan gang" of Mary Kearney, John Smith, and Candy Lakin were there, plus a couple he had earlier met briefly—Helen Anne Hickey and Graeme Sephtan. Peter was missing, and Susan Ramsay was not in sight.

"Susan hasn't arrived?" he said.

"Ve vent to get guitar. Then Peter and Susan vent to get strings," Renate said.

Bob didn't understand, and JJ said that Renate and Peter had earlier gone into town to see if they could borrow a guitar from someone. They had come back unsuccessful, but a little while later two teenagers in a jeep had come to the hostel, guitar in hand—but without strings. Susan and Peter had gone back into town to buy strings.

"Susan vants to have a songfest for your homecoming," Renate added.

Bob could feel his face spread in a grin fully as broad as the dam at Fontana.

"So—you got doctored up and beat us to Damascus after all," Bob said.

"I am very vell, thank you. And the sing-song vas my idea first."

There was a mild chilliness to Renate's voice, he noticed. It took him a moment to figure why, and he said just under his breath, "Women."

He, Dave, and Frank hit the showers. The hot suds provided such a feeling of luxury that Bob felt that he could fly the remaining distance of the AT. He began to sing until somebody called out.

"We passed a herd of bleating sheep in Shady Valley that made a better noise than that, Mountford!"

It sounded like nurse Candy Lakin's voice coming from the porch.

"Jealousy, Candy. Jealousy! I know that I should have gone on TV long ago!"

He dressed and took note that he had used the last of the clean underwear and jeans. He would definitely have to do a wash in Damascus.

He had gone back out to the porch and suffered more putdowns on his best witticisms when things suddenly got quiet. Instinctively he turned around. Susan stood there deadpan with Peter behind her.

A slow, unsure smile formed on her pretty face, and he felt himself responding in kind. For a moment it seemed that neither knew what to do. Her long dark blond hair hung loose. It appeared that the tresses were in motion before she moved, but he saw the distance closing and met her. It was kind of like a clumsy bear-hug.

"There for a while, I thought you'd chickened out," Bob said.

"For once I'm on schedule," she replied.

Her brown eyes were dancing, and he could see the excited anticipation in her countenance. She looked almost trail-ready in jeans and well-fitted cotton shirt with sleeves rolled to the elbows.

"How long have you got . . . . how much vacation?" Bob asked.

"A week. Then it's back to our favorite salt mines."

She explained the stop-offs and the quick trip home.

"Jeez, we can't cover much ground in a week! Can't you get an extension?"

"I don't know. Maybe."

"It'll take us a week to get to Pearisburg. And I wanted to take you by to see the Desjardins in Blacksburg; then for a ways, at least, up the valley of Virginia . . ."

"I'll call Pat Moore and ask for another week if you say so."

"Consider it said!"

Bob had every confidence that the Executive Director would be cooperative.

"Any of you mountain goats that want to make the PO, it closes before twelve," Frank sang out.

The screened porch began to clear, and on the way they all looked like a scout troop in trail formation.

Susan brought him up to date on happenings in Ellsworth, shared details of the Oberlin affair, and conveyed her parents' good wishes for their Trail journey.

"Gotta meet these Ramsays some time," Bob said casually. "They as free-spirited as their daughter?"

"On the contrary. They're liberal and open sometimes. Not quite like me, though, I guess. They're coming up to Ellsworth for my birthday. Too bad, you'll still be on the trail."

At the modern brick post office, there were long lines. Hikers and residents were buying stamps. In turn, each hiker called for his held mail. Postmaster "GP" Grindstaff was well known for his helpfulness and general friendliness.

Having mailed an assortment of cards and letters and finally having gotten his incoming stuff, Bob began ripping open letters. Old friends, fellow counselors at Homestead, and several of the members brought him up to date on happenings. A couple of letters contained news clippings about the walkathon, but they were outdated. According to them, he was still in North Carolina.

"They knew you'd be a slow walker," Susan teased. "Stopping at every farmer's house to chew the fat and argue politics."

"You remember me so well, don't you?"

"It's only been six weeks."

Six weeks since what? He remembered. She had the time element down pat. Had she missed him? He thought so. He, too, remembered with unusual clarity the tender moments, the quiet dinners they had shared at her cabin by the water, the hikes and jogging, and the cross-country ski trips down the frozen lake. Yet, it was not quite the same here. His weeks on the trail had put distance between them somehow and had brought changes in him that were not easily explained.

The line was almost as long at the public phone booth on the corner.

When their turn came, Bob let Susan make her call first. She reached Pat Moore in Ellsworth and jumped for joy when Pat said, "Yes."

"Done!" She told Bob. "But I've got to be back at work on May 26."

Susan shared her good news with hikers in the rear of the line while he began placing his own calls.

He reached Jackie first and found her more excited than ever about a reunion on the Trail in Pennsylvania; he thanked her for the little "care packages" and notes he had received from her at a couple of mail drops along the way, gave a brief rundown of the Trail experience, and sent barrages of hugs and kisses across the wires.

He began to sound like a stuck record repeating the same thoughts and information about the hike to Joanne. When Joanne expressed concern about his safety, he laughed at her. "If you could see and feel the beauty and serenity of the trail, you'd know that thoughts of violence are impossible! The only real danger is starving to death," he added and then confessed that lonely moments on the trail made him obsessed with thoughts of savory food. Joanne brought him up to date on Press Secretary Jim Brady's condition in the aftermath of the Presidential assassination attempt; she said that a long letter was on the way to the Pearisburg mail drop and that she missed him. Bob echoed the sentiment and asked for a meeting in the fall at the Trail's end so that he could really tell her what the AT was all about.

"Meanwhile—send food—anything edible. And Joanne, I am going to marry you one day, you know."

There was the same familiar pause before she promised another mail drop of nuts, carrot-coated things, but no sugary snacks. He groaned and said goodbye.

The call to Dover-Foxcroft was even more lengthy, and growls of impatience began to resound at his back. He rang off and rejoined Susan before he remembered that he had forgotten a matter of importance.

"Damn! I forgot to wish Mom happy Mother's Day."

"You can call her back tonight or tomorrow," Susan said. "I've already done my daughterly duties."

"They may be getting tired of my long distance, collect, phone bills. Anyway, we'll be hitting the Trail first thing in the morning—no phone booths there."

"Your friend Frank Maguire wants us to stay over. Go with him and a couple of others to his daughter's house in Kingsport. Steaks and a big party, he promises. Interested?"

Bob felt his digestive juices already in motion.

"I think you just said the magic word."

Susan wanted to buy beer for everyone while they were in Damascus, and a number of other hikers had taken up collections for the needed ingredients of a Mexican-style feast. Amply supplied with chili beans, cheeses, lettuce, tomatoes, chips, dips, and other ingredients, the feast was well under way shortly after midday.

Full of good food and cold beer at last, a few of the hikers took to the hostel lawn for a frisbee-throwing contest. Susan and JJ came out the champions. Bob parked his food/beer-logged body in a chair on the screened-in porch, picked up the guitar, and began to serenade them with a waggish ditty of his own invention. When Bob ran out of steam, Peter took the battered flat-top guitar and played and sang a few numbers. His deep, impassioned voice seemed to bring on a mood change within the group, and soon a full-scale singalong was in progress. They did hiking songs, country and western, folk tunes, protest lyrics, and the latest in popular fare. Renate introduced some Old Country ballads of her own.

The mood changed again when Susan took her turn with the guitar. It was immediately apparent that she had a kind of gentle mastery over the instrument in a way quickly discernible but not easily explained. She sang a number of her own compositions before she went into a rendition of *Dona Nobis Pacem*—"Give Us Peace"—which afterwards she taught the group to sing in the round.

There was a haunting, lasting quality in that final song. It said something to all of them—not just about the ideal of peace but about the serenity and the holiness of nature, and human relationships and brotherly love. It summarized the essence of life, especially trail life.

Later that afternoon, Frank Maguire's daughter, Kathleen Shaw, and her young sons, ages four and six, arrived in her Chevy Impala. In her early thirties, Kathleen was a pretty brunette, nearly as tall as her father and more outgoing. It was well that Kingsport—in Tennessee—was only fifty miles away since five additional bodies were now piled into the car. Frank, claiming the right front seat, held the youngest grandchild on his lap and wedged the other boy between himself and Kathleen. In the back seat, Bob, Susan, John Smith, and Candy Lakin were packed like sardines.

At Kathleen's house Bob retrieved the guitar they had used at "The Place." Susan's playing—and her own compositions especially—had done something to him. He didn't want that something to stop. He wanted that mesmerizing music to eddy along his spine long after he had devoured the good steaks and cold beer and the fellowship wore down. Then, some time during the quiet of night, he would have a chance to really hold her and tell her how glad he was that she had come to share the trail experience with him, to lie under the stars with him and feel the cleansing, renewing power of nature invade their beings, fuse their souls.

Somewhere in between the lines of Susan's latest compositions was a message for him. He had felt it and had seen it in her eyes as she seemed to play for him alone — a message too complex and discreet to be picked up by anybody other than him.

Next morning, Frank decided to stay in Kingsport with his daughter and grandsons for a day or so. He would catch up, he said. Kathleen drove the others back to Damascus and said goodbye.

There were all sorts of chores to do. Susan helped him wash clothes, pack fresh supplies, and give all his gear a good cleaning. Without Susan's prodding he remembered to call his mother and wish her happy Mother's Day. Mim commented on his timing and how "up" he sounded.

"Why shouldn't I be 'up'," he asked her. "It *is* Mother's Day, and I've got the world's greatest mom. Besides, it's spring in Virginia, and you ought to see the redbuds and the dogwoods!"

Mim's sigh of appreciation was long and distinct. To lessen her pain of longing to share it all, he said, "I won't tempt you with more elaborate details of the beauty in every direction, but I'm counting on seeing the Mountfords — and Jackie — when I reach Pennsylvania. Don't blow it this time!"

Many of the hikers at "The Place" had already hit the trail. Dave Tice had been anxious to get an early start. Pearisburg was not many days away, and he lived there. Peter, JJ, and Don Farrell were gone as were some of the friends Bob had first encountered at Fontana Dam. A few hikers prepared to attend the Methodist service next door.

Newcomers off the trail were arriving as others shipped out. It was the same old story of quick but fleeting friendships. As if to provide background music for this happy - yet sad - scene, the church organist went into action: "Amazing grace! How sweet the sound That saved a wretch like me . . ." The powerful strains of the hymn brought thoughts of Mountford senior. How his father loved that ancient old Newton classic!

A dense drizzle came down as they headed for the Trail, and it wasn't long before they all—Bob, Susan, John, Candy, Mary Kearney, and Renate—looked like windswept nomads. At Laurel Creek four of them began to stretch out, their heavily laden multicolored backpacks adding new hues to the misty landscape. He kept close to Susan. Although she was an experienced outdoorsperson who had hiked the northern end of the AT many times, she had been away from it long enough to need disciplined breaking in. He teased her unmercifully about her tenderfoot status.

"Then leave me and let the bears eat me up." She feigned a pout.

After a couple of miles through a series of switchbacks, they reached the crest of Feathercamp Ridge. Susan was not even puffing when they stopped for the view of Damascus below.

With amazing stamina Susan led off, and they soon passed through the saddle of the mountain near Cuckoo Knob. At the junction where the yellow-blazed Iron Mountain Trail (earlier routing of the AT) led to Sandy Flats shelter, they sat for a swig of water. The drizzle had kept them cool, but the upward climb seemed to dissipate mouth and throat moisture, and the height was reaching the three-thousand-foot level again. Susan soon hopped up, eager to go. Her braided hair was wet and dripping.

"You're some kind of girl" he said, the words trailing off.

"I didn't do daily six-mile jogs for nothing!"

"*That* kind of girl, but the other kind too. Y'know, the soft, cuddly kind."

"I hoped you'd remember," she said, watching his eyes.

"I could hardly forget. I think we almost had something going."

"Almost?"

"I'm screwed up in a lot of ways, Susan. Got a lot of things hanging. Think I'm in some kind of transition state—mind, body, soul."

"The body looks good. Twenty pounds lighter, I'd say." She ran wet fingers through his lengthening beard. "I like this too. Makes you look rugged and virile."

He waited for her to go on, but she didn't. Obviously, she had been told by the others that Jackie didn't make it to the Smokies, and she would be unsure whether that implied anything. He decided to broach the third subject again himself.

"I've been thinking a lot about belief lately. Maybe I ought to add that spiritualism has been intruding itself upon me a lot lately. You know — I've had three transcendental experiences in the last four years; the most recent spectral was only days ago after I'd ascended Clingman's Dome. Some One or Something is trying to send me a message. I don't know whether I ever told you this, but when I entered college, my aptitudes indicated that I had some ministerial leanings. The truth is I've long had an interest in finding and exploring my deeper self."

"You've exercised that to a point, I think. Isn't our work a kind of ministry?"

"Yes, but only to the degree that a cartoonist is a fine artist."

"That's stretching the comparison a little, isn't it?"

"Maybe. Let's forget it. The Trail does strange things to you. Damn strange things if you're alone too long."

"Maybe we ought not to forget it —" She stopped short.

He didn't know what she meant, and he searched her face for meaning. Susan Ramsay wasn't usually so somber-looking; at Homestead she was the school pixie, clown, cheerful art therapist, jolly woodland companion, and warm, unselfish friend to everybody.

"We ought not to forget what?" he prompted.

"The soul-searching. I've had some experiences of my own in the last three or four years. I use to go out with a waitress during my stranded days in South Dakota. Some gal, Betty. She used to take me to her Pentecostal church. I had some feelings there I've never been able to share with anyone. Maybe —" but again she held back.

"Maybe it's something we can share, you were about to say? Jeez," he laughed. "This sojourn is taking all kinds of twists and turns."

"I always did want to do a weird number on you like you did to me: like having two girls show up for the New Year's holiday with you in Dover-Foxcroft."

"That wasn't any weird number. I wanted you both. What the hell's wrong with that?"

"Knowing one Bob Mountford as I'm beginning to, nothing, I guess — at least for now. I've missed you, y'know."

"Well, you ain't seen or imagined anything yet. I'm taking you deep into

127

a wonderland you're never going to forget."

"Sleeping Beauty and Prince Charming lost in the Appalachian woods?"

"At Homestead you'd have said Beauty and The Beast. You're slipping."

"I'll try to do better here," she said. "Be on my best behavior."

"Why? I like you the way you were."

"I want this little outing to be meaningful and memorable, I guess. Thanks for inviting me."

He leaned over and kissed her wet lips. Her arms were at her sides, and she didn't move.

"That have any meaning for you?"

"Not bad for an inexperienced, bearded mountaineer." Her smile was challenging.

He took her in his arms then, felt her own tighten around his neck, and kissed her hard. Rain dribbled down her nose and onto his cheek before he let go.

"Wow," he said breathlessly. "Did lightning strike or did I just imagine it?"

Her eyes opened and focused slowly on him.

"Like you said, maybe the wilderness does play tricks, but I felt it, too."

They had not moved until other hikers had come across the backbone of the ridge toward them. Then they walked on.

Late in the day when they had reached Bear Tree Gap, the rain was coming down for real. Tentless, Dave Tice was already encamped under his tarp, cozy in his sleeping bag. John, Candy, Renate, and Mary Tierney were already busy setting up their tents. In spite of the rain, Bob was in no hurry, and he took Susan over to the nearby pond. They watched the raindrops bombard the pond water for a few minutes before looking for frogs along the bank.

"How about frog legs for supper?" he asked.

Horror struck at the very thought of injuring any creature of the wilds, she threatened to push him into the muddy pond if he so much as touched a tadpole.

They set up their own tent and waited out the rain before attempting to prepare food. The rain stopped before dark, and Bob made a fire and started sloppy joes. Somebody else made trail hash, and Susan helped Renate and Mary make hot chocolate.

When it was all ready, Renate sampled everything.

"I vill predict that it von't sell in East or Vest Germany, either. I have tested better spoiled sauerkraut!"

In spite of Renate's critique, everyone was soon full, and the campfire brought warmth and cheer back in good measure. Susan went to her backpack and brought back a bottle.

"Champagne? Champagne!" Candy exclaimed.

"We bought it to celebrate our first day on the trail," Bob said. "Get your cups and gather 'round."

Dave Tice proposed the first toast:

"Welcome, Susan Ramsay, to the great state of Virginia, mother of Presidents, home of women fair beyond compare; where lofty mountains rise to kiss the skies; where peace and enlightenment dwell!"

"Jeez, Tice. You getting ready to run for office? Mayor of Pearisburg or something?" Bob asked.

"Definitely a Rebel with a forked tongue," somebody else said.

When the others finished their own toasts and the bottle was empty, Dave took even more of a ribbing. He was the only Southerner present.

When it started to rain again, everybody ran for shelter. To the hissing sound of rain extinguishing the campfire, night came and thunder and lightning shook the landscape.

Morning dawned cold, wet, and foggy. Dave Tice was the first to be on his way. Those remaining fired up stoves under tents to heat water for tea or instant coffee and to wash down muffins, pop tarts, or the like.

Breaking camp was a mess. Everything was wet, and it was a grumpy bunch that headed into the wilderness once again. Bob and Susan were soon left behind.

The going was slow. Rain came and went. Once visibility was so poor that they had trouble finding the stile over a split rail fence; then there were swollen creeks to cross and finally a barbed wire fence.

The rain ceased as they began to follow switchbacks and ascend a long gradual grade along the south slope of Beech Mountain. A mile or so farther, a large rock outcropping appeared out of the haze. Susan stopped to look and he caught up.

"It's called Buzzard Rock," he said.

"Reminds me of the time I was hiking in Maine and came to a spot like this. I heard a flutter and discovered I'd interrupted a bald eagle's lunch of fish. It was like no other bird I'd ever seen in my life — a monster, but so commandingly graceful."

"Sounds like one of Grampy Bill's bear tales to me."

"It's true. I swear. I remember the way the eagle looked at me. Our eyes met, and there was some kind of communion. Beautiful. I even thought about climbing back up there, finding its nest, studying its ways. . ."

"I thought you told me you'd once spent a whole winter studying the habits of osprey in Michigan. You didn't get your fill?

"Not really, but I was driving everybody bonkers with my reports and observations, not to mention the smelly samplings of bird-shit I brought into the house for analysis."

When they began to ascend White Top Mountain, the fog was rolling in heavier than ever. Soon it was difficult to see more than twenty or thirty feet ahead. White Top Mountain rose more than a mile into the sky; according to the Trail Guide, a Federal Aviation guidance transmitter and other electronic installations perched on top. If so, Bob couldn't see them. The pea soup was thick enough to cut with a knife.

"Our crowd's not going to hike all day in this stuff," Bob said. "Why don't we try and make Deep Gap shelter and call it a day? The others probably have the same idea."

Susan agreed, but then he remembered the necessary side trip in to the village post office. Since she was developing foot blisters, he didn't want her to walk extra distance.

"Can you make it on your own to Deep Gap? I'll fetch my mail drop and catch up."

"I am an experienced hiker, you know."

Later it was like a whole different world after Bob made the circle and approached Deep Gap shelter. The sky cleared, the sun popped out, and the earth smelled of freshness. A scattering of mountain laurel was in early bloom, but the bushes were stunted, victims of the great height. In spite of the beauty, he was irritated with himself. Caught up in the excitement of receiving another package from home, he had left White Top village without his trusty walking stick and was miles away when he remembered. In camp Susan picked up on his mood instantly.

"It's only a stick. I'll cut you a new one."

"Dammit, it was more than a stick. It was a Maine stick. My companion since Boston station. Kept me safe. Funny, but it had some kind of staff-of-life feel about it. Damn! And it's too far back."

"It's not that far. You could go back. I'll go with you."

"No. You don't play with blisters on the trail. We've got to doctor those feet of yours."

Susan went off, determined to cut him a new stick anyway, and he made the rounds, checking on the camp arrivals.

Dave Tice had called it a day, and Renate had arrived shortly after Tice. Bob couldn't figure that; then he learned that Renate had gone off the trail and hitchhiked part of the way. Bob had earlier heard murmurings about Renate's bent to hitch rides, cover distances quickly, or avoid rough terrain; doing so cut into one's credibility as a through hiker. Even so, he couldn't be too irritated about her behavior. During the intimate moments they had shared along the way, he had learned the source of her moods. At the age of eighteen she had married an American serviceman and had come to the U.S. The marriage had lasted a brief year and a half. Furthermore, she was burnt out in her most recent job and had no better place to go. Inside her was more anguish than she wanted to show. Little wonder the pain in her unguarded countenance showed so plainly.

John, Candy, and Mary were about, but the biggest surprise of all was seeing Pete Gallager. Pete had been at Damascus when they left, and here he had covered the whole distance in record time. Scarcely post-college age and as well-toned as a long-distance runner, Gallager was evidently a formidable hiker.

After supper, everybody got into the act of doctoring Susan's feet. Powdered, salved, and bandaged, she complained of feeling like a war casualty. In a way she was. Bob knew that she wasn't ready yet to keep the through hiker's pace and that the two of them would have to hold back now.

That night the other six occupied the small shelter while Bob pitched his tent nearby. Susan snuggled against him under the bright moon, but he could tell that she was a little down. Susan could be a humble person, and yet she had her share of pride: pride in her healthy body and physical accomplishments as well as in her fertile mind. He held her tighter and offered words of encouragement.

"So — what does it matter? We'll see them all again in Pennsylvania or Maine or some place."

"I was just getting to know them, to like them. It's a little sad."

"Welcome to the club. The feeling's part of trail life."

"But I'm holding you back, too."

"Maybe that's a bonus. We really haven't had much privacy."

Her body stirred and then she rolled over and faced him. The whites of her eyes were the only distinct facial feature in the dim nocturnal light.

"When you put it that way . . ."

Somewhere in the distance a high-pitched yap or bark echoed through the trees. Probably a fox. A mating call? The thought was warming. Perhaps on such a pleasant spring night it was a universal urge.

CHAPTER XVI

"What do you mean, 'I quit'?" Larry Stowers shot back, though Randall Lee Smith had declared his intentions calmly even though a little fearfully.

Randall tried to meet the piercing blue eyes of the plant superintendent bravely, but there was too much power there to out-stare the stocky man. Randall stood taller than his middle-aged boss by three or four inches, but that didn't help either. Randall looked away and lowered his gaze.

"I said, 'I quit,' " he repeated softly.

"What's the problem?"

"Don't seem like I can suit anybody. The line foreman's on my back all the time and I saw him talking to you about me."

"Yeah, he talked to me about you, but I wasn't going to fire you. He just wants you to shape up. You're a good welder, Smith, if you'd just keep your mind on your work. Your foreman says you walk around in a dream world of your own. You got some kind of problem?"

"He ought to mind his own business; they all ought to mind their own business. Always trying to look into people's heads."

"Your performance on the job is his business. Your work is getting sloppy. And you don't pay attention. Quit if you want to, but according to your record, you've been through too many jobs. You may run out of chances one day. Any employer'll be gun shy of a man who's had a dozen jobs and keeps moving on. How old are you, Smith?"

"Twenty-seven."

"Give it some thought. Now, are you quitting or not?"

"I quit."

"Do as you want. Work out the shift and pick up your check."

Randall turned and walked out of the small cubicle that served as the super's office. The whole place was a slip-shod rat's hole anyway; it was just a small pilot plant of the Long-Airdox Corporation that had been set up five years previously in an old Kroger grocery store outlet. The company's main plant and headquarters were at Oak Hill, West Virginia, but if they were such a hot-shot company with new plants opening everywhere like his fellow workers said, how come the Pearisburg, Virginia, operation was crammed in an airless old food chain building where you could still smell rotten produce? Making parts for mining equipment, the company's main product line, was dull business anyway. He should have stayed in eastern Virginia with the Newport News Ship Building and Drydock Company, where he'd gone after high school. That was a company. But he'd gotten so homesick for his mother and his home town of Pearisburg after a few months. It'd been just him and Loretta, his mother, for so long. His father had deserted them before Randall was two. People didn't know what he and Loretta had been through. Didn't even give a damn.

He walked down the center aisle of the assembly area toward the back of the building and his work station.

"What's the matter, Snuffy? The super callin' you in on the carpet?" an assembler called out.

"Cram a brass bushing up your ass," Randall said. "He didn't fire me. I quit."

The assembler wasn't a good friend—Randall didn't claim any close friendships with anyone at Long-Airdox—and Randall resented anyone's calling him after a cartoon character. He wasn't the sawed-off little runt like Snuffy Smith of the funny papers anyway. He was just under six feet though he knew he didn't look it. Loretta and his teachers had always railed at him for his drooping posture, his bent shoulders. But he'd shown them. He'd quit high school in the eleventh grade. Some of his teachers had said that he was smart, but he'd shown them anyway. Just walked out without telling anybody. They hadn't even missed him. Wouldn't have mattered anyway. He didn't associate with any of them except for one or two guys like himself, and most of his classmates didn't know his name. Didn't know he existed; in fact, they probably couldn't identify him in a room full of sheep.

The shift ended at 4:00 P.M. He made no effort to leave his work area in a neat and orderly condition. There was a sense of satisfaction in leaving welding rods, tools, and his welding helmet in the middle of the floor. In the washroom he cleaned the grime from his hands and combed his shoulder length brown hair.

Most of the thirty or so employees had hit the street by the time the payroll clerk had handed him his check. He tried to calcuate the money due him. But six dollars an hour was considered big money in this rural Virginia town, and the check was big enough to tide him over. The young payroll clerk seemed to sense his frustration. She was young and pretty though a bit overweight, and she liked to paste comical signs around the walls of her desk. *I Fight Poverty—I Work,* one of them said. *You Don't Have To Be Crazy To Work Here, But It Helps,* said another.

"The check is correct," she said a little nervously. "I figured it twice."

He looked at her and said nothing. She winced. Did she think he was going to snap her head off or something? He wasn't like that. They should all know that by now. He left people alone, and they left him alone.

As he turned to leave, Larry Stowers came to him. The super extended his hand.

"Good luck, Smith. You planning on leaving Giles County?"

Randall gave his hand but felt a sense of offense when the super dropped it so quickly. Even so, he knew his palm was clammy. He could feel it, and it always was when something ate at his gut.

"Don't know where I'm goin'," Randall said. "Might go to New River Community College over at Dublin. Take up draftin', auto mechanics, or somethin'."

"Well, good luck whatever works out. I believe you could do good at anything if you apply yourself and get your head on straight."

Randall walked out into the mid-afternoon sun and half-circled the brick building to the parking lot out back. The middle of May was just around the corner, and the day was almost like summer. He unlocked the door of his '78 Ford pickup, backing off a couple of steps to admire the sheen of the two-tone green paint and the oversized Goodyear Wrangler tires he had tire-blacked to a rich ebony. That big four-wheel-drive was his whole life. It was better than any woman, better than the best buddy he had, admitting that his buddies were few.

He cranked the engine and let it warm up slowly. People were so dumb. They'd rev up an engine even in zero weather before the oil had time to circulate among the rods and the pistons. It was murder on moving parts before the oil had time to circulate.

After another moment he did rev the Ford just slightly until the hum of power was like a lion's low growl. He loved that big Ford; it was an extension of his personality somehow. Where he lacked power, aggression, a certainty of purpose, that trusty machine made up for it. The Ford had never failed him, and he had taken it up every hill and hollow of his native Giles County over rocky creeks and soggy bottoms of more distant territory and to the most challenging roads of Jefferson National Forest. The Ford had easily taken inclines that threatened to tilt the truck over backwards, and still its raw power seemed scarcely tested. Even if he bogged the vehicle down in mud, as he sometimes did, the trusty winch on the front could yank him out like a fisherman landing a trout.

Once out of the parking lot, he drove slowly through the center of town. Pearisburg—the county seat of Giles—was small enough at five or six thousand people so that he knew by sight a good segment of the population his own age and above. At mid-block he saw Wade Shannon, who tried to wave him down. Wade would be wanting money for drugs; some "speckled bird," or "black beauties"; or he would be trying to get a bunch together for some wild party. Randall didn't dislike Wade exactly; he just didn't like for people to push him. And Wade could get spaced out so quick and start getting loud, vulgar, and bossy.

He had first met Wade at a Saturday afternoon gathering at White Rock Park in the eastern end of the county in the summer of '76. The occasion was a going-away party for some of the workers of an out-of-state construction company, a firm that did contract work around the gypsum mines and stone quarries of the county. The company had a lot of nationalities working on its crews; he had met some of the Mexicans,

South Americans, and Canadians, and liked them. They were down-to-earth people as poor and lost as he himself had always felt. He hated to see them go, but they had to move on to some other job just as grimy and dangerous.

Anyhow, that gathering at White Rock had been well planned, and a couple hundred people showed up. There was every kind of drug imaginable, and liquor came in by the truck load. Undoubtedly company officials were unaware of it, but some of the construction foremen were the biggest drug dealers in the area. They used their high wages as investment capital for bulk drug purchases and then doled out their supplies to company workmen and others throughout the area who would pay the high street prices. Two foremen in particular, whose regular incomes and bonuses ran to high figures, boasted of incomes over two hundred thousand dollars a year. Randall didn't doubt it. He had been to their homes, made purchases now and then and seen them in action. They were cool operators, but now they were gone. Life hadn't been the same since. That group of workers and foremen had been the only bunch that gave any light to his life. The whole scene saddened him. He hadn't mingled with the crowd much on that day. He had simply sat on the tailgate of his Ford and taken slowly a handful of "F-40 reds," chasing them with frequent intakes of Jack Daniels.

He had kept pace with the best of them, staying at it all afternoon and into the night until the party was over at 2:30 A.M. He didn't like crowds, and that's why he had kept watch from the sidelines. He hadn't moved from the tailgate—or fallen off—except to go into the woods and relieve himself.

He hadn't been long into the drug scene; in many ways he was still an amateur. He had started on grass, prodded by his roommate in a rundown boarding house in Newport News when he had worked in the shipyards. Not long after coming back to the southwest part of the state, he was introduced to coke, quaaludes, a dozen varieties of uppers and downers, and other drugs he didn't know how to identify. At the going away party, and later at the home of a foreman, he had seen people shooting heroin, smoking killer weed, and gobbling brown-barrel LSD like it was going out of style. He had been offered angel dust and he had almost tried some, but he had balked. He didn't know why he had, but it had something to do with Loretta. He lived at home and owed her something. It didn't make sense then or now.

He headed east toward the old high school—now the middle school—and when traffic thinned, reached for a half-full bottle of Jack Daniels. Watching the rear view mirror, he took a quick drink and put the bottle back.

At the eatern outskirts of town a few moments later he slowed and turned onto the driveway of John's Garage. John Spaur, a young man his own age, ran the place, and on occasion Randall had done small welding jobs for him. Spaur was one of the few people in the world that Randall

135

liked and trusted. Spaur had gone to New River Community College and had ambitions to be a teacher. As a student John had worked at this same garage and later bought it. Since returning to Giles County, Randall had always got John to inspect and service the Ford.

He cut the engine and walked toward the opened overhead door. Pausing along the way, he looked about. Just over the hill to the south was Giles Memorial Hospital, where his mother worked as a housekeeper and linen service maid—then finally she was promoted to a nurses' aide. She would be at work now—three-to-eleven shift. Farther to the east was Giles High, the consolidated school where he had spent too many years.

Entering the building, he saw John Spaur scraping an inspection sticker from a customer's windshield. Three or four people stood around as they always did. Among them was Marty Haley, a man younger than he, who had attended the party at White Rock Park. Marty was most always spaced out. It was rare that milky spittle didn't drool from the corners of his mouth, the residue of some kind of pill. Everybody was welcome at John's Garage, for John Spaur was a friendly, well-liked man.

Spaur put the new sticker on the windshield, pocketed the fee, saw his customer safely backed outside, and came over. "You're outta luck, Randall. Haven't had a welding job in a week."

"Not lookin' for welding work. Quit my job today. Gonna take off. Maybe go to Canada or Mexico. Might even go back to Michigan and look for that woman I had up there."

Marty, hearing it, came over and laughed.

"LR, you never had a woman in your life and everybody knows it. Bet you never been to Michigan either."

"Don't you call me that, or I'll take a tire tool to your fucked-up head!"

Randall faked a movement, and Marty's dull blue eyes brightened. Marty was just a red-haired, freckle-faced kid barely over twenty, but Randall was in no mood to take his shit. He knew that others called him LR—Lying Randall—behind his back, but Marty was getting a little brave to use the term in public.

"Cool it," Spaur said when the other loafers rushed over in anticipation of a fight. "Can't have any brawlin' in my place of business."

As Randall turned to leave, John called him back.

"Did you really quit again? Jobs around here are hard to find."

"Yeah, I quit. Been gettin' restless. Four months is long enough."

"You stayed at Commonwealth Bolt longer than that," John said.

"Yeah. They was nice to me."

"I thought you went to work for Celanese," a loafer, whose truck frame Randall had welded, said.

"Been all around," Randall boasted.

Talking about it, Randall felt himself growing melancholy. Funny how it worked. It'd start coming and swept over him slowly. Roll like the ocean waves at Virginia Beach had done, once, when he'd been between shifts at Newport News and gone there alone to lay on the sand. On that occasion, all those skimpily-clad women parading by him in their bikini suits had brought on the melancholy. Only it was worse then. He'd never gone back to the beach.

"Look," John Spaur said. "I can give you a few days work here 'til you get somethin'."

"Don't want to weld no more," Randall said. "The light's blindin' me, giving me headaches."

"You can change oil and do some lube jobs for me, then," John said.

"Think I'll go and work at the Bluefield airport," Randall said. "Been thinkin' about goin' to West Virginia. There's a woman up there that keeps writin' me."

"There he goes again," Marty snickered, but when Randall reached for a wrench, Marty ran for the street. The other loafers moved off.

"Don't pay any attention to him," John said. "Come on in tomorrow, and I'll put you to work at somethin'."

"I'll think about it. You're good to me, John."

"No reason I shouldn't be."

There was no patronizing smile on John's face. He was a true friend, Randall thought. John never laughed at people or made fun at them. Let people say their fantasies out loud without comment or condemnation. Good man. True blue.

Randall turned again to leave.

"Think about my offer," John called out. "Don't go and do something stupid now! You hear?"

Randall wheeled about. Like a jolt from his welding machine, a great idea flashed across his brain.

"I'm gonna save my last check. Hold it back and buy groceries."

"Loretta'll appreciate that. She needs all the help she can get."

"It's not for her. It's for me. When the weather gets a little hotter, I'm gonna head for Jefferson National. Camp out and give my Ford a work out on the fire trails. Maybe think about some things."

"Watch out for those Appalachian Trail hikers coming through," John called. "They might cart you off to Maine!"

By May 18, the warm nights invited sleeping under the stars. Randall retrieved the hoarded money and headed for the Kroger supermarket. He parked carefully so as not to bump the curb too hard. People were so stupid. You could knock the front end of a vehicle out of alignment by bumping the curb, and ever after, the front wheels would wobble and tires wear improperly. He read *Hot Rod Magazine* and most of the other automotive journals as some people read the daily newspaper; he couldn't think of anything more enjoyable than having Queenie, his big flour-white cat, sit in his lap while he studied how to overhaul an engine or customize a body.

Kenny Sharp, one of his few friends from high school days, worked in the dairy and meat department, and once in the store, Randall headed in that direction. In the old days Kenny, Jimmy Niece, and Randall had been a threesome, cruising town, drinking beer, trying to get up nerve enough to pick up some women. He'd always made excuses and tried to fight off the cold sweats. They'd see his agony and let him off the hook. They'd understood and didn't push him. Both of them were married now with kids, and during the past year, Kenny had taken his son to Jefferson National for a campout and invited Randall along. Randall had been moved by the invitation, but he couldn't get up the nerve to go for the first few days. When he had finally got there—on the last two days of their vacation—he'd taken Kenny and his son and their other guests for a thrilling ride up the steepest fire trails. They'd all thought that he was brave and expert at the wheel of his Ford. The joy of it all was better than any drug high ever had been.

At the meat department he asked for Kenny but was disappointed to learn Kenny was off duty. Randall began his shopping.

"May I help you?" the clerk asked.

Randall looked deep into the eyes of the older man and decided he didn't like him. His blackish eyes were too penetrating. He'd be one of those people who were secretly trying to look into other people's heads.

"Naw. I'll wait on myself," Randall said.

He got a cart but did ask another clerk what kind of meats would last longest in the out-of-doors without spoiling.

"Nothing will last except canned meats—or maybe some beef jerky and salt pork," the clerk said with an amused chuckle.

Did he think Randall didn't know that? Smart-ass. Another one of those cocksure people who made other folks feel like they were shitty worms.

At the checkout the price of the contents of the cart left only eleven dollars and a few cents from the money he had brought with him.

"You must have a family," the skinny blond cashier said cheerfully, bagging the groceries.

"Yeah," Randall said. "A big boy and a set of girl twins. And my wife's pregnant again."

"What if she has another set of twins!" The cashier laughed.

"I'd get rid of her."

The cashier finished, looking up ready to laugh again. After a study of his face, she focused her eyes quickly back to the register.

Outside again, the groceries on the seat beside him, he watched the activity in the parking lot—the people coming and going. Looked like a big spread-out anthill. He'd like to step on them and give his foot a twist and crush them all. Surplus people. He didn't need them. If they knew how dumb they looked rushing around. His skin began to itch, and he cranked the Ford and tore out of the parking lot.

At the south limits of town he turned off Route 100 into Ingram Village. The village was a working-class neighborhood of small white-frame houses, and he and Loretta had lived there most of his life.

At home he didn't know whether to leave Loretta a note or not. She had been on him too much lately about the length of his hair anyway. Couldn't she see that the way the soft brown strands framed his face and accented his moist brown eyes made him all the more attractive to women?

He decided against leaving a note. Most times he didn't, and he would often be gone for weeks at a time. And when he did come home, nothing would have changed. Same old routine.

In his bedroom he went to the disorganized bureau and searched through assorted garments for his sleeping bag. It was worn and ratty looking from frequent use, and though it was the cheapest thing he could find at the time of purchase, it had lasted well. Uncoiled, it looked worse than he remembered. He shook it and the dust flew. First laying his H & R .22 caliber revolver, a carton of cartridges, and the sheathed Buck knife upon it, he rolled the sleeping bag into a tight bundle and tied it.

Having deposited the roll in the truck, he returned to the house. He was not about to head for the woods wilderness without his most prized possessions. From under his mattress he withdrew the collection of Playboy, Penthouse, and Hustler nudes. Some of them he had had laminated, and others he had placed between plastic photo holders. Still others were too recently purchased to have been preserved more carefully. He laid them all out on the unmade bed. Each was a favorite for a different reason. He had no redheads or strawberry blondes. Red hair and lipstick clashed. And red pubic hair and the pink texture of spread genitals didn't go together at all. The combination was sickening. Black crotch-hair and pink, moist flesh was a different matter; the combination that made him tremble and lose his breath —— made him stare for lost hours and caused his flesh to sweat slowly until his armpits and thighs wanted to stick together.

He couldn't understand how some men had more women than they could handle—women practically hanging around their necks all the time. The thought of it scared him but excited him, too. He wondered how other men "did it" —— not the men in the porno film that he kept hidden in the cellar up over the floor joists but the guys around town. A woman's tits did strange things to him. Maybe if they were left covered when you did the other thing, then maybe it would make things better. It wasn't that he didn't like to look at the soft flesh but that they wiggled like jello, and it made him sick to his stomach. The thought that there might be milk inside the jello had always made him all the sicker. But he didn't know if women without babies had milk in their boobs or not.

He couldn't bring himself to pick up the pictures and be on his way. With an index finger he traced the implied mounds and crevices of the naked bodies before him. All the women had high, erect breasts, and he liked that. He'd thrown away all the pictures of women whose boobs drooped. It disgusted him that in some of the pictures the nipples had focused downward, pointing—like some pink-stemmed, dead melon—at the ground. Why weren't they proud and erect—sticking straight out to meet a man, welcome him?

The longer he waited and savored, the more he began to tremble and sweat. Why didn't women go for him like they did for some men? He forced himself to turn away; he went to the dresser drawer and rolled himself a joint. A few drags later he began to feel relief. He then remembered that he hadn't got the playing cards out of the dresser drawer. He'd bought the poker deck from a sailor in Newport News, and on the back of each card was a different pornographic scene. He hadn't known until the pictures that people did things like that to one another. It looked like fun, but the descriptions of what was going on were in French or Italian or something. The sailor had offered the cards free if Randall would do some of the things illustrated in the men-with-men scenes, but it hadn't worked out. The sailor had called him a dead wet rag, demanded five dollars for the cards, and walked out of the boarding house.

When the joint burned down, he stuffed the remaining pouch of grass in his hip pocket, picked up the nudes and cards, and left the house. Everything was in order now except that before leaving town he would need to buy Cola, rum, and beer. You never knew when another loner like himself might wander into camp, and he wanted something to share. And if the ocean waves started rolling in on him again, there was a small supply of coke under the truck seat and a bigger supply of THC in the glove box. But he wasn't like Marty and some of the others who lived on the stuff. He could go for weeks and never touch drugs. It all depended on how the waves rolled in and on whether they hit him from behind or in front, and whether after it was all over, people stood looking at him, trying to see inside his head.

Maybe he wouldn't need anything. Jefferson National would be peaceful and quiet, and there was a lot in his mind to get straight.

He cranked the Ford and dug dirt. The dusty spray obscured the front door of the two-bedroom house; he chuckled as his spirits rose. It was always like this when he'd headed for the wilds in the truck: the good feeling of freedom, wild adventure, and escape from the terrible oppression of people. One time he'd thought about entering the forest, abandoning his truck, and just keeping on walking forever.

Maybe this time he'd really do it.

CHAPTER XVII

By May 17 Susan and Bob had reached the Big Walker Mountain range well within Jefferson National Forest. At 4:00 p.m. they decided to call it a day after finding a scenic camping area in distant sight of Big Walker Lookout Tower, a commercial enterprise operated in conjunction with a craft shop/snake pit/ski lift. *See Five States* the owner/promoter advertised via road signs,. bumper stickers, and colorful brochures. On a clear day the gigantic steel tower perched atop thirty-five-hundred-feet-high Big Walker Mountain did indeed allow a distant view of parts of West Virginia, Kentucky, Tennessee, North Carolina, and Virginia.

While Susan got food and cooking utensils from the packs, Bob busied himself with setting up the tent. Both were hungry as wolves, and the hot day had taken a toll on their bodies. After Susan had laid her food selections out on the picnic table, he lit the gas stove.

"How does vegetable patties with potatoes and dried fruit hit you?" she called out.

"If you can't serve red snapper and tartar sauce, it'll have to do." Bob said.

"It's Sunday, not Friday."

"So? You couldn't think for a minute I'm a traditionalist? Oh, for some shrimp scampi!"

"Wait'll we get off the trail for Blacksburg. I'll treat you."

"Hello, there! Bob Mountford?"

Susan looked up in the direction of the intruding voice. The tall young man coming down the trail toward them had vaguely familiar features, and his dark hair and beard accented friendly, deep-set brown eyes. The visitor's face spread into a broad grin as he approached them.

"Aren't you Bob Mountford?"

"Yeah. And you're ___ ?"

"Steve Skinner. Sandy's brother. I knew I was catching up with you. Been watching the trail registers and asking about you."

"Where the hell you been? Where's Neil and Sandy? With the side trips and delays we've had, I thought you'd all catch up days ago."

"Sandy had some bad ankle and foot problems. They had to go off the

141

trail and see a doctor. Then they decided to go into Gatlinburg, Tennessee, and rest up and see some sights. They'll be along."

Susan introduced herself.

"I've heard Sandy and Neil speak of you. As they probably told you, both Bob and I worked with Neil when he was at the Homestead. You and Sandy share a strong resemblance."

"She's a midget compared to me." Steve grinned as he straightened his hundred-seventy-pound body. "Everybody says we look alike, though."

Bob offered to share their food, but Steve heated his own soup, ate cheese and crackers with it, and talked excitedly all the while about the Trail.

"You out of college? Working? What goes?" Susan said.

"No college yet. I'm working for Dad in his home improvement and painting business. Everett, Massachusetts, my home town. I'd like to go to college and get into social or religious work of some kind."

"Must be a disease among hikers," Bob said.

"One thing I've thought about is being a counselor with the Quest Wagon Train group in New Hampshire. Don't know if I could go along with railing and swearing at the kids, though," Steve said.

"It's not as cruel as it sounds," Bob said. "It's just a method of making the kids face up and get their hostilities out into the open. Some kind of confrontation has to take place. You've got to make them show you the inside of their heads."

"Don't know if I could take the explosions though," Steve said. "I'm kind of chickenhearted. Don't like to see people's pain."

"Then you don't want Homestead-type work," Bob said. "I've seen kids erupt in such fury they damn near foamed at the mouth and banged their heads on the wall and rolled on the floor. Real anguish, man. Scars, bitterness, hatred, self-loathing—the whole bit."

"Maybe I ought to train for religious work, then," Steve said. "I like what the charismatic groups are doing, but I don't see myself as preacher material. I want to work with young people. Spend time out-of-doors."

Susan questioned Steve at length about his experience with the charismatics. He expressed his ideas well, his sincerity was obvious, and she was moved by his frank and sympathetic testimony in the charismatics' behalf. She saw in Steve a young man of unusual piety and humility, a quality not unlike that possessed by her friend Betty in Rapid City. Whether the youth faced up to it or not, the ministerial calling was in him she felt.

The conversation got more in-depth until darkness began to close in. Steve set up his own tent, and they all turned in. In the quietness of night, she could hear Steve softly humming a song or repeating a prayer. There was something about Skinner that seemed to make Bob more thoughtful, but Mountford said nothing as he lay back, donning his miner's lamp, reading his Bible.

Bob's concentration was short-lived Susan noticed. He kept looking in the direction of Steve's darkened tent. For Susan the whole evening of fellowship had been restful and good; yet there was something about it that was unusual. She felt it strongly and knew that Bob reacted similarly.

"The guy's too calm. Too damn peaceful," Bob muttered. "It can't be for real."

Susan thought the remark a strange one, but Bob wouldn't elaborate. But that was it: Bob couldn't take too much peace at a long stretch. Undoubtedly he had enjoyed long periods of tranquility during the long hike, but there was a side of him that rebelled against it. The boundless energy within him was bottled up, demanding an outlet. Skinner was probably not the type for verbal combat. He was a good conversationalist, nice guy, but most likely uninterested in intellectual fisticuffs. Maybe Bob missed the old job at Homestead and longed for a heated emotional exchange at which he usually emerged a quick victor.

With her sleeping bag drawn near to Bob, she slept fitfully. In the very early morning hours, the rain came down gently, and the soothing sound seemed only to make Bob snore more contentedly.

The morning broke overcast and foggy, but the temperature was not uncomfortably chill. After a hasty breakfast of gorp, granola bars, and hot tea, the three of them headed north. The earth seemed to exude a fresh, washed-clean aroma, and blooming things were everywhere. Birds chirped and when they could see the pastured earth, fields glistened in wet emerald green. Susan pointed to scenery here and there as excitedly as a child.

"Maybe we've all died, gone to paradise, and just don't know it," she laughed gleefully.

"Did you side-trail to the rim of Burkes Garden?" Bob asked Steve.

"Yeah. Now there's your paradise. It looks like some huge bowl cut out in the earth. You suppose a giant meteorite carved out such a big hole?"

"Could be."

Bob said they'd done a fifteen-mile day when they reached a deserted cabin near an old fire tower. *Cabin* was stretching the word. The structure was maybe eight by ten feet, but it did have two bunks, a former forest ranger's quarters, undoubtedly. Steve was nowhere in sight.

Susan sat down on one of the bunks and started eating gorp. Bob helped himself from her supply.

"This is okay for a snack, but we've got to have something substantial tonight. Got any ideas—like squab and wild rice or roast duck with asparagus hollandaise?"

"Holy Toledo! Can't you get food off your mind?"

"When you've been on the Trail as long as I have, it damn near gets to be an obsession. You begin to have visions of every kind of dish, fixed a thousand different ways."

"When you get your Pearisburg mail drop, maybe Mim will have surprised you with a hunk of salt-cured ham for frying."

"Don't torture me!"

Bob began to pace outside. Out of the corner of her eye, she could see him rubbing his belly as he walked. She couldn't help chuckling: Mountford loved good food with a passion which she'd observed in few people. And he could prepare the same with a skill and touch not often excelled. As for her, she often fasted, not alone for attempted weight control. Sometimes her fasting derived from spiritual need; sometimes, from the good feeling of self-mastery. Occasionally, she'd do it for a sensual experience. A few times she'd fasted for a twenty-four hour stretch, and before breaking the fast had gone swimming in the buff. For some reason the water against her skin at such times had an entirely different feel as if every pore in her body were being tenderly kissed and caressed; her breasts would seem to float in grateful freedom; her mind, set free as if she could actually soar toward the sunset that cast fading rays down upon her in the water. Such peace. Pity to those who had never had such an experience or lived even for a day in a setting like her own in a little rustic two-room cabin in the Maine woods by a lake.

Steve came into camp and shared the details of his side trail wanderings. She could see in him an especial tenderness for all forms of life. Just watching a grey squirrel scurry up a tall hickory was evidently a memorable adventure. And she had earlier seen his trail diary lying open; she had seen on the exposed page a simple notation: "Thank you, Lord, for the scenery and sunshine. Thank You for Your Love and protection today ___ "

Bob brought up the subject of supper again.

"I'm all fixed. A farm lady down the blue-blaze gave me two pork chops between homemade bread. Sorry about you guys," Steve said.

Mountford went into a frenzy.

"Show them to me! Let me smell 'em!"

Steve did so with tantalizing slowness.

Bob inhaled deeply.

"I'm floating—I'm drifting on a soft cloud of gastronomic euphoria. Steve, old friend, you know, of course, the law of the Trail is to share all things: hardship, injury, sorrow, delight ___ "

"And food?" Steve said.

"I think that's what he has in mind," Susan said.

Steve dutifully cut the two fat sandwiches into three equal portions and shared his last macaroni and cheese dinner as well. Bob contributed soybean burgers, dried peaches and prunes; Susan fished in her pack for dehydrated potatoes and powdered milk.

In record time Bob had his stove going, his big pot in place. Soon he was offering a passable serving of spiced-up mashed potatoes.

After the feast was over, each of them found quiet sanctuary; Bob on one bunk, Steve on the other, and Susan propped against the door jamb. Steve began writing post cards; Bob was reading his Bible; Susan turned back to the final book of her Alexandria Quartet series, *Clea*. She had found the

Lawrence Durrell tetralogy enthralling: an illusion full of bright colors that worked beautifully. The story of life, love, politics, and intrigue in war-time Egypt was compelling enough on its own terms, and she had, like so many other readers, been beguiled by all the characters and the sheer power of the narratives. Yet, in this final book of the series, it was the artistic Clea herself who captivated Susan. Amid the nightly World War II bombings by the Germans, Clea had sat serenely in her Alexandria studio, painting. Perhaps Susan was reading into the narrative something more than the author had intended, but she saw in those scenes a symbolism with which she could identify. Was not Clea—in the very midst of turmoil—saying that beauty had to survive the ashes and that personal spiritual victory was possible even in the throes of chaos? In fact, the whole book seemed to say that shallow is the man, or woman, who succumbs to fear or to undervaluation of himself, who blames Fate and circumstances for his failure to realize the impossible dream. Love—both *agape* and *eros*—fused to the highest idealism must survive all things; it must overshadow the most catastrophic events, else what is the value of life?

She continued to read, oblivious as possible to the small talk in the background. Author Durrell fascinated her. Uncanny how he could delineate interesting facts and details, yet always convey to the reader the necessity of looking much deeper, thereby discovering archetypal beauties just beneath surface fact.

Finally Bob's and Steve's cross-chatter became interesting enough to compel her attention. Bob was reading aloud from the Acts of the Apostles and making a point about the experience of the Holy Spirit's descent upon Peter and other apostles at the time of Pentecost: a great misconception— Bob said—was still held by numerous, if not by most, Bible readers.

"The fact that many people from many lands heard Peter's sermon that day in a 'tongue' they could understand has no relationship to 'speaking in tongues' as defined by some charismatics and other groups. Peter simply was given the power to speak in a way in which Romans, Greeks, Hebrews, Parthians, and Cappadocians heard him in their own mother language."

"I don't disagree with that," Steve said.

"Dammit, I thought I could get a rise out of you with such an astute observation. A lot of charismatics will tell you that the day of Pentecost was the first instance of 'speaking in tongues.' "

Unopposed, Bob began to read again in silence. For a moment Susan watched him. In many ways Bob Mountford was a strange guy. There had been times since she'd known him that he would pick the Christian faith to pieces. And he could do it with consummate skill. At other times he would defend it with even greater fervor until his rapid-fire mouth and boiling brain had the power of a modern-day Saint Augustine. It was logic, secular humanism, and intellectualism fighting a simple act of trusting faith, Susan suspected.

It was the same with her—this matter of the spiritual realm—although they took slightly different approaches to the Big Question. She wondered whether Bob realized just how much they had in common. Wondered whether on another subject—love—he had begun to care for her as much as she cared for him. He hadn't said so as clearly as she'd like, but some good signs were on the horizon. They shared a wonderful companionship and sexual compatibility, but success in recreational lovemaking was no real gauge of a long-term commitment. Not in this day. Maybe during the era of Bud and Ginny Ramsay when the illusion of the happily-ever-after romance was in vogue. But so saying, she knew that a bit of that old-fashioned romance dwelled in her own breast. Hadn't she cried for days in the privacy of her cabin when Mountford had left for the AT?

Without notice in typically Mountford fashion, Bob hopped up enthusiastically from his bunk.

"Anyone want some popcorn?"

Bob fired up his stove, emptied a little cooking oil into the big pot and held it over the flames.

He doctored his and Susan's portion with cheese oil. Steve took his with a sparse addition of salt.

"Not bad if we had some beer," Susan said.

"I was dreaming of a frosty Mountain Dew," Steve said.

"We're in an area where, historically, a lot of it's been made," Bob said. "Land of moonshiners, bear hunters, and feuds."

"Not that kind of mountain dew. Wouldn't mind trying a slab of bear meat or some venison, though."

"How come you're not a vegetarian like Sandy and Neil?" Bob asked.

"Haven't been bitten by the bug, I guess."

"Speaking of Sandy and Neil," Susan said, "you think they're coming up pretty close behind? Maybe Frank Maguire and some of the others we left at Damascus are closing in too."

"I'd say they're getting closer," Steve said. "I'd like to hike a while with two of my buddies that are coming up behind, too. Stephen and Bret from Indianapolis. Brothers. Maybe I'll hang back in the morning. Let you two go ahead. We'll catch you at Wapiti shelter or at the Pearisburg hostel."

"Whatever you say," Bob said. "Tell those two Ellsworth turkeys that I'm anxious to see them. Tell 'em if they'd put a little red meat in their gut, these mountains wouldn't seem so formidable. Y'know—a little rare filet with mushroom gravy and green peas . . . "

". . . Holy shit! Not food again," Susan said. "You're driving me bananas. I think I'm getting attuned to the trail diet and you keep coming up with these gastronomic visions!"

Bob popped a second batch of popcorn, and when they had finished it off, darkness was creeping in.

She gave them the bunks and laid her own sleeping bag on the floor. Her spine hadn't adjusted to the heavy weight of her backpack. Maybe firm, straight back support would ease the ache.

Somewhere in the distance a whippoorwill's voice pierced the night. The aroma of pine and hemlock invaded her nostrils, and the aura of peace made her relax quickly. Let me live to be a hundred, she half-prayed, half-dreamed. Let me experience it again and again until I'm washed clean of all hypocrisy, greed, unconcern. Keep me out of the swift current of mediocrity and materialism until I'm whole and sincerely compassionate. . . .

When morning came, no sun peeped over the horizon to greet the day. The sky was grey and brooding. Susan gave the report, but Steve and Bob only groaned and lay back in their bunks. She cooked some cream-of-wheat with powdered milk.

Finished, she packed her utensils and gear away, readying the backpack.

"I'm getting an early start," she called in Bob's direction. "You'll catch up with me anyway by lunchtime."

"Which way you going?" Bob grunted. "The trail's been rerouted. Taking the new trail to Wapiti II or the old trail to Wapiti I?"

"Don't know yet. I'll play it by sight and sound. I'll leave you notes. Either way, we'll end up in the same general area."

Bob rolled over. Before she had cleared the cabin opening, he was snoring loudly.

At the point where the trail dropped into Lick Skillet Hollow, she looked back to the northwest and saw the sky darkening. Rain was in those clouds, and she could picture Mountford moaning when he rolled out of his warm sleeping bag and faced the downpour. He could be so damn cute doing his little acts of melodrama. She could hear him now.

"Steve, talk me out of it! I don't want to go! I'm tender. I'll melt in the rain. Y'know. Sugar and spice and everything nice. Tell me to get back in the sack and sleep a while longer! Steve?"

"And Steve would probably say, "Only girls are made of sugar and spice. Get going. Your lady love waits in the dark woods. What if timber rattlers are hiding beside the trail or bobcats spring from the swamps? Get going, Mountford."

And Bob would reply, "No, Steve, talk me out of it. Susan's as good a woodsman as I am. Maybe better. And I haven't had breakfast yet. Talk me out of it, Stevie! The rain looks wet and cold . . . "

She walked on. Bob would come shortly. Something was growing between them. She could feel it now as powerfully as she could feel the fresh breath of life this beautiful Virginia countryside exuded from every hill and valley.

The exhilaration of the trail was mounting in her though it had only been ten days since she'd alighted from the Trailways Bus in Damascus. She tried mentally to define what the AT had already meant to her. It was like climbing a vast tower and seeing all things, not just terrain and the panorama, in broader perspective. But it was also a humbling experience, for one saw his individual insignificance and mortality. Yet hadn't Betty's pastor said that not a single sparrow would fall uncounted?

147

She'd left the Homestead on vacation partly to get away from the members, and now a rush of feeling came over her, a wishing for their presence. Every one of them. Here was some element of their healing to be found. She couldn't quite articulate it, but she'd seen it work in small doses at times when groups of them had taken a brief few days together in the wilds or down the river. But just as it had begun to work, it was time to get back to the "home" again. Nature. Sweet, sweet nature ____ healer of wounds; giver of strength in place of weakness; mother of resolve; cleanser of apathetic souls; warmer of cold hearts; mirthful goddess laughing, loving, warming with sunray darts and gentle breezes.

The sheets of rain clearly visible in the distance soon swept down upon her. The trail turned before reaching the first bridge over Kimberling Creek, but she headed for the bridge anyway, got down under, waited for the storm to pass. Great drops peppered the creek water like volleys of birdshot. A mild wind arose; the air got chillier. Her bare legs grew goose bumps. The shorts most hikers preferred for freedom of movement and general comfort suddenly felt inadequate. She opened the pack and took out a pair of jeans and pulled them on. A light knit shirt advertising the Michigan "10K Run" that Renate had lent her for hiking comfort was also overcovered with a long-sleeved one. Warmth returned, but the rain came down harder.

In half an hour the grey-white curtain moved on down the valley as though pushed by a powerful hand, leaving puffy white clouds, seemingly perched on the mountaintops.

Back at the trail intersection, she left a note for Bob, impaling it on a broken walnut tree limb. She had walked a ways before remembering that he could have passed her by while she waited out the storm under the bridge. No matter. They'd probably converge on Bernard's Store or Trent's Store at about the same time, and the stores were only a few miles apart. Bob was a fast walker when he was alone. She remembered also that she was their money keeper. If Bob wanted ice cream, beer, or other supplies, he was out of luck without her.

Rhododendron thickets lay along the slopes above Kimberling Creek. An old summer cottage sat farther along to the right, and though the blooming bushes gradually thinned, the cottage looked dwarfed among the heavy greenery. The setting was hypnotic. She paused to munch on a granola bar. Once the place must have been the original "vine-covered cottage." She wondered who might have honeymooned there or might have breathed in the feint aroma of the blooming rhododendron through open windows while they were making love.

She took a deep swallow of water from the canteen and moved on. The trail soon turned onto an old woods road and passed through deep shade and mossy banks interspersed here and there with johnny jumpups. The fertile crescent began to turn barren after a half mile or so, and she began the ascent of Brushy Mountain.

At the top the Trail Guide said twenty-four-hundred-sixty feet high; it was a little more than a third the height of Clingman's Dome that Bob had told her about. He had spoken in such awe of the soaring peak that like a giant's arm had lifted him toward Heaven's door. So, too, had he shared with a few of them the experience of feeling there that he had been in God's presence. Giddiness from height? Vertigo? Imagination? She didn't know, and he had seemed reluctant to discuss it a second time.

The descent from the mountain was over a broken, rocky footpath suitable to the agility of a mountain goat. At the bottom the trail merged with the bed of an old logging road. Once out of the woods, she entered upon an open field with a breathtaking vista of lush green farmland in the valley below. Mountain ridges lined the perimeter to the south.

She walked in to Bernard's Store, inquired about Bob, and getting a negative answer from the middle-aged female clerk, left two dollars for a snack when Bob did arrive. "I'm our treasurer," Susan said as she finished her own snack. In minutes she was back on the trail.

Down in the lowlands she crossed a split rail fence at the stile and came out on Route 42. After crossing Kimberling Creek via the bridge, she turned north on Route 606 and walked parallel to Kimberling Creek. The narrow meandering stream ran over and between big limestone boulders, giving the water a lyrical sound. Except for the backpack weight, she might have skipped like a school girl along the paved highway.

The Trail turned again in the woods just behind Trent's Store. She could smell the sawmill operation across the road before she actually saw it. The aroma of cedar and hemlock shavings and sawdust was rich and refreshing, and the whine of the big circular saw eating its way through the logs was like a serenade of personal welcome.

Welcome or not, the several mill hands hardly looked up. Undoubtedly the sight of hikers was too commonplace to matter much. A couple of workers finally looked her way, and raised an arm in greeting. They waved back and smiled, and she was sorely tempted to go over and greet them and to learn of their life and work. Once, when she'd gone on her infamous jaunt to Portland, Oregon, she'd seriously considered seeking employment at a big lumber mill operation. If she told these locals about the size of Pacific Northwest logs, they'd swear she was telling a Paul Bunyan tale. The biggest of the mountain of cut trees surrounding this mill looked like toothpicks in comparison.

She dropped the backpack at the front door of the modern brick store and went inside. A fiftyish woman, attractive, dark-haired, of medium height and build, stood behind the counter.

"This is a nice little store," Susan said, smiling. "Bet you serve lots of hikers this time of year?"

"They come in droves sometimes," the woman said routinely.

"Many come by today?"

"Hard to remember, but four or five, maybe."

Seeing that the woman was busy, Susan began to look around for the makings of lunch. She selected a couple of packaged sandwiches, a package of potato chips, a cold Schlitz, and paid the tab. She used the restroom to freshen up, then went outside to a picnic table under a shade tree.

As she ate, her eyes focused on workers across the road. She was drawn to any industry that used wood, clay, stones, or any of nature's gifts. She was lost in the reverie of Portland and her days there when a voice behind her sounded but was lost in the whine of the saw blade.

Two middleaged men stopped at her table.

"I was sayin' you better eat more than a sandwich," the older of the two continued. "You've got a good climb ahead of you if you're goin' north. I talk to lots of hikers and they say it takes plenty of body fuel."

"Pearisburg is our next stop," she replied. "After my hiking companion catches up — or shows up, we'll have a feast.."

"I'm Tom Thornhill," the speaker said. "My buddy, here, is Bill Breedlove."

Susan extended a hand to each man in turn. "I'm Susan Ramsay from Ohio and Maine. Beautiful country around here. You both lived here all your lives?"

"Mostly," Breedlove said. "We're just gettin' ready to go to work at Radford Arsenal—the Powder Plant most people call it."

"Gunpowder?" Susan asked.

"Mostly rocket fuel—big guns, missiles, stuff like that," Breedlove said.

"Wow! Don't point anything in this direction before we hike past the area," Susan said.

"No danger there," Thornhill said, "but we do have an accidental blow-up now and then. Touchy stuff, powder."

Susan had just begun to enjoy the conversation about powder making, when both men had to leave for work.

She stood up, stretched, and walked across the road to the log yard and watched the operation for a while. The mill was semi-automated, and she was impressed by the efficiency with which the logs were fed onto the carriage. She tired of the scene and began walking northwest along the highway until a big rustic sign saying JEFFERSON NATIONAL FOREST could be seen close-up. As an artist, she appreciated the artistry of others, and the large wooden plaque appeared in total compatibility with its forbidding surroundings. She walked back to the picnic table and sat down. Growing impatient after a half hour had passed, and no sighting of Bob on the horizon, she threaded arms into her backpack and moved off.

She walked back down the road and entered the woods. It had grown warm again; the sun was shining. She removed the jeans and over-shirt and stored them. The freedom of being in hiking shorts again was uplifting, and she started off again with renewed vigor.

Once up the northwestern slope of Brushy Mountain and down a gully, then skirting the Dismal Creek bank and ascending again, she came to the blue-blaze that led to the overlook of Dismal Falls. Since the Trail Guide indicated that the side trip was only a third of a mile, she decided to take it.

Before reaching the overlook, she could hear the rushing, churning water. The first view of it took her breath. Dismal Creek was a narrow stream; yet at this point a broad expanse of flat rock, layer upon layer, fanned out from bank to wooded bank, and then emptied the water over craggy ledges to the pool below. With a childish impulse, she wanted to drop her clothes in a heap and run for the water. But the overlook was too steep. Getting back up without a rope would be chancy and dangerous. All she needed to ruin it for Mountford was a broken leg or back.

She simply stood in awestruck wonder. The whole scene freaked her out, with visions of fantasyland. The longer she looked, the more a feeling of tenderness and appreciation came over her. Without warning she felt her eyes misting. The gorge, the pool, the surrounding circle of trees, the shaded dimness taken as a whole suggested a vast womb.

"Give me new life," she whispered. "Expel me from darkness. Show me light."

She took a deep, lingered breath, trying to hold in the aroma of wild mint, sundry blossoms, and the ever-present pine. Below the pool on either bank, a dense growth of sourwood and Judas trees rose above purplish-and-pink blooms of lush rhododendron. While she lingered, four whitetailed deer came to water. She removed her Pentax camera from the pack and took a couple of shots. One of the deer looked up, stamping a foot indignantly. Perhaps they had smelled her. She backed away from the ledge. There was something unholy about her intrusion on their domain. She left the peaceful scene with regret and headed back to the white-blaze.

Seemingly she walked forever. A quick drizzle swept in from nowhere, but the forest was so dense that prolonged views of the sky had not been possible. She was feeling the fatigue of a long day and just wanted to be with him. The white-blaze marks were too far apart, and for the first time she felt a sense of confusion and uncertainty. A vehicle horn to the east provided a sense of comfort. Four-wheelers tearing up the mountain turf along a fire trail, no doubt. Shame!

She walked on, the backpack getting oppressively heavy now. In the distance the slope of a new mountain loomed. Then she saw it through the trees: a spanking new log shelter. It had to be Wapiti II.

A man stood at the corner of the building. He was wearing cut-offs, but it wasn't Mountford. Mountford had a bushy beard. This man was clean-shaven, but his hair fell to his slightly stooped shoulders.

She came closer, shedding the pack. The sight of anybody was welcome.

"Hi. I'm Susan Ramsay from Maine. Anybody else around?"

"No."

"You seen a heavy-set guy with a beard and moppish dark hair?"

"No."

She looked into his dull brown eyes and wondered at the reason for his reluctance to communicate. On second look she noted that the pupils of his eyes were enlarged.

He ran a long-fingernailed hand through his grimy hair and gave his head a quick toss.

"You didn't introduce yourself. What's your name?"

"Billy Joe."

He straightened his drooping shoulders proudly for a moment. He would be five-ten or so, she thought. Maybe a hundred-seventy or-eighty pounds. Older than she.

"Billy Joe what?"

"Just Billy Joe."

She moved a few steps, looking around.

"You hiking or what? I don't see your backpack."

"Didn't have time to get a pack. Just flew in from Ohio. Me and my wife."

"I come from Ohio. Aurora. Near Cleveland. What part were you in?"

"Up north."

"You work in Ohio or just vacationing?"

"I'm a helicopter pilot. Fly racecar drivers all around."

She looked at him more penetratingly. She doubted it. Definitely not the type.

"What's your wife's name? What does she do?"

"Name's Reanna. She's a model. Y'know—pictures, magazines, stuff like that."

"She must be really pretty."

"Yeah. Women like that go for me. Bother me a lot all the time."

He looked at her in a strange way ⸺ not a leering look, but a look that seemed to gauge whether she believed him or not. He walked a half-circle around her without averting his eyes: eyes that had brightened considerably. Was he on drugs? He wasn't really spaced out, and yet some of the symptoms were present.

"Billy Joe—I think I'll wander a little farther along the trail and look for my friend. Will you be all right?"

He didn't answer, and she reached casually for her backpack.

"No! Don't leave! I mean stay here with me a while. The waves been rollin' over me all day. How long I been here under the trees?"

"I don't know how long you've been here. Are you feeling all right, Billy Joe?"

"Yeah. I feel good. Reanna'll be mad though."

"Why don't you go on home to her?"

"No. I got to push the sand back in the water."

"I don't understand, Billy Joe."

"If I put the sand back, it stops the waves—and I don't have to watch the women in their little suits."

"You don't like women? But Reanna sounds so beautiful and sweet."

"Yeah. But she looked ugly when she was pregnant with the twins."

"Oh, you're a father—and twins! I have a little niece."

"Yeah, but if she gets that way again, I'm goin' to leave her."

She looked again into his eyes and saw the pain and the hatred; she began to feel the onset of fear in the pit of her stomach.

Again she got a little foot movement going and stooped for her pack. He beat her to the draw, but instead of helping her lace arms, he laid the backpack on the floor under the shelter. When she tried casually to pull it back out, he moved closer, sort of hemming her in.

"Billy Joe, I've enjoyed meeting and talking with you, but I really ought to go. If I don't, my friends will be backtracking down the trail to find me."

"I thought you said you was lookin' for a man."

"Yes, but others are in our group."

Billy Joe grinned a little for the first time; his unbrushed teeth, barely revealed, were yellow and stained.

"You've been so nice to me ___ "

"I like meeting people on the trail. I've made a lot of friends that way. Do you like meeting new people, Billy Joe?"

He didn't answer. Looked away. Far away. Hung his head.

"You've been so nice to me."

"I'll bet you're a nice person when people get to know you."

"People don't like me. Everybody looks down on me. Call me Snuffy and things like that ___ "

"Sometimes a nickname is a form of affection. You know— friendliness."

"No. They did it in school. Before they even knew me."

"You want to talk about it, Billy Joe?"

He plopped down on one end of the slab seat under the shelter. She was to the outside and could run if she wanted, but there seemed less of a need to now. And she thought that she'd left the Homestead and Homestead-like problems behind.

Still she hesitated. How did one reconcile the two opposing voices— when professionalism said "No," and the example of the Good Samaritan cried "Yes"? Everything in her said that people were more important than rules.

"Billy Joe, I work with young people all the time who have fears and troubles. I wish I could help you."

"You a doctor? Where?"

She decided against telling him too much about the members or naming the institution.

"No, I'm not a doctor. I'm an art therapist. I help people draw and paint, and sometimes they express the things that trouble them in the pictures."

"They draw their troubles? How is that?"

"Not exactly draw their troubles, but sometimes if a person is very sad, he'll draw a picture in only black crayons or paint, and draw trees stark and leafless—things like that."

"I like that," he said, and then reached for one of the paperbacks visible in her backpack.

He fidgeted on the seat a minute, stood, sat down, turned the pages. She hoped that the increased animation was a good sign.

They talked on for a few minutes. Once she got him to chuckle; he was opening up still more when the tramp of boots interrupted the discussion.

Five uniformed Forest Service workers came upon the scene. All were young, early twentyish; one of them was a very pretty girl. Susan introduced herself and Billy Joe, and commented on the youthfulness of the visitors. The girl, Robin, introduced herself and companions, saying that they were all working under a government program that President Reagan was about to discontinue. They were all fearful of losing their jobs. Susan asked more questions about the scope of their work and learned to her surprise that this same team had built Wapiti II. She complimented them on the workmanship and asked about construction details. The rapport with all of them was quick and pleasurable, and surprisingly, Billy Joe got in on the conversation and talked about the AT.

She debated the thought of getting Robin or one of the guys aside and relating Billy Joe's strange behavior. She tried it with Robin, but Billy Joe stood and came closer. The other girl failed to pick up on the signal, and two of the guys were calling to move out; they still had work to do; and the sky was darkening. Susan looked at her watch: nearly two o'clock.

She was tempted to go off with the team, but what about Bob? And she'd just been getting to a point that allowed Billy Joe to open up when the Forest Service Workers arrived. Damn! Small fears still eddied through her, but she fought back against her instincts. Compared with some of the kids she and Bob had worked with at Homestead, Billy Joe was a docile lamb. Indecision lingered as Robin said, "Enjoy the trail. Good to meet you."

The other workers echoed the sentiment routinely.

A flash of irritation hit Susan. Couldn't these people see that Billy Joe had no backpack? That his demeanor was odd? That he didn't come close to resembling the average hiker?

Of course, they didn't. They were woodsworkers—not hikers. Besides, it probably wasn't in the least unusual for all types of people to be in this particular area. Dismal Falls probably attracted sundry visitors, and she had heard evidence of vehicle activity at several points—four-wheelers and weekend campers most likely.

One last crazy idea hit her before Robin moved off.

"Hey, Robin. Take our picture before you leave."

Susan got the Pentax from the pack, and Billy Joe headed for the slab under the shelter. He scooted to the farthest end.

Robin took the camera.

"It's dim in there. Both of you come out in the light."

Susan waited, but Billy Joe refused to move. Susan sat down beside him, pulled the book from before his eyes.

"This'll do. It'll get your handiwork in the picture."

"Billy Joe's face is shaded," Robin said. "Have him move your way."

Billy Joe refused to budge.

"Robin, you move over—change your angle. Maybe you're causing the shadow."

"I still can't get you both very well."

"I want us *both* in the picture, Robin. Take your time. *Take care* ___"

Robin returned a quizzical look, aimed, and snapped.

"That ought to do it," she said.

"No, take another shot to make sure you got us," Susan insisted.

Robin focused and shot again.

Susan stood to receive the camera, and Billy Joe followed.

"See you," Robin said and ran to catch up with her co-workers.

At first Billy Joe was noncommunicative again, and she tried a variety of approaches to get back on track. It began to work; Billy Joe revealed a few more seemingly insignificant facts about himself. But were they facts? She sensed that much of what he said was a fabric of lies or fantasies.

It started to drizzle again. Billy Joe got up, walked out, looked skyward; the drizzle splattered his face momentarily. Now he moved off around the building. She waited for him to return.

Oh, Bob, where are you?

When Billy Joe came back, he worked his tongue against his inner cheeks. Had he popped a pill? He sat down, pulled out a pack of Merits, and lit one. As an afterthought he pointed the pack her way.

"No, thank you," she said.

"You don't like grass either?"

"It's a bad trip for me."

He grinned slightly as if to show appreciation for her understanding of the terminology.

"I got a bottle in the truck. Want me to go and get it?"

The rules said, "No." But to say "no" under the circumstances might mean social rejection to him. To say "Yes" was to invite a degree of intimacy. To say "Yes" also meant buying time—might even allow him to become engaged with somebody else down among other four-wheelers if that's where his truck was parked. Might even ensure his not coming back. She debated. *Dammit, Bob, get here!*

She stalled and got him talking again. His whole personality began to change, and she couldn't understand it. If he had popped a pill, it hadn't had time to work yet.

"You seem happier than when I first came, Billy Joe. Are you feeling better?"

"I feel real good. You're so nice to me. You and me make a good pair. Want to go for a ride in my truck? Got a big Ford. Four-wheel drive."

"I'd rather stay and talk. Billy Joe, if I asked you to draw a picture of your mother, father, and Reanna, how would you illustrate them?"

"Don't have no father. Can't draw pictures anyway. Before I started weld ___ flyin' planes and stuff, I thought about takin' draftin'. You know—blueprints and stuff."

"What happened to your father? Was he killed? I don't mean to pry, but I really care about you."

"Don't want to talk about it."

"Is your mother living?"

"Yeah."

She waited. Nothing came.

"Tell me when you and Reanna first got together. Did you meet her in service maybe? Or was she your high-school girlfriend?"

"Yeah, that's it."

"Which?"

He took a long drag and ducked the cigarette.

"I was a pilot. She kept pestering me. She looked good in her uniform."

"She was a stewardess, you mean? Or was she in service too?"

"Yeah, that's it. It was at Newport News, I think. She used to go to the beach a lot. Wore a little yellow suit."

"If I get pen and paper from my pack, would you try and draw the design of the yellow suit for me?"

A flicker of enthusiasm crossed his face. She got the material. He laid the paper on the slab; thinking deeply for a moment. He drew a match-stem figure hardly credible to a third grader and then paused. Quickly he sketched not a swimsuit but a long-to-the-ankles "A" line skirt.

"That's very good, Billy Joe. Now do a picture of your mother for me."

He drew identically the same figure and the same dress, but this time he inked in the "A" line from top to bottom until it was as black as the ace of spades.

She praised him, and he responded like a grateful child. It was uncanny. She was actually treating him like a grade-school student—but new light had come to his eyes.

"Now do a drawing of the school you went to."

He looked at her as if to say something but then thought better of it.

"Go ahead. Do the school," she prompted. "You're doing fine.

He drew slowly with exaggerated care this time, though she saw that his hands were beginning to tremble slightly.

He drew a broad rectangular building and then tried to add an ell. The single door he drew was excessively tall and very narrow. He left the entire building windowless. As a seeming afterthought, he sketched a crudely shaped shrub and match-stem figure peeping out from behind the bush.

"That's excellent, Billy Joe! I'm proud of you!"

He beamed like a victorious quarterback. Then the smile disintegrated in slow motion.

"Why are you so nice to me?"

"Because I like you. I like all people. Once I taught a retarded boy to swim. You should have seen his face!"

"Yeah? How'd you do that?"

She explained the long, patient, hours it had taken. Billy Joe looked awestruck. His mouth hung open with attentiveness. When she had finished, he said, "I'm goin' and get the bottle. We'll have a party. I feel good."

Panic surged through her again. She couldn't bring herself to agree, but whatever it took to keep the upbeat in forward motion had to be maintained. A "no" would destroy everything. *Mountford, where in the hell are you!*

He'd already got up and cleared the opening.

"Take your time, Billy Joe. If you run into some of your friends, it's okay."

"Don't have any friends. I'll be back in a minute."

She watched his bent back disappear into the trees. A few precious minutes. What to do with them? She could run, but with the weight of her pack, he could catch her quickly. His probable fury would propel him with the speed of an antelope. Without the pack if she had to hide out more deeply in the dense undergrowth off the trail, she'd die of hunger. Was she exaggerating the situation? And she had made so much progress with him in a short time. He was probably on quaaludes. The in-and-out personality. The up-and-down moods. The fantasy-to-reality, back and forth. Maybe it was a mixture of drugs. Bob would know. It was one of his specialties. *Damn you, Bob, get here!*

Billy Joe hadn't exaggerated much for once. He was back, brown bag in hand, in twenty minutes. That must mean that the truck was not far away. What a patchwork of paths, fire roads, cross trails, and dense woods Jefferson National was! Mountford was probably lost.

Billy Joe reached in the bag and extracted a Cola and a one-fifth sized bottle of rum; he set it down carefully as if it were a jar of TNT. Even his movements were unusual: excessively controlled when there was no need for it. Anticipating him, she broke the seal on the rum and poured a short drink in her sierra cup. He swigged from the bottle. A new awareness of the foolhardiness of the situation hit her like a bomb. The alcohol added to the probable drugs in his system ___ .

Feigning a refill of her cup, she purposely knocked over the bottle. It failed to break. The shelter floor was of thick wood boards. Only a part was lost until he reached for and capped the bottle. In the act he looked at her with fleeting hatred but said nothing.

He sensed that she had done it purposely. She could see it in his expression. He finally muttered something under his breath; then he pushed the bottle away from him and toward her as if it had been contaminated. His eyes focused on the contours of her breasts. She knew the damp material clung, and she shifted positions. She wondered what to say next.

Then she heard it: the muffled sound of approaching boots. Was it her imagination? *Oh, God, let it be!* She leaned outwardly and listened. The sound was coming closer. She dashed out. Billy Joe was at her heels.

Bob flashed a big grin.

"Louse! And you were supposed to be the leader!" She ran for him, hugging his neck. Her act sent a wave of confusion across his face.

He shed his pack beside the opening. His eyes lingered on the bottle.

"Hey! You guys got a party going already? May I have a little snort?"

Billy Joe was silent. She gave the permission. Bob downed a quick shot and let out a long sigh of appreciation.

"Where you been?"

He covered his face with a shame-shielding hand. He still hadn't seen the look on her face that she knew was there.

"It gripes the hell out of me to admit it, but I got lost. Me—the trail hotshot. Ramsay, if you ever tell anybody, I'll murder you!"

"Bob. This is Billy Joe."

Bob shot out the usual friendly hand.

"Bob Mountford from Maine, Billy Joe. Where you hail from?"

"Michigan."

"Detroit? Lansing?"

"Yeah."

Bob did a double take, studying Billy Joe's face carefully for the first time.

"Where'd you get on the AT?" Bob said.

"Billy Joe isn't hiking," Susan said. "He just flew in from *Ohio*."

Bob did see her face at last. Their eyes held. Bob gave his shoulders the slightest shrug.

She ventured a few casual steps toward the outside of the shelter. Bob followed.

"Space cadet?" Bob whispered.

"I don't know. I think so," she whispered back.

Billy Joe was quickly at their side.

Bob tried a few pointed questions. Billy Joe was clearly rattled.

Bob, obviously confused, took an oblique direction; he laid on the smooth professional kindness Susan had seen him use many times to good effect. As Billy Joe seemed to drop his defenses, Bob led him into talking about camping and hiking. Billy Joe soon switched to talk of engines and four-wheel-drive vehicles. When the short conversation petered out, Bob attacked from the rear.

"You got a problem I can help you with, Billy Joe?"

"I don't have problems."

"I thought you might have. Been dropping a few pills? Snorting anything?"

"You're tryin' to see in my head!" Billy Joe's lower lip curled.

"Just want to help," Bob said calmly.

Color rose in Billy Joe's face. Bob placed an arm around his shoulder.

The power of touch. Caring. Something Susan had not dared use for fear of misinterpretation.

"Something's eating at your gut, Billy Joe. Why don't you get it out?" Bob asked.

A fury was rising in the "member." She could see it. Bob was coming on too fast; the Mountford exuberance intent on the goal.

She tried to catch Bob's eye to warn him. This wasn't the Homestead with all of its back-up counselors.

"Who do you hate? What have you got the guilts about?" Bob pressed.

"Fuck you!" Billy Joe hissed. "You're tryin' to see inside my head!"

We're in the wrong place for confrontation therapy, she wanted to call out.

But Bob backed off on his own and shot one from left field: "Why don't you question me, Billy Joe? I'll tell you anything you ask me."

"Don't want to know nothin' you know. All you foreign hikers keep comin' through laughin' and talkin', tearin' up the woods ___ "

"Does it bother you that other people have fun?"

"People. Screw 'um all."

Bob probed more with utmost gentleness, but Billy Joe went into a pout. He wouldn't respond to any question.

"Maybe if we gave Billy Joe something to eat ___ " Susan suggested.

There was no positive response. But he hung around. She and Bob made small talk and tried code words to suggest ways to rid themselves of the visitor without angering him further.

Susan gathered a hodge-podge of food as quickly as she could. They were running low on supplies. The Pearisburg food drop from Dover-Foxcroft was just a day away. She opened containers of peas, cube-cut potatoes, and corn, and fired up the gas stove to heat the offerings. While waiting she laid out some crackers and opened a package of dried apricots.

Billy Joe watched the food heat with interest. He leaned so close to the small appliance that the flicker of fire was reflected in his eyes. Maybe only the viewed flame was doing it, but his pupils seemed intermittently to grow from pinpoints to enlarged black/brown orbs before going back again. Finally he sat Indian style on the ground.

At the picnic table she served Billy Joe in her own cup, poured Bob a helping in his, took her own portion in an empty can. Billy Joe took a couple of slurping spoonfuls. Mountford watched him intently; then after a while he posed a few routine questions about Billy Joe's background. The answers Billy Joe gave were in direct contrast to what he had earlier told Susan. Bob hadn't heard those earlier responses, but she could see in Mountford's eyes his quick perception that Billy Joe's explanations were fantasy or even lies. Still Bob listened patiently as the hot food had seemed to loosen Billy Joe's tongue. Bob let him run down.

"It's all a lot of bullshit. You're making up everything you've said. No more bullshit. Why don't you just level with us?" Bob said.

"Both Bob and I are experienced in talking with people who have problems," Susan said. "We really do care."

Billy Joe flung his spoon to the ground and ceremoniously poured his food in three little puddles upon the table.

"I don't have no problems, and I told you to stop messin' with my brains!"

"I've dealt with hundreds of people like you," Bob said. "You've got a cancer in your gut, man. A big sore that's grown a long time. If you'll let us, we want to help you get it out."

Billy Joe pondered for a moment. His breathing grew more rapid until his chest swelled with each breath. He reached for some crackers and stuffed two whole ones in his mouth. He chewed a moment, started to speak, but sucked the words back in.

"We care about you, Billy Joe," Susan prompted.

"Let's just talk," Bob said. "But this time, no fantasy crap and no lies. Just tell us who Billy Joe really is."

Billy Joe jumped to a standing position.

"Fuck you," he said with such vehemence that cracker spray rained down upon them. "You're still tryin' to see inside my head!"

"If we don't understand where you're coming from, we sure can't help you," Bob said calmly.

"You're the ones that're all screwed up. I'm gettin' away from here. You're both makin' the waves roll over me again."

Billy Joe stalked off toward the tree line like a pride-wounded child.

"Wow!" Susan exclaimed under her breath.

Bob watched the retreating figure, a worried look still creasing his brow. "I don't think he's really left yet."

Susan looked, and she, too, saw Billy Joe, standing under the first row of trees well within the shade and shadows but not as well hidden as he supposed. He faced them. Watching.

"Come on back, Billy Joe, and let's talk," Bob called.

With the labored steps of an old man, Billy Joe returned.

Before he spoke, Susan could sense the total absence of hostility now. There was something about him docile as a lamb.

"You've both been so good to me," Billy Joe said. "And you fed me and all."

"Sit back down and we'll talk," Bob said.

"Want more food?" Susan said.

"No. I'm goin' this time. Couldn't leave without tellin' you how nice you've been."

Susan could swear that Billy Joe's eyes had moistened; but if not, they had grown warmer and a little sleepy looking. He turned without another word, walked off, and disappeared into the trees.

She was hardly conscious of half-holding her breath. Bob was sparse with words, too, until they heard a vehicle engine come to life in the distance. Then the grind of digging wheels sending gravel spray into the trees faded gradually until only the sounds of birds and breeze-ruffled leaves prevailed.

"For God sake, tell me what's been going on here," Bob said at last.

She related everything in minute detail; she knew she was going on forever. At last she finished.

"He's not your usual, run-of-the-mill pothead, that's for sure," Bob said.

"I'd bet that he's been switching back and forth on ludes and krystal or cactus."

"But it's more complicated than drugs."

"I agree," Bob said. "Wish we could have gotten him to talk, cry, anything."

"I think we forgot that this isn't exactly The Homestead."

Bob stood and began to clean up.

"Just another Trail adventure to tell about. Forget it."

Susan couldn't tear her eyes away from the route Billy Joe had taken in departure. She didn't answer Bob.

She started as his arms, from the rear, encircled her waist.

"Hey—you're still a little shaken, aren't you?"

"Yes."

"Why didn't you just go off with the Forestry Service workers when he started acting bananas?"

"Dammit, I don't know." She wrestled free. "You were coming. I knew that. I couldn't leave you. But I guess it was more than that. Somehow, Billy Joe needed me—and for a while he was beginning to open up."

"Next time, just go."

She shuddered at the thought of "next time."

"At one point I did start to run out on you. But Billy Joe kept close at my heels. I did have the presence of mind to have one of the forestry workers take Billy Joe's and my picture together just in case."

"Small comfort. If Billy Joe had had any evil designs, he could just as well have destroyed the film."

The logic chilled her anew.

"Let's not even talk about it anymore," she said. "The whole scene freaks me out."

"As you say."

"Do you really think he's gone?"

"I thought we weren't going to talk about it any more."

"Let's go and check to make sure. He could just pull a weird number, y'know."

He came to her, drew her close, and kissed her lightly.

"Whatever makes you feel good."

"*This* makes me feel good."

"That was some greeting you gave me when I got into camp. Can't you do a rerun?"

She held on like a bear.

"I was never so glad to see you in my life. And I promise, on Scout's honor, never to tell anyone that the Great Mountford got lost in Jefferson National Forest."

"You probably never were a Scout, but that only reminds me I have a lot to learn about you."

"Some of it may be dull and disappointing."

"Let me be the judge. Let's get the chores done and settle in early."

His kiss was prolonged and probing this time.

"I just want to be held close tonight. Nothing more," she said. "Guess I still feel a little wiped out."

The vehicle road was farther away than they had supposed. Yet earlier vehicle sounds seemed close by. The road lay to the east/southeast of them, a narrow dirt passage littered with trash and beer cans. Sound traveled clearly in the usual quietness of the forest. Not a vehicle was in sight when they reached it, but they could see the digging wheelprints left by Billy Joe's truck as he had sped away in a cloud of clay dust.

Relieved, she began her chores in earnest: she laid out the sleeping bags to air, took a foot/legs bath, using the piped-in spring water that new Wapiti II boasted, changed into clean dry kneesocks, and swept out the shelter floor. She reheated the food they hadn't had the stomach to finish while Billy Joe was with them.

Later, Bob washed their utensils and then took his own feet-and-legs bath after screaming in protest at the chilliness of the water.

As daylight faded, they placed their sleeping bags on the clean shelter floor. The damp ground all about exuded a chill, moisture-laden airiness. It took no prompting for Bob to build a fire as near to them as safety would allow. She reclined nearest to the firelight, with her head propped on a makeshift pillow, as the dancing flames illuminated adequately the unfinished pages of *Clea*. Bob donned his miner's lamp and read from his Bible.

Try as she might, concentration eluded her. Something delayed, yet meaningful, in the day's experience had only superficially registered. Now that something was trying to worm its way back into her consciousness. She dropped the book, causing Bob to look over.

"He wants to rape me."

"He what? You didn't mention anything like that earlier."

"It just hit me. He wants to rape me."

"What makes you think so? Did he make advances you didn't tell me about?"

"No. He looked at me lustfully only once. And it was just a fleeting sweep of his eyes."

"Then how do you know? Sure you're not imagining things?"

"I know it instinctively. It may sound flaky, but women have a fine-tuned sixth sense about such things."

"Well, he sure as hell wouldn't try it now. I could wrap that seedy-looking specimen around a tree and tie him in a knot with one hand."

"Thank God for small favors."

She rolled over and laid a grateful hand against his bearded face. He held it there against the bristles, sand-papered her soft skin until it itched and she wrenched away.

She started reading again. Concentration was good enough to keep her at it until the fire was dying out. She laid the book aside and started to get up and add more wood. At sitting position she froze. Deep in the woods, something snapped.

"Bob, did you hear that?"

"Hear what?"

"A snapping, breaking sound?"

He rose in concentration. The night was suddenly so quiet that a lone cricket far away sounded like a chorus.

"Bob, I know it's crazy, but while you've got your miner's lamp on, let's check the service road again."

He looked at her strangely but said nothing for a moment.

"Forget it. Guess I am acting a little far out," she said.

She picked up the book again and read until her eyelids grew stiff. Casting the book aside, she lay back. A renewed sense of peace and well-being slowly crept over her. She reached out for Bob's arm. It was hairy and she stroked it.

"Finished *Clea?* Want me to read to you from Doctor Luke? He was quite a fellow. The only one to remain loyal to Paul while Paul languished in a Roman prison awaiting death. Touching."

"Thanks, but no thanks. That sounds a little heavy. We've got the rest of our lives to deal with the heavy stuff."

"How about a poem then?"

"You brought a book of poetry?"

"No, but I taped one that I like in the back of my Bible. Before the hike I read everything I could find with a nature theme. You know—kind of psyching myself up for the Great Adventure."

"I'll bite. Knowing you, I would say it's probably something zany from Woody Allen."

Bob turned to the back cover. "Not Woody Allen. Longfellow's 'Nature.' "

> 'As a fond mother, when the day is o'er,
> Leads by the hand her little child to bed,
> Half willing, half reluctant to be led,
> And leave his broken playthings on the floor,
> Still gazing at them through the open door,
> Nor wholly reassured and comforted
> By promises of others in their stead,
> Which, though more splendid, may not please him more;
> So Nature deals with us, and takes away
> Our playthings one by one, and by the hand
> Leads us to rest so gently, that we go
> Scarce knowing if we wish to go or stay,
> Being too full of sleep to understand
> How far the unknown transcends the what we know.

Like fine old wine, the words reached some secret crevice in her soul and lingered there; yet something in the poem gave her cause for disquiet.

"Bob—why did you select that particular poem?"

"I told you. I was looking for nature themes."

The answer was unsatisfactory, and she contemplated a response. There must be in print, she thought, five thousand poems with nature themes.

"It's saying something I'm not sure I like."

"Now who's getting heavy? Didn't I hear somebody say that all she wanted at the end of the day was to be held tightly?"

He laid his Book aside and reached for her. They had no woolen blanket; the blazing fire felt good.

He could both sense and feel that she was still jumpy in spite of his cuddling. Remembering the bottles of rum and Cola Billy Joe had left in his hasty departure, he got up to get them. Neither he nor Susan had a preference for cola and rum, but the wilderness was not a place to be choosy. Tonight, it might be just what the doctor ordered.

They swigged on the fiery liquid until Susan not only calmed but began to slur a word or two. He, too, was getting buzzed, but it had never felt so good. The fire crackled in harmony.

After a while Bob began to feel giddy. "Here's to Billy Joe," he said as the liquid got close to bottom. "It was a great party. Thanks for the free likker!"

"Keep your voice down," Susan giggled. "He may remember and come back for it."

"I don't think so. Don't believe he's the partying type."

"Weird," she said.

Bob got up a little wobbly, discarded the bottles; he washed and returned their drinking cups to the backpacks. He came back and wiggled up to her.

"We've shared a lot during these ten days," he said. "Maybe it's a new beginning of something."

"But I'll be leaving you after Pearisburg and the visit with the Desjardins at Blacksburg. I've got to be back at work on the twenty-sixth. Remember?"

"Fate—if it's meant to be—always put the pieces of her puzzle together again," he whispered. "And I'll be coming down Mount Katahdin before you know it."

She accepted his assurances and snuggled closer. It felt so good; but in the pit of her stomach, the empty feeling she'd felt when he'd first left for the AT began to eddy through her. *"How far the unknown transcends the what we know—"* the last line of the poem intruded itself upon her consciousness. One day at a time, she thought. The sounds of a thousand katydids and a nightbird soloist saluted the deepening darkness. Bob's warmth meshed with her own, but as the night aged into dawn and the fire faded, they'd have to nest in their separate sleeping bags. That or roll up the pine-needle-earth-blanket with its rich aroma and polkadot patterns of blooming things and pull it over themselves. The thought was strangely comforting.

CHAPTER XVIII

The hikers' hostel at Pearisburg, sponsored and maintained by the Holy Family Roman Catholic Church, was not as spacious and luxurious as the facility at Damascus. The hostel—a rehabilitated sixty-year-old grain barn, was only a hundred yards from the new brick church. Perched on one of the highest hills in town, both church and hostel in a park-like setting, commanded a spectacular view. Although the old barn was rustic, various civic clubs, social agencies, hikers and friends of hikers had improved it with a crude kitchen, shower facilities, a small book nook, and bunks in the loft. A gazebo and fireplace had been built near the barn, and the surrounding lawn, rich in thick, trimmed grass and dotted with shade trees, made the ideal camping site.

Oblate Father Harry Winter, the parish priest, was proud of the contribution Holy Family Church and others had made toward a resting and stopping-off place for Appalachian Trail enthusiasts. He saw in most of the hikers an unusual awareness of and sensitivity to the world's ills, a general reverence for life, and a fierce protectiveness toward Nature's gifts.

He was pleased also that the diocese of Richmond had adopted the Pearisburg hostel ministry as an official diocesan program and supported it financially. He himself preferred the term "hospice" to "hostel." Hospice meant hospitality, rest, healing—not just a place to stay overnight. He was proud, too, that of the five church-related accommodations along the two-thousand-mile trail, his Roman Catholic brothers maintained three. Even so, he had no interest in denominational supremacy. He had visions of how all churches might render general assistance and maintain unique ministries: ministries of simply listening, for example. He wanted a closer relationship with the Methodists at Damascus, a sharing of ideas. And his support of the Presbyterians was equally enthusiastic. That group had long investigated the feasibility of training leaders who would use campers' retreat facilities and thus be enabled to share Christian values with hikers. He wanted also to involve the Southern Baptist Special Mission Ministries and the American Bible Society in the trailside distribution of their reading materials. The Presbyterians had already developed a small journal-diary that had caught on with hikers; it was both a practical need and a wonderful tool for evangelization.

Father Winter also envisioned hostels as a center for wilderness survival schools, partly for the benefit of scouts, community action groups, and troubled teenagers. He hoped that this use could be enjoyed without interference with the regular hikers. He had the feeling that the American people had not yet grasped the magnitude of the Appalachian Trail movement. A new appreciation of Nature and the discovery of one's deeper personhood were themes near and dear to the hearts of millions of Americans and foreigners now. It was possible—if not probable—that within the decade ten million people would be hiking annually some part of the historic footpath.

Every spring he felt the urge to strike out with boots and backpack, but free time for woods-walking was scarce amid the numerous responsibilities of his parish. He took small comfort in the fact that he was still lean at forty-three and had, he believed, the necessary stamina of a through hiker. In any event he identified strongly with the hikers and relished the all-too-brief individual association that always enriched his own soul. He had met few who were not making first a journey into self and secondarily a hike into the challenging wilderness.

John Smith and Candy Lakin had agreed to wait in Pearisburg at the Holy Family hostel and have a celebration party with Bob and Susan. Maybe the occasion would even top the night of celebration the four of them had shared with Frank Maguire and his daughter and grandchildren in Tennessee.

It was Wednesday, May 20, the agreed meeting date, but the day passed and Bob and Susan hadn't shown. Frank Maguire and Renate Lillifors also waited. Dave Tice had checked in, but since he lived in Pearisburg, he had gone on home where he'd meet his brother John and resume the trek northward. According to the register, Peter Butryn and John "JJ" Juczynski had checked in earlier, but they had soon hit the Trail again.

Steve Skinner and the Robinson brothers came in late in the day. Questioned, they could cast no light on Bob and Susan's whereabouts. They—Steve and the brothers—had spent the night of May 19 at the old Wapiti shelter. Steve reiterated, however, that he had spent the night of May 18 with Bob and Susan, that the next morning he had been the last to leave camp, and that he had not seen them since.

At dusk other hikers filtered in. But all questions generated the same answer: Bob's and Susan's names had been seen on various shelter registers, but Steve Skinner had evidently been the last to see them, on the morning of May 19.

That night as a group of hikers sat around "tent city," Frank Maguire broke the thoughtful silence he had imposed on himself.

"They've sacked out in a motel somewhere. Maybe they've even eloped!"

Some of the group agreed that such could be the case; that romantic, impulsive Mountford would be just the type to pull such a switch.

166

That night, however, Frank slept fitfully with a groggy sense of trepidation.

Next morning, Frank, Steve Skinner, Renate, John Smith, Candy Lakin, and a few others decided to wait around for a while.

Don Farrell came to the hostel. He, too, could report that he had seen only Bob's and Susan's names on various shelter registers, not them in person.

At mid-day John Smith suddenly recalled:

"Mountford said something about going on into Blacksburg to visit some doctor—a friend of his family, I think. That's where they are. Still, it's not like Bob to skip out on the party we talked about . . . "

"You're right," Frank said. "He told us about the doctor back down the trail. He had a funny name I can't remember. I think this doctor delivered him into the world or something."

"But wasn't Susan supposed to catch a bus here in Pearisburg and head back to her job at Ellsworth?" Candy asked.

"Yeah," John said, "but don't you see—that what they're doing. Bob probably took her for a quick trip to Blacksburg before he had to put her on the bus. We might as well hit the trail. He'll catch up. We can postpone our party for farther along the trail."

"I wanted to say goodbye to Susan," Candy lamented. "Now I'll never see her again."

"I vanted to say goodbye, too," Renate said. "I vill go to Ellsworth sometime and see her."

Shortly after lunch, Frank, Renate, John, Candy, and most of those that had remained hit the trail. Steve Skinner and the Robinson brothers stayed on. Steve had hoped that his sister and Neal Chivington would catch up. He loved Sandy deeply. He wanted to be with her and wanted the Robinsons to meet her. He was concerned, too, that she might still be having foot and leg problems.

The next day, Neal and Sandy hadn't shown. Neither had Bob Mountford. Steve hadn't really expected Bob to make an appearance. He had seen enough while with Bob and Susan to know that romance was in the air and that a spark was obviously turning to hot flame. The motel idea—though not an elopment—sounded entirely plausible. And he had heard both Susan and Bob promise each other a feast the moment they hit the town limits.

The Robinson brothers were getting itchy feet by mid-morning. Steve told them to go on, for he'd soon catch up. They left at 9:30. Steve hung around the hostel until 1:30; then he decided he was playing a guessing game. Sandy and Neal could be a week behind him. He left a note for them, and one for Bob, on the register, and noted that Frank had left a note for Bob, too.

As a new string of unknown hikers began to come in to the hostel grounds, Steve made one final inquiry about Neal, Sandy, Susan, and Bob. Nothing. He laced arms into his backpack and hit the Trail alone.

By May 23 Steve and the Robinson brothers had caught up with Frank and Renate, who had left Pearisburg first, south of the town of Cloverdale. One of Frank's and Renate's first questions was whether the newcomers had heard anything about Bob.

"Nothing," Steve answered, "but I've left him almost as many notes along the way as I noticed you have."

"Yeah," Frank said. "A couple of times I told him that it was good to be rid of his lousy cooking and that I knew he was slow as granny, but that granny was ninety. I miss that loud mouth of his. I wish he'd catch up. Probably he broke a leg or something after he did get going."

"Maybe ve should call back and check. Maybe ve should ask Father Vinter if he heard anything," Renate said.

"A good idea," Frank agreed. "We'll do it when we hit Cloverdale. And while we're at it, it won't hurt to call back to the post office at Pearisburg and see if Mountford picked up his mail drop."

It was a hard stretch of miles over rough terrain to Cloverdale, but the beautiful valley of Virginia now lay before them. Since they had to come into town for phone service, a motel looked all the more appealing. The counter calendar now said May 25. Before eating or showering, Frank was on the phone to Father Winter. The priest had heard nothing, but he had received calls of inquiry about the couple.

Since it was Memorial Day, calling the Pearisburg post office was out. That would have to wait until morning.

Everyone showered and went to a hamburger joint for supper. Frank was unusually quiet.

Prodded, he finally spoke up: "Something's wrong. Bad wrong. I've got a nose for this kind of thing."

Back at the motel, Frank decided to call Bob Mountford, Sr., in Dover-Foxcroft. When the Maine number answered, he tried to sound casual, and Mountford made it easy. There was instant warmth in the man's voice. Frank asked if he had heard from Bob Jr. Bob Jr., hadn't called; neither had Susan Ramsay, the elder Mountford added; then he went on to explain that the girl had been scheduled to call her folks before she boarded the bus in Pearisburg for the trip back to work in Ellsworth. Susan hadn't called on May 20 or 21 as scheduled, and Bud and Ginny Ramsay had called Dover-Foxcroft to find out what the Mountfords had heard. Also, nobody at The Homestead had received a call from Susan since she called for an extension of vacation leave.

"Bobby was scheduled to visit Dr. Richard Desjardins in Blacksburg," Mountford added. "I think they're just running behind schedule. I don't think there's any cause for worry. Bobby's tough and experienced. He can handle any situation, and even if they're temporarily lost, he'll find his way out. I've never seen him fail. . ."

168

Frank listened patiently as Mountford reiterated his own points and shared even more background, but Frank had the sinking feeling that his own sixth sense was not lying to him and that something tragic— something sinister—might have happened. Since it was Memorial Day, Mountford said he had not been able to call the Pearisburg post office but that he did have a call in to the Desjardins. He had also called Father Winter but had learned nothing.

He gave Frank the phone numbers of the Ramsays, the Desjardins, and the Pearisburg post office and suggested that he call them all for any last-minute news.

Frank hung up, but he soon had the receiver in his hand again. The others looked on, the same concern in their faces that he felt deep in his gut.

He placed the Aurora call, introduced himself to Bud Ramsay, and stated his connection with Bob and Susan. Ramsay was calm and businesslike but confessed his disquiet. Susan would not ordinarily have postponed by days her obligatory phone call home, Ramsay insisted. Frank relayed all that he and the others knew, emphasizing a second time that Steve Skinner had been with Susan and Bob as recently as the morning of May 19. Frank could hear Ramsay's sigh of appreciation; then came the question Frank dreaded.

"How do you size up the situation?" Ramsay asked.

Frank paused unduly long. He didn't want to get into the romance angle, and he didn't want to convey the sense of alarm that he himself was already feeling. For the moment there was only one way to keep the matter in perspective.

"I don't have an answer just now. Fact is, I think we'd better wait until the Pearisburg post office opens tomorrow morning and see if Bob and Susan made the pick-ups. Bob's father has already tried to reach a Dr. Desjardins in nearby Blacksburg to see if Bob might be there."

Ramsay asked more questions, sharing speculations of his own. He mentioned that Dianne Collins from the Homestead had called again, saying that they had heard nothing via phone but that they had received a card from Bob and Susan postmarked May 20, from Sugar Grove, Virginia.

"That's impossible," Frank said. "Sugar Grove's too far south for a May 20 postmark from Bob and Susan. You can forget that."

Ramsay asked for an explanation.

"Sometimes a hiker will leave stamped, addressed cards on the trail register, and the next person going into the village will act as mailman. Sometimes a letter will be given to another hiker, and he'll carry it for days before he remembers to mail it. That card at that address has to be a delayed mailing."

Ramsay added: "Susan did say on the card that she and Bob would be arriving at the Pearisburg hostel on May 20 and that she'd call the Homestead from there. Does that sound on target?"

"Yes," Frank said.

"Obviously, they didn't make it." Ramsay's voice trailed off.

"If Bob and Susan didn't pick up their mail and food drop at the post office and if they haven't made contact with the doctor, I think you should insist on a search party at once and cover the area of Jefferson National Forest where they were last seen," Frank suggested.

"A few of us are getting ready to head up the valley of Virginia, but I'll be calling you back if we hear anything." Frank moved to ring off. "Try not to worry. This kind of mix-up is nothing new along the Trail."

Ramsay's pause was so long that Frank could hear his breathing.

"Yeah. Thanks for your help," Ramsay said finally.

With a sense of foreboding, Frank picked up the receiver again and placed a call to the Desjardins in Blacksburg. Each ring began to sound like a death knell. Betty Desjardins said that Bob had not arrived in Blacksburg, nor had he called.

Again the little group assembled in Frank's room could do nothing but stare at each other in confused silence.

"I am going back to Pearisburg. I vant to know vhat is going on."

"We can't do any more there than we're doing here," Frank said.

The others debated the necessity and the wisdom of going back. What could they do? Steve Skinner confessed that he didn't have the money to spare for motels or bus fare. The Robinson brothers hadn't even met the couple in question.

Next morning Frank called the Pearisburg post office. Bob had not picked up his mail and food drop. Neither had Susan claimed her letters.

Frank wrestled with his dilemma. Should he, too, go back to Pearisburg? He could join a search party that was now almost a certainty, but perhaps he could do more along the trail by spreading the word and interviewing those who had bypassed the Pearisburg hostel and who might have seen or talked with Susan and Bob. Besides, he had an appointment in Shenandoah National Park to meet some friends, and he was behind schedule now. There was no way to call them, either. They were already on the Trail, walking north to south. Maybe he and his fellow hikers were jumping to panicky conclusions anyway. He had been on many a wild goose chase. Events that seemingly raised complex questions often had simple answers. Bob and Susan were not greenhorn amateurs. Both were professionals. The probability of the romance thing began to weasel into his consciousness again.

He called Father Winter once more and learned that the phone lines had been kept hot between the Church office, Dover-Foxcroft, The Homestead, and Aurora. Also, he learned that although John and Martina Linnehan had checked in the previous day, they knew nothing, for they had not even seen Bob since North Carolina. They were staying over in a local motel. "In spite of the new wave of hikers arriving at the hostel," Father Winter said, "no one can offer any vital information."

Steve Skinner and his friends headed for the trail and planned to continue northward. They promised to keep in touch via phone to the Pearisburg hostel. Still determined to go back, Renate prepared to leave for the bus station.

Frank was still undecided.

"Do you think they could have eloped?" Frank said.

"Not a chance. Vhat age vere you born in? Nobody vorries about veddings anymore."

The reminder that he was of an older generation stung a little, but he knew that Renate was right. After he had promised to call her at the hostel, they said goodbye. He checked out and headed for the trail.

CHAPTER XIX

Bob Mountford, Sr. signed the last of a half-dozen letters on his desk, but the task didn't bring him up to date. There was still a pile of unanswered correspondence plus receipts and thank-you notes he had agreed to help Mim with, relative to incoming contributions for The Little Red School House. Thus far there had been only the briefest mention in the TV and print media about Bobby's and Susan's overdue status. Up to now he himself had not been that worried. And Jackie Hilton supported him in this view. Bobby could take care of himself in any situation, for he had all the needed skills of survival. He might have been temporarily lost in the woods because of the impulse to take a blue-blaze sightseeing trip to someplace interesting, but he was not in trouble. Still, Susan was now one day tardy at work. It was May 27.

Later in the day, he could fight the anxiety no longer. The agony of uncertainty already showed in Mim's face. It was time to worry. She was more quiet than tearful; it was Grampy Bill that paced the floor, mumbling the same phrase over and over: "Something's wrong. Bad wrong. Something's wrong. Bad wrong."

Grampy Bill refused to leave the house and take sanctuary in his mobile home out back. Just as they too responded, every ring of the phone visibly jarred Grampy Bill like a jolt of electricity. For seeming hours all the calls were routine. Bob could see the energy from his normally jovial father-in-law draining away. His face was taking on an ashen look, and his big two-hundred-twenty-pound body drooped until his powerful shoulders were half-mooned.

"If anything happens to that boy. . ." Grampy Bill's shaky voice became lost in the next jangle of the phone.

Mim picked up the receiver. After two sentences Bob could tell that it was Bud Ramsay she was speaking to and that he had no fresh news either.

When Bob took the receiver, it was a grimmer Bud Ramsay than he had spoken to previously. Ramsay advised that he had already made contact with Deputy John Greever of the county sheriff's office at Pearisburg and that he had contacted officials at Appalachian Trail Conference Headquarters at Harpers Ferry, West Virginia, as well. Ramsay proposed that Giles County authorities be put on notice in order that a full-scale search might be requested the following day unless encouraging news of some kind was forthcoming.

Bob agreed, and after dinner when they had finally gotten Grampy Bill to go back to the mobile home and to his own bed, they placed calls to the children again. Carolyn in Orlando answered at once, but the time zone difference delayed contact with Scott and Catherine in Houston. Bachelor Steve lived in Orlando also, but finding him at home was another matter. Carolyn promised to run him down. This time, Bob and Mim pulled no punches. Their first call, when Bobby was simply overdue, was more a progress report. Now, they had to report Bobby as missing.

Before bedtime, Bob placed another call to Father Winter in Pearisburg. The priest had already told him to call at any hour because his living quarters were attached to the church. To his dismay, Bob learned that not one person who had been interviewed or contacted had seen or talked with his son or Susan Ramsay since the morning of May 19.

"There have been rumors afloat about unsavory-looking characters here and there along the Trail," Father Winter added. "And somebody mentioned what might be interpreted as threatening notes along the southern end. There was something about a 'ninety-five-pounder.' None of it would seem to have any bearing on Bob and Susan's delay, though."

Bob lay in bed that night, fighting against his fears and trying to play down the multitude of apprehensions Mim had thrice repeated. They lay there holding hands like two lost, frightened children bedded down in the dark, leafy woods. Bobby and Susan couldn't be in danger. They couldn't be. Bobby had made it across country to California, hitchhiking the return journey; he had been to England, to Russia, and to a dozen Slavic countries. All went without a hitch. And Bud Ramsay had left no doubt that Susan was a top-flight wilderness survival enthusiast and first-rate hiker in her own right. Of course, Bob and Mim knew that. Susan had been a house guest several times. She had spent a few days with them just before Bobby had gone to Georgia.

The morning of May 28 came in so clear and bright that Bob suspected every photographer in the picture post card business would be out taking shots of spring in Maine. The very atmosphere had a good feeling. Strangely, he was happy, without any particular reason. God was good. "This is the day the Lord hath made. Let us rejoice and be glad in it."

Mim went off to her duties at The Little Red School House. Life had to go on. Sometimes routine could be the most soothing of balms. Bob worked at getting his own affairs in order. It might prove necessary that he go to Virginia, but what function could he serve? He knew the procedures of a search. There would be dozens, if not hundreds, of volunteers, rescue squad members, forestry people, and local and State police. But even so, he could just picture Bobby emerging from the woods with a perfectly plausible explanation, laughing at all of them. It was all going to end as a big joke.

At 9:30 that night, the Ramsays called to say they were leaving Aurora for Virginia. Frank Maguire had called an hour earlier to advise that a search be delayed no longer. Though he was without any important new facts, every instinct he had, every shred of training he had learned as a law enforcement officer, told him that something was indeed wrong. Maguire had come off the Trail in a rainstorm, Ramsay added, and they were going to call him again enroute at his motel in Buchanan, Virginia.

Bob mentioned his indecision about going to Pearisburg, and Ramsay promised to call from the sheriff's office once he had reached Virginia.

The next day had begun as routinely as possible under the circumstances. A few close friends had been told that Bobby and Susan were overdue and that present circumstances indicated they were now unofficially missing. Sean Stitham, home from college, had been one of those called. Stitham volunteered his services, including chauffeuring Bob, Sr. to Virginia if the latter wanted to go. Bob still stalled. They were all jumping to conclusions. Bobby would emerge from the woods any hour now. He might be hobbling along with a homemade splint supporting a broken leg, but that would be the extent of it. Or so the older Bob told himself. He fought against the rationale that if such were the case, other hikers would have come upon Bobby and stretcher-carried him out of the forest.

Grampy Bill had not been purposely ignored during the morning hours, but both Bob and Mim were feeling the pressure of heart-aching worry and numbing distraction. And Grampy had been so quiet for the last two days that if you didn't see him moping around the house and grounds, it was easy to forget him. Bob headed for the mobile home to ask Grampy Bill to join him and Mim for lunch.

The entrance door was ajar, the TV set was on and Grampy Bill sat in his favorite chair in front of the screen. Bob issued the invitation and started to retreat, but he was suddenly aware that not even a flicker of movement had come from his father-in-law. Bob did a double-take and saw that while the eyes of the elder man were open, life had fled them. Loyd "Bill" Rideout sat there with his hands folded in his lap, a peaceful expression on his still-handsome but well-lined face as if he had just repudiated life on his own terms. Bob was momentarily mesmerized by this unexpected death scene. He reached for the hand of the dead man. All the warmth had already gone. The mirth-filled, tired old heart had stopped forever; the last bear tale had been told.

Bob held onto the lifeless hand, feeling his eyes moisten. He had not always felt a warmth for Mim's father. In the early days there had been some difficult times, but as the years had gone by, both men had mellowed and found a new respect and affection for each other. And it was in Dover-Foxcroft that Grampy had chosen to spend his last days.

Bob went back to Mim with the sad news. He held her tightly as the impact of the event sank in and she started to tremble. She wept softly as he tightened his grip; after a moment she wanted to go to her father.

They went back to the mobile home, and after a time Mim unfolded a clean sheet and covered the lifeless form.

"He was so worried about Bobby . . .," Mim's words gave way to sobs. He held her again.

"I've got to go to Virginia after I help make the arrangements here. Don't know what I can do, but I've got to go," Bob said.

While Mim went back to the house to begin the barrage of calls the situation required, Bob stayed in the mobile home to use Grampy's phone. He called the funeral home, Grampy's pastor, his physician, and a few of his friends. The whole scene was becoming unreal. He kept walking circles around the sheet-covered form, doing this chore or that or going back to the phone to make another call or searching for paper and pen to jot down obituary information.

After the hearse had come and gone, the rest of the day became even more unreal. Both Mim and he would forget whom they had or hadn't called; as word of Grampy's death had spread by word of mouth, people by the dozens began to arrive. He and Mim moved about like robots, their thoughts shifting from imagined scenes along the Appalachian Trail to the present reality in Dover-Foxcroft. But what was reality? Bob asked himself. Until five days previously, life had been so peaceful, so routine.

When morning came, Bob got out the lawnmower. The grass was badly in need of trimming, and still more people would be coming by. But aside from the need of the chore, he himself needed to work up a good sweat and purge the morose spirit from his body.

He finished the task by ten-thirty and went inside to shower. When he emerged from the bathroom, he picked up the phone and dialed Sean Stitham's number. When Sean answered, Bob said: "If the offer's still good, let's head for Virginia as soon as possible."

Shortly before noon, Sean arrived and they were soon headed south.

CHAPTER XX

Bud and Ginny Ramsay had left Aurora on May 28 at 9:30 P.M. They arrived at Marietta, Ohio, at 1:00 A.M. and checked into a motel. As previously agreed, they called Frank Maguire at his motel in Buchanan, Virginia. Frank could still offer nothing new, but his gut feeling was more than ever that the evidence was overwhelming: something was wrong. According to hikers coming up behind him, Maguire said, the notes he had left for Mountford along the trail had not been taken down.

At 7:00 the next morning, Bud and Ginny left Marietta for Pearisburg, Virginia.

It was a six-hour drive. On arrival at the post office, Bud explained their mission and offered to furnish identification. The young clerk with a GI haircut left his post momentarily to clear the release of Susan's mail with his superior. The clerk retrieved a packet of letters, and both postal workers approached the window. The elder of the two said that many people had called to ascertain whether Susan's and Bob Mountford's mail drops had been picked up. Had the couple been located yet?

"Afraid not," Ginny said.

"Try not to worry," the younger clerk said with feeling. "It's happened before. Some of the hikers give up, leave the trail, and go home. We stamp their mail 'undeliverable' and send it back."

"We just came from home," Bud said. "No word on that end either."

The postal workers seemed genuinely concerned, and Bud brought them up to date on all that was known. Ginny answered more questions as best she could and then asked directions to the sheriff's office.

The elder clerk walked out to the street with them and pointed. The back of the courthouse could be seen over the top of the one-story bank building.

"The sheriff's office and jail are just across the alley from the east end of the courthouse," he said.

As they thanked him and turned to go, a college-age boy-girl pair of hikers laden with heavy backpacks came down the sidewalk toward them. Bud saw Ginny's face go expressionless. Like a sleep walker, she took measured steps toward the pair. The girl's hair was short and black. The boy had frizzled red hair going in all directions. Not a chance.

When the young couple came abreast, Ginny asked, "Have you heard anything along the trail about Susan Ramsay and Bob Mountford? They might have been temporarily lost, perhaps one of them suffered an injury."

Neither hiker had ever heard the names, and they had heard of no mishaps. Both asked quickly how they might help if there was a problem. Bud went into the long story one more time, feeling a twinge of anger when the couple told them that it would be impossible for harm to have come to his daughter and her friend.

"There are too many people on the AT who would help in any situation," the boy said. "Even if they'd gotten lost, they'd eventually find their way out to a farmhouse, a road, a blue-blaze — something."

"And if they'd been injured," the girl said, "somebody would have come along — this time of year — within a few hours or a day at most."

"We've heard that so much we want to scream," Ginny said.

"Yeah — with all this help, where are they?" Bud added.

He realized the remark sounded hostile, and he told of his and Ginny's sleepless nights.

They moved the car to the courthouse parking lot. Close up, the ancient red brick building was larger than it had first appeared. The usual white cupola sat on top, gleaming in the bright sunlight. To the west the mammoth termination of a mountain — column-shaped and flanged at the bottom — looked as if it might fall across the small town and squash it. No flat Ohio, this; they could see hills and mountains in every direction.

They traversed the alley dividing the two buildings, walked by barred windows, and entered a side door. A row of cells lay to their left; the dispatcher's office to their right.

Bud introduced himself to the young officer and said they had just hit town.

"Deputy Lawson's been expecting you, Mr. Ramsay. Follow me."

As they entered the small, unpretentious second-floor office, Deputy Tommy Lawson rose to greet them. His youthful good looks and slender six-foot frame were momentarily disarming. Lawson had to be under thirty-five; even his handshake somehow conveyed the eagerness and enthusiasm of youth.

Lawson pointed to worn wooden chairs to the right of his desk.

"Sorry the sheriff isn't here to meet you," Lawson said. "He's on vacation in South Carolina with his wife and child. Myrtle Beach."

"You a family man?" Bud said.

"Yeah." Lawson grinned through straight teeth. "A boy thirteen and a girl eleven."

"Then you know how we feel just now," Ginny said.

"Yeah."

"Any new word at all?" Bud said.

"No. We've kept a close check with the post office and the local hostel. Not a word. A lot of people are trying to help, though. Other hikers. Father Winter. Friends of your daughter and her companion."

"We just came from the post office," Ginny said. "Her mail was still there."

"Let's get the ball rolling and find them," Lawson suggested and reached for a form in his desk. "I want you to file a missing person report and then go over to the rescue squad building and meet with Steve Davis. Steve's captain of the team. Good man. Knows what he's doing."

"Will you be in on the search? Sending other deputies?" Bud asked.

"We'll be on standby. Since the search will be concentrated in Jefferson National, the Forest Service people have jurisdiction. Buford Belcher is the district law enforcement officer. He's got a good team, too. I'll give you directions to his office."

Deputy Lawson paused to dial Steve Davis to tell him that Bud and Ginny Ramsay were on their way over.

"We'll all be working together," Lawson said, rising from his chair. "Try not to worry. A few days overdue is not so unusual among hikers, I'm told."

"You're forgetting that our daughter was due to report for work on May 26," Ginny said. "She wouldn't have missed that deadline without good reason. And she would have called her employer if events dictated otherwise. SuSu hasn't called anyone to our knowledge."

"If they're out there, we'll find them," Lawson promised.

"I hope we're not sending an army of people on a wild goose chase." Ginny hedged a little.

"All in a day's work," Lawson said. "If you want to join the search team, come by in the morning, and we'll provide an escort."

The Giles County Rescue Squad headquarters was scarcely six blocks away, a large masonry building with rescue vehicles within and an older model jeep and a pickup truck without. They entered by the front door and went into a space that looked like a squad room. A couple of short wave receivers were alive with squawks, whistles, and garbled voices. A short, rotund man in his thirties with a handlebar mustache moved from behind his desk, reached for the controls and turned down the volume before he approached them.

"I'm Steve Davis. You'd be the Ramsays?"

"Yes," Ginny said, accepting the extended hand.

Davis motioned them to chairs around the squad room table.

"Can I get you coffee? Or a Coke?"

Both of them accepted black coffee. As they sipped, Davis slid his portly bulk onto a chair opposite and advised that the search had been anticipated as a result of their earlier phone calls to the sheriff's office.

"In addition to us and the U.S. Forest people, I'm callin' in the Bland County Rescue Squad, too," Davis said.

He explained that Bland was the adjoining county to the west, and that they shared a boundary with Giles deep inside Jefferson National Forest.

"With so many people involved, do you think it'll take long?" Bud asked.

"Even with a small army, it's still not goin' to be any snap," Davis said. "We don't have much to go on. All we know — from what you and others have passed on to the sheriff's department — is that they were last seen by a certain Steve Skinner, enterin' Jefferson National, and that they never came out and checked in at the hostel here in Pearisburg."

"What's your plan?" Bud asked.

"Set up base camps and search a twenty-mile-long grid from northeast of Trent's Store in Bland County to the crest of Angel's Rest Mountain."

Bud heaved a sign of appreciation for the magnitude of such a painstaking search.

"Yeah," Davis agreed. "Pretty big task. Even bigger than you think considerin' the blue-blaze trails along the way — all the fire trails, log roads, and deserted homesteads down each side of the mountain. We could end up coverin' hundreds of square miles."

Ginny's thoughts were lingering on the strange name of the mountain — Angel's Rest. Maybe SuSu waited there for rescuers. Maybe she and Bob had taken a blue-blaze, fallen, sprained their ankles — or, at worst, just had a pair of broken legs. Surely they would have enough food and water to survive. Angel's Rest. Such a peaceful-sounding place to wait and rest until somebody came.

"Angel's Rest?" she said. "Is that the jutting pedestal we saw just west of town?"

"Yes," Davis said.

"Do you think they could be up there?" Ginny said.

"I don't know, Ma'am, but if they're anywhere in Jefferson National, we'll find 'em."

After Davis had gone into more intricate detail as to his plans, Bud and Ginny took leave.

In the car once more, they headed toward the town's eastern limits and the church and hostel upon a summit as Steve Davis had instructed them. They talked about the two men they had just met. Both Lawson and Davis were young and definitely small-town, but each had exuded confidence in himself and his fellow workers. A genuine aura of integrity definitely shone through, and feeling it, both Bud and Ginny expressed feelings of new hope.

With some difficulty they found the church to which they had been directed after winding through a web of residential streets and attractive middle-class homes. As high as the hill was, it still looked little higher than the base of Angel's Rest Mountain, to the west.

The church was new-looking, of modern design, with a sanctuary built in the round. They knocked at the study door and a tall, slender man in clerical attire responded; he was bespectacled, early fortyish, with fine graying hair.

"Father Winter?" Ginny said.

"Yes. May I help you?"

"You're just as I pictured you by your voice. We're the Ramsays," Ginny said.

"Come in! We'll talk, and then I'll take you outside to the hospice and you can see how we operate. We're full almost every night now. And we have inquiry sheets posted about Bob and Susan. I'm sorry to report they haven't helped much."

Bud told the priest of their meeting with Deputy Tommy Lawson and Steve Davis, commenting that groundwork was properly laid for the search to begin.

"Hope we're not getting panicky without just cause," Ginny added.

"I think you've done the right thing," Father Winter said. "There are too many unanswered questions. I wish that I could answer some of them, but it appears that no one can. Let me serve you tea—cookies, too, if you care for some—and we'll compare notes again."

Father Winter started to leave through a side door and paused.

"My living quarters adjoin the study, but since I'm without help today, perhaps we'd best take our refreshment here. Something is always going on — and the phone, you know."

After more talk and refreshments, the priest led the way to the hostel. The rustic structure sat a hundred yards or so east of the church and Father Winter walked toward it with a look of pride on his serene face. From their first phone contact Ginny had felt great compassion in this man. Like so many priests she had known across the years, there was the right blend of scholarliness and humility, quiet strength and gentleness, Christian idealist and practical, laboring servant. She could see and sense through his "hospice" that he was confident that his church rendered a true and good service to youthful humanity.

A dozen or more hikers lounged about even though the sun was two hours or more from setting. Some were doing laundry. Some were reading or writing letters; others brought food from the hostel kitchen. The whole scene was surprisingly like Girl Scout and Boy Scout outings Ginny had observed or participated in during her girlhood.

"Most of the through hikers like to get in to camp early and leave early the next morning," Father Winter explained.

Since the hostel was filling up already, the tour was a quick one, self-introductions brief, and then they were shown the hostel register. Bud thumbed through it first and pointed out to Ginny names and addresses of hikers who had added comic little notes meant for Bob or Susan or both. Frank Maguire had said: "I've waited on you long enough. I'm headed out, but I will slow down to a crawl on my knees so you can catch up."

Reading the notes, Ginny felt first a sinking feeling in her stomach and then a strange joy in her heart. Susan and Bob might well come up over the hump of the hill before the sinking sun winked from behind Angel's Rest Mountain if she and Bud just waited long enough. She kept rereading the register, and looking down the hill. The messages seemed so current—so fresh as if written only moments rather than days ago.

180

Bud eased her away gently. It was the first time during this exhausting day that she had allowed tears to come. But the feeling was so real. SuSu should be here. She would be coming any moment now. She would be dirty and tired, maybe, but her urchin face would be aglow with the day's challenge over and won.

The two men walked on either side of her back to the church. Father Winter asked whether they would like to see several hikers who had walked part of the distance with Bob — and perhaps Susan — and who had stayed over a few days in local motels. He mentioned John and Martina Linnehan, Renate Lillifors, and others, but added that some of them had said they could wait no longer.

"I couldn't give them any reason to wait," the priest said softly. "Most of the hikers — they're all so self-confident and so sure that Bob and Susan could handle themselves that they think there's a rational explanation for the long delay."

"I hope they're right," Bud said. "Regarding the waiting hikers, maybe we can see them later. Don't see that it would help now, and you've already questioned them all. We've got to stop by the U.S. Forest Service office and check in with a Mr. Belcher there, and then we want to find a motel and get some rest. We're joining the rescue teams in the morning."

Father Winter suggested some of the better motels in the general area and saw them to the car. He made no canned speeches nor offered religious cliches seemingly appropriate to the occasion. His simple caring seemed to say it all. Bud and Ginny thanked him for his help and drove away.

At nearby Blacksburg, they checked in at the Marriott Motel. Bud fixed drinks, and both tried to shake the fatigue of the long day from their bodies. While Bud stood and paced, Ginny placed calls to Kelly in Aurora, and Richard in Indianapolis to appraise them of the day's events. She also asked Kelly to mail photos of SuSu directly to Steve Davis, which he had requested.

After showers and dinner in the motel's elegant dining room, for which they had little appetite, they gave up and took a walk.

Outside to the southeast, the vast campus of Virginia Polytechnic Institute and State University lay spread before them like a colossal spider, dwarfing the town and overpowering the night-time horizon in a mosaic of artificial lights and forms. Somehow, Ginny thought, all college campuses were alike: vast, impersonal — even cold. It was the young people who brought the breath of life to them and gave heart and pulse to the corpses of masonry and steel. But she quickly remembered that SuSu had not gone off to Denison with a happy heart. She had wanted desperately to enter Michigan School of Music and had flunked her audition because of a lack of sufficient formal training. And it had been the same at Oberlin. And to add insult to injury, her short suspension at high school — because of the underground newspaper incident — had been on her record and ultimately worked against her. But finally had come SuSu's chance to work summers at Interlochen, and her heart and soul had floated.

Bud squeezed his wife's hand and broke her reverie.

"No reminiscing," he said, "I know what you're thinking: Denison. Interlochen."

"Guilty." She said, "But they were such pleasant thoughts. You know, we lost our little girl at Interlochen. She became a young woman there — so inspired and challenged, so quickly aware that the world was so much bigger and brighter and promising than she had ever dared dream. Somehow the thing in the Maine woods and the Appalachian Trail venture is an extension of that. I want her back, Bud. I want her back tonight —"

Bud took his wife's tear-streaked face in his hands, and drew her to him.

"There'll be a hundred, maybe even two hundred, people in those woods at daybreak. If she's in there, they'll find her. And we'll all probably be eating dinner together about this same time tomorrow, laughing about the whole incident!"

Ginny wanted so desperately to believe it, and she clung all the harder, holding onto her husband's warmth and strength, till passersby took too much notice of them.

Bud gently held her at arm's length. "Let's go in now and talk with the Mountfords to see if Bob is on his way."

The search was already under way when they reached Pearisburg next morning. A deputy sheriff and a Giles Rescue Squad member brought them up to date on the activities, and led them out of town.

It was an eighteen-mile drive to the best access point into Jefferson National: a narrow road that entered the trees just north of Trent's Store and ran parallel to the meandering waters of Dismal Creek. The narrow road was paved, and Bud followed his guide close on until the mountain road wound its way along the west side of Dismal Falls and on toward the top of the mountain. At the junction—of dirt roads, the dust forced him to hold his distance. The forest seemed to close in from all sides, screening off civilization, engulfing the intruders. The grey company Cadillac seemed strangely out of place. Ginny commented that perhaps they needed a four-wheel-drive vehicle.

Another two miles and they began to see numerous vehicles: some parked and others moving slowly through the woods. Their escort pulled off the narrow dirt road adjacent to a picnic area in a clearing.

Before they left the car, Steve Davis strode in their direction. Davis extended a hand in greeting; in the other a small transmitter-receiver cracked alive with a report too garbled for Bud and Ginny fully to understand.

"Where are we?" Ginny said.

"This area is called Horse Camp," Davis replied. "Seemed the best place to set up our first base headquarters. Right after daylight, we did a quick search of the Honey Springs and the Doc's Knob Shelter locations. No helpful signs, and your daughter's and Bob Mountford's names were not on the registers, I'm sorry to report. We're searchin' north and south since

182

we've had such a good turnout of volunteers. We've got between eighty-five and a hundred men in here now and more comin'."

Davis paused to receive an incoming radio message; then he barked a series of orders into his own transmitter.

Bud looked at his watch: 10:15 A.M. The morning sun shot oblique rays of light here and there into the dense woods. Individual trees seemed to be blinking on and off. Dust motes randomly appeared against the backdrop of evergreens, the result most likely of all the movement from vehicles and men. The aroma of the forest, however, was still one of uninterrupted purity, a glaring contrast to the surreal scene of green-emblemed rescue vehicles, squawking instruments of communication, and hurried men weaving in and out like army ants.

Ginny sidled over to her husband, feeling that they were out of place somehow. Under other circumstances the wilderness might have given birth to serenity, but now its overpowering vastness seemed a threatening menace; the trees with their spidery roots and graceful boughs like some gigantic octopus with life-crushing tentacles.

Momentarily, Buford Belcher, the Forest Service officer whom they had met the previous day, moved to their side. In contrast to short, rotund Steve Davis, Boots Belcher was better than six feet tall and carried his 200-pound frame like a robust logger. Belcher was a young forty-one in spite of the salt and pepper hair that seemed to belie his youthful physique — a body kept trim by the rigors of frequent, long jaunts over rugged terrain.

"Are we making any headway?" Bud asked absently.

Belcher's walkie-talkie crackled alive, and Bud heard part of the answer for himself.

"That was J.C. Link reporting in," Boots said. "His crew was checking out the Warspur and Bailey's Gap shelters. Nothing. And no signatures on the shelter logs that come close to your daughter's or Mountford's."

Belcher was joined by another Forest Service officer whom he introduced as Bruce Lagniel. Lagniel paused only as long as courtesy demanded; he then suggested that he and Belcher and other Forestry Department people head across the mountain and check out Wapiti II and Wapiti I shelters.

"The circle is closing," Belcher said as he started to move off. He paused longer and showed Bud and Ginny the map of Jefferson National and the red ring enclosing the land area first to be covered.

Alone again, Bud and Ginny wandered about the base camp. Belcher and Davis obviously had not had time to introduce them around, and occasionally their presence drew questioning stares. They continued to feel as out of place as they surely looked.

Bud drew a cup of water for Ginny and himself from a cooler in a rescue vehicle, and they sat down on a log. Ginny sipped lazily, her thoughts deeply submerged.

"If you were lost in this kind of vast wilderness, what would you do?" she asked her husband.

"Probably wander around in circles," Bud confessed.

"Let's try to think like SuSu would think. Who knows her better than we?"

"True," Bud said. "But you think as a situation demands. And we don't know what her situation was."

Ginny knew he was right, yet she struggled to contribute something.

"If she'd been hurt — or Bob — one or the other would go for help. If they got lost, they'd leave signs — send up smoke signals or something. If somebody did them injury, someone must know . . . must have heard . . . oh, Bud, don't even let me think in that direction!"

In the valley to the southeast of them, the sawmill whistle near Trent's Store sounded off, grotesquely suggesting that her most fearful supposition had been confirmed.

It was lunchtime, of course. Sawmill workers would invade their lunch pails ravenously. She hadn't the slightest pang of hunger, and Bud couldn't even empty his small cup of cool water. Nobody in the search group would pause to eat either. She knew that. She had already sensed in all of them an unspoken, yet discernible, fear that the revelation of some great evil might be facing them. Still, maybe her imagination was going as wild as the timberland about her.

Down on Route 606 — the paved highway that ran along the creek in the direction of Trent's Store and the sawmill—a threesome of hikers came in view of the sawmill and grocery. Neal Chivington and Sandy Skinner had encountered Matt Savitz from Boston on the trail, and the three of them had hiked together since entering Bland County.

They stopped at the store, dropped backpacks, and bought refreshments and snacks. Outside, each became vaguely aware of contrasting conditions. The mill workers ate leisurely, throwing in rounds of banter between bites, but a variety of rescue vehicles were coming and going up and down the highway. Momentarily, a Bland County Sheriff's office vehicle pulled in. Neal sidled over and asked what was going on.

The young deputy looked Neal over with a scrutinizing eye. "We're looking for a couple of overdue hikers. One of the parents put out a missing persons. . ."

"Who are they? They might have passed us on the trail. We've been traveling pretty slowly."

The deputy reached for his pad.

"Robert Tatton Mountford, Jr., and Laura Susan Ramsay. Ever hear of them?"

"They're our friends!"

Neal explained the connections at work, their mutual trail plans, the fact that Steve Skinner, Sandy's brother, had hiked on ahead and should have caught up with Bob and Susan. He added, "We've been left notes by Bob and Susan all along the trail from as far back as North Carolina. We couldn't have been many days behind them!"

"Well, they never made it to Pearisburg. If you want to join in the search and offer any help you can, we'd be obliged. The base camp's up ahead. Above Dismal Falls at Horse Camp. Check in with Steve Davis with the Giles Rescue Squad."

Neal relayed the news to Sandy and Matt. Matt had not met Bob and Susan anywhere along the southern trail, but Sandy's face reflected the same look of startled wonder that Neal himself was feeling. They both had expected to catch up with them any day now. And they fully expected that Steve Skinner would be with the pair. After a few moments of conversation, all of them agreed that lost — really lost — was out of the question. Both Neal and Sandy knew the impeccable credentials that Bob and Susan possessed when it came to backpacking and wilderness survival.

Hurriedly, the threesome finished lunch. More rescue teams and vehicles were suddenly pouring into the area, some taking the road into Jefferson National north-west of the store, and others continuing along Route 606 to enter the vast forest at points along the northwest perimeter.

As the threesome hiked toward Dismal Falls, it was decided that Neal would join the search party at Horse Gap and that Sandy and Matt would stay on the trail to Pearisburg. Sandy, still having leg and foot problems, could contribute nothing in the way of off-trail searching.

At Horse Camp Steve Davis was not to be found, but Neal recognized Ginny and Bud Ramsay immediately. He had once been a guest of Susan's at the Ramsay home in Aurora.

After all that Bud and Ginny could offer about the situation, the whole thing still seemed so incredible that Neal found himself fighting his disbelief.

"You say that Sandy's brother was with Bob and Susan as recently as the 18th or 19th?"

"That's what we've been told," Ginny said.

"But why didn't he wait at Pearisburg? For Bob and Susan? For us?"

"Father Winter — he's the parish priest at the Catholic church beside the hikers' hostel — said that Steve and others had done so," Bud said. "Guess everybody thought young Bob and Susan had just been delayed or gone off the trail, and everybody hiked on.

"Frank Maguire, Steve, and some of the others apparently didn't really begin to worry until they got farther north along the trail. They called back to Pearisburg, and when Bob and Susan still hadn't checked in, Frank Maguire called us in Aurora and insisted that we do some checking. When the Homestead had heard nothing either — and Susan was overdue at work — we knew something was amiss."

"Unbelievable," Neal muttered to nobody in particular. "We were just days apart on the trail. We were close enough at times that it was almost like reaching out and touching them."

"Let's hope we still can," Bud said.

A tingle traversed Neal's spine. The Appalachian Trail was adventure and tranquility. It was ridiculous to think a hiker in need could really come to harm or be in serious need and go unhelped.

"I've got to find Steve Davis and join the effort," Neal remembered suddenly.

"Davis and some of his volunteers have gone to check the country stores in the area," Bud said. "They're hopeful of finding a clerk or two who will remember seeing the kids pass through. Small chance, of course, but SuSu and Bob might have gone in somewhere for refreshments or supplies. Some of the Forest Service people have gone to search the area of the Wapiti shelters, wherever they are. You might want to join them if you know the location."

Neal knew vaguely, but he got his trail map out and studied it.

"Sandy and our trail companion are hiking on to Pearisburg — she's too lame to help much — but I'll stay as long as I can help."

"Thank you," Ginny said. "Maybe it'll all turn out to be a Keystone Cops kind of joke," she said lightly, but there was a quiver in her voice.

Neal moved off toward two of the rescue squadsmen who were hanging close to the vehicle radios. Double-checking his position with their help relative to the Wapiti shelter location, he strode off through the woods. There was no reason in the world why Bob Mountford and Susan Ramsay would still be in that area unless they had taken shelter from the rain in a cave, been snake-bitten and died quickly or were being held secretly against their will or some other unthinkable and far-fetched reason. Any thought that they might be long dead and buried was too absurd to consider, but Neal felt a wave of apprehension. Fear was always "out there" somewhere, but the heavy thudding of his trail boots told him instinctively that he came near to something — something of awesome proportions.

CHAPTER XXI

By midafternoon the base camp had been moved from Horse Camp to Walnut Flats. As the perimeter of search expanded, so did the rescue teams. Besides the Forest Service group, there were now five separate rescue squads, including the Virginia Polytechnic Institute squad from Blacksburg. Volunteer horseback-mounted searchers had reached the area, and so had members of the Virginia Search and Rescue Dog Association. Founder Alice Stanley, a robust woman, wise in woodland savvy, brought four mature dogs, each with a handler, and she herself had a pup-in-training under leash.

Various AT hikers also were coming upon the scene, and many of them joined the effort. Steve Davis and Boots Belcher had by then one solid clue relative to the missing pair. Earlier, they had interviewed Louise Trent, owner of Trent's Store and Mrs. Bernard at Bernard's Grocery in the neighborhood of Crandon, just nine miles farther southwest along the AT. Mrs. Bernard had been certain that both a boy and a girl meeting the description of the overdue pair had been in her store days earlier. She remembered the occasion in particular because the two had not been hiking together — the girl ahead of the boy by two hours — and the girl had left money for "Bob." Bob had come to the store, picked up his money, bought a few items, and left. Mrs. Bernard reported also that shortly thereafter two or three male hikers had come into the store, lounged about, had refreshments, and then followed Bob. Louise Trent had only vague recollections of a girl meeting the description.

The first woman's information was entirely believable. Both Steve and Boots were convinced now beyond any shadow of a doubt that Bob Mountford and Susan Ramsay, dead or alive, were lost or buried somewhere between the eastern Bland County line and Angel's Rest Mountain overlooking the town of Pearisburg. Even so, that was a twenty-five-mile stretch of some of the most rugged mountain terrain imaginable.

Many questions lingered in Davis's mind. Who were the three male hikers who had left Bernard's Store just behind Bob Mountford? Were they friends, foes, or just hikers passing through? And could they be found now or, if needed, in the future?

As the afternoon wore on, only negative reports came in to base camp from the various teams. Bud and Ginny were bone weary. From all indications the search could go on for days.

Still later, when the sky darkened and a drizzle began, they decided to head back to their motel in Blacksburg, wash the woodland dust from their bodies, and call Kelly and Richard with an update.

Once out of the woods and back on Route 606, Bud stopped to pick up a middle-aged AT hiker. The heavy backpack was arching the shoulders of the trail traveler, and little effort was required to convince him that a ride to the Pearisburg hostel was simpler than twenty-odd miles of rock-ribbed footpaths to the same destination.

Ginny spoke of SuSu and Bob and the effort being made to locate them and got in return those same assurances they had heard so often: that help for troubled hikers along the AT was just around the next corner.

Once in Pearisburg, they dropped the senior hiker at the crowded hostel and went to Father Winter's study to give him a progress report.

The priest listened patiently as weariness and dejection invaded the voices of his visitors. One of his parishioners had been listening in on the rescue channel via his own short-wave radio, Father Winter told them, and thus some of the hikers and church staff had glimpses of what was going on inside Jefferson National.

"I know that some of the hikers have joined the search, but others, learning something unusual was afoot, skirted the area and caught rides to the hostel here. Some of them are frightened — many feel that if foul play on the trail is proved or suspected, an evildoer may be still lurking out there somewhere in the bushes."

"Let's hope that possibility comes to naught," Ginny said.

"If the fear does become reality," Bud asked, "what can you do?"

"Call Appalachian Trail Conference Headquarters and have that section of the trail put off limits," Father Winter said.

Bud sensed in the priest's voice — that Father Winter had considered that such a course of action was already advisable. Bud wondered what, if anything, was being held back. He began to probe.

"I know nothing I haven't shared with you," Father Winter said, "but one thing still bothers me. For days now, various hikers have mentioned again what appears to be threatening notes along the trail, signed by the one who calls himself 'the ninety-five-pounder.' "

"Maybe the authorities ought to know about this." Ginny said.

"Except that it would seem to have no bearing on this area," Father Winter explained. "The notes have only been found much farther south, originating in northern Georgia or North Carolina, I believe."

"The guy could be working his way north. Maybe he's stopped leaving notes; maybe he's playing a cat-and-mouse game with somebody approaching this area. I agree it doesn't seem to fit here, though."

"As you saw, we're beginning to have a full house every night now," Father Winter said. "I'll continue to quiz each incoming group."

Little more than an hour and a half after the Ramsays had departed, the phone rang in Father Winter's study. His parishioner with the short-wave radio was calling: a mobile unit of the Giles County Rescue Squad had called in to headquarters for two body bags. The message had not been elaborated upon, the parishioner said, but the situation seemed self-explanatory.

Father Winter rang off, looked up the number of the Appalachian Trail Conference Headquarters in Harpers Ferry, West Virginia, and began to dial. He dreaded the next move; nor did he welcome the task of going out to the hostel and breaking the tragic news to the hikers. *That* duty would have to wait until the Ramsays knew, but he was surer than ever that AT headquarters had to act to warn all hikers that skirting the area of the tragedy might be wise. Before the mechanism stopped spinning, the priest noticed his hands had begun to shake. But was he premature? Indeed, had even a single body been discovered?

Back in a dense section of Jefferson National, Steve Davis, Boots Belcher, and their crews had drawn blanks all afternoon in their continuing search. The teams had each used a search dog and a handler, but for men and canines alike, it was a needle-in-a-haystack matter.

Just after 5:00 P.M. the Virginia Tech group, along with Forest Service Officer Bill Basset, had come up with something highly suspicious. The group had searched the area from Honey Springs to old Wapiti and back to the road intersection above new Wapiti II shelter. Regardless of how many searchers might have examined the area, Basset and his group looked with a more scrutinizing eye. A closer look revealed that the floorboards of Wapiti II had been scratched over with the ends of burnt campfire wood. The charcoal smudges had not done the job. Still visible were dark red stains underneath. Basset noted, too, that the shelter logbook was missing.

Notified of the finds by radio at base camp, Davis, Belcher, and others converged on the scene.

As Basset, dog, and handler continued their search, a hiker-volunteer encountered them — for a moment too shaken to speak. Basset looked at the man's pale face and knew that the frightened, youthful eyes had beheld something of horror.

"I found a sleeping bag covered with leaves," the hiker said haltingly. "A foot's sticking out. . ."

Basset walked with the youth to a spot some seventy-five yards southwest of the shelter and saw for himself. The sleeping bag had been placed between a large hickory tree and a rotting chestnut log. It had not even been laid in a shallow grave; only leaves and dirt had been piled upon it. Two small sticks lay upon the leaf pile, their southernmost points joined at the ends as if to indicate an arrow, a point of direction.

When Belcher and Davis arrived on the scene, they noticed quickly that no drag marks from the shelter to the place of body hiding were visible. As the leaves were carefully brushed away, both feet appeared. The feet and lower legs were covered with long blue knee socks perfectly in place. The body had, however, been stuffed head first into the ratty green-and-olive-drab-plaid-lined sleeping bag. Fully unzipped, the opened bag revealed that a plastic bag had been pulled over the head and down the body. Torn away, the trash bag exposed the full form of a young woman. Her tightened, decaying flesh had pulled her lips upward and downward from her teeth, leaving a grotesque smile on a once-pretty face. Above the socks to the waist was no clothing save for white panties that had a large puncture mark over the vagina. On the upper body a blue hooded sweatshirt was zipped to the top. The girl lay face up, her dark, reddish blond hair in pigtails, badly matted. Her wounded left hand was folded over her heart. The right hand was fully extended along her body. A thin gold chain encircled her neck.

Davis guessed the woman to be mid-to-late twenties, five-six to five-eight in height, and one sixty to seventy pounds.

For a person missing so short a time, he was surprised at the degree of body decay. But on second thought, Davis pointed out, she had not actually been buried—just covered with the plastic bag, sleeping bag, and a shallow scattering of dirt and leaves. Exposure to heat and air had done a quick job of early decomposition. Belcher agreed and added that recent rains and the resultant soaking had contributed to rapid deterioration.

Skin slippage was most noticeable in the hands; the face revealed the girl's earlier beating. Large bruise spots still stood out. Penetrating the sweatshirt over the left breast were a large elongated hole and two smaller ones. The holes were possibly stab wounds since large areas of blood clotting were visible.

Both the team leaders stepped back, and pondered. One never became accustomed to such a sight, no matter how long a veteran of search and rescue service. Searchers, converging from all directions now, came to a silent halt before the tragic scene. For moments no one moved. Each in his own way seemed to be giving tribute to a young life ended, to the tragedy of unlived years and happy moments she should have experienced and now never would.

The silent tribute lingered. Like so many in his profession, Steve Davis had read volumes on the subject of death — homicides, freak accidents, suicides, the whole lot — and yet a lifeless body was still a mystery to him. Once he read that a Swedish parapsychologist had theorized that after a violent murder, the gaseous form of the murderer — or his soul, spirit, or whatever — tarried for a while at the scene of his crime and that the properly endowed and receptive criminologist could see and feel the assailant's aura.

Davis could neither feel nor envision any evil presence or glowing aura, but he did for a moment experience a feeling of absolute peace. The earlier drizzle had seemed to add to the sweet essence of the towering pines, hemlocks, and hardwoods above and around them, and it was as if they all stood, mourners, heads lowered, within a majestic cathedral witnessing a service of solemn burial.

Belcher moved first and issued orders to seal off the area. Official photographs were taken from every angle and direction, and then Davis radioed in to Pearisburg for instructions. Would the county medical examiner prefer to view the body on the scene or might the rescue squad bring the corpse in for examination?

Awaiting official word, Davis and Belcher got the search teams busy again. No second body was discovered, but just in case, Davis radioed in for two body bags.

After an hour little more had been found. One of the dog handlers came up with a Bacardi rum bottle, an empty bottle and a full bottle of Coke, and a Pearisburg liquor store receipt, all inside a brown paper bag. It was small evidence, but it was a start.

Where was the other body? Was there another body? All of them were weary. Already it had been a twelve-hour day. Maybe they all were stumbling over vital signs, too lacking in alertness to see the obvious.

The word by radio finally came back: "Bring her in to the hospital."

Davis helped load the corpse and ordered the ambulance on its way. With the area cordoned off and the searchers fatigued almost beyond endurance, Belcher agreed that they should all call it quits and resume the following day. Darkness was approaching, the searchers were dispersing, but both Davis and Belcher stayed put. Perhaps the question struck them both at the same time, but it was the same question: If Mountford and Ramsay had been hiking together and if only Ramsay had been found murdered, where was Mountford? Could it be that he was the murderer? It was a possibility, and a strong one, that the authorities would have to deal with.

On the way back to Pearisburg, Davis wrestled with another question: his own opinion of AT hikers in general. Most of them, he knew, were clean college kids, or respectable business and professional people out for an adventure; but a few of them — and he had encountered both kinds — were what his fellow Giles Countians would call "the scrapings of the earth." Where in these categories did Mountford and Ramsey fit.

He prided himself on reading character and character types. He had met the Ramsays — nice, upper middle class — and he had already gotten the feeling that their SuSu was maybe the liberated woman type, headstrong perhaps, but solid and respectable. But what was Mountford's type? Was the hiker from Maine capable of murder, and if so, for what possible motive?

Doing a job like this and wondering afterward seemed to be the story of Davis's life. The authorities would have to take over from here. Still, he might render a contribution that would make their job easier, and a feeling of enthusiasm for the morrow surged through him. For now, the day had caught up with him. He would stop by the sheriff's office, file his report, and go home. He acknowledged his growling hunger and remembered that he had already missed Karen's usual good dinner. But tired or not, he had a story to tell his wife and the three pre-teenagers who shared his table.

Once Bud and Ginny were back at the Marriott in Blacksburg, hot showers, and a cold drink put new vitality into their tired bones. Just talking with their children had been uplifting. Kelly had sent the requested photos of SuSu special delivery, and Richard was ready to come and aid in the search if Bud thought it advisable.

As Ginny placed other calls, the motel operator broke in on the line: Frank Maguire had been trying to get through.

Connected with Frank, Bud thought the hiker's voice sounded a million miles away. Frank was hoarse; he had come off the trail in the rain, and he had hiked up the valley of Virginia as far as Buchanan. Bud gave his own routine and nearly factless report; then he listened to Frank's. The ex-police chief had only second-hand rumors. "I keep hearing stories from hikers coming up behind me that some flaky-acting character was seen in Jefferson National. Not a hiker, I gather. More like a local, I'd say. The guy's supposed to be wild looking, five-ten or—eleven, with long dark brown hair; supposedly he has no hiking gear and he 'acts queer' to quote my sources. Better call it in just in case." Bud promised to relay the information, and Frank prepared to ring off.

"Trailway rumors have a way of getting blown out of proportion, but you never know. I wouldn't be surprised if a weirdo did figure into this fiasco somewhere. Take care," Frank said.

At nine o'clock, Bud and Ginny went down to the motel dining room. Ginny thought the waitress's demeanor a little odd. The girl looked at them in a strange way and seemed overly solicitous. Possibly the motel staff did know who they were and why they were in Virginia. But was it more than that? Did they know something Bud and Ginny hadn't yet been told? The small town grapevine? Information passed quickly by CB radio, word-of-mouth, hushed telephone calls?

They tried to eat but couldn't. Something was not only in the wind, but the wind carried with it dark clouds and sinister shadows. The waitress appeared again. There was a phone call for Mr. Ramsay. Could he please come to the front desk?

The caller identified himself as Investigator Mike Meyer at the Giles County Sheriff's office. "We need you to come to Giles Memorial Hospital. We'll meet you there," the terse voice announced.

"Have you found our daughter?"

The pause seemed endless.

"We're not sure. We've found a body. A young woman's body. That's all we know at this point. Do you need directions?"

Bud couldn't answer the question. His vocal cords had tied themselves in knots, and his hand wouldn't let go of the receiver. He heard a gurgle come from deep in his throat; felt his legs go weak.

"Do you need directions, sir?" the voice insisted.

"I know where the hospital is. We saw it from the hilltop near the hikers' hostel. Was there a second body found?"

"No."

"They're still searching?"

"They've roped off the area for the night, but at daylight they'll go at it again. Mr. Ramsay, how well did you and your wife know Robert Mountford?"

Bud let the question — its implications — sink in and wind its way through the maze of contradictions that seemed to be flooding his brain.

"Not well. Not at all. We've never met him. Only knew of him through our daughter. She worked with him, but you know that . . . "

"On your way over," the investigator said, "recall as many facts as you can about him. We'll be talking with you more along these lines."

Bud laid the receiver down on the counter. The desk clerk returned it to its cradle.

"Is there anything I can do, sir?"

"No," Bud said. "Nothing anyone can do. Thank you."

He stood there an actor in a silent film. And the reel had stopped turning. His body shook a little, and he tried to tighten his flesh.

On his return Ginny would take one look at his face and know. She would see it even before then in his stride. There was moment of cowardice when he wanted to circle and come up behind her; but then he took a bee line, moving closer and closer with measured steps.

She saw him from afar and straightened her back. When she saw his face clearly, her hands shot up quickly to mask her own.

Having confirmed with the sheriff's office that the earlier radio interception did indeed mean that a corpse had been discovered, Father Winter was still puzzled that only a young woman's body had been found and that no further information would be forthcoming prior to positive identification. But Bud and Ginny Ramsay — if the body now at the local hospital morgue was Susan's — must be spared the agony of identifying their own child, the priest thought.

He went out to the hostel to break the news. A pall of silence fell over the group, and there was fear mixed with sadness in the eyes of many. He told them that he had already called Appalachian Trail Conference headquarters and had suggested that all hikers going north or south be appraised of the possibility of existing danger.

After he had thrice repeated everything he knew, Father Winter asked whether others in the group of newcomers had known either Susan Ramsay or Bob Mountford. Renate Lillifors, who had arrived back in Pearisburg earlier and kept a vigil at the hostel, had already taken her own poll. Only Neal Chivington, just in from the search himself and previously unknown to Renate, knew the missing pair.

"Only Neal and myself," Renate said.

"Then come with me," Father Winter said. "I think we can render a service."

Both Renate and Neal were pleased with the thought that their identification of the body — if it was Susan — might spare the Ramsays the ordeal. At the hospital their volunteer mission explained, Investigator Meyer, a short chunky man with blond hair and mustache, ushered them into the office of Dr. Kenneth Walker, staff doctor and county medical examiner. The investigator and the physician questioned Neal and Renate briefly and asked again whether both volunteers were sure they could go through with what would be an unpleasant task.

Neal went first. The thud of his hiking boots against the tiled masonry floor sounded to him like muffled thunder as he followed the tall, young physician down the corridor. He lost his breath as the long body drawer was pulled from its slot in the wall of the small cold room. For a moment he couldn't look, and then his eyes swept slowly up the length of the partially opened body bag. Only her head and shoulders were visible. As they all had, he fully expected the form to be the remains of Susan Ramsay, but, incredibly, he could not recognize one feature of the swollen, bruised face that he could positively identify. Only the long, pig-tailed, dark reddish-blond hair might have belonged to Susan.

Neal looked again, more bravely this time, until he had done a thorough and repetitious study, and still he wasn't sure. Incredible. The word kept intruding itself, but as many times as he had been with Susan and Bob, and had seen her jogging, skiing, crouching over her guitar, engaged in a host of activities, that which he had seen and observed before was not now before him. Many times at various parties and dinners — and once around the Ramsay family table in Ohio — he had looked close into the wine-brightened eyes of Susan Ramsay, but the opened, glassy orbs of the form now before him were inanimate and languid, suggestive of melting wax.

Renate took her turn, and neither could she be absolutely sure. Only days before she had walked along the trail with Bob and Susan, sat with them in camp, heard their funny stories, and told her own around the firelight, sung ribald and sentimental songs with them, broken bread, and shared dreams with them; even so, this thing in the metal box was some drunken potter's attempt at a life-sized clay doll, its features still in the rough and undetailed.

Renate wanted to turn away and leave the antiseptic-smelling room. Something about the place was suggestive of the death and destruction of war-torn Germany her parents and grandparents had often told her about and of the death scenes from Auschwitz, Buchenwald, and Treblinka she had learned about later as an adult.

The room was closing in on her, and she turned to leave. She paused to light a cigarette.

"Would you look at her clothing?" Dr. Walker asked. "Maybe that would help you . . ."

Renate shuddered as he unzipped the outer sweatshirt so that the

194

undershirt could be seen. She recognized it immediately. She had given Susan the blue T-shirt the dead girl wore. Renate had brought it from Michigan, and silk-screened across the chest area was "Cadillac, Michigan, 1980 . . . Labor Day 10K Run." It was unmistakable.

"Yes — yes — that vas the shirt I gave her. It's her. It's Susan Ramsay."

"You're sure?"

"Yes. Positive."

"Must have been damp or chilly on the night___"

He needn't finish. She could see for herself three holes in the shirt that looked like the punctures of a sharp hunting knife.

"But aside from the T-shirt, you're not positive the body is that of Susan Ramsay, are you?"

"I can't be absolutely sure, but I'm almost certain ___"

"We've got to be sure. I had hoped her parents wouldn't have to view the remains in this condition."

As she walked unsteadily back to the doctor's office, Renate had the uncomfortable feeling that she was letting somebody down. And if she and some of the others had stayed closer on the heels of Susan and Bob, maybe the safety of numbers would've helped. Still, people went their own way. And there was the romance thing. Everybody saw it deepening, but there would still be a lot of hikers who would feel a sense of responsibility for not helping prevent the tragedy.

Renate told Father Winter about the T-shirt. She was sure it was the remains of Susan that she saw. When she finally broke down, the priest held her comfortingly until her tears had subsided.

"It is so vild and crazy. Ve vere friends just a little vhile ago."

Dr. Walker turned to his work, and Investigator Meyer led them upstairs to the main waiting room so that he could watch for the arrival of the Ramsays.

Neal noticed that the stocky officer watched him and Renate with more than casual glimpses. Even as Neal made small talk to Renate or said something to Father Winter, the officer cocked an unusually interested ear.

Neal got up and moved to the entrance door and back. The strain of the day, the hard climbs in the woods during the search, the trauma of seeing the decaying body — all of it had begun to make him irritable and jumpy. And what animal would have beaten Susan Ramsay to a pulp anyway?

When Neal finally came back and sat down, Meyer said, "I'll want you and Miss Lillifors to come by the sheriff's office. We need to get a few things straight. Anybody else up there that knew Mountford and Ramsay or hiked with them?"

Father Winter assured him that there were none and that all of those save Renate who were with Bob's and Susan's group had hiked on.

The Investigator pumped the priest for all he could offer, listened patiently to the cleric's information and opinion and then he began to pace and twist his mustache.

When Bud and Ginny Ramsay came through the front door, Neal and Father Winter rose to meet them. The priest introduced them to Investigator Meyer and Renate.

"We had hoped to spare you this," Father Winter began, "but neither Neal nor Renate was absolutely positive after the viewing."

"Thank you," Ginny whispered.

Renate looked at the older woman's face. Her rosy cheeks were obviously tear-stained earlier and now not quite wiped dry. Spontaneously Renate sprang and embraced Ginny.

"I vas sure of the shirt, but I vasn't sure about the body. Maybe it vasn't your Susan," Renate whispered to the woman in her embrace. "Nobody vould hurt your Susan; she vas so nice."

"We're about out of hope." Bud's voice broke.

When Renate released her, Ginny stood rigid as if she had entered a strange house and knew she didn't belong there. Deep pain registered on her face, a cheek quivered for a moment, but she fought for control and gained it. She moved with quiet dignity across the expanse, and Father Winter guided her to a chair. Bud, indecisive, stood and walked in little circles. Investigator Meyer disappeared for a moment and returned.

"Would you come with me, please?" he asked Bud.

Ginny started to stand and follow.

"Just Mr. Ramsay, please. Dr. Walker told me, 'Just Mr. Ramsay,' " Meyer said.

The Ramsays' eyes met. Ginny still took measured steps toward her husband. Father Winter had her quickly by the arm.

"May I get you some coffee or hot tea? I'm sure the kitchen is still functioning, and one of the nurses ___"

"Thank you," Ginny said, and allowed the priest to seat her.

Meyer introduced Bud to the medical examiner. Kenneth Walker grasped Bud's hand unusually long. Bud looked equally long into the physician's compassionate blue eyes.

"No parent is ever prepared to do what you must do. Are you up to it?"

"I'm not sure," Bud said honestly. "Tell me it's a nightmare."

Dr. Walker made no reply and led the way.

En route, Bud tried to sort out the mixture of smells, the quick views through this doorway or that. It was a bad movie, the little scenes of drama disjointed and sad. The actors and the actresses returned his glances first blankly and then sorrowfully as if he walked a last mile to an execution chamber. Perhaps he did.

Once in the small room, two unrelated but spontaneous thoughts crossed his mind: first, how to summons the military courage he once possessed when he had worn a Marine Corps officer's uniform; and second, an almost-forgotten letter SuSu had written them after her return from Italy. In the letter, she expressed how good she felt about herself but had ended with some doubts. "How do you perceive Me? — and I'm not begging praise," she had written. For a horrifying moment he couldn't remember whether he had answered her, and now the question seemed to take on monumental proportions. On the one hand, this most precious child had always begged approval; on the other hand, she had fought tooth and nail for her independence and individuality.

The groaning, grinding sound of the body locker being withdrawn from the wall cubicle interrupted his reverie. Another oppressive silence began. He stiffened. Dr. Walker stood motionless to one side of the compartment, his eyes alone imploring. Bud inched forward and before he allowed his eyes to move upward toward the head, a flash of anger darted through him. He had expected her body to be wrapped in a clean sheet, the grime of her dried blood and woodland dust to have already been washed away. Impractical thought. Of course, she had to remain as found until the chief district medical examiner and the authorities had completed their work; even her clothing and crude wrapping were evidence.

He stepped closer. He wondered whether his breathing was as loud to Dr. Walker as the physician's was to him. Bud let his eyes begin again at where the rigid feet would be; and then, at the waist level, they balked on him. Only his peripheral vision had seen a pasty facial image in the distance. In one final burst of courage, he forced his eyes to confront those other eyes, staring, lifeless and discolored, at the ceiling.

His knees buckled, and he held onto the locker. Dr. Walker was quickly at his side.

"Are you all right?"

The doctor's supporting hand to Bud's elbow assisted him upward again.

"Are you all right?"

"Yes."

Now Bud could not keep his eyes from the bruised, grayish mass that had once been the pink, cherubic face of his favorite child. All revulsion fled. With the lightest touch, he laid a hand upon the unbruised cheek. He tried to stroke and felt the rubbery flesh giving way under his touch.

"Well done, Susypie—well done, Sweetheart," he whispered as the tears came.

He walked unsteadily to the other side of the locker, adjusting the position of her hair. He pulled the fragment of a leaf from a strand and discarded it.

"You have no doubt? You're sure?" Dr. Walker asked.

"Yes. Positive."

"Do you want to be alone with her?"

"No. It's all finished."

"You're a brave man."

"Yeah."

"I see no need of your wife's—I don't think it would be advisable."

"No. I agree."

"Death was evidently caused by multiple stab wounds and a fractured skull."

"Rape?"

"We're not sure yet. It'll take a lot of work. We get outside help on homicides."

Dr. Walker pushed the locker slowly home, but the clang of metal against metal still rang out with the authority of a closing bank vault.

The physician's guiding hand reached for Bud's arm, and they moved from the room and up the corridor.

"Now that the identification is not in doubt, we'll be sending her on to Roanoke to Dr. Oxley. He's the chief medical examiner for this district. Just to make it official, he'll be requesting dental records. Will you authorize her dentist to take care of this? In such cases the body is usually cremated after the autopsy is complete and the body released. I can give you a list of the funeral homes in Roanoke."

"Thank you. Can't bring myself to believe it's all happening, though."

"I know. I see too much of it myself. Don't understand what's happening in the world anymore. Crazy. Mad. Less and less regard for the sanctity of human life. What kind of fellow was her hiking companion—Mountford, wasn't it?"

"Yeah. We don't really know. We're beginning to wonder ourselves."

"I understand he hasn't been found dead or alive."

"Not from the last account we had."

They turned a corner and ascended the stairs to the waiting room. Ginny sat surrounded by the others, but when Bud and Dr. Walker approached, she rose to meet them. Bud gave one affirmative nod of his head and reached for her.

"Oh, Bud. Oh, Bud," she cried softly.

They clung tightly; the others moved to the far side of the deserted room. The hour was growing late—it was nearing midnight.

Dr. Walker and Father Winter chatted briefly, and then the physician went to the Ramsays.

"Would your wife like to have a sedative?"

"No. I'm all right," Ginny said.

"If you'll come to my office, there are a few things to get out of the way."

Investigator Meyer had matters of his own to attend to and asked Neal and Renate to accompany him to the sheriff's office. Neal wondered whether Sandy's presence would also be required. But she and Matt Savitz were still on the trail somewhere between Pearisburg and Trent's Store. After helping with the search for a time, he had caught a ride to the hostel—they would be until morning getting in.

Once seated in the sheriff's second-floor office, Neal found himself talking nonstop. Investigator Meyer and Deputy Tommy Lawson took turns during the grilling. Meyer was the shorter and the older of the two— early forties, Neal guessed—but Lawson seemed the more perceptive. The willowy Lawson paced as he probed. Myers was quieter; he sat calmly twisting at the ends of his blond mustache.

When Neal had finished the whole story of his relationship to young Bob Mountford and the plans they had made relative to the AT hike, he began to get the impression that he himself was suspect. It was wild, but he and Sandy hadn't been closer than fifty miles to Bob, or to Bob and Susan since hitting the AT in Georgia. Somehow he couldn't get that across.

The officers had a go at Renate. Up to a point Neal was allowed to listen in. Then he was asked to wait outside.

His watch said 1:10 A.M. Sunday morning. This incredibly bizarre matter was getting more bizarre by the hour. How in God's name could anyone suspect him? Bob and Susan were his friends!

Inside Renate squirmed in her chair. Neal caught occasional glances through the glass door. She knew a lot that he didn't—she had filled him in at the hostel and at the hospital, but surely the sheriff's department didn't think she had any part in the murder. The only thing Neal had noticed in his conversations with the girl was an evasiveness about her true feelings for Bob and Susan as individuals. There was some emotion there—some hint of conflict—just beneath the surface.

Neal was asked to come back inside. Renate was shaken. He could see that. They let her breathe easily for a moment and asked Neal for a more thorough character analysis of Bob Mountford. Was Mountford capable of an uncontrolled outburst of temper? Did he show anger quickly? Was he on drugs? Were drugs a routine part of trail life? When Neal said that he had seen little use of drugs on the trail, Meyer's perceptive blue eyes searched the speaker's own with a gleam of cynical doubt. But Neal told the truth. Mountford had never been anything more than an experimental, or casual, drug user, and Susan couldn't tolerate drugs. If the implication was that every trailside shelter was the scene of a drug and sex party and that Susan was a victim of such an orgy, then somebody was way off cue.

For a brief moment under more pointed questioning, Renate got testy.

"Are ve suspects? Do you think ve had anything to do vith it? This is an absurdity."

"Everybody on and off the trail that was in spittin' distance of Ramsay and Mountford is a suspect for the time being," Meyer said. "Includin' Bob Mountford himself."

As the grilling continued, Neal better understood the frustrations the authorities must feel. They were grasping at straws, but a beginning had to start somewhere.

"There vere veirdos several times along the trail. Vhy don't you ask some of them?"

"That's being implemented right now," Lawson countered. "We'll be pulling a lot of people off the trail. North and south. And while I'm thinking about it, don't either of you leave the area without notice."

It was after 2 A.M. when Neal and Renate were taken back to the hostel. Nobody had gone to sleep. The whole camp was alive with rumor, speculation, and a degree of fear. The same question kept being repeated among the hikers: what if the killer, or killers, were still hiding along the trail?

Renate sought Neal's exclusive company. Knowing she had been interrogated at the sheriff's office, some of the hikers were staring at her she said. Outside the circle of ongoing chatter, Neal and Renate compared notes again. Renate said the officers had shown an unusual interest in what she had told them about Frank Maguire.

At some ungodly hour, Neal finally fell back on his sleeping bag and felt relief creeping over him. The night was warm; the sky above him, clear. He watched the stars twinkle and tried to sort it all out. He thought he knew Bob Mountford like a brother, but was his friend capable of murder? And for what reason? You never really knew a person—never knew what major or minor thing could light the fatal fuse. If Susan was dead and Mountford on the run, what other conclusion could anyone draw?

He wanted to see Sandy's brother. Surely Steve could cast some light on the mystery. But Steve would be way up the valley of Virginia by now, and it would be no small task to find him and to bring him in off the trail.

Back in Blacksburg, Bud and Ginny had stopped and tarried at an all-night restaurant. At the motel the bedside phone would stare back at them suggestively. There was no hurry. Each of them had to come to terms with himself before another could be told and comforted.

Ginny sipped at her black coffee; still on her eyelids was the dew of innumerable floods that came up without warning. SuSu gone. Gone. Right up until she saw Bud's moist eyes as he returned from the morgue, she had held out hope that it was a big mistake. No, that was a delusion. She had known since the phone call during dinner. Maybe even before that. Mothers and daughters were on a very special wave-length. And amid the towering trees of Jefferson National, she had heard the murmurs of discord. The very breezes whispering through the trees had said: "Mother and daughter are no more —— no more —— no more."

Her eyes began to flood again. Bud reached for her hand. His other hand, still holding his own cup, trembled ever so slightly until the coffee spilled and he set the cup down.

"The reality of it comes at me in waves," she said.

"Me, too."

As quickly as she shed new tears, her eyes now brightened with inspiration.

"Bud—let's scatter her ashes at Au Gres. The cabin — there's no place she'd rather be than there. Bless her heart. She loved the Michigan woods as if they were a holy shrine."

"To her, they were."

The inevitable began to rush in on them again; the memories that already seemed dearer than ever before; the special times that could be magnified now out of all reality; the replay of infant wails, childhood blubberings, teenage tears of real or imagined devastation, and the silent tears of adult hurts and disappointments.

Afterwards, they went for a walk on the lush green of the Virginia Polytechnic Institute campus. Ginny carried her shoes—let the cool grass tickle her feet and the rising dew saturate her toes. There was renewal in the act—as if she were drawing strength from the soul of the earth itself.

The sun was not now far from rising. "Death is dawn": an obscure line from somewhere intruded itself.

They walked and walked. Past the War Memorial, by the shadowy height of Burruss Hall, over and around the lower quadrangle, and back to the high side of the campus nearest their motel.

Bud looked out across the vast complex and remembered. He had taken SuSu—bag and baggage—to Denison that first year, and she had been both scared and excited, and he had felt so helpless to assuage the one and curb the other. In the space of that single day, it had seemed that she changed personalities ten times. In the end when the time had come to leave her, it had appeared that she had not been sure of her own identity. On the one hand, she wanted to be rid of him; on the other hand, she didn't want him to depart. He had been willing to leave it so, but when he had turned to go, she'd sprung at him like a tiger. "I love you, Daddy," she said during the crushing embrace that totally ignored any skeptical eyes. "I'll make you proud of me!"

"The sun's getting ready to rise." Ginny broke his reverie.

He looked and saw the gilded rim begin to peep over the horizon. In minutes more the earth began to glow in a soft orange light, and the rising disk looked like the eyeball of a giant, cocked up over the realm of his domain, checking to see that all was well.

"We can't put it off much longer," he said.

Ginny looked at her watch. The hand had not yet reached six. Let them sleep a little longer, she thought.

Kelly would have to call their minister. Ginny herself preferred to call her sister and their parents in Scottsdale.

When they got back to the room, it was after six. Ginny dialed Kelly's number first, trying to begin the dreaded task and stumbled. Kelly caught on all too quickly before Ginny had finished a sentence. Ginny could hear—see—her daughter breaking down, and then the words gave way to mutual weeping.

Bud called his son, and so it was again.

After they made the other calls, they went down to the motel dining room. Both managed to drink a glass of juice and sip at coffee.

They had run out of conversation, reminiscences, and energy. Reality was coming in waves again. Bud remembered the tasks of the day.

"Would you rather stay here while I go to the sheriff's office? The funeral home in Roanoke?"

"No, I want to go with you. And then I want to go home."

After Bud paid the check and they entered the lobby, the newspaper deliveries were just being made. They watched as the newsboy propped various newspapers in the display rack. It was too soon, of course, for extensive story coverage about SuSu, but very soon the whole country would hear about murder on the Appalachian Trail.

CHAPTER XXII

Bob Mountford, Sr., and Sean Stitham left Interstate 81 at the Blacksburg, Virginia, exit. It was 9:50 A.M. Sunday, May 31. They had driven eleven hundred miles nonstop except for food and fuel. Though each had taken catnaps while the other drove, a kind of groggy weariness had settled on both of them. The airwaves had been strangely quiet about the missing hikers, and Bob had decided not to make frequent stops and call this person or that for the latest word. Getting to Pearisburg fast had been his priority.

Once in downtown Blacksburg, Bob asked directions to the police station. He went in to talk with the dispatcher and got routing directions to Pearisburg. He got more information he had dreaded hearing: Susan Ramsay's body had been found early the previous evening in Jefferson National Forest, and her father and friends had identified the body just before midnight. No, a second body had not been found. At the police station he dialed the Marriott, but the Ramsays had checked out.

Bob gave the report to Sean as they headed out of town toward Pearisburg. Sean rubbed the reddish/blond stubble on his chin and was thoughtful for a moment.

"Where does that leave us? Do we allow ourselves to believe that Bob's still alive somewhere?"

"Dear God, I hope so, but right now I know what the Ramsays are going through __ "

In Pearisburg they located the Holy Family Catholic Church with a minimum of difficulty. The hikers' hostel to the east of the church was obviously jam packed with an auxiliary tent city at the southern and eastern flanks. Morning mass was just over, and families filed routinely from the sanctuary-in-the-round.

When the bespectacled priest concluded his obligatory handshakes at the door and the crowd had dispersed, Bob and Sean approached the slender, robed cleric and introduced themselves.

"I'm Father Harry Winter, and I guess you've already heard __ "

"Yes, at the police station in Blacksburg," Bob said.

"I called your wife with a full report while you were en route. She wants you to call her, of course. Come on into my study, and I'll bring you up to date; then you can use my phone."

Bob and Sean listened to the terrifying details, but Bob found his mind rebelling at the thought of a knife being repeatedly raised and plunged into Susan Ramsay's young body. And what beast calling himself a human being would have finished the job by crushing her skull and beating her brutally without a shred of mercy? And which atrocity had come first? He would wager that the beating had come first; that Susan had put up a monumental and heroic struggle to defend her body, her life.

"The hikers are badly frightened," Father Winter said. "As you can see outside, they've all come to a grinding halt __ here. We've requested that this section of the trail have warning signs posted. At least we can avoid the chance of another tragedy."

"Are the search parties out again today?" Sean said.

"Yes, in force. Some of my parishioners picked up radio communications before Mass. Nothing new, though. We still don't know anything about your Bob."

Father Winter continued the briefing, adding that a variety of stories had come from the hikers about the sighting of strange-looking and suspiciously-acting people along the AT at one point or another and that separating fact from fantasy was impossible. Still, the priest said, he hadn't discounted any of the reports and had duly passed them on to the authorities.

"We have a hiker here—Dave Christoffersen from Oregon—who came through Jefferson National before Susan's body was found, and stayed overnight near where the corpse was buried. Throughout the whole night he said that he felt the overwhelming presence of evil and couldn't sleep. It was as if the spirit of the murderer hovered over the area, or something, and he still has an eerie feeling about it. A few of the hikers have suggested a service of exorcism at Wapiti II. In any event we've decided to take a group of hikers and have a memorial service at the shelter after lunch. Would you care to attend with us? I assume you'll be going to the search site anyway."

Bob and Sean accepted the invitation.

"Incidentally, John and Edna Schohn of our church want you to use their home as your base here. It's the least we can do."

Bob called home, and after giving his own report, found out from Mim that, having learned of Susan's murder, his sons had decided to fly to Virginia and join the search for Bobby. But their arrival might be delayed by hours since Steve would be coming from Orlando and Scott from Houston. Without prior reservations they would have to hop any plane by any routing to get to Virginia in a hurry. Even so, the knowledge that his remaining two sons would be at his side during the continuing search was a warming thought. But why had his brain selected the word "remaining"? Bobby was not dead. Wounded, hiding out from a killer or killers, maybe even kidnapped, but not dead. *Not dead.*

Back in Jefferson National, the woods were alive with activity. With the discovery of Susan Ramsay's body, the Virginia State Police had entered the case. Cecil Wyatt, of the Criminal Investigation Division at nearby Wytheville, had arrived on the scene early that morning, and so had the Police Mobile Lab Unit.

It was not long before the combined efforts of all searchers began to turn up a duke's mixture of findings. A number of dark red stains were found on tree trunks, bushes, and ground leaves. Somebody had put up a valiant but very bloody fight. In addition, an odd assembly of items started surfacing: a carton containing three full, and one partial box of .22 caliber cartridges; a roll of nylon cord; a roll of adhesive tape; and a packet of Protex condoms.

Oblate Father Jim MacGee, pastor of the neighboring Monroe County (West Virginia) parish, volunteered the use of his four-wheel-drive Scout. After lunchtime he, Father Winter, Bob Mountford, Sr., Sean, Neal Chivington, Sandy Skinner, Dave Christoffersen, and Gene Rischer loaded up and drove to Jefferson National, arriving about 2:30. Renate had gone to the search site earlier with personnel from the sheriff's department.

The heavily-laden Scout took the steep mountain roads effortlessly, but finding the access road to Wapiti II—in the midst of a whole network of log roads and cross trails—proved more difficult than originally supposed. The group finally found old Wapiti shelter.

Although Neal, Sandy, and Dave had earlier hiked in the general area, finding Wapiti II by vehicle roads was another matter. After a fruitless search, they all backtracked to old Wapiti shelter, tried new routes, and finally arrived at Wapiti II about 4:00.

Well away from the searching activities, under a particularly magnificient hemlock tree, Father Winter assembled the little flock of mourners.

"We all do fade as a leaf . . . ' " the priest began.

Bob listened attentively to the words from Isaiah, but during the service, his mind began to wander. He twisted his heel in the carpet of leaves and tried to fight the increasingly hollow feeling that Bobby was indeed out *there* somewhere, having already become a part of the firmament.

Father Winter ended the service with prayer—a prayer for the dead, for the living, and for those who would be tempted to hate in the aftermath of the tragedy.

The prayer, and especially the last part of it, struck a resounding note in Bob's heart. He had long ago—since that unforgettable day in his own bedroom—overcome the need or desire to hate. Even now, he did not hate Susan Ramsay's killer or killers. And if his Bobby lay dead upon or under the forest's carpet, there would be no hatred, no grudge—only infinite sadness. Then and there he prayed his own silent prayer that Bobby by some Divine Providence might have been spared and that Susan's killer had already begun his own prayers of reconciliation with the Maker and lover of all mankind.

The service was scarcely over when Bob became aware that some of the officers and rescue squad leaders were mildly resentful of the church group. No one said anything, but Bob could see it later in their eyes and manner. It was not that the memorial service was inappropriate, but Bob guessed that the searchers felt it an impediment to the investigation.

Save for the church group, no one knew who he was, Bob realized. Not that it mattered. He was content to let the professionals do their jobs. He, Sean, and the church group moved off a ways to a small clearing, while Father Winter approached an officer to make inquiries and offer the group's help if needed.

The Virginia Search and Rescue Dog Association team had also returned to the search. Alice Stanley had the utmost faith in her canines, but every search and rescue mission had its own set of obstacles. A body or bodies sealed in air-proof containers, or buried, posed special problems. Dogs had to get close enough to smell.

With Bambi, the same pup-in-training she had under leash the previous day, she kept up her own searching. Just before 2:30 she had circled to a point west/southwest of Wapiti II shelter. She started in toward the shelter, giving her dog his head. Before reaching the shelter, she decided that it was foolish to search over ground that obviously had been gone over a dozen times by as many groups. She had already turned to change directions, but Bambi was not ready to turn with her. His interest, and the point of his nose, centered on a small clump of mountain laurel bushes. Again she gave the animal his head, and he came to a halt beside a large fallen tree adjacent to the bushes. An abrupt stop, a quick freeze, and a lifted nose told Alice that Bambi was "on alert." Alice peered at the spot, saw that the earth had been disturbed, or at least looked unlike some of the earth at the fringes of the area. She felt the soil. It was soft. Too soft. Something had to be underneath. She watched Bambi. The young dog's nose was still locked in the alert position.

"Good, Bambi, good," Alice cooed.

She felt her own heart race as it always did on such occasions. Bambi's mother Danka had completed thirty-five missions before her death from gastric torsion. Perhaps Bambi would live to beat her record.

Alice called in, and Investigator Mike Meyer was the first at her side. Meyer scraped the top layer of the area away and dug down until his hand came in contact with fabric. Lifting gently he caught a glimpse of red. Tugging, he saw that the red material was a section of sleeping bag. After a few exploratory probes with his hand, it was evident that the bag was filled. Something mildly pulpy responded to his grasps.

State Police Investigator Cecil Wyatt with his Criminal Investigation team, Bland Rescue Squad members, and Deputy Sheriff Melvin Cox, Steve Davis with his Rescue Squad members, and Boots Belcher, Jim Lagniel, and George Martin of the Forest Service converged on the scene.

It was easy digging. In minutes, the full length of the dark red sleeping bag was exposed.

There was a tear in the material, but the bag was zipped up fully, and the drawstring pulled tight and tied in a neat bow. Officer Wyatt untied the drawstring, unzipped the bag, and exposed the head area. A plastic garbage bag of the same type that had covered Susan Ramsay's head was visible; but this time the bag had been tied tightly with nylon cord around the victim's throat. As the bag was cut away, a more gruesome sight awaited the onlookers. The murderer had tied more of the same cord around the victim's bloodied, bearded chin, drawing his mouth wide open. The bloated, purplish-black tongue protruded from the cavernous opening in one final gasp for life. Well below the left eye was a small hole resembling a gunshot wound. The head was too bloodied for anyone to see other bullet wounds if there were more.

The body was clad in a green T-shirt and khaki trousers; the feet were without shoes or socks. The victim's hands and arms were folded in an upward "X" over his chest. One more feature was particularly outstanding: the victim had a small gold earring in his left ear. And although the grave was a shallow one, the good covering of cool dirt had preserved the body well.

"Don't guess there's much doubt about who he is," Wyatt said. "And he sure fits the description."

"The German girl—Lillifors—is up ahead. I'll go get her. She knew him," Meyer said. "And if that group from the church is still around, two or three of them knew Mountford, too."

Steve Davis volunteered to go inquire.

The church group still kept its vigil. Davis approached them: "Will those of you who knew Mountford personally please come with me?"

For a moment nobody responded or stepped forward. The question was also an answer.

Bob saw respectful glances on either side fall upon him. He heard the squadsman's question, but every fiber of his being rejected it. A deep moan escaped his throat and his knees gave way. Father MacGee caught him.

"We need someone's help if any of you would volunteer," Davis repeated.

"I knew him. Worked with him," Neal said. "And we planned the hike together."

"We've been friends since boyhood," Sean said.

Bob stepped out from the group, but then he returned to Sean's side and embraced the young physician-to-be.

"I can't go. I don't want to see Bobby like this. You've been a friend of our family since you and Bobby were boys. Will you do this for me?" he whispered.

Sean stepped forth. "I'll go with you."

Neal followed.

Renate already stood beside the grave, her head lowered, her cheeks wet.

Sean approached the crude opening in the earth.

At the grave site, the onlookers kept silence, but some of them lit cigarettes to assuage their disquiet. The various men—and Allison Stanley—stood so still that, save for the uniformed men, their bodies seemed to blend with the tree trunks. With Sean's nearer approach to the scene, the young dog evidently caught the whiff of a new smell and let out a low whine.

As a medical student, he had seen his share of blood, performed countless autopsies on now faceless cadavers, but all of his background had not prepared him for this gruesome view of his lifelong friend. His breath left him momentarily, but his vision was locked upon the eyes that now looked dully heavenward through the overhanging tree limbs. He searched the bloodied, contorted face in every detail before his focus dropped to the left ear lobe. The small gold earring. He had pierced that beloved ear—put the jewelry in place. His and Bob's anti-macho statement. Bob's special badge for the hike on the Appalachian Trail. There was no doubt.

"It's Bob," Sean said and let his vision sweep from Wyatt to Meyer to Belcher.

Neal came forward. He, too, recognized the moppish hair and bearded face of Bob Mountford in spite of the mask of dried blood and twisted features.

"Yes, it's him," Neal said softly to nobody in particular.

Sean talked briefly with Cecil Wyatt, and as Sean, Renate, and Neal moved away, a police photographer moved in. Then a rescue squadsman brought a body bag to the grave.

Among the remaining church group the waiting had become unbearable. Bob Mountford drifted away among the trees. What he was feeling was a contradiction in terms. He must walk—had to walk—and sort it all out. How was it possible amid this forest wonderland with its sweet essences and pure air that the specter of violent death and serene nature co-existed? The stately trees, their graceful boughs lifted now and then in the slight breeze, spoke only of tranquility and God's grace.

He wanted to run. And run. And run. But there was no energy in him. His rubbery legs balked, and he sat down on the fluted edge of a limestone boulder. He peeled a small slab of moss away from the great stone and held it in his hand, stroking it like a kitten. Green. Life. Not death.

His eyes welled over. The spongy mass caught the drippings, absorbed them. Again, he got up and started to walk ____ just had to be in motion. For a moment he walked in the direction Sean and the others had gone, but then he turned back. He wanted to go to the grave or wherever they had Bobby, but he couldn't. He had last seen his son jubilant and eagerly preparing to begin the long hike—the foremost dream of his young life, and the father had dreamed the dream with him, longed to see the radiant face of the son when the latter had come down off Mount Katahdin happy and victorious. To see his decaying body in a makeshift grave now was a mockery.

Even so, the urge to go struck him again, and he reversed direction. Yes, he would go and lift the body from the womb of the soft earth and cradle it in his arms and it wouldn't matter. They would have their reunion after all, and the grief would pass and he would tell Mim how sweet the final parting had been that day when he had found the Hunter of Dreams fallen in his beloved woods.

Along the way he met Sean, Renate, and Neal. He saw in their faces what they each had seen.

"I'm going to him," Bob said.

"Mr. Mountford, do you *really* want to go?" Sean asked softly.

Bob searched Sean's eyes. Bobby's friend—their friend—had always had a certain depth, a strong presence that was both youthful and mature. Sean was really saying, "Don't go—please."

Bob reached for the younger man, letting his own tears spill unashamedly on the younger's neck.

"Maybe it's best I don't go . . . better I remember him like he was—so full of life, and fun, and . . . always on the go. Not like this ___ "

"Bob would like to be remembered like that," Sean said.

"How did he die? I need to know that."

"There's a bullet wound in the left side of his face. Perhaps other bullet wounds in the head also," Sean said.

"Then it was quick."

"Yes," Sean said.

"Since he had no shoes or socks on, it must have been while he slept," Neal added comfortingly.

They all stood there mixing speculation with old memories, and Bob felt better until new waves of grief swept in on him again with new intensity.

"Ve need to go tell the others," Renate said to break the tension.

"Yes, you're right," Bob said. "You've all been too kind."

After Bob told the others, Father Winter suggested that they all go back to the hostel and break the news to the waiting hikers.

But nobody could move. It was as if the magnetic pull of the earth held, compelled them to ponder more deeply what had transpired. All eyes had spilled over, and one by one, hands found hands until a tight circle formed. Father MacGee and Father Winter again offered prayers.

Bob was not yet ready to leave their woodland sactuary. Somehow, he was deserting his son.

"What will they do now?" Bob asked Sean.

"I talked with the ranking policeman. The body will be taken to the local hospital as Susan's was. They'll send it on to Dr. Oxley in Roanoke. He's the District Medical Examiner, I believe. If you change your mind about wanting to see Bobby . . . maybe while he's at the local hospital. Or in Roanoke ___ "

"No. It's all over. It's done," Bob said. "He'll have to be cremated, of course. We'll have to stop in Roanoke on the way home and make arrangements to have his ashes shipped. Dread calling Mim ___ "

Officers Meyer, Wyatt, and Belcher came by as the church group began to split up. Each offered a firm hand of condolence.

"We hate to burden you further, Mr. Mountford," Wyatt said, "but we'll need to talk with you about a number of things when you feel up to it. Officer Meyer will set up the appointment at his office, and some of our people will meet with you, too."

"The sooner the better," Bob said. "I want to get all this over with and get home."

Each of the officers in turn tried to assuage Bob's hurt, give assurances that no stone would be left unturned in finding the killer or killers, and that if his present state of mind would allow it, he—Bob—should be thinking about anything, however remote, that would shed any light on the case.

Small chance he could help them at all, Bob thought. So far as he knew, Bobby hadn't a real enemy in the world. If he'd ever seriously angered anybody, it could only have been in the execution of a practical joke, for which Bobby was famous. But maybe Bobby *had* invited the wrath of some of the parents or guardians of his court wards at the Homestead. No, that was too much of a long shot. There could be no connection between Bobby's psychiatric social work and his murder on the Appalachian Trail.

"Could I meet you all first thing in the morning?" Bob asked. "My two sons are flying in to Roanoke some time this evening—or tonight—so I can't plan anything for now."

A morning hour was agreed to, and Bob joined the church group as they headed for the Scout. The loaded Scout moved slowly out of the dense woods and along the narrow dirt roads until at last they reached a wider, graveled road. They passed Dismal Falls, and after Father Winter had identified the natural wonder, Bob looked back. Except for the white birches which were missing here, the picturesque scene was beautiful and much like the landscapes of Maine. How often across the earlier years he and Mim had stood before such a scene with Carolyn, Bobby, Cathy, Scott, and Steve—their children—in tow. All of them were growing in love with nature in every experience, and their young minds were fascinated by the bee on the blossom. Those days had been the real beginning of Bobby's love of the great outdoors and of his determination to hike the Appalachian Trail.

Bob let his head fall back on the seat headrest and his eyelids close. The memories were so dear. So sweet.

"Both you and Sean need a break," Father Winter suggested to Bob. "After we meet with the hikers, you must go to the Schohns' home and rest."

"There'll be no argument from me," Sean said, but Bob made no answer. His mind had formed and held onto the image of a cross-eyed boy, his front teeth missing, with the most mischievous of grins on his fat little face.

Although the second body had been found—May 31, the day after Susan's—and sent on its way to Giles Memorial, the search for evidence was still on. Heretofore, the concentration had been on finding people. Now the focus was different. Every leaf and rock would have to be overturned in the search for the smallest clue regarding the murders. The authorities had roped off the area around Susan Ramsay's death site to prevent unwanted visitors, late volunteers, and sightseers who might muddy the water. Now the same was done around the Bob Mountford grave site. Ramsay's body had been found 225 feet southwest of the Wapiti II log shelter; Mountford's nearly 500 feet west/southwest. Now, at last, the area to be gone over with a fine-tooth comb had narrowed to manageable proportions.

With Mountford accounted for, it was a whole new ball game anyway. As far as Steve Davis was concerned, the search for evidence was already taking on some strange twists. When 5:00 P.M. had rolled around, a number of items had been found, but few of them made any sense. An old padlock, an 8-inch Crescent wrench, a roll of plastic tape, an 8-inch mill file, a pair of pliers—these were items that any of the numerous visitors over the months might have left. Where was the critical stuff? Susan's expensive Pentax camera, which her parents had assured Mike Meyer was in her backpack? If that camera still had film in it and could be found, it might prove the first big break in the case.

And what of Mountford's diary, which Renate had seen him keeping faithfully? That might reveal important names and make references to incidents along the trail. And where was the Wapiti II log book? Who had been the last to sign in?

At 6:30, Mike Meyer pulled a roll of slick paper from a hollow log.

"Look at this," he called to workers nearby. He fully unrolled the glossy magazine pages and a choice dozen centerfold nudes stared back at him.

"Looks like somebody subscribes to *Hustler* and *Playboy*," a squadsman chortled.

Steve Davis came over, too, and he saw something the others hadn't seen. On top of the log from which the paper roll had been extracted were two thin sticks, their ends joined to form an arrow, pointing southwest. A point of direction? He remembered the same pattern on Susan Ramsay's makeshift grave. Quickly, he went back to the girl's gravesite, took a sighting to the log where the magazine nudes had been found. His compass said 243 degrees southwest. Dead in his sights beyond the log was a rotten tree stump. He hurried to the place and found on top of the stump two more sticks—their points joined. Like a hungry dog after a ham bone, he started digging. He soon came out with a hiker's canteen. He still kept on course to a suspicious-looking pile of leaves and sticks. Once removed, the covering revealed a Texas catheter. A Texas catheter? Davis scratched his head. What was a hospital item like that doing in Jefferson National?

"Meyer, you and Wyatt come over here."

He held up the rubbery object but it occupied his interest only briefly.

What held his attention was his compass. Everything he was finding seemed to be on a 243-degree heading.

When the officers got nearer, Davis queried, "Who would be most likely to play games with a compass? You know—an Easter-egg-hunt kind of thing?"

One of the men called back, "Somebody with a military background, probably. Why?"

Davis revealed the odd set of circumstances he had discovered.

Later, on the same heading, Davis and others found more items, but not the big bonuses they all waited for. Even so, somebody was playing games with them, showing them the way. The compass heading proved it so.

Again, it had been a long day, but there was not a man present who didn't look forward to the day to come. There was still a lot of woodlands left in which to glean, but somewhere in this stump or that, under a rock, or in the hollow of the hundreds of fallen and standing trees, the true diamonds in the mine were waiting to be found.

Bob had managed only a short, fitful nap after he and Sean had gone to the home of their hosts. After his call to Mim, he had been unable to settle down. She had taken the news bravely; but was it news anyway, or just a foregone conclusion after the knowledge of Susan's death? There had been no uncontrolled weeping on the part of either of them. They both believed without reservation that earthy death — even premature death was really the beginning of life.

He had just started to doze off again about 7:00 when John Schohn came in to advise that Father Winter was calling. The son from Orlando had just called from the Roanoke Airport and needed to be picked up. Should somebody from the church meet him? Bob said that Sean had already planned to do so.

Bob shook Sean awake.

"Ready to do taxi service?"

Sean rubbed his leadened lids. "Both of them?"

"Just Steve. No word on Scott. Bad routing from Houston, probably. Check while you're there and see if anything's incoming shortly that Scott might have connected with. It might save you an hour's trip back. I'll call and have you paged if I get any word after you've gone."

Still later—400 miles away to the south—Scott Mountford's plane was approaching Charleston, South Carolina. He had had incredibly bad luck. One standby after another in Houston had proved fruitless until at last the flight to Charleston had opened up.

On the ground once more, a dash to the various ticket counters set the pattern in motion again. And only Piedmont Airlines served Woodrum Field at Roanoke, Virginia. And it would be tomorrow, the ticket clerk said, before a possible cancellation. He considered the bus lines, but a stretch of twelve or fourteen hours up and down the mountain roads of North Carolina and Virginia was not welcomed —— not welcomed unless, for some reason unknown to him, he was desperately needed in Virginia.

What was the situation? Had Bobby been found? He must get to the phone and call the number his mother had given him. Bag in hand, he darted to a pay station, readied his coins, and dialed person-to-person. Father Winter answered and referred the operator to another number. Another male voice, and then his father was on the line. He started talking before the operator cut him, asking for the toll.

"Dad?"

"Yes, Scotty. I'm back on."

"Have you found Bobby?"

"Where are you, Son?"

"Charleston, South Carolina."

"Steve's here now. Sean Stitham picked him up in Roanoke."

"Did you find Bobby? Is he all right?"

The silence was momentarily deafening.

"Come on; you're holding out on me. Tell me!"

"The news isn't good, Son."

"Oh, God! Is he alive? Is he still breathing?"

"We found his body this afternoon. He'd been shot—"

"Whatdoya mean, shot! Bobby could take any two men with one hand tied! Whatdoya mean shot?"

"He was shot in the head, Son. Some of the people think he was murdered while he slept."

"Oh, God __ oh, God __ oh God! I want my hands around the neck of the guy that did it. I want to watch his eyes pop out while I squeeze him and squeeze him! The bastard. The inhuman bastard!"

The phone went silent again, but Scott could hear the seeming feedback of his own breathing and feel the rising, the receding tide of his anger. People at other pay stations to each side were watching him strangely.

"You mustn't feel like that, Scotty. The Lord loves us all __ even the person or persons who killed your brother."

"Don't talk to me like that! You ought to have a ball bat in one hand and a pistol in the other, going through the woods looking for that guy! I'm coming in tomorrow. I'll find out something. I'll do it for Bobby."

"There's no point now in your coming here. Get a good night's rest. Sleep late. We've got some rough days ahead. Just catch a plane to Maine as soon as you can."

Scott listened to his father's voice still longer, only vaguely aware that his own cheeks shone with wetness.

Finally both ran out of words, starting to repeat themselves. Scott hung up and went out into the night to search for a motel.

Once in his room, he called their apartment in Houston. He and Gail had decided to formalize their relationship in July, and the wedding was set for the fourteenth.

Gail listened to his sad story and soothed him as best she could when he began to break. It seemed such a short time ago that all the family had met in Houston for the big Thanksgiving/Christmas reunion, and Bobby and Jackie Hilton had stayed at their apartment. And then they had all gone as a family unit to The Church of the Redeemer. That day was still talked about—it was a milestone in all their lives.

Scott made calls to Dover-Foxcroft and to Orlando. Everybody tried bravely to comfort one another.

Scott plopped his rugged five-nine body on the bed. Normally, he was a big sports fan with an athletic record at Dover-Foxcroft Academy to equal Bobby's. But he left the TV sports channel black, just wanting to lie back and think. God, what a waste! Bobby was only two years older than he. Scott was grateful for his own blue-collar oil company job, but Bobby, the college man, was destined for greater things than Scott dared dream about. Bobby, the brain. The great outdoorsman. The sports enthusiast, friend, brother in all senses and master of comradeship. The thoughts themselves began to lull Scott to sleep and to be the source of peace his turbulent mind begged for.

Before dawn, a nightmare brought him out of a shallow slumber. In the dream Bobby was being dragged at the end of a rope over jagged rocks by a black-hooded horseman. Bobby was crying out, but nobody would help him.

"I'm coming, Bobby! I'm coming!" Scott's voice reverberated about the room before full wakefulness came.

He got up and took a single swallow of the stale beer on the bedside table. His watch said 4:08 A.M. He flipped on the TV. When the tube brightened, a running cavalryman was just feeling the sting of an Indian's arrow. Dear God—the suggestions were everywhere! He turned off the set and reached for pen and paper. Sprawled across the bed, he ran his hand repeatedly through his thick blond hair and struggled with the beginning. He decided to print a heading for his proclamation.

BOBBY—My Great Big Brother
Lying here in my lonely closed-in four walls, I don't know what to think. I'm totally confused. I think of the past, but not too much. I think of the future, but not too much. I love you, Bobby. I love you.

I know, Bobby, you've had a good life because I have, too, and I'm a MOUNTFORD. I do know this, Bobby: I do promise you TWO things as I'm lying here. I promise to find out WHO DID THIS as I know you would if the shoe were on the other foot. And second, our baby will be named either Robert Tatton Mountford III, or Roberta, AFTER MY BIG BROTHER.
Bobby, I lie here thinking of shit you've done, but you know what really hurts is that I TOLD you I was going to make part of your walk with you and I DID NOT. We were supposed to keep in touch more. REMEMBER, Bobby, I will hold you

closer to my heart than anyone. All we have is memories, and I hope one day soon you will get back in touch with me. Please, Bobby. I will not be frightened by you in whatever form you come back, but, please for me, let me know more than I understand now. Please. I know God helps those who help themselves, but Bobby, He also says AN EYE FOR AN EYE, AND A TOOTH FOR A TOOTH.

I know it's late for writing, but I'm sorry, Bobby, I'm so truly sorry.

Your loving brother,
Scott Michael

Scott read and re-read his own epistle and felt a great sense of peace. He laid the paper aside and covered himself with the blanket. If he could only sleep now, for a day. A week. A year ___

At 9:00 A.M., Bob, Steve, and Sean kept the appointment at the Giles County Sheriff's office. Investigator Mike Meyer, Deputy Tommy Lawson, and State Police Investigator John Ratliff took turns in the questioning. It had already been determined from interviews with the Ramsays, Officer Lawson stated, that the green sleeping bag in which Susan Ramsay had been found was not her own. Was the dark red sleeping bag Bob Mountford's?

"Yes," Bob said. "He left home with a dark red bag."

"Camera? Personal diary or log book?"

"Yes—both," Bob said, and elaborated.

"Any other personal items aside from the normal camping gear that would be unique to your son?"

"Yes. A Bible we'd given him. I'd like to have that back if you find it."

The questioning began to get more personal. Did Bobby use drugs? Was he a heavy drinker? Did he have known enemies? If so, were any of them known to have been on the trail in front of or behind him? What was his temperament? What was the true relationship between Bob and Susan? Were love triangles involved on the part of either party?

On the last two points, Bob confessed he wasn't sure on point one, and on point two, his son *was* engaged to another girl and previously he had been engaged to still another. As to Susan Ramsay's love life, he had only smatterings of information.

The probing seemed endless; yet every question had intriguing logic and might somehow fit in.

"Hope we can find those cameras," Meyer said. "We may just have a photo of the murderer—or murderers—in natural color."

"Small chance," Steve Mountford said cynically. "Odds are that the dude that killed my brother hocked them in some pawn shop."

"That's possible," Deputy Lawson agreed, "but we'll be checking that angle, too."

The lanky deputy ran out of questions for the moment, and John Ratliff, the state police office, focused penetrating grey-eyes-behind- glasses on Bob. The officer was middleaged and large of statue, and his dark hair had receded noticeably.

"We've got our work cut out for us in lots of ways," Investigator Ratliff began. "We've already started pulling hikers off the trail at every forestry station for miles around, not to mention a number of them here at the local hostel we want to talk with again. This one's got the makings of a tough case—real tough."

"As decomposed as I understand Susan Ramsay's body was, you're going to have a difficult time proving the girl was raped if indeed she was," Sean said.

The perceptiveness of the opinion took Ratliff off guard, but he smiled in appreciation.

"We've already thought of that obstacle," he agreed, "and it's only one of many. Try this one on for size: What could possibly be the motive of a killer or killers who from all evidence decided to do away with total strangers? Any logic in that?"

The brief exchange inspired a new round of questions, opinions, speculations.

"One more thing," Ratliff asked. "What do you know about this alleged ex-police chief we've been hearing so much about? Maguire—Frank Maguire, I believe his name is."

"Nothing other than what Bobby told us in his letters and phone calls. Bobby liked the guy. He hiked with him off and on since Georgia or North Carolina. He's sure been helpful—to us and the Ramsays," Bob said.

"Possibly too helpful," one of the other officers half mumbled. "And we have only his word that he's an ex-police chief."

Before they all parted, Bob left his Maine phone number and got from Meyer a reminder to send Bobby's dental records directly to Dr. Oxley.

Leaving town, they stopped by the hostel. Tent city had thinned considerably. Many of the hikers who had not been asked to wait over by the authorities had moved on, though under a cloud of sadness and apprehension. Nearly all of them, Father Winter said, had decided to follow the highways until they were well out of the area.

Bob took the opportunity to say goodbye to Neal and Renate.

"Neal and I have decided to continue the hike in your Bobby's name," Renate said. "Ve vill go the whole vay as a memorial to him."

Bob embraced her.

"Bless you. It's a fine gesture. Stop in to see us when you come down Mount Katahdin. We're only a short distance from the trail's end."

"Maybe I vill leave the trail long enough to come to the funeral. I vill call."

Bob shook Neal's hand.

"Thanks for everything you've done. Will you and Sandy be coming to the funeral?"

"Haven't made up my mind," Neal said. "Completing the walk for Bob comes first. But I'm sending Sandy on home by bus. Her feet and legs have about given out. She'll only slow me down."

At last Bob embraced Father Winter in parting.

"We Episcopals and you Catholics already have a special kinship," Bob said, "but you have bridged any faint crack that ever existed between us. I won't soon forget you."

"Nor I you. 'All things work together . . . ' "

"Yes," Bob said. "Yes."

When they were back on northbound Interstate 81, Bob heaved a sigh of relief.

"One more stop at the funeral home in Roanoke, and we'll be ready for the long drive," he said.

"You're not riding," Sean said. "I made reservations for you and Steve to fly home, and Mim will pick you up at Bangor. And you'll have lunch on the plane. We're running out of time."

When Bob and Steve landed in Boston, an unexpected surprise awaited them. It hadn't been planned that way, but as the passengers for Bangor began to assemble in the preflight waiting room, who was to appear but the other three of his children. First through the door was sometimes-fashion-model Carolyn—his first-born—dark, brown-eyed, and beautiful like Mim; then Scott Michael, rugged and blue-eyed, looking worn-out and angry; and finally, Cathy, as pert and bouncy as she'd been as a teenager. Bob gathered Steve—as handsome as his brother Scott and nearly like a twin to him—and the others in a small circle and embraced them all. All of their eyes glistened as they released one another, but now they were all going home, all save one.

As if to remind him it wasn't a dream after all, the little entourage brushed by a young executive whose briefcase-on-knees supported a Boston paper. A headline read: "Two Maine Hikers Murdered on the Appalachian Trail in Virginia."

At the airport in Bangor, the reporters and a TV crew were waiting. Momentarily defensive, Bob gathered his clan to him. Respectfully, the reporters held their cameras in check as they had in Pearisburg and Jefferson National, but their barrage of questions echoed their personal anger and dismay at the loss of two young lives.

"Do you favor the death penalty," a young reporter asked, "if the killer is found and convicted?"

"I have no desire for revenge. No hatred. Only pity for the sick soul who did this horrible thing," Bob said.

A murmur traversed the media group.

"Surely you want justice," another reporter ventured. "To millions of people, and certainly those in Maine, the Appalachian Trail is holy ground. How do we put an end to this defilement before another such tragedy happens?"

"How do we stop the evil of mankind's hatred and violence against each other everywhere?" Bob said. "Will it not be through love rather than retribution?"

They pressed him more, and he spoke briefly, adding details that filled in the gaps of the hastily-prepared news flashes and newspaper stories.

They asked permission to take pictures then, and Bob gathered his family to him and granted the request.

"I have one more thing to say," Bob added. "In your stories tell not so much *who* he was, but *what* he did. He loved people—especially people who had little chance in life—and *to* them he was dedicated, and *for* them, in part at least, he was walking the historic trail that we all revere so much. Bobby will soon be coming home now, and we'll scatter his ashes upon this land of Maine that he loved so much. Thank you for your concern."

CHAPTER XXIII

Outside the main entrance door to the Kroger Supermarket in Pearisburg, the newspaper vending machines were well patronized and emptying fast. The local *Virginian-Leader* had devoted a whole page to the murders, heading one three-column spread *"Double Murders on the AT Probed";* another three-column segment, *"Dead Hikers Were Talented and Caring People";* still another three-column story on the current fears and mixed emotions of the trail hikers in general. Days before—when Susan Ramsay's body had been found—the favorite daily of the area, the *Roanoke Times and World News,* had got the jump on the weekly papers with pictures and indepth stories about the two Maine social workers. Now with both victims identified, the *Bluefield (W.Va.) Daily Telegraph,* the *Richmond Times-Dispatch,* the *Washington Post,* and other newspapers began to give daily coverage to the "mountain massacre" as a town barber had termed the tragedy. Local subscribers to *The New York Times* and *Boston Globe* discovered that all the gory details had survived intact as big city papers picked up on the wire service accounts of the dead New Englanders, who had suddenly become martyrs to a noble cause. The sad story spread equally fast among the TV and broadcast media up and down the east coast until the citizens and county leaders of Giles and Bland began to feel a sense of personal responsibility for the deaths of Ramsay and Mountford. The same big city newspapers and TV stations that had covered Bob Mountford's daily progress in his fund-raising walk now took up the issue of the ugliness and the needlessness of violence everywhere especially in what should be areas of serene retreat into nature.

Inside the Kroger building in the back, Kenny Sharp went about his daily duties of keeping the meat and dairy cases well stocked. He sensed more than he saw somebody drawing close and just standing there. He placed the final armload of items and turned about. Randall Smith stood before him with an expression on his face that Kenny—in all their years of acquaintanceship—had never seen before. Kenny had always thought that Randall possessed the softest liquid brown eyes he had ever seen on a woman or a man. Normally there was a kind of pleading gentleness and innocence in them, but what Kenny now saw was fright or hostility or both; yet Randall's manner was controlled, if not calm. Kenny rarely called his friend Snuffy or LR as some of their mutual acquaintances did, but today for some reason the reunion seemed to call for lightness.

"Snuff, what the hell's going on? You look like you've seen a ghost."

"You still want to buy that winch off my truck?" Randall said brusquely.

"You said before that you wouldn't part with it for nothing. Why are you interested in selling now?"

"Need some money. Headin' out for Connecticut. Got the promise of a big welding job. Just got back from up there."

Kenny studied his friend's face. Even after years he couldn't tell when Randall told the truth or when he fantasized. He just accepted him as he was.

"You really going? Leave Giles?"

"Yeah, I'm goin'. What about it—a hundred-and-a-quarter okay?"

"Whatever's fair. Even a hundred twenty-five won't last you long in Connecticut."

Randall pondered the opinion, running his fingers through his long hair. He was clean shaven, Kenny noticed, and wore clean slacks and shirt.

"It'll do," Randall said. "Is it a deal or not? I gotta get goin'."

"What's the hurry? It's a deal, but I don't get paid till tomorrow."

Randall ignored the first part of the question.

"I'll have the winch off. You be at the house tomorrow after work, and be sure you got the money."

Randall wheeled about and stalked off in long strides like a lumberjack, his clean long hair flagging out behind him.

Kenny was on time the next day. On the graveled drive, Randall's two-tone green Ford truck sat polished and gleaming in the late afternoon sun. The exchange was made and Kenny said, "You sure you know what you're doin'? You never did make it outside Giles County—you always came back like a bad penny; you say there is no place like Pearisburg."

"I said I was goin'. They need me up there."

Kenny gave a friendly slap to the hunched shoulders of his friend.

"See you around then. You'll be back. Hang in there and watch those Yankee women. Hear they're fast and loose."

Randall grinned reservedly. Kenny could see that Randall relished the suggestion that protection from an onslaught of females would be necessary.

Just before 6:00 P.M., Randall pointed the Ford southward for Interstate 81. Near Dublin he approached New River Community College where he once planned to study drafting. He stopped the truck and looked longingly at the campus. He had wanted to attend, but he couldn't bring himself around. Other students would be sitting all around him. Surrounded like a sheep dog. The oppressive heat of strange bodies crowding and stifling him.

"Shit," he said, jerking the truck in gear.

On I-81 at last, he headed southwest until 81 intersected with Interstate 77 near Wytheville. Route 77 cut through the southern Virginia mountains and headed for the heartland of the Carolinas, and that's where he was heading.

He popped his favorite road tune into the tape player and pressed down on the gas pedal. He loved hearing Bob Seeger and the Silver Bullet Band's version of "On the Road Again." He played it endlessly—had worn out two tapes of it. Something in the song spoke to him, resonating with the hum of the Ford's big engine; it blended all things into a sort of harmony and held back the waves when they threatened to roll over him.

Near Fancy Gap—just before the highway began to drop over the vast Blue Ridge mountain crest into Mt. Airy, North Carolina—he spotted a hitchhiker. He never picked up hitchhikers. And didn't the dumb fart know that you couldn't thumb on the Interstate? Randall whizzed past the bedraggled-looking youth, but he found himself hitting the brakes. Something in the quick view Randall had got of him suggested some weird hint of brotherhood. He debated as he continued looking back and watching the youth run for the stopped truck. Randall had plenty of time to take off again if he needed to. He thought about waiting until the hitchhiker got within a few feet and then digging dirt and letting the grass, road tar, and gravel spray the other's face. Randall had done that before many times. Doing it pacified some deep longing beyond his understanding. This time, he waited until the youth threw an old bag in the back and took his seat.

Randall dug out, made the tires squeal, and then turned down the tape player only slightly. He didn't say a word though the passenger mumbled something.

"Ain't you gonna say nothin'?" the passenger queried.

"What's to say?" Randall said without looking at the questioner.

The silence lingered save for the tape player repeating the music over and over, and the passenger began to squirm.

"You got a name? No reason why we can't get acquainted."

"Yeah, I got a name."

The passenger waited.

"Well—what is it?"

"Call me Billy Joe."

"My name's Torrence. Torrence Townley. But everybody calls me Toe."

Silence lingered again for miles.

"Don't you never change that tape? It must be wore thin as a hair."

Randall gave his passenger a withering look, seeing him distinctly for the first time. He was a short, half-starved-looking kid of nineteen or twenty with stringy blond hair almost as long as Randall's own. His blue eyes were dull and outlined with dark half-circles. The smell of grass clung to his frail body and clothing of dirty jeans and print shirt. Randall recognized the signs of a junk food diet with drugs for dessert.

"It's my tape and my truck," Randall finally said. "Get the hell out if you don't like it."

But Randall didn't slow the truck.

"I didn't mean nothin', Billy Joe. Just don't like hearin' it over and over."

Randall lit a Merit, took a deep drag, and extracted the tape. He plugged in another—"Two for the Show" by the Kansas Band.

"That's more like it," Toe said.

"Got some Marshall Tucker tapes, too. Got everything."

"I can tell you're somebody important," Toe said. "What do you do?"

"I'm a talent scout."

"I knew it. You probably know all the musicians—the whole Nashville scene."

"All of 'em. Crystal Gayle and me were just talkin' on the phone the other day."

"Hot damn! I knew I was flaggin' a winner."

Toe watched Randall drag on the Merit.

"You wouldn't mind if I rolled a joint? I feel good just ridin' in the same truck with you."

"You can roll one. Roll one for me, too."

They smoked and Randall drove, turning the tape player louder. He re-plugged Seeger's "On the Road Again."

"I like you, Billy Joe. I like you a lot. You got somethin' I can't put my finger on. You got a kind of Willie Nelson thing about you."

Randall took a deep drag and held it. The birth of a smile parted his lips, and the faint residue of smoke exited his mouth and drifted in twin ribbons from his nose.

"Toe—me and you ought to team up. Whatta you do?"

"Most everything and nothin' __ play a little guitar. Me and my folks work the fruit pickin' trade __ start in Florida and Georgia early, then hit the Carolinas for the early apples—and stay on for the peach crop—then work on north for the fall apple pickin'."

"You like workin'—climbin' trees, I mean?"

"Hell, no. I wasn't made for no monkey. But my old man's spent more time in the pen than he has feedin' my mother and sisters. Somebody's got to keep 'em goin'."

"What'd your old man pull time for?"

"Murder. Assault. Robbed a likker store. You name it."

"You ever been in trouble?"

"What the hell business is it of yours?"

The grass was making Toe brave all of a sudden. Randall smiled appreciation.

"Don't matter," Randall said. "I'd like you anyway. You're all right, Toe."

"Well, I've never been in no bad trouble if that's what you mean. A little thievin' now and then to keep me in stuff. And I knocked up a girl in Georgia. Her old man took a shot at me when I wouldn't marry her. Stuff like that."

Randall pondered it, saying nothing in reply.

Toe said as the silence hung; "You ever been in trouble?"

222

"No. Never as much as got a parkin' ticket in my life."

"I see what a good driver you are. Careful. Stay on the speed limit."

Randall looked down at the speedometer to confirm it. An even fifty-five. He was careful and lawful about his driving. Always had been. Respectful and careful for his vehicle, most times. Had to show off sometimes and had to make the Ford strain a gut in four-wheel drive on occasion, but it was made for that. Loved that machine. Its hum and his heartbeat were one and the same thing.

The gas gauge showed "low" near Pilot Mountain. He turned off onto a service road and pulled in at a station. Toe went to the rest room and returned. Randall was getting ready to pay the bill when he noticed gas was two cents a gallon higher than in Pearisburg. It infuriated him.

"Gas is higher here than in Virginia," he growled.

"I just work here, Buddy," the burly attendant said.

Nevertheless, Randall threw the money at his feet rather than hand it over.

The attendant stooped to pick it up. "You some kind of nut?"

Randall said nothing and headed for the rest room.

When he returned, Toe had changed the "On the Road Again" tape for another and had the volume high enough to cave the roof in.

"Leave my fuggin' tapes alone!" Randall yelled and switched them back.

"I did't mean nothin', Billy Joe. Just thought it'd be all right ___ "

"Well, it's not all right. You remember that good, you hear?"

Toe shrunk back to his side of the truck and rolled another joint. Randall had to ask for his. The mood lightened again.

"Didn't you say your name was Billy Joe?"

"Yeah. What about it?"

"While you was in the rest room I looked over and saw *this* envelope layin' on the dashboard. It says Randall Lee Smith. This ain't a stole truck, is it?"

"It's my truck."

"Randall—Billy Joe—you ain't on the run, are you?"

"If I was on the run, I'd be on the back roads, wouldn't I?"

The logic seemed to satisfy Toe.

"That'd be crazy, wouldn't it? A big Nashville talent scout on the run? And Dolly Parton chasin' after you!"

Toe laughed at his own humor, but Randall didn't crack a smile. Toe added that he could understand how a big-time talent scout might want to travel "in-cog-nito" so's not to be bothered by amateurs.

Randall had his eyes on Pilot Mountain in the distance. It was a whole lot bigger around and taller than Angel's Rest. But he tried not to think of home or to think of how Loretta would bawl and miss him and not know where he was. He didn't tell anybody about his comings and goings. That would take the fun away and diminish some savored sweetness he felt in being secretive.

Suddenly he didn't want to think about it anymore. Thinking sometimes caused him agonizing pain. Must talk to Toe instead.

"Where *you* headin' for?"

"No place in particular. Wherever you're goin'," Toe said.

"Y'was bound to be goin' somewhere?"

"Don't matter. When I'm between jobs, I just start thumbin' and go whicheverway. It's sorta fun not to know where you're headin' and just end up there. Know what I mean?"

"Yeah."

"I guess when we hit Statesville, you'll be hittin' I-40 west for Nashville? Settin' in on a big band session somewhere, I'll bet?"

"No," Randall said.

"Where *are* you goin'?"

Randall didn't answer for a long time.

"Got to stop in and see Tammy Wynette and Glen Campbell while I'm down south, but I need a rest first. Been hittin' it too hard. Guess I'll pull in to Myrtle Beach for a spell."

"Hot damn! Now you're talkin'. A hundred miles of white beach and truckloads of womanflesh. Damn! Them little bikinis get skimpier every year, don't they! De-lic-ious!"

Toe had to roll another joint just thinking about it. Randall said nothing until Toe handed him another joint and prompted him.

"Can't you see 'em, man? Them creamy white tits floatin' over the top?"

"I don't like women," Randall said coldly.

"Then what the hell's all these nudie magazines all about? They been spillin' out from under the seat all the way down."

"Somebody must of left them there."

"You screwin' me? Everybody likes womanflesh."

"Forget it."

"But everybody —— "

"Shut your fuggin' mouth."

Toe sank back, resting his head on the seat.

North of Charlotte, they turned off the interstate and finally found a cheap motel. Randall had driven around for an hour. He didn't want one that had any wood construction. It had to be brick or cinderblock. Fire. Wood burned like Hell if fire broke out. Before checking in, they bought hamburgers, milk shakes, and french fries to take to the room.

Inside, Randall turned on the TV, propped himself up on the bed, and bit down with such force that tomato and mayonnaise squirted crosswise and landed on the nightstand. He got up, brushed it to the floor, and changed channels to a country music show.

"You find any of *those* people?" Toe pointed at the colored screen. "But I guess you call it 'discovering.' "

"Naw. They're small time."

Toe looked at him funny. Maybe Toe was really thinking that a big-time talent scout didn't stay in cheap motels and drive a '78 four-wheel. Maybe tomorrow he'd get rid of Toe.

The musical program was soon over, and Toe got interested in a detective drama. Randall went barefooted out to the truck and got a copy of *Hustler*. Toe stole side glances at Randall as he flipped the pages but said nothing. When Randall finished with one magazine, he would go barefoot out to the truck and bring in another. He did it a half-dozen times until his feet were blackened, and Toe couldn't resist.

"Why don't you bring 'em all in at one time? Your feet look like a Georgia nigger's."

Randall sprang like a tiger and swatted Toe's face with a magazine as though it were a horsefly.

"Don't you ever call me one of them! Don't you ever. You hear?"

"Okay, man. Back off. I was just teasin' you. If you want to get your whole ass bl___ dirty, that's your business."

Randall lay back down. Toe eyed him. Randall Joe didn't like women, huh? But he practically slobbered over those nudie magazines. What kind of crazy had he hooked up with, Toe wondered.

Randall went out again barefooted for a walk and stayed till the one o'clock movie came on. Toe rolled another joint, nursed it, and began to space out and then to cave in.

Sometime later in the night, Toe woke up. The TV was still on with some local country group doing a fiddle and banjo tune, and Randall was doing a comic version of the clog. Toe raised up on an elbow and watched. He was scared to laugh or comment unfavorably.

"You come alive after midnight, Randall Joe. You must be one of them 'night people.' "

"Yeah, I like the nighttime. Can't sleep most times anyway. Guess that makes me a 'night people.' Right?"

Randall's personality was changing. Toe could see it coming out like the slow movement of a turtle neck from out of the shell. There was the hint of more gaiety now, and Toe began to ride him cautiously about women. Randall laughed a little.

"You ever been to Myrtle Beach before?" Toe asked.

"Yeah. Last year me and Mark Coker—he's a boy I used to work with— came down. We got us a motel on the beach ___"

"Where you could watch those big boobs jigglin' by. Right? Man, the girls are endless. They go by all day and half the night. A feller can get diarrhea of the eyeballs and rheumatism of the neck just watchin' them pass."

Toe laughed at his own humor again, and he looked over and Randall had stopped dancing. Randall had a damp glow on his face, and Toe could soon see the sweat droplets.

Randall went to the bathroom and stayed a long time. Toe tried to drift off again but couldn't. He reached into his bag and got a mustard-colored pill out of an aspirin bottle.

Randall came out of the john, wiping his face. Something in his expression warned Toe. The old Randall was clearly back.

225

"I got to get some sleep ___ but I can't," Randall said.

"When I get all uptight and can't sleep, I reach for these little pills ___ "

"Who the hell said I was uptight?"

"I just meant if something was botherin' you, you could have one of *these*."

"Well, nothin' is botherin' me. What are they?"

"Yellow jackets."

"Yeah. I've had 'em. Rainbows, too."

"Come on." Toe rattled the container.

Randall swallowed two, downing them with a swig of Bacardi rum and Coke he had brought along.

"I'm no addict," Randall said after the gulp.

"Me, neither," Toe said and laughed a little.

"You want to stay with me at the Beach?"

"Yeah. I might for a while. Got a week to spare before I have to get back."

"No more shit about my feet bein' dirty? Sand in my toes?"

"Hell, no. What's a beach for?"

"I like to walk along the water late at night."

"Walk all you want."

"Me and you ought to hook up, Toe. Somethin' stopped me back up the road. I don't pick up people thumbin'."

"We're still five hours from Myrtle. Let's get some shut-eye."

Randall undressed in the dark. He crawled under the covers and started to shake. Toe heard the bed vibrating and, before remembering that the old Randall was back, he said, "What you doin'? Jerking off?"

Randall didn't answer for so long that Toe started to tremble.

Finally, Randall's low voice penetrated the darkness:

"I wonder if sharks like shitass meat? I may just knock you in the head one night and feed you to the sharks."

Toe didn't answer. He just lay there and tried to sound like he was snoring; but between breaths, he listened for any hint of movement from Randall Joe, any unevenness in his breathing. Finally, Randall began to wheeze as the yellow jackets took over. Toe thought once about getting up and seeing if he could find the truck keys. But he decided to gamble, and he hadn't walked the sands of Myrtle for two years.

Investigator Al Crane from the Virginia State Police Criminal Investigation Division had not been assigned to the Ramsay/Mountford murder case until Monday, June 1. His friend and colleague, Cecil Wyatt, had pulled first duty a day earlier. It was good to have a weekend free without complications and interruptions. At thirty-four he was still a bachelor. But that was in the process of changing. Things were getting serious between him and Glenda, and their busy lives allowed too little time together. Glenda—a willowy beauty with shoulder-length auburn hair—was a tax auditor for the state, and she at least understood the demands of his job.

He had come up through the ranks. In '66, after high school, he had trained for a dispatcher's job in Richmond. He made another move to the Salem Division as a full-fledged dispatcher, later training for a trooper's post in '69 when he turned twenty-one. A move to Martinsville in '72 had exposed him to narcotics undercover work; then, he served a short stint in Henry County before moving to the far western part of the state at Richlands, where he saw first-hand the tough conditions around the coalfields. The area was a melting pot of people and troubles. Virginia, Tennessee, and Kentucky merged not far from the area, and all the elements of race, nationality, politics, poverty, and unionism, came together in rugged terrain. It had been unusual duty, to say the least, but it proved a boon to his career. In July of '76, he was promoted to Investigator. He worked in narcotics enforcement until April of '81 before the transfer back to Wytheville came.

He was a big man—six-four, two-hundred-forty pounds—and his salt and pepper hair, and glasses, made him look a little older than he was. He knew he didn't project the image of a tough, dour lawman. His manner was naturally outgoing. He liked people ___ even people in trouble though he had to get away from them on occasion and escape to a good fishing hole or piddle around with his hobby of electronics.

His arrival in Jefferson National on that Monday seemed to coincide with an explosion of new developments. No leaf had been left unturned, and a virtual bonanza of things were being found. The Mobile Lab Unit was still on station, and a refreshed and expanded crew went at the continuing search with new ideas and vigor.

At the close of day, the list of new items was impressive: pocket knife, bloody bandage, large spike nail (could that have been the instrument that penetrated Ramsay's body?); two blood-stained paperback books with thumbprints in blood entitled *Clea* and *Mountolive;* a big cooking pot; a woman's blouse and panties, and a back-pack reasonably intact with routine contents. There were also four Merit cigarette packs and an assortment of Merit butts, two handkerchiefs, a raincoat, a bag containing a tent, *Thermo Keep* bag and food, set of playing cards faced with porno photos, a blue-topped canteen, three unused picture postcards, a silver canteen with green cover, a can of *Optimus* LP cooking gas, and four small plastic bottles.

The real bonus had seemed in grasp when Ramsay's Pentax camera was found buried deep in a rotten stump. But the film had been ripped out with such force that the holders were splintered. Shortly thereafter, the film itself had been found, but it was uncoiled and already browned-out by light exposure.

The Wapiti II log book turned up under a moss-covered flat rock. The last two pages of entries, however, had been torn out.

Mountford's camera—a Canon AT-I—was located with film intact. A searcher had found it in a depression, covered with leaves and dirt, down near the service road that came near Wapiti II shelter. A strange pattern had seemed to develop during the search. What appeared to be Susan Ramsay's possessions were hidden in a seeming straight line out from her grave site. Mountford's probable possessions were buried and otherwise concealed in a large expanding circle from his gravesite with his camera and some other objects disposed of on a line with the service road. Steve Davis's theory of buried treasure on a set compass heading didn't hold up entirely. If the killer simply walked in a straight line and hid items, most any compass heading would have sufficed, some of Steve's fellow searchers argued.

But nobody could explain the frequent sticks joined together, forming a point, seemingly aiding the searchers. Did the killer or killers want to be caught? Did some deep psychological need of discovery and frequent self-condemnation lurk in the murderer's breast? And why hadn't he—they—kept the expensive cameras for resale?

With all that he knew thus far, Al Crane was leaning toward a lone assailant. Yet there were questions. Since there had been no drag marks from the shelter—where Mountford at least had been shot, judging from the bloodstains and the charcoal overmarkings—to Mountford's grave site, was a lone killer able to carry the victim's body by himself for so great a distance? The killer, if acting alone, would have to be a fairly large, strong man. The same reasoning applied to Ramsay's body disposal though she had not been carried so great a distance from the shelter area. You couldn't always reason like that, however. Under conditions of extreme excitement or mortal fear, even a small man—or a woman—could perform amazing and unbelievable feats of strength and daring.

Another bonus came about when a searcher, not Crane, found a long iron rod of the serrated kind used to reenforce concrete. It took little imagination to conclude that forestry workers had used the rods in constructing the concrete footings for the new Wapiti II shelter and had cast the unused piece aside or had lost it in the leaf-rich, wooded terrain. The searcher had found the object plunged deep in the ashes of the campfire residue. If there had been blood and hair on the instrument, they had burned away. As everybody nearby gathered around to inspect the deadly-looking instrument, there was little doubt in the group that the rod had been the instrument used to batter the dead woman's skull.

Other known items belonging to Ramsay and Mountford were conspicuously missing: Mountford's Bible, the hiking boots of both victims, the diaries or logs of both, Ramsay's sleeping bag, their billfolds, their wristwatches, and Mountford's reading light.

On another front John Ratliff and Mike Meyer were taking a different tack. They had interviewed several local people and listened to theories advanced by town residents, former resident hikers, and newcomers to the local hostel. They had used Father Winter's help in reviewing the hostel log book for names, addresses, phone numbers, and general comments of hikers signing in and out. They had also radioed park rangers as far away as Maryland to pull certain northbound hikers off the trail for questioning.

On Tuesday morning, June 2, the biggest break of all unfolded. The morning dailies ran more photos of Ramsay and Mountford. Robin Cunningham had seen them and come to the Sheriff's office to make a startling statement. Residing in a remote section of Giles near Mountain Lake, she did not always see a daily paper or keep close tabs on current news, but seeing the photos of Susan Ramsay struck a sensitive nerve. Robin, as member of a temporarily-employed park service construction team, had met the murdered girl briefly less than two weeks previously. She had even taken Susan's picture with the girl's own camera. And in addition she had observed that Susan's companion was both camera-shy and a little strange to boot.

Could she describe the "strange" male with Susan Ramsay at the time, the Sheriff had asked? She gave the description and then used the office phone to call in John Hairfield, her friend and co-worker on the Park Service construction team. He and others had seen Ramsay and Mr. X on the same occasion.

Hairfield's description was nearly identical to Robin Cunningham's. Coincidentally, their description closely paralleled those of earlier hikers who had reported observing or hearing of a strange-looking, strange-acting male somewhere in Jefferson National.

The more Officers Myers and Ratcliff reviewed the notes from interviews with hikers Father Winter had sent by or descriptions second hand relayed by telephone, the more convinced they were that one and the same suspect emerged.

Don Flinchum, a State Police artist, was called in to do a composite of the man Robin had seen with Susan Ramsay for inter-intrastate circulation and media release.

When VSP investigator Cecil Wyatt and Tommy Lawson returned from Dr. Oxley's office in Roanoke, they had the first preliminary autopsy reports. Susan Ramsay had suffered twenty-three major stab wounds and half as many more "defensive" minor wounds about the hands, fingers, and wrist. In addition, nine blunt-force lacerations appeared on her body. The doctor's report ended:

"... Four potentially fatal wounds are present. These are the three stab wounds on the anterior chest and one stab wound of the left upper back. The other stab wounds are superficial and not potentially fatal. The occipital skull fracture is a potentially fatal injury. The deepest of the stab wounds measures approximately 4.5 inches from the skin, while the shallowest of the fatal stab wounds measures approximately $3\frac{1}{4}$ inches in depth. The non-fatal wounds are superficial and do not enter the body cavities." The CAUSE OF DEATH column read: "Stab wounds of chest with perforation of heart and left lung and hemothorax and hemopericardium."

What a fight the young woman had apparently put up! Mortally wounded from the face and body blows, she must have fought on until the vicious onslaught of a knife had cut her to ribbons. Then, most likely, the skull fracture had finished the job.

Mountford's autopsy was less lengthy: "Three gunshot wounds of the head and brain."

There were both surprises and disappointments in the reports. The stomachs of both victims contained undigested food, implying that they had eaten shortly before death. Peas, cube-cut potatoes, corn, and dried apricots were still identifiable. The blood alcohol was .11, suggesting that both victims had enjoyed a considerable amount of alcohol—enough in fact to constitute drunk driving under Virginia law.

The big disappointment was the removal of the bullets from Mountford's skull. The projectiles were easily identified as .22 caliber, but they were either shattered or mangled beyond accurate ballistics testing.

As they all sat in the sheriff's office going over the reports, Tommy Lawson commented wryly: "If you want to kill somebody, do it with a .22. Don't know that I've ever seen a case where a .22 slug didn't disintegrate if it hit bone."

But the bullet holes themselves were helpful for analytical purposes. One bullet had pierced the left cheek and gone backwards, downward, and toward the right, fracturing the left maxilla and right mandible. Two of the bullets passed from left face to right and angled backward, passing through both cerebral hemispheres. Judging from the angles, the officers concluded that the bullets had been fired from a standing or crouched position into a victim sleeping on his right side. On the other hand, they could roughly draw the same conclusion if the killer was kneeling and shot into the left face of a standing victim. But the former was more likely, Lawson wagered.

As to the matter of rape in Ramsay's case, everyone had expected to prove rape quickly if the body had not deteriorated too badly to destroy the evidence. Fly eggs and innumerable small maggots were already present in body orifices, and the lab work had not been easy.

In conclusion, however, the examiner seemed to be writing the death knell to a possible capital murders/rape/commission of a felony-with-a-firearm charge. The INTERNAL DESCRIPTION REPORT ending read:

". . . The vaginal and perineal areas are examined. There is no
physical evidence of sexual abuse and the vaginal vault shows
no evidence of laceration or bruising, nor does the rectum.
Swabs are taken from the vaginal vault, rectum, and oral
cavities for further examination."

But extensive lab tests were yet to be done. Evidence of spermatozoa could still show up.

It had been a foregone conclusion among state police investigators, the sheriff's office, the forestry service officers, the various rescue service personnel, and most certainly among the print and broadcast media that rape was the motive for the killings. Mountford had simply been an obstacle in the rapist's—or rapists'—way.

As the little group of assembled lawmen continued to hash and rehash all the facts at hand, they began to see many, if not most, of their earlier suppositions fail. Even the suspicion of rape *and* robbery as the motive for murder lost validity. A robber—or robbers—certainly wouldn't have left two very expensive cameras—the cream of the victims' meager possessions—in the mountain to gather rust. And more intriguing still was the fact that the film had been left intact in one camera and yet ripped from the other. What did that signal? Knowledge on the part of the killer or killers that nothing on the one roll of film was incriminating, but that roll number two was indeed accusatory? Robin Cunningham's testimony certainly reenforced that assumption.

The meeting began to break up. And as they had every day, reporters and TV crews hovered around the courthouse and sheriff's office like hungry vultures.

"Best just hand them a small tidbit today," Meyer said. "Who's gonna be the star this time?"

John Ratliff was elected since he had attended and actually witnessed the preliminary autopsy, and, Ratliff was affable by nature and a good talker under any circumstances. The group rose, and Ratliff squared his broad shoulders and headed for the door. Like his colleague, Al Crane, Ratliff was a big man, topping six feet and looked overpowering at two hundred pounds, and every inch the football player he had once been during college days. At age fifty-five, however, his long years of law enforcement were winding down.

He opened the door and walked into a barrage of TV cameras and anxious reporters. He knew that in no way must he weaken the Commonwealth's case with a premature revelation of vital information. He would skirt the issue of rape and simply confirm that Mountford had been shot three times in the head with a .22 caliber weapon and that Ramsay had suffered twenty-three stab wounds and a brutal beating, one blow of which had fractured her skull.

"But was she sexually molested?" staccato voices rang out.

"Tests are being continued," Ratliff replied calmly.

"But if there was no rape, what other motives are suspected?" a TV reporter pressed while his cameraman backup moved in closer.

"That's a big question mark right now. I don't have to tell you that this case has the markings of a bizarre, psychopathic killing," Ratliff said, instantly sorry that he had made the statement.

"Would you elaborate on that, sir?" sundry voices insisted, and reporters crowded in still closer.

"For obvious reasons, there is nothing more I can tell you now," Ratliff pushed on through to his car.

Once in his car and on the way back to Wytheville, Ratliff remembered an old axiom from his earlier days as a young trooper. A classroom

231

instructor had once said that all homicides sprang initially from character weakness on the part of the killer. Across the years Ratliff had found that to be true. And now he wondered what was the particular weakness of the murderer of Susan Ramsay and Bob Mountford. He sensed more than knew that somehow the "weakness" in this case was infinitely complex.

CHAPTER XXIV

"Why is it every time the family and I go on vacation, all hell breaks loose?" Sheriff John Hopkins III playfully growled to the group of lawmen assembled in his office. It was day four after both bodies had been found—June 4.

Al Crane, Tommy Lawson, Mike Meyer, John Ratliff, Deputy Sterling Greever, Cecil Wyatt, and Boots Belcher sat in a half-circle about the worn desk. Each took turns complimenting the sheriff on his tanned, rested-looking face and asking whether the bikinis at Myrtle Beach were more scandalous than ever.

"I don't know," Hopkins said deadpan. "Sarah Jane wouldn't let me look."

There was a round of guffaws. Hopkins was a man of brief and infrequent humor. His dark brown eyes were rarely mirth-filled though his youthful face could break out in a broad grin on occasion. Some of his friends and associates even considered him aloof. His enemies used the term "arrogant." But be that as it might, he ran a tight ship. His chief desire in life was to give Giles County a top-notch law enforcement team. He had twenty-three deputies now—an all-time high for the county.

And north and east Giles was no longer just a rural county of farmers, merchants, and timber cutters; it was diversified with light industry, modern schools, a shopping center, and all the current ills of society-at-large. Drugs and crime had invaded the once-placid hills and valleys in the same way—if not to the same degree—that other localities had experienced.

Colleges, too, surrounded the county: Virginia Polytechnic Institute and State University to the east; New River Community College and Radford University to the south; Wytheville Community College to the west; and Concord College and Bluefield College, across the state line in West Virginia, on the northwest. Although all of the educational institutions were an asset, they nevertheless had a negative side. Drugs, drug trafficking, liquor, and a small element of wild, uninhibited, law-breaking students and school dropouts posed a recurring problem. To many, it seemed that Giles had burst into the twentieth century overnight. Certainly the young people were changing fast. The drug dealing and boozing had reached into the high schools via the colleges, and only a minority of the area's students seemed to have any sympathies for the time-honored values, traditions, and mores of the older generation of Giles Countians.

In a manner of speaking, Hopkins had succeeded his father as high sheriff. John Hopkins, Jr., had served three terms—'56-60, '60-64, and '72-74—as the county's top lawman. He had died in office before completing the last four-year term. But even then, John III had been gaining valuable experience as a deputy under his father.

Before that, the younger Hopkins had graduated from high school in Narrows, the second largest town in the county, gone on to a two-year stint in the army artillery, and married Sarah Jane Caldwell, his school sweetheart. The union had produced a boy now aged five, John Hopkins IV.

The Sheriff's credentials were solid: member of the local Kiwanis Club, active member of Narrows Christian Church, and avid sports fan of local and state teams. He was on the right side of the political fence. Giles County had always been a hotbed of Byrd Democrats from the courthouse hierarchy down to the smallest post office in the county.

Thus had his father's old office and duties evolved from a horse-and-buggy operation to a sheriff's office with the aid of electronics, computers, and modern scientific techniques of criminal investigation. And more and more, the deputies would be coming from the ranks of police science majors at the local colleges.

And now at the advanced age of thirty-three with not a strand of grey among the well-groomed brown locks, he looked five years younger than his age according to his friends. John Hopkins III reigned over his home county. It was a role in which he felt comfortable and challenged to do a good job. He knew, too, that his demeanor was that of a much older and wiser man, but that's the way he was and had always been. And the reserved, unexcitable, always-in-command stature he maintained for himself could only help in keeping the proper distance and engender the necessary respect. His medium height of five-eight, his slender build, and the boyish good looks he was sometimes teased about didn't always coincide with the image of high sheriff; but the attitude made the man, not the physical make-up.

Hopkins looked about the room. All the men around him were professionals. He had worked with all of them before on one case or another. Traditionally, the Virginia State Police or the F.B.I. came into a case at the request of the sheriff's department and to "assist" the county officers. In truth, the combined effort was almost automatic and taken for granted; certainly, all county enforcement officers everywhere would be lost without the highly trained personnel and technical expertise of outside agencies.

"Since being back, I've looked over the reports, talked with some of you, but I think it's advisable to summarize and make sure our collective efforts are well coordinated," Hopkins said. "Now what have we got?"

John Ratliff led off: "Lawson and myself handled the interview with Frank Maguire. Park rangers pulled him off the trail at the Peaks of Otter the night after the first body was found. The guy was who he said he was. The matter of his leaving the trail at Damascus to spend a few days with his daughter and grandchildren at Kingsport, Tennessee, checked out. Maguire and Lawson had a few sharp words, but I think it was age versus youth or retired chief versus young deputy or something. All in all, Maguire was professional, knowledgeable, and very helpful. He seemed to have all the loose ends of people and places tied together except for those few days when none of us has a very clear picture. Maguire was impressive in his grasp of things. His years of police service kind of put him in our league."

Lawson gave his version of the interview, adding that at first Maguire's former employment had been in doubt. But the wrong Princeton (the wrong Princeton in the wrong state) mayor's office had been contacted, and when told that Frank Maguire was unknown and that they had never had a police chief by that name, little wonder questions had arisen. But then the current police chief of Princeton Junction, New Jersey had verified Maguire's story.

Lawson continued: "Not only did Maguire give us a good picture of trail life and a complete run-down on Mountford and Ramsay, but he gave us a whole list of hikers that had traveled in roughly the same group. He told us we'd get essentially the same information from everybody else, at least up until the time the victims actually entered Jefferson National. He was right. Every hiker's story has been pretty consistent."

"What of this fellow Steve Skinner?" Hopkins prompted.

"For a while we thought he'd skipped the country," Al Crane said, "but we found out later that he'd backtracked into Roanoke to visit a cousin. Anyway, the park rangers got wind of him being on the Blue Ridge Parkway south of Glasgow. As it happened, other hikers who'd been stopped and questioned started leaving notes for Skinner. He didn't even know about the deaths, he said, until he had gone into a store for change to make a phone call to the ranger station. A ranger came by, questioned him, and put him in touch with me. He confirmed that he'd spent the night of May 19 with Ramsay and Mountford and that both had left the next morning while he was still in camp waiting for friends."

"Any reason to doubt this story?" Hopkins asked.

"No," Crane said. "His short stopover in Roanoke checked out. His concern about the victims and his layover here in the local hostel have been confirmed. He seems like a really nice kid. He nearly broke down on me during the phone conversation. Said he had a hard time living with himself when he realized that he and his two friends slept only two miles away—at old Wapiti shelter—from Ramsay and Mountford on the night they were apparently murdered. Didn't hear a shot—or a sound, he said __ kept saying it over and over: 'We didn't hear anything. Not a scream. Not a shot.

Not even a tree limb breaking.' I ended up feeling sorry for the kid. He seemed anxious to come back when we wanted him. He plans to finish the trail hike as a memorial to Mountford."

Hopkins began to shuffle the papers on his desk. "I see you got a statement from our local hikers, Dave and John Tice?"

"Yeah," Lawson said. "Dave laid over here at home; then he and his brother skipped up to Shenandoah National Park. The rangers pulled them off. They hadn't heard about the murders either. Anyway, both the Tice boys came home immediately and joined in the search for evidence. In fact, Dave helped find the missing pages of the Wapiti II logbook. Another strange thing about that logbook: Frank Maguire's name was the last registry. But Tice admitted he'd been at Wapiti II when Maguire had arrived, and that he—Tice—hadn't signed the logbook. He couldn't give an explanation why he hadn't. He usually signed all shelter logbooks. Strange, but he's local with a spotless record and from a good family here."

"Did Maguire mention signing in on the Wapiti II logbook?" Wyatt said.

"I believe he did," Crane said, "but he didn't mention whether Tice did or didn't. Just said Tice was a clean college kid."

"What about Neal Chivington?" Hopkins shifted papers.

"Everything he said checks out," Meyer said. "We checked trail logs on him and his girlfriend—Steve Skinner's sister—back to Georgia. And he and both victims had a good relationship of long duration."

"And the German girl?"

Meyer smoothed the curly blond hair at the back of his crown. "A little bit of mystery here. My information is from a personal interview with her and talks with people that hiked with her. Actually we may need a report from her employer in Michigan and possibly a report from Immigration Service to verify all her story. Anyway she was always goin' on and off the trail accordin' to some of the hikers. Some of them apparently resented her takin' 'the easy way' as they put it and skirtin' some of the really hard climbs. Accordin' to my information, she and Mountford had a thing goin'. When Susan Ramsay arrived on the scene, there was some jealousy on Renate's part."

Hopkins's ears pricked up. "You're saying Mountford and the German girl slept together?"

"Some of the hikers swear to two instances when Renate and Mountford were in bed together. My informants don't think Susan Ramsay ever caught wind of it. I guess the jealousy was on Renate's part, but it was there."

"Strong enough to kill somebody?" Hopkins mused aloud. "But I don't guess that makes much sense when the object of her affection was put away, too."

"Love and hate—rejection—sometimes go hand in hand, the scriptwriters tell us," Belcher said.

"Of course we're straying away from what may turn out to be our strongest evidence," Crane said. "The various fingerprints. The one impressed in blood on the back of one of the girl's books may be what we're looking for."

"Why do you say 'the girl's book'?" Hopkins asked.

"Her folks in Ohio confirmed it. Susan was reading one of the books in the series while she was at Aurora, and she took the remaining two—the two we found—along on her hike."

"I'll be anxious to see the lab report on the quality of those prints," Hopkins said.

"Even with good prints, a match-up may not be so easy. Let's hope the guy, the girl, the gang, whatever, has a nice little match on file with the F.B.I.," Crane said.

Deputy Sterling Greever handed his boss another stack of reports, recorded interviews, and miscellaneous notes. The group weighed the merits of each bit of information and character insight, compared notes and shared opinions until the noon hour arrived. Before they began to break for lunch, Hopkins posed one more question.

"How much response have we gotten from the composite drawing that was released?"

"A lot. But most of the responses either muddy the water or bring out the crackpots," Meyer said. "One respondent wanted to know why we'd use a picture of Devil Anse Hatfield in his youth, as a model for the composite. Another one said he had a brother-in-law that looked like the composite, and since the whole family wanted to get rid of him, would he do?"

"What about this one?" Greever asked. "A woman called in and said she'd seen the man of the composite in Dayton, Ohio, at a ball game in 1976. Good memory, huh?"

"But aside from the far-out stuff," Wyatt said, "we have six or eight responses that may help us."

Hopkins stood and stretched. "We may as well admit that with all our wheel-spinning, we're not much closer to finding the killer—or killers—than we were four days ago."

It was true, yet it was a routine state of affairs in most homicide cases. The quick and easy ones were few and far between. Every man present knew the endless tasks involved in putting all the puzzle pieces together for the big picture. In fact, the big picture was almost never put together completely, but if enough of it fell into place to gain a confession or a conviction, that's all one could hope for.

"And what is the consensus?" Hopkins continued. "Are we talking about a person acting alone, or were two or more involved?"

The question opened up a new barrage of opinions and counter-opinions. The group was almost equally split on the one-person/more-than-one-person controversy.

Hopkins took a phone call his dispatcher said wouldn't wait and afterwards rubbed his belly. It was 1:30.

"The sheriff's office buying today?" Al Crane jibed.

"On my budget?" Hopkins countered. "I can't even get new radios for my squad cars, and God knows this office needs remodeling."

Later that same day in Ohio, The Church in Aurora had filled to capacity by 4:00 P.M. The entire town had felt a profound loss in the person of Susan Ramsay. Her work relative to the city's summer recreation programs of yesteryear, her former popularity at Aurora High School, and her accomplishments at Denison University had engendered media recognition that helped to swell the ranks of mourners.

The memorial service began with a lighting of the altar candles.

Bud Ramsay could not escape the cruel irony of the event. Candles. June 4 was his fifty-fourth birthday.

As Bill VanAuken, their pastor, began his opening remarks, Bud found his thoughts straying, his eyes drawn magnetically to the flickering flame. He remembered many birthday candles: SuSu's first, and second, and third—and seemingly, all the rest.

"Susan professed her Christian faith before this church on March 23, 1967," the pastor continued, "and through her music especially she contributed an eternal gift to the Church's ministry ___ "

The congregation stood and sang "Fairest Lord Jesus." When the hymn was over, there began a reading in unison:

". . . eye hath not seen, nor ear heard, neither have entered into the heart of man, the things which God hath prepared for them that love Him."

Afterwards, the pastor looked out over the congregation unduly long as if he wished them all to separate themselves entirely from the cares of the day and the distractions of personal problems or thoughts and enter into a communion of souls.

He reached for the eulogy he, with Ginny's and Bud's help, had written and began: "Laura Susan Ramsay. If there was only one word to describe her, it would be the word Love. It shone from her like a beacon and enriched the lives of everyone she touched."

The pastor found that he could not finish the eulogy before his voice wavered, his eyes flooded, and his voice faltered. Momentarily winning the battle, he continued: ". . . She loved the out-of-doors. The beauty of nature was everywhere for her and in her . . . in the jargon of today, she was into the majesty of God's world . . . And who but our SuSu would bring back a special chunk of wood from her trip to Italy so that the family dog would have an 'imported' stick to chew on. May God hold her in the palm of His hand."

As the story of their loved one's life unfolded through her pastor's lips, the hands of Ginny, Bud, Kelly, and Richard linked together.

Too soon the eulogy was over, coming to a quick end just as SuSu's life had gone.

There was another hymn and then the congregation prayed in unison: "Savior, again to thy dear name we raise/With one accord our parting hymn of praise/We stand to bless thee ere our worship cease/Then, lowly kneeling, wait thy word of peace."

The candles were extinguished, and little trails of smoke, like miniature campfires, drifted into the cathedral ceiling. Throughout the benediction, Ginny's eyes were drawn to the disappearing vapors. Somehow they were a curtain—not a curtain lowered after the grand finale but a curtain raised for the beginning of a new drama ___

Later in the afternoon of the same day, Jackie Hilton prepared to go to Bob Mountford's memorial service at Dover-Foxcroft. It was an occasion that she both looked forward to and dreaded. She had not yet come to terms with Bob's death, and almost daily she had read and reread the last letter he had sent her. The words still so fresh, so alive, so strength-giving.

She stopped her preparations, reached across her dressing table, and retrieved the well-worn sheets once more. The letter was dated May 9.

Dear Jacqueline,

I miss you sweetie! I'm lying in a leanto forty miles south of Damascus, Virginia, writing this by candlelight as a light rain falls. I so wish you could be here to share this with me. It will be difficult to convey to you what this adventure had been up to this point—400 miles from Springer Mountain, Georgia, and still over 1700 miles from my beloved Maine and my beloved you. I think of you every day and hope all is well with you and Jennifer, and look forward to holding you and touching and kissing you when I see you in June. The beauty and ruggedness of these Southern mountains reminds me so much of you and our Allagash trip—such sweet memories!

Today I went swimming for the first time this year in a beautiful deep gorge reminiscent of Gulf Hagas under a waterfall. So cold, yet refreshing! The dogwood and the mountain laurel are just beginning to bloom in bright whites and pinks, scattered between bright green. Blooming rhododendrons, budding hardwoods, and virgin conifers are everywhere about. The forest floor is covered with hundreds of multicolored wildflowers. I wish I were more educated in botany. There's a kind of wild onion/garlic (very strong) which I've learned to identify, and I pull them whenever I can and add them to my dinners. Very delicious! Also, there's a mushroom called "Morel" which is easy to identify, and "branch lettuce" which goes well in a stew.

My first 37 days have gone by so quickly and so much unexpected has happened to me. The people on and along the trail have been exceedingly helpful and friendly. I've made many new friends whom I hope some, at least, you'll be able to

239

meet this fall in Maine. Some, you won't be able to meet—like the bootlegger in Sam's Gap, North Carolina. And the man who drove me all around Irwin, Tennessee, looking for my friend, Frank Maguire, and doing errands for us. And the woman in Elk Park, North Carolina, who stopped me and Renate on our way out of town and fed us breakfast. I hope you will have a chance to meet Frank Maguire. He's 57, and a retired chief of police from Princeton Junction, New Jersey, whom I've been hiking with from south of Fontana Dam. Also, the "Michigan" group . . .

Please keep writing, sweetie. I so look forward to your letters. I hope things go well re: Jen's school, and you don't need to start a new, messy litigation thing. I'll pray for you, honey.

I've spent a lot of time thus far considering what I might like to do after I finish the hike. I really have a lot of options in terms of employment and travel, and it's exciting to be open to them all. I often wonder how you fit into all this in terms of your hopes and dreams, and responsibilities, and it's quite confusing. I love you very much. I don't want to get into this in a letter, but I do look forward to being able to talk with you in June.

Well, I've got a long day ahead of me tomorrow so I'll wrap up for now. Susan is supposed to meet me in Damascus on May 9 which is the closest place I can mail this. So I'll end for now and try to write more before then. I love you sweetie, and I hope to dream of you tonight . . .

Later—

Sweetie, I have more to say, but I'm at the post office so I want to send this now. I love you! I love you! Can't wait til June when I see you. Could you send $20.00 to Pearisburg for me? I won't be there 'til May 20-23. Give my love to Jen ——

She laid the letter aside, wondering whether there was any more moisture in her body to give, but again her vision clouded.

In the aftermath of the tragedy, she had not sat nursing her grief. She had wanted to do something positive. And she had been frustrated by the local news stories—wire service reports that originated in Virginia—that clearly indicated Virginia authorities were doing everything they could but essentially were accomplishing no break-throughs. Not a single suspect had been arrested. Then her grand idea had been born. She had heard about a local medium—an older woman with startling powers—who had a good track record in helping enforcement authorities "picture" the features of sought killers.

The woman had gone through an impressive ritual of crystal gazing, card readings, and another "procedure" Jackie had never heard of.

240

Toward the end of the session, the woman had laid out a silk cloth embroidered with letters and figures arranged within small circles—a sort of checkerboard arrangement. At various points on the silk, she placed sewing needles which pointed to random letters and figures. Incredibly Jackie had seemed to see those needles rotate—and yes, even move—to indicate a letter or a figure.

Finally, the woman had reached a conclusion: "The person who killed your friend is dark-skinned—perhaps a foreigner who is in this country illegally—and he has light brown, bushy hair, and a mustache. He is between twenty-four and twenty-six years old. His eyes protrude slightly, he is medium-tall, and the color green has special meaning to him. I am sorry to report that if he is not caught, he will repeat his crime in August of this year."

Jackie had been so impressed with the woman's insights that she herself was having visions by then of exactly what the killer looked like, and she had rushed home to get it all down. Those "facts" were now on the way to the Giles County Sheriff's office.

Having left Portland earlier in the day, Joanne Irace was already enroute to Dover-Foxcroft for the memorial service. As she wound her way northward along I-95 to Bangor, the sweet memories became overwhelming: University of Maine at Orono, and all that she and Bob had experienced there; the coast to the southeast, and Bar Harbor, and the unforgettable times they had walked along the shore picking up shells and dreaming their dreams; mountain climbing in Baxter State Park, when the exhilarating heights and virgin air had only added to the intoxication both already felt when in each other's presence. All were gone save for the memories.

News of Bob's death had come to her as the coldest kind of shock. On that morning—the morning after his body had been found —she had crawled groggily from bed only to learn from her mother that the early morning newscast told of Bob's death along the AT in Virginia. Her mother had already begun to weep before Joanne herself had recovered enough breath to utter the sounds of her own anguish.

The newscast—and a later one—had not been clear on the cause of death. For some reason Joanne had thought of poison mushrooms. Bob had mentioned during their correspondence and telephone conversations the various herbs and plants which he had gleaned along the trail and how he had used them in his cooking.

As her remorse had deepened she longed to know whether Bob had died alone. She had whispered an hourly prayer that he had not died alone or suddenly, that he had died in the company of people dear to him, and that he had had time to make whatever peace with God his turbulent soul required.

Somehow, she trudged off to work. While awaiting her own career decisions, she had taken a temporary job in her father's business.

All day long—on the hour—the newscasts were more explicit. Mr. Mountford's voice had come over the radio, saying that no hatred and vengeance should be harbored among the people in Maine because his son had been murdered. Murdered? Joanne left her desk and endured another siege of salty tears. She had at first heard, "killed", and now it was "murdered".

For the rest of the day, diarrhea had threatened to consume her; yet she hadn't wanted to go home. Depression descended like a wet blanket, and then, unaccountably, her spirit seemed to soar as if strength and power were coming from an unseen Somewhere.

A still-later newscast made mention of Susan Ramsay's stabbing and Bob's death by gunshot wounds. Joanne had tried to create in her mind the setting and the possible details of the killings. But her mind had rebelled at coming to terms with the vision of blood and the sounds of exploding bullets. Bob *had not* had a chance to cry out to God, and yet she had felt— and still felt—a sense of peace about it. Unexplainably verses of Scripture had entered her consciousness—words from "The Acts," having to do with the martyrdom of Stephen after the young Christian had accused the unbelieving Jews and suffered stoning to death.

Saul of Tarsus—later to become the Apostle Paul—the man who had held the coats of the stone-throwers, had later recorded a graphic picture of the closing moments of Stephen's life. It was those words that had come to Joanne.

She saw Bob's dying moments like that. Saw him lifted up. Loved, held in saving, caring arms that lifted, lifted, lifted. There was capacity in her even to be angry with him: he had departed this troubled world while he was still young, healthy, and happy. He would never suffer old age, arthritis, wars, or the fading glories of earthly existence, that she and most of his friends would have to endure.

Every kind of thought and emotion had invaded her mind that first day. And each hour she had wanted to go and be with the Mountfords. They had assumed, of course, that mutual friends had got word to her. She loved Bob and Mim, and they loved her.

Now she was on her way—the ending chapter—on earth—of "her" Bob. Nothing —save for the joy of the living Jesus in her heart—had lighted her life so brightly as Bob had.

After clearing Bangor and turning onto Route 15 for Dover-Foxcroft, she searched the radio dial for her favorite FM station. Every song seemed to be a song of love, saying something that had a personal meaning. And she wondered whether that was the way it would always be: she would see him in music, along the woodland paths, and on the horizon as the sun sank low. Dared she believe that somewhere—some time—they two might wake together to a glorious dawn too wonderful to imagine, too magnificent to describe?

The Mountfords' Episcopal church was not large enough to accommodate the anticipated crowd, and thus St. Thomas Catholic Church had been chosen. Bob's ashes had not arrived from Roanoke, but in the place of an urn, a walnut casket had been substituted. The casket was laden with a pall, and before the casket, an inordinately large photo of the deceased, framed by flowers. At its lower edge was printed in large letters: "God, grant me the serenity to accept the things I cannot change, courage to change the things I can, and the wisdom to know the difference."

242

The full sanctuary of people was as silent as the death they had all come to commemorate.

Before the family and the clergy entered, Jackie Hilton, guitar in hand, took her place before the altar. Her rich, pure voice lifted the words of her selection with mounting majesty that seemed itself the eulogy: *". . . To everything turn, turn, turn; there is a season, turn, turn, turn . . . and a time for every purpose under heaven. A time to be born, a time to die . . . ."*

Afterwards silence again lingered. The clergymen appeared and took their stations. Shortly Bob, Mim, their children, and near relatives filed down the center aisle. Occasional hands reached from pews here and there to grasp Mim's or Bob's. Father Sprague of the Mountford's Episcopal church at Dexter, Father O'Toole of St. Thomas, Bishop Wolf, Father Whitt, and Father McCall met the family and seated them.

After a time Father O'Toole relinquished the pulpit to his Episcopal counterpart and retired. Father Sprague led the congregation in The Ministry of the Word: "Blessed be God: Father, Son, and Holy Spirit." The People responded: "And blessed be his kingdom, now and for ever. Amen."

Father Sprague led the recitation of the Gospel Rite: "I am the resurrection and the life, saith the Lord; he that believeth in me, though he were dead, yet shall he live; and whosoever liveth and believeth in me shall never die . . . "

Bishop Wolf began the homily: "Reality. What is Reality? Jesus died, was entombed, yet was resurrected from the dead. Robert Tatton Mountford, Jr., whose memory we here assembled, commemorate, is the heir to that same Reality. Dostoevsky, in his *Brothers Karamazov,* said: '. . .

On earth, indeed, we are, as it were, astray, and if it were not for the precious image of Christ before us, we should be undone and altogether lost, as was the human race before the flood. Much on earth is hidden from us, but to make up for that we have been given a precious mystic sense of our living bond with the other world, with the higher heavenly world, and the roots of our thoughts and feelings are not here but in other worlds. That is why the philosophers say that we cannot apprehend the reality of things on earth.' And so it is that while we cannot begin to understand or quickly come to terms with the loss of Bobby Mountford's earthly existence, the true Reality is that we are here to celebrate life—not to mourn death. Let our service be a holy and mystic communion of the living with the living . . . "

After the reading of the Creed and the Intercessory Prayers, Father Sprague said: "While hiking along the Appalachian Trail, Bobby's favorite hiking verse was Isaiah 55:12: 'For ye shall go out with joy, and be led forth with peace: the mountains and the hills shall break forth before you into singing, and all the trees of the field shall clap their hands.' If we can recapture the essence of that joy Bobby surely felt in the arms of nature, we will, I think, experience the faintest shadow of what it means to be immortal . . . ."

A hymn was sung, and then the Offertory preceded open Communion. During the celebration of the Eucharist, a nun played guitar and two other singers sang "On Eagles' Wings."

When Communion was finished, the congregation sang "Our God, Our Help in Ages Past." Father Whitt then offered a prayer. Sean Stitham followed him, and read an excerpt from Bob's last letter to Jackie, and then Bob's favorite poem, "The Trial by Existence," by Robert Frost:

> Even the bravest that are slain
> shall not dissemble their surprise
> On waking to find valor reign,
> Even as on earth, in Paradise.
>
> Nor is there wanting in the press
> some spirit to stand simply forth
> Heroic in its nakedness
> Against the uttermost of earth.
> The tale of earth's unhonored things
> sounds nobler there than 'neath the sun
> And the mind whirls and the heart sings
> And a shout greets the daring one.

Sean took his final words from Shakespeare's *Julius Caesar:* "His life was gentle, and the elements/So mix'd in him that Nature might stand up/And say to all the world, This was a man!"

Congregational singing of "Without Clouds" concluded the service.

Outside on the wheelchair ramp near the church's front door, Bob and Mim stood and greeted each person. When the seemingly endless line had passed, they went home.

The house was anything but a shroud of gloom. A songfest was already in session with Jackie on guitar, Sean on flute, and Debbie Hardie on violin. Strains of "She'll Be Comin' 'Round the Mountain" resounded as Mim and Bob entered the living room, and they both got in on the "Whoa back!" part. It was the most re-invigorating laughter that either had heard in weeks.

But somebody in the crowded room soon began to cry, and the mood was one of total transition. A group hand-holding prayer session ensued, and then the mood swung back to one of cheer. Why was it that grief came in waves, releasing its captives momentarily before crashing in again with more fury than ever?

Bob and Mim made the rounds. Bobby's friends from all stages of life seemed to be there: high school, college, State of Maine Human Services, The Homestead, and all periods in between. John and Martina Linnehan and Renate Lillifors also had come off the trail to attend the memorial service.

Mim went to the kitchen to check on refreshments. As she could have guessed, everything had been done for her. In fact, since Bobby's death, a mini-staff of volunteers had been a godsend. A two-shift receptionist, telephone operator/coordinator, secretary, cook, and several errand persons and taxi drivers had been required to handle matters. The outpouring had been only one of many things that had sustained the Mountford family. And though Bobby would never conclude the hike he had set out to attain, it was clear that his nationwide supporters would not forget one of the goals of his hike. Already a new wave of donations in support of The Little Red School House had begun to come in.

Seeing that all was well, Mim started to retreat to the living room, but her big kitchen was filling as fast. For a moment the chatter seemed subdued. Mim turned about. Joanne Irace entered, paused momentarily, and went to Jackie Hilton, where Jackie was pouring coffee.

"I'm so sorry for you," Joanne whispered.

"He loved you, too," Jackie said.

The two women embraced and clung to each other.

The scene-in-microcosm gave birth to misty eyes among numerous onlookers, but Debbie Hardie became the rescuing, wandering fiddle player again and had the entire household following her own rendition of "Old Macdonald Had a Farm."

Over coffee and cake, the tale-telling threatened to go far beyond the bounds of probable reality: Mountford's antics in England (Stitham); Mountford's practical jokes in high school (Hardy); Mountford's losing his pants while going up the side of a rock cliff (Koch); Mountford's perfect mimicry at Homestead of a notorious gangster, complete with period clothes (Collins); Mountford's toe-to-toe and eyeball-to-eyeball confrontation with a Russian professor in Russia (McGinn); Mountford's invention of a new deodorant made from ramps and guaranteed to annilate Appalachian Trail mosquitoes (Linnehan). Then Bobby's brothers and sisters got into the act. After each had told his favorite story, the rafters were in danger of collapsing.

The good laughter lingered on well into the night, but one by one, and two by two, the guests departed.

Later that night in bed, Mim fought for sleep. It was not the loss of Bobby entirely. She had made some progress in that way even on this night of nights. Worming its way back into her mind was a tragic family incident almost forty years old. She had been nearly nine at the time ___ a time of family hardship when her father had been forced to leave Millinocket for Yarmouth—near Portland—to find work. World War II was raging, and her father found work as a shipyard painter. The family had stayed behind, the older children helping with the younger, and generally making do. Their unpretentious, semi-rural home sat on a small acreage, and behind the house was a hay barn.

One day Jimmy, Mim's four-year-old brother, and a playmate had climbed up into the barn loft with a supply of matches. Before any of the family realized it, fire was raging. A quick rush to the barn and attempts at ascending the loft ladder were of no avail; the children had started the fire between themselves and their only means of escape. Mim's mother had had to be restrained from her suicidal attempts at reaching the second story through licking flames. There had not even been time to run for ladders, and the loft had no windows. Even so, the other children had been paralyzed with terror. From the moment of seeing the fire and smoke, they had heard their little brother crying out repeatedly: "Momma, help me! Momma, help me!"

In spite of their own—and their neighbors'—heroics, the blistering heat and dense smoke were in seeming seconds victorious. They all had watched in horror the little boys' cremation. Lucy Rideout never really recovered from her son's untimely death; for years she remained withdrawn and spiritless, and in time Mim became a surrogate mother to her younger siblings.

On this night, Mim again heard the anguished cries of her little brother with the clarity of yesterday's happenings. She wondered whether Bobby, too, had cried out, and there had been no one to help him.

Across town, two others also remained awake, talking. At the home of Mountford friends, Joanne Irace and Renate Lillifors had been housed in an upstairs bedroom. They quickly discovered mutual interests.

Renate told in great detail and with European animation many of the adventures she had shared with Bob and the others along the Appalachian Trail.

"He wanted to lose weight so badly—and I know he stopped smoking; he wrote about that," Joanne added.

"He vas pulling your leg." Renate laughed a throaty laugh. "He started smoking again vith Frank Maguire."

"And he probably started drinking beer again, when he knows—knew—it would only accentuate the weight problem!"

"Yes, that too. But you must understand, at the vorst times vhen everybody hiked alone, it vould get very lonely. It vas easy to fall back into the old vays."

"I am so mad at him. He is so strong—yet so weak," Joanne said, only remotely realizing that she still thought and spoke in the present tense.

Without warning Joanne's eyes spilled over.

"You loved him—once?" Renate said.

"Yes."

"He vas an easy man to love. I vill finish the hike in his memory."

"You told me earlier that you helped identify the body. Wasn't that terribly hard for you to do? Hiking with him—getting to know him?"

"I come from a country vhere the shadow of death and the stories of var are still too fresh. I vas raised on tales of suffering and dying. Maybe I have grown hard. Neither has America been good to me; and frustrations about vork, about people . . . you know . . . "

Renate went on at length, and when she had finished, Joanne said: "May

I share some of the experiences of my life with you? Perhaps there is something in them to give you new courage."

Renate listened with interest to the story of one pilgrim's progress. Dawn had almost arrived when each woman slid under the sheets. No covers were needed—the night air was still warm and hinting of another hot day.

For a moment Joanne lay rigidly still. Then it came. The memory of Bob's reading Ruskin's poetry to her that day long ago beside Pusham Lake: "No day is without its innocent hope . . . ."

With a smile on her lips, she closed her eyes and began a silent prayer.

CHAPTER XXV

Day six. June 6. John Hopkins sat in his office with Mike Meyer tallying the score. Things were looking up. Evidence gathered at the scene of the murders had yielded a half-dozen suspect prints; the thumbprint in blood on the paperback was the most perfect of the lot. Now, if its counterpart could just be found.

Hopkins' buzzer sounded, and he picked up the phone. Lieutenant Catron from the Galax Police Department was on the line. Galax was a city to the southwest, two counties removed from Giles.

"Hold onto your badge, Sheriff," Catron began.

Sensing the importance of the call, Hopkins motioned Meyer to another extension.

"I've got my hand right on it," Hopkins said.

"How'd you like to have a prime suspect in the AT killings dumped right in your lap?"

"Anything to get off the hotseat for awhile. The press and the public are about to drive us nuts. The State Police, too. Crane tells me Delp and Duff—his bosses—have been forced to play the role of full-time public relations men. What've you got?"

"We picked up a guy and his girl friend, and they had a car full of what appears to be stolen property. Among the stuff was camping gear, and get this—two butcher knives. One of the knives is still blood-stained. We haven't had a chance to check his alibis thoroughly, but we did run an APB on him through NCIC. Guess what? The dude's a fugitive from the state of Maine."

Hopkins's blood pressure surged. A grudge killing? Some recent or ancient trouble between residents of the same state? But how would Susan Ramsay fit in?

"Hope the State boys can join you on this right away. You may just have something," Hopkins said.

Catron tossed off a couple of theories of his own.

Hopkins rang off. Meyer was quickly at his side.

"Sounds good," Meyer said, "but it could be another Knoxville thing."

It could at that. The "Knoxville thing" was another hot tip that had fizzled. Two men in a bar in Knoxville, Tennessee, had overheard a third man bragging about what a sweet job he had done "blowing away" two Appalachian Trail hikers. The eavesdroppers had called Virginia State Police. The half-drunk braggart was found later to be on an ego trip, and nowhere near the state of Virginia at the critical time.

Way up the Valley of Virginia, Peter Butryn and John "JJ" Jurczynski hiked on. Before many days now, they would be approaching the Virginia/Maryland state line. Earlier, near the city of Waynesboro, they had come off the trail for a good breakfast at a Sambo's Restaurant. While sipping juice and waiting for hot pancakes, JJ had retrieved an outdated newspaper from under the booth and with nothing better to do started scanning the pages. The front page had been folded inward, but once in order, photos of Bob Mountford and Susan Ramsay stared back at him.

When he had recovered from his shock and shown the story to Peter, both hikers could only stare, unbelieving, into each other's eyes. So recent had been the camaraderie with Ramsay and Mountford that their deaths were incomprehensible. Their *violent* deaths, Peter reminded.

In spite of all the questions the issue of violence raised, JJ's thoughts turned in a different direction. He loved Mountford as a brother though he had only known him for a brief time. The know-it-all, loudmouth Mainelander had wormed his way into everybody's heart.

As he read the story yet again, tears dribbled down his face and dripped onto his pancakes, and he made no attempt to hide his grief. The pancakes were left largely uneaten, but he tore the news story away, folded it, and put it in his pocket.

Strangely, rangers hadn't stopped Peter and him on the trail, but they called the Pearisburg hostel anyway to offer any help they could.

Back on the trail, a strange thing had happened. From out of nowhere, a young shepherd pup showed up at JJ's heels. His attempts at scaring or coaxing the animal back in the direction from which he had come were fruitless. Just when JJ thought he had won the struggle of wills, the dog would sneak back more determined than ever. JJ thought he had prevailed until one night after he had sacked out and settled into a deep, exhausted sleep. A sudden cold nose against his neck sent him into spasms of momentary terror as, more wakeful, he reasoned that a ferocious bear had smelled the honey JJ had consumed as a bedtime snack. It was the dog, of course, and he decided that separation was now totally out of the question. Since man and beast had met in the Blue Ridge, he decided that if the name was good enough for a mountain chain, it was good enough for a dog.

All the next day and most of the night, JJ sensed something about "Blue Ridge" that he simply couldn't shake—even as weird as it would sound if verbally expressed. In some uncanny way, Bob Mountford was manifested in the dog. The feeling had nothing to do with anything Blue Ridge had or hadn't done. Still, there was the undeniable "presence" of a human spirit in the animal. And as the fellowship of man and dog deepened, JJ felt at times along the trail that he carried on a conversation, not with Blue Ridge but with the invisible Mountford himself.

He began to dream at night that he and Mountford spoke to each other without the need of words. He questioned his own sanity. Was the isolation of the trail doing him in? Or was the awesome woodland stillness opening his consciousness to a higher level of life in which the spirit world and the mortal overcame the chasm?

He honestly didn't know. It was, after all, the first and only time he had ever shed tears over a death. He began to feel the need to share his experience with others beside Peter, and he toyed with the idea of going to Bob's parents after he and Peter had reached the end of the trail. But maybe he shouldn't—maybe it would only increase the Mountfords' grief.

Al Crane was taking a different tack. The film taken from the murdered Mountford's camera had proven highly interesting. The people in some of the photos were quickly identified since state police, sheriff's department personnel, or forest rangers had personally met Maguire, Lillifors, Skinner, Tice, John Smith, Candy Lakin, and others. There were still more hikers in some of the photos that no one could identify. The most interesting photo, however, was of Susan Ramsay, firing a revolver at a target behind a picnic table. Unfortunately, the angle and the distance in the photo didn't allow a close-up view of the revolver. It was a long shot, indeed, but Crane couldn't help wondering whether there was any kinship between the revolver in the photo and the one used to end the life of Bob Mountford. Even if there was, it wouldn't be an easy fact to prove since the bullets taken from Mountford's skull were too fragmented for ballistics testing.

The photo of Ramsay with the revolver showed a limited amount of peripheral landscape, but after making the rounds of ranger stations, interviewing hikers coming out of Carolina toward Jefferson National, and inquiries at The Place in Damascus, the state police had successfully identified the location where Susan Ramsay took potshots at beer cans: Houndshell Campground in the Mount Rogers preserve.

Once at Houndshell Campground—a privately owned camping site with a small, rustic grocery—Crane hit seeming pay dirt. Mike Sims, storekeeper and manager of the campground, was one of the unidentified young persons in the photographs. And Sims' girlfriend, Donna Perkins, had given a ride to Mountford and Ramsay to the campground store.

"They'd run low on groceries, they said," Donna continued, "and they looked so tired walking along the highway, I just stopped and picked them up. After I dropped them at the store here, I went on home."

Between customers, Mike Sims filled in other details: "They were a friendly couple—y'know, real-with-it kind of people—and we hit it off good."

Donna agreed. "There was something about them that sort of latched on to you. You felt good with them. They could get excited about simple little things. They were different from us ___ that's for sure."

"Anyway, they must have liked us, too," Sims said, "and they talked to a lot of people comin' in and out. Talked about what a good hike they were havin'—things that happened to them on the AT. Stuff like that."

"And this revolver in the photograph?" Crane said.

"That's mine," Sims said. "A .32 caliber H & R. I set up some beer cans out by the picnic tables and let Susan try her luck. She couldn't hit a bull in the rear end, but she got as excited tryin' as a little kid. Mountford was busy takin' her picture."

"May I see the weapon?" Crane said.

"Sure," Sims said, and reached under the counter.

Crane hoped the disappointment didn't show in his face. He studied the photo and the weapon. As best he could tell, they matched, but even so, he would have the police lab do a blow-up of the photo to be sure. He handed the revolver back. A .32 was the wrong caliber. Another lead gone sour.

"Anything you can tell me of a helpful nature?" Crane asked. "Did Mountford have any run-ins with anybody here? Say anything that would lead you both to believe any trouble had happened on the trail? Were they hiding out from anybody during their layover in Mount Rogers?"

"Like I told you earlier," Sims said, "they hung around the campground the rest of the afternoon, camped out overnight, and hit the trail the next morning. They never said a thing about any trouble of any kind. Just a couple of happy hikers havin' a real blast. We couldn't believe it when we read in the papers they'd been murdered . . . like losin' a couple of good friends . . . everybody liked 'em."

"If you ask me," Donna said, "I think some real weirdo did them in. They wouldn't have hurt a flea."

The pert young woman's opinion was one that Crane was coming more and more to accept.

On the way back, Crane checked in with headquarters to see how the Galax lead was shaping up. It was still hanging, but thus far, the suspect's alibis were checking out, and the blood on the butcher knife was beef blood.

Next day, Crane headed for Pearisburg and Sheriff Hopkins' office.

Hopkins looked dejected when Crane entered.

"I can tell it's bad news," Crane speculated.

"Yeah. Catron just called from Galax. Our Maine fugitive—who has ties in Chesterfield County, Virginia, I just learned—has iron-clad alibis for the whole week the murders took place. The suspect and his girlfriend were heading from eastern Virginia to Kingsport, Tennessee, and among other things can apparently prove their stops en route. As for the camping gear, none of it matches what we're looking for."

"I caught part of the developments on radio traffic after I left headquarters," Crane said.

251

Tommy Lawson came in, and the three of them began to rehash some of the lesser points of the case. The Bacardi rum bottle found at the murder scene had been purchased at the state liquor store right in Pearisburg. That had been easy enough to trace simply by the stamp label. The Coke found with the rum bottle bore the imprint of a West Virginia distributor that serviced the Pearisburg territory. But what did that prove? Although Mountford's and Ramsay's autopsy reports showed high blood-alcohol content, that didn't prove that they had drunk from the Barcardi purchased in Pearisburg. The sweating, sun-baked bottles bore no usable comparative fingerprints. The Texas catheter had been traced to Giles Memorial Hospital, but again, what did it prove? And what was the use of the catheter and by whom? The drinks and the catheter could have been left, or lost, by anybody, although it seemed unlikely that anyone requiring the use of a catheter would be running around in Jefferson National. So many people used and had access to all areas of Jefferson National that dozens, if not hundreds, could have left one or many of the items. What had actually happened, Crane and Hopkins agreed, was that the minute search in the mountain had uncovered months' of debris, much of which was not connected with the murders at all. That was one way to look at it, but Tommy Lawson reminded that much of the "stuff"—as it had come to be collectively called—had been buried, or otherwise hidden, not just discarded.

"That catheter bugs me," Lawson added.

"Maybe the user-owner found a new way of getting the jollies for himself," Crane said. "And do we have anything to tie even a remote suspect to employment at Giles Memorial, or to a friend's or relative's employment?"

Nobody could think of one. And as for "remote suspects," between responses to the composite drawing, various hikers' suspicions, a battery of phone calls from anonymous tipsters that were mostly crank calls, the "remote suspects" list was growing daily. In addition, a dozen mediums— including the woman working with Jackie Hilton—had offered assistance.

"Speaking of the composite," Crane said, "we got a call from a hiker named Meitzler—from Connecticut—who said that he saw a strange-acting man matching the drawing, at Doc's Knob Shelter, on May 17 or 18. I don't have to remind you that Doc's Knob is in spitting distance of Wapiti II. And the date of the sighting was just one or two days before the murders. This makes the fourth good ID that seems to stand up from hikers through the area at the time."

"If that is true, it means our murderer—alone or with friends—had probably hung around that section of Jefferson National for several days," Hopkins said. "It's the only way all the alleged sightings and encounters match up."

They ran that subject dry and got back to more of the odds and ends found at the murder scene. The boxes of .22 caliber cartridges had been traced to Ched's Discount Store right in town, by the price labels, but while

252

sales of guns were strictly regulated and records kept, the same was not true of ammunition. Another stone wall. But the rum, the Coke, the catheter, and the cartridges — all originating right in Pearisburg — hinted of a homicide by a local person or persons.

"Do we say that the owner of the catheter and the Protex condoms we found was one and the same person?" Hopkins asked.

"Who knows?" Crane admitted. "If he *was* getting his jollies by some perverted use of the device, maybe he liked to try on regular rubbers for thrills as well."

"And just maybe he was waiting for someone to come along to try one out on," Lawson said.

"Yeah, but if we're speaking of one and the same person, there's something distinctly wrong here," Crane said. "There's a suggestion of perversion or certainly abnormality."

"And the package of fishhooks we found? How do they fit in?" Hopkins asked.

"God knows," Crane said, "but I'll bet my reputation on the fact that those nude pictures, the rubbers, the cartridges, and the catheter all fit together somehow."

"The cigarette butts your crew on the Mobile Lab collected? Did they show narcotics residue?" Hopkins asked. "Ours came back from the lab with an inconclusive test report."

"There was some evidence on some butts of drug residue—Smack, Blue Velvet, Yellow Jackets—something of the sort—but not enough to be absolutely certain about and certainly not enough to support an evidence exhibit in court if and when the time comes," Crane said. "And anyway, who's to say that contaminated butts and the murderer have anything in common?"

"And we haven't gotten a thing from the pawn shops, flea markets, and second-hand stores," Lawson added. "If the killer sold Ramsay's and Mountford's hiking boots, watches, and so forth, he did it well out of the area, or to friends or other individuals."

"None of it makes sense," Hopkins said. "If robbery were part of the motive, why would the thief be more interested in twenty dollars for used boots, another twenty-five for each watch, and then leave two cameras that would've brought him at least fifty dollars apiece? Crazy. Where's the logic?"

"Maybe that's part of the picture," Crane said. "Maybe our man is short on logic or at least on clear rational thought."

When each began to repeat his theory, they decided to give it up. Let a new day come and see what it brought.

That night, sometime after midnight, John Hopkins had just drifted into a deep sleep. The jangle of the bedside phone shot through his tired body like a splash of ice water. Still half asleep, he reached for the receiver. Mike

Meyer on night watch had to repeat his words before Hopkins came fully alive.

"I won't believe what?" Hopkins growled.

"It's the damnedest thing I've ever seen." Meyer's voice rose to a high pitch. "I've got the twins of both Bob Mountford and Susan Ramsay waiting downstairs in the dispatcher's office!"

"What!" Hopkins sat bolt upright.

Sarah Jane, accustomed to nightly interruptions and quickly recognizing the difference between the mundane and the important, likewise sprang to attention.

"The girl's a dead ringer for Susan Ramsay, and the guy is a duplicate of Bob Mountford if I ever saw one." Meyer's voice was going still higher.

"You better run all this by me slowly," Hopkins said.

Meyer slowed down, articulating each word, and continued; "Earlier tonight, some hikers from the local hostel called me and said two other hikers—Peggy Wheeler and Isaac "Ike" Charlton—had come in just before nightfall. While they were all sittin' around talkin' about their trail experiences, the subject of the murders surfaced. The more everybody talked, my informants said, the more uneasy this Peggy Wheeler and Ike Charlton became."

"This Wheeler and Charlton hadn't heard about the murders?"

"No, apparently not. They've been hikin' alone—comin' northward along the trail out of Carolina. Anyway, as everybody brought the couple up-to-date on what had happened, the Wheeler girl got real shook up. When copies of news stories and photos were shown to Wheeler and Charlton, the girl started breakin' down. By then half the hostel residents were lookin' back and forth between news photos and the newly arrived couple, seein' at once the unbelievable similarity. The Wheeler girl was fallin' apart by then, and she told some of her fellow hikers a wild tale about bein' pursued along the trail by an ex-lover who wanted to kill her. She told me the same story a little while ago, and it's damn convincin'. Her alleged pursuer supposedly left threatenin' notes along the trail for her. Called himself "the ninety-five pounder" or somethin'; an ex-army sergeant."

"Did she and Charlton actually encounter this 'ninety-five pounder'?"

"No. He seemed to stay just out of reach. The girl's still too shaken to be very coherent. I think she had to be talked into comin' out here. Father Winter, or somebody, had a hand in convincin' her—and Charlton—to come out and tell us what they knew."

"I think we've got something," Hopkins said.

"You haven't heard the end yet. The big macho man, Ned Shires, was seen at the hostel just before she left to come out here. She spotted him walkin' around among the tents. She was gettin' close to hysterical when she first got here. She's better now, but I think you ought to get up here."

"You already sent somebody out to the hostel to see if this Shires is still around?"

254

"Yeah. All this suggest anything to you?"

"Yeah. I'll be there shortly."

Hopkins sprang out of bed and began to dress.

Sarah Jane offered to make coffee and said, "What's up?"

"I think we may have a mistaken identity murder."

Before she could pry additional information from him, he was gone.

Hopkins made the five-mile distance between his home in Narrows and his office in record time. He came to a screeching halt in the alley, flipped the switch of his blue flasher, and entered the building.

"They're upstairs," the dispatcher said.

When Hopkins entered his office, the others stood. His eyes locked onto Peggy Wheeler and Ike Charlton. It was startling. Absolutely incredible. The girl would go a hundred-fifty-five or sixty pounds, her height was right, her dark reddish-blond hair was done up in a long pigtail, her fair face was pretty but not quite as round as Ramsay's; the likeness was unbelievable.

And Ike Charlton was indeed a dead ringer for Mountford, right down to the heavy beard and moppish hair.

Meyer introduced his superior. Hopkins asked the visitors to be seated. Peggy folded her hands in her lap, but they were still shaking. She asked permission to smoke and attempted to light a Winston. The match danced around the cigarette tip like a firefly before landing on target.

Hopkins could hardly pry his eyes away, but he suddenly remembered others matters: "What's the report from the hostel? Any sign of this ___ this Shires?"

"No," Meyer said. "He was long gone when we got there. Must have just buzzed in and out."

"Well, he buzzed near enough to our tent that I could've spit on him," Peggy said. "Somebody told me that he was looking for a short guy— nicknamed The Midget—that he'd hiked with earlier."

"But he didn't see you?" Hopkins asked.

"No. I was petrified at the sight of him. I hid under the tent."

"And you?" Hopkins focused his vision on Ike Charlton.

"I was at another tent, talking with a hiker we met at Damascus."

"Do you think Shires was really looking for The Midget?" Hopkins prompted.

"I think he was there trying to find some friends he'd earlier made along the trail—somebody that could vouch for his whereabouts the days he laid low for us. Especially the day he thought he'd killed us."

"Wait a minute," Hopkins said. "You're just now getting in to the hostel, and so, apparently, are some of his former hiking acquaintances. The murders happened more than two weeks ago. How do you square that?"

"There for a while he was playing tag with us, and us with him," Ike said. "After a while we had no idea where he was along the trail, and the same was true for him."

"Yes," Peggy said. "We think he suspected that we'd left the trail, which we did. We took a bus to get farther northward in a hurry, and rid ourselves of him entirely."

"Then if he suspected it, and did the same, each of you was leap-froggin' the other? Meyer asked.

"Probably," Peggy said, "but then I got a case of bad blisters and had to go off the trail again for medical attention. We rested a few days in a motel and hit the trail again. Never knew from then on where Ned might be, but we were back with some of the same group we'd started with."

"Yeah, but we stayed away from them, kept away from hostels, and hiked alone, so we could cut down on the chance of Shires gettin' word as to where we were," Ike added.

"We're moving too fast for me," Hopkins said. "Start over. I want to hear the whole thing from beginning to end."

Hopkins had emptied his ash tray twice before Peggy finished. The way she told it, her story was jarringly amazing and almost totally believable. Two points bothered Hopkins. The girl had not fully convinced him that Ned Shires's jealousy—obsession, vendetta, whatever—was fervent or twisted enough to make Peggy and Ike the objects of murder. On the other hand, Hopkins had known of similar homicide cases with shallower motivation. And the longer he stayed in law enforcement, the more convinced he was that the woodwork was ever fuller of strange worms.

"And I'm still confused about those notes signed by 'The Ninety-Five Pounder,'" Hopkins said. "What was the last place coming northward on the trail *you* actually *saw* one?"

Peggy and Ike stole a quick glance at each other.

"We heard about them and listened to other people talk about them all the way to Virginia," Peggy said.

"But where did you *see* the last one?" Hopkins insisted.

"We didn't—personally—see any more after we got out of Georgia," Peggy said. "But we heard . . . "

"Isn't it possible rumor was breedin' on rumor?" Meyer queried. "Maybe the story got bigger the farther north everybody got."

"Ned Shires is no rumor," Peggy flared. "He wanted—wants—to kill Ike and me, and he thinks he has!"

"Why can't he just go and find another woman?" Meyer asked.

"I don't know why! He wants to possess me. And if he can't have me, he wants me dead. He always has. I don't know why he's got the fixation. I certainly didn't encourage it!"

"How well do you know Shires?" Hopkins asked Ike Charlton.

"Only saw him once. He used to trail Peggy or Peggy and me in our home town. I caught him once, but he slipped me before I could get to him. Don't take any genius, though, to figure out the guy's a quart low."

The observation had logic, and the four of them backtracked at considerable length, reviewing every aspect of Shires's life that Peggy could remember.

"Was Shires ever institutionalized?" Hopkins asked.

"When he was in high school, I think he had brief psychiatric counseling, but I'm not positive."

"Did he ever assault you—other women?" Meyer asked.

Peggy told of one personal incident when Ned Shires had abused her. She added, "His brutality was more directed against men. He liked to pick a bar fight, even with men much bigger and stronger than himself, just for the chance to prove his superiority. I never saw it personally, but he had the reputation of making bloodly pulps out of guys twice his size."

"Heavy drinker? Drugs?" Hopkins asked.

"Neither," Peggy said. "An occasional glass of wine. That was it."

Every new direction explored led to still another avenue. The night was turning to dawn.

"Before you leave, we need all the helpful names and addresses you can give us," Hopkins said. "I'm sure you don't have any more idea than we do where Shires might be found, but think of all the places he might go. I'm sending you back to the hostel now, but we'll need you to meet with us again tomorrow."

"I can tell you one thing," Peggy said. "Father Winter is going to have a house guest even if we have to sleep on the floor or in the baptismal pool. We're not sleeping out in the open!"

It was tomorrow already, Meyer observed after the two hikers had left with a deputy.

"Well, what do you think?" Hopkins said.

"I can tell you this much: if I was Ned Shires stalkin' my ex-lover and her new boyfriend and came up on them at dusk—or, on a moonlit night—I couldn't have told the difference between Peggy-Ike and Susan-Bob."

"I'll buy that. Even by campfire light, distinguishing between the couples wouldn't have been easy."

"And bein' furious at the time wouldn't have helped much."

"Get a call in to the State Police dispatcher and alert Crane," Hopkins said. "Looks like it's going to be a busy day."

The media picked up quickly that something new was in the air. Maybe the first leak had come from the local hostel. Hopkins hadn't forbidden Peggy and Ike to discuss the matter further: after all, the couple had already told their story to three or four dozen hikers and to church personnel. Both Hopkins and Meyer had, however, advised the couple of the seriousness of accusation against anyone without solid proof.

In any event when state police arrived to join in further questioning of Peggy and Ike, Hopkins noticed reporters and TV crews closing in on the courthouse and the jail building. Funny, but when something was in the air, even the elected county officials and their various staffs seemed to feel the shifting winds. And leaks from some of those quarters were not historically unheard of. It was amazing in a small town: whose aunt had connections to what secretary who dated whose son; whose mother patronized what beauty shop or bridge club. And the short-wave interceptors and CB radios in Giles County already constituted an underground network of unbelievable proportions.

Peggy and Ike stuck solidly to their earlier story; they enlarged on it with facts about Shires's encounters with others along the trail while he was still in Georgia. Even so, there was something in the girl's manner that was giving pause to some of the officers present. Allowing that anyone seemingly a target for murder would be unnerved, the girl appeared unusually excitable and excessively high-strung. Ike, on the other hand, seemed not excitable at all; he was willing without protest or a simple difference of opinion to go along.

New questions—or old questions presented differently—made the rounds.

"Suppose Shires was simply playing cat-and-mouse with you. Would each night in the mountains have blown the seriousness of his intent toward you out of proportion?"

"Two people that closely resemble us are dead. Murdered. According to the news stories we've just read, they were from Maine; unknown in the area; had no enemies—'wouldn't hurt a fly' according to their friends, and now they're dead. Does that sound like I'm imagining things?" Peggy asked.

It was the kind of answer that made even the pros smile in appreciation.

The couple was advised that interviews with the media might not be wise after all, because too many volunteered details, names, and places might hinder the investigation. The couple would not be asked to stay in Giles County so long as they kept authorities advised of their whereabouts. In fact, if their theory was right and the killer thought he had gotten away with it, they would be better off skipping way up the trail and starting anew.

The couple was escorted out a rear entrance and whisked away, but inside, debated continued.

"I think she's a little flaky," a state officer said.

"I'm inclined to believe her," a deputy countered.

The group was almost equally split but still open and cautious. A lot of things no longer fitted. If the story had merit, one thing might just fit: Ned Shires's thumbprint and the one in blood on the back of Susan Ramsay's book.

"It's the hottest thing we've got. Let's get on it," Crane said.

Outside, the media closed in. They were hungry for news. With the initial story played out, the newshounds had run thin and concentrated on bio pieces about both victims, their aspirations, their interests, and work history. Now they wanted something new and hot.

The state policemen were on tight rein. Official responses would henceforth come from headquarters at Wytheville, but Hopkins gave them a morsel.

"We've got a new suspect. That's all I can tell you for now. You'll know when we know."

Hopkins found himself fighting them off like flies, but he kept his cool and weathered the storm. Holding back everything too long from the local papers might not be so easy. Furious local editors and publishers made formidable enemies especially at election time.

Nevertheless, the following morning several dailies ran front-page stories: "New Suspect Sought in Slaying of Two Maine Hikers." The stories contained an amazing array of accurate facts about Ned Shires, but prudently, the papers had refrained from mentioning names.

It was too late to worry about leaks. A mountain of investigation remained to be done, and Hopkins had the feeling that it wasn't going to be as easy as it sounded. In his career, it never had been.

CHAPTER XXVI

On June 7 Randall Joe was down to his last eighteen dollars. Even a sleazy room in a dilapidated rooming house anywhere near the beach was now out of the question. They had to eat, and Toe had less than five dollars.

It was just before noon, and for a time they cruised in Randall Joe's truck up and down Ocean Drive. The cab was like an oven, and Randall Joe's face dripped with sweat. The hot seat fabric was like an iron against their bare thighs.

After miles—and repeated miles—of it, Toe said, "What we running all the gas out for? We don't have money for no more gas."

"Shut up!"

Randall Joe pressed down on the accelerator pedal. The tape player, blaring out that same damnable song, was going full blast. Toe wished that the unbearable heat would melt it. They were soon speeding, and Randall Joe was having to swerve in and out among the mixture of swimsuit-clad pedestrians and slow-moving ocean-front traffic that crowded the narrow thoroughfare. Finally Randall Joe slowed the vehicle, and Toe hoped that he would stop and they could lounge on the beach.

"Along here looks good," Toe ventured. "Look at that gang of girls headin' for the water. Man—look at those buns shimmy . . . "

"I'm not stoppin'," Randall Joe said—and didn't. "Don't like walkin' on the beach in the middle of the day. Too hot."

Toe tried to reason through Randall Joe's thinking. It was twenty degrees hotter in the truck. But every day Randall Joe had lain around—in bed, mostly—until midafternoon before he would venture out on the beach. Not until night did Randall Joe's personality change, and he would soften, laugh, and joke about the most insignificant things.

And Randall Joe loved to stay up late. When midnight came and he had had a couple of joints—and they had gotten some really good grass from a couple of beachbums—Randall Joe relished going down to the water and running in and out of the crashing waves like a child. It was obvious that he had a terror of the big swells, but he didn't mind if Toe went for a swim. Toe would come out of the water, and Randall Joe would be sitting on the sand near motel lights, making a minute study of newly found seashells.

One night Randall Joe had stayed out until the sun came up. When they were riding again, Randall Joe at the wheel, and Toe had asked where he had been, Randall Joe flared up.

"You one of those fuggin' people always tryin' to see in other people's heads?"

Toe had calmed him: "I was worried about you. Thought maybe some of those college girls might of raped you and left you layin' or somethin'."

"Yeah, they hemmed me in, but I got away from them. Bunch of sex maniacs."

Toe had quickly figured out that any suggestion of Randall Joe's appeal to women calmed and pleased him.

"Long about here okay?" Randall Joe said, easing up on the accelerator.

Toe did a double take. One minute Randall Joe was against something. A split second later, he was all for it.

"This looks good. And look at those two beauties comin' toward us! Ever seen two sets of knockers jigglin' any better than that?"

Randall Joe said nothing but parked the truck quickly. They followed the two girls across a motel parking lot and down toward the beach.

The women spread a blanket and started to lie down on their stomachs. Toe gasped at the generous view of hanging cleavage. Randall Joe looked longingly for a moment before averting his eyes.

"Wouldn't you just love to play windshield wiper with your nose?" Toe said. "I could drown myself between those big boobs and die happy."

"Shut up. You got outhouse soup for brains. They might be some kid's mother."

Toe couldn't quite cipher the strange, disjointed remark. So their tits had been sucked on. So what? When Randall wouldn't comment further and got sulky, in fact, Toe ran for the water.

Toe played in the surf for a time. Looking back toward the beach, he could tell that Randall Joe wanted to venture out, for he would approach the water and wade in, but the curling swells seemed to frighten him and he would jump back.

Toe came out of the water and joined his companion. They had no blanket ____ no oil, no towels, no nothing. Randall Joe sat on a discarded pizza box. Toe stood, dancing barefoot in the hot sand.

"Wanna walk or what?" Toe said.

Randall Joe only grunted, but he kept looking sideways at the two women they had followed down to the beach. Toe had a sudden inspiration: he felt instinctively that Randall Joe needed something special.

The beach was crowded with people of all shapes and sizes. Toe looked about, saw a little boy of four or five, and went to talk with him. The child laughed in delight at Toe's idea and ran to execute it.

Not until two women called out did Randall Joe take notice. The little boy jerked the two women's bras down, and making a circle, had exposed the breasts of half a dozen other women before anyone knew what was going on. The boy ran for safety with a swimsuit top in each hand but in seeming danger of his life as one woman chased him, her bare breasts cupped in her hands, until the object of her hostility had taken refuge with his parents. The child pointed toward Toe and Randall Joe.

Toe suggested that the two of them move on up the beach in a hurry.

As they were moving off, Randall Joe said, "I saw you talkin' to that kid. What the hell did you make him do that for?"

"I thought you needed it, Randall Joe. Honest to God, I did."

Randall Joe walked with his head down for a moment. An ill-concealed grin began to form on his face.

"You're good to me, Toe. I'm going to buy you a big supper tonight. You're all right, Toe."

"But we're about broke."

"It don't matter. I'd give you my last dollar. You're all right in my book, Toe."

Toe beamed with his newfound approval. Wished he could stay with Randall Joe always. But it was all winding down. He just had to get back to North Carolina. His mother and sisters might be hungry—might need him in a lot of ways.

That night they entered a nice restaurant in South Myrtle Beach. They stood in line a long time, and when their time came, a hostess led them to a window table; but there was some reluctance in the woman's eyes. True, he and Randall didn't look very presentable—they had changed clothes in Randall Joe's truck, but their long hair was sand-matted.

Randall Joe studied the menu, and Toe could tell that his friend was unprepared for the prices. Toe would make it easy on him. When the waitress came, Toe ordered a hamburger and fries. Randall Joe ordered oyster stew. The young waitress eyed them as suspiciously as had the hostess, but she was polite and helpful.

"This means a whole lot to me, Toe. You're just all right."

"Me and you together," Toe agreed.

When the waitress returned with the food, and Randall Joe's oyster stew was placed in front of him, he stared dumbfounded at it for a moment and said to the waitress:

"What's this?"

"It's oyster stew, sir."

"It's some kind of fuggin' soup."

"This is the way oyster stew is served, sir."

"Everybody knows oyster stew is kind of like a seafood plate—fried oysters, clams, and stuff . . . "

"No, sir. Maybe you're thinking of a seafood platter. But you ordered oyster stew."

Randall Joe looked down at his serving questioningly and then back at her. His face flushed and his eyes grew hostile.

"Would you like for me to take it back and bring you a seafood platter?" the waitress asked sweetly.

"No!" Randall Joe growled.

Diners at tables nearby stopped eating and watched intently.

"I'll be glad to take it back."

"Forget it," Randall Joe snapped.

The girl stood, indecisive and embarrassed.

"Get lost," Randall Joe said between gritted teeth.

"That stuff's good," Toe said. "Had some once when we was working in Louisiana."

Randall Joe didn't answer; he just sat there, staring into the bowl like he was hypnotized. Toe didn't know whether to eat or not. Finally he poured ketchup over his fries and began.

Randall Joe's eyes didn't move. They were locked onto the stew as if they were glued there. Still without eye movement, Randall Joe reached for the ketchup.

He must have poured half a cupful into the stew. Then he used salt and pepper. He stirred the mixture with infinite care but didn't take a spoonful until he had smelled it. One taste and he threw the spoon down, rattling the other silverware, drawing more attention to their table.

Toe ate as fast as he could. Fury was rising in Randall Joe's face; the pupils in his brown eyes growing large and shiney.

"Let's get out of here," Toe said. "I've had better horse meat than this burger. Let's go back up the beach where we were. That blond in the white bathing suit might still be there. You know—the one that kept eyin' you? I believe she likes your long hair."

Randall Joe ignored him. Toe left a small tip as they got up to leave. At the cash register, Randall Joe paid the bill without comment and bought a candy bar with his change.

Randall Joe wouldn't go back to the beach; they drove around instead and came to a stop at a deserted strip of undeveloped land at Yaupan and Twenty-Fifth Street. The broad expanse of scrub trees and thick brush looked forbidding and out-of-place against the backdrop of tall buildings in the far distance. The spot was probably swamp land, not fit for development, Toe reasoned. Randall Joe found an opening—a dirt drive almost too narrow to get the truck through, but he gunned the Ford and forced it between two scrub pines and farther along the path.

"What are we doin' this for?" Toe asked.

"This is where we're stayin'."

"The mosquitoes will eat us alive. The snakes, too."

"You can sleep in the cab."

"But what about you? The mosquitoes ___ "

"I'll bite 'em back! Shut up."

They sat there a moment in silence. Toe rolled himself a joint. Randall Joe reached for the grass and cigarette paper. After both had lit up and taken a few drags, Toe said, "You're no talent scout, are you?"

Randall knew the facade had held up only briefly. Now Toe wanted him to admit it. Randall didn't answer.

A few more drags made Toe braver still.

"I said, you're no talent scout, are you?"

"No, I'm no fuggin' talent scout."

"And you're on the run, aren't you?"

"None of your fuggin' business."

"It wouldn't matter none," Toe said.

"Then it don't matter."

"What's it all about? You can trust me."

Randall Joe rolled down a window to let some of the smoke out. A squadron of mosquitoes seemed instantly to take advantage of the opening. Both of them slapped at the insects.

"I said ___ "

"I heard what you said," Randall replied.

"I'm no loudmouth. You told me I was all right. You said ___ "

"I know what I said. But I was just feelin' a big high when I said it. Now just shut up."

Randall Joe finished his joint and got out of the truck. He walked down through the trees. He was gone a long time, but finally Toe could see him inching his way back through the thick brush, silhouetted by the distant lights.

When Randall Joe was back and sitting on the truck hood, Toe said, "Why don't we get out of here in the morning? We're about out of money, and I got to get back. If you'll take me home, I'll buy the gas."

"With what?"

"I know a few tricks. How to steal food without gettin' caught. How to club a gas station operator over the ear—but not hard enough to kill him. Just hard enough to put him out. Things like that."

"I don't steal, and I don't hurt people unless they hurt me first," Randall Joe said.

Toe hadn't expected that kind of answer, but somehow he felt Randall Joe was telling the truth.

Later that night, Toe walked down toward the beach to a quickie food place and to a Seven-Eleven store. With the last of his money, he bought two hamburgers, Cokes, and a spray can of mosquito repellent.

Randall Joe ate hungrily; he threw the wrapper and Coke can over his shoulder into the brush.

"Litterbug," Toe teased.

"You see any fuggin' trash barrel?"

There was none, of course, and Toe had already seen that the ground was littered with paper plates, beer, and soft drink cans.

Even with the mosquito spray—none of which Randall Joe would use— Toe found that he couldn't sleep. In the cab with the windows rolled up, it was stifling hot. With the windows down, the insects pounced on his flesh as if the repellent were strawberry ice cream. He'd never seen such monstrous mosquitoes and other insects. The swamp had to be a regular breeding ground, and he'd bet there were snakes everywhere, six feet long.

When morning finally came, he'd had it. Great welts were all over his neck, face, and arms. He was cutting out, with or without Randall Joe. But where was he?

Toe walked all around the truck; he saw Randall Joe squatting in the distance. He had to laugh at the scene, thinking it funny that the squatter would end up with bites on his ass as well as everywhere else.

When Randall Joe came back, Toe said, "You're the only one left with a few dollars. How about us gettin' some breakfast."

"Don't have any money."

Toe knew that he did —— a little, at least.

"You're goin' to stay around here in this swamp with no money?"

"Yeah."

Toe knew that he meant it. Toe walked out of the island of trees and brush and down toward a fruit stand and a small grocery. He would have to steal breakfast. Might as well sharpen his skills, he thought. He would be stealing all the way back to North Carolina.

In half an hour Toe was back with bananas, apples, and a package of cookies. He didn't know why he didn't just keep going. He didn't owe Randall Joe a damn thing. Still, there was something about the odd Virginian that drew him.

A bright warm sun flooded the woodland as they ate. Birds sang sweetly, and the traffic noise out along the highway even sounded melodious.

Toe thought he'd try one more time.

"Gonna tell me why you're on the run?"

"Nothin' to tell."

"Like hell," Toe said.

"Just shut up."

"You don't need me no more, Randall Joe. I'm cuttin' out. Goin' home."

"Then go home."

Randall Joe never raised his eyes. Just like that, it ended. Toe walked out of the brush toward the highway. He looked back once, and Randall Joe was slapping at mosquitoes as if a swarm of bees had alighted on him. By day's end the Virginian would look like somebody had filled him full of birdshot.

All morning, the phone on Al Crane's desk had rung off the hook. It was June 7. He closed the folder, pushed his glasses up the bridge of his nose, handed the file to the pool secretary, and prepared to leave for Giles County. Before he could clear the door, the phone rang again. He listened to yet another report; this one caused a shot of adrenalin to surge through him. He asked a few lingering questions before ringing off. "Not the answer we'd hoped for, but thanks anyway," he sighed.

He walked down the hall to his boss's office. Gene Duff was a pro in the same sense that Crane and Carroll Delp—the other ranking administrator in Criminal Investigation Division—were. They had all come up through the ranks of dispatcher, trooper—the whole works. But Duff, a no-

nonsense man of forty-seven, and the father of four teenagers, had begun to tire of the onslaught of public and media inquiry regarding the AT murder cases. It was all part of the job, of course, and he and Carroll Delp had been as helpful and open as they could be under the circumstances. The public—and even the media—seemed slow to learn that what was for them good information and hot copy was not necessarily efficient police work. The Virginia State Police worked under rigid guidelines in such matters. The Department walked a tightrope from a number of points of view. The bottom line was the maintenance of public confidence and good public relations while not revealing a shred of information that might prove erroneous, or damaging to the State's case.

The latest suspect in the Mountford-Ramsay affair was a case in point. The media had printed or broadcast everything but the size of the suspect's shorts and then afterwards tried to confirm more speculative information via State Police sources. The nightmare from the Department's point of view was, of course, pointing—or helping to point—a finger at an ultimately innocent suspect.

The Department had always managed to live with the local and state media reps. In this case it was the eastern and northeastern media that kept the heat on, especially the New England papers. The suggestion that Virginia authorities were dragging their feet had hit a sensitive nerve. Both Duff and Delp had diplomatically reminded the callers that the murderer, or murderers, had had nearly a two-week head start on the authorities.

Where some of the state and local papers—not to mention half a dozen TV stations and the Associated Press—had got some of their information was a mystery. Undoubtedly Peggy Wheeler and Ike Charlton, or other hikers they had told their story to, had talked openly. But even so, some of the media had reported other facts about the case with amazing accuracy, facts the Department had thought were generally unknown. At least the name of Ned Shires had not yet been printed or broadcast.

"I'm headed out," Crane said. "Hate to tell Hopkins the prints don't match. Every one of us was betting his last dollar that the thumbprint on the back of Ramsay's book and Ned Shires's print were one and the same."

Once in his car, Crane began mentally toying with all the puzzle pieces again. Since Ned Shires was a former military man, it had been easy enough to get quick comparative print checks from the FBI. The fact that a mismatch rather than the expected match resulted did not necessarily eliminate Shires. The fact might simply give evidence to the more-than-one murderer theory. Maybe Shires was smart enough to have someone else do his dirty work for him.

State police agents had pinpointed Shires's whereabouts fairly quickly after Peggy Wheeler's and Ike Charlton's testimony, but the decision had been made not to bring Shires in for questioning prematurely. A lot of ducks needed to be put in a row before closing in.

At Pearisburg "the Board of Directors Meeting," as they called the almost daily sessions, got under way. When he told them of the print mismatch, Crane could see the wind escape the sails of Hopkins and his deputies.

"The problem now is to prove that Shires—and an accomplice or accomplices—were in Jefferson National at the time of the murders," Crane said, "and you know where the complications come in about that."

Hopkins and the others knew only too well. When the first APB had gone out on Shires, a quick and unexpected response had occurred. Ned Shires had not actually hiked the AT all the way from Springer Mountain, Georgia, to Jefferson National in Virginia. Shires had been arrested in Helen, Georgia, on a Virginia warrant charging larceny and brought back to the area. The case had not yet come to trial, and Shires had not spent one night in jail, having been bailed out by his family. The point was, Shires could not have left threatening notes along the AT any farther north than the Georgia-Carolina border since he had been arrested in Georgia and brought home. Unless ___

"And now the question is, after being bailed out on the larceny charge, did Shires go back, get on the AT again, and continue his hike?" Hopkins said.

"Exactly," Crane replied.

"And he could've gotten back on at any point. Or even waited around Jefferson National for his prey to come to him?" Tommy Lawson offered.

"Yes, and there's still another complication," Crane said. "Our people have been doing a more minute study of the various eyewitness reports, with regard to the 'weird' man supposedly seen in or near the critical section of Jefferson National. What we're coming up with is not one man but two. The long-haired, stoop-shouldered man Robin Cunningham saw with Susan Ramsay at Wapiti II shelter is not the man hiker Barry Newsome and others saw. There seems to be a difference in clothing, hair length, height, and general build."

"Maybe the two men were a team or joined forces later," Meyer suggested.

"That's the sixty-four-dollar question," Crane agreed.

"Maybe it's time we moved on Shires," Hopkins said. "Let him give us his answers to some of these questions."

"Maybe. But then again, maybe not," Crane said. "It may be interesting to keep him under surveillance a while longer. His movements, who he sees, his general behavior—all of it might point to something better than bringing him in."

They all debated the pros and cons and decided to live with the status quo for another forty-eight hours.

That night, Mike Meyer stayed on to supervise the night shift. Things were unusually quiet, and for that he was grateful. For days now, he had been deprived of adequate sleep, and the sheer tension of a big case and the pressure from all sides were in themselves fatiguing.

He had put his head down on his desk for a quick catnap when the door burst open.

"You're not gonna believe this," the dispatcher said excitedly.

"Right now, I'd believe most anything." Meyer lifted leaden eyelids.

"Ned Shires just left a packet of photos with the Blacksburg Police Department. He said he wanted to help in the AT murder case. And he thought the photos might aid authorities to identify various people. Apparently, he took a whole bunch of shots at Springer Mountain and later on the trail."

"Helpful dude, isn't he? He sensin' the heat."

"With all the newspaper stuff, he's got to be making some comparisons."

Meyer started to reach for the phone, but then decided against it.

"It's not important enough to wake Hopkins. Let him get his sleep. Looks like all our tails are goin' to be draggin' in the next few days."

Contrary to his usual practice, Randall was on the beach well before midday. Toe had been gone only one day. He missed Toe with a terrible emptiness. And the churning surf as he walked along the beach reminded him of the waves inside himself that pounded unmercifully.

He gathered a handful of seashells and sat down in the cool, wet sand near the edge of the water to sort them out. The twisting, erratic lines within some of the shells reminded him of the pathway of his own life. The evenly placed spirals at the base of the shell implied the normal beginning of his existence—those peaceful days when he had been a child, little aware that he and Loretta had been deserted by his father. But soon he had become aware of their miserable, poverty-stricken existence. How he hated the sonofabitch that gave seed to him!

He got up and with a vengeful fury threw the shells into the surf.

"Hey! Watch out! You almost hit my kid!" a young father shouted.

Randall strode off up the beach. Big deal. Maybe the kid would be better off dead anyway. Might save him a lot of pain. Could rescue him from the terrible waves that might roll over him all through his life.

Shortly after noon, he bought a hot dog for lunch. The waitress looked at him strangely—let her eyes linger on the numerous mosquito bites that made his flesh look as if he had chickenpox. He moved away from the snack bar and her condemning eyes. He could tell. She was one of those fuggin' people that liked to look into people's heads.

As he put the change in the pocket of his cut-offs, he realized more than ever that his money was almost gone. He'd have to cut down to one snack a day. Maybe he'd have to rob garbage cans. Unlike Toe, he wouldn't steal to survive. He was no thief.

He'd wandered aimlessly up and down the beach forever it seemed. It was midafternoon, and his bare back was blistering. He could feel the heat with such intensity that it began to make him sick. He headed back toward the isolated grove.

Along the way he picked up a bag of rags somebody had discarded and decided to use them to polish his truck. Even hidden among the scrub trees, the vehicle had lost its sheen and became dull and cruddy-looking under a film of dust.

Back at the truck, he tried to rest a while to help the nausea pass. In spite of the shade, it seemed even hotter in the swamp land than on the beach, and sand flies had joined ranks with the mosquitoes, invading his ears and eyes. He plugged in the "On the Road Again" tape, but kept it low.

When he had finished the polishing, the job was less than satisfactory. Streaks here and there still showed. The truck needed washing, but money for the car wash was out. Besides he dare not move the truck now. Deep inside, something told him that time was running out, that yet another intrusion into his life was about to unfold. "Unfold and roll, roll and unfold." He tried to make up some kind of rhyme, but it wouldn't work; it only made the waves start to surge bad over him again.

He got pliers and screwdriver from the glovebox and took the license tags off. In a soft spot well off to the west of the truck, he dug a hole with a stick, rolled the plates like a slab of bologna, and stuffed them in. After he had filled the hole, stamped the dirt tight, and covered the area with leaves and pine needles, he went back to the truck and gathered his meager belongings. He found a piece of note paper and pencil, laid the sheet flat on a copy of *Hustler* magazine, and began writing a message. Finished, he stuck the note in the ashtray. He gave every part of the truck he had touched a final polishing with the cloth and then used the fabric for a mitten. He rolled up each window tightly, locked the doors, gathered his tapes and other things, and walked deeper into the swampy woodland.

Late that same day, Patrolman Rick Shafer of the Myrtle Beach Police Department had gone on duty and begun routine cruising. Summers were tough in Myrtle Beach when the area grew suddenly from small-city status to a city accommodating over five hundred thousand people at the height of the tourist season. And the influx brought its own problems: drugs, drunkenness, major and minor theft, assaults, murder, rape, accidents, and all things in between.

Shafer headed toward Yaupan and Twenty-Fifth. The vast wooded area was the occasional hideout of drug dealers or users. Furthermore, the ground was alive with snakes, rats, mosquitoes, and insects of every kind. No human could stand more than a few hours of the onslaught.

He drove slowly along Twenty-Fifth and then on Yaupan. He started to accelerate when a shaft of sinking sunlight reflected off something shiny among the trees. He backed up, parked, and got out of the cruiser. Along a narrow drive just inside the treeline, the source of the reflection was apparent: the polished chrome bumper of a pick-up truck. He closed on the two-tone green Ford with caution. The vehicle was out of place. There was no place to "four-wheel" in the immediate area. Neither was the truck hidden well if concealment was the owner's intent. He circled cautiously, saw a reflection of his own young, tanned face in the door glass, but no one else was in sight. Coming closer, he noticed something missing: license plates—front and back. Abandonment was nothing new. Both youth and adults stole vehicles just to get to the beach resort and then abandoned them with disdain. Even so, it was a little strange that the possible thief had removed the tags.

He tried the doors without success. One vital thing had not been removed from the truck: the Virginia inspection sticker on the windshield. But the vehicle serial number—atop the dash—was covered by a piece of scrap paper.

Four hours later when Detective Captain Wayne Player had authorized forced entry into the vehicle, Officer Rick Piersal and a fellow officer using "slim-jims" quickly got the vital number.

The cab was clean: no guns, no blood, no drugs, no alcohol—nothing. Then Piersal reached for a scrap of paper sticking out of the ash tray. The note, scarcely six-by-four inches, was hard to read.

"This boy and girl have been so nice to me. You would to if it meant your neck. All the money they gave me is almost gone. It's going to be a real shame for them when the time comes to get rid of them. He sold parts off the truck and gave me all of his hunting guns and knifs and fishing stuff. His girl friend has gave me her car so its time I dump his truck and take her car. Its bad that I have to get rid of them. His girl friend is so pretty and nice. I will be far away before truck and these people are found."

Player studied the poorly written note in his office. It was somehow saying more than the simple words could convey; it had a chillingly sinister ring to it. For such things as this note, Player had a nose that had been sharpened across the fourteen years of his career—from station dispatcher to detective captain with army service in between.

He read and reread the crudely formed words and tried to figure what single thing was most disquieting about them. The composition had obviously come in jerks and surges—a jumble of thoughts and emotions that seemed strangely incongruous.

Player showed the note to Stanley Bird, Player's boss and long-term chief of the department. The note was either a confession or an attempted diversion—or maybe a mixture, the chief agreed.

Player paced as the older man read and reread. When Player's mind was about to give birth to something, he found himself combing his curly hairdo with outstretched fingers. His quickened pacing betrayed his nervous energy, his edgy, impatient nature.

Bird's brow furrowed under his silver mane, then he handed the note back and said: "Can't see it any other way."

Later, when the Vehicle Identification Number (VIN) had been traced, the owner was ascertained. Why had Randall Lee Smith of Pearisburg, Virginia, removed his tags and apparently abandoned his vehicle? A check with National Crime Information Center revealed no stolen vehicle meeting the description.

Player went back to his office, but before he had seated his six-foot frame, an article he had read two days previously at breakfast in the local paper came to mind. The page 2 story centered on the continuing search for the murderer of two Appalachian Trail hikers in Virginia's Jefferson National Forest.

He sent for the earlier VIN report on the abandoned vehicle and studied it again. It was a long shot, but he reached for the phone and dialed Virginia State Police.

CHAPTER XXVII

The dispatch out of Myrtle Beach resounded like a bullet smacking the bullseye of a metal target. Two things hit Crane at once: Randall Lee Smith was a Giles Countian, and the first, third, and last three lines of the note found in the truck seemed to be a sort of confession.

After the wording of the note had been tape recorded and transcribed, Crane and his superiors studied it minutely. All agreed that the wording appeared to be a mixture of fact and fantasy and that two or more interpretations could be applied to the total message. But those critical lines stood out like a red flag: "This Boy and girl have been so nice to me ... It's going to be a real shame for them when the time comes to get rid of them ... It's bad that I have to get rid of them. His girl friend is so pretty and nice. I will be far far away before the truck and these people are found."

Still, the lines implied that the "getting rid of," though contemplated, had not yet taken place. But when had the note been written? Had it been penned in Giles County before the trip to Myrtle Beach or at Myrtle Beach at the time of vehicle abandonment? And did it matter? Had the act of "getting rid of" actually occurred apart from either time or location? Had the killer not yet fully faced the magnitude of his act, and was he thus not playing psychological games with himself?

The more remote interpretation of the note was that Smith himself— and a female companion—had been a victim of kidnapping and murder and that the note was a third-person confession, the truth of which would begin to unfold with the finding of the truck and note with the bodies.

Crane set the machinery in motion for a criminal history check on Smith and headed for Giles County.

With his big body hunched forward for the incline, Crane bounded up the stairs to Hopkins' office, merging with Mike Meyer on the way in.

"You've got vengeance in your blood today. I can tell," Meyer jibed. "We're movin' on Ned Shires?"

Hopkins, too, awaited Crane's answer.

"We can put Shires on the back burner, for the time being, at least. We've got a new suspect, a real live one."

Crane brought Meyer and Hopkins up to date, laying the transcript of the note on the desk before the sheriff. Meyer read over Hopkins' shoulder.

The irony was not lost on Hopkins. He had just returned from Myrtle Beach, might even have walked by Randall Lee Smith along the sandy shores.

"You know him?" Crane asked. "Neighbor of yours?"

"Never heard of him," Hopkins said.

"Me, either," Meyer agreed.

Hopkins' and Meyer's eyes went back to the wording of the note. Each caught the disjointed complexity of the message and questioned Crane as to his interpretation. They hashed and rehashed the implications; and afterwards Meyer went downstairs to check with some of the deputies and the dispatcher to ascertain whether any of them knew Smith.

When Meyer came back, Crane said, "I've already got a criminal record check going on him."

"One of our men knows him," Meyer said. "Apparently Smith is sort of a loner. Doesn't have much to say to anybody."

"Never been in any trouble?" Crane said.

"No. Not that they know of," Meyer said.

"I don't ever recall hearing the name," Hopkins said. "As small as this town is, I'm sure we'd have some inkling of it if Smith was any kind of troublemaker—major or minor."

"Something askew here, fellows," Crane said. "You mean to tell me one of your hometown boys who keeps his nose clean and goes to church on Sunday runs out and murders two innocent people he probably never met before?"

"Stranger things have happened," Meyer quipped.

Crane knew the truth of that. Hopkins stood. They all looked at one another in silence and began to pace.

Then Meyer said, "It fits. Who could better purchase the rum, the .22 cartridges, the Coke—all with local identification—any better than a hometown boy? And if he has a tie-in to Giles Memorial Hospital where that Texas catheter came from, it might prove an intriguin' coincidence."

"That still doesn't prove anything," Crane remarked. "It looks interesting, as does the catheter thing, though I don't think we'll ever know how that fits into the picture. The icing on the cake's going to be if Smith's print matches anything we've got."

Hopkins kept scratching his head. He had been a deputy and sheriff long enough that he thought he knew all the rats in the holes of Giles County pretty well, and yet he didn't have a flicker of memory about a Randall Lee Smith.

"I'll bet you a steak dinner your suspect doesn't even have a traffic ticket against him," Hopkins said suddenly.

"Let's get busy and see if you're right," Crane said. "The VIN information gives an address of Ingram Village. Where's that?"

"South of town almost under the southern overhang of Angel's Rest Mountain," Meyer said. "Only angels live there, of course."

"Looks like a devil may have invaded paradise," Crane countered.

No one was to be found at the address, but neighbors advised that Loretta Smith worked the three-to-eleven shift at Giles Memorial Hospital and would not be home until the late hour. With the information bells went off simultaneously in all three lawmen's heads.

Hopkins, Crane, and Meyer headed for Giles Memorial, checked in with the hospital administrator, arranged private conference space, and sent for Randall's mother.

The small, frail-looking woman, dressed in a white work smock, entered the room with apprehension written on her pinched face. The faded eyes behind rimmed glasses searched each man's face momentarily. Hopkins introduced himself and his two associates and asked her to be seated.

"We need to ask you a few questions, Mrs. Smith," Hopkins began. "Do you know the whereabouts of Randall Lee?"

"Why do you want to know? Is he in some kind of trouble?"

"We're conducting an investigation, and his name has come to our attention," Crane said.

She studied the face of each man again and lit a long filtertip cigarette with trembling hands. She lowered her eyes and took a series of deep drags.

"Would you answer the question, please," Hopkins said.

"Of course I know where he is. Randall left home on June 1. That afternoon. He got a job in Connecticut—welding. He went up there."

"Have you heard from him since he left?" Crane asked.

"No. He don't write much when he goes away."

"Does he go and come a lot?" Meyer said. "Where's he been workin'?"

"He takes it by spells. He did work—until the middle of May—at Long-Airdox here in town. He quit and then got this job in Connecticut."

Questioned further, the woman gave a brief history of her son's employment at Commonwealth Bolt Company in the county and of his earlier employment at the eastern end of the state with Newport News Shipbuilding and Drydock Company.

"But how did your son get a new job so quickly, and so far away? Do you have relatives there?" Crane asked.

"No, we don't have relatives. Randall's just good at finding jobs, and he travels around a lot."

She paused, seemingly sensing the implausibility the officers attached to her answers.

Crane took oblique directions to other vital questions, and in turn Hopkins and Meyer did likewise. Strangely, the woman seemed to forget momentarily that they all were talking about her son rather than about some mutual acquaintance.

"Randall's not hurt or anything, is he?"

"We can't answer that," Crane said. "We don't know exactly where he is at the moment. We'd hoped you could help us."

"Don't understand the boy myself, sometimes," she said with unexpected candor. "Strange boy, but I guess you'd be too if you ___ "

The statement trailed off; the room grew silent. The woman adjusted her greying hair with bony fingers, and sucked on the cigarette. When she lifted her eyes, there was an infinite sadness in them.

"All Randall and me's ever had is hard times."

"I'm afraid we'll need to go through some of your son's things," Hopkins said.

"Some of my nosey neighbors been shootin' their mouths off?"

"This has nothing to do with your neighbors," Hopkins said. "Will you agree voluntarily to a search of your premises? We want to avoid search warrant procedure if we can."

"I don't know what you're looking for. You're not going to find anything anyway."

"What time do you get off work?" Crane asked.

"Eleven. I get home about eleven-twenty. What are you looking for? If you're talking about this drug business, Randall don't fool around with that crowd. Likes to be by himself."

"We'll meet you at the house," Hopkins said. "You do agree to sign a Consent-To-Search form?"

"Don't appear like I have much choice in the matter. Yes. I'll sign."

During the afternoon the all-too-familiar brick wall rose again. The general manager at Long Airdox confirmed Randall's voluntary severance from the company, but the application procedures there did not require fingerprint data. The same was true at Commonwealth Bolt. At Newport News Shipbuilding & Drydock, a company doing business with the government, Crane hoped it would be a different story. And what about military records?

Hopkins had been right. Locally, at least, Smith's record was as clean as a hound's tooth.

That night the three officers headed out of town. Ingram Village was what the name implied—a small village subdivision of seventy-five to one-hundred houses, mostly of modest white frame construction on narrow lots, likely of World War II vintage. A number of larger, more expensive brick homes were scattered here and there as were mobile homes.

The Smith residence was off a paved street and lay at the northernmost point of the village, accessible only by a short, narrow dirt-and-gravel driveway. The house was clearly one of the oldest and most humble of the compact frame dwellings.

Loretta arrived on schedule, and the four of them ascended the steep wooden steps to the front door.

Inside, in the small living room, Hopkins presented the consent form for the woman's signature. She signed with a painstaking scrawl.

"I forgot to ask you. Was your son ever in the military?" Crane asked.

She weighed the implications of the question.

"No. What's that got to do with it?"

"We always get background information," Crane said.

Nobody sat down. A roly-poly cat, its fur as white as snow, sauntered across the floor and rubbed against Crane's leg. He bent down and stroked it.

"Pretty cat."

"It's Randall's," she said. "Queenie. He worships that animal."

The moment was awkward, and she picked up the slack.

"There's not much to search. *That's* his room," she pointed and wandered off toward the kitchen as if to avoid the humiliation. The house appeared to contain only four small rooms and bath, but the walls were freshly painted; the floors, clean.

Meyer started searching under the bed, beneath the mattress, and along the adjacent wall; Hopkins examined the hanging clothing; Crane searched the dresser drawers. Crane came up with a 1973 driver's license, and an ID tag with Randall's photo, dating to his employment at Newport News Shipbuilding & Drydock. He studied the photo at length—his first glimpse of the suspect's likeness. Smith had the softest eyes Crane had ever seen in a man. And the face suggested kindness, even looked a little innocent and babyish.

"Look here," Crane said.

The other two joined him. They, too, studied the image.

"Yeah, I think I have seen him," Meyer said, "but with longer hair."

On a wall rack a deer rifle and shotgun were displayed. Loretta identified them as Randall's hunting weapons.

There appeared to be nothing else to find. They went through Loretta's room with equal care and searched the living room as well. Crane stepped into the kitchen. The woman had made herself coffee and stood chain-smoking. She watched him with silent hostility as he went into this cabinet or that.

Hopkins came in. "Is there a basement?"

"You have to get in from the outside. It's just a dirt basement," she said hesitantly.

When Crane joined his co-workers below ground, they had already found in a metal cabinet something highly interesting: a relatively new blue sleeping bag, a waterproof rain cape like the ones hikers use, and a small roll of red cloth. The red cloth had little meaning, but each man present knew that Susan Ramsay's body had been stuffed into a ratty green bag, not her own; her parents had described their daughter's sleeping bag as a fairly new one, blue in color. That bag—or her cape—had never been found—unless . . .

They spread the bag out on the dirt floor. No name was stenciled onto the material.

"What do you think?" Meyer said.

"No name, and blue's blue," Crane said with a sigh.

The basement search continued, but in various areas the searcher had to crawl. Quarters were cramped. "Basement" was stretching the point. It was more like a dug-out root cellar. They went through numerous storage boxes, shelves of jars and paint cans, and old vehicle tires, dislodging a multitude of spiders. The whole basement/root cellar area, as small as it was, still resembled a mammoth rat's nest. A minute examination would require additional lighting.

They rolled the sleeping bag, rain cape, and red cloth for carrying. Hopkins wrote a receipt for Loretta for the various items being taken, and all prepared to depart. Back upstairs, Hopkins presented the receipt and held out the bag and cape for viewing.

"Are these Randall's possessions?"

"Of course, they are, or they wouldn't be here," she snapped.

"They look fairly new," Crane said. "Would you know where he might have purchased them?"

She said she had no idea but elaborated on how Randall had been an outdoorsman all his life, camping with uncles and others since childhood. Maybe he had purchased the items from some of them.

Back in Hopkins' office, they studied the ID photo again. Smith just didn't look like the type. But that was an oft-repeated phrase in law enforcement circles; besides, that implied innocence, as reflected in the photo, and the actual man represented, could have changed radically in the eight years since the photo/ID date. In any event Crane would get the photo blown up and circulated.

They were all getting bleary-eyed anyway. It was nearly 2:00 A.M.

"We'd better go back out there," Crane said. "We must have overlooked something. I'm bringing Cecil Wyatt with me in the morning. He's our house expert on search and detection."

On the way back to Wytheville, Crane found the image of Loretta Smith hard to erase from his mind. She was evidently a simple, hard-working woman of limited means, no more hostile under the circumstances than any protective parent would be, but there was a deep-seated melancholy about her. She was not old—no more than late forties or early fifties, he'd guess—yet her face was drawn, her countenance projecting suppressed bitterness and general negativism. Somewhere along the line the story of her life would have to come out before a profile of Randall was complete. But Hopkins would have that information in a day or two.

The next day, the media had begun to smell pay dirt. It was strange how well they could put two and two together and, adding to their own innumerable sources, come up with amazingly accurate reporting. Jim Lettner, Assistant Chief of General Investigation at Wytheville, was handling PR duty. His phone was ringing itself off the desk as Al Crane stuck his head in the doorway.

". . . Sorry, but we're limited in what information can be released." Lettner rolled his eyes but remained composed. "Surely you understand that premature information hinders the police in their investigation."

Lettner cradled the phone for the umpteenth time.

"If you guys don't soon wrap this thing . . . "

"Hang in there," Crane said. "We may be ready to go public before the day's over. Seen Wyatt? We're running late."

Wyatt, too, had been called back to his desk Crane learned. Calls were coming from everywhere. Everybody wanted the jump on the story.

When Crane and Wyatt got to Pearisburg, Hopkins, Meyer and Lawson had surprisingly little new information on Smith. Smith's former co-workers at Long-Airdox and at Commonwealth Bolt—all painted the same general picture: Smith was basically a loner with a fluctuating personality that was sometimes high, sometimes low and depressed. And yes, Smith was capable of deep hostility or great kindness, depending on his moods. A store owner near the suspect's home reported that though Smith frequented the establishment, his transactions were made quickly, often without an extra word uttered.

In the afternoon Crane called Loretta at work, saying they wanted back in the house at her convenience. She suggested that they go without her, and that her sister, who lived next door, would let them in after Loretta had cleared it by phone.

Loretta's sister, Bernice Kincer, awaited Crane, Wyatt, Hopkins, and Meyer. The woman was healthier looking than her sister; obviously more fearful, she tried to project pleasant cooperativeness. Hopkins and Crane could tell that she anticipated—and dreaded—being pumped, but for the meantime they refrained from questioning her in depth. All four officers headed for the basement, and this time they had additional lighting.

Wyatt knew where the nooks and crannies were. Building construction had been a part of his recent training—that, and case studies of where people usually hid things. He was soon finding a multitude of things behind this header or that floor joist, but it was all miscellaneous trash.

Each officer was conducting his own Easter-egg hunt. Wyatt struck a match to better illuninate a constricted space, then used the flame to fire his dead pipe. He then called out, "Bring another light over here."

They converged. Wyatt was pulling a plastic bucket from a tight area between the water heater and an exterior wall. Bright light revealed clothing soaking in water. Wyatt carefully lifted out a pair of jeans. Dark stains appeared on both legs and near the front belt loops.

"Blood?" Hopkins said.

"I'll bet on it," Wyatt said.

"Yeah—but in soapy water?" Crane countered. "That's going to give the lab boys a fit."

"No chance of blood-typin' those stains," Meyer speculated.

Further searching in the same area turned up a pair of cut-offs and a pastel-colored T-shirt that somebody had stuffed behind a workbench. Unrolled, the garments were stained in several places down the front.

The men carefully wrapped the clothing in plastic garbage bags. When they all got back to Hopkins' office, the sheriff immediately dispatched a deputy with the new evidence to the State's forensic lab in Roanoke.

"Looks like we've got our work cut out for us," Crane said. "Maybe we'll get a break on the latent prints angle at Newport News, and Myrtle Beach may have some goodies for us by tonight."

"When can we expect the F.B.I. report on whether Smith has prints on file?" Hopkins asked.

"Tomorrow—or, next day at the latest. I think we're beginning to see light at the end of the tunnel," Crane said.

"Guess I'd better put a couple of deputies on standby ready to go to Myrtle Beach," Hopkins said. "Those boys can probably use some help."

On this same afternoon, a memorial service was in progress at The Homestead in Ellsworth, Maine. Near the main building, staff and members had established a sort of minipark along the shores of Graham Lake. It was here that the group assembled around the newly planted evergreens, flower beds, and stone memorial.

Jackie Hilton and Homestead staffer Tom Taylor played guitars and sang; afterwards a series of young speakers took their places before the portable lectern to recite poems several had written or to express halting eulogies. Those "members," unable to express themselves verbally, had painted pictures appropriate to the occasion and displayed them on nearby trees. Some of the scenes depicted woodland hikes, canoe trips, or skiing outings they had experienced with Mountford and Ramsay.

Jeff Raymond, a Homestead staffer, read a dedicatory poem selected by Karen, the girl who had stabbed herself when Susan Ramsay was preparing to join Mountford on the trail:

Do not stand at my grave and weep.
I am not there, I do not sleep.
I am a thousand winds that blow;
I am the diamond glints on snow.
I am sunlight on ripened grain;
I am the gentle autumn's rain.
When you awaken in the morning's hush,
I am the swift uplighting rush
Of quiet birds in circled flight.
I am the soft star that shines at night.
Do not stand at my grave and cry.
I am not there.
I did not die.

The Reverend Reginald Couture then offered a prayer, and the Reverend Stanley Haskell read from the Scriptures:

We know that all things work together for good to them that love God, to them who are called according to *his* purpose. For those whom he did foreknow, he also predestined to be conformed to the image of his Son, that he might be the firstborn among the brethren. Moreover, those whom he predestined, them he also called; and whom he called, them he also justified: and whom he justified, them he also glorified.

What shall we then say to these things? If God be for us, who can be against us?

When Bob Mountford's turn came, he re-enforced the truth of the minister's words ____ that indeed good could, and did, rise from the ashes of evil, that lives had been changed for the better as a result of his son's death, and that many had sent donations to be used for the betterment of the retarded and to aid in the rehabilitation of troubled youth who needed a new start in life.

As Bud Ramsay stood to share his thoughts, his eyes swept across the vast expanse of water, to the sun-drenched mountains beyond.

"It is difficult to stand in this place surrounded by the beauty and serenity of nature in all her glory and not conclude that we are all blessed beyond our ability to understand or accept. As I look across the water and see the breeze-stirred boughs of the trees, I feel that some loving, caring, ever-present Spirit is here with us. Perhaps it would not be inappropriate to say that in some way beyond our understanding, Bob and SuSu are witnesses to this day—see in some new perspective this place that they loved and served. I would like to believe that at this moment my daughter in angelic form might be standing upon the water before us hearing our tribute. Perhaps just for today her Creator might allow her to be the top angel ____ "

Dianne Collins, standing at the fringe of the group, was glad that the service had been meaningful yet brief. All of the "members" had suffered remorse, even depression in some instances, with the violent deaths of the two counselors. It would not be an easy thing for outsiders to understand the degree of attachment and dependency that existed between members and counselors. For many of the youth, their counselors were parent substitutes. But even so, strangely, those members who themsleves had been guilty of violence could not draw the proper parallel between their own violence and the violence done to Bob and Susan.

That observation was not the only strange phenomenon. News of the murders had descended on The Homestead like a black cloud, but there was one among them that by some uncanny intuition knew long before anyone else that tragedy had struck. On May 26, when Susan had not returned to work on time, Susan's golden labrador Silica began acting strangely. The next day, Silica retreated under a table in Dianne's office and refused to come out. In spite of the fact that the animal and her newborn pups were the home mascots and were adored and pampered, all the coaxing directed at Silica would not assuage the apparent depression and reclusive behavior. Then the dog stopped eating and had to be force-fed.

In retrospect, Dianne wondered if Silica had understood dark undertones in the conversations of concern about Susan; yet there had been other instances when Susan had been late returning from an official woods outing or a long canoe journey, and Silica had shown no concern.

With all her reasoning, Dianne knew that this time it was different. Silica knew in some way beyond human understanding that her mistress was dead and had known it almost from the moment of occurrence.

After the service, Dianne took the Mountfords and the Ramsays and their daughter Kelly on a tour of the facility and shared Silica's story with them. As Ginny cradled the canine in her arms in Dianne's upstairs office, it was almost as if she held a grandchild.

"Silica's fine now," Dianne offered. "She and her brood are loved and spoiled to the point of rottenness!"

"I want the kids to keep her," Ginny said. "Maybe in this way some part of SuSu will always be with them."

Both families paid their final respects to Peter Rees, The Homestead's clinical director.

"It was a moving service. You did a fine job directing it," Bob Mountford said, extending his hand.

His sentiments were echoed by the others.

"The Homestead will never be the same again," Rees said. "Bob was a pro with the most uncanny ability to see into the psyche of a person, and his good humor and vitality always drove him to get to the seat of a problem instantly. And in Susan, we've lost the epitome of love and concern for others, and the example of unselfishness and sacrifice. I wish there was something I could do ___ "

"You just have," Bud Ramsay said.

Later, at an Ellsworth restaurant, Ginny, Mim, Kelly, Bud and Bob had dinner together. They had met this day for the first time, and yet a friendship had previously developed via the numerous telephone calls and the tragedy both families were heir to.

Conversation centered on outpourings of concern from across nation, especially from Virginians. Both families had realized that the people of the state felt a responsibility—perhaps a sense of shame—in the act that had occurred within their borders. The Giles County Board of Supervisors had passed a resolution as to their concerns and sympathies as had other county and state officials and bodies. Equally thoughtful words had come from officials at Appalachian Trail Conference headquarters in Harpers Ferry. And all over the country there had been newspaper and TV editorials about the senselessness and horror of violence.

Perhaps even more meaningful were the letters each family had received from the ordinary people of Virginia and elsewhere.

And there had been those whose life Bobby had touched in another way. A New England mother wrote: "Had not it been for your son, my daughter would still be in reform school. He helped her so much, and she now has a part-time job and a new interest in school. I don't have the words to tell you how grateful we are and how blessed the whole family has been just for having known Bob ___ "

And still another letter: " . . . With deepest regret I am returning a package to you. Our entire staff conveys our heartfelt sympathy. I personally know what you are enduring. I, too, lost a boy about your son's age some years ago." Signed: R. C. Montgomery, Postmaster, Buchanan, Virginia.

Another unusual tribute occurred that had moved Mim and Bob to the depths: the Mitchell Finn family of Bangor had donated the price of a memorial tree to be planted in the Myer Minsky Forest in Israel.

Bud, Ginny, and Kelly shared similar experiences.

"Even Father Winter still calls us often and checks on us as though we were of his parish. Bless him," Bob added.

The conversation shifted to the killing and the killer. Al Crane, both families agreed, had gone far above and beyond the call of duty in maintaining contact, keeping them advised, and making no effort to conceal his humanistic concerns.

Crane's latest call to Dover-Foxcroft—scarcely an hour before the Mountfords had left for the Homestead memorial service—had brought Bob up to date on the latest information about the suspect. The F.B.I.'s involvement was now imminent. Randall Lee Smith would soon have the largest federal, state, and county wolfpack after him of any recent case in Virginia history.

"Crane says that Smith's father in Maryland has been warned. Apparently the boy has a pathological hatred for his dad. Guess the authorities think Smith may be headed for Maryland," Bob said.

When Bud, Ginny, and Kelly began to take leave, the Mountfords offered their home for a day or two of rest before the Ramsays headed back for Ohio, but the Ramsays declined.

"I don't think we can stand familiar scenes much longer. Thanks," Ginny said, "we'll do it another time—under better circumstances. For now, we have the dreaded task of cleaning out SuSu's cabin and shipping the stuff back home. Don't look forward to it ___ " Her voice began to break.

They all embraced and said goodbye.

CHAPTER XXVIII

Special Agent R. P. "Buddy" Grimmet of the Norfolk Division of the Virginia State Police was butting headlong into his own brick wall at Newport News. Having started his investigation at the personnel offices of Newport News Shipbuilding & Drydock, he found out quickly that no prints of Randall Lee Smith were on file. Although such had been required beginning with Smith's first employment at the Company in August of '71—and again when he had been re-hired in June '73—the Company did not retain and file prints after an employee was discharged or quit. In fact, the personnel manager elaborated that potential employees were also checked out with the F.B.I. prior to employment as a security and criminal record precaution.

Smith had been fired in January of 1975 for unsatisfactory attendance and "a bad attitude." It was not a particularly unfavorable record as work histories of shipyard laborers, mechanics, and welders went. From the profile furnished by the Giles County Sheriff's Office/Wytheville Division VSP, it was noted that Smith had become extremely homesick during his work tenure at Newport News, a possible reason for absenteeism and lack of attentiveness to his job.

Smith's residence was traced backwards through occupancy at three boarding houses, and the Colony Hotel on Washington Avenue, where he had stayed nine days after first arriving in Newport News. The investigation was colorful only by the repetition of gaping mouths asking "Who?" Few people seemed to remember the name or the man __ understandable perhaps had the time lapse been thirty years rather than six. On the other hand, transient workers in Newport News came and went by the thousands.

Grimmet started calling the object of his search The Shadow. The cognomen seemed more apt with each passing hour. In the final analysis the only detrimental information collected was the report of one boarding-house manager that Smith had been visited occasionally in his room by unsavory-looking characters, a rather dubious observation when the whole area had its share of unsavory characters. The bottom line was that Smith hadn't as much as a recorded misdemeanor against him or, for that matter, a traceable complaint.

Myrtle Beach police were doing little better. Apparently Smith's truck had been dry-polished inside and out just hours before discovery. The sand-and-dust residue between the polishing cloth and metal had done a good job of destroying any latent prints. The owner had previously polished the steering wheel, the gearshift lever, and the dash as well.

"You'd better add to your APB that the suspect is a fanatical polisher," the reporting officer had told his Virginian counterpart. "Whoever he is, he must love that truck better than his old lady—if he's got one."

But Myrtle Beach police had got one break: between the seat and the backrest on the driver's side, they found thirty-one playing cards. Maybe, just maybe, helpful prints would be found on them as well as the "confession" note.

On June 13, the latest word from the F.B.I. was equally discouraging: there was no Randall Lee Smith of Pearisburg, Virginia, on record. They did, however, forward by Special Delivery three copies of the fingerprint card of a Randall Lee Smith from Parkersburg, West Virginia—an Air Force serviceman—for comparative purposes. The State Forensic Lab at Roanoke quickly determined that the comparison prints did not match the best latent prints they had—the prints from Susan Ramsay's blood-stained book, *Mountolive,* and the print from the blue Sterno stove found at the murder scene.

Allen McCreight, Special Agent in charge of the F.B.I.'s Richmond, Virginia, office, had handled the request for assistance from Giles County Sheriff John Hopkins. With the federal warrant in order, charging Smith with illegal interstate flight to avoid prosecution, the wheels of F.B.I. involvement began to turn.

Enlargements of Smith's ID photo had been well circulated and made available to the media, and before the week was over, Smith's pleading eyes would be staring back at millions of readers and viewers. Maybe just one of them would know Smith's whereabouts and point a helpful finger or make a hurried phone call.

Acting on the federal warrant, Don Myers, Chief Resident Agent of the F.B.I.'s Myrtle Beach office, readied his own team. While the Bureau stretched out its tenacles into other cities and states, Myers would concentrate his efforts in eastern South Carolina and Myrtle Beach in particular. When all profile and evidence material was in hand, Myers formed some positive opinions, one of which was that Smith would not be the daring, innovative type of criminal. Myers was by nature a soft-spoken, methodical man; he had even been accused by friends and associates of being a frustrated would-be college professor. There was still time for a change of careers at age forty, but the truth was that like so many other agents he had gotten his law degree and liked working for the Bureau.

Believing that Smith might still be in Myrtle Beach, Myers decided on a massive sweep of the swamp and wasteland areas around where Smith's truck had been found. Although Myrtle Beach police had made searches, perhaps they hadn't thoroughly combed the dense underbrush. Perhaps, too, they had accepted the theory that Smith had fled the state.

Myers assigned two of his agents to the case. Jon Armstrong, a former Washingtonian, was older than his boss by three years; at six-one he was built like an athlete.

Tom Reynolds, at thirty-two and six-three, also looked like good basketball player material. His youthful handsomeness was marred only by a prematurely receding hairline. Having been reared in Miami, he was accustomed to the Myrtle Beach heat.

Both possessed a law degree and the clean-cut, professional-man-on-the-street look that the Bureau liked. In a crowd either would not stand out as anything more than an ordinary citizen.

At a strategy conference with MB police Chief Stanley Bird, Detective Captain Wayne Player, and other officers, Reynolds and Armstrong offered their suggestion: a wide sweep of *all* the wooded territory from Yaupan and Twenty-fifth, running southward, to short of Garden City.

"If he's been holed up in that jungle all this time," Chief Bird said, "his bones have been picked dry. The swamp flies alone would suck the blood out of him in two or three days."

"He couldn't have lasted in there this long," Player agreed. "The heat is stifling. If he'd been coming in and out for food and water, I don't believe he could have evaded us every time."

"Maybe he has an errand boy—or girl—with him," Armstrong said.

Various theories and speculations made the rounds, and the concensus was that if Smith had a companion, he or she was holed up with him. Otherwise, the companion, if coming or going from any area of the woods, would have been observed by the tight patrols still being maintained around the section in question.

"He doesn't have a companion," Reynolds ventured. "Everything we know about him tells us he's basically a loner."

"Well, if you federal guys are right, and he *is* still in Myrtle Beach, we'll soon know, won't we?" Bird said.

"And if he's sneaked over into Horry County and can live in their swamps off of crawfish, lizards, and frogs, we may never find him," Player said.

While plans were being readied, F.B.I. and Myrtle Beach personnel went over the confiscated truck one more time. Even if they could find dirt up under the frame or in the fender walls of the truck—dirt that could be positively identified as soil from Jefferson National Forest—it might prove helpful. But it was no go. The long trip from Virginia or contamination by salt sea air and Myrtle Beach sand had confused any reliable analysis.

The carpet and the floormats from the truck were minutely examined; then they were marked for forwarding to Virginia. Sometimes a simple thread of fiber could prove crucial in a major case.

For all the renewed effort, not a single good print resulted. Getting good latent prints was a hit-or-miss proposition anyway under the best of circumstances. So much had to be right: temperature, moisture content, object surface, finger/palm pressure, and other conditions.

With Smith's photo in hand, the police continued to make frequent checks of the city's seemingly endless hotels and motels and beaches. And there had been dozens of leads—all fruitless thus far—to be checked out as a result of local publication of Randall Smith's photo. At the end of a particularly tiring day, Armstrong and Reynolds heard a new theory from their superior.

"The Bureau's latest profile study points to Smith as being a potential suicide candidate," Myers elaborated. "They believe you'll find him dead."

"That ought to simplify things," Armstrong agreed.

"Dr. Sexton, the Myrtle Beach medical examiner, says that at some point all you'll have to do is follow your nose," Myers added. "A decaying body in this heat can be smelled half a mile away, he says. Looks like we're going to have to do it the hard way. Too bad the undergrowth is too dense for helicopter assistance."

In Pearisburg, Hopkins first heard the theory when state police and F.B.I. asked his assistance in locating Smith's dental records.

The towns of Pearisburg and Narrows didn't have many dentists. Record checks were made among all of them in a matter of hours. The score was zero. Either Smith had never had dental work done, or he had it done away from Giles County.

Area newspapers jumped on the latest theory. The following morning regional newspaper headlines read: "POLICE SAY MAN CHARGED IN KILLINGS MAY BE DEAD."

Heading the various search teams for the second day were F.B.I. agents Reynolds and Armstrong; Myrtle Beach Detective Captain Player, Patrolman David Smith and Rick Piersal (who had helped open Smith's truck); and Bill Knowles and other deputies of the Horry County Police Department. Giles County, Virginia, deputies Lawson and Epling had also arrived and joined the search parties.

It was early on the morning of June 22 when the combined force closed from four directions on the suspected swampy, wooded area. They accidentally flushed a foursome of druggies who evidently thought an army had been sent for them and took off like jack rabbits. From the start it was tough going, and the mosquitoes obviously didn't sleep. They were like dive bombers with icepicks for snouts. Some of the men on Player's team slapped at the insects as if battling hornets until Player reminded them of the noise.

Over on the north side, Don Armstrong and his team soon came upon a household garbage bag that seemed out of place in the dense woods. They examined the bag, saw that no discarded foodstuffs—had there been any—

remained. Perhaps there had been none, but if so, it might explain Smith's survival methods: Smith could have dashed in and out of the woods in darkness to neighboring residences, drunk from a garden hose, stolen from garbage cans, and satisfied what must by now be ravenous hunger and thirst. The team slowed their pace and walked as silently as possible.

Bill Knowles and a fellow Horry County deputy, and the Giles County deputies were moving in slowly from the east. Their progress had been slowed when Knowles nearly stepped on a swamp viper. He had killed the reptile with a broken tree limb, but his breath was slow in returning after the experience. He had also lost his walkie-talkie temporarily in the excitement.

Other Horry County deputies coming in from the west were experiencing nothing but impossible walking conditions. The underbrush was matted and interlaced with sand briars, twisted vines, and some kind of thorny bush that, having pricked the skin, stung like corn worms.

"Why in the hell didn't somebody think of machetes?" a deputy growled.

At 9:15 A.M. Player thought he saw movement in the distance. If he wasn't seeing things, so much for the "smell" theory. But they *were* smelling things—anything and everything—a conglomerate of the putrid and the rancid and the sweet aroma of flowering bushes and woodland plants.

Player crested a hump in the earth, and then he saw it—a human form, squatting, resting on heels, back against the base of an old, twisted pine tree. Player stopped dead and threw up his arms to signal, but patrolman David Smith was still advancing, and he snapped a dead tree limb. The squatting form saw the human intruder, lunged upward, hesitated, then ran. Patrolman Smith caught the action instantly and began pursuit. Player and Piersal were not far behind in the footrace, but Patrolman Smith's prey changed directions when he saw another team dead ahead.

The object of pursuit tired quickly. Even as he tried to run, there was a certain weariness in his stride; Player could see the contortions of the gaunt, bearded face. Patrolman Smith soon had his prey hemmed in against a thorn thicket. Knowles, too, was closing in. Smith prepared to tackle, if necessary, but with one quick lunge he had the man by the arm.

When Player and the others moved in, they saw a sickening sight. The prisoner—a man of twenty-five to thirty—had bites and welts over every visible inch of his body. The long hair and scraggly beard were matted with sand; his torn Adidas T-shirt and cut-off jeans caked with dirt. The sockless feet were clad in Adidas tennis shoes, and above the right ankle was a swollen reddish lump that possibly implied snakebite.

"Are you Randall Lee Smith?" Player said.

The dull eyes were uncomprehending.

"I said, are you Randall Lee Smith?"

The parched lips and yellow teeth parted: "I don't know."

"Who are you?" Player pressed.

"I don't know."

Player studied the pained face more carefully. Take away the probable two-week-old beard and cut the hair, and what did he have? Even so, he was unsure. The prisoner still didn't look like the official photo.

Patrolmen Smith and Piersal began shouting into their walkie-talkies more loudly than necessary, "We've found him. We've found him. Over here!" The loud voices caused the prisoner to cringe slightly, and he began to tremble.

"You mean to tell me, you don't know who you are?" Player said.

"What am I doing here?" the other returned dully.

"Come off it!" Player growled. "You know what the hell you're doing here!"

"What's my name?"

Player searched the dull eyes again. They hadn't brightened one iota. It was incredible. Maybe the guy *had* been in the woods so long that heat, hunger, and countless insect bites had baked his brain and sucked his blood until he really didn't know who or where he was.

More searchers converged, and Armstrong and Reynolds studied the prisoner intently.

Player questioned the two, "What do you think?"

"Maybe."

"I don't know."

The F.B.I. men ventured a few questions of attempted identity and got the same broken-record answers.

"Better read him his rights," Armstrong said.

Player recited the Miranda. The prisoner seemed not to hear. Then he said, "You got anything to eat?"

"That'll come later. After you tell us who you are," Player said. He dropped the questioning. He had begun to sound like a broken record, too.

When the Virginia deputies arrived, they too, were uncertain.

They viewed the makeshift campsite the prisoner had fashioned near the base of the venerable tree, and it was pitiful indeed.

Once out of the woods, Player, Smith, and the Virginia deputies took the prisoner to Myrtle Beach General Hospital. Disrobed, Smith—if it was he—looked like a human pin-cushion. Countless chiggers had invaded his armpits and under his beltline, leaving great knots of bulging flesh. The raking paths of thorns and briars had overlaid the filthy flesh with gashed and crimson lines.

"He's badly dehydrated," the examining physician mumbled.

"What do we do about that?" Player said.

"Give him everything and anything he wants to eat. And lots of liquids. Juices. Milk."

The nurse assistant, trying to remain detached and professional, was nevertheless turning pale at the odor and the sight.

Under Player's watchful eye, Smith showered and shaved. When the physician had ordered shots and the nurse had completed the application

288

of ointments, the doctor, at Player's whispered suggestion, tried his own line of questioning. He, too, got nowhere.

Aside, Player said, "Is he faking it, you think? Does he really have amnesia?"

The physician shrugged. "Who knows? It'll take some digging to tell."

The physician studied the patient silently for a moment.

"Any recommendations?" Player said.

"Just feed him well, get some clean clothes on him as soon as you can, and watch him. You never know with a case like this. I've been following the story in the papers. If it's him, I know a lot of people will rest easier."

Player signed the John Doe release. Patrolman Smith handcuffed the prisoner in the hall, and they left the hospital. Outside, reporters and TV crews—tipped no doubt by someone in the hospital or by communication intercepts had started to gather. As more of them arrived, came to a screeching halt, and aimed cameras on the run, the prisoner attempted to shield his face with his free hand.

In the squad car, Player said to the Virginia deputies, "You guys call back home while we were doing our thing?"

"Yeah," Lawson said. "Sheriff Hopkins has an idea. One of our deputies, Dicey Shaver, is the only one of us that really knows Randall Smith. Shaver is sacked out on vacation here at the beach now. We'll call his motel number and get him to come down for a positive ID."

"Good thinking. Your sheriff and some of the State boys coming down?"

"Yeah. They're planning to fly down late today or tonight if they can lasso a State plane."

At the Myrtle Beach police station, the man they thought was Smith was fingerprinted, given clean clothes, and lodged in a TV-monitored holding cell. For nearly two hours the prisoner kept a deputy busy carrying in hamburgers, fries, and orange juice, two at a time. The eating was so ravenous and prolonged that a cellful of busted teenage druggies across the corridor had begun to giggle at the sight. The dispatcher—also charged with watching the TV monitor—began to think he was seeing a televised situation comedy.

At mid-afternoon Virginia deputy Dicey Shaver came in and tried his hand at conversation, but it was the same broken record again. The act—if it was an act—was good. "Smith" showed not a flicker of recognition. But there was no doubt in Shaver's mind; the ID was positive beyond any doubt. It was Randall Smith all right.

Having commandeered a VSP plane, Hopkins, Mike Myers, and Al Crane landed at Myrtle Beach airport early that same night.

At the MBP station, Crane read Smith the Miranda a second time and attempted to question him. The broken record went round again, but adding to it, Smith said, "I'm not sayin' nothin'. I want to talk to a lawyer."

Then he turned sulky. Even the broken record stopped.

Crane and Hopkins wanted a fresh set of prints to take back with them, and Randall was once again brought to the records room.

"We're probably going to have to send him over to the Horry County jail. We're spilling over. Peak of the tourist season as you can see and looks like every year we get more druggies, car thieves, drunks, robbers, and rapists, to name a few," Player remarked when the printing was over.

"Guess you'd be glad to get rid of the extradition thing anyway," Hopkins said. "Wish we didn't have to go through with it either. Like to get on with it. Just about paralyzed my office for weeks now."

"Good luck." Player extended a hand to Crane also. "It's been a long day. Your ride's on standby when you're ready to head back to the airport."

Within the hour all the Virginia officers were airborne.

Next morning, every city paper on display at the newsstands was headlined with SUSPECT ARRESTED IN HIKER DEATHS or some variety of the essential data.

Father Winter had caught the development on a late-night news flash, but he studied the newspaper story for more details. It occurred to him that since perhaps the New England papers had not got the story in time for the morning edition, he ought to call the Mountfords.

Crane had already called, Bob Mountford said, and the Ramsays had likewise been called at their summer cabin in Michigan. Mountford and Father Winter talked at length. Mountford expressed gratitude, but not jubilation, that the killer had been captured; and the hope that the minds of all hikers would be at rest.

After they had rung off, Father Winter sipped at his morning coffee and dwelt on that thought. The AT around Wapiti II had not actually been closed, but many hikers were still bypassing the area. Maybe this new development would clear the air, although the more-than-one-murderer theory was still commonly held. Since there had been no drag marks at the scene of the murders, could one killer have literally carried Bob Mountford's husky body to the distant grave site, or would it have taken two or more men to do so. And Susan Ramsay had been no lightweight. Neither had the burying, disposal of evidence, and tantalizing guide markers been an easy task for one person.

Two days previously, the area dailies had carried an inner-page story headed: "Police Say Ex-Student No Longer Suspect." Not only had Ned Shires brought in all his trail photographs voluntarily; he made a personal appearance before local authorities as well, obviously doing a good job of convincing them of his innocence of any wrongdoing and providing provable alibis.

Shires had been quoted as saying that he didn't deny his antics on the lower southern part of the trail in pursuit of the woman he still loved but that she, others, the media, and even the authorities had blown the affair totally out of proportion in the hysteria of the times. Neither did he deny the larceny and consequent arrest on which charges were still pending.

Rumor also had it that Shires was going to sue a series of newspapers and TV stations for premature release of information and accusation about him.

But Father Winter and others, including some Rescue Squad members, were still dubious about protestations. Shires's participation in the murders still seemed too logical—too many things fitted too well to be dismissed. An awful thought occurred to the priest: Had Shires and Smith somehow got together on the trail and had Smith, on drugs or not, been talked or coerced into participating in the crime? Smith might just be a scapegoat.

CHAPTER XXIX

"It's a match!" Richard Taylor from the Bureau of Forensic Science Lab cried into the telephone. "The print on Ramsay's *Mountolive* matches your man's with unbelievable perfection. We're working on the other things. I'll call you back and then get everything in the mail."

"Bingo!" Hopkins said and hung up.

The officers were punch drunk from the frantic activities of the previous day and night, but Crane and Meyer, sitting around Hopkins' desk, "read" the message before Hopkins repeated it.

Not all the previous news from the lab was so positive as the three of them had tallied score. There had been no spermatozoa found in the vaginal, rectal, or oral specimens from the female victim, no semen on the victim's panties, nor on other panties discovered at the murder site. And Ramsay's blood had been too deteriorated to type.

Many tests remained incomplete. The lab technicians needed head and pubic hair from the prisoner for comparative purposes to finish their tasks.

On the positive side Mountford's blood had been in good analytical condition and typed "B." Blood on the boards of Wapiti II shelter was also identified as "B" type.

The clothing taken from the Smith home needed additional lab work, and the results on the soaked jeans did not look promising. The case was shaping up as the authorities had suspected. A charge of capital murder—with rape and the commission of murder-with-a-firearm—was definitely out the window. A sympathetic and impassioned jury might return a murder-in-the-first-degree verdict, but as things stood thus far, even that—or conviction period—might be hanging by a thread.

Loretta Smith was on break at home, but when Crane, Myers, and Hopkins got there in the afternoon, she was pouty. She resented, she said, having deputies come to her house the night before, asking more questions when they knew her son had already been captured in South Carolina and hadn't told her. Even the neighbors knew, she maintained, but she had been kept in the dark.

It was not a charge totally without foundation, but there were good reasons at least from the police's point of view.

"Want to tell us your version again of when Randall left Pearisburg and where he went to?" Crane led off.

She sucked on the ever-present cigarette and pouted still more.

"I believe you'd be wise to cooperate," Hopkins prompted.

"All right. I'll tell you the truth this time. Randall left home the night of May 17 about bedtime. I don't know who he went off with, and I believed he walked away alone. But I think he left the truck here. I was on vacation that week, I'm pretty sure. He was gone for the whole week. Late Saturday evening on the twenty-third, he was back. I asked him where he'd been and he said, 'In Connecticut.' I told him that his friend Kenny Sharp had called, but Randall didn't say much. He stayed around the house for a few days, and then on the thirty-first of May—or maybe it was June first—he said: "I'm going back to Connecticut and take that job." I'd gone back to work by then, and when I got home, he was gone. I haven't seen or heard from him from that day on."

She now knew the whole story of her son's pursuit and capture from friends, TV, and newspaper accounts, but out of courtesy Crane and Hopkins offered to fill in any gaps they could discuss.

"When can I see him?"

Crane explained the probable delay in getting Randall back to Virginia, especially if he fought extradition. He added that she could visit him in jail in South Carolina and that the truck would be released to her custody.

Later, Crane, Hopkins, and Meyer agreed that the woman's reaction to her son's arrest was not that of a typically bereaved mother. It was a strange mother/son relationship anyway, they had learned from relatives and neighbors. There had been reports Randall sometimes threatened his mother and his aunt and uncle next door. If investigators read the implications correctly, the woman loved the boy, but she was secretly glad that somebody had him under control.

Meanwhile, as the extradition thing evolved, there was still work to do, and there were loose ends to tie together if that was uniformly possible. Hopkins was determined to pass on to county Commonwealth Attorney Hez Osborne as neat a package as possible.

A part of the wrap-up was convincing the public that Ned Shires had not been dropped as a suspect without concrete reasons. In retrospect the Ned Shires episode had been blown totally out of proportion although most of the team had thought at the time that everything was falling into place. The mistaken-identity-murder angle just seemed to fit perfectly. But Shires, feeling the heat from a number of directions, had presented himself voluntarily, and made a good, and an intelligent, case for himself. And most of it had checked out. The whole Shires affair could be explained in one sentence: The story of a man in love with an attractive and sensuous woman who had thrown him over, doing some crazy things to win her back even if he had to scare the wits out of her to get her attention.

It was going to be a difficult case to prosecute. Hopkins felt sorry for

Hez Osborne already. The State had some good ammunition but not nearly enough.

After a night in Myrtle Beach, Randall had been moved to Conway, county seat of Horry County, South Carolina. Sheriff Matthew L. "Junior" Brown took possession of the prisoner and housed him on the first floor of the three-story jail. Brown, a middle-aged man with gray-streaked hair parted down the middle, had been sheriff of Horry County for fourteen years. He had also been a county coroner for four. His manner was friendly, quiet, and courteous, and some said that he had the countenance of a lay preacher. He himself believed that his varied experience made him a good judge of human character. If he was that, Randall Smith was a poor specimen of a killer. The Virginian was docile, disoriented, and confused as a child. He even mixed all his food together in one big pile of multi-colored hash and gulped his continuing heavy dosage of orange juice like a two-year-old. His body was still covered with welts, and he insisted that he didn't know who he was, where he was, and how he got here. Brown believed him. It was true, or else Smith was the world's best actor.

Smith was closely watched at the jail. A suicide attempt was still anticipated. The Virginian did, however, summons the presence of mind to contemplate the pros and cons of fighting versus waiving extradition. For a time he had leaned toward the latter; but he changed his confused mind—or had trouble deciding anything—and thus received a court-appointed attorney, Horry County Circuit Judge Dan Laney having so ruled.

Phillip Dyches Sasser was that attorney. He was of old Southern stock, son of a medical doctor and brother of three other physicians. He had an undergraduate degree from Davidson and a law degree from University of South Carolina. He was a family man with a beautiful wife and four children. He was a Baptist deacon and had served in the State Legislature from '68-'72 on the Democrat ticket. He believed in capital punishment if he was convinced that it was warranted.

It wasn't his specialty, but he had defended murderers before. A recent case had the makings of a soap opera. Someone's wife had hired someone else's handyman to play sniper and kill someone else's husband so that several romantic triangles could be made square and eternally blissful. Sasser had defended one of the conspirators, and the client had been found guilty.

Sasser was a stocky man with a football-player build, a mildly leathery and friendly face, and the winning smile of a politican.

Sheriff Brown was present when Smith met his attorney for the first time. Smith told Sasser that he did not know how he got to Myrtle Beach, but he said that he remembered begging food from people on the beach. Smith's demeanor was odd, as if his mind was far away, and his body movement was sometimes spastic. After the lengthy conference was over and a deputy had taken the prisoner back to his cell, Sasser agreed that the Virginian was confused and disoriented, and that as the prisoner's attorney, he had no choice but to fight extradition on behalf of his client.

Back in Virginia, Hezekiah "Hez" Osborne lost no time in getting to work on the extradition documents. It was not a particularly exciting task, but it was part of the job he had asked the voters of Giles County to allow him to perform. He had come from the neighboring city of Radford to Giles in 1972, practiced law for a time, and then had run for Commonwealth Attorney in 1976 and lost. The second try in 1979 was successful.

He also had an appreciation for evidence gathering and crime detection; he had been an F.B.I. agent for three and one-half years in the New England area. He was originally a Southerner from Big Stone Gap, Virginia, and he had gone to undergraduate school at King College, Bristol, Tennessee, and taken his law degree at Cumberland University School of Law at Lebanon, Tennessee. At fifty-eight he was in good health but bore one burden that weighed on him unmercifully: he had lost the love of his life three years before. The split with Betsy had left him devastated, but all three of their children remained with him, and he had retained their love and support and a measure of normal family life.

There was going to be one hang-up in the extradition proceedings: Governor John Dalton, a long-time friend and colleague from Radford days, was in Europe on a trade mission. If Dalton didn't get back in time, was the Lieutenant Governor empowered to sign the document?

Osborne had decided, when the time came, to ask revocation of bail for Smith. But when the magistrate set bail, it would probably be so high that the family could not raise it anyway. And it wasn't possible, as hoped, to hold preliminary hearings and prepare to seek indictments against Smith by the July 14 meeting of the Giles County Grand Jury. The next possible meeting date would not be until October.

As almost daily area newspapers and TV stations carried the stories from South Carolina of Randall Smith's amnesia, disorientation, and innocence of what was transpiring, the subject became the favorite topic of conversation around Pearisburg and most certainly at the town watering hole, the Virginian Cafe. A few of the habitual bar-stool occupants had bets going as to conviction for Smith versus his beating the rap, pools as to how many years he would get if convicted and more pools as to whether the trial would prove Smith had done it alone or had had an accomplice. The case sure livened things up in the sleepy town. Everyone agreed on that, but the chief source of amusement was Smith's apparently successful amnesia act.

"Ain't they heard everybody around here calls him 'Lying Randall'?" an old wino chortled.

Meanwhile, Randall was languishing in jail. A woman and a man had come for a visit and to take somebody's truck back. The woman said she was Randall's mother. He didn't know her or the man. He didn't know who this "Randall" was. He had listened to her rantings and saw her tears, but he didn't know what she was talking about. Still not long after she had left, big waves started to roll over him, knocking him flat. He would get up, but the waves would roll in again, slapping him down, sucking his breath out, and making him dizzy and sick in his gut.

He spent the lonesome hours picking at the sores on his body. Every other bite had produced a scab. How long had he been in that fuggin' jungle anyway? He'd lost count. Whether anybody believed him or not, nothing was very clear to him. He remembered somebody named Toe vaguely, but where was Toe now when he needed him?

In the next few days—Randall didn't know how many—some of it began to come back slowly. The fuggin' heat had made the jungle like an oven—baked his brain. That was it. But he'd loved the loneliness. Solitude always made the waves be still, but the heat must have done him in. The heat and forty million mosquitoes. He'd got so dry one day that his pasty lips had stuck together and his tongue glued to his throat. He'd had to pry his teeth apart and moisten his mouth with his own piss.

But it was all coming back. Best not to let anybody know it, though. Nobody could be trusted. His enemies were everywhere. He could rely only on himself and give his mind its head. Float free. Why, even now he could get in his private plane and fly out of South Carolina, give his fuggin' lawyer the finger and flash the bird to the cops as he roared down the runway.

His cell smelled like a hospital. What kind of goo did they use to wash the floors with anyway? And he'd never seen such fuggin' windows. They were slits. And the slits were covered with hair—heavy wire mesh. He looped his fingers in the hair, looked out into the hot sky.

Enzor—Captain Herman Enzor, the head jailer—came down the corridor a ways and looked into Randall's cell. Randall let loose his grip. What did the fuggin' jailer think—that his prisoner was going to climb out through one of those little slits? Why was everybody watching him every five minutes anyway?

When the big man with the crossed eye went away, Randall went back to the window. Wasn't much to see anyway. Was he supposed to pay a quarter? The slit/window opened on an alley, and beyond was a building that said, "Horry County School District Office."

Fuggin' schools. He hated them. They tried to look in people's heads. Change their brains. Take the peace away and put trouble back in. One day in elementary school—about the sixth or seventh grade it was—he'd come close to hitting a teacher in the head. He'd played hookey again and she'd climbed his frame about it.

He had come up behind his teacher and casually balled up his fist. The teacher had grabbed for his hand and held it, looking into his eyes. Although she'd earlier fussed at him for playing hooky, her eyes were kind and sweet. She held his hand. He'd never forgot how soft and warm her hands were as she held his. He never wanted her to let go. She was so young and pretty and nice.

For days the warmth of her touch stayed with him. And the waves were away for several weeks. But in the back of his mind, he knew he'd failed himself in his weakness.

Governor John Dalton returned to the State Capitol the first week in July and signed the request for extradition documents. In a Keystone Kops turn of events, however, the Post Office Department had failed to deliver them to South Carolina after six days had passed. Time was running out; the law required filing within twenty days after the initial arrest.

A duplicate set of documents was sent by delivery courier, and the hearing was scheduled for Thursday, July 18.

The Horry County courthouse was an imposing structure. The ancient-looking two-story brick building, faced with four huge white columns, sat majestically amid a sea of green grass and stately trees.

Al Crane and John Hopkins strode up the walk and entered the front door. Once inside, they were met by an imposing wall-hung painting of Confederate General Peter Horry for whom the county was named. The red, white, and blue predominance of colors the artist had selected was a little overwhelming but admittedly eye-catching.

In the courtroom, William Moore, Assistant Attorney General for the State of South Carolina, acted as hearing officer. The extradition hearing in the case at hand was more of a formality than any kind of contest, Crane and Hopkins had thought. The Virginians presented their warrant, evidence of positive identification of Smith, and other papers. After thorough examination the hearing officer stated that Virginia's documents were in order and that the burden was on the accused to offer any testimony to show why he should not be extradited.

Smith's attorney took issue with the ruling. "Our position is," Sasser said, "that the burden of proof is up to the State of Virginia to show certain things: that a crime was committed and, more importantly, that my client was in Virginia on the day the crimes *were* committed."

Although Hearing Officer Moore disagreed, he did allow Sasser to put Hopkins and Crane on the stand for questioning. Hopkins and Crane presented enough of their case to support their position, but Sasser called it all hearsay.

"I have stated before and so state again," Sasser continued, "that this young man was, and still is, incompetent to protect his own interests. He doesn't know who he is; he doesn't know where he is from or how he got here; and he doesn't know how long he's been here. He doesn't know anything about the murders. His mother came down to see him, and he didn't know her. My client is a very mild individual who doesn't know what's going on around him. I've met with him ten or twelve times, and he can't even remember my name. I asked him once what my name was. He said, "Dick." We've talked about the murders many times, and each time it's like he's heard about it for the first time. Before this hearing began, I tried to prepare him for it—told him again what it was all about. You know what he said? He said, 'I sure am sorry to hear about those people getting hurt. ' "

The impassioned and impressive speech continued, but in the end the Hearing Officer maintained that no burden of proof was required of the State of Virginia, only that their documents be in order and that the identification of the prisoner at the bar be firmly established.

Smith was at his attorney's side in the courtroom, but he did not testify. From all appearances he was not even listening; he just picked at lint on his socks and maintained the most bored of looks.

Within forty-five minutes it was all over. The courtroom cleared and participants went outside to face a barrage of media people. Smith covered his face with his hands; he went cuffed and stumbling across the courtyard back to his cell. Crane, seeing the prisoner disappear into the jail, wondered why a man who didn't know who he was, where he was, or what he'd done, would be so self-protective.

On the assumption that the paperwork would take several days, Crane and Hopkins flew home. The two Virginia officers could have waited. By the next afternoon South Carolina Governor Richard Riley had signed the extradition warrants turning Randall Lee Smith over to the Commonwealth of Virginia.

On Sunday Mike Meyer and Tommy Lawson, along with local flyer Ben Robinson, who had volunteered his plane, flew back to South Carolina and took possession of the prisoner.

Back in the air, Randall sat in a window seat and crouched so tightly against the bulkhead that a flea would have been crushed. The prisoner didn't talk, and Lawson and Meyer didn't push him.

Once over the North Carolina mountains when turbulence shook the small craft, Randall came alive.

"I don't like this flying business . . . slow it down."

It was a good sign. If the prisoner *was* suicide prone, he certainly didn't want to die in a plane crash.

They landed at Dublin Airport, just twenty miles from Pearisburg, loaded Randall in the squad car, and headed home. Route 100 from Dublin to Pearisburg ran past Ingram Village.

Meyer was sitting in the back seat with the prisoner. As they passed the white houses of the village, Randall turned his sight from the scene, scooted away from his window and toward Meyer, and asked for a cigarette. If Meyer had had any illusions about Randall's alleged amnesia, there were none now. Smith had recognized home ground and had shrunk away at the thought of facing his neighbors and his crime.

At 3:00 p.m. Randall was safely in the Pearisburg jail.

That same Sunday night, the circuit judge set bail at $200,000.

It was a figure Hez Osborne felt comfortable with, but he still didn't drop off to sleep easily. A new milestone in his career had begun. He and his adopted county would be the focus of national news for months to come. He was not at all sure that he was anywhere near to being ready for it.

CHAPTER XXX

While Randall had been in the South Carolina jail, neglected and left to rot, Loretta hadn't been sitting still. Anybody with half a brain knew you didn't keep a person locked up like a mad dog for nearly a month without proper food and medical care. And why had her boy been retained there? He hadn't done anything.

She had contacted a lawyer, and later she had called Frederick Gray, Secretary to the Commonwealth, in Richmond, to make a personal plea for her son's immediate return home from South Carolina. She had also lodged a complaint that Randall was sick and infected, not getting the medical attention and diet he needed. And not for a minute had she believed that it was Randall who had refused voluntary extradition. She didn't understand such things, but it smelled of the usual crookedness she had become accustomed to when she was dealing with officials of any persuasion. Didn't the sky-high bail prove it? Where in God's name was she to get $200,000? Even $2,000?

Couldn't everybody see that Randall was still sick? On none of her jail visits since his return, had he shown total recognition of her. On her very first visit at the local jail, she had asked him how he felt; she told him that it was good he was home again. He had replied, "I wish it would stop raining so hard outside!" At the time he couldn't even see the outside. And neither had it been raining.

Loretta had a theory about the whole mess anyway. She was on duty the weekend the bodies of the murdered hikers were brought in. She had seen the girl's parents in the hospital, how torn up they were; and she'd felt for them. She'd also seen the German girl, and the young man who'd come to help identify the body.

If the police were so smart, they'd better be taking a closer look at those hikers, especially that German girl. For days on end, the German girl was pictured in every newspaper and on TV for miles around, telling how much she knew about everything and everybody, bragging about how she was going to hike all the way to Canada or some place in memory of the dead people. The truth was, Loretta would bet, the girl wanted to get out of the country so *she* wouldn't have to stand trial for murder. And you could tell how she ate up the publicity; she loved having her name and picture spread all over the place and talked about on TV.

It was an abomination anyway that unmarried people of a different sex walked in the woods together, slept in the same tent or shelter, and took baths in the open for everybody to see without a chaperone in two hundred miles. In Loretta's day a girl would have been chased out of town for wearing a T-shirt and no bra, and with her nipples poking out like two grapes waiting to be plucked. Even the lowest-down white trash had sense enough to stay off the pathway—the Appalachian Trail—that was the road to iniquity.

Loretta claimed no perfection or sainthood for herself, but she *had* tried to live a Christian life. She read her Bible faithfully and attended church when she was off duty at the hospital; and Randall, too, had gone to Sunday school and summer Bible school during his childhood.

Nobody until this day could know and appreciate how hard the struggle had been. When she'd been deserted with a baby less than two years old in her arms, she'd been terrified. And though family and friends had helped her as best they could for a time, the day soon came when she was on her own. She was trained for nothing. Her meager schooling had taught her no skills adequate for doing office work. And the depression and the hopelessness she'd felt during those early years had crippled her so severely that she couldn't have functioned at a regular job anyway.

For over ten years she'd barely kept body and soul together by babysitting hordes of snotty-nosed kids in her little house. And it was not the house she lived in now—a mansion by comparison. The former house had been much less comfortable with plumbing that didn't always work and without insulation to keep the winter winds at bay.

The children she'd kept were often dumped at her door, sick and hungry. They'd bawled and vomited on her doorstep plenty of times as their mothers rushed off in tears, afraid and unable to miss a day's work. Many of the families represented were as poor and helpless as she had been.

She'd always known how much Randall resented the endless stream of other children invading and taking over his home. And in truth, there had been countless times she'd pushed her own child aside to attend others more in need. Randall had not fought her or the other children as often as he'd had the right to; he seemed in some childish way to understand in part at least. But the day had come, early in his elementary school years— when he'd given up the battle of daily competition and retreated into himself. Sometimes, maybe he was in a room corner or under the dinette table—he got so quiet that she didn't miss him for hours. Other times he retreated so far into his own dream world that she'd have to shake him to bring him back. On occasion Randall would get angry and accuse her of interrupting a "train ride" he was taking to some far-off place.

At age seven he'd gone to school and liked it. But when school was over, and he came home, the bevy of small children still filling his house made it difficult for him to study. By bedtime, both she and Randall were too exhausted to study, talk, or do anything but prepare for and dread another day that would be exactly the same as the previous one.

It wasn't as if Randall had been penned up like a sheep in a flock all the time. Within her means she'd tried to give him other things. And the boy's uncles had occasionally taken him out for a day. At eight Randall had gone deer hunting with an uncle. The hunt had been successful, but when they returned from Jefferson National and hung the doe by the feet from a tree behind the house, Randall had burst into bitter tears. Wrapping his little arms around the deer's crimson-streaked neck, the child had refused to let go and stood there blood-soaked, crying out, "You've killed it! You've killed it! You've killed it and it's so pretty!" He had to be dragged away from the dead animal, and for several nights, Loretta remembered, Randall had slept fitfully.

Some of Randall's teachers had said that the boy showed flashes of being a good student. She didn't know whether that was true or not. She did remember that in the late elementary years he began to play hooky and get into minor scrapes. After a year he had hated high school. The class he hated most was biology. Frog cadavers repelled him. To touch one or attempt to dissect one with a scalpel, unnerved him, suggesting the realm of the dead. He would join no organizations; he didn't participate in many school activities. What friends ever came to the house could be counted on the fingers of one hand. That wasn't any surprise. The Smiths, she knew, weren't the most popular folks in town. Once when she asked him why he didn't play sports or join some clubs, he replied, "Everybody thinks I've got the itch or something."

By the time Randall was in high school, a noticeable change in him began. As a junior, he decided to quit school. By 1970 he was out for good. But Randall hadn't changed radically until his second time at Newport News. The first time, he'd gotten homesick quickly and had come back. When he'd come back the second time, there was a viciousness about him that frightened her. That viciousness often manifested itself in his fits of anger. Periodically, he'd barge into the house, leaving the front door open, slam something down, knock over furniture, walk right out the back door without shutting it, and be gone for hours or days. And by then she knew that her son was smoking marijuana and taking other drugs, too, at times.

Whispered phone conversations became regular. She guessed that he conversed with drug dealers. He began to talk about a number of women. Several names were mentioned repeatedly, but Loretta never met any of them or saw him with any of them. The most favored names were Reanna, Adrienne, and Cindy. Adrienne was a teacher; Reanna, an airline stewardess; and Cindy—and sometimes the other two—played a number of occupational roles. Loretta came painfully to realize that the women were figments entirely of her son's imagination or they were women by other names whom Randall knew casually or admired from a distance.

Loretta's lawyer had been helpful and honest enough to tell her that she had no hope of financing her son's defense from her limited income and savings. He strongly advised that she and her son asked for a court-appointed attorney. If she didn't, the mammoth legal fees and probable appeals—appeals that might last for years—would bankrupt her. And she would probably lose her home as well. For the first time since the ordeal had begun, she felt a flicker of hope that somebody was willing to help her.

Later in the week, as Loretta and Randall sat in General District Court, all eyes were upon them. She knew that her son looked gaunt and a lot older than the ID picture the media had used widely, but he was dressed neatly now in a blue striped shirt and checked pants.

As proceedings got under way, Substitute Judge Jim Cornwell asked the prisoner whether he understood the charge against him. Randall nodded; then, prompted, he answered with a weak "Yes." The judge asked whether the accused could afford to hire his own attorney.

"I don't have no job." After glancing at his mother, he added, "I—we—don't have nothin'."

"You're an adult. Your mother's assets are not at issue," the Judge said. Finding Smith indigent, Judge Cornwell then appointed J. Livingstone Dillow and Michael Davis, Pearisburg attorneys, as Randall's counsel.

The Commonwealth Attorney made a motion to revoke the prisoner's bail, arguing that the violent nature of the crimes and the flight to South Carolina made Smith a continuing danger to society and a bad risk if he should be released on bond of any amount.

Judge Cornwell ruled that a bail hearing would be held as soon as the accused's attorneys had the proper time to prepare for it.

After fighting their way through a battery of reporters and camera crews back to the jail building and again as she left the barred edifice for her car, Loretta drove back to Ingram Village in a better frame of mind. She'd lived in Giles County long enough to know that Dillow was considered one of the best defense attorneys in the area, well known throughout the state.

John Livingstone Dillow was seventy-six years old, a family man with two daughters and a native of Giles County. He was a large man—not quite six feet—well proportioned, and younger and healthier looking by ten years than his actual age. Even his critics conceded that if his sharp mind had faded, it didn't show in the courtroom or out. His piercing gray eyes under a flowing mane of silver hair were as inquiring and perceptive as ever.

Friends and enemies alike called him The Silver Fox. He had practiced law for fifty-five years, having opened his first office in his home town of Narrows in 1926 immediately after graduation from T. C. Williams Law School in Richmond. Dillow knew well the task Hez Osborne faced. Dillow, too, had served as Giles Commonwealth Attorney, beginning in

1927. He had been re-elected to that office for a total tenure of sixteen years, ending in 1942. Since then he had enjoyed a booming private practice and active participation in the Republican Party; and once he had reached for the State's attorney general office. During Eisenhower's second term, he had allowed his name to be placed on the ticket along with that of governor aspirant Ted Dalton of Radford and Horace "Hunk" Henderson as the lieutenant governor aspirant. It had seemed the ideal time for a Republican victory over Democrat control in Virginia since the National Guard and seemingly the whole Federal Government bureaucracy, had swooped down on Arkansas at Little Rock relative to the school segregation issue. Among others, Virginians were fearful that they would be next. The Republicans believed—and worked diligently to prove—that they could best guide the state through the impending difficult times.

Dillow, Dalton, and Henderson had lost very narrowly. But Dillow had continued as a power in state and Republican politics, and Dalton had gone on to a Federal judgeship, and his son John, to a later governorship. Since that time Dillow had seen his law practice grow and prosper, and he had headed defense teams in some of the region's most notorious murder cases.

Young bachelor Mike Davis had no such credentials—yet. Having taken his undergraduate degree at Radford University, he had gone on to University of Virginia Law School and graduated in '79. After passing the bar, he had set up his first law office in Pearisburg (in the same building with Dillow) in May of the current year, and was now eager to get into the thick of practice. He was a large man at six-one, two hundred forty pounds, and being a culinary artist and connoisseur of good food and drink, he was constantly fighting the battle of the bulge.

As matters got under way, it occurred to Dillow that at his age, should anything happen to him, young Mike Davis might find himself in a difficult position: changing horses in the middle of the stream was risky business indeed. Did they need a third attorney to ensure that Randall Smith would have uninterrupted and totally competent counsel throughout the ordeal to come?

Dillow and Davis talked it over, deciding a third attorney would be prudent. Even so, a third member of the defense team should not convey the idea to the Commonwealth Attorney that he was being overwhelmed by design. Then, too, Dillow believed that the possibilities were good that the Mountford and Ramsay families would employ legal assistance to aid the prosecution if Osborne felt the need of it. Maybe they would insist whether Hez felt the need of assistance or not.

Dillow and Davis talked the matter over with Osborne and, later, before the circuit judge (with Randall present); the third attorney, Keith Neely, was added to the defense team by mutual consent and judicial approval.

Keith Neely was young also, having graduated in '75 from Dillow's old alma mater, T. C. Williams Law School, now part of the University of Richmond. He had celebrated graduation by getting married five days later. He and wife Elizabeth—a "retired" medical assisant—were parents of a little girl, and another child was on the way. At five-seven he was short of stature and small of build, but his eagerness and quick intellect made up for any size deficiency.

As a native of Montgomery County (adjoining Giles on the east), Neely had come back to his home town of Christiansburg to attorney Kenneth DeVore's office, where he had long been employed during his student years. It was a matter of returning to familiar ground, but when DeVore won judicial appointment as a circuit judge, Neely established his own office.

In his brief practice, Neely had been associated in a number of lucrative criminal cases. He wanted, in fact, to specialize in homicide and felony cases, feeling especially challenged by courtroom appearances. Perhaps one day after years of broadened experience, he would turn out to be the F. Lee Bailey of the South.

The threesome of the defense team thus made for good balance: the old head, experienced and shrewd; the enthusiastic young attorney, eager for the battle; and the recent law school graduate, fresh from the books.

They lost no time in getting down to work. At the outset they recognized the case as being fraught with snags, pitfalls, and unanswered questions. Was Smith guilty? Not that it mattered—they were bound to give him the best counsel of which they were capable. At this stage, they hadn't the faintest idea of all the incriminating evidence the State had, but the odds were even that Hez Osborne was already sweating blood about what he didn't have. In late July the Defendant by counsel petitioned the Court for access to any photographs, written information, or confessions made by the accused. Such access to include autopsies, ballistic tests, finger-print analyses, and other scientific reports.

From the defense point of view, the amnesia issue was a good place to begin. The South Carolina authorities—all of them, from the police chief, captain of detectives, right on down to Phil Sasser, Randall's South Carolina court-appointed attorney—had declared Smith confused and unknowing as to his whereabouts or actions.

And as for the "confession" note found in the truck, that evidence was full of holes from a number of viewpoints. First off, the interpretation that Randall and an unnamed girl were the victims, rather than Randall's confession to killing "this boy and this girl" was the stronger. Besides, whether the truck had truly been abandoned, even if hidden and its tags removed, was an intricate legal question. The chances were good that somewhere down the road a judge would rule in favor of illegal entry; he might even rule to suppress the note's content as being prejudicial and unlawfully obtained. There was no denial that Randall had hidden the truck and removed the plates, but if he had intended returning to the vehicle and driving away later, the vehicle had not been abandoned.

Whatever latent prints, murder weapon or weapons, and other incriminating evidence the State might possess was another matter. The defense would not know all of that before the discovery hearing. But for now, the direction of attack would be a court-ordered sanity hearing for Randall. If the psychiatrists would support a mental incompetency position, then the ball game was won before it started. Randall Smith would then be sent away to some sanitarium to drop from view and be slowly forgotten by the public and the victims' families.

The court-ordered physical and psychiatric examination was imposed on July 9. Local physician Dr. Kenneth Walker of Giles Memorial was named as the "committee to make such investigation . . . and determine whether more extensive evaluation and observation is required . . . "

In carrying out the assignment, Dr. Walker was first struck by the ironies of the situation. He was not a native of the area (having come from New York state) but he loved jogging along the scenic byways of Giles; enjoyed the small town life and the demands it made on him. The small-town physician was often the wearer of many hats, and just a few weeks previously he had stood by the side of Bud Ramsay, painfully observing the agony of the dead girl's father as he identified her. Now Walker faced the task of examination and evaluation of the alleged murderer. Walker wondered whether the time would ever come in his practice when he could understand, even remotely, what humanity really was; what sinister designs, what amalgamation of genes, what duke's mixture of chemistry, what hostile or peaceful environments made up the human psyche, thus shaping the man or the woman.

After comprehensive examination of Randall Smith, Walker rendered his report on July 30. It began: " . . . Patient complained of numbness in the left arm and occasional frontal headaches. At the time the vital signs were normal. Examinations of the head, eyes, ears, nose, throat, pharynx, neck, chest, abdomen, genitalia, and skin were completely normal.

The report went on to state:

"ALERTNESS: Patient was alert and responsive. He sat quietly, answering questions with little emotion, and was smoking a cigarette during the entire examination.

"MEMORY: Short-term memory was very poor. He could not recall, after four minutes, a blue shirt or gold wedding band which I had asked him specifically to remember. Recent memory was good. He remembered what he ate for dinner. Ancient memory was extremely poor. He could not give his mother's first name. He did not know that he previously lived in Pearisburg. He did not know any of his former friends. He could not name the current or last President of the United States.

"ABSTRACTION: Three proverbs were given to the patient; i.e., a bird in the hand, people in glass houses, and a stitch in time. Patient was not able to abstract any of these for one proverb. He said, 'I saw a bird on the window.'

"CONCENTRATION CALCULATION: Patient was unable to multiply 2 x 2 was unable to multiply 2 x 4; he was able to add 2 + 2 and get the correct answer. He said he did not know what it meant when he was asked to multiply 2 x 4.

"ORIENTATION: Patient was oriented to person, giving his correct name. When asked what place he was in, he said he was locked in a room but could not seem to conceptualize that he was in jail. He did not know the county where he was located but said that he was told that he is in the town of Pearisburg. Patient was disoriented to time; he could not name the month, season or year. He guessed the time of day was evening.

"JUDGMENT: Two simple judgment questions were asked; i.e., What would you do with a stamped, addressed letter that you found on the street? The second question was, what would you do in a packed movie theatre if you discovered a small fire? His answer to the first question was, 'That must be Willard's letter.' The answer to the second question was, 'I don't know what a theatre is.'

"AFFECT: Patient's affect during the entire examination was very flat. He showed almost no emotion in answering questions.

"On the basis of this examination, it is my medical opinion that more extensive examination, evaluation, and observation by professionals with expertise in psychiatry is required and indicated. I also feel that CAT/CMI scan of brain is indicated to rule out any introcerebral pathology in light of complaints of headache and left arm numbness."

Round One for the Defense. On motion to the Court and recommendation of Dr. Walker, the Defense received a favorable ruling from Judge Bondurant. Randall was ordered confined to Central State Hospital in Petersburg, Virginia, for further mental competency testing, determination of his ability to understand the charges against him, and his ability to assist his attorneys in his own defense.

On September 2, Randall was taken to the opposite end of the State.

As the weeks of Randall Smith's evaluation dragged by, it seemed for Bob and Mim Mountford one of the most painful periods of the tragedy. Was the mental competency angle merely a defense ruse or was the killer authentically deranged? Both Bob and Mim had trouble believing that any person totally in control of his faculties could ever kill anybody for any reason. In a sense a ruling of mental incompetency would be a relief. It might even give some shape and sense to the unexplainable. Yet justice must be done; society protected.

There was absolutely no cry for revenge in their minds. Bob and Mim had searched their hearts deeply on that point and passed the test. On the contrary, they were motivated not only by a forgiving spirit, but also by a profound need to do something that would be affirmative and sacrificial, attesting to the desired substitution of love in place of hatred.

It was then that they had decided on a course of action: For one day each month they would fast, using for the support of a Nigerian child the funds that would have been allotted to food. Working through the Christian Children's Fund in Niamey, Nigeria, they adopted Moudi Allo, a seven-year-old boy. As days passed, a correspondence was under way. The Mountfords received the photograph of a grinning, chocolate-faced child, and they had an adopted member of the family. The photograph was framed and displayed proudly among the gallery of loved ones in Bob's study. Life was full of surprises: twists, turns, and serendipitous adventures with each dawning day.

Meanwhile to the north of Dover-Foxcroft still more hikers had reached Baxter State Park, the end of the trail. Coming down off Mount Katahdin in September with the status of end-to-enders were Frank Maguire, John Smith, Candy Lakin, Woody Rambo, Peter Butryn, John Pearson, and others who had been trail friends of young Bob Mountford.

But of all of them, JJ Jurczynski believed that he alone had had the most unforgettable experience. Bob Mountford *had* continued his trek along the trail—not on two legs, but on four. Somehow, Mountford *was* manifested in Blue Ridge. JJ was sure of it. The pup even had eye contact, expressions, and mannerisms like Mountford's. During the hike through Bear Mountain State Park in New York, JJ had been interviewed by reporter David Bird, and the story—and a picture of JJ with Blue Ridge perched atop JJ's backpack—had made the July 27 issue of *The New York Times*. At a village farther along the trail, JJ had got a copy of the story. Again it struck him that the expression in Blue Ridge's eyes was the same warm, mischievous, inquiring look that JJ had observed in Bob Mountford numerous times.

It was all so crazy/unreal that JJ was reluctant to talk about it, and yet the trail had taught him so many things. God's providence was so much more vast than humankind could ever grasp. All that could be seen was not all there was. The smallest flower, the tallest oak, the fluttering hummingbird, the soaring eagle, the countless babbling brooks, the towering mountains—all of them were friends and God's special gifts— that attested to a broader dimension of life too often missed by the unfeeling modern man caught up in the hustle of modern living. Yes, even dogs that acted like people—they too were a dimension of the real.

At the pinnacle of Mount Katahdin, JJ had gathered the pup in his arms. As he and Blue Ridge had stood awestruck and gazed out over the vast landscape toward Dover-Foxcroft to the south, somehow JJ knew that Bob Mountford had made it to the end of the trail and had in partnership with JJ became an end-to-ender.

Last of the once-close-knit group to reach the final peak were John and Martina Linnehan. Martina's delicate—a term young Bob Mountford had once used—ankles were no less delicate, and she had overcome the foot, ankle, and leg problems that had plagued her earlier on the trail. Atop Katahdin, Florida had seemed so far away, almost as if life there had been in another age. Was it all real? Had they, in fact, basked in the warm sea of human personality along the way, met a vibrant young man named Bob Mountford so eager for life and full of dreams, or had it all been an illusion? If so, it was an illusion both wanted to cling to always.

Sandy Skinner had gone home from Virginia, plagued by leg problems; and Neal Chivington, too, had given up before reaching New York and had taken a bus back to Ellsworth.

Although Renate Lillifors had rejoined her hiking companions, she, too, fell victim to physical problems—and problems of memory and spirit. She gave up the quest at Harpers Ferry, West Virginia and headed back to Michigan.

Steve Skinner would require additional time to gain trail's end. He had already been called back to Giles County, and he knew also that he would be called back for the main trial. But some day he'd go all the way; gain the status of end-to-ender.

At Central State Hospital back in Petersburg, Virginia, Randall was being observed around the clock. Forensic Unit Administrator Sue Lewis sought still more background information about the patient: Did he have a history of drug abuse? Was there a history of any previous treatment? Was he previously a sex offender? Were the Hospital staff at liberty to discuss sucn matters with the accused? And specifically, from the defense counsel position, were they allowed to touch upon the facts pertaining to the charges against him in their overall evaluation?

Finally, as October neared, Dr. James Dimitris, Forensic Unit Director, and Dr. Henry Gwaltney, Clinical Psychologist, rendered a joint report. The pertinent parts read:

" ... It is the consensus of our professional team that Mr. Smith is neither feebleminded nor mentally disorganized (insane). He is utilizing a selective, self-serving memory. For example, he does not know what time of the day or night it is, but he knows the time that he can call his mother with whom he can talk incessantly and fluently in an ongoing, meaningful conversation. He can complain about headaches, if he is receiving or not receiving medication; yet, on the other hand, he is not aware of the charges, the pending procedures, pleadings and options for trial, and he is requesting for his release home.

"It is our definite observation and opinion that Mr. Smith is not a brain-damaged person who has deficient or eliminated memory. He is intelligent enough; he is organized and is capable enough to participate in any necessary legal procedures if he so wishes. Because of the enormity of the case, though, we anticipate that Mr. Smith will be deliberately antagonistic to such an invitation as to participate in the legal procedures ... "

Dillow knew before he opened the letter that contained his copy of the report what the evaluation said. He had just passed Hez Osborne in the Post Office, and on the way out, the commonwealth's attorney was wearing an unusually broad smile.

Back at his office, Dillow studied the report once again; he had his secretary go down the hall to Mike Davis's office and fetch the young attorney.

Dillow, his glasses way down on his nose, was still reading when Davis came in.

"They say our boy is 'utilizing a selective, self-serving memory,' whatever the hell that is."

Dillow handed the report to Davis and paced as the other read. When he was concentrating deeply, Dillow had the habit of squinching his eyes and grinding his teeth. The grating sound was exaggerated in the long silence.

"At least we blocked direct interviews about the murders per se, and the report does leave the door open on one vital point: they concede Randall's inability to understand fully what he's facing. That's still mental incompetency of a degree. We may want a second evaluation," Dillow said.

"This business about long phone conversations with Loretta, whom he's not supposed to know or recognize, doesn't help his claims much," Davis said. "You get the feeling there may be even more of a dependency complex there than we've suspected up to now?"

"Looks like it. We'd better get hopping. We'll be finding out a lot of things we don't know. And we damn well don't want to get caught with our pants down."

Judge Bondurant allowed media access to the report, and newspaper headlines up and down the East Coast read: "Suspect Ruled Fit for Trial in Hiker Deaths."

At the Virginian Cafe on Main Street in Pearisburg, the news was greeted with mixed emotions.

"I told you ole Randall couldn't fool 'em," a young bar-stool regular gloated. "What kind of idiots did he think them doctors was? He's been tellin' us his big tales so long thinkin' we believe 'em that he can't see everybody ain't so easy hoodwinked."

"It's not over yet," speaker two said. He took a deep swig of beer, swallowed, and paused unduly long for effect. "Just you wait. Dillow'll get him off even if ten witnesses saw the murders in broad daylight."

"I'd hate to see him get the chair. Or life behind bars," a third man said.

"I went to high school with him. He's not a bad guy. Just a little mixed up, maybe. Don't believe he'd hurt ___ "

"Like hell," a fourth man at the end growled. "My brother-in-law worked with him at Commonwealth Bolt. Smith threatened to kill Paul one day for not gettin' out of his way quick enough. Everybody knew Smith meant it. Not a bad guy, my ass! The killer instinct's been in the sonofabitch for years!"

CHAPTER XXXI

As November 2, the date set for the beginning of preliminary hearings, neared, Dillow, Nelly, and Davis met again for a strategy session. They suspected that heading off a "probable cause" ruling from the judge was an exercise in futility, but they would put up the most vigorous fight possible. The best ammunition they had lay in three areas. From the autopsy reports, it was known that both murder victims had a high alcohol content in their blood—high enough in fact that under Virginia law they could have been classified as drunk. Had a drunken party gone on in Jefferson National? An orgy, even? Had killer and victims been so boozed up that nobody knew exactly what had happened or how the conflict had come about?

Secondly, the fingerprint cards the FBI forwarded to the Bureau of Forensic Science Lab at Roanoke were not the prints of Randall Lee Smith of Pearisburg but those of a man by the same name from West Virginia. Could they capitalize on that little mix-up?

Thirdly, everything the defense knew thus far indicated that no one had actually seen Bob Mountford at Wapiti II shelter, and without witnesses to place Mountford on the murder scene, the State would be hard pressed to prove all the points they would have to nail down.

As the defense team saw the case shaping up, the State's case against their client regarding Mountford was weak indeed. The evidence pertaining to Susan Ramsay's murder was a more worrisome matter. Separate trials were, therefore, a must. Even if Randall was convicted on one count, beating the second might save him years in the penitentiary. If conviction on both counts occurred and if two sentences were to be imposed, Smith would never again see Giles County as a free man.

November 2 dawned chilly, and all of Pearisburg was fog-shrouded. To the west of the county courthouse, the tip of Angel's Rest Mountain was only faintly visible. A large crowd had assembled along the walks and on the grass; reporters, TV camera crews, and free-lance writers stood at the fringes waiting for the preliminaries to begin.

As the 10:00 A.M. hour neared, the bulk of the crowd headed for the second-floor courtroom. TV cameramen waited in the alley between the jail and the courthouse, anxious for the prisoner to be brought out.

The courtroom soon filled, but the business of the day was slow to start. The seats to the front of the double aisles were reserved for the media and accredited free-lancers. Nearly all the media people were young, save for Bob Kane, local owner/publisher of the *Virginian-Leader,* who had long passed the half-century mark. He had seen too many small-town and rural county trials to believe even this one would start on time. Small-town law practice and courtroom procedure still bore the shadings of an earlier era when a trial resembled a town meeting and bore a shade of informality.

Finally, at just after 10:10, a few of the principals came into the courtroom from the rear and side entrances. In a large conference room to the left, a door opened partially, and a host of subpoenaed witnesses, state police, sheriff's deputies, and others could be seen. At mid-section of the courtroom, Bud and Ginny Ramsay took seats; many in the crowd seemed to recognize the pair. Bob and Mim Mountford and Jackie Hilton had not come for the occasion, but in the rear Loretta Smith had taken a seat so unobtrusively that few people took notice.

Eula Bott-Naff, free-lance court reporter—short, with close-cropped blond hair—took her seat before the dais and readied her recording equipment. She was dressed attractively in a navy blue skirt and sweater and wore a single strand of pearls. Chores done, she struck an attentive pose and sat rigidly upright with a look of anticipation on her pretty face.

Almost simultaneously Hez Osborne and Livingstone Dillow entered the courtroom from opposite sides; then Lois Mahaffey, General District Court Clerk entered. Sheriff John Hopkins wandered in and out of the room, seemingly keeping an eye on everything.

Dillow began to pace, his grinding teeth already in motion. He stole quick glances at his adversary. Hez Osborne, however, kept his eyes on the voluminous stack of papers on his table.

"What are we waiting for? Are we going to try this matter without the defendant?" Dillow finally said.

"He's your client," Osborne quipped. "We're ready when you are."

"He's in the Commonwealth's custody," Dillow countered. "It's up to you to get him in here."

The courtroom observers were obviously enjoying the informal banter. A khaki-clad farmer near the front said, "They act like they're goin' to cut each other's throats, in here, but I'll betcha they go out later and take dinner together."

Dillow continued pacing, finger-combing his silver locks in the process. He was dressed in a brown suit, blue button-down-collar shirt, and a red polka-dot tie.

A low gasp rose from the crowd as Randall Smith was led into the courtroom then unshackled, and seated at the defense table. He shifted weight to one hip to ease the pain of his hemorrhoid flare-up. A deputy sheriff sat just behind him. Keith Neely and Mike Davis left their conference room and joined Dillow and Smith. A hushed silence ensued, and the air was suddenly electric.

While the judge was still absent, defense attorneys began a whispered conversation with one another. Randall Smith looked bored by the whole matter. He rested his clean-shaven chin on the heel of one hand; with the other he picked at lint on his maroon trousers and light brown sweater. His hair had grown long again during confinement, reaching his shoulders, but it was clean and combed.

"All rise!" A deputy sheriff stepped through the door nearest the dais and intoned his order. Judge Thomas Bondurant, black-robed, stout and tall, with thinning white hair and black horn-rimmed glasses, followed, smiling, close behind.

When the deputy had finished the announcement that court was now in formal session and after the presiding judge was properly introduced, everybody sat down in an uneven, noisy wave of shifting feet upon the floor.

Randall Smith was still clearly bored by the proceedings, his eyes not yet meeting those of the judge but searching the wall plaques to his right that said: "William Bane Snidow, 1877-1950; Martin Pence Farrier, 1869-1946; John Summerfield Andrews, 1902-1953"—all former judges thus memorialized. Indeed, the venerable courtroom even smelled of antiquity, and—especially around the judge's station, looked like a church chancel, so rich and beautiful was the woodwork.

Judge Bondurant explained briefly that the occasion was a preliminary hearing only, held to certify, or not certify, the case to a grand jury; he elaborated on the necessity of the proceedings and asked whether the two cases were to be dealt with back-to-back.

"Back to back, Your Honor," Osborne answered. "Defense counsel has so suggested, and the Susan Ramsay case will be first."

"Is that all right with *you*?" Judge Bondurant asked.

"Yes, sir," Osborne replied.

The Judge seemed almost too jovial. But such was clearly the personality of Tom Bondurant. He could not hide his natural outgoing nature. The stereotype of the severe, frowning jurist was simply not his style.

After the court reporter was sworn, Judge Bondurant directed his attention to the defendant. Neely half-lifted his client to a standing position.

"Are you Randall Lee Smith?"

"Yes, sir," the defendant answered timidly.

"Randall Lee Smith, you are charged in Giles County, Virginia, on or about May 19, 1981, that you did unlawfully and feloniously kill and murder one Laura Susan Ramsay, in violation of Section 18.2-31 of the Code of Virginia . . . "

When the judge finished his oration, defense counselor Neely was on his feet asking that all witnesses in the case be sequestered. It was determined that Loretta Smith also be asked to retire inasmuch as she had been summoned by the Commonwealth.

In the interim deputies continued adding to the already impressive display of State's evidence. Visible to everybody were the blood-stained floor boards from Wapiti II shelter, various pieces of clothing, camping gear, lab exhibits, and numerous small items.

"We have agreed to stipulate that Laura Susan Ramsay died not of natural causes but of multiple stab wounds," Osborne began.

"That is our understanding of the stipulation, Your Honor," Neely concurred.

"All right, Mr. Osborne, you may call your first witness," Judge Bondurant said.

Osborne stood, moving his six-foot-plus, two-hundred-twenty pound frame around the corner of his table. His hooded eyes were more tired-looking than usual, but his ruddy face reflected confidence and warmth. A double chin had begun to show, but he looked sporty in a dark green jacket, light green-checked trousers and matching tie.

"My first witness will be Deputy John Sterling Greever, Your Honor."

The witness duly sworn, Osborne began to lay his groundwork. Greever, a tall young man with one impaired eye, had been the dispatcher on duty the day Bud and Ginny Ramsay had called, reporting their daughter overdue.

Testimony progressed with only an occasional objection from the Defense team until Deputy Greever began to enlarge upon his knowledge of the case.

"Objection!" Neely interrupted. "I think this witness is trying to get into certain things that would not be admissible!"

"No, sir, we're not trying to pull any trick on you. We want to get a logical story of what has transpired in this case, in sequence," Osborne countered.

"We would just like to know what this officer did, not what he thinks," Neely barked.

"Well, we'll tell you what he did if you will be quiet a minute!"

Ginny Ramsay was the next witness called and sworn. Osborne led her into a revelation of all that she knew about her daughter's plans to hike the trail with Bob Mountford and then into her knowledge of what books Susan had taken along for reading.

Dillow interrupted: "Now, if the Court pleases, I don't believe that is admissible."

"If she *knows* her daughter was reading ____, " Osborne began.

"If she knows of *her own personal knowledge* then . . ., " Neely interposed.

"I'll withdraw the question and approach it in another way," Osborne said.

Finally the point was made that Susan Ramsay had purchased the four books in the Alexandria Quartet series: three of the four books had been brought to Ohio during Susan's visit there. One of the three had been read there and mailed back to The Homestead, and the other two—*Mountolive* and *Clea*—had been packed in Susan Ramsay's backpack, preparatory to the trail hike.

Steve Skinner was the next witness, and Osborne was able to establish that Skinner was the last hiker to have spent a night with the victims and to have him relate the circumstances of the threesome's mutual parting the following morning of May 19.

Neely's cross examination became long and tedious; at times Skinner was required to go over and over fine points. Of particular interest to the Defense attorney was why Skinner and the Robinson brothers—Bret and Steve—had stayed at old Wapiti shelter rather than New Wapiti (Wapiti II) on the night of May 19.

"And you don't know whether you passed Mountford and Ramsay or got ahead of them or whether you were still behind them after May 19?" Neely pressed.

"I only know that on May 20, the Robinson brothers and myself hiked into Pearisburg, and Bob and Susan were not there," Skinner insisted.

Forestry worker Robin Cunningham was next on the stand; her testimony was quickly devastating. She told of coming upon Susan Ramsay and a male called Billy Joe at Wapiti II on May 19.

"Do you see this Billy Joe in the courtroom this morning?" Osborne asked.

"Yes, I do."

"Where is he?"

Robin pointed at the defendant. "He's sitting right over *there*."

After more questioning Robin related her conversation with the female victim and elaborated on the picture-taking session and on "Billy Joe's" peculiar behavior on the occasion.

On cross-examination, Neely began gently. Robin Cunningham was an especially petite and pretty young woman with long dark hair—a contradiction in terms as regards the stereotype of the ax-wielding woods worker—and the young, handsome Neely seemed to respond to her beauty as did the courtroom spectators. Neely dwelt on Cunningham's background—and that of her fellow workers—with the Forestry Service; then he led on toward more fertile ground. Had she and her fellow workers seen other hikers that same critical day?

"Yes, after we left Susan Ramsay and Billy Joe—Randall Smith—we saw three hikers coming out of Trent's Store."

"Did you know them? Ever see them before?" Neely asked. "Have you since seen them?"

"No."

"Did you see this particular individual who just left the witness stand—Steve Skinner? Was he one of the three hikers you saw coming out of the store on that particular day?"

316

"I can't be sure."

"Your Honor, may we have Mr. Skinner brought back out?" Neely asked.

"I don't know what purpose that'll serve, your Honor," Osborne protested.

"For whatever it's worth, have Skinner brought back," Judge Bondurant ordered.

Cunningham and Skinner faced each other and Robin studied Steve minutely.

"He could have been one of the three. He does look very familiar," Robin said. "But I'm still not sure. They all had backpacks on and bandanas around their heads, and it was difficult . . . I just can't be sure."

Neely squared the shoulders of his short body. He was clearly frustrated; but he tried not to let his fustrations show. After Skinner was again dismissed, he led Robin back into a repeat of her testimony about the picture-taking session and the conversation with Susan Ramsay and Billy Joe; and then to her identification of Billy Joe as Randall Lee Smith from photographs shown her by the Sheriff and the State Police.

"When they brought you and John Hairfield, your co-worker, to the sheriff's office, how many different pictures did you view before identifying the defendant?" Neely asked.

"About twenty."

"And you picked out the photo of Randall Smith?"

"Yes."

"And you were looking at these by youself or in the company of two or three other people?"

"In the company of three other people."

"So would it be fair to say that the three of you separated the pictures out and all three of you came to the conclusion that one particular photograph was the same person as the person who identified himself as Billy Joe?"

"I did it myself. The three others present were law officers."

"So when you looked at the photos, you didn't say anything to start off with?"

"That's right. I didn't want to say anything until John Hairfield looked at them."

"And when John looked at them, he identified the correct picture?" Neely said.

"Yes."

"Let's go back a moment. You said it had drizzled earlier on the critical day and that the sky was overcast. You saw Billy Joe first, sitting in the Wapiti II shelter. Is the shelter fairly small?"

"About fifteen feet wide, and maybe six feet deep."

"Where, exactly, in the shelter were Ramsay and Billy Joe?"

"Well, if you face the opening of the shelter, Susan was on my left and Randall - Billy Joe - was on my right."

"In the corners?"

"Susan was directly on one side, and he was directly on the other side. They were just both kind of - she was laid down on her sleeping bag and he was kind of just sitting there."

"And it was about two o'clock in the afternoon?"

"Two or two-thirty. We must have left about three."

"What did Miss Ramsay say about Mountford?"

"That she was waiting for him to catch up, that he might be as much as an hour behind her."

Neely grilled Robin at length about each aspect of their conversation with both Ramsay and Smith.

"Did Billy Joe have any hiking gear with him?"

"He had an old sleeping bag and just a little pack: it wasn't really a hiker's sleeping bag. It was kind of a big heavy thing . . ."

"While you were there, was anybody consuming alcohol or anything like that?"

"Not that I observed," Robin said.

Neely asked for the witness's memory of every move Smith and Ramsay had made.

"When you took the picture with Susan Ramsay's camera, Randall Smith made no effort to move out of the shelter or camera range?"

"No."

When it appeared that Neely was getting ready to dismiss the witness, Judge Bondurant interrupted: "Did the defendant have *any* camping equipment with him?"

"No, he didn't. That's what we thought was a little bit strange. He didn't have a tent or anything like that, and we just thought that he must have spent some pretty rough nights during the weather that we were having. Billy Joe—Randall—told us he'd never been in the area before, but he did know that there was a Blue Blaze trail which takes you to a wildlife cabin that we have up on top of Flat Mountain. If he didn't know the area, how did he know about the cabin? It was all a little strange."

When Neely did finally excuse the witness, Osborne said, "I have no questions, but I can't excuse this witness, Your Honor. I might need her again."

After being called, John Hairfield corroborated his co-worker's testimony almost perfectly, save for the number of photographs the sheriff had shown him and Robin to aid in identifying Randall Smith. Hairfield remembered seeing only six to twelve. Questioned further, Hairfield did add details about Billy Joe's appearance.

"He was wearing fatigues, like a fatigue jacket, jeans, and not steel-toed boots, but maybe an Army issue boot. Something like you'd get in the military."

"Was the fatigue jacket tucked in?" Neely asked.

"No, sir. It was hanging loose."

"Were you able to observe and see—did he have any gun on him?"

"No, sir. Not that I noticed."

"Did you see a knife?"

"I thought that maybe I did see a case knife—the kind of folding knife that you wear on your hip. I can't be positive; it's just that I thought so."

"Are you certain it was a knife?"

"No, sir. I couldn't be certain of that at all."

"You could not testify under oath that he did, in fact, have a knife?"

"No, sir. I could not."

Buford "Boots" Belcher, district law enforcement officer, U.S. Forestry Service, was next on the stand, relating his part in the search for the missing hikers. Additionally, Belcher was called upon by the Court to locate and explain the position of Wapiti II on a large map with particular emphasis on the many roads, paths, and fire trails leading into and out of the area. Belcher ended his testimony with his role in the discovery of the bodies of the victims.

Steve Davis, captain of the Giles Rescue Squad, was then sworn and found himself repeating Boots Belcher's testimony.

In the cross-examination, Neely dwelt long and intricately on discovery of the Ramsay body, taking of the on-scene photographs, exact position of the body, details about the search effort, and seemingly endless other facts. Just as Neely's voice seemed to be running down, his eyes took on a perceptive gleam.

"If you went in a straight line from the opening of Wapiti II shelter to where Susan Ramsay's body was found, were there any indications of marks or disturbances between the two points?"

"No, sir. We had looked for drag marks in all directions from the shelter area and did not find any."

"You saw none?"

"We saw none."

"You particularly looked for drag marks, is that correct?"

"Yes, sir," Davis said.

Noon hour had come and passed. Judge Bondurant looked at his watch, and after warning all witnesses not to speak to one another about matters pending, said, "Ladies and gentlemen, we are going to recess for lunch until 1:15."

Ironically, Ginny, Bud, and a local friend ended up at the restaurant obviously patronized by the prosecution, the defense attorneys, and a few of the witnesses.

Ginny looked around disbelievingly.

"What is this? Old home week?"

"It's a small town," said the friend.

"Something tells me a lot of lawsuits have been settled right here over coffee," Bud chortled.

"Probably," the friend said. "Well, what do you think? You've seen Osborne in action now. Are you going all the way with him, or do you think he'll need help?"

"I'm impressed," Bud said. "He's holding his own. Seems on top of things although I know the actual trial will test him more severely."

"The Mountfords said for us to size up the situation, and if advisable, they'd help finance legal assistance for Osborne," Ginny added. "But I agree with Bud. I think Osborne can weather any storms."

"There haven't been many storms this morning," Bud said. "Part of the proceedings would almost put one to sleep."

"I found my attention diverted at times from the testimony because I couldn't take my eyes from 'Billy Joe.' He sat there looking bored and put-upon all morning as if we were all inconveniencing *him*. I didn't once see him look at the judge, the attorneys, or a witness. Just stared at the ceiling or picked lint from his clothing," Ginny said.

"He was hearing, all right," said the friend. "And if the truth be known, probably reliving everything that happened."

"I still found myself wanting to get my hands around his worthless throat," Ginny said. "He looked so smug. So damn self-assured ___ "

The waitress brought a round of club sandwiches and coffee. As the three ate, the friend caught Dillow—seated in the next booth—eyeing the Ramsays with interest. Presently, Ginny caught it too.

"Want me to introduce you?" the friend said.

"Maybe after it's all over. If justice has been done ___ " Ginny said.

Ginny ate less than half her sandwich but managed to down most of the coffee. It was incredible. Here they all sat, she thought, just like it was time for parlor games. Everybody so calm. Opposing attorneys breaking bread under the same roof. Witnesses oblivious to everything but their own bellies. And here the parents of Susan Ramsay sat among the horde. Time marches on. SuSu's ashes had long been swallowed by the earth. All that remained was a memory and imagined images that flashed on the mind at unexpected moments and painful times. Ginny tried to eat more of the sandwich but couldn't. She lit a cigarette and sipped at her coffee.

"When do we get to see more of the actual evidence?" Bud asked in the void.

"You won't see any more of it than the Commonwealth's Attorney deems necessary to help establish probable cause," the friend said.

When court resumed, Deputy Tommy Lawson was the first witness called. Osborne led him quickly to the evidence of the blood-stained boards from Wapiti II shelter. The stained wood was fully visible to the spectators, and a discernible murmur came from some in the crowd.

"Your Honor, we would like to introduce these boards as Commonwealth's Exhibit Numbers 1, 2, and 3," Osborne intoned.

The evidence was duly received, and Dillow and Neely came closer for an inspection. The third defense attorney, Mike Davis, hastily scribbled some notes on his legal pad while Randall Smith's eyes still searched the ceiling.

Osborne next went to other items in his evidence display. He picked up two cards and showed them to Lawson.

"Do you recognize these?" Osborne asked.

"Yes, sir, I do," the lanky, confident deputy said emphatically.

"What are they?"

"Two fingerprint cards that I picked up at the State Forensic Lab in Roanoke," Lawson said.

"Whose fingerprints are they?"

"The prints of Randall Lee Smith."

"I would like to introduce this into evidence, Your Honor, as Commonwealth's Exhibit #4."

"Your Honor, the Commonwealth's Attorney has not made the proper connection in this matter," Neely said.

"We'll connect it up later on, along with other similar items."

With the judge's permission, Osborne went full steam ahead and with Lawson's help introduced Exhibit B—a paperback book entitled *Mountolive,* Exhibit 6—another paperback entitled *Clea,* Exhibit 7—a pair of blue jeans, and Exhibit 8—a cooking pot.

"We would like to reserve objection to all of this, Your Honor," Neely said.

"The evidence will be received," Judge Bondurant repeated.

Osborne kept up his retrieval from the evidence display. In each case, Lawson explained the origin of the item.

A pair of cut-off blue jeans became Exhibit 9; a plaid shirt, Exhibit 10.

"And all of these items have been under lock and key since you personally picked them up sealed at the forensic lab in Roanoke and brought them back to the evidence lockers at the jail here in Pearisburg?" Osborne asked.

"Yes, sir," Lawson said.

Neely was already poised like a hungry tiger before Osborne finished with the witness. On cross-examination Neely hit at the issue of evidence security.

"Deputy Lawson, you testified that all sealed evidence from the forensic lab was stored in your evidence lockers under lock and key. Does anybody other than yourself have the key to that storage area?"

"Sheriff Hopkins, I believe."

"Anybody else?"

"I know of no one personally. No."

"Is it possible—a possibility that other people could have a key—or access to a key—to the evidence lockers?" Neely pressed.

"Possibly other deputies."

"Do you have any log for the evidence locker?"

"No," Lawson said.

Neely through Lawson's repeated testimony retraced the origin, the disposition, the transportation, and the storage of all the exhibited evidence over and over again. Even the judge began to yawn.

Before Lawson was excused, Neely again hit on the issue of drag marks.

"Yes sir. We searched the whole area for anything out of the way and found no drag marks," Lawson said.

"None anywhere?"

"No, sir."

"That's all I have at this time, Your Honor," Neely concluded.

Investigator Mike Meyer was next in line.

After quizzing Meyer on his part in the search for Ramsay and Mountford, Osborne got to the issue of the two paperback books—Exhibits 6 and 7.

"And where did you find the books?" Osborne asked.

"Under a log approximately one hundred and fifty feet from where Miss Ramsay's body was found."

"And the titles?"

"*Mountolive* and *Clea.*"

"And did you personally do anything with these books?"

"I moved the leaves from them and called over Cecil Wyatt, the State Police investigator, who was the receiver of all evidence on the scene that day. We marked the items with orange ribbon, and he recorded it and took it from there."

On cross-examination, Neely's brow was furrowed.

"You said both books were found together under a log, 150 feet from Miss Ramsay's body. I'm a little confused as to exactly where her body was found. I've heard about three different locations during today's testimony. Could you identify where the book was located in relationship to the shelter?"

Meyer straightened his short, stocky body and pondered. The wheels going around were easily envisioned as he twisted his blond mustache.

"Yes, sir," he said. "It would have been approximately 325 feet from the shelter opening."

"Did you take any actual measurements?"

"Officer Wyatt did. I didn't."

"And if you were inside the shelter, facing out from the opening, in which direction would the books be located?"

"Stepping out of the shelter, you would take a right, and it would be southwest."

"Southwest, and then a straight line approximately 325 feet?"

"Yes, sir."

"That's all I have of this witness at this time, Your Honor," Neely said.

Cecil Wyatt, always brimming over with energy and enthusiasm, was up next, chart in hand, and Osborne put him through the evidence relating to *Mountolive* and *Clea,* and other vital points. Except for minor details, Wyatt's and Meyer's testimony jelled nicely.

On cross-examination Neely said, "Mr. Wyatt, the chart—or drawing—that you've just used to show Wapiti II shelter and the relative locations of the paperback books in question—when did you prepare that chart?"

"Last week."

"Last week?"

"Yes, sir."

Neely let a moment of silence hang.

"Suppose we go over the chart point by point."

The officer did so repeatedly, showing relative distances, points of vital evidence collection, and burial locations.

"Did you personally find Miss Ramsay's body?" Neely asked.

"No, sir."

"Then you don't know where, of your own knowledge, the body was found?"

"No, sir. I didn't see—all I know I was shown where the body was found. When I got there, it was the day after the young woman's body was found."

The point made, Neely suddenly changed directions.

"Do you know Lieutenant D. V. Catron of the Galax Police Department?"

"I know of him as an officer."

"Well, he submitted Items 14 and 15 shown on the Supplemental Certificate of Analysis—items that were examined by the forensic lab in Roanoke. The items were two knives. Have you had any contact with Officer Catron?"

"No, sir. I have not."

Neely was clearly confused about how Catron and the knives fit in. He approached the problem from all angles and got nowhere.

"How did an officer from the city of Galax play a part in this investigation?" Neely pressed.

"I don't personally know, sir."

"Your Honor, defense counsel has asked the same questions about five times and gotten the same answers," Osborne protested.

"Mr. Osborne, please," Dillow interrupted. "It is a strange situation and please let's find out if we can."

Judge Bondurant allowed Neely to proceed, but Neely still got nowhere.

Neely excused the witness, but Osborne said, "I want to lay some groundwork first, but I'll need to bring this witness back on the stand."

The new groundwork centered around Al Crane and his testimony with particular emphasis on the search of Loretta Smith's house, Officer Wyatt's help, and the finding of clothing in the cellar of that residence. The Consent-to-Search form was entered as Commonwealth's Exhibit 11. Then Crane testified to his trip to Myrtle Beach, where he met Randall Smith for the first time and had him fingerprinted; he testified that State's Exhibit 4 was the fingerprint cards thus obtained.

"At the time you visited Randall Smith in the Myrtle Beach jail, could you describe his condition?" Osborne asked.

Neely was quickly on his feet. "Your Honor, I don't know what this has to do with the crime. I know there has been a question as far as our client's competency to stand trial is concerned. It has been determined thus far that he is competent to stand trial, and I would object to anything as far as what his condition was after those alleged offenses."

"It's a very, very valid question, and I don't see why the officer can't testify as to the defendant's condition," Osborne argued.

Dillow, too, got into the fray. Supporting his colleague vigorously. The judge was patient only for a moment.

"Mr. Osborne, Defense Counsel is saying they are not now raising any defense in this area ___ "

"I'm not planning to ask the officer if the defendant looked or acted crazy," Osborne said. "I'm asking him to tell us Randall Smith's condition when he was first seen at Myrtle Beach City Jail."

"Physical, emotional, or what?" Judge Bondurant asked.

"The defendant's physical condition," Osborne explained. "I don't see why Officer Crane can't testify as to the defendant's physical condition."

"What materiality has it to the issue?" Dillow demanded.

"It may *become* material, Mr. Dillow," Osborne answered.

"I'll allow the question," Judge Bondurant said, "subject to Defense objection."

"The defendant had scratches and bite marks on all of his skin that I could see," Crane began; and he elaborated at length.

Getting all too well the drift of things, Neely took a new direction on cross-examination.

"Officer Crane, when the defendant refused to answer any questions, he was simply exercising his Constitutional right to remain silent. Is that not correct?"

"Yes, sir."

"Did he have an attorney at that time?"

"No, sir."

"When you talked to Randall Smith, did you advise him of his Constitutional right to remain silent based on the Miranda decision?"

"Yes, sir, I did."

"Did he waive his rights?"

"No, sir," Crane said. "He said he wished to talk to an attorney."

"And knowing this, you still went ahead and got the defendant's fingerprints?"

"Right."

"You did that without the defendant's having consulted an attorney?"

"Right."

Neely next went into the matter of the search of Loretta Smith's home; a search, which Neely noted, was carried on late at night.

"And did you inform Loretta Smith that she did not have to consent to a search?" Neely asked.

"Yes, sir."

"That she could refuse . . . "

"Yes, sir, and her right of refusal is also listed on the Consent-to-Search form. I read the fine points to her and informed her that at any time she wanted me to stop searching she had the right to tell me and that we would quit looking at things in her house."

Neely chewed on the point until all possible effect was exhausted; then he moved on to the items found in Loretta Smith's house.

"Is there any reason why you would not have found the Levi jeans in the pot of liquid—behind the basement water heater, I believe you testified—on the first day of search rather than on the second day's search?" Neely asked.

"We just didn't find them the first day."

"You looked all over, didn't you?"

"We were all looking in different parts of the house—yes, sir."

"Would it be a fair statement to say that the Levi jeans in the pot weren't there the first day?"

"No, sir, it wouldn't be a fair statement."

"Well, you didn't find the jeans the first time when you searched the house from top to bottom."

"No, sir."

"You also found a pair of Wrangler cut-offs that second day. Would you elaborate on that?"

Crane did so at length.

"And you also found some film—or film tape—later?" Neely prompted.

"That was 8-millimeter movie film."

"It was 8-millimeter film?"

"Yes, sir."

"And you didn't find that the first day although you searched the house from top to bottom? Is that correct?"

Round and round the matter went until every item found in Loretta Smith's house had been identified and the place of finding accurately pinpointed. Neely got back to the matter of Randall Smith's truck, clothing taken from the defendant at the time of capture, the whereabouts of the garments now; and finally the matter of Lieutenant Catron with the Galax Police Department. Again Neely was getting nowhere.

"I would just like to know who has talked to this man in Galax," Neely insisted. "Wouldn't it be fair to say that you, Officer Crane, and Special Agent Wyatt are the chief investigators in this particular case?"

Osborne's ruddy face was turning beet red. "Your Honor, I don't think it makes any difference who is in charge of the investigation and who is responsible for what!"

"I would just like to know who has talked to this Galax police lieutenant," Neely retorted.

"Well, I know you would like to know, but what has it got to do with the case?" Osborne said.

"The knives submitted in evidence to the Roanoke forensic lab surely—"

"Well, if they had anything to do with the case today, you know they would be here on display," Osborne barked and sat down.

Neely got to the matter of photo identification by Cunningham and Hairfield. He wanted to know what Crane knew about that and whether all or any of the photos viewed had names written on them.

Crane came from the witness chair well-drained, and Special Agent Wyatt replaced him at Osborne's recall. The whole search procedure at Loretta Smith's house—and the evidence found there after Wyatt had joined the effort—was brought out.

On cross-examination both Neely and Judge Bondurant had trouble keeping straight the exhibit numbers as applied to specific items of evidence. At one point the courtroom's spectators burst out in laughter.

Neely wouldn't let drop the matter of evidence found at Loretta Smith's on the first day versus second day. It was too good a morsel to hang onto. How could one team on one day find so little and then on the second day come up with a bonanza of suspicious items? Neely got to the matter of how many doors and windows opened into the basement/cellar and asked if they might have been unlocked all the while. Thus suggesting that evidence might have been planted, Neely played that theme fully.

He then turned to Wyatt's part in the search and to the discovery of the body in Jefferson National and to evidence that Wyatt had responsibility for at that time.

Any hope that the Ramsay and Mountford cases could be heard back-to-back was now diminishing. It was almost three o'clock.

Richard Taylor, tall, bald and bearded, from the Bureau of Forensic Science, Western Regional Laboratory in Roanoke, was next sworn.

"What is your specialty, Mr. Taylor?" Osborne asked.

"I specialize in latent print identification."

Osborne had the witness state his qualifications and established that Taylor had tenures of service with the Washington Metropolitan Police and with the FBI.

"Now I ask you, Mr. Taylor," Osborne continued, "have you seen and had occasion to examine Commonwealth's Exhibits 5 and 6—books entitled *Mountolive* and *Clea*?"

"Yes, sir."

"And what were your findings concerning these books?"

"There was one latent print of value for identification purposes on the book called *Mountolive*."

"And to whom did that print belong?"

"It was identified as the number three—or right-middle finger on the

326

fingerprint card—Commonwealth's Exhibit 4—bearing the name Randall Lee Smith."

The testimony sent a shock wave across the faces of all three defense attorneys. Recovering, Neely asked the Court's indulgence for a brief recess.

The defense team conferred for nearly a quarter hour; then Neely began the cross-examination.

In spite of the fact that Osborne had extracted all of Taylor's impressive qualifications, Neely put the fingerprint expert through the mill again, obviously trying desperately to find a flaw somewhere. Getting nowhere, Neely dwelt on the damaging print analysis itself.

"Did you work from a blow-up of the critical print?" Neely asked.

"No, sir."

"You did not?"

"No, sir."

"Okay, how many points of comparison did you have in your analysis?"

"Somewhere between nine and eleven."

"That would be about the minimum amount of points that are acceptable to afford a comparison, would it not?" Neely asked.

"There is no set number required. Each case is judged on its own merits."

"What is the least number of comparative points you ever heard of being successfully used in a case?"

"Six or seven," Taylor said.

It was around the barn all over again as swirls, loops, dots, islands, ridges, and so forth were discussed ad infinitum. Finally, Neely took a different tack.

"Mr. Taylor, do you recall filing a report, a Certificate of Analysis, dealing with thirty-one playing cards containing forty latent prints, taken from the suspect's truck in Myrtle Beach?"

"Yes, sir."

"Okay, and on all those cards, you could not identify any of the prints as matching the allegedly incriminating print on the book entitled *Mountolive*. Is that correct?"

"That is correct."

"Do a person's fingerprints change in a matter of days? Weeks? Months? Years?"

"Only if mutilated or if the skin is stripped away below the second layer," Taylor said. "Approximately from the fourth or fifth fetal month of life until a body decays after death, a person's fingerprint changes only in size."

Neely tried to capitalize on the implied mismatch, skirting the fact that the prints on the playing cards need not necessarily be Randall Smith's at all.

"Mr. Taylor, do you recall receiving fingerprint cards by Special

327

Delivery from the FBI, on June 12, bearing the identification of Randall Lee Smith?"

"Yes, sir."

"And did you examine these cards?"

"Yes, sir. I made a comparison."

"But a while ago you denied having a second set of prints on Randall Lee Smith."

"The two sets of cards do not apply to the same Randall Lee Smith."

"You mean there are two Randall Lee Smiths?"

"There are four—possibly more—on file at the FBI."

"But you did make a comparison of the FBI cards and the ones made at Myrtle Beach, and they did not match up?"

"No, sir. The cards belonged to two totally different people."

"Different prints anyway?"

Taylor refused to be led. He remained silent.

"Same name? Different prints," Neely mused. "As far as you know, it could have been the same person but different prints?"

"No, sir, that's impossible," Taylor insisted.

"Your Honor," Osborne cut in, "I think I've been very patient with Mr. Neely. I think he has gone a little bit too far. He's been suggesting answers he hopes the witness will confirm."

"Your Honor, we have the results of a fingerprint examination by this witness dealing with Randall Lee Smith, and I don't know but one Randall Lee Smith."

"The testimony is clear. His testimony is that two different people of the same name have come into play here," Judge Bondurant said.

Elmer Gist, also from the Bureau of Forenic Science Lab at Roanoke, was next on the stand. The red-haired witness exuded a scholarly demeanor and possessed impressive credentials and educational background.

"And what do you do specifically?" Osborne asked.

"I'm responsible for isolation and identification and typing of blood and body fluid stains and the isolation and the identification and comparison of hairs and fibers."

"Mr. Gist, I would like to show you State's Exhibit 7. Did you examine these blue jeans?" Osborne asked.

"I examined these particular blue jeans for blood stains. I found numerous blood staining on the jeans, many of which are indicated by arrows pointing to the large, more conspicuous stains, especially the upper right area near the pocket and then down the right leg and also down the left leg, the front, and further staining on the upper back right area and down the leg. Also down the leg on the left-leg-rear of the garment."

"And were you able to type these stains?"

"No, sir, I was not. The test to determine the blood type was inconclusive. I could determine, however, that the stains were human blood."

"The jeans in question are listed as Item 60 on the State's Certificate of Analysis?" Judge Bondurant asked.

"Yes, Your Honor," Osborne said. "And now, Mr. Gist, I ask you to look at Commonwealth's Exhibit 9. Have you examined these cut-offs?"

"Yes, sir. I found human blood on them, but again I was not able—the stains were too slight—for blood type determination."

"And Exhibit 10—the plaid shirt? What did you find?"

"On this garment, too, I found human blood, but too limited for blood type determination," Gist said.

"All right. Now we get to the floor boards from Wapiti II shelter—Exhibits 1, 2, and 3. Did you analyze these?"

"Yes, sir. I found human blood on all three boards. The blood type was Type B."

"Now, I have one more item, Mr. Gist. It's *this* book. Did you examine it?"

"I did. I found human blood also of Type B. A fingerprint in blood is also present on the book."

On cross-examination, Neely pounced on the fact that Gist had been unable to type blood on the three garments.

"Did you ever have a blood sample of Randall Lee Smith's submitted to you?"

"No, sir. I did not."

"You don't know whether he has B, A, O, AB, or what?"

"No, sir. I have no idea."

"How much blood would you say was on the long pants?" Neely asked.

"There had been a great deal, but they were very wet—totally saturated with water—at the time I received them. The numerous stains appeared to be diluted, and I could only surmise that at one time they had been quite bloody."

"But as far as what you were able to do regarding an examination, you couldn't determine how much blood was on them, could you?"

"I couldn't determine how much, but there had been a lot on them at one time," Gist insisted.

"A couple of vials? A gallon bucket full?"

"I have no idea. The garment had been soaked."

"Based on your experience as an expert, you could not testify that the amount of blood on these jeans was enough to cause a person to die from loss of blood, could you?"

"No, sir. People can lose a great deal of blood and still survive."

"Could the stains on the jeans have been there a year? Two? Three? Even if soaking?"

"Yes, sir. The stains could remain until the pants rotted away."

Neely was riding a crest on all the garment evidence, and he went the full distance. Even regarding the floorboards from Wapiti II, Gist testified that an accurate time frame of how long the stains had been upon them was impossible to determine with accuracy.

When the Commonwealth finally rested, the dapper Neely was on his feet again, waiting.

"Does the defense desire to offer any evidence of its own at this time?" Judge Bondurant asked.

"Your Honor, at this time, we would like to make a motion to strike this testimony. In spite of the impressive display of evidence shown to the benefit of the Commonwealth, this evidence does not in any way connect the defendant, Randall Lee Smith, with the death of Susan Ramsay, except for the fact that he was seen with Miss Ramsay some ten days prior to the date she was found dead."

Neely went to great length in explaining all of the points not properly and convincingly connected to his client: that the blood-stained garments had not been proven even to belong to Randall Smith; that the blood on *Mountolive* was not proven to be Ramsay's or Smith's; that the forensic lab had not in fact been able to type Susan Ramsay's deteriorated blood.

Judge Bondurant looked the young attorney straight in the eye.

"I overrule your motion to strike."

"Your Honor, we would then like to call Investigator Crane back on the stand as an adverse witness," Neely said.

Crane reappeared and Neely began his questioning.

"Investigator Crane, I would like to ask you one question. As a result of your investigtion into the death of Laura Susan Ramsay, were you able to determine what type blood she had?"

"From her mother, yes, sir."

"And what was her blood type?"

"Her mother told me that Susan's blood type was Type O negative."

"O negative?"

"Right."

"That's all we have, Your Honor," Neely said.

"No questions, Your Honor," Osborne said.

Neely called Elmer Gist back on the stand.

"Mr. Gist, you examined the blood on *Mountolive*. Based on that analysis, let me give you a hypothetical question. If you knew that the blood type of Susan Ramsay was O-type blood, could you make a determination whether or not the blood on this book was hers?"

"Yes, sir."

"And given the fact that the blood on the book in question has already been identified as Type B, what are your conclusions?"

"If her blood type was O and if the blood type on the book is B, then the blood on the book was obviously not hers."

"That's all I have," Neely sauntered away triumphantly.

"I would like to ask the witness a question, Your Honor," Osborne said.

"You may do so," Judge Bondurant replied.

"Mr. Gist, I will give you a similar hypothetical question: If Susan Ramsay's blood is type O negative, could you say whether or not the blood on the soaked jeans might have been hers?"

"As I testified, the blood typing tests were inconclusive. I've got a reaction that I can't report, but the reaction I've got is not inconsistent with type O. It was just that it was such that I couldn't identify it."

"Thank you. That's all," Osborne said.

Neely sprang forward for the redirect.

"Let me see if I can get this straight. Given Susan Ramsay's blood type O, could you testify that the blood found on any of the garments at issue was in fact her blood?"

"No, sir. I've indicated that there either was insufficient blood or that the tests were inconclusive."

"Okay. And it could have been anybody's blood as far as you know. Is that correct?" Neely pressed.

"Yes, sir. With the results that I was able to report, that is correct."

"It could have been a person with B, AB, O, or whatever?"

"That is correct. yes, sir," Gist said.

Dramatic silence hung for a moment.

"Is the State's case concluded, Mr. Osborne?" the Judge asked.

"Yes, sir."

The Defense thought otherwise.

"We renew our motion to strike," Dillow stood and said, "and I wish to be heard briefly."

The Judge was agreeable.

"Your Honor, I understood that you had already overruled the motion to strike," Osborne protested.

"But we've introduced new evidence via the two witnesses just excused," Dillow said. "Our motion is renewed."

"The situation is still the same as it was," Osborne held firm.

The merry-go-round turned repeatedly, tempers rising.

Judge Bondurant indulged Dillow as Dillow gave a flowery, Socratic oration on the advantage of the preliminary-hearing kind of procedure— which spectators had today witnessed. He emphasized, however, that the State had failed to prove anything against Randall Lee Smith other than casting a degree of suspicion upon him and that mere suspicion was not "probable cause." Dillow quoted a recent Virginia Supreme Court ruling wherein the court had found mere circumstance and suspicion "utterly insufficient" as grounds for probable cause. Dillow thus tried to give the ruling applicable meaning to the case at hand.

The impromptu speech was so dramatic and impressive that for a moment the spectators were tempted to applaud.

"I don't think the Court ought to send this case to a grand jury," Dillow pleaded.

"Mr. Osborne, do you wish to reply to those remarks?" Judge Bondurant asked.

"No, not really, Your Honor, but I will."

Osborne, not nearly so eloquent in speech as Dillow, nevertheless refuted defense assertions and arguments with skill and good command of facts. Concluding, he was happy for the chance just to sit down. A discernible weariness had begun to permeate participants and spectators alike. Randall Smith seemed the only one present who was relaxed; his attention focused on a plaster crack in the side wall.

When all was quiet at last, Judge Bondurant sat deep in thought.

"I'm not going into all this evidence, obviously; it is getting late," Judge Bondurant remarked. "There was a stipulation to the fact that Laura Susan Ramsay died of multiple stab wounds. Numerous inferences can be drawn from the evidence. It appears that Randall Lee Smith was at the Wapiti shelter on May 19 and that she was due in Pearisburg the next day and failed to show up."

Judge Bondurant continued: "Her body was found several days later, and inferences can be drawn that she met an unnatural death by the stab wounds on or about May 19. The evidence shows that the defendant was placed at the scene of the crime, which is a very isolated area; that the defendant's fingerprint was found on the victim's book; that the defendant was seen there with the victim, somewhat suspiciously, giving a wrong name and denying knowledge of the area to the witnesses; that the defendant was the last person seen with the victim in the general time frame of her death; and that sometime later the blood-stained garments, several of them, were found soaking at the home of the defendant. And shortly after the body was found, for some strange reason the defendant was located in South Carolina. I do find probable cause to believe that the defendant committed the crime alleged in the warrant, and I do certify this case to the Grand Jury of the Circuit Court of Giles County."

CHAPTER XXXII

The preliminary hearing in the Mountford case got underway on November 30. The crowd had grown, and the weather was for once clear and crisp.

Prosecution and Defense had agreed to stipulate that the male victim had died from multiple gunshot wounds to the head, and the case was off and running. With minor variations the hearing was a replay of the Ramsay hearing, but with Steve Skinner on the stand, Neely began a new line of attack.

"Mr. Skinner, you have testified that on the morning you parted company with Mr. Mountford, Miss Ramsay had already departed camp and that Mountford set off two hours later. Did you observe in which direction they traveled?"

Steve Skinner was momentarily startled. Bob and Sue went north, of course—toward Pearisburg, yet he hadn't actually seen them go north. He had been still sacked out in the cabin.

"No," Steve said.

"As far as you know, she could have gone south? He could have gone south?"

"It's doubtful . . . and their bodies ___ "

"But you didn't see them leave either way? Is that correct?"

"Yes, that's correct."

"As far as you know, one or the other—or both—could have backtracked for some reason. You just don't know of your own personal knowledge?"

"No, I don't."

Neely got into distance between points on the Appalachian Trail and then to personal relationships.

"When you were traveling with Miss Ramsay and Mr. Mountford, did they have any problems with one another as far as you know?"

"None whatever," Skinner said emphatically.

"Did you notice whether they had any alcohol with them?"

"Not to my knowledge."

"Did they open their backpacks sufficiently where you could see their possessions?"

"Yeah."

"Did either of them have any firearms, to the best of your knowledge?"

"No."

The Robin Cunningham testimony was essentially the same as previously, but Neely did pin her down this time on whether she saw a firearm in the possession of the man who had identified himself as Billy Joe.

"No, I didn't," Robin said clearly.

"And were you actually in the shelter itself while Billy Joe and Susan Ramsay were there? Did you ever look closely at the left side of the shelter?"

"Well, I don't know how close ___ "

"At the floor itself?" Neely said.

"Yeah, I looked around. I didn't examine it. They were sitting—you know, he was sitting there not moving much, and I didn't exactly ___ "

"So you didn't examine to see whether there were any stains or anything?"

"No."

"There could have been and may not have been as far as you know?"

"Well, Susan told us—I mean Susan told us when we got to the shelter that she had examined it."

"Well, I'm going to object to that." Neely's face flushed.

Hairfield backed co-worker Cunningham; he reaffirmed that neither did he see a weapon on or near Randall Smith.

"But you did say that Smith was reading something. Could it have been a book?" Neely queried.

"I suppose so. Yes, sir. I think I remember it to be some type of paperback maybe."

"You didn't look very closely at the book? Its condition?"

"No, sir. I didn't look closely at all."

"It could have been that it was soiled? Right?"

"I really couldn't say," Hairfield said. "Like I said, I didn't look very closely."

"But he was handling the book? Reading it? He had it in his grasp?"

"It was in his lap, more or less."

Mike Meyer was next on the stand, telling of his role in helping to find Mountford's body, its position and relationship to the shelter, and certain evidence he had helped uncover. Deputy Tommy Lawson followed him. Osborne got quickly to the critical evidence officer Lawson had personally submitted and transported to the forensic lab.

"Would you tell the Court what is in this package?" Osborne asked.

"This package contains items listed on the various Certificates of Analysis. Item 23 is a paperback book entitled *Mountolive;* Item 72 is a fingerprint card labeled Randall Lee Smith."

"Are these the same items that were presented in the preliminary hearing in the Susan Ramsay case?" Osborne asked.

"Yes, sir, they are."

Osborne managed to get across that the critical evidence had been under lock and key, but after Osborne introduced it as Commonwealth's Exhibit 1, Neely was rapidly on his feet.

"I'm going to object to that, Your Honor. There has been no showing in any way that this book is connected with this case."

"I'll allow the evidence subject to Defense objection," Judge Bondurant said.

"Your Honor, we can't show everything all at one time!" Osborne said.

Osborne continued one submission after another to repeated Defense objections, and the Judge intoned just as often, "Same ruling."

Osborne got to the matter of the floor boards from Wapiti II shelter without delay. He managed to convey that the same had been subjected to the most infinite testing and that the evidence had been all the while under lock and key.

Neely, on cross-examination, found little to argue about; he did take notice, however, that the stains on the top side of the boards were darker than down the narrow sides. He asked whether the boards before removal had been nailed flush or left with breather cracks and which side of the shelter the boards had come from.

Crane and Wyatt did their replay, and a brief recess was held.

Under way again Osborne called Richard Taylor, latent print expert from the Bureau of Forensic Science Lab.

Even Dillow was willing to stipulate Taylor's qualifications, having heard the same in the Ramsay case. Again Taylor identified the fingerprint cards on Randall Smith.

"And I show you Commonwealth's Exhibit 1 and ask you if you have seen this before?" Osborne asked.

"Yes, sir."

"Did you examine this book, entitled *Mountolive?*"

"Yes, sir."

"Did you find any fingerprints on this book?"

"Yes, sir."

"Did you find any fingerprints on this book that matched any of the prints on Randall Lee Smith's fingerprint card?"

"Yes, sir."

Osborne looked over to the defense table. For the first time he saw that there was a flicker of emotion on Randall Smith's face and that his legs had begun to tremble.

On cross-examination Neely tried the confused-fingerprint-cards ruse again.

"Okay, now, the cards that you examined from the FBI bearing the name of Randall Lee Smith, did they in any way match any of the prints found on this *Mountolive* exhibit?"

"Which Randall Lee Smith?"

"Your Honor, I asked him a simple yes or no question."

"Let him answer it," Judge Bondurant ordered. "Did the prints on the book match the earlier prints?"

"No, sir."

With Judge Bondurant's leading, the witness did finally get across that the correct print cards had ultimately been matched with the print on *Mountolive*.

Elmer Gist, the blood, fluid, and fiber expert of the forensic lab, began to tie the needed knots nicely by identification of the blood on *Mountolive* and on the Wapiti II floor boards as type B.

"And were you able to type Robert Mountford's blood?" Osborne next asked.

"Objection, Your Honor!" Neely barked. "There's been no showing that this man ever saw Robert Mountford or that he ever took any blood samples from him. And there has been no evidence introduced that Mr. Gist received any blood of Mountford's for analysis. Until the Commonwealth's attorney can make the proper link-up, we've got to object."

"Mr. Osborne, do you have any evidence you are going to offer today linking the blood with Mountford?" Judge Bondurant asked.

"I was going to ask you if . . . I think he can testify as to whether or not Gist typed Robert Mountford's blood. If he didn't, then he can't testify."

"I don't think he can because ___ " Neely's voice trailed off.

"*Do* you have any evidence linking up the blood that Mr. Gist tested with Robert Mountford?" Judge Bondurant reemphasized.

"The only way I can do that is to ask him, Your Honor," Osborne said.

"Your Honor, if ___ ," Neely began.

"Well, I will let you ask him ___" Judge Bondurant hesitated.

"I can ask him. I don't see why I can't ask him whether or not he ___" Osborne seized the initiative.

"I will overrule you for now, Mr. Neely, and let you renew your motion later. Go ahead, Mr. Osborne, and ask him," the Judge said.

Osborne turned his attention back to the witness.

"Mr. Gist, did you have an occasion to type Robert Mountford's blood?"

"I examined a sample reportedly from Robert Mountford. Yes, sir."

"But you didn't type it yourself?"

"I typed it. I just said it's 'reportedly' from him. I didn't take it from him."

"Your Honor, again, I object," Neely pleaded.

"Your objection is overruled. Go ahead. Mr. Osborne, is there anything else you want to ask? Judge Bondurant said.

Osborne resumed: "Mr. Gist, what type was the blood you analyzed?"

"Type B."

· "That's all I have, Your Honor," Osborne concluded.

"All right, now," Judge Bondurant began. "I will sustain the objection to strike all this unless there is evidence offered showing that the blood

336

sample given to Mr. Gist was, in fact, taken from Robert Mountford."

On cross-examination of Gist, Neely extracted again the fact that the blood on the floorboards, on the books, and on the clothing, could be many years old and also that Gist had never received a blood sample from the defendant.

Osborne called Loretta Smith next, and a low murmur traversed the crowd. After being sworn and seated, mother stole one brief look at son, but the son averted his eyes.

Osborne quickly established that mother and son did share the same household and had shared it for months—information that Osborne had not gotten across in the first hearing and that Neely had pounced on in his first motion to strike.

Loretta Smith confessed again that her son had been strangely absent from May 18 until his reappearance on May 23. She stoutly maintained, however, that her son's truck had not been moved from the driveway for the entire period. She further stated that he then remained at home for the period of May 23 until May 28. Again she stated that he left— reputedly for a job interview in Connecticut—but came back again on May 31, stayed overnight and left on June 1. She did not see him again until he was imprisoned in South Carolina.

On cross-examination of the witness, Neely zeroed in on what had so intrigued him during the previous hearing: Loretta Smith's basement/cellar.

"Mrs. Smith, in your basement, I believe, the only door stays open? Is that correct?"

"That's right."

"It stays unlocked?"

"That's right up until all this happened. Then afterwards, I put a lock on it myself."

"Okay, when did you put a lock on it?"

"I don't know what date it was, but after all that stuff was put in my basement I put a lock on it."

"After the stuff was *put* in your basement?"

"That's right."

"Are these articles of clothing and other evidence from your basement what you're talking about?"

"All they showed me that they took from my basement was a sleeping bag, some red material, and maybe some fishing stuff."

"These long pants? Jeans?"

"No, I did not see those. I was not at home every time they came."

"How about this shirt? These cut-offs?"

"I did not see those."

"How often do you go in the basement?"

"Very often."

"When Randall left on June 1, did you see any of these articles in your basement?"

"No, I did not. I searched my basement."

"You searched your basement?"

"I searched my basement on the first of June right after Randall left," she insisted.

"Okay, and you didn't see any of these articles of clothing at that time."

"No, sir."

"Did Randall ever return to your home after June 1?"

"No, sir."

"And was your basement unlocked at that time?"

"That's right, it was."

When Neely had finished, Judge Bondurant had one final question: "Mrs. Smith, do you recognize the checked shirt?"

"No, sir, I do not."

Osborne on redirect picked up the large pot in which the soaking jeans had been found.

"Mrs. Smith, have you ever seen this pot before?"

"I couldn't even say that pot came from the house."

"Could you say that it *did not?*"

"I could not say that it did."

"That's not what I'm asking you, Mrs. Smith. Can you say that it did not come from your house?"

"I could not say because they come to my house and got stuff that I did not know they got."

"You're not answering my question. Can you say that that pot did not come from your house?

"I do not know."

The question and the evasion went round and round until Neely intervened.

"Your Honor, I believe she has tried to answer the question."

"Not very well," Osborne shot back.

"Not to your satisfaction certainly," Dillow added.

Osborne relinquished the witness, and Neely took up again on recross. He guided the witness into the issue of all her son's clothing and got her to state that she had washed and been familiar with her son's wardrobe and that it was questionable as to whether any of the garments credited to him were in fact possessions of her son.

"And you are sure that none of these items were in your basement on June 1 after your son left home?" Neely began to wind down.

"That's right."

Loretta stepped down, and Dillow asked the Judge for a a brief recess. After the recess Neely came back swinging.

"Your Honor, the first thing I'd like the Court to rule on is a renewal of my motion to strike the evidence of Mr. Gist as to the blood sample and typing allegedly from Mountford's own blood. There has been no showing that the said blood was, in fact, Mountford's blood."

"All right, I sustain that motion," Judge Bondurant said.

Osborne cringed. He had failed to subpoena Dr. Oxley, the area Medical Examiner, and have him establish the chain of circumstances of how samples of Mountford's blood had been drawn and given to the forensic lab for analysis.

"And I would move to strike evidence as far as the blood-stained boards and clothing are concerned," Neely continued. "There has been no showing that Mr. Mountford was ever at Wapiti II shelter ___ "

"I overrule that motion," Judge Bondurant said firmly.

"And as far as the items found in Mrs. Smith's basement are concerned," Neely continued, "I would ask the Court to strike and disallow. The Commonwealth through its own evidence has shown no connection whatsoever that the defendant was the owner of said garments, and the Commonwealth can rise no higher than its own evidence."

"I overrule your motion," Judge Bondurant repeated.

Neely pulled all the stops and used every angle, but each time like an unwelcome echo the words, "I overrule," resounded.

Dillow got into the act, and for a time it appeared that he might sway the judge. Courtroom spectators leaned forward to the strange terms of "corpus delicti," "death stipulation," "detrimental repercussions to the defendant," and other high-sounding phrases. But in the end all the oratory fell on deaf ears. Judge Bondurant found probable cause and certified the case to the grand jury.

In his office the next day, as Osborne helped file and give order to the mounds of reports, certificates, handwritten notes, and subpoenas he had used in the preliminary, he realized more than ever the woeful lack of ironclad evidence by which Randall Smith could be convicted on two counts of murder in the first degree.

From the Bureau of Forensic Science, he had ten long pages of itemized evidence listings and applicable analyses. Many of the items and their analyses were valueless to the case. Still more were only marginally helpful. The really solid stuff could be counted on the fingers of both hands. And the Defense had been right: except for the fact that Mountford's body had been found buried at Wapiti II and that type B blood of Mountford's type had been found on the floorboards and on the paperback book, there was no way to prove that Mountford had ever arrived to join Susan Ramsay at Wapiti II shelter. If Robin Cunningham and her co-workers had just seen Mountford, too, arriving on the scene ___

But Osborne believed that as sparse as his solid evidence was, he could get a murder-one conviction in the Ramsay case. Smith's bloody print on *Mountolive* and Cunningham's testimony, coupled with all the strong circumstantial evidence, would do it.

Osborne knew—or thought he knew—a Giles County jury well. The middle-aged-and-above juror was white and Protestant with a strong work ethic, basically conservative, and strong on law-and-order justice. And such a jury might just convict Smith in the Mountford case, based on the reasoning that if the killer did away with one victim, he had killed the other hiker as well. It was the kind of logic Osborne had witnessed before. Yet he couldn't be sure. Those same types of jurors believed in honesty and fair play, and would they, seeing the lack of convincing evidence, let Randall go free in the Mountford case? Would the time-honored phrase, "beyond reasonable doubt" echo in the heads of every juror until he had no choice but to vote "not guilty"?

And would the cases be tried in Giles County after all? With the mountain of local, state, and national publicity the case had wrought, the Defense would fight hard for a change of venue.

During the preliminaries, both sides had made mistakes, done foolish things, and missed vital points. But all that had been just a warm-up before the real thing, Osborne well knew, and the actual trial would separate the men from the boys. The crafty Dillow would use all his time-tested skills; the ambitious Neely would burn the midnight oil, laying his plan of attack, getting everything into the record nice and smooth, and plotting countless pitfalls for Osborne along the way. And brainy Mike Davis would be digging ever deeper into the books for just one more precedent that might help turn the tide.

Maybe the Ramsays and the Mountfords had placed too much faith in Osborne's abilities, Hez thought. He had kept in close touch, feeling the two families to be close friends now. Did he need help? Perhaps. Yet in spite of everything, he felt confident, even eager to get on with the trial.

He would be even more eager, he knew, if additional and stronger evidence could be uncovered before trial date. Maybe the State Police and the Sheriff's Department would yet come up with something vital like possessions of the victims that had been pawned by Smith, the weapon that killed Bob Mountford tied irrefutably to the defendant's ownership, or any eyewitness to the murders or hasty burials who hadn't yet stepped forth. Osborne dreamed of a dozen things that could yet happen to put the ball safely in his court.

The grand jury hearing got under way December 7. Judge Robert Powell—a TV-star-Steve Allen lookalike of approximate age—presided.

Judge Powell, after brief opening remarks, addressed the neatly dressed Smith in somber tones.

"Does the accused understand that he is charged with the murder of Laura Susan Ramsay and Robert Tatton Mountford, Jr., on or about May 20, 1981?"

Randall nodded his head slightly and answered, "Yes."

The defense, obviously searching for straws, made a motion to throw out the grand jury, pointing out to the Court that the jury had been improperly seated; *this* jury, having been empaneled for the October term of circuit court and having completed their work, should not have been called back for the December term. A totally new jury should have been called.

Judge Powell overruled the defense motion.

Judge Powell overruled the defense motion.

The grand jury members retired to their chambers and after a time, called in one witness after another. Al Crane and Cecil Wyatt, Deputies Mike Myers and Tommy Lawson, gave graphic descriptions of the crime committed in Jefferson National. Forest worker Robin Cunningham—looking straight at the jury—told how she had seen Smith in Susan Ramsay's presence at Wapiti shelter about the time the murders had taken place; her co-worker, John Hairfield, reaffirmed her story. After still more lengthy and detailed testimony, the jury began a final deliberation, and after two hours came back into the courtroom solemn-faced.

"How do you find?" Judge Powell asked.

Jury Foreman Betty Freeman, trembling slightly, spoke clearly: "In the case of Laura Susan Ramsay, a True Bill. In the case of Robert Tatton Mountford, Jr., a True Bill."

Judge Powell thanked the jury and dismissed it.

With court over, reporters and other media people who had been courtroom observers hustled outside for a final look at the shackled prisoner being returned to jail.

A TV reporter spotted a juror and queried: "What took you so long in there? We all thought it was cut and dried."

With unexpected candor the juror replied: "It bugged us a little that maybe Randall was taking the rap by himself when others might be involved. We got to talking ___ "

But before the speaker had finished, a fellow juror hearing the untimely conversation had his counterpart by the arm, easing him away.

Afterwards, when a couple of TV newscasters had made slanted references to the lingering public opinion that more than one murderer was involved, Hopkins, Crane, and Hez Osborne went into orbit. There was simply no foundation whatever to believe that two or more killers were involved. And no person would take the rap alone if others had had a part in the murders. Yet, some of the public, they knew, still harbored belief in multiple participation. That feeling was especially strong among hikers and among those having a close connection to the local hikers' hostel.

From Hopkins' and Crane's points of view, the investigation was still ongoing, and not even a hint of a new development had surfaced.

Then it happened. A call came from a farmer out in the Sugar Run section of the county. The farmer's son Chris, aged twelve, and daughter Laurie, aged nineteen, had been out walking, picking up discarded drink cans, and had found a .22 caliber revolver barely hidden in a ditch along the road. The weapon appeared to have been exposed to the weather for a long time, judging by the appearance of rust, farmer Fletcher reported. Did the Sheriff's Department think the weapon had any connection to the recent murders?

Hopkins' and Meyer's ears would not have pricked up so suddenly except that one routing back from Wapiti shelter to town was via the secondary road throughout the Sugar Run community.

When Hopkins, Crane, and Meyer got out to the farm, Fletcher confessed that his children had found some of his own cartridges, had loaded the revolver, and fired it a total of nine times.

Clearly Fletcher had grasped belatedly the implications of not having left the discovered weapon untouched and unfired, but his offsprings' actions had been innocent and unthinking. But Crane had little hope that the discovery would prove anything new unless the weapon could be successfully traced. Certainly the rust and the weather exposure would have obliterated vital fingerprints even before the children had touched the weapon. Neither would ballistics tests be successful since the slugs from Mountford's skull were fragmented. Nevertheless, Crane took the rusty revolver and prepared to go on yet another witch hunt.

Hopkins' revelation to the Commonwealth Attorney of the new discovery brought forth Hez Osborne's usual friendly grin and a cryptic comment.

"Maybe we'll get lucky! We sure need more than we've got."

"Is it looking *that* bad?"

"We just got word from Dianne Collins—The Homestead—that she remembered the color of Susan Ramsay's sleeping bag and the shop where Susan had purchased it. The bag was a green and blue sectional—not a solid blue like you guys found in Loretta Smith's basement."

"Oh, God," Hopkins groaned.

"Yeah," Osborne said and returned to the stack of work on his overburdened desk.

A week later, Crane called Hopkins with bad news about the revolver. Hopkins dreaded relaying the word to the Commonwealth Attorney. Osborne was in the County Clerk's office when Hopkins found him.

"I'm not sure you're ready for this," Hopkins led off.

The warm, hooded eyes of Osborne that normally sparkled with friendliness and mirth looked tired and a little bloodshot from long nights of preparation, but he forced an optimistic grin.

"Looks like it's time for anything. Lay it on me."

"The State boys with ATF help have traced the revolver to Chandler Hardware Company in Mars Hill, North Carolina. But that just tells us what firm the manufacturer shipped the weapon to for re-sale. No records were kept as to what individual purchased the gun. The sale was made in 1958. As you know, before 1968 the law didn't require purchaser registry."

Osborne shook his head disbelievingly; his double chin dropped.

"That's all I need," he groaned.

"Even if we had the original purchaser's name, it would be a long shot. That gun's maybe twenty years old. It's probably had twenty owners by now."

"Maybe. But maybe it had only two or three," Osborne said.

"We'll never know, will we?"

Osborne was tempted to say that if he were to guess, that guess would be that the revolver was indeed the murder weapon and that Randall Smith had come into possession of it while he was an employee at Newport News Shipbuilding and Drydock. Most probably he had gotten it from another welder or mechanic from North Carolina who had come to the eastern shore just as Randall had. But speculation was speculation. The Commonwealth's Attorney's office dealt only in facts.

"Well—you just made my day," Osborne said. "Why don't you give me a wide berth until there's some good news?"

"I'm not done with the bad yet. Randall's on a hunger strike. Won't eat. Won't say anything to anybody. His cellmate is scared to death of him. Some of the other inmates—even though they're separated from Randall—are scared of him. They claim Smith has 'some weird spirit coming out of him.' "

"That's a rather odd observation if Randall's on a silence and hunger strike."

"They said he doesn't have to say anything. It's the way he looks at them. And the 'way he moves,' according to them. Some combination of Randall's eye contact and hand and arm gyrations seem to mesmerize them."

"Maybe he ought to be in a cell by himself," Osborne said.

"What about the suicide angle?"

That possibility, having originated from the FBI profile while Randall was still in South Carolina, was still a matter of concern. And the Giles County jail had no TV monitoring facilities. Randall's cellmate was to a degree an around-the-clock guard or, at least, a reporter.

"Maybe we ought to leave things as they are," Osborne said.

When Hopkins went back to his office after lunch of the same day, there was another opinion in the matter. Zeb Songer, incarcerated and awaiting trial on bank robbery charges and Randall's cellmate, had asked for a conference with the sheriff. Hopkins sent for Songer. Standing before Hopkins' desk, Songer was shaking like the proverbial leaf.

"That crazy sonofabitch is scarin' the hell out of me," Songer began. "I can't sleep—not even a catnap—without wakin' up to find him standin' over me. Sometimes he's grinnin'. Other times, he's got this weird look in his eyes. What am I supposed to do? Wait 'til I feel his hands around my throat? Or a shiv plunged into my belly? I want the hell out of there!"

Hopkins sent him back, promising he would take care of the matter. Like most rural county jails, the Giles facility lacked much to be desired and was overcrowded.

Just before Christmas, Randall broke his hunger strike. No one seemed to know what twist in the mind of the prisoner had plotted a new direction. However, Marie French, the pretty, dark-haired jail cook, attributed the breaking of the fast to the savory meals she had prepared, leading up to the holiday with the turkey and all the trimmings that prisoners were allowed on December 25.

In spite of the fact that the jailed men—and women—were lawbreakers to one degree or another, Marie felt sorry for them, especially during the festive days. The prisoners didn't seem all that different, save for Smith. She didn't have direct daily contact with the jail population, but she got to know them by their eating habits, by second-hand reports of what they said or did, and by comments made by the jailor or the various deputies. People were still people, in jail or out, dreaming their dreams, hoping their hopes, longing once again to be free and getting on with their lives. Perhaps this was the key to Smith's breaking his hunger strike. Maybe Randall *did* have a girl somewhere, and had decided that a hunger-starved body wouldn't hold much attraction for her. Maybe it wasn't Marie's cooking after all.

Randall Smith was an enigma. Marie knew people who knew Smith and who had known him for years. And the small-town grapevine chatter had gone full circle so many times that every interested citizen knew Randall's life story from the time he had cut his first tooth right down to the latest news about his hunger strike.

Marie felt sorrier for Loretta Smith than for anyone else. The woman came often to visit and had brought her son a Christmas gift. Under the watchful eyes of a deputy, mother and son would sometimes talk briefly, sometimes just sit and stare at each other, and then Loretta would leave as stone-faced as she had come. Only once had Marie seen tears in the other woman's eyes; those apparently came from her frustration at a wordless session.

Loretta Smith was not the only one having communication difficulties. Dillow, Neely, and Davis were getting little cooperation from their sulky client. Randall seemed more inclined to talk to Davis. Maybe it was because of the age similarity, but whatever the reason, Davis was liaison man. The defense strategy was shaping up; just before New Year, Davis tried another session with Randall. They were seated in the visitors' room. Randall chain-smoked, and his eyes were dull and disinterested; and most of the time they were focused on the floor.

"We've asked for a change of venue—want you tried in another county and town," Davis continued. "We don't believe with all the publicity you'll get a fair trail in Giles."

Davis waited for a response, and when he got none, he continued: "We're doing everything we can for you, and you've got to cooperate."

"You're just like all the rest. Tryin' to see in my head."

"We're trying to save your life. Can't you see that? The court has appointed us to defend you and to help you in every legal way we can. Whether you're guilty or not, it doesn't matter. We're duty bound to give you every defense we can."

"Don't need defendin'. Never done nothin'."

"You wouldn't be here if the State didn't have some pretty convincing evidence. It's time for you to wake up and give us all the help you can. We're not going to know all the evidence they've got against you until the discovery hearing—that's when they've got to reveal everything—but let's get a head start on this thing. What about the note you left in your truck? What did you mean when you wrote it?"

"Don't know nothin' about any note."

"Oh, come on!"

"Toe must have wrote it."

"Who?"

"Never mind."

"Did someone from here go to Myrtle Beach with you? Are you saying that someone was with you at Myrtle Beach?"

"No. Nobody from here went with me."

"What did you tell the psychiatrists at Central State Hospital?"

"Who?"

"Dr. Dimitris and Dr. Gwaltney at Petersburg? What did you all talk about?"

"Nothin'."

"Randall, you couldn't have been in eastern Virginia all that time and not talked about plenty of things."

"Don't you know?"

"We have a copy of the report that says you remember what you want to and forget what you want to. Looks like they were right on another point: You're not showing any willingness to help us. And we're trying to help *you*."

"You just want to see in my head."

"No, dammit, we're trying to help you! Yes, we are trying to see everything we can. We can help you better that way."

Randall lit another cigarette with the old butt that had burned down to the filter line. The hot ash had burned his fingers yellow. He looked up, a mischievious gleam now in his eyes.

"Can I go back now?"

"You might as well. I'll talk to you later. Maybe we'll get the change of venue; maybe we won't."

Back in his cell, Randall paced. He lived alone now. That's the way he liked it. Alone. But alone wasn't exactly the way it was. True, no one was in his cell, but from every direction other prisoners had only to look through their own bars. It was a fucked-up jail anyway. The second-floor cells were like a big bunch of lions' cages all jammed together in the center of a big room with an observation walkway around the whole complex—between the cells and the outer walls. During the hot months, the exterior wall windows had been opened, and the sounds of civilization had filtered up from the alley and parking lot below. Now, the only sounds were the voices of the other prisoners or the sounds of music coming from the radios of the prisoners who were allowed such privileges.

He wished somebody would play "On the Road Again." That song made him feel good—kept the waves back better than anything. He'd give his right hand if one Willie Nelson could shake it first. Willie would understand. Willie was true blue. Local friends, John Spaur and Kenny Sharp, had come to visit, and they used to be true blue, but it wasn't the same now. They, too, had looked at him strangely.

Loretta was all that he had now. And God, he hated her. But he loved her, too. Couldn't make it away from her for very long 'til the worst kind of waves came crashing down. But no sooner would he come home than they'd fight, and off he'd go for hours or days or weeks to get away from it. The memory of all that had gone on across the years—years that for the most part were filled with visions of the packs of brats and bullies that had come to his house, stolen or broken his toys, and driven him under his bed to get away from them. And most times Loretta hadn't even noticed. And when she had, it was "Don't be selfish now. Share your things. Help me with the children. Do this. Do that. Be nice, now."

But weren't those fuggin' little monsters supposed to be nice, too? He remembered a girl named Pearl that had pulled her pants down and crapped on his favorite book that he'd left open when Loretta'd made him go attend some other sick kid. When he'd come back and saw what Pearl had done—dumped her pile right on top of the picture of a silver jet plane—he'd picked up the whole mess and pushed it into her face. He had got a whipping, and the other children had laughed.

Why had their house become a shed full of squealing pigs anyway? Why hadn't Loretta found a rich man to marry—a man that could've given them things? Taken them places? She was a fuggin' failure. And she wallowed in it. Made him wallow in it. He'd needed a father so bad; used to lay under the covers at night with a flashlight and a Sears-Roebuck catalog. He'd flip the pages in the men's section and find a face that looked friendly and loving and imagine what it would be like to go with him to a ball game or to the circus. But the image wouldn't last long. Then he'd find himself flipping the pages back to the women's section, and his eyes would lock onto the models wearing low-cut brassieres and underpants, and strange things would start to happen to him. It was during those early days when the waves had first begun to come, and they'd driven him to go and look in the photo album at the pictures of "Smith." Everybody referred to his real father as "Smith." Randall would study the photographs by the hour, but in the end he'd want to reach deep into the pages and get his hands around the neck of the grinning bastard and choke him until his eyes bulged and popped out.

Even now Randall entertained visions of the multiple ways "Smith" could be made to pay. His favorite fantasy was hanging "Smith" by his balls. While he was upside down, filling his nose full of acid, and while "Smith" screamed from the agony of it, he—Randall—would stick the blade of his pocketknife into each eyeball and into "Smith's" worthless belly. Plunging a knife into soft flesh was high drama anyway. It was like opening a surprise package. Cutting into people was like discovering a secret. When everything spilled out, the secret could be kept no longer.

346

Why had the fuggin' bastard left his son and his wife? Didn't he know that running out like that would leave them helpless and frightened? Even hungry and cold and in dread of facing a screwed-up world of people that didn't give a damn?

"Smith? You in some kind of trance?" a jailmate across the way called out.

The surname Randall was loathing in his thoughts, but now applied to himself, caused him to jump from the cot on which he sat. Randall looked in the direction of the voice. It was Jerry Rainey, the only prisoner that had showed any friendliness, a man four or five years younger than Randall with wavy black hair and a broken front tooth.

"Cheer up. You're gonna beat this shitty rap," Jerry said.

"You think so?"

"Yeah. Dillow's gonna get me off, too."

"Don't need him. Never done nothin'."

A few chuckles filtered through the open cells. Prisoners could see into the cell of the others. Randall's eyes met briefly those of Zeb Songer, but the view was somewhat obscured by two sets of bars between them. Songer looked another way.

"I know you snitched on me, you fugging scab!" Randall yelled. "They better not put you back in here."

"Cool, it man," Jerry said. "Listen up. Something's coming over the radio about you."

The volume went high. All the inmates listened. It was about the change of venue angle.

"Where they going to move the trial to? Maybe they'll have it in Bland County. Isn't that where you told me your girl, the school teacher's, from? Adri — Adrianne or something like that?" Jerry asked.

"Yeah. That's her," Randall said.

But he said no more. Just wanted to savor the vision of her: the flowing brown hair that fell to her shoulders, the long shapely legs, and the plump breasts that had freckles down the valley between them.

"Tell us about her again," another jailmate called out.

"Shut up!" Randall yelled.

Save for the radio, the cellblock got quiet. Randall lay back on the cot, turned his back to them, pulled the blanket over himself, and felt for his spinning head.

CHAPTER XXXIII

Judge Powell set January 29, 1982, for the discovery hearing and March 22 as the first trial date. The judge did not, however, rule on the defense motion for change of venue.

From Dillow's, Neely's, and Davis' points of view,.there was still time to work on that maneuver. For now, seeing *everything* Hez Osborne had up his sleeve—and in his evidence lockers—took priority.

Dillow, Neely, Davis, and Osborne were thinking more alike than any of them realized at the time. Barring the remote chance of a mistrial for some reason, a change of venue to a really distant location, or an unforeseen lucky break of some kind, the Defense was reconciled to a long fight on home ground and was imagining a Giles County jury in about the same light as Osborne had. If the Commonwealth's Attorney played his cards right, Randall Smith might well be given life in the Ramsay case, Dillow conceded. Osborne didn't stand a chance of getting a conviction in the Mountford case unless the jury decided on guilt by association of events; then the defendant could draw two life sentences. And Judge Powell could possibly decide that such sentences run consecutively, and thus a prison term would be longer.

Dillow had seen Giles County juries, as well as Giles County judges, do crazy things. He had seen them make moral decisions—based on their own concept of what morality was—rather than legal decisions, judicially guided, based on guilt beyond reasonable doubt. Hell, you didn't dare allow a Baptist or a Methodist to sit on the jury in a simple drunk driving case. A helpless defendant was convicted in the minds of such a jury before the case was even heard.

Dillow was convinced his team could get the so-called confession note suppressed; surely the Defense could make a good case about illegal entry of Randall Smith's truck. At this point Dillow and his team viewed the note as a hot potato, fraught with all kinds of snags. If the note was finally allowed into evidence, the jury might give any kind of interpretation to it, and the State could use it against the Defense as an argument supporting abandonment of the vehicle.

And the Defense attorneys had more maneuvers up their sleeves. There was still the matter of Smith's competency. At no time had the defendant shown the proper degree of understanding or cooperation. It would not be hard to convince a judge that a more extensive examination was needed. And perhaps the Defense could move successfully to quash the murder indictments altogether.

On January 13 Judge Powell heard the Motion to Suppress (the "confession" note) in closed chambers. It was a highly ticklish issue with legal complications and of vital interest to both sides. The day ended with the judge hearing preliminary arguments but making no ruling for the time being.

Nevertheless, Hez Osborne under judicidal order had to show everything save for police reports, and on February 12 (not January 29 as originally set—numerous delays had been encountered) he prepared to do so. The day was bitterly cold, and snow flurries hinted of more winter weather to come. The scene was set in the main courtroom at 9:30 a.m., and Osborne and Dillow went through the same familiar routine before court opened.

"Old White Head—listen! Do you want Randall or not?" Osborne said.

"Do *you* want him?" Dillow asked.

"He's your client."

"Better wait awhile. Don't be running the Sheriff around needlessly until my associate's ready. Neely is just getting here."

The spectators loved it; they felt somehow that they, too, were a part of the action.

After more delays, Neely, Davis, and Dillow finally went back into their respective conference rooms, re-emerging after a time. Neely looked dapper as usual in plaid shirt, maroon tie, and flashy suit; Dillow and Davis were more conservatively dressed.

The first witness was Fred Webb, a large, handsome, middleaged man of confident demeanor, who was a handwriting expert with former F.B.I. credentials, now with the Bureau of Forensic Science Lab, at Merryfield, Virginia.

Webb revealed how he had been given the note taken from the defendant's truck, blown it up, and made comparisons to various employment applications filled out by Randall Lee Smith. Thus he established positive identification of Smith's handwriting.

Neely was anxious to know how and by whom such applications had been obtained.

"Special Agent Crane of the State Police, via certified mail," Webb said. "The applications were from Long-Airdox Corporation, Celanese Fibers Company, and Commonwealth Bolt Company," Webb explained.

Neely laid down a barrage of questions as to how the positive ID worked in practice.

Webb patiently went over his blow-up; he explained the fine points of his craft involving stroke, letter comparison, disguise methods, hand pressure, and speed-of-writing details.

Both Dillow and Neely were intrigued by the testimony and the obvious skill of the witness.

"May I have a copy of your enlargement?" Neely said.

"Why?" Webb asked.

"So the Defense can think up new questions," Osborne cracked.

Randall Smith, sitting at the defense table in gray trousers, yellow-and-white striped T-shirt, looked decidedly uncomfortable in the exchange. He shifted positions several times, looking behind him in the direction of his mother who was seated near the front of the courtroom. Loretta Smith was dressed attractively in aqua slacks, white blouse, and gray jacket, but her normal stoic calm was betrayed as Fred Webb's testimony brought a look of pain to her face.

Elmer Gist was next on the stand, laying all that he had before the onlookers. His detailed lab analysis lists covered everything from semen tests to minute examination of hairs. He had done anal smear tests, vaginal smears, panty examinations—the whole works—and had found no evidence of spermatozoa. Although he had received a vial of Susan Ramsay's blood from Dr. Oxley, he had been unable to type the deteriorated fluid. Mountford's blood, also from Dr. Oxley, had been successfuly typed.

"Why weren't you able to type both?" Neely asked.

"Mountford's body was in better condition. Apparently, he had been buried deeper than the girl. The damp earth kept his body cooler."

"How about if one body had been dead for days longer than the other?" Neely seized the opportunity.

"Possible, but not probable in this case," Gist admittedly grudgingly.

Gist went down a list of thirteen other items, and after each one Neely had a long string of questions. What items had human blood of what type on them; what were their origins; who had transported them to and from the lab, and when? Finally, Gist got to the knives submitted by the Galax Police Department. Neely, Davis, and Dillow smiled at the answers they had long awaited: how Captain Catron and his Galax Police Department first believed that they had captured the possible murderer of Ramsay and Mountford.

When Gist got to the blood-print-stained *Mountolive,* Neely was intrigued to know why the recorded days of rain during which the book had obviously lain somewhat exposed to the elements—or, moisture, at least—hadn't obliterated or damaged the prints.

"The book's coated enamel-and-varnished cover will hold a print—and blood—an unusually long time," Gist said.

When Gist got to the recently found .22 caliber revolver, Neely held his breath.

"There was no discernible blood on the weapon," Gist said.

The item-by-item analysis droned on: *no* blood on the concrete enforcement rod; blood *on* a cooking pan but not enough to type; type B blood on a pair of panties (not those the female victim was wearing); no blood on the Buck knife; type B blood on the checked shirt; blood on the sleeping bags into which each victim had been stuffed but not typeable.

Richard Taylor was next, responding to Neely's queries about this item or that.

"No prints on the Buck knife, no prints on the concrete re-enforcement rod, no prints on the plastic water bottle," Taylor answered in turn. "Item 71? The playing cards? Five latent prints, fourteen latent palm prints, one latent finger joint."

"And the .22 caliber revolver? Item #74?" Neely asked.

"No prints that matched the defendant's," Taylor said.

Taylor continued until the long list of Certificate of Analysis items was fully covered.

The Defense asked for a recess. Upon returning, Dillow asked Taylor—on the record—for a blow-up of all critical prints.

"Why on the record?" Osborne queried.

"I want to cross-examine Mr. Taylor in court," Neely said. "I will have some questions as to how he arrived at his conclusions about certain things."

Dr. James Dimitris, Forensic Unit Director, Central State Hospital, Petersburg, Virginia, was next called to the stand. He was solidly built with penetrating dark eyes and olive complexion, and did a thorough recap of the evaluation Randall Smith had received at Central State, but nothing dramatically new was added to the earlier written report. After lengthy Defense questioning, however, it was clear that the Defense was not yet finished with the issue of mental competency.

After lunch recess the long day dragged on with only occasional spurts of dialogue or facts that snapped the media to attention. When it was all over, Pam Chesser, feisty and attractive reporter for *The Roanoke Times and World News,* buttonholed Dillow and asked for a copy of the confession note.

"It belongs to the Commonwealth," Dillow said pointedly. "Ask Osborne."

Chesser did so.

"No," Osborne said politely. "It would be improper."

Chesser hung around, and her nimble brain was already in motion. Too much about the Randall Smith case was shrouded in mystery or kept under tight wrap. There were ways to meet the public's right to know. Her newspaper had intervened via legal process before in such cases. Maybe it would again. She began to envision the full contents of that infamous document printed on page one of *The Roanoke Times and World News.*

Having seen now all the ammunition the prosecution possessed, the defense team broadened its counterattack with a motion to quash the murder indictments, a revised motion to suppress certain of the State's evidence, a motion for a Bill of Particulars, and a new motion for additional mental competency testing of their client.

Dr. James Dimitris supported the move for additional testing and wrote to Judge Powell, Osborne, and Dillow, Neely, and Davis:

> We realize after our latest visit to Giles County, during the hearings, and from the defense attorneys, that Mr. Smith is not showing the necessary inclination and eagerness to work with his attorneys in the preparation of his defense. In spite of our professional opinion that Mr. Smith is mentally capable of understanding and participating in his own defense, because of the seriousness of the case we strongly recommend that the Court consider another comprehensive evaluation from the University of Virginia Forensic Clinic, under the direction of Doctor Robert Showalter and his associates.

Acting in accord with the recommendation, Judge Powell issued the order. On a snowy day in late February, Randall was transported by two deputy sheriffs to Charlottesville, Virginia.

It was suggested that Loretta also present herself for evaluation and testing at the same psychiatric clinic. It would be embarrassing to reveal all the details of her unfortunate and unhappy life, Loretta thought, but if the result would be a tool the defense could use to her son's advantage—one that might even cause a jury to take especial pity on Randall—then it might be worth the humiliation. Still she debated the matter.

She talked it over with Bernice Kincer, her sister, next door.

Over coffee and her umpteenth cigarette of the day, Loretta said, "I don't know whether I want to make a guinea pig out of myself or not. If it'll help Randall, that's one thing, but if that bunch of quacks wants to make up some kind of filthy tale, then I'm not going to be a party to it."

"Everybody—around here, at least—knows more about you than you think," Bernice reminded her. "There's been all kinds of snooping around. Neighbors, relatives, and Randall's teachers and his friends have been questioned. I heard word of it every day or two before and after Randall was brought back."

Loretta inhaled a deep drag. "I know. People look at me now all the time with kind of a dumb stare. Don't know whether they believe everything they're hearin' or not. Even at work, you'd think I had some kind of pox the way people run clear of me."

Bernice gave her sister an affectionate pat on the shoulder. They were close, although Randall's behavior—and particularly his threats of violence toward his aunt and uncle—had strained the relationship.

Loretta lit another cigarette and stared into her coffee cup.

"Are you going to Charlottesville?" Bernice asked again.

"I guess so. Don't guess much of anything can hurt now . . . and it might help. Don't understand that boy. Honest to God, I don't. If he did it—and maybe he did—I don't know what made him do it. Don't make sense. What'll I do if Randall has to spend the rest of his life behind ____."

As Loretta's voice broke, Bernice came to her sister's side.

"Maybe it won't be for long. They get paroled pretty quick now. Jails overcrowded. Good behavior. Things like that."

"This local bunch'll lock him up for life if they can," Loretta muttered. "What's a poor woman to do?"

"Hope and pray," Bernice said.

"Yeah. After almost thirty years of it, I ought to be good at that." On March 1, Loretta headed for Charlottesville.

Meanwhile, the defense team kept up the heat. In the defense motion to quash the murder indictments, it was argued before Judge Powell that the selection of the grand jury had not met State code requirements; thus the indictments were illegal. With the motion to quash, the motion for a change of venue, the motion to suppress certain evidence, and the motion for closure of the continuing hearings, the case was further complicated: Two more motions—one by attorneys for *The Roanoke Times and World News* and one by WDBJ Television—to intervene with the purpose of legally forcing the Court to keep all hearings open to the public and the media.

Another hearing was scheduled for March 8. Judge Robert Powell heard the intervenors first. Carter Magee, attorney for the *Roanoke Times and World News* and Samuel Wilson, attorney for WDBJ, led off.

"We are entitled to know all the facts, and we have the responsibility to make such facts known to our viewing public," Wilson argued. "In the public interest, there must be no suppression."

Magee reminded the Court that if closure was granted, accurate media reporting would be impeded if not made impossible and that in a recent case—similar to the case at hand—between *Richmond Newspapers, Inc.* vs. The Commonwealth of Virginia, the court had ruled that such hearings must be open to the public. "What is unknown is often more important to the public than what is known," Magee concluded.

When his turn came, Neely rebuffed the claims.

"The Constitution says that a defendant shall receive an impartial trial. How can my client's trial be impartial if prejudicial publicity has the effect of convicting him before a jury hears the case?"

"But measures—such as change of venue—do exist to protect the defendant's right to a fair trail," Wilson argued.

As the hearing progressed, Neely pounced on the illegal entry of Randall Smith's truck by police in South Carolina.

"The Court is unaware of points supporting illegal search," Judge Powell retorted.

Neely went to his notes and read the check-off: No search warrant before entry of the vehicle. No proof of actual abandonment. No attempt to contact the truck's owner.

As the long, tiring day wore on, it was clear that the judge was in the mood to grant only limited concessions. His final decree was to allow open hearings on the entry of Randall Smith's truck, but the hearings with regard to the confession note, its content, and its allowability as evidence would be closed to the media and the public. "Closure in this instance must be granted in the interest of the defendant," Judge Powell reiterated. Quashing of the original indictments and the change of venue motion would remain before the court for further consideration. Evidently Judge Powell was not going to consider a change of venue until it was determined whether or not a qualified and impartial jury could be seated in Pearisburg.

The hearings continued on March 15. The sky was gray, and an icy drizzle periodically chilled pedestrians to the bone. Judge Powell opened court by first hearing arguments on the motion to quash.

Neely went into a long tirade about jurors who had been given the responsibility to serve for one term of court and then been called back to serve yet another term, rather than being replaced by new jurors as the Virginia code required.

"The wrong jury was reconvened! A new jury should have been chosen." Neely's voice rose. "This is a Constitutional point. The grand jury's seating and subsequent actions violate the Fourteenth Amendment!"

The courtroom crowd and the media had seemed bored with a mere technicality in grand jury selection; but everybody snapped to attention when several officers wearing uniforms of the Myrtle Beach Police Department were brought out from the witness rooms, paraded before Judge Powell, and sworn en masse.

Osborne led off, laying the groundwork for the South Carolina police involvement. Neely's counterattack was spirited and calculated to draw from one officer or another that the truck had been illegally entered with no probable cause to do so and that impoundment was totally outside the scope of South Carolina authority.

"Officer Shafer, you keep using the word, 'suspicious,' " Neely snapped. "What is suspicious about a truck parked in the shade?"

"*That* area has always been a lovers' lane, a hideout for drug dealers and thieves, and a staging point for burglars that prey on nearby motels," the deeply—tanned young officer replied.

Shafer went on to explain how he had first spotted the truck and reported it to his superior; then how, during Officer Piersal's watch, Piersal had investigated and found that the tags were still missing and had taken steps to identify the owner.

"Couldn't it have been possible that Randall Smith was a guest of the land owner? For all you know, permission to park the truck there had been granted. Right?" Neely surmised.

"Your Honor, he's leading the witness," Osborne protested.

"I withdraw the question," Neely barked.

Osborne kept Shafer on the stand.

"Did you suspect that the vehicle in question might have been stolen?" Osborne questioned.

"Yes, sir. We get a hundred-fifty to two hundred stolen vehicles each summer in Myrtle Beach."

Officer Piersal, with a neatly trimmed black mustache and as tanned and clean-cut as Shafer, was next called. Osborne had him confirm and enlarge upon the earlier testimony.

"And how did you enter the truck?" Neely asked on cross-examination.

"With a slim-jim."

"What's a slim-jim?" Neely asked.

The officer explained the device—a long, sliver of metal that could be inserted between the vehicle door and the doorpost to disengage the latch.

"Did you have a search warrant?" Neely pressed.

"Under the circumstances, we didn't need one."

"Did you contact the owner of the wooded property?"

"That wasn't the issue," Piersal said. "We first needed to identify the truck's owner. Had to get inside to get serial numbers. Get numbers off the inspection sticker."

Neely probed in every direction: Were the tags found? Didn't South Carolina vehicles have only one tag? (Maybe one tag *was* in place, and brush had obscured it.) Neely's efforts proved negative.

Lieutenant Carter, a short, blond-haired Myrtle Beach officer, was called next, and in his turn Neely asked: "After you impounded the truck, did you then obtain a search warrant?"

"Yes, sir. The warrant was issued by Judge Lam."   Neely was taken aback by the answer.

"And you had this warrant before you searched and removed other articles from the truck after its impoundment?" Neely pressed.

"Yes, sir."

"Is what you and your associates have described your standard procedure in South Carolina in regard to stolen vehicles?" Neely asked.

"Yes, sir. We handle hundreds of such cases each year."

"After the ID and trace, did you attempt to locate the truck's owner?"

"We couldn't identify the owner quickly. The trace took some time." "Did you make any sort of press release?" Neel asked.

"That's not our area of responsibility."

Neely asked for a conference at the bench. Osborne joined Neely before the Judge. It was agreed that Piersal could be recalled to clarify a vital point. Piersal took the stand again.

"You did not really consider the truck abandoned until you found the note in the ashtray. Is that right? Until the press got hold of the situation, the truck might have been just another stolen vehicle?" Neely pressed.

"No, sir. We considered the truck abandoned when we found the tags had been removed—from the way it was parked—more or less hidden."

Neely went round and round with the officer until Osborne objected to the badgering repetition. Neely was undaunted.

"Other than the missing tags from the vehicle, not one thing was improper. No one had reported that the vehicle or its owner was trespassing; neither the truck nor its owner had been accused of anything. No officer in any jurisdiction had probable cause to break into the vehicle. Beyond the act of simple identification of the truck and its owner, normal guidelines should have been adhered to: a search warrant must always be obtained in such instances before the first lock or doorglass is broken! The law is clear in this matter! What will officers of the law do next? Break into houses just to see who lives there?"

When Neely wound down, Osborne stood up swinging.

"The truck was clearly abandoned! It was hidden. The serial number was covered. The tags had been removed. Of course, it had to be entered and searched! Is the defense claiming that the truck's owner hid the vehicle and removed the tags just to go out and sun bathe? Probable cause need not be shown in the case of an abandoned vehicle. A residence is a totally different matter. A vehicle owner has absolutely no claims once that vehicle has been abandoned!" Osborne exclaimed.

"We've made a *prima facie* case in this matter!" Neely's voice was quivering with emotion. "Those truck doors were locked, signifying the owner's intent to ensure the sanctity of his property and its content. The State did not have the slightest hint that the truck or its owner had been involved in any way with a crime in this state or in South Carolina! The State has not—and cannot—prove abandonment!"

But Osborne had done his homework and found a precedent. An amazingly similar case. Osborne cited it and gave the references.

Neely tried futilely to pick the precedent apart. It was no use. He was losing the battle and he knew it.

After the arguments were over, Judge Powell paused just long enough for the exhausted adversaries to catch their breaths; then he rendered his decision.

"It is clear to the Court that Randall Lee Smith did, in fact, abandon his vehicle and thus has no legal standing to challenge its search ___ "

Judge Powell discussed at length the motion to quash the murder indictments; he overruled, and had the order entered on the record.

In Dillow's office later, members of the defense team were still nursing their wounds.

Although he was the junior member of the team, Mike Davis, felt sure that he knew in which direction the case was heading.

"Anybody besides me thinking the words 'plea bargain'?"

Dillow and Neely looked at each other momentarily, and Davis could see Dillow's jowl muscle tighten and hear faintly the grinding teeth.

"Does look like the matter is coming down to a draw," Dillow agreed.

"Well, I'm not so sure we don't still have a good shot with the right jury," Neely said.

"The 'right jury,' " Dillow mused. "Those are the magic words."

Dillow, pacing for a moment, came to rest at his wall calendar. Davis could imagine the wheels going around in the silver-thatched head. The trial date in the Ramsay case was less than ten days away.

"When's Randall due back?" Dillow asked.

The defendant was being shuttled back and forth between Charlottesville and Pearisburg for the various hearings, and Davis knew that the interruptions had delayed the work of the Forensic Psychiatry Clinic doctor.

"The last contact I had, they expected to be done with him by midweek."

"They'd better be," Dillow said. "The clock's running out, and if they give us any ammunition at all, we're going to have to move on it fast."

"Don't know how much it can help us, whatever comes, when Randall's not turning a finger to aid in his own defense," Davis said.

They all had been frustrated by the defendant's obstinacy or unconcern, whichever it was.

"He's not helping because he's guilty as hell and we all know it. And he knows we know it," Dillow said. "That doesn't change our obligation to him, of course, but you'd think he'd wake up to the reality of things."

The three of them talked a while longer; then they parted company. Each of them had other cases to try on the morrow. It had begun to seem, however, that each had lived with the Randall Smith case for half a lifetime. In fact, it had been just ten months.

Later in the week in Judge Bondurant's court, Davis was waging war in the defense of another client. He noticed a messenger come into the courtroom and whisper to the court clerk, who in turn handed the Judge a note. Judge Bondurant interrupted the proceedings and summoned Davis to the bench.

Davis—still new enough at the game to wonder if he had somehow goofed—came forward a little nervously.

"Yes, sir?"

"You have an urgent call," Judge Bondurant said. "Think it's from Charlottesville. The Smith matter. Take all the time you need. We'll wait."

Davis took the call in the court clerk's office. He listened as the Forensic Psychiatry Clinic's legal adviser apologized for interrupting him in court: she had been unable to reach Dillow or Neely, and the Clinic staff urgently needed some guidance.

"About what?" Davis asked.

"Mr. Smith is on the verge of opening up. He says that he does know something after all about the Appalachian Trail murders. Our question: shall we let him proceed or stop the testing? We don't know what else he may say, but it's possible he may make a full confession."

The information so jarred Davis that momentarily he just stood there, feeling his palms moisten.

"Let me think a moment," he said finally.

Both Dillow and Neely were in distant cities with little chance of being reached. Davis recalled that Judge Powell in his court order had been clear on what Randall Smith's commitment to the UVA Forensic Psychiatry Clinic was supposed to accomplish: " . . . shall address itself to the competency of the defendant to stand trial, as well as the competency of the defendant at the time of the alleged offenses"—that was the way Davis remembered it. The order asked—allowed—nothing more. Anything beyond that opened up big and little cans of worms.

"Stop it where you are," Davis finally said into the phone, "as long as you've got specifically what the court order asked for. It doesn't appear to be to the defense's advantage for you to go any further. It's certainly not to our advantage to have anything on the record beyond the Judge's order."

"If that's your instructions ___ "

"I'll contact my associates as quickly as I can run them down. If there are further instructions, I'll get back to you promptly."

"Yes, sir."

"I trust that anything above and beyond what is required by the Order can be forwarded in written form to our office alone," Davis said. "Any problem with that?"

"No, sir."

Davis went back into the courtroom. All the Defense needed was a witnessed confession by Randall, neatly recorded in the official report. Still another round was lost. Whether the Judge would allow more information than he had asked for was beside the point. The very fact that Randall might confess—or indicate that he was ready to confess— would be devastating on its own terms.

Davis got through his own case in a daze and rushed from the courtroom.

It took him hours to reach Dillow and Neely. When he finally got in touch with them, each backed Davis' decision and instructions.

On the morning of March 17, copies of the competency evaluation reached Pearisburg. In accordance with the judicial order, copies had been sent to the Court, the Prosecution, and the Defense. Dillow's secretary summoned the other two members of the defense team quickly, and well before lunch they met in Dillow's office.

"Guess you've both read your own copies?" Dillow began.

"Looks like we've been shot down again," Neely said.

"All the time I spent with the guy, and he tells the psychiatrists, 'He's against me,' " Davis said. "Did you two catch that line? Neely, apparently you're the only one of us Randall trusts!"

"Keith's the one with the big mouth," Dillow quipped. "Maybe Randall trusts the one of us who has talked the most. I notice the defendant gave me about the same score as Mike got."

When they all got to the meat of the report, they went over each line in scrutinizing detail. The critical portion of the five-page document reported:

MENTAL STATUS EXAMINATION

Mr. Smith was presented at the Forensic Psychiatry Clinic as a stocky man of medium height who appeared older than his stated age. He was oriented to time, place, and person. He stated at first that he did not understand the purpose of the evaluation, reporting that he thought it was to help him with his headaches. However, his initial concern to talk to his attorney before he participated in the evaluation suggests that his assertion about his understanding of its purpose was not candid. After an explanation he appeared to understand the purpose. Mr. Smith continued to be suspicious of the evaluation and frequently declined to answer questions stating "I don't know about that." He expressed difficulty trusting the evaluators, his attorneys, and others, reporting that "everyone in Giles County" wanted to see him convicted. Mr. Smith's suspiciousness was reflected also in his assertion that he was being "framed." He was evasive in his response to questions; however, it did not appear that he did not understand the meaning of the questions.

Mr. Smith did not exhibit significant anxiety during the evaluation. He did appear to be somewhat depressed, and he expressed a hopelessness about the outcome of his trial and a resignation about the disposition. He assumes he will be convicted and sent to prison. There was no evidence, however, of any suicidal ideation.

At times during the evaluation, Mr. Smith reported auditory (running water) and visual (lights, a tree) hallucinations and delusions (his mother was a policewoman). Although hallucinations may be associated with psychosis (a state of being out of touch with reality) and may reflect a severe thought disorder in the Clinic's opinion, Mr. Smith's reports of hallucinations and delusions were probably fabricated. There was no other evidence of psychosis, and he subsequently acknowledged that the delusion about his mother was not real. He exhibited no bizarre behavior during the evaluation.

Mr. Smith appeared to be of a low average intelligence, a clinical impression which was supported by the school records. Psychological testing of his intelligence during the evaluation was not viewed to be accurate given Mr. Smith's reported unfamiliarity with many basic objects and concepts.

Mr. Smith reported varying degrees of memory loss during the Forensic Clinic evaluation. He initially reported a global amnesia, for not only all the events and persons of his life before he was in jail but for certain skills such as reading, writing, knowledge of colors, etc. The psychological testing revealed no evidence of brain damage. This confirmed earlier tests at Central State Hospital and supported the Clinic's opinion that the amnesia was feigned. During the course of the evaluation, Mr. Smith acknowledged that this amnesia was largely not genuine although he continued to report a spotty memory for certain events and skills. He continued to claim very vague memories of his childhood and for other events; however, he admitted that he did not like to recall these things. Mr. Smith's short-term memory was unimpaired. His insight and judgment were thought to be within normal limits.

COMPETENCY TO STAND TRIAL

Mr. Smith was aware of the identity of his defense attorneys and recalled speaking with them on occasion. He reported that he did not trust two of his attorneys because of his suspicion that everyone in Pearisburg, including Mr. Dillow and Mr. Davis, was against him. The clinic does not believe that Mr. Smith's distrust would make him unable to work with his attorneys on his defense. Mr. Smith understood who the judge was and what his role is. He recalled having been in court. He does not know what a commonwealth's attorney is and reported that he is unaware that there would be attorneys involved in the trial who would be "against" him. It is believed that this lack of understanding reflects a lack of information, not an inability to understand this issue. Similarly, he reported not to know what a jury is although there is no evidence that he is unable to understand this. Mr. Smith understands the meaning of pleading "not guilty"; he also understands the consequences of a guilty plea. He is aware that he is charged with "killing some people" and was able to describe accurately the specifics of the crime with which he is charged. He understands the consequences of being convicted of the offense, and he anticipates that conviction will result in a long prison term. He does seem to have some misconception about the possibility of getting the electric chair and believes that the death penalty is a possible disposition of this case. Again, this appears to be more a lack of information than of comprehension.

CONCLUSIONS CONCERNING COMPETENCY TO STAND TRIAL

It is our opinion that as we understand the legal standard of Virginia Code 19.2-69, Mr. Smith is competent to stand trial. He understands the nature of the charges against him and comprehends the proceedings. There are no psychological or cognitive impairments which should inhibit his ability to work with his attorneys. It does appear that he is extremely suspicious of his attorneys and may need some persuasion that their concern is to represent his interests. He also may need some additional information about the courtroom proceedings to increase understanding of the roles of the different participants.

"Well, gentlemen," Dillow said. "As Mike previously mentioned, maybe the time for a plea has come. We'll have to talk it over with Randall first, of course, make him understand as fully as possible what he's up against. Anybody have any trouble with that?"

"You think Hez will go for it?" Neely asked.

"I would," Dillow said. "I've been there. Haven't forgotten by commonwealth attorney days. Hez can't get a conviction in the Mountford case, and he knows it—that is, unless the jury simply concludes, without supporting evidence, that if Randall killed Ramsay, he must have killed Mountford. It could happen. We've got to wrestle with that possibility. As you well know, our only concern now is the defendant's best interest."

"I'd still like to try the case," Neely said. "Sometimes the breaks come right out of the blue. If we did a good research job on the jury members, we could strike our share of the diehard conservatives and hope for a few bleeding heart liberals."

"You live on the fringes of Blacksburg—a university town," Davis countered. "Such a jury might be seated in your area, but here ___ "

"Mike's right," Dillow said. "Getting your bleeding heart liberal jury in this county would be a miracle. Hell, there's so many Baptists, Methodists, and hard rock fundamentalists of every persuasion in this county that the state liquor store was twenty years late in passing local option."

"Guess we can assume the change of venue is out, or at least the judge is going down to the wire on it," Neely mused. "But I'd still like to try the case here or elsewhere."

"We still may have to," Dillow interrupted. "Osborne may feel as confident as a bucksheep. I don't see how he could, but he might. He may not be open to a plea of any kind. And, of course, he'd prefer some backing from the parents of both victims before he entertained any offers."

"Let's play it both ways," Neely suggested. "If Randall can see the handwriting on the wall, let's get our heads together on what we feel prepared to offer in Randall's best interest and then make the overture. But we'll be prepared to go all the way just in case."

They chewed it over at length and decided that pleading Randall guilty on two counts of first degree with a twenty-year sentence on each count, the two to run *concurrently,* would be the plea target.

But what would they do if the defendant insisted on going the trial route? But maybe he wouldn't since he had faced reality enough to begin talking truthfully to the psychiatrists at Charlottesville.

As for Loretta's evaluation, nothing dramatic had come from it that would help change the direction of things.

"It's agreed then?" Dillow said. "I'll feel Hez out—see if we can get the drift of his thinking?"

They all agreed, and Davis volunteered again to be liaison man to Randall, who had been returned to Pearisburg two days previously.

"Maybe I ought to go with you since I'm the only one Randall likes—and trusts," Neely said, rubbing it in. "Don't know what good it'll do, but let's keep the record clean."

Just before ten next morning, Davis and Neely had Randall brought from his cell and faced him across the conference table. The long stay in Charlottesville had taken its toll. Randall moved—even sat—with weariness, and his sallow face looked drawn. Davis could tell from the way Randall tended to lean and favor one hip that Randall's hemorrhoids were acting up as they had during two of the previous hearings.

"You feeling all right, Randall?" Davis said. "Your hemorrhoids bothering you again?"

"Yeah. The doctor gave me some stuff."

"Did they treat you well in Charlottesville?" Neely said.

"I didn't like it up there."

"Why not?" Neely probed. "They were trying to help us—help you—understand what we're all up against."

"I didn't tell 'um nothin'."

"Come on, Randall. We're your attorneys," Davis growled. "When are you going to face reality? Dammit, man. Wake up! We're just a few days from going to trial. Aren't you tired of playing games?"

Randall lowered his head timidly. Davis had tried every approach in the book to draw his client out. The two of them had played Good Guy—Bad Guy; Davis had tried shouting, pleading, play-acting—the whole bit.

Finally Randall looked up. He reached for and lit a cigarette in a slow, trembling motion.

"Are they goin' to give me the chair?"

"The State is not even asking for the death penalty," Davis said. "We explained that to you repeatedly."

Once again Davis and Neely explained the Bill of Particulars wording in the simplest language they could devise.

"The doctor at Charlottesville. He said there was a lawyer or somebody against me," Randall said.

"The Commonwealth Attorney, you mean?" Davis asked. "Osborne?"

"Yeah."

"Of course he's 'against you.' The whole state of Virginia is against you.

I've explained all that. Mr. Dillow and Mr. Neely explained all that," Davis said.

"I never done nothin'. Why they against me?"

"For God's sake, Randall," Neely barked. "You started to tell the psychiatrists in Charlottesville that you *did* know about the killings."

"Some times I remember things. Some times I don't."

"Whether you remember or don't remember is beside the point," Davis said. "We're duty bound to protect your interests as best we can. We are out of time! You're going to be standing before a judge and a jury in a matter of hours."

"They've got some strong evidence in the Susan Ramsay murder," Neely said. "And a jury might decide that if you killed one of the hikers, you killed them both. It may be to your advantage to plea bargain."

"They think I killed both of 'em?"

"You know very well they think you killed them both," Davis said.

"How much time would I get?"

"A conviction on both counts you mean?" Neely said. "Two counts of first degree?"

"Yeah."

"If it goes to trial and we lose, and you're convicted and get two life sentences running consecutively—one after the other—you'd get forty years or more in prison," Neely said.

Randall started to shake all over.

"There *is* another way," Davis said. "If we plead you guilty to both murders, maybe we can make a deal with the Commonwealth Attorney and get shorter sentences. We would plead you on first degree counts and ask that the sentences run concurrently—not one after the other, but at the same time. You could get out of prison in four or five years *if* you got early parole."

"Say that again," Randall perked up slightly.

"What do you want?" Davis pressed. "If you want the trial, we'll do everything we can for you. But there's a strong possibility you'll get a life sentence in the Ramsay case. If that happens, at the least you'll spend fifteen years in prison even if you beat the Mountford case."

"It could work out that way," Neely agreed.

Randall sat sucking on his cigarette, but it took both hands to guide the cigarette to his mouth.

"We think it might be wise to go for a plea bargain," Davis said. "Make the best deal we can for you. Even if the judge ruled that your sentences had to run consecutively, you could be out in seven or eight years if you got early parole."

"And the time you've already spent in jail will count toward your time," Neely added.

"I'd just like to get out of here. Go home. Maybe go on a long campin' trip," Randall said.

"Of course you'd like to get out, but you're not going to get out!" Davis exclaimed. "Wake up, man. We're talking about murder."

Neely was growing as exasperated as his associate.

"Randall, we're just going around in circles. Do you want to think about it for a while?" questioned Neely.

"Yeah."

Randall was ushered back upstairs to the cellblock, and as the cell door locked behind him, Jerry Rainey called out: "What's happenin', man? You been gone a long time."

"I'm gettin' out of here. They found some people that killed those hikers," Randall said. "I'm goin' free."

A ripple of guffaws sounded down the line.

Jerry didn't laugh, but he offered no congratulations.

"Too bad about the judge draggin' his feet on the change of venue, but maybe that teacher from Bland will come anyway and stick by you."

"Yeah. She'll be here," Randall said.

"Sure. She might even ask the judge to marry you both after the trial's over," a prisoner a safe distance away snickered.

"Fuck you all!" Randall lunged at his bars.

Jerry tried to cheer him, but Randall made no response. He began to mull over all his lawyers had said. The words he remembered best had to do with *time*. Prison time. Eight years. Fifteen years. A lifetime. Loretta might have to sell his truck. Maybe she was thinking about it already. Maybe she was even getting used to the idea of his long imprisonment. He'd miss the truck more than anything, or anybody. As he tried to come to terms with it, big waves started to roll in, and he covered his head with the pillow.

CHAPTER XXXIV

Liv Dillow sought his opportunity and cornered Hez Osborne along the corridor of the Giles General District Court building.

Dillow led off. "The Smith case? We ought to bargain out the matter."

"What do you have in mind?"

"How about a plea of first degree on both counts: twenty years on each to run concurrently?"

"The last word I don't like."

"The three of us think that's a just resolution to the matter," Dillow said.

"I'll think on it, but I won't do anything before talking with the Ramsays and the Mountfords."

"That sounds reasonable. Of course, I needn't remind you that we're just three days removed from jury selection."

"How well I know," Osborne sighed, then grinned a little.

"I know what you're feeling. I stood in your shoes a long time. The burden is all on the Commonwealth. *We* can make a mistake and wiggle out of it, but you ___ "

"You guys *do* have the easy side."

They walked the length of the building. Outside, the formalities ceased as if professional conversation had been cut off with a knife. Both men genuinely liked each other. Small town life encouraged, if not demanded, peaceful and respectful coexistence. As Dillow walked toward his car, Osborne watched him. There was still vigor in the older man's legs. The posture was straight and proud. And Osborne, above all people, knew that his adversary's mind was still as sharp as a steel trap. "The burden is on the Commonwealth. We can make a mistake and wiggle out of it, but you ___ " Dillow's words resounded like an echo.

On the way home Hez began to feel a degree of elation. Maybe Dillow's offer was a good one for all concerned. A dual plea of guilty now rather than a long drawn-out trial in the case—then still another in April for the Mountford case—looked all the more appealing if justice could be done in the bargain.

But there were others besides the Mountfords and the Ramsays with whom the matter should be discussed. Sheriff Hopkins and his men had done an outstanding job in the case as had the state police, and all of them had a stake in the matter. And so did the public at large. Hez began to slump as he drove. It was as if the weight of the world were suddenly on his shoulders.

Pulling into the driveway of the brick ranch in the southern suburbs of town he and his three sons shared (though oldest son Tommy was presently away at law school), Hez decided to call the Ramsays and the Mountfords before dinner.

He paused long enough in the kitchen to have a cold beer and to get son Jeff, a senior at Giles High, and son Josh, a sixth grader at Giles Elementary, going on the meal preparations and then headed for his study.

He dialed Ohio but got no answer. It was only six-fifteen. Maybe the Ramsays—both workaholics, Hez suspected—were still at the office. He tried that number. No luck. It suddenly registered again that indeed time was running out. Maybe the Ramsays were already enroute to Virginia for the trial.

On the call to Dover-Foxcroft, Bob Mountford's exuberant voice answered after the second ring. Every time they talked, Osborne had felt uplifted by the sense of joy Mountford always conveyed.

After a few pleasantries, Hez repeated Dillow's offer verbatim. Mountford asked a number of questions, and Hez answered them as best he could. Then Mim came on the line, and Hez began to repeat the offer. After Hez had explained the difficulties the State faced in the case, he reminded them that under Virginia law all murder charges were assumed to be second degree unless the State could prove that death was caused deliberately and willfully.

"I'm not at all sure that I can prove premeditation in either case," Hez added. "It would seem simple enough that Smith crept up on the victims late at night most probably while they slept and killed your son to get him out of the way, and then had in mind raping Susan—and that he planned this hours—or minutes—in advance; but proving it is another matter. The law and the courts don't operate on logic as you know. A jury might buy it, but then again, they might look at the whole episode as a campsite brawl with no premeditation or malice aforethought involved. There *was* drinking involved as the blood-alcohol content in the autopsy reports revealed."

There was a long pause when all Hez could hear was heavy breathing.

"The burden is all on the Commonwealth to prove its case," Hez said. "I wanted to get your—and the Ramsays'—feelings about the matter."

Mountford asked if the Ramsays had been reached.

"Not yet. I'll keep trying," Hez said.

"I think we're willing to leave it in your hands," Bob said finally. "We hold no malice. Bear no grudges. If justice can be done by way of a plea, we'll be satisfied with that."

"What do *you* think?" Mim asked.

"I want to talk to others who've assisted me in the case, but I'm somewhat inclined to go with a plea. For one thing we resolve most of the lingering questions that way. We get a guilty plea in both cases—lay to rest any more speculation that more than one murderer was involved. And no long wearisome trials. And last, but certainly not least, there will be no appeals that could go on for years. Everything will be over and done with, and the murderer will be behind bars for a long time to come."

"But how many years?" Mim asked.

"On a twenty-year concurrent sentence, the earliest Smith could be considered for parole is about five. But I don't think the Parole Board would even consider it the first time up. I can't be sure of that, of course, but it's my strong opinion."

The Mountfords went silent again.

"Do you plan to be here for Susan's case?" Hez asked.

"No, we hadn't," Bob said. "We're not even sure we want to come for Bobby's case. Jackie Hilton feels the same way. Sometimes we all think that we will; then we all agree it's like opening an old wound. And our coming would really serve no purpose since none of us will be witnesses. We're just not sure. Bobby's case still set for April?"

"Yes. As matters now stand—if we go on with the trials. If we accept the plea, then it's all over. A few more days, and it's all over."

All over. The words seemed to echo and re-echo along the line like a ghostly voice.

Again the silence hung.

"Would you like to think about it more? Talk among yourselves and your family?" Hez asked. "There's still time. Jury selection doesn't start until Monday, March 22."

"We'll do that," Bob agreed. "You'll have reached the Ramsays before then and heard their opinions. But if it'll make you sleep better, I think we'll still be inclined to go with whatever you think best. You're the man in the arena."

The vote of confidence made Hez feel a lump in his throat.

"And I feel like I'm up against a very large and ferocious bull."

They chatted a moment more about mundane things, and when Hez cradled the receiver, he had that same uplifted feeling again. By some uncanny means, Bob and Mim Mountford had a way of infusing light amid shadows, and yet the source of it escaped Hez completely.

He left the study and made his way back to the kitchen where his sons were piling spaghetti on the plates and putting the final touches on the tossed salad. It all looked so appetizing, and yet Hez felt his stomach begin to knot. More and more he sensed that, whatever the outcome of the cases of the murder on the Appalachian Trail, a lot of questions would linger for years.

Sleep that night was spasmodic. The next morning at the first opportunity, Hez made his way up to John Hopkins' office and told the sheriff of Dillow's offer.

At first, Hopkins, the most serious-minded of all the enforcement officers, said nothing. Osborne began to feel as if Hopkins thought it foolhardy to even consider a plea.

"I'm no lawyer," Hopkins began, "but I can see the pitfalls in the cases. We have a revolver we think might be the murder weapon but can't prove it. We have a Buck knife we think may be an instrument of Susan Ramsay's death, but can't prove it; there was no provable rape, and the confession note if allowed into evidence may not convince the jury of anything. It's a nightmare of a case for you. I can see that. What do you think? You inclined to accept the plea? Get it all over with?"

"Yeah. Especially if the Ramsays will go along. I've already talked with the Mountfords."

"Guess you ought to talk with Crane. Those boys have busted their butts on this case."

"Yeah. Seems like we've all got years of our lives invested, and it's been less than a year."

"It's still your decision," Hopkins said. "I'll go along if you think a plea is best. Can you second guess Judge Powell? Will he buy it?"

"I believe he will, but we'll just have to wait until the time comes. All sorts of things can go wrong. Randall may back out at the last minute. May decide to plead not guilty. If he does, there's not a thing anybody, including his own attorneys, can do about it. That'd be a hell of an anti-climax, wouldn't it?"

"It could happen," Hopkins agreed.

"Nothing we can do but proceed as if we're going the full distance. Of course, you know the irony in all this?"

"Yeah. If Smith hadn't run to South Carolina, had just stayed put, and if he could've avoided ever seeing Robin Cunningham and her coworkers again—after their meeting Susan Ramsay and a male called Billy Joe at Wapiti as she testified here—he'd still be a free man. The case would have gone unsolved for years. Maybe never solved. Funny how things work out."

"We should have kept a diary down through the years." Osborne allowed himself a moment of lightness. "Maybe we could have written a book in our old age."

"Who's to say either one of us will stay in office long enough to fill many pages?"

"God, don't remind me of the voters. I've got enough on my mind right now. And how do they think anyway? Ever figured that out?"

"When I do, I'll share the secret of my long success with you," Hopkins said dryly.

Back in his own office, Osborne scanned his mail and speed-read a few of the letters that had continued to come in relative to the Smith trials. In every major case there were always letters from concerned citizens, cranks, meddlers, political aspirants—and in this case, Appalachian Trial enthusiasts. Some of the writers were obviously under the illusion that the State was asking the death penalty for Randall Smith, and some thought that such an end was just what the prisoner deserved. Others pleaded for mercy in Smith's behalf—lamented long and vehemently against the inhuman treatment experienced by criminals at the hands of the State. Crazy. Half the populace wanted to hang everybody from the petty thief to the murderer; the other half was against anything but the mildest form of retribution, feeling that society, not the criminal, was to blame.

All the mail dispensed with, Osborne made and took a few phone calls. He then had his secretary try the Ramsays' business number in Aurora. In the waiting he circled his desk. Would the Ramsays go for blood, or be willing to compromise? What would he do if the victims had been his children?

"The Ramsays are on their way to Virginia," the secretary called through the open door rather than use the intercom.

Life was full of ironies. Barbara Smith, the young blond-haired beauty who had been Hez's secretary for two years, lived in Ingram Village just as Randall Smith had. Although she had been able to provide insights about Smith and his family (to whom she was not related), she, too, had been as shocked and surprised when the case broke as many of the other neighbors were. Randall Smith had always been a loner, Barbara had said, and there had been problems in the Smith family, but murder of strangers? Something didn't fit, she felt. Something about the incident was unusual; some factor was present in the tragedy that was obscure but important.

At lunch time, Hez avoided the usual restaurant where most of the professional people gathered for the noonday meal. He wasn't ready to run into Dillow just yet. On the way home he stopped and touched base with Hopkins and learned that Mike Davis had again visited Randall. Was Smith holding out for a trial?

Thus far, no word about a possible plea bargain had leaked out. Secrecy was vital. If a leak occurred and if the bargaining fell through, it could possibly affect a jury's disposition of its duties and weaken the State's case.

It was four in the afternoon before Hez reached the Ramsays at the Marriott in Blacksburg. Again, he laid it all out, talking first with Bud and then with Ginny.

"What I want most is to hear him utter the word 'guilty.' " Ginny said. "However he comes to that moment is beside the point. I must hear him say, 'Guilty.' "

When she had finished, Bud came back on the line. "You know the situation better than we do. We know a part of what you're up against. Doesn't take a genius to see the maze of obstacles you're confronted with, and we've already anticipated that the Mountford trial could go in any number of directions. We're with you if you recommend a plea, but let's just hear him stand up and tell the world he did it."

Hez heard himself going through it all one last time. It occurred to him that maybe he was trying harder to sell it to himself than to them.

Hez hung up. The work day was winding down. He supposed the Ramsays had arrived early in order that Ginny might rest up before the trial started on Monday. She was scheduled as a witness. She might still have to serve in that capacity.

At ten of five, Hez dialed Dillow's office. Surprisingly, Dillow himself answered.

"You've sent everybody home early for the weekend?" Hez said lightly.

"No, but I should have. Everybody's running errands. Things are getting too hectic around here. We'll probably be here all weekend. Part of it depends on you. What have you decided?"

Hez didn't know why he paused so long, but he did. "I believe a plea is the best way to resolve the matter, but instead of concurrent sentences, I'll need two twenty-year terms to run consecutively."

"No dice."

"Even with forty years, your client can conceivably be out on parole in ten or less. Isn't that better than two full life terms handed down by a jury?"

"You don't stand a chance in the Mountford case, and you know it," Dillow said.

"I'll take my chances. This whole county and people all over the state are still shamed by these senseless murders, and besides, they're in a law-and-order mood right now with all the crime and drug cases that are keeping you and me running all day and half the night. A jury may just fool you. I'll wager they'll put Smith away for life on both counts and never bat an eyelash."

"Maybe, but what I'm offering may be the best deal you can get." Dillow was gambling.

Hez again found himself pausing unduly long. "Maybe I still ought to take my chances."

"Wouldn't you rather have a sure thing?"

"What if Smith himself decides to scrap the whole deal? He may foul up the works at the last moment."

"We've used every approach to explain the options," Dillow said. "He's definitely inclined to go with the plea as we've offered it. We think it's a just resolution of the matter."

"The potential short prison time bothers me. What's 'just' about the chance that he'd be free in five years? What's 'just' to the State and society about that?"

"None of us can answer the parole issue. That's out of our hands."

Hez felt his throat constrict and his tongue go dry. He hesitated until Dillow prompted impatiently,

"Well? What do you say?"

"I guess we'll go with the plea as you've offered it. We need to close the book permanently on this thing."

"I agree completely. We'll proceed accordingly and get right to the paperwork. That way, on Monday we can let the potential jury members and all the witnesses go home sooner than they expected."

The phone went dead, and Hez sat at his desk in kind of a daze, not sure at all that he'd done the right thing.

On Saturday morning Hez went to his office as if it were a normal work day. His modest quarters at Bluff City—a village one mile removed from Pearisburg proper but now within the corporate limits—were part of a commercial building on the site of what once had been a motel, but the location was isolated somewhat from the noise and movement of Main Street. It was a historic old village aptly named, for to the front and rear of his office vast limestome bluffs overhung the narrow valley below. But the area was scenic, and New River was almost in spitting distance from the front door. Once Indian camping grounds had lain along the riverbanks, all the way into Ohio and beyond. New River, if Osborne remembered his history correctly, was the only large stream east of the Mississippi that flowed northward. And those same Indians had been the first users of parts of what was now called the Appalachian Trail.

He had never hiked the trail; he hadn't really had the desire even in college when the urge for most people seemed to be most predominant. But even now he wondered what it would be like to shoulder a backpack and know that a thousand miles or more lay footstep-by-footstep ahead. Mentally, he caught the thrill and the adventure of it; he knew more strongly than ever that it took a very special person to believe in himself and in his physical prowess enough to try it. Throughout the whole ordeal of the investigations, he thought often how much he'd like to have known Bobby Mountford and Susan Ramsay. Some part of them yet lingered here in Virginia where their young lives had been snuffed out.

His thoughts shifted, and he began idly to sort through the stack of documents, lab reports, police files, photos, and copious notes he had assembled in preparation for the first trial. Before the day was over—or certainly tomorrow, subpoenaed witnesses would be coming into town from South Carolina, eastern Virginia, Charlottesville, and the northern states; hikers and others who had had contact along the trail with the victims or knew something helpful about the tragedy. Didn't he owe all of them something also?

He began to have second thoughts about the plea bargaining. The sentence agreed to simply was not stiff enough; Randall Smith could not pay his debt to society unless a healthy hunk of the twenty years was actually served. If parole was granted in five, it would be a mockery of justice—a further crime against the victims and a betrayal to all of those who had worked so hard to see that justice was done.

He reached for the phone and dialed Dover-Foxcroft. Again, Bob Mountford answered promptly.

"You folks having any second thoughts about the plea bargaining?" Hez questioned, once small talk was out of the way.

371

"The children—especially the boys—are a little leary, but we can allow for their youthful sense of wrath, I suppose. It's only natural they'd want revenge, but maybe in time they'll see that love is much more powerful. Are you having second thoughts, Brother Hez?"

"I still think the plea bargain is the best solution, but I've decided that we must get more prison time or go to trial and do the best we can."

"We're still with you whatever you decide."

They talked on, getting away from the trial subject completely, and finally Hez began to ring off.

"The Lord be with you," Mountford returned. "We'll be praying for you and for Randall Lee."

Mountford's signoff lingered momentarily in Hez's mind, and the New Englander's accent seemed to give new meaning to the ancient words.

Hez started to dial the Ramsays in Blacksburg, but he then decided to wait until he stood face to face with them. As for Dillow, Hez debated the wisdom of telling the defense team just yet that he had changed his mind, and that the ante would have to be upped. That, too, could best be handled eyeball-to-eyeball, and it would work best just before court opened on Monday.

When Monday came, the sky was clear, but the air was bitterly cold. Hez entered the courthouse before the spectators had begun to gather, but not before the various TV camera crews had begun to unload their trucks and to make ready.

He unpacked and arranged his papers and pads but found it hard to concentrate.

Mike Davis was the first defense attorney to appear, and Hez went over to him.

"Your ship is not going to sail," Osborne said grimly.

Davis stared back unbelievingly; his mouth dropped open slightly. "You're calling it off?"

"Yeah. It's not justice. And I represent a lot of different people."

"What's your counterproposal? I'll take it to my associates."

"I'll accept the plea as offered with one exception: the prison terms must run consecutively."

"It won't happen." Davis' body stiffened behind the freshly pressed brown suit he wore for the occasion. "And Neely's downstairs right now in the Clerk's office putting the finishing touches on the plea agreement— or what we thought the plea agreement was!"

"You know me well enough to know I haven't dealt with you in a duplicitous manner, no matter how it looks. It's just that I owe too much to too many people not to ensure that justice is done."

Davis still looked dumbfounded. But he wasn't angry. Here, too, stood two friends as well as two adversaries.

Davis walked off, entered the Defense conference room and closed the door. Soon he reappeared, walked the length of the courtroom, and disappeared down the stairway.

Osborne was talking with Hopkins when he saw the defense team come in and go directly to their conference room. Dillow and Neely hadn't so much as cast a respectful glance Osborne's way. Dillow's white hair was in wild disarray, his grinding teeth already in gear; Osborne could see the clean-shaven jowls in motion.

When Osborne had finished bringing Hopkins up to date, the sheriff said: "Whatever happens from here on out, it's been the best kept secret so far in Giles County history."

Al Crane, Cecil Wyatt, Tommy Lawson, Mike Meyer, and three Myrtle Beach officers entered the chamber and headed for one of the large witness rooms. Osborne motioned Crane into a corner, but before Hez had finished talking, Davis had called Osborne aside.

"Will you meet with us for a moment?"

Osborne followed, and when he entered the Defense conference room, Neely was smiling and jovial, but Dillow kept his eyes on the papers upon the table.

"Well, Hezekiah, I understand you've said our ship won't sail," Dillow began.

Dillow used Hez's full name only when he was miffed at the Commonwealth's Attorney or otherwise displeased with the workings of the State in Giles County.

"You heard right," Osborne said calmly. "The sentence is too lenient. I've thought about it all weekend. In good conscience and in the interest of justice, I can't accept it. The sentences have got to run consecutively."

"No way!" Dillow barked. Then he looked up with piercing eyes that were angry but controlled.

"We thought about backing out, too," Neely said. "We were handing it to you too easily."

Neely was grinning triumphantly. Osborne tried to gauge the seriousness of the assertion. But from Neely's point of view, it was serious. Clearly, Neely wanted—hungered—to try the case. How else did one become the Marvin Belli and F. Lee Bailey of the South?

"You're now totally intractable in the matter?" Dillow said.

"Absolutely," Osborne said.

"Then we'll try it," Dillow said to the nodding heads of his associates.

Osborne left the room and closed the door behind him. The court room was filling for real now, and the front rows were lined with media people, pads and recorders in hand. Eula Bott-Naff, the court reporter, readied her equipment and began checking it out. Bud and Ginny Ramsay came in, but before they sat down, Hez asked a deputy to bring them to the Prosecution conference room. "Have Hopkins join us," Hez called to the departing deputy.

When all four of them were seated, Osborne began: "Looks like we're going to try it after all. I've agonized over this thing all weekend. A twenty-year concurrent sentence is just not enough. I asked for a consecutive agreement and was refused. Now we've got to lay it before the judge—let him know what's going on. Normally, the judge just approves or disapproves what's brought to him by the Prosecution and the Defense. He has nothing to do with the actual bargaining, but you can understand his need to know what's in the background."

"We're still with you," Bud said. "You are the professionals, and if you don't know what you're doing, we certainly don't."

"But if a plea works out somewhere along the way," Ginny said, "I won't be at rest until I hear from that murderer's mouth—however illiterately—the word 'guilty.' "

"We'll do our best," Osborne promised. "Now I'll leave you in the sheriff's good care and see if the Judge has arrived."

Just momemts before ten, two deputies ushered in the prisoner, seated him alone at the defense table, unshackled him, and sat just behind. Randall slouched, kept his head down except for one fleeting rearwise glance toward his mother seated on the outside right aisle.

The courtroom had grown deathly quiet, and though court had not been officially opened, the silence prevailed. Osborne and his adversaries re-entered the courtroom and took their seats. A few minutes after ten, deputy Jim Spicer did the call to order. Judge Powell entered and took his seat. The judge looked particularly grim as he uttered his opening remarks in measured tones. When the judge had finished explaining to the spectators what jury selection was all about and declared the court ready for business, Dillow was on his feet.

"Your Honor, the Defense requests a conference with the Commonwealth's Attorney in chambers."

The request was granted, and Judge, Prosecution, and Defense deserted courtroom and spectators.

In the Judge's chambers Powell removed his robe, sat down, and pointed to chairs for the other four.

"Any reason we can't be comfortable?" Powell said lightly as if to discharge the electric air suddenly about him.

"Your Honor," Dillow began, "you have heard the Commonwealth's side of the plea matter. We'd like you to hear ours."

Dillow went on at length, adding that a deal made should be a deal carried out.

Osborne tried to justify—and believed that he did justify—his change of mind. Powell commended the Commonwealth Attorney's integrity on behalf of society and the various law enforcement officers who had worked so long and hard on the case.

Neely and Davis took their turns; Davis hit hard on the matter of ethics when a deal was made between fellow members of the bar and the sacred nature of such agreements.

"You all know that I cannot enter into the negotiations. When both sides have come to an agreement acceptable to all, then I'll hear it and rule accordingly," Powell said.

"But we did have an agreement acceptable to all," Dillow insisted. "We're asking you to rule on that agreement."

"Gentlemen, since there obviously is not an agreement acceptable to all, I suggest that we get back to the courtroom and get on with it. We've been out now for an hour and one-half."

Once back in the courtroom, Judge, Prosecution, and Defense, alike, could see impatience if not weariness on the faces of spectators and the media. Witness rooms, their doors opened to the main courtroom, revealed numerous witnesses peeking out, trying to discern what was happening or not happening.

Getting back to the case, Judge Powell called on the Commonwealth to present the list of eligible jurors. Osborne did so, and in turn Neely was on his feet, his eyes afire.

"Your Honor, you have before you a motion to dismiss the jury panel. It is the Defense's contention that the State and the Jury Commissioners are not in compliance with the selection of jurors pursuant to Section 8.01-342 of the Code of Virginia and in addition are not in compliance with the procedures of drawing, selecting, and summoning this jury panel."

Osborne could hardly contain himself as the glowing Neely ranted on about yet another obscure technicality. First it had been the grand jury selection. What would come next? The Judge's robe was the wrong color? That black suggested mourning, and thus the defendant's case was prejudiced?

Neely was having a ball—totally in his element. All the media people were leaning forward, hanging on every maneuver. Neely wanted to try this case. That was abundantly clear.

Osborne called the three jury commissioners, one at a time, and Byron Skeens, one of the senior members, related the commission's procedure with such painstaking skill and clarity that Osborne felt the matter had been dealt with completely and truthfully.

"But Your Honor," Neely protested, "the jury list should have been made up from the general voters' register, not from the list of the Clerk of Court. There must be a completely random selection. The clerk did not draw the names in accord with State statutes!"

The judge, obviously feeling now as weary as the spectators, witnesses, and media, glanced at his watch and called a lunch recess.

Osborne tried to get away from his station quickly. He was being goaded and he knew it. Before he could gather his papers and leave, a half-dozen reporters had cornered him.

"What is going on in *there*? In here?" a West Virginia reporter queried.

"A trial—what else?" Osborne snapped.

Twelve more questions seemed to come at once, but Osborne wheeled about, said "Excuse me," and headed for the parking lot.

In the afternoon the issue of jury selection continued. In all his years of practice as an attorney and as a state's attorney, Osborne felt that never had he witnessed a duller, more fruitless day. Even Randall Smith had almost dozed off. The one positive thing that finally came of it was the Judge's overruling of the motion to dismiss.

"I don't know why you could have a more random selection of jurors than that compiled by the jury commissioners as presented today," Judge Powell had said.

Osborne again tried to get away quickly. Most of the reporters and all of the camera crews had followed Randall back to the jail, but afterwards a few back-tracked. Osborne was polite but noncommital.

Heading for the stairs, Osborne hit the traffic jam at the bottom. TV cameras were focused on the emerging crowd pouring out the front door. Davis caught up with his adversary.

Neither could withhold a poorly suppressed grin. They were out of the arena now—out on the street, practically.

"Why don't we all sleep on it?" Davis suggested. "Talk again in the morning."

"There may not be anything to talk about. Randall may hang himself from sheer boredom; he'd save us all the trouble."

The humor didn't escape the extroverted defense attorney and Davis chuckled. "It *wasn't* one of our better days, was it?"

"Does Neely ever miss the chance to squeeze something in that may later be used in the appeals process?" Osborne said.

"Guess I'd better pass on that one."

"Forget that I asked. I'm just a little more bushed than usual."

In spite of himself, Osborne had to admire Neely's tenacity, his innate shrewdness.

The big double doorway cleared at last. Both attorneys walked into the camera lens.

"See you in the morning," Davis called out.

Osborne didn't sleep at all. He got up a half dozen times; in fact he saw the tail end of a movie on TV in which Henry Fonda played the part of a juror who swung an entire jury around from an eleven-to-one vote for a guilty verdict to a unanimous vote of acquittal. If there had been any chance for sleep before, Hez thought, that kind of reminder scuttled it.

He drank a glass of milk to settle his stomach before going back to the bedroom. He lit what must have been his fiftieth cigarette of the day and saw the twin ribbons of smoke from his nose rise against the window and the street lights beyond.

How much could he compromise? Would the Defense team go for *fifteen* years to run consecutively?

Hez did catnap briefly. Shortly after seven-thirty, he got up, showered, shaved, had a farmer's breakfast, and felt the surge of new energy and expectation.

Again he tried to beat everybody to the courtroom; but the day had turned milder, and spectators were already gathering on the courthouse lawn. In passing, he saw a reporter and a camerman hem in a local farmer and ask the man his opinion of what the trial outcome might be. Hez didn't hear all the answer but the words . . . ."I don't believe the boy done it," sent chills up the attorney's spine.

Osborne took the stairs two at a time and walked down the long aisle of the courtroom. It was almost like walking down the aisle of a cathedral. The venerable courtroom reflected history and tradition, its good craftsmanship indicative of a time unrushed and less complex. Just when he thought himself totally alone, the door of the Defense conference room opened. Davis stood in the doorway, and Hez could see Dillow and Neely seated within.

"Want to join us for a minute?" Davis called out, his voice bouncing around the empty chamber.

Hez accepted the invitation. Once Hez was inside, Dillow looked up cheerfully.

"Well, Hezekiah, did you sleep well last night?"

"You know damn well I didn 't" Hez smiled back.

"Oh, the woes and the tribulations of being a Commonwealth's Attorney," Neely teased.

"Well, I slept extremely well." Dillow took it up again. "I do my best thinking while lying in bed. My thinking tells me there's no reason why honorable men can't come to a fair and equitable agreement regarding the matter before us."

"That sounds good so far—and in your usual eloquent terms," Hez said.

"Give us your best counter offer and let us respond to it," Dillow said.

"Two counts of first degree. Fifteen years on each, to run consecutively."

"No first degree," Dillow insisted. "We've got to get *some* concessions."

"Besides, you can't prove deliberate and willful premeditation," Neely said.

"Shooting a man in his sleep? Picking up a knife and going after a helpless girl? That's not premeditation?" Hez barked.

"Mere supposition, counselor," Dillow mocked. "Mere supposition. Can you prove that Mountford was shot in his sleep? Or that Smith was not merely defending himself?"

"All the evidence suggests that Mountford was shot in his sleep to prevent his interference with the act of rape upon Susan."

"Suggestions are not proof," Dillow interrupted. "All you can prove is that Randall Lee Smith was seen with Susan Ramsay alone, that his fingerprints appear upon a paperback book and a few other items, and that he took a trip to South Carolina and left his truck among the trees. And where's the proof that Randall Lee even attempted to rape the girl?"

"And I suppose bloodstained clothing in his mother's basement suggests nothing?" Hez added.

"Suggestion, yes. Irrefutable proof, no," Neely said. "No positive blood type—remember?"

"Juries have been known to hand down stiff sentences on strong circumstantial evidence," Hez argued.

"Gentlemen, we're just going around in circles," Dillow said calmly. "Playing old records that are getting scratchy indeed."

"*You* make an offer," Hez filled the void.

"Our client will plead guilty to two counts of *second* degree with a fifteen-year sentence on each count to run consecutively."

Hez momentarily lost his breath. It was close to the compromise he himself had envisioned.

"Thirty years," Hez said almost in a whisper. "Thirty years. I think we can live with that."

"Then let's take it to the judge," Dillow said.

When they left the conference room and crossed the main courtroom, four faces froze in startled realization: They had been in conference so long that the courtroom had filled and witnesses and spectators alike were in place, waiting. Hez caught the eyes of Hopkins and Crane and gave one nod.

In the Judge's chamber, Hez informed Powell that at last they had reached agreement. Powell questioned both sides at length.

"I see no reason why the Court should not approve this agreement," Powell said presently. "It's a difficult case for both sides. We'll not be above criticism, but I believe your joint proposal is fair in the interest of society and in behalf of the defendant and the victims ' families."

"Your Honor, I'll need a few minutes to go downstairs to use the Clerk's typewriter and make the appropriate changes in the original plea agreement," Neely said.

"Take your time. We'll wait," Powell said.

Outside in the courtroom, media people had begun to smell a rat. They had watched their timepieces tick off the minutes, quarter—and half-hours. Court was supposed to have opened at ten sharp. It was now eleven-twenty. Deputies, the court clerk, state policemen, and others wandered in and out. Tired spectators left for a quick smoke and then came back. Everybody seemed in motion, but nothing was happening.

"What is going on?" a TV reporter asked Bob Kane, publisher of the local *Virginian-Leader*.

"Who knows?" The older man shrugged his shoulders. But the truth was, he did know—or thought he knew. In addition to being head man at the hometown paper, he had also practiced law earlier in his career. All the movement clearly signaled plea bargaining. Kane smiled in appreciation. The bargaining had probably been in motion for hours, if not days, and the participants had kept it neatly under wrap. That was no small feat in the small town of Pearisburg.

Neely came in and out a couple of times, once for a lawbook and again for a stack of papers. His steps were vigorous, but his handsome face was a little pained. He was clearly disappointed about something.

Several reporters scooted closer to one another and speculated. Could there possibly be a plea under consideration?

Seemingly out of nowhere, Dillow, Neely, Davis, and Randall Smith suddenly appeared and took seats at the defense table. Osborne went quickly to his own station. To the left of the dais, Deputy Jim Spicer stepped through the door, and like a blaring radio snapped on suddenly, began the recitation of the call to order. Judge Powell entered, gathered in his robe, and took a seat. His Steve Allen look-alike face was relaxed this time as if something pleased him.

The whole room was suddenly charged. Media representatives inched forward in their seats.

Judge Powell's gaze swept the jammed courtroom but came back and lingered on the person of the accused. Randall's eyes were lowered, his body in the usual slump.

The smallest sound seemed magnified during the exceedingly long pause.

"The Commonwealth of Virginia against Randall Lee Smith. Is the Commonwealth ready?" the Judge asked finally.

"The Commonwealth is ready, Your Honor," Hez said.

"Is the Defense ready?"

"The Defense is ready, Your Honor," Dillow said.

"There are two indictments pending against Randall Lee Smith," the Judge began. "One charging that he did feloniously kill and murder one Robert Tatton Mountford, Jr., and one charging that he did feloniously kill and murder one Laura Susan Ramsay. What is your client's plea to the indictments?"

"May it please the court," Dillow began in stentorian voice, "Counsel for the defendant respectfully advises the court that it is the desire of the defendant, Randall Lee Smith, to interpose a plea of guilty to the charge of second degree murder to each of the indictments which the court has mentioned."

A prolonged gasp traversed the courtroom. The media people lining the front rows were suddenly astir. A few of the reporters looked as if they might rise, their gaping mouths making them look all the more off guard.

Dillow turned and looked toward the crowd but did not waver from the stately demeanor with which he had begun the pleading. As the rustle of surprise and shock waned, he again faced Judge Powell.

"The defendant will, of course, for the record, make his own plea, but Counsel tenders the pleas with the approval of the defendant. I might advise the Court that pursuant to negotiations which have been going on for the last few days, a plea bargaining agreement has been consummated. It has been signed by the Attorney for the Commonwealth, by each of the counsel for the accused, and by the defendant. At the proper time, this agreement will be presented to the Court. The defendant is now ready to plead and does plead guilty to the charges of second degree murder."

"May I see the agreement?" Powell asked.

Dillow complied. "I might add, Your Honor, that *this* document is the one finally agreed to. There was previously a plea bargaining arrangement which had been discussed with the Court, and it is our understanding that the order of this case will show that the first plea was rejected by the Court. The pleas I now submit are tendered to the Court as the final and consummated agreement."

"Mr. Dillow, with regard to the agreement shown to the Court yesterday, the Court indicated its displeasure. There was no actual ruling as far as that particular agreement was concerned," Powell said.

"Your Honor is correct. The order to be entered in this case would, of course, show that."

Osborne agreed. Neely sat stone-faced, the disappointment of the way matters were proceeding clearly registering on his face. Davis looked on with a faint smile of approval. Media eyes focused back and forth from Judge to Dillow to Neely, trying to figure it all out.

"Let Mr. Smith approach the bench, and I will take his plea," Powell said.

For a man who had slumped, dozed, and acted generally bored throughout the whole proceedings, Randall got up quickly and walked with surprising agility. He attempted to straighten his stooped back and stepped briskly before Judge Powell.

The Judge asked the accused his age, place of residence, educational background, and place of schooling. Finally he asked if Smith understood the two pending indictments.

"Yes, sir," Smith intoned clearly.

"And what is your pleading to the first indictment?"

"Guilty."

"And to the second indictment?"

"Guilty."

"Mr. Smith, before accepting your pleas, I want to ask you these questions: Do you feel that you had ample time to discuss these indictments fully with your attorneys?"

"Yes, sir."

"And you have had a good line of communication with your attorneys?"

"Yes, sir."

"And did you discuss with them the plea of not guilty as well as a plea of guilty?"

"Yes, sir."

"Do you feel that you made up your own mind to enter the plea of guilty to each of the indictments?"

"Yes, sir."

"Was that after a full and frank discussion with your attorneys?"

"Yes, sir."

"You have presented to the Court a plea agreement. Has anyone made any threat to you or any promise to you other than that embodied in the document before me?"

"No, sir."

"So you feel satisified that your plea to each indictment is entered into freely and voluntarily on your part?"

"Yes."

"Do you understand that on your plea of guilty to the indictments, you admit that you did commit the offense with which you are charged?"

"Yes."

"Do you understand what the range of punishment is that you are subject to upon a conviction?"

"Yes."

Randall's knees continued to shake as the judge droned on point by point: that the Commonwealth needed proof to effect conviction; that those elements had been discussed with defense attorneys; a trial by jury was being forfeited; and that the right of an appeal was given up.

"Do you feel satisfied that you fully understand the effect of your plea of guilty?" Powell continued.

"Yes, sir."

"Do you understand that your plea of guilty is an unconditional admission and that you waive any objection to matters that have gone on throughout all the proceedings?"

"Yes, sir."

"Are you completely satisfied that your plea of guilty to each indictment is entered into freely and voluntarily on your part?"

"Yes, sir."

"Do you have questions of the Court at this time? Would you like to ask questions of your attorneys at this time?"

"No, sir."

"You may be seated. Let the record show that the Court is of the opinion that Mr. Smith does understand the nature and the consequences of this proceeding today and the effect of his plea of guilty and that his plea is entered freely and voluntarily on his part. The Court, therefore, accepts his plea to each of the two indictments."

Ginny and Bud had clasped hands during these final proceedings. They had been among the number of nine people here present who had known in advance what was coming. There were no tears, and the victory was shallow. Smith had said, "Guilty" so many times and in so many different ways that the impact of it faded away like melting snow. Perhaps now the need for revenge and justice was giving way to sickening pity.

Judge Powell allowed Osborne and Dillow to enter matters necessary for the record.

"Mr. Osborne, I would like to ask you further, what is the feeling of the officers who investigated this matter?" Powell questioned.

"I have talked with Officer Crane and Sheriff Hopkins, and they feel the pleas as presented and agreed to is an appropriate disposition of this case."

By now Neely sat at the defense table reading the morning issue of *The Roanoke Times and World News,* oblivious to uninteresting chatter. Momentarily he closed the outspread pages with a loud rustle and began to fill his briefcase.

Dillow made a conciliatory statement in behalf of the Defense and took no exception to the Commonwealth Attorney's statements for the record.

"All right, then," Powell said. "As to the plea agreement, if the Defense and the Commonwealth are in agreement with the Court, let the record show that the Court did not participate in any way in the draft of the said agreement."

Dillow and Hez concurred.

Powell gave a lengthy resume of the concerns of the Court throughout the entire length of the case, and his especial concern that the parents of the victims felt that justice was being done.

"Let Mr. Smith again come forward."

This time, Randall came front and center docilely with bowed head.

"Mr. Smith, do you have anything to offer at this time? Is there any reason the Court should not pronounce judgment upon you?"

"No, sir."

"All right, then. Upon the Court's finding of guilty, it is the judgment of the Court that you serve the term of fifteen years in the State Penitentiary under each of the two findings of guilty under second degree murder. Those sentences will run consecutively so that you will have a total of thirty years in the state Penitentiary."

Just like that, it was over. A kind of controlled pandemonium seemed to break out in all directions. Keith Neely stalked out of the courtroom ahead of everybody, evidently signaling that he was not about to be interviewed and that he had begun to feel a certain distaste in his mouth.

Reporters were visibly in a state of stark surprise if not in shock. Deputies whisked Smith away quickly down the back stairs. Loretta stood alone at the rear of the courtroom, her face tear-streaked. A reporter headed in her direction but then thought better of it.

Osborne and the two remaining Defense attorneys stayed at their stations; Judge Powell also remained on the scene and talked congenially with several spectators and reporters. Osborne accepted the congratulatory handshake of several officers; he then gave Al Crane a friendly slap on the back.

"Can you believe it's all over?" Osborne said.

"No," Crane said with a broad grin. "I've eaten with it, slept with it, puzzled over it so long. No, I can't believe it."

Osborne thanked the officers from Myrtle Beach for their contribution and wished them well.

The courtroom finally began to clear except for a group of well-wishers gathered around Bud and Ginny. Osborne gathered his papers once more. His bulging briefcase in hand, he walked down the winding stairs and out the front foor. A few cameras were already sighting in on his exit, and other cameramen rushed over from the jail building to catch the new action.

A reporter thrust a microphone almost into Hez's face. With Randall safe in jail and out of sight, Osborne became the focal point for all the media.

The questions came hard and fast.

"How did you and the Defense keep the bargaining so successfully secret?" "Do you think the plea agreement is fair for the State? The victims' families?" "What did the plea really accomplish?"

Hez braced himself, faced the cameras, and began to give the best answers he could.

"My critics will be the people who don't understand all the ins and outs of the law, and what the Commonwealth can and cannot do. The plea bargain brings to an end the speculation that more than one murderer was involved. You heard Randall Lee Smith stand before the judge and confess. You heard the word 'guilty'. As to the sentencing, the maximum second-degree term under Virginia law would have been twenty years on each count. The plea is for fifteen years on each count. It was, and is, doubtful that I could have convinced a jury that the murders were deliberate, willful, and premeditated—a position necessary for a first-degree conviction. The evidence simply was not strong enough to convince twelve men and women unless they threw to the winds the time-honored guidelines of *guilt beyond a reasonable doubt."*

After Hez took the bombardment still longer, dealing with each probe as best he could, his captors set him free and latched onto Mike Davis for the defense viewpoint.

Ginny and Bud Ramsay emerged from the courthouse, and again there was a mad scramble, a barrage of questions.

"Yes, we are satisfied with the plea bargain," Bud led off. "It lays to rest, I think, many unanswered questions."

"We really do think it's fair under the circumstances," Ginny added.

While the Ramsays were still being interviewed, Hez and Mike Davis bantered for a few moments until Hopkins, his deputies, Al Crane, and his fellow officers, came on the scene.

"You guys going somewhere to give thanks?" Hez asked.

"Yeah. Over to the luxury of my office," Hopkins said. "Want to join us?"

"No," Hez said. "I'd be outclassed. You guys did a helluva job. Go on

383

and re-live it. Talk about what could have been rather than what was—like you always do."

"I know *I'm* in the wrong camp," Mike Davis said and took his leave.

Hez hung back and lit another cigarette. When Ginny and Bud had finished the interview, Hez stepped forward, extending his hand.

"I wish it wasn't under these circumstances, but I've enjoyed meeting and getting to know you both."

"Same here," Bud said.

"If you ever come to Ohio, look us up," Ginny said.

"Small chance. You can see what my life's like here. Wish things like this didn't happen, but every few months it's the same old ball game with new batters or with new knives or guns, I should say."

"Will Randall ever tell what really happened, you think?" Ginny asked.

"Yeah. Before long he'll tell," Hez said. "Most likely someone of his own kind. And with a mixture of truth and fantasy."

"So strange," Bud mumbled. "The Judge reminded us again upstairs that Smith had no record. Strange indeed."

"Will you call the Mountfords?" Ginny asked Hez.

"Yes. I'm headed for the office to do that just now. Hope the news will bring them a new sense of peace. Maybe they can forget."

Wednesday dawned warmer still, and Giles residents got the first hint that spring might really be just around the corner. There was a general upsurge in the collective outlook: merchants and shoppers alike made mention of it. Offices and plants buzzed with increased efficiency.

The trial was over. The people of Giles and the residents of Virginia could show their faces to the world again, reclaim the title of Mother of Presidents, gentlest of the genteel and purveyor of Southern hospitality in the finest tradition. That was one side of the issue. The other was that scores of Giles Countians and Virginians, at large, were outraged by the plea agreement.

Later in the day, shopowners closing their doors, workers heading home, tourists passing down Main Street, were confronted by a strange sight. A lone man—one Warren Doyle—picketed in front of the county courthouse. The large sign he wore about his body said:

> DID BOB & SUE PLEA FOR THEIR
> LIVES?
> DID RANDALL LEE SMITH GIVE
> THEM A BARGAIN?
> Shame on the murderer!
> Shame on the judicial system!

Doyle, aged thirty-two was an Appalachian Trail hiker, a West Virginia resident with a doctorate in Appalachian studies, and he held a professorship at a West Virginia college. He had also hiked the full length of the AT four times and was preparing for his fifth walk. But he would delay it, he promised, if local residents who stopped to talk would stage a protest rally. There were no takers.

"My protest won't change anything," Doyle confessed to those who paused to inquire what was going on, "but if there is a next time—God forbid—better the matter be heard before a jury, not decided upon by judicial powers."

Doyle was not the only protestor. Steve Mountford, after the impact of the plea, and the chance of early parole for Smith, had weighed on his mind—became hostile and vocal about the matter.

Through interviews by some of the New England dailies—a few of which had editorially lambasted the Virginia plea arrangement— Mountford had threatened to come to Giles County and do some questioning of his own.

"If Randall Smith goes out in seven or eight years, will that help bring my brother back? Is that justice?" he was quoted as saying.

For days on end, the trial resolution was debated in the editorial press and on TV. Both Judge Powell and Hez Osborne received a share of hate mail, or—in some cases—well articulated criticism written on engraved stationery.

But in a few weeks, the press, the letters, the TV faded into nothingness. Justice, or the next best thing, had been done.

In Dover-Foxcroft, Bob and Mim tried to get on with their busy lives. With the money received in their son's memory, they planned the enlargement and modernization of The Little Red School House. It would take months, but their son's death would provide new life for countless unfortunates.

Jackie Hilton, too, had picked up the pieces of her life and started a new relationship with a friend who had helped her through the bad times. Her wounds would be a long time healing, and perhaps they never would heal entirely, but each day she won small battles over memory. Jennifer, once so close to "Big Bob," had begun to forget and to lose herself entirely in the activities of school.

Joanne Irace moved into a new apartment near her school in Windham. She still felt the pang of loneliness and of a void that would never be filled. She kept in close contact with the Mountfords, especially on days of special meaning. She had no serious male interests at present and yet it had been a time of growth—a time of growing closer to God— of feeling His sustaining power and love.

"And it came to pass." She thought often of the much-used Biblical terminology that now was analogous to Bob Mountford's life and to the life that the two of them had shared.

"And it came to pass." Not to stay but to pass.

CHAPTER XXXV

Ordinarily, a prisoner such as Randall Smith was transported out of the county in a matter of a few days, but Hopkins learned that the state prison facilities were overcrowded and backlogged from the Tennessee line to the Atlantic Ocean. He would be forced to house Smith longer than normal. And Smith had become very restless after the trial had ended. It almost seemed as if Randall wanted to get on with his confinement—or out of Giles County, at least.

Loretta came faithfully to visit on weekends, but it was evident that some of those visits went sour. The whole aftermath was growing hairy. It was akin to paying off the bill collector only to have him return, saying more money was owed.

And Loretta had accused the sheriff's department of not turning over all of her son's things unto her keeping. The air was getting frostier by the day.

As for Randall, he had swings from apparent depression to orneriness. Some of the deputies predicted that he would soon go on another hunger strike. That's all Giles County needed: a grandstand play that might draw the media back and put Pearisburg in the spotlight again.

Deputy Tommy Lawson, the best amateur psychologist in the department, concluded that the prisoner was lonesome for his old cellmates. Most all of the short-termers in the jail since Smith's incarceration had been transferred or set free or had concluded their own long-awaited trials.

"We've got to get Randall a neighbor that he'll talk to," someone suggested at coffee break. "Wouldn't that be better than a hunger strike?"

Hopkins listened to other suggestions as well and pondered them. He felt a certain uneasiness about the whole situation. The Charlottesville doctors had earlier discounted the possibility of a suicide attempt in Randall's case, but Hopkins wasn't so sure. He just wanted to be rid of Smith.

Randall's incoming mail picked up. Most of it was hate mail, the dispatcher—whose task it was to examine such before passing it on— discovered. But a few letters could be classified as fan letters. In either event everything had to be examined in case a sender tried to slip in a small file, drugs, bribe money, or any other tiny, but dangerous, items.

Bigger packages also arrived for Randall. Some people sent gospel tracts, Bibles, and other inspirational books. Randall appeared to ignore all of these, but his spirits soared when a female writer followed up her initial correspondence. Randall showed the letter to a deputy jailer as if it were the first letter he had ever received; he mouthed the girl's name like a dying fish gasping for air: M-a-s-e-l. M-a-s-e-l. M-a-s-e-l.

It took Randall two days to compose a return letter, but after he had written it, he started repeating the girl's name out loud.

Colby Shaffer, a new inmate one cell removed, tired quickly of the mumblings.

"If you're prayin', hurry up. If you're groanin', shut the hell up! I'm trying to read."

Randall ignored him. Didn't waste his time on fat old slobs. He put Masel's letter under his pillow and lay back. What did she look like? Big boobs like cantaloupes? Shapely hips held tight in jeans? Red hai—No! No! Why had he let himself think red hair?

Black hair. Dark eyes. A little on the tanned side. Thinking about it further caused him to start shaking.

"You sick or somethin'? Runnin' a fever?" Shaffer called out.

"Mind your own business," Randall growled.

"Hey, neighbor, I didn't mean what I said 'while ago. I can't read good, and I was tryin' to cipher this western book. If you're sick, I'll call for somebody."

"I'm not sick I told you!"

"Then what you shakin' for? You scared or somethin'?"

"Just shut up. Shut up! Shut up!"

"Don't know why we can't be buddies. What are you in for anyway?"

Randall sat up. "None of your business."

"They got me for stealin' a little ole can of diesel fuel out of a dozer parked along the street. What else is a broke trucker from Kentuck supposed to do when he runs out of juice?"

"You're not from around here?"

"I said I was from Kentucky. Hazard. Things are bad out there. No way to keep bread on the table. I was hopin' construction was better around here. What do you do?"

"Used to be a welder."

"Used to be? You lost the touch?"

"Didn't lose the touch. Lost my fuggin' freedom. Landed in this screwed up, fuggin' jail."

"What happened?"

"Never mind. Get back to your horseshit western."

"I'm here if you need me, neighbor. Ain't you ever heard how jolly and friendly fat folks are?"

Randall clammed up. Fat people sickened him. Their flesh wiggled, and their breathing was always heavy—always as if they were drawing a last breath.

The hate-thoughts ran dry and Randall stood up; he rested his chest against the bars.

"You said you was a trucker?"

The fat man lowered his book and stood up opposite.

"Yeah. Lumber. Coal, dirt, bricks. Anythin' to make a dollar."

"What's a '78 Ford pickup worth? Four-wheel drive."

"Well, now. That depends on who wants it, how much he wants it, and whether he's livin' in the lap of prosperity or poverty. Where the money's at, I'd say about forty-eight hundred. Where the money ain't, about twenty-five hundred."

"Shit. What kind of answer is that?"

"A true answer. You buyin' or sellin'?"

"It'll be a long time before I need one."

"You in for that long?"

"Long enough."

"Speakin' of four-wheels, I used to have a Toyota when I was flush. Took to the mountains with it on weekends. Fished. Hunted. Just generally tore up the sod. Had to let it go. Got so I couldn't keep beans on the table and the light bill paid."

"Used to do that, too. The huntin', fishin', and four-wheelin', I mean."

"Hey, neighbor, I knowed you and me would get on. No use us sittin' across from each other like dummies when we can visit a spell and tell fish tales. When I get out of here and get prosperous agin, I'm goin' to get me a new Chevy Blazer and head right for the Tennessee River and stay for a month!"

"Wish I could go with you."

"No reason why you can't when you get out. My old lady's a good cook and my kids—all but one—has left home. Be glad to put you up for a night or two—take you where the real bass are."

"Not gettin' out for a long time. Drew thirty years, worth."

Shaffer, not knowing what to say, decided to say nothing. He just backed away, and Randall did likewise.

Randall lay back down, reached for and read Masel's letter again:

Dear Randall Smith. I feel for you. I know how lonely you must be. I get lonely too sometimes. I wonder if you get as lonely as me? It seems like there never was a time I wasn't lonely. I work in a garment factory in Christiansburg and even when the machines are humming and people are all around me I still get blue. I read all about your trouble. I don't believe you did it. In the papers you looked so kind and sweet in the face. I'll be thinking of you. Do you want to know what I look like? I know what you look like, but you don't know what I look like. Maybe you won't like me but it doesn't matter. I care about you anyway. Goodbye for now. Love, Masel.

He asked for the offered picture in his own letter. He couldn't wait. The jailer made his rounds before the evening meal trays were emptied. Shaffer smacked his mouth until Randall stopped eating and watched him. Two cells nearest them were empty, and the sound kind of bounced back; it sounded like a fish flopping in shallow water.

"Not bad eatin'," Shaffer chuckled. "Not bad a'tall."

"You eat much jail food before?" Randall said.

"Nope. Ain't been in the pokey for a right long time. Pulled a short stretch for moonshinin' when I was younger and just a while back for stealin' a car battery. Nothin' serious."

"Was it in Kentucky? They good to you there?"

"Yeah, it was in old Kentuck. But they ain't good to you no place. Behind bars is no place for a man or a dog."

It was four days later at Tuesday's mail call when Randall received Masel's return letter. The flap was already unsealed, and he cursed the person unknown who had censored the letter.

"They're just doin' their job, neighbor," Shaffer consoled. "All guards ain't bad. Some of 'um are downright friendly."

Randall ignored the remark and removed the contents of the envelope carefully. His hands shook, and a photograph fell to the floor. He picked it up and looked. The longer he studied it, the more fury in him rose. It was only a head-and-shoulders shot, but he could see that the puff-cheeked girl with the bullish neck was as broad as a bathtub all the way down. Her beady eyes were lost below frizzled short hair that was as orange-red as clay.

What difference did it make if she had boobs as big as watermelons? They'd be swallowed up by her bloated body.

He ripped the picture in half, threw it on the floor, and stomped it repeatedly.

"I don't know what's goin' on, neighbor, but you don't look like a happy man."

"The fuggin' deputies—they switched the pictures. She's tall and slender, and her hair's got to be long. They switched the fuggin' pictures!"

"They ain't got no reason to do that. You sure you ain't sick? Imaginin' things?"

"They're the ones that's sick. Enjoy makin' the waves roll over me. Like to see me slapped down. Drownin'. Drownin'."

"You ain't makin' sense to me, neighbor, but whatever is botherin' you, maybe you ought to read the letter. Maybe it'll clear things up."

Randall stuck the unread letter under his mattress and pouted. Shaffer tried to draw him out, but he got nowhere. Randall just kept talking to himself.

"You know, pardner, looks in a woman ain't everything. Sex ain't either. Bein' a young feller, you wouldn't agree with that, but it's so. Take me and Opal, my old lady. We ain't made love in three years. She's bigger than I am. We'd be plum funny lookin' just tryin' to connect up. Don't matter none. We're still like school sweethearts. She's stuck with me through thick and thin though I gotta say she's in a better humor when I'm flush. You listenin' to me?"

"Don't look like I have much choice."

"What I'm sayin' is, looks wear off pretty quick. It's what's under the skin that matters. Somebody you can count on. Somebody to come hom—somebody that'll cheer a feller up when he gets blue."

"Where I'm goin', no woman would want me."

"I wouldn't bet on that. A good woman'll wait. By the way—where are they sendin' you?"

"I don't know yet."

"You never did tell me about it."

Randall lay back, put both hands behind his head, and stared at the ceiling.

"Sometimes you just got to get things out of your system," Shaffer said.

"It ain't me anyway," Randall said in a low voice.

"Whatdoya' mean, neighbor?"

"It was that fuggin' Smith."

"Smith? I thought that was your name?"

"I'm talkin' about another Smith. A real sonofabitch. Left his wife and kid when the kid was just a baby. Left them to scrape and starve for theirselves."

"That's a sonofabitch if I ever heard of one."

"I saw him do some things. That's why I'm in here."

"You're a—how they say it—a 'material' witness or somethin'? But how'd you draw thirty years?"

Randall sat up and lit a cigarette and looked down at his bare feet.

"I seen Smith do it. I can testify against him. They're puttin' me away for protection."

"I don't cipher it," Shaffer said. "What did he do?"

"These two people were tryin' to see in Smith's head. They thought they'd chased him off, but he came back to their camp in the woods that night and watched them. Got so close up he could hear every word they said. They didn't even see him or hear him. They were drinkin' his likker and just havin' a good time. Afterwards, they just laid there all cuddled up by the fire and Smith could hear them breathin'."

"Slow it down. Slow it down. Whatdoya mean they tried to see in Smith's head?"

"They kept lookin' at him and sayin' funny things. Askin' strange questions. And the girl made Smith draw some pictures. She was nice all right, but she was lookin' too deep. She saw some things she shouldn't of never seen. Sooner or later she'd have to pay."

"But wait a minute. Who were these people?"

"Trail hikers. Out tearin' up the woods. The man with the girl—he saw in Smith's head, too. He was nice a little bit, but he knew the answers to everything. Had a fuggin' answer whether Smith asked him anything or not. Smith just wanted to close his mouth permanent—make him stop spoutin' off all his smartass answers."

"I still don't understand the part about lookin' in Smith's head."

"Then shut up and listen." Randall almost leaped from the bed. He took a bar in each hand and gripped it. Shaffer could see Randall's knuckles grow white.

"When Smith couldn't take it no more," Randall continued, "he left, but he came back that night and waited. The ground was soft and wet in the woods, and they couldn't hear him. He just sat there for a long time 'til he thought they was goin' to make love, but they didn't, and Smith got madder than he'd ever been. Wanted to see 'em undress and play with each other, but they didn't. They just started to go to sleep and the man started snorin' with a funny-like sound. Kind of like a chucklin' noise. He was laughin' in his sleep about seein' into Smith's head."

"What did Smith do next?"

"What else could he do? Had to shoot that fuggin' loudmouth. Quiet him down forever. He'd saw everything in Smith's head. Stripped him bare like bark off a poplar saplin'."

"But you said the girl'd seen in his head, too?"

"She did, but she was nicer. She'd have to pay, but Smith didn't want to kill her. Just wanted to shame her. Make her pay that way."

"But did he kill her?"

"Yeah, but he didn't mean to. She made him. She wouldn't lay down. Fought him."

"I still don't get it. You say Smith killed this man. When? How?"

"Both of 'em. They was stretched out in a little cabinlike place on the floor. Smith pulled out his .22 and shot the man in the head three times. Bang! Bang! Bang! The girl got up screamin'. Started to run. Smith chased her. He just wanted her to lay down and take her clothes off, but she wouldn't. She was wild and strong, and she knocked Smith down. He picked up a long stick and started hitting her, but she just kept comin' on. Smith drew the Buck knife at his belt and stabbed her. He didn't mean to do it, but she kept pilin' on. She kept screamin', 'But why? But why? But why?' Even after he stabbed her agin and agin, she just wouldn't quit. She was squirtin' blood all over Smith and everything, and he could taste the hot salty flavor of it. She just kept fightin', and she knocked him down—and his hand found a stiff rod and he got up and beat her head 'til she was helpless."

"She was dead?"

"No. She laid there quiverin', and Smith took her clothes off and did some things I can't tell you about. Smith wouldn't like it. But when she got real still, Smith put some of her clothes back on. He didn't want to do it. I know he didn't ___ just wanted to shame her. Make her pay for seein' inside his head."

"You're tellin' the gospel truth, ain't you?"

"Yeah, I seen it all. Smith ran away. Couldn't stand to watch them quiverin' like that. He went and changed his clothes 'cause the blood was stickin' to him. When he came back they was stretched out and still. Then Smith carried them off in the woods and put dirt and stuff over 'em. But he tied the man's mouth open with rope first. Smith just had to tie that loud mouth open so it wouldn't spout off no more. He carried 'em like they was light as pillows. Seemed like he had power to spare. He'd never felt so high. It was just like the first time he ever smoked a joint of grass."

"Did they catch Smith right away?"

"No. He outsmarted 'em. He hid everything he could find in the moonlight, and when daylight came, he tried to do it up better. But he had to hurry because hikers come along every few hours."

"And you saw all this?"

"Yeah." Randall sighed and sat down exhausted on his bed.

"And now you're bein' kept outta Smith's reach?"

"Yeah. Smith would kill me if I ever testified about him."

"But if Smith's still free, and the law can't find him, what's the use of keepin' you penned up?"

"It's in case they ever find out."

"Huh?" Shaffer did a double take.

"They gotta keep me and Smith apart. Can't you see?"

"Not exactly. Maybe we'd better talk about fishin' or four wheelin' or somethin'."

"You won't tell anybody, will you? What all I told you about Smith?"

"No, unless it'll buy me a meal ticket and a full tank of juice back to Kentuck. Guess it don't matter anyway, does it? I mean since they ain't never found Smith and probably never will?"

"No. I don't guess it matters. He's too smart for 'em. Somebody said he went up to Connecticut. Goin' to learn to fly one of those moon rockets probably."

"Yeah," Shaffer said, backing away from the bars slowly.

Randall stood up again, looked down, stooped, and picked up the pieces of the photograph. He did it in such slow motion that Shaffer was mesmerized. Randall licked the torn edges of the photo and tried to stick them together. It didn't work. Childish frustration registered on his face.

"Get the jailer to bring you some of that sticky tape," Shaffer suggested.

"You really think a fat, ugly woman is worth havin'?"

"Some of 'em is the sweetest plums in the world; just eat a feller up with affection. Good cooks. Faithful and true. The right one could turn a man's life teetotally around."

"Even if a man was behind bars?"

"Yep. She'd write and tell him things; she'd tell him she'd be waitin', workin', and savin' money so you both could have a little house sometime."

"Do fat women like cats?"

Shaffer chuckled. "I don't know about all of 'em, but my wife's got a whole passel. Like to see her sittin' in front of the TV watchin' her soap operas and them cats swarmin' all over her lap. Real peaceful."

Randall reached for the unread letter from beneath his mattress and read with visible effort.

Shaffer waited. And waited.

"Well?"

"She says she's got fourteen hundred dollars saved up if I need it for lawyers. Appeals. Stuff like that. Course I—Smith don't have no chance of appeals."

"Didn't I tell you the plump gals had a heart of gold? Didn't I tell you?"

Randall stood there grinning like a child with a Christmas toy. Shaffer saw him slip the torn photograph into his shirt pocket and pat it a couple of times.

Two days later when Shaffer returned from his own hearing, Randall Smith was gone. He looked into the bare cell and shivered.

Randall lost his long brown locks while at Powatan Correction Center near Richmond and began learning there the ins and outs of what prison life was all about.

For the prisoner who had future hopes of living in a free society once again, there was much to learn about how to become a model inmate and build up point privileges and how to establish a controlled behavior pattern and good conduct record that at some distant date might mean the difference between early parole and sweating out unnecessary years behind prison walls.

After his sixth week of confinement at Powatan, Loretta visited him. He told her things there about certain memories he'd had: memories about being in Jefferson National and being chased off the mountain by a whole band of trail hikers. Loretta listened patiently—tried to sort it out; to read between the words. When he'd run down, she tried to share the hometown news with him.

"And Dr. Love died," she added, hoping Randall would remember with affection their family physician.

"Who killed him?" Randall asked.

"Nobody killed him. He died of a stroke."

Randall had little interest in the hometown news. Loretta thought him incapable of even understanding it. At some moments her son was like a man in a daze.

Before visiting hours had ended, however, Randall did convince her that he could have a TV set.

On her way out, she inquired and found that such was permissible under certain conditions and only if the set came by direct factory or mail-order shipment.

She took care of the shipment and later he called to thank her.

Something about him began to change after that. There was a flicker of enthusiasm in his voice during calls home, a kind of new interest in everything. She didn't understand it all, but unbelievably, prison life seemed to be helping him.

Later in the summer, Randall's letters bore a new address. He'd been reassigned to Brunswick Correctional Center in Lawrenceville, Virginia, a brand new center that looked like a college campus he said; and he had been assigned to the farm machinery maintenance shop as a welder, a job his counselor had helped him get.

Loretta looked for the location on the map. It was in the flat country near Suffolk, not far from Newport News.

It was as if Randall had gone off again as he had for that first job at Newport News. Maybe he was being given a new start in almost the same place—a chance to live his life all over again so that he could do it differently.

Susan Ramsay and Bob Mountford were finally committed to the earth by those most dear to them. Far away to the north in Au Gres, Michigan, Bud and Ginny Ramsay, Kelly and Dan Sucher, Richard and Kathy Ramsay had gathered with various relations and neighbors at the family's summer cottage.

The little group moved from the cottage to the Sims Cemetery, their family burial ground, a mile away. It was a sunny day with a comfortable breeze blowing in from the lake.

Frank Paniccia, a Catholic deacon and Bud's brother-in-law, conducted the service. After a brief eulogy and group participation in The Lord's Prayer, Frank flipped the switch of the tape recorder he had brought along. The voices of singing nuns permeated the respectful silence and drifted into the forest.

Afterwards Ginny reached into the urn they had brought and scattered a handful of ashes among the trees. The remainder of the urn's contents were buried in a flowering corner of the cemetery.

Each parent, brother, and sister knew it was a place they would be compelled to pay homage to often.

In Maine, the time had come when Bobby's ashes must be relinquished to the past.

The elder Mountfords knew that what they had planned to do with these precious remains was illegal, and yet they felt it was a righteous infringement of the law.

With food, water, and hiking attire, fourteen of them ascended the slopes of Mount Katahdin. Besides Bob and Mim, there were daughter Carolyn and husband Dan Carver, Jackie Hilton, Scott and Steve Mountford, Sean Stitham, Debbie Hardie, friends Holly Clark, Sandy Wright, John Stanquist, and Mim's sister and her son, Gail and Scott Pender.

The name which Thoreau had given Katahdin—"a cloud factory"—proved not so accurate as the group topped Baxter Peak. Only a few clouds floated aloft, the wind was only mildly fickle and the air as fresh as mint. The wooden sign at the summit read 5,267 feet, and the less experienced hikers in the group had counted every foot of the journey.

Each refreshed himself, and then Bob led them single file among the massive greyish-brown boulders along the pinnacle. Near the Knife Edge they gathered in a circle of embrace. They sang a song, Bob said a prayer, then he lifted his son's ashes heavenward.

"Dust thou art, and unto dust shalt thou return," Bob quoted, and flung the plastic bag's contents to the wind. For a moment the powdery matter seemed to hang suspended; then it dispersed into a million birds in flight. The last of the residue swirled into a crevice along the Knife Edge, escaped in part, and disintegrated in the direction of Daicey Pond.

Scott Pender placed a painted stone he had brought along atop a moss-covered boulder. The writing on his small marker said simply:

Bobby Mountford

1954-1981

He died climbing

The group looked at the crude memorial and smiled. The young boy had captured more of the essence of truth appropriate to the occasion than he would know for many years to come.

As the others still pondered the tribute, Bob turned away. His vision swept over the vast forests on the plains below, then to the tall wind-stirred trees in every direction. Soon some of those trees, or others like them, would be sawed into boards, shingles, and framing. As a result of the memorial contributions from all across the nation in Bobby's and Susan's names, the architects were already at work, and before long a skeletal outline of the new arts and crafts center at The Little Red School House would rise against the skyline. For reasons beyond his ability to explain or to fully understand, there was meaning in what seemed to be a kind of grand plan in which all things were aright again. He tried to mentally articulate the feeling and couldn't.

He turned back to the others. Each was smiling and radiant. A great gust of wind came as if to remind them all that perhaps they had overstayed their welcome; that Nature, after all, was in command of her pinnacles and with one mighty breath could sweep them all, like so much dust, from the face of the earth.

AN AFTERWORD

Murder on the Appalachian Trail attempts to be as accurate as is humanly possible in the depiction of the life of Randall Lee Smith before, during, and after his conviction for the murders of Robert Tatton Mountford, Jr., and Laura Susan Ramsay, in March 1982. No less an effort will be made in the case of other major characters in the story. Therefore, the book is directly based on numerous interviews, documents, records and tape recordings of court proceedings, conferences with all attorneys on both sides of the issue, as well as the presiding judges, and from other original material: the result of research trips to Aurora, Ohio; Ellsworth, Maine; Dover-Foxcroft, Maine; Myrtle Beach, South Carolina; Conway, South Carolina; extensive areas of Bland and Giles counties, Virginia; several locations along the Appalachian Trail; and author attendance at every hearing and court proceeding at the Giles County Courthouse in Pearisburg, Virginia, the location of legal jurisdiction in the case.

In addition, uncounted hours were spent with various officers of the Virginia State Police, who were most courteous and cooperative in allowing the author access to all official records and photographs pertinent to the crime. Of equal assistance were: The Federal Bureau of Investigation; City of Myrtle Beach Police Department; The Sheriff's Department, Horry County, South Carolina; The Giles County Sheriff's Department, Pearisburg, Virginia; Central State Hospital, Petersburg, Virginia, and other offices and agencies.

Out of such a wealth of information, one side of the story began to take shape. The other side evolved, in part, as a result of help from some of the childhood friends, schoolmates, coworkers, employers, friends, acquaintances, relatives, and teachers of Randall Lee Smith, most of whom insisted upon — and will receive — anonymity. All testimony as to Randall Smith's movements, habits, hangups, general temperament, interests, prejudices, lifestyle, and such, at any given age and before, during, and after his conviction, did not always agree, and on occasion, the author was left to make a choice. He did so on the basis of what rang true and what seemed in character. The author makes no claim to being right in every instance.

More than eighty people were interviewed face to face, and as many more by telephone and correspondence. Some critical testimony was received on tape, requiring transcription and careful analysis. Five separate interviews with Loretta Smith plus follow-up phone calls that, all together, spanned a period of eighteen months, provided insights the author could have gained in no other way. The author is in her debt for the patience she demonstrated in telling and retelling of bad times, painful situations, and for having to face again and again circumstances repugnant to her.

Establishing the sequence of events relative to the pre- and post-crime time frames was a writer's nightmare alleviated only by the splendid cooperation of numerous AT hikers, rescue squad personnel, U.S. Forest Service personnel, and law enforcement authorities on the county, state, and national levels. But even so, the frailty of human memory, the faulty recordation and/or retention of every vital fact required exhaustive review until most of the pieces fit together like a jigsaw puzzle.

Material used from Randall Smith's various court hearings, and transcripts of the trial itself, are as verbatim as literary transcription will allow. During the proceedings, Defense attorneys, the attorney for the Commonwealth, and the presiding judges were, of course, not free to discuss the case. Afterwards, however, no group of men could have been more patient and helpful in defining every point in the lengthy legal procedure.

Where required, most of the principal characters in the story are identified — with their permission — by their real names. The names of Peggy Wheeler, Isaac Charlton, and Ned Shires (and their places of residence as depicted in the novel) who play such a pivotal part in the drama, are fictitious. From the beginning, their help and cooperation was conditioned upon this anonymity. All principals, including Randall Smith, were given the opportunity to read the manuscript, or, the parts referring to their parts in the story.

So many are to be thanked for their contributions, whether large or small, to this epic undertaking that spanned almost forty months. To complicate matters, at the halfway point in commiting the novel to typescript, the author was hospitalized for major surgery. For the innumerable phone calls, cards, letters, personal visits, and prayers, his eternal gratitude is here expressed again, and more especially to those people who believed in his project and encouraged him quickly back to the typewriter. It was not that easy. Weeks after the recouperation period was over, the words just wouldn't come. The juices were sour, the brain fuzzy, the stamina nonexistent, and the wheels just wouldn't go back on track. Then, one day, a tide of words and thoughts began to flow, but sans quality and hence, on paper, excellent wastecan fillers. A little later still, that hum of resonance, that poetic tension — or whatever other writers call it — came back to stay.

In the following list of names, being first or last carries no intended implication of rank or importance, personally, or to the individual contribution regarding the book. And so the litany of thanks begins thus:

From the area of South Carolina: Detective Captain Wayne Player, Patrolmen Rick Shafer and Rick Piersal, Chief Stanley Bird, City of Myrtle Beach Police Department. Don Myers, Chief Resident Agent, Jon Armstrong, Special Agent, and Tom Reynolds, Special Agent, Federal Bureau of Investigation. Horry County Sheriff Matthew "Junior" Brown, Deputy Bill Knowles, Captain Herman Enzor (who, among other things, showed the author Randall Smith's South Carolina jail cell). Phillip Dyches Sasser, colorful Southern gentleman, who was Randall Smith's South Carolina attorney.

In Virginia: Federal Judges Jim Turk and Ted Dalton, who, though uninvolved in the Smith case, helped provide the author with insights and answers to the complexities of courtroom procedure and the fine points of the law; attorney Dick Davis, for the same reasons, plus his willingness to read and evaluate the manuscript when he'd rather have been playing poker; attorney Max Jenkins, who viewed the Smith case with interest from afar, and who provided some keen observations and predictions.

Specific officers of the Virginia State Police are hereby recognized: Jay Cochran, Jr., Director, Bureau of Criminal Investigation, VSP, Richmond, for giving the author a green light on all fronts; Carroll Delp, Special Agent-in-Charge, Wytheville, Division; E.A. Duff, Assistant Special Agent-in-Charge; Special Agents Al Crane, John Ratliff, Cecil Wyatt.

And from the U.S. Forest Service, Blacksburg, Virginia Division, Buford "Boots" Belcher and Robin Cunningham provided invaluable help as did their associates.

In the Giles County section of Virginia, there were many helpers. Namely: Ted Johnson, County Clerk, and his staff, who must have felt, at times, that the chore of producing and copying documents for the author would never end. Bill Bane, County Treasurer and lifelong friend, for encouragement and beneficial insights. Kenneth Walker, M.D., for help beyond the call of duty, who wears so many hats so well. Steve Davis, a man's man and of that breed of volunteers never properly thanked by authors or the public, and all his Giles Rescue Squadsmen.

A special word of appreciation to Father Harry Winter (then) of Holy Family Church. His help and enthusiasm were without limit, and his belief in the Appalachian Trail movement, inspirational. He is to be thanked also for one of the most perceptive and in-depth critiques received from those burdened with reading the semi-final draft of the manuscript. The following men I came to know like fellow soldiers at battle: Hez Osborne, Giles County Commonwealth Attorney, who as weary as he was from the long ordeal, was never too tired to answer one more question; Livingstone

398

Dillow, heading the Defense team, and still the epitome of the colorful and wise small-town attorney at his best; Mike Davis, also of the Defense team, and a good manuscript critic and a promising young lawyer; Keith Neely, the third Defense team member, who helped me see between the lines, and who may, after all, become one day the F. Lee Bailey of the South; Sheriff John Hopkins III, Deputies Sterling Greever, Dicey Shaver, and most of all, Investigators Tommy Lawson and Mike Meyer of that office, who worked untiringly with the author in order that he might get it all down right.

Eula Boff-Naff, freelance court reporter was an angel for getting official approval and making available the use of her tapes.

Many thanks to Alice Stanley of the Virginia Search and Rescue Dog Association, Inc., for a short course in dog search and rescue work.

Judge Tom Bondurant, and Judge Robert Powell, of the 29th Circuit of Virginia, offered insights that could come only from the impartial viewpoint, and the author was immeasurable helped by Judge Powell's analysis and perceptions after the trial was concluded.

And now, a special category of helpful people are to be recognized: My personal secretary, Bonnie Clark, for a thousand tasks done for the author, and always pleasantly. Manuscript secretary, and assistant researcher Liz Barkovitch, who is a joy to work with and the world's best typist. And thanks to Bonnie DiRico and Kaye Conner, who are whizzes at the keyboard of a word processor. Reference librarians at Virginia Polytechnic Institute and State University, Blacksburg; Radford University, Radford; University of Virginia, Charlottesville, Virginia; Virginia State Library, Richmond; City of Radford Public Library, Virginia, and many other individuals and institutions who offered everything from news clippings, pertinent articles, useful equipment, medical and technological information, and a great deal of moral support.

Profound appreciation goes out to hikers Peter Butryn, John "JJ" Jurcznski, John and Martina Linnehan, Frank Maguire, Neil Chivington, Sandy Skinner, Steve Skinner, Renate Lillifors, John Smith, Candy Lakin, Dave Tice, John E. Pearson, Don Farrell, Woody Rambo, and others from throughout the country, all of whom embody the true frontier spirit.

For advance readings of the manuscript, and for general editing advice and helpful critiquing, the author thanks: Jack Davis, Rage Young, and Jean Willcox. Flossie Hart and Marguerite Gunn, the author's mother and sister, respectively, and his Number One fans and severest critics, are hereby recognized for their outstanding proofeading ability. And to Lois, Kate, Susan, and Marsha, the author's wife and daughters, a hearty cheer for their patience, longsuffering, and belief in a country-boy-come-novelist.

Other advance readers were Al Crane, Mary Alice Davis, Harry Winter, Mike Meyer, Steve Skinner, and Barbara Hunley, whose constructive criticism was beneficial and appreciated.

Special recognition goes out to Lawrence VanMeter, Executive Director of the Appalachian Trail Conference Association, and his staff, for advice, manuscript evaluation and criticism, and a handy supply of Trail Guides, maps, and other data.

Thanks to Dr. Sean Stitham, one of young Bob Mountford's closest life-long friends, for his help and special insights. The same gratitude goes out to Chris Labun for his recollections regarding Mountford-at-work. Jan Waterson helped with information about Susan Ramsay's trip to Italy. Gary Henson provided guidance for the author relating to trail life in general, and the use of the Trail Guide.

Only through the splendid cooperation of many of the staff of The Homestead Project at Ellsworth, Maine, was the author enabled to understand the range of services that insititution offered to its troubled young members. And too, the help was invaluable in seeing the work place of Bob Mountford, Jr., Jackie Hilton, Susan Ramsay, and others.

The following staff members made my stay delightful as well as informative: Mitchell Gelber, Dianne Collins, Tom Collins, Pam Damon, Chris Lavin, Tom Taylor and Jeff Raymond.

Dianne and Tom Collins went out of their way to show me the whole area, including a visit to Susan Ramsay's lakeside cottage, and to the tract of land Susan had planned to buy from Dianne and Tom, on which to construct her own wilderness cottage.

Alan McKelvy, far away in Michigan, must not be overlooked for the contribution he made. Without complaint, he filled out a twenty-page questionnaire — as did many of the friends and associates of both he and Susan Ramsay — endured a half-dozen lengthy phone conversations, and made contributions unasked for. Perhaps the hardest of these for him, was the surrender of the letters between Susan Ramsay and himself. He read the manuscript — and it was often uncomplimentary to him — without the insistence of a single change.

The following group to be acknowledged are very special people indeed: Bud, Ginny, and Kelly Ramsay (Sucher), who even while the black cloud of bereavement yet hovered over them, offered every assistance, and were the perfect host and hostesses during the author's brief residence with them. And to have shared SuSu's, diary, personal correspondence, and the most intimate details of her life — that the author and his reading audience might more fully understand and appreciate her — was an act of magnitude and literary charity quite awe-inspiring. For the pain they each endured while reading the manuscript, and thus having to live the tragedy all over again — that sacrifice, too, is a contribution here recorded.

To Bob and Mim Mountford, and to their remaining children — Scott,

Steve, Carolyn, and Cathy — you showed the author the real meaning of courage; and from Bob and Mim, the Christian definition-in-practice of what forgiveness really means. In your home, you treated your visiting novelist like a member of the family, held nothing of truth and literary value from him, and bared your souls for the benefit of those who wanted to hear the full story of the deaths on the Appalachian Trail. It is the author's most fervent hope that, as a result of this book, an outpouring beyond your wildest dreams in support of The Little Red School House will benefit the retarded children whom you nurture, serve, and love.

Jackie Hilton, what a void in the story there would have been without your help and support! There were times your mind, your emotions, your instincts wavered. The pain was so deep; the intimate moments so hurtful to recall and discuss, and yet all that you ultimately offered put flesh on bone, and surging blood into stagnant veins, giving life and personality to a real man and woman a reading public might be anxious to know, even at the sacrifice of information otherwise deeply personal.

And to Joanne Irace: You did the impossible. You made a vast contribution in helping the author to see into the psyche of one of his principal characters and in the sharing of your hopes and dreams with that character, until a most unforgettable love story was revealed. The little touches, the deep insights you provided were like the final brush strokes upon a fine portrait.

Regrettably, the many individuals who contributed in other ways cannot all be thanked by name. But those who made a phone call, ran an errand, double-checked a fact, made one or one-hundred photocopies, acted as an intermediary, friend, advisor, critic, or whatever, hats off to every one.

The author met many people from the print, radio and TV media, and was enriched by their friendship, helped by their sharing of ideas, suggestions, and notes (all of them copied faster than the author, as we all shared the front benches in the venerable courthouse), and may God bless them all with a sense of tender mercy when the time comes to review this mountain of words.

Finally, to the hundreds of you who have kept the author on his toes and at his typewriter by your constant letters and phone queries of, "when is it going to be ready?" — it is, as good as he can make it, at last.

J.C.
Radford,
Virginia
1984